Praise for *Ours*

"[An] ambitious debut . . . In lush, ornamental prose, Williams, who is also a poet, traces many characters' entwined journeys as they seek to understand the forces that assemble and separate them."

—*The New Yorker*

"Deeply absorbing . . . *Ours*, for all its elements of magic, fantasy, and mythology, is a realistic depiction of how we might arrive at utopia: through people who are always trying to become, always finding ways to navigate and survive harsh realities, always reaching for moments of joy and intimacy."

—*Los Angeles Times*

"*Ours* enthralls from its earliest pages. . . . Written in distilled, distinct prose . . . *Ours* reads like mythology or folklore paired with ethnography. The inhabitants of the town, their relationships and routines, feel specific, lived-in, and complex. Questions about how to form a utopian community—if such an ideal is even attainable—reverberate throughout. Unlike many stories that grapple with slavery, *Ours* is refreshingly focused on freedom."

—Buy Side, *The Wall Street Journal*

"Williams finds new ways to ask age-old questions: How do we have both safety and freedom? What makes a ragtag group into a community? And most important, how do we find the missing parts of ourselves in other people?"

—*The Washington Post*

"There's nothing that hits like a truly magnetic work of magical realism, and *Ours* by Phillip B. Williams has all the makings of a stunner. . . . Williams is unabashedly brilliant."

—*Elle*

"A transcendent and lyrical exploration of freedom that delivers a fluid, spiritual, and empowering meditation on the complexities of reclaiming identity … Williams has assembled a vivid and theatrical ensemble in *Ours* and given them plenty of room to access their humanity as their lives intersect and intertwine. The result is a spiritual, redemptive, and stirring look at the numerous shapes autonomy takes."

—*The Atlanta Journal-Constitution*

"*Ours* is so vivid a glimpse into the lives of formerly enslaved people that it reads with the beauty and urgency of a spoken-word poem. … This is an important novel, peopled with vivid characters literally and figuratively hidden from view. Every scene portrays a people trying to understand themselves, individuals trying to give and receive love, attempting to balance hope with trauma."

—*Star Tribune*

"A sweeping, epic novel … Remarkable."

—*Town & Country*

"By taking such care to document the horrors of slavery alongside the 'freedom [his characters] deserve,' Williams seems to offer the possibility of a world beyond trauma."

—*Financial Times*

"A multigenerational epic that will sweep you off of your feet … Williams possesses a brilliant imagination and understanding of storytelling. … [He] uses his poet's ear in crafting his prose, and the words shine on every page."

—*Book Riot*

"Phillip B. Williams establishes that his lyrical gifts, which work so well in poetry, have the strength to support a nearly six-hundred-page tome in his debut novel. … *Ours* is a novel that touches several centuries, exploring the nature of freedom, the limitations of safety, and the ways that love traps and frees a soul."

—*The Rumpus*

"Shot through with themes of freedom versus bondage and empowerment versus protection, *Ours* explores what happens when community members dare to ask if their newfound safety is just a new type of entrapment."

—*Reader's Digest*

"Williams has crafted a mesmerizing, mythical, multilayered portrait of a unique Black American community. . . . Williams's prose is graceful and eloquent in a story that is big and beautiful as it probes the terms and conditions of true freedom. Don't miss it."

—*Bay Area Reporter*

"Now, this, this is the one. . . . The narrative, bolstered by effervescent prose, Black spirituality, mythology, and surrealism, sweeps over four decades, showing what love can do to you."

—*Book Riot*

"Williams has a voice that soars across each page, breathing life into his dazzling array of characters—the lovers and the malcontents, the queer and the mystical, the brazen and the cautious. At an incredible six hundred pages long, *Ours* is nevertheless a novel worth savoring."

—*Shelf Awareness* (starred review)

"A gorgeously written, evocative saga of Black American survival and transcendence . . . Resonant [and] wildly imaginative . . . As in the magical realist sagas of Latin America or the grand fictions of Russian literature, time itself becomes a morphing, enigmatic character in Williams's novel. . . . What keeps you attentive, and the sweeping narrative anchored, are the rich characterizations and, most of all, the often-startling impact of Williams's poetically illuminated language. A multilayered, enrapturing chronicle of freedom that interrogates the nature of freedom itself."

—*Kirkus Reviews* (starred review)

"Ambitious and lyrical . . . Williams's accomplished narrative leaves readers with much to ponder."

—*Publishers Weekly*

"*Ours* is the epic and lyrical debut novel by poet Phillip B. Williams, featuring unforgettable characters woven together with folklore and humanity's search for freedom."

—*B&N Reads*

"A beautifully written and ambitious epic about the complexity of freedom. Williams crafts an expansive, original world filled with characters who linger long after the final page."

—Brit Bennett, *New York Times* bestselling author of *The Vanishing Half*

"In *Ours*, Phillip B. Williams creates a fictional town with a complicated, magical history that is as thrilling to explore as the Macondo of Gabriel García Márquez's *One Hundred Years of Solitude.* The mysteries at the heart of this novel are deeply considered, as is the concept of freedom itself. With a poet's precision of language and a seasoned storyteller's attention to character, Williams has written a truly one-of-a-kind epic."

—Angela Flournoy, author of *The Turner House*

"As consummate and compelling a storyteller as he is a poet, in *Ours* Phillip B. Williams spins a stellar tale of resistance and reconstruction that could school any US history book. Crossing rivers and decades, involving folk culture and the miraculous as a matter of course, and centering on the mysterious Saint and the secret community she creates in the midst of nineteenth-century chattel slavery and the long battle for Black freedom, *Ours* speaks to our past, present, and future with incomparable poetic verve."

—John Keene, National Book Award–winning author of *Punks: New & Selected Poems*

"*Ours* is a radical re-creation of our pasts. With a keen eye to historical detail and the expansive imagination of a poet, Williams has constructed a jewel of a novel, a deeply felt exploration of the strengthening ties and broken cords of kith and kin under the weight of complicated histories. In the uncertain future that awaits us, *Ours* illuminates a greater understanding of what it means to be human and the complex, tangled lives and afterlives of enslavement."

—Kaitlyn Greenidge, author of *Libertie*

"Phillip B. Williams is loved by language; I know this because language opens to him. Within this fortress of a novel, what Williams builds is far from paradise but something richer, realer, more fragile. Oh, is this story alive."

—Danez Smith, author of *Homie*

PENGUIN BOOKS

OURS

Phillip B. Williams is from Chicago, Illinois, and is the author of two collections of poetry: *Thief in the Interior*, which was the winner of the Kate Tufts Discovery Award and a Lambda Literary Award, and *Mutiny*, which was a finalist for the PEN/Voelcker Award for Poetry Collection and the winner of a 2022 American Book Award. Williams is also the recipient of a Whiting Award and fellowships from the Radcliffe Institute for Advanced Study at Harvard University and the National Endowment for the Arts. He currently teaches in the MFA in creative writing program at New York University and the Randolph College low-residency MFA.

Also by Phillip B. Williams

Mutiny

Thief in the Interior

Ours
PHILLIP B. WILLIAMS

PENGUIN BOOKS

PENGUIN BOOKS
An imprint of Penguin Random House LLC
1745 Broadway, New York, NY 10019
penguinrandomhouse.com

Designed by Amanda Dewey

ISBN 9780593654842 (paperback)

THE LIBRARY OF CONGRESS HAS CATALOGED THE HARDCOVER EDITION AS FOLLOWS:
Names: Williams, Phillip B., author.
Title: Ours / Phillip B. Williams.
Description: [New York] : Viking, 2024.
Identifiers: LCCN 2023010345 (print) | LCCN 2023010346 (ebook) |
ISBN 9780593654828 (hardcover) | ISBN 9780593654835 (ebook) |
ISBN 9780593832226 (international edition)
Subjects: LCGFT: Novels.
Classification: LCC PS3623.I5593 O97 2024 (print) |
LCC PS3623.I5593 (ebook) | DDC 811/.6—dc23/eng/20230310
LC record available at https://lccn.loc.gov/2023010345
LC ebook record available at https://lccn.loc.gov/2023010346

First published in the United States of America by Viking,
an imprint of Penguin Random House LLC, 2024
Published in Penguin Books 2025

Printed in the United States of America
1st Printing

The authorized representative in the EU for product safety and compliance is Penguin Random House Ireland, Morrison Chambers, 32 Nassau Street, Dublin D02 YH68, Ireland, https://eu-contact.penguin.ie.

For my grandparents, on the Otherside.

For my mother, in the Here and Now.

Part One

· CHAPTER 1 ·

Blood and Light

[1]

Nearly two centuries before the boy who was shot dead at the intersection of First and Bank stood up in his own blood and spoke his name as if it were just given to him, there was a town named Ours, founded by a mysterious and fearsome woman right where the boy had been shot. But perhaps this story begins centuries before then, at the muddy waters of the Apalachicola River, or further back on a ship named the *Divider* carrying those misunderstood to be the future of slavery to the Western World.

To begin in any of those three places would lead back here, to this boy, age seventeen, fresh out of his junior year in high school, a bottle of orange Fanta rolling and emptying onto the street just feet away from his body from which blood spilled until it stopped, until the boy with his closed eyes opened them with a new mind and breath and understanding that shook him. He had been lying in the middle of the street for three hours with police tape squaring him off from his neighbors, friends, and family. The whole hood had rocked at the sound of the bullets popping off. Then he dropped and they all gathered, hymn-less and weathered, to see yet another one of their youngest take his last breath.

But he stood, his wounds no more than memories as he touched himself where he had been shot, a resonance of pain still there until it, too, departed, the smell of burnt corn bread in the air that someone had abandoned so that he wouldn't have to lie there for hours alone. Yes, they had all left something behind to stand in that street together, blocked off from touching him and told to "Back up," had it yelled at them as though they were to have as little care and consideration for the boy as the ones who had shot him.

He dusted himself off and looked around at the faces looking back at him, "What the fuck? My nigga . . ." peeling from a mouth astounded into a beautiful circle. The whole block went quiet except for that question and the loud suddenly sparked up in the crowd despite the cops right there, but who could give a fuck now when the dead have risen?

And he heard his name screamed from someone in the crowd, the voice bright and familiar, but a part of him didn't recall exactly who had said it. He had two minds now: one in the future and one from the past.

To begin this journey, move backward. The boy's body returns to the hot asphalt; the orange soda slides back into the bottle, and the blood back into the boy's warming body; then the boy's corpse rises and the bullets spin out from the right lung, the neck, the back of the head, the left hamstring, the right buttock, the right triceps, the left scapula, the—; his corpse becomes a living him as flecks of bone restructure and reenter the red-black wound, the broken wet resealed, the white meat sucked back into unbroken muscle, uncooked fat, and closing behind the retreat of the backward-flying bullet; the air the bullets once displaced returns from the curve of its displacement; the silver bullets return into the black gun like an unspeakable organ moving back into its dark element, the explosion of gunfire now the sound of wind hissing, then roaring, then suddenly silent; and the brown finger lifts from its trigger; the boy with his back to the police as the Fanta rises back into his pocket; and further back, weeks ago, the boy is asleep in bed and a small circle of light leaves his body. The legend begins where that light leads. At the end, the boy may teach you his name.

· CHAPTER 2 ·

Go Down, Moses

[1]

Ours was founded by a single incident. Several white families established themselves in what was then called Graysville. The entire town relied on Graysville-Flint Bank, headed by a Mr. George Flint, who had already made hundreds of thousands of dollars in real estate somewhere in Maine, as rumors had it. He founded Graysville on a whim. With a sudden need for adventure, he packed up all he owned and sent for the rest once he made it across the Mississippi River and found himself in St. Louis, Missouri.

Banking there became a hassle; already-established branches offered little to no room for a new executive and showed no interest in his cut-throat procedure of lending to those most in need who also carried the smallest possibility of paying anything back, taking from them their very bed if debts weren't paid on time.

Word of his arrival preceded him with the force of a plague and the entire banking community refused to have anything to do with him. With no other choice, Mr. Flint headed just a few miles north of St. Louis, discovering a nothing place burdened by woods and orioles. He used his fortune to tear down every piece of nature that challenged his financial vision. He bought up the land and divided it into plots he sold to anyone able to pay between $130 and $200.

Word got around in 1832 that a new development had started just north of St. Louis with cheap prices for large plots of land. Mr. Flint made a name for himself and his business, calling it the Oriole Street Realty Corporation. Between 1833 and 1834, more than 120 people moved into Graysville, bringing with them over three dozen businesses.

In the summer of 1834, a dark-skinned woman and man appeared on the outskirts of town. They were watched from the moment they arrived to the moment they reached the newly built branch of the Graysville-Flint Bank. It hadn't been open for a full two years before the two opened the door and the woman asked to speak with "the superior of this bank." Everyone working stared at her, one man so anxious he sweated the pen from behind his ear till it slid to the floor, the clink across the wood making him jump. She cleared her throat and repeated her request. Someone stood and ran to the back.

Moments later, Mr. Flint approached, a gun in his holster. People ducked beneath desks. Some of his bankers left the establishment to wait for shots to go off and for two bodies to be dragged out. He glared at the woman and then spoke to the towering, broad man who came with her.

"Your business here?" Mr. Flint said.

"I caught word that you have a few plots of land left for purchasing. I'm looking to buy one. Build myself a home," the woman said. The man who accompanied her stood a couple of feet off to the side and behind her, meaning Mr. Flint had to turn around to see the woman he had briskly passed.

He didn't like the height difference between the woman and man, she of average height but her head top reaching just under his chin. Mr. Flint stood about three inches shorter than the man, and the man's silence paired with his daunting size and intense stare toward nothing felt deliberately hostile.

"Is this man your husband?" Mr. Flint said. "If so, he should have told you that we do not sell to coloreds here. It is illegal. There is a sign out front. If he is not your husband, then he should have told you anyway. Much time would have been saved for the both of us if you two would have"—he paused—"could have read the sign."

"But, sir, I have money for—"

"It is impossible," he said, and headed back to his office. "Please, let yourselves out."

"Even with this?" The woman reached into a large mismatch pocket sewn into her dress and pulled out $1,500 in cash tied in a tight bundle with sprigs of jasmine. Mr. Flint laughed uncontrollably, and seemingly out of his mind with humor, he smiled broad as a dog's mouth. With a "Follow me" he led her into his office.

It was true that selling to her as a realtor carried legal repercussions, but with the amount of money she carried, Mr. Flint couldn't let her leave unattended. He was jovial, almost feeling accountable to find room for this woman and her silent companion. He decided that she would purchase her plot from an independent seller, someone who would purchase the land in their own name and legally sell it to her without any ties to a realtor. Mr. Flint said the land cost more because it came with a house already built, though that was untrue. She agreed to the price of $1,500 for 2,500 square feet and moved in right away. In less than three months the entire town evacuated, the white residents moving south to St. Louis or, in much smaller numbers, north to Delacroix. The fleeing white residents sold their properties, houses and furniture included, to Negroes for triple the price they had purchased them. They gave a third of the profits to Mr. Flint and used the rest of their earnings elsewhere. Graysville became Ours and its new citizens were thereafter called the Ouhmey.

After the woman and man arrived and settled, more and more Negroes from all over the south came to Ours led by hearsay, both freedmen and soon-to-be freedmen, around forty in total. Many found themselves running away from undesirable pasts, including slave work that had killed everyone they loved and surely would kill them next.

Negroes occupied the houses abandoned by their once-ago residents. Mr. Flint, though no longer a part of the community, visited from time to time to mark which houses had new occupants. He took copious notes of faces and names, the day they said they arrived, and where they came from. Once a week he visited Ours to collect money owed. Those who had moved in during his absence were told to buy the house immediately for $250 or pay Mr. Flint $35 a week for two months straight. Whoever couldn't pay him what he requested within a month's time were to be forced from the houses at gunpoint by St. Louis officers, but of course this never happened.

Mr. Flint died of a stroke one month after Ours had been named. No one bothered charging them anything thereafter, not even the government that took over all property in Mr. Flint's name, as he had no children and left no will. Mysteriously, no evidence existed that either Graysville or Ours was ever affiliated with Mr. Flint. Allegedly, the room he died in smelled like jasmine for months after they removed his body.

[2]

The woman who pioneered the migration called herself Eleanor to Mr. Flint, no surname, and this not her actual name at all. To the no-longer-slaves she called herself Saint. The man that traveled with her was nameless and speechless.

When they reached town, Saint told those who followed her, "Wait somewhere in the wilderness until you hear word from me that you can come. When you come, bring the amount of money I gave you before we left. Keep yourselves covered in jasmine. Keep it in your pockets and rub it on your skin. We gambling here and need all the luck we can get."

The newly freed had traveled with her from plantations all around Arkansas, plantations that she single-handedly ruined without any bloodshed but plenty of death, so most of them trusted her without question after having seen her power to liberate them.

It began on the Ross plantation in Hinton, Arkansas. One night, Saint seemed to appear out of their combined suffering taking shape in the form of a woman dressed just like they were. In one of the slave quarters, she whispered something that made everyone wake up at the same time. They all thought she was a spirit. Some hid their faces from her while others sat in awe and listened: "In three days, your self-proclaimed master will be dead, and you will follow me to freedom." Then she walked out the door, reappearing at each place the enslaved slept.

The second night at the plantation, Saint and her companion tore down white fists of cotton and destroyed a garden reserved for the so-called master and his family. They trampled a pattern into the land that if seen from above resembled a pitchfork. Sunrise, and the mistress of the house broke into a violent fever. Every doctor that visited, three in nine hours, failed to relieve her, and everything they tried seemed to worsen her illness. It wasn't until the mistress threatened to kill herself and everyone in the house if one more doctor tended to her that the requests for doctors ceased.

On the third night, Saint carved symbols into flat stones. When she finished carving, her companion took the stones to four different locations around the plantation and hid them beneath bushes. That following morning, the so-called master discovered every crop had withered overnight or sat soft and blackened on the ground.

Ross, the so-called master, took his rifle and, out of anger, shot at the nearest black face he saw. When he missed, his angry expression became mournful. Defeated, he grumbled as he returned to his sick wife.

On the fourth and final night, Saint and her companion rotated the location of each stone clockwise so that the southern stone became the western stone, the western the north, and so forth. That morning Ross, the so-called master, and his wife died in their sleep, both discovered in their bedroom by Ren, an enslaved cook, when neither showed up for breakfast. The three overseers were all dead, too, mouth-gaped and blank-staring at the ceiling of their cabin. Slobber slid down the sides of their cheeks like translucent worms.

Ren stumbled backward as though resisting the inward pull of the open mouths before her. She deserted the stiff corpses, running to her quarters to share the news with thirty-one enslaved Africans suddenly without a master. However, whatever joy Ren expected to feel crumbled before her because the so-called master's son and the son's wife appeared up the lane, their surrey growing larger over the horizon.

Saint stood on the steps of the house and watched the couple approach, led by two horses guided by a young Negro man. The so-called master's son, enraged to see her standing on the steps of the mansion, wearing his mother's emerald dress that he had purchased for her only months ago, rushed out of the surrey, and dropped dead the moment his feet touched ground. Panicked to see her husband fall and not get up, the wife demanded the Negro driver to help her get out of the surrey.

"Paton, open this door this instant, since you do not have sense enough to assist your master." Paton opened the door and the woman slapped him hard, then reached for Paton's hand. Her gloved hand in his, she stepped onto the ground and dropped dead. Paton leaned down to see her more closely.

"You touch them, and you die," Saint said without anger. Her stolen elegant dress swiped the steps behind her like a receding wave as she made her way toward Paton. What a beautiful day: clouds, puffed up like bloated bodies, slipped between the old trees—the sight made Saint tear up, all that amorphous white, midair and aimless. When she got close enough, she touched Paton's face with a gentleness he had never felt before and said, "This way." She turned and walked to the field, speaking to Paton as he followed her. "Don't ever try to touch your chains again. You might get rust on your priceless skin."

She did this on five more plantations, emptying the houses of anything valuable she found, including money and food, clothes and tools, books and legal documents, animals, ledgers, and deeds. They took everything except the receipts of payment for the purchased slaves. Those were burned immediately, unfortunate only because they documented what may have been correct birthdays for the soon-to-be-freed, many of whom wanted to know if they were lied to about their births, forced to believe in whatever myth about themselves they were given. Saint knew, however, that those dates were mostly false and the new selves the just-freed obtained through fire was a new birth.

She gathered herself a parade of ex-slaves and guided them north to Missouri. That they were never caught by or even saw a living thing—not even a bird—throughout their entire journey proved to them that Saint was their savior, though some never fully trusted her and considered her with suspicion because they feared both her and the man who said nothing and always smelled like the earth.

[3]

One early morning in Ours, just days after Mr. Flint died, Saint left her house, wearing a large blue dress with a train of several feet. She held a wood staff carved to bear a nest of thirteen serpent mouths at the top, their heads all facing the sky, the length of the staff made of the outstretched bodies of each serpent. She descended the steps of her home at the west end of Tanager Street, and everyone stopped and smiled at her. She hid her hair beneath a hat of fabric wrapped such that it made a ring of cloth on top of her head like a fat halo of dough, not a strand of hair poking out. Her companion walked by her side, staring ahead, his hair cropped low and face hairless. He wore black trousers and a black vest with a white shirt underneath. His black shoes were shined, as glossy as his eyes that floated in the bony cradles of their sockets.

Saint told everyone to come to Creek's Bridge at sunset and to bring whatever meal they can to share. "Everything you can spare and even what you can't," she said. The musicians were to bring their instruments. She told everyone to dress in something to dance in. As soon as she finished speaking, wild strawberry pies went into the oven and someone started roasting a pig, boiling turnip and collard greens, enough to feed the entire town. The children searched for clothes to wear and waved garments over their laughter like flags.

When time came to head over to Creek's Bridge, they went straight to the water. Lanterns hanging on pikes arranged in a circle, a large bonfire in the center, made it bright enough that they saw everything in front of and all around them. Food furnished a few tables farther from the creek and the fiddlers began to play.

Saint had changed into a small white dress with a large yellow ribbon wrapped around and knotted at the back. She wore no shoes and encouraged everyone to take off their own. She went to the bonfire and started clapping. Soon everyone clapped with her in unison *clap clap clap* and she began to dance, to twirl, and laugh. The children joined her first, then the women, hopping up and down and spinning about. The summer night had not cooled much since daytime, but they moved in the heat, the fire yanking sweat from their bodies, their naked feet sliding on the grass, their arms spinning above their heads. They touched their faces, put their fingers in their mouths, tugged on their ears and stomped the ground, their bodies moving and creating a new rhythm that the men had to change their claps to fit, the claps now being determined by the dancers moving, while the men got to stomping and shouting joyfully, syncopating their palms to the women and children and if the men got off beat they fixed that by paying close attention to the feet blurring and kicking and stomping near the fire so they laid down their instruments and played a song with their bodies and their heads got to nodding and hips to rocking to gyrating to the claps pulsating around them changing changing changing and their mouths open and the funk of the body let loose the sweat the stink all in the hair until somebody hollered something beyond a word and they kept on hollering it the sound leading into another sound into a new sound loud from the mouth like a spirit trying to answer the bodies or the bodies trying to answer the spirit that wouldn't be contained as their legs kicked and their heads rolled until their movements spoke in Tongues and the throat got to letting out a moan here and a groan there and the sound of pain left their flesh while their muscular bodies and their thin bodies and their fat bodies and their sickly bodies glistened in the fire and every child screamed as they jumped and spun and every man clapped moaned and testified with their feet to what sounded like it hurt so bad must have hurt them so bad coming up out the body out the burning well of the throat out the wet of their spit wailing lifting up from the bodies now contortion-flexed and contracting on the ground eyes fluttering in their heads the body creating a new way of being a new way of thinking creating a new knowledge that belonged to them—then Saint stopped moving and stood up; her body shook and shined. Her companion brought her a rooster and a knife. She struggled to keep herself still and raised her arms in the air, the rooster in one hand and the knife in the other, and screamed as she separated the rooster's head from its body in one clean swipe. At that moment, Saint felt The Gate, the breach between the living realm and the spiritual realm, swing open over the creek. Everyone stopped moving. Their bodies heaved in the flame-bent light, in the grooves they made in the earth with their feet.

Without much thought, they all went to the creek and let the water's flow rinse first their feet, then their knees as they knelt, then their faces, their entire bodies cleansed in the running water, the water taking with it all that wasn't theirs to carry: their bruises, their traumas, their hardened melancholy. They returned to the fire to dry off and admire each other's faces in the warm light. Out of breath, they sat and reclined, naked, and none rushed to hide themselves while the ground, the earth that had once haunted them, felt softer beneath them.

[4]

The lay of the land in Ours: four horizontal roads stretching west to east, the northernmost street being Tanager, followed by Oriole, Freedom, and then Bank at the southern end of town. Intersecting those roads were unnamed roads that became First, Second, and Third, moving from the most western road to the most eastern.

Everyone decided if they wanted to change their own names or keep the ones they had. Someone said, "If our masters not no more our masters then they names our belonging anyway." That seemed to settle it for some. They had their names for as long as they could remember and had shared those names with loved ones for just as long. But one woman did want to change her name. She said, "From now on my name is Miss. Not Ren. Miss. And my second name is Love." Miss Love they called her from there on out.

This caused a small commotion because not everyone had used the word "miss" as an honorific. "Mistress" or "master" they had used for any white woman, while a few Ouhmey had never spoken to a white woman before in their life, thus never needing an honorific for them. There were even some who never used "miss" amongst each other, choosing "mother," "maman," "gammy," "sister," "ma'am," "nene," or "elder" instead. So, when Miss Love shared her new name, they wondered why she would want to call herself a name absent of love or lonesome for it.

"What she want to miss love for?"

"Maybe she lost her husband years back. Or some children. Poor thing."

"Then why not call herself Have so she can have her some new love?"

"She got the right to miss it if the kind she want not here. I might call myself Miss. Miss Wife, cause I shole miss her. She was selled a year after we was married."

And that's how Paton became Miss Wife.

THE CITY OF DELACROIX neither encouraged nor discouraged Negroes from working there as long as they arrived on time, behaved themselves, and left when time to leave. Plenty of work needed doing, and the white population would pay; they would usually pay less, but they would pay.

The distance between Ours and Delacroix was walkable, tested by Franklin Chisholm, a wiry man with a penchant for keeping to himself, who acted as guardian of Thylias Chisholm, a heavyset and reticent fifteen-year-old girl, though she and the rest of Ours thought she was older. Franklin headed north to find work, to see if he would be accepted in some fashion. "What you good at?" he asked himself, and responded that he could handle any animal and butcher it just as easily. That is the job he found for himself at York's Butchery. When he returned to Ours, he said it took him an hour to get there. "Took no time at all and with a horse it be quicker," he said.

Before anyone headed north, Saint had placed a stone with a dollar coin tied to it beneath a bush behind her house. She covered the stone in lemon grass and grain alcohol a week prior to everyone's travel. The Ouhmey went up a few at a time and many found something to do: watching the young ones, cleaning houses, cobbler work and shoe shining, baking, and farming. Saint smiled when each one returned successful.

Miss Wife had the most difficulty finding work. When he gave his name to interested parties, they thought he wanted to make a fool of them.

"First name," they would ask.

"Miss, sir," Miss would respond.

"Pardon?"

"Miss."

"Spell it."

"M-I-S-S."

"Is that short for something?"

"Miss my name."

"Last name, then."

"Wife."

They sent him home that moment. After several tries over the course of several days, he returned each time more dejected than before. Ours, then, would be where he worked, and he wouldn't be the only one. Miss Love worked in Ours, too, as a baker, offering her skills in exchange for carpentry, some sewing, a week's worth of foot rubs.

"Whatever you want, I'll make it right," she would say, and kept her word.

Her sincerity made her popular. "I'll make it right," she said each time, and each time it felt as though she knew exactly the burden her customers needed lifted, believing her baking would get the job done. Corn bread muffins, pound cakes, small loaves with dried fruit and chocolate in them. Each seemed to be their own remedy for her customer's tribulations.

Miss Wife had no skills of his own. He was a young man, registered in the so-called master's burned ledger of slaves as being twenty years old for better to sell him if needed, but he was actually twenty-seven. He wasn't very handsome and boomed when he spoke, so there was no superficial reason to want to be near him and he knew it. He punched the ground and cried into the road after Delacroix made it clear they wouldn't allow him to work within its town limits. No one in Ours needed to work because Ours had everything they needed, but pride was on the line and to be a working people meant a lot to them.

Miss Love took pity on the man. In her thirty-three years she had never seen someone so distinctly useless. She understood even more why he missed his wife so. 'He may never get another,' she thought, and invited him in to teach him a different way to use his hands.

The man Miss Love had legally married in a two-window cabin, witnessed by her then so-called master, a few enslaved Africans, and a frenzied menagerie of farm animals, wasn't the man she loved, and she was thankful he didn't stay with her. Whatever happened to him she had no clue, just assumed he had run away or been sold off. The latter made her terribly sad, so she decided only to assume he ran off in the middle of night into the surrounding woods and did so because he wanted freedom more than a wife who didn't want him.

She tended to the world with this ambivalence, doing things for love of mankind with zero interest in loving a specific man, though not minding if a specific man loved on her enough to convince her he should be allowed to stick around for the time being. Specificity bored her, such that when her husband went missing, she then started to have feelings for him again as if his no longer being there somehow made him larger than he had been and therefore more possible in his largeness. Miss Wife, with the changing of his name into pure longing, confused Miss Love with his determination to be with a woman forever, a woman who would be there, just be there and nothing more.

It didn't take long for Miss Wife to propose to Miss Love and it took even less time for her to reject him. In 1840, he tried again. He had been baking with her for five years by then and secretly developed his own recipe during that time. On the days Miss Love spent hours at the Delacroix market, Miss Wife managed the bakery, cooking milk down with sugar and butter. He discovered for himself caramel but called it brown cream. By the time Miss Love returned, Miss Wife had spilled hot brown cream on his arm that left a burn in the shape of a smile. More importantly, though, he had baked a three-tier cake covered in brown cream.

"You made caramel," she said. "You made a whole caramel cake. Who taught you that?"

"A what? This here brown cream," Miss Wife said.

"What you made is caramel and"—Miss Love swiped her pinky across the top of the cake and collected a generous lump and tasted—"Oh, Miss."

"I made it for you," he said.

Miss Love teared up. The last time someone gave her something, she didn't want it. Her legal husband had given it to her, her legal husband to whom she was still married but hadn't seen in years, so much time gone by that she couldn't recall his face. He had meaningfully but immaturely brought to her a gift. "This for you," he had said, and held his palm open to reveal a light gray stone. She rubbed and rubbed that stone to calm her nerves, its smoothness to her the best gift anyone could've given her. She put it under her pillow and rubbed it until she fell asleep each night. But then he went missing and the stone with him, which let her know that he meant to keep the stone with him always and had simply loaned it to her. He left his wife but kept the rock.

"Miss Love," Miss Wife said, but she had already walked away, shaking her head as she exited the front door and scurried down the road.

Thereafter, Miss Wife left his home in the morning and came to work face-to-face with Miss Love's silence. They didn't speak and the sound of dough slapping across the table and pans clanking into the oven were heightened into torture by this silence. Miss Wife stole glances of Miss Love, hoping to catch her doing the same, but she spent the day looking past him as though he were a tree—baffling, intrusive, but a nonevent after all—that had grown in the middle of the bakery, as though he didn't make brown cream just for her the day before.

On the third day of silence, Miss Wife asked his friend Aba for advice and received a shave. Aba, who sold most of the fruit in Ours, was sitting outside on his porch, cutting up small apples into halves and eating them seeds and all. People thought him strange but wise, the closest thing to a confidant Saint had, and besides bartering and selling meticulously picked fruit already washed in a bucket beneath the selling table, he passed along advice that often made little sense to those who received it.

While Aba rubbed Miss Wife's face with oak ash soap, Miss Wife complained about the silence he had been receiving from Miss Love. Aba slid the blade down Miss Wife's cheek and tufts of curly black hair followed. The glossy curls landed on Aba's porch and Miss Wife's bare shoulders, the dark brown cheek smoothed and shining.

"You was looking wolfish," Aba said, turning Miss Wife's face by the chin to observe his work. He smiled. "Now you just look mannish." Aba carried over a bucket of water for Miss Wife to use as a mirror. "See yourself as yourself and tell yourself nice things."

"That's me?" Miss Wife asked. It had been years since he had a proper shave by skilled hands. He knew Aba was a friend because of how beautiful Aba made him feel. A good friend will show you the good they see in you.

"See what she say tomorrow about today's you," Aba said. "If she got a pea of sense, she'll lose her senses and be with you."

On the fourth day of silence between the two, Miss Love left the last business hour of the bakery in Miss Wife's hands and took an evening stroll, flustered by Miss Wife's new appearance that broke her into a sweat as she stole glances while sweeping flour from table to hand but missing her hand. She returned just before dark with creek water at the hem of her dress and all about her legs. 'Just a dip,' she thought when she arrived at Creek's Bridge. 'Just a toe.'

The walk had been tiring but necessary. It was a warm March day, warmer than natural, but the water still ran cold with winter. By the time she reached her home, the sun had arced down into a basket of trees, one tree much larger than the others. She wouldn't live to see the day when the children named that tree God's Place.

The creek lay east, just outside of town, and ran north to south like a minor Mississippi River. Someone decades before had built a small but beautiful open-air bridge. No intricate railings and no baroque deck. Just a swift cobblestone arch over a trench of shallow, moving water. It was out of the ordinary to see stonework in a place where everything, even teeth, was made from wood, as though the bridge itself were a gateway to another world. She wondered if during her brief stay in that other world she saw Miss Wife naked amongst the rest of her neighbors. It seemed recent that she and everyone else had sat nude as opossums down there in the wet with Saint. Would she be able to remember seeing a man of whom, at the time, she had no awareness?

Many of the folks in Ours still carried with them a broken-mirror self they were figuring out how to piece back together. They saw the shards of who they were and couldn't fathom how to make themselves whole again. 'Just pick one,' Miss Love thought, 'just pick up a shard and know that be you looking back at you.' It made sense when she first thought it, but now, seeing all the stones in the creek, so many smooth stones but none of them her original gift, she realized they were once part of a larger stone. The entire mirror needed fixing, every shard in its place to make the whole. That's when she understood the truth about her hurt. It wasn't her legal husband taking the stone that had affected her so; it was that the taking had attached to it a part of her that was hollow, and now even the hollow was gone.

SUNSET LIKE A halved blood orange, and Miss Wife was sitting in a chair in front of Miss Love's home. She had to let him know that during business hours he could linger all he wanted, but when night came waltzing down the road, the bakery became her house again, like a fairy tale, and he had to waltz down the road as well, back to his own private space in the world.

"We closed now," she said, which were the first words spoken between them in days. "We closed," she repeated. And he sat there as though he didn't hear her, staring off to the west as the sun dropped, and it seemed to him that the sun bled in the sky like that because of Miss Love's disapproval.

Miss Wife investigated Miss Love's face, wanting to see if his feelings made sense. For all he knew, he only wanted to pull his old wife out of a property ledger that had moved her name from one column into another, consequently moving her from one plantation to another roughly one hundred miles away. Clotho. 'Her name was Clotho,' he thought, summoning her into himself, then imagining her image beside Miss Love, not to compare but just to be sure they didn't favor and that he wasn't stuck trying to force alive a dead thing.

Up there, the bleeding in the sky neared its end and purpled behind

Miss Love. 'She can even bruise God,' Miss Wife thought, then said to Miss Love, "I was just waiting to make sure you got back safe. I be on my way," and stood and walked home. Miss Love lingered outside until he shrank to nothing in the distance.

It had grown dark when they met up accidentally in the middle of Oriole Street on Second Street. They both saw a wobbling light approach them from the opposite direction and when they got upon each other, they were surprised to see that they both had the same idea. Miss Wife had decided to visit Miss Love and Miss Love had thought to do the same to Miss Wife. Shocked into stupor, they settled on standing close for a little while without talking, just standing there softly gazing at each other, then going back to their separate homes.

When Miss Wife next proposed, Miss Love said yes. From their marriage came baby Luther-Philip Wife, born April 2, 1841.

[5]

Saint spent most of her days walking around Ours alone, her companion waiting somewhere in the darkest room of her house. She greeted everyone and knew everyone by name. Thylias once said about Saint that she could see everybody's seeing, and this carried some truth, considering Saint had grown accustomed to conjuring for the entire town, even if it meant one conjure contradicted another. In many ways, she had become a resource toward better understanding a world they had been locked away from, but more importantly she helped them retrieve parts of themselves they had forgotten belonged to them, beginning first with resolve. If they wanted something done, do it. If they needed help, just ask. Saint made herself available for the asking, and the more they knew they could ask for anything, the more they learned that they could receive. Even if she rejected their requests, the rejection belonged to them. For this, they were grateful to Saint.

For her own sanity, Saint refused to do more than that. She conjured but did not lead, gave advice but was no mentor. Ours didn't have a mayor. Wasn't even a discussion about getting someone to do it. Had they asked her, there was no telling how loud she would've laughed in their faces. They wanted her around more, to do things with them, an appeal for her to allow them to fall in love with her. Saint knew all about love, and she believed her refusal to give it protected both herself and Ours.

· CHAPTER 3 ·

Plague of Arrogance

[1]

Eventually, the corpses of white folks appeared miles away from Ours, making a strange and inexplicable perimeter of death. Patrollers marked where the bodies were found with red flags. Few people were unaffected by whatever killed off folks, but theirs was a minuscule number. Soon, white folks started heeding the red flags, not wanting to test if they had immunity to whatever disease floated up that way.

Walking just an inch within the red flags' border caused severe sickness. Some noticed that this sickness didn't yet happen to any Negroes but did affect some of the Indigenous Americans, discovered only when a white patroller who scanned those death grounds noticed the body of, in his own words, "an Indian without breath or color."

When all the flags were put into place, a St. Louisan schoolteacher noticed that within the rectangular perimeter existed a single town, a recently "colored" town as he had put it, and that the source of this white death was more than likely in Ours. Flyers went around explaining the "White Plague," and no new Negro was allowed into St. Louis for all of 1841, purchased or not; it took that long for Saint to realize that she had marked the stones she placed around Ours with the wrong symbol, meaning only to deter those whom she deemed potential problems for Ours's residents, including sheriffs, politicians, patrollers, anyone dealing with the law and enslavement; and to kill those who at any point in time had enslaved others. Instead, her stones were set to destroy anyone who had ever thought at any time that Negroes were less than human, for which she felt little pity, more so mortification that she had made a mistake like that after having so long dealt with stonework. It wasn't until a day or so before she decided to change the stones that Negroes started to drop dead where once they hadn't.

"I see," she said to herself when told by some of her people that they found Negroes dead on a path a few miles north. The Ouhmey didn't have what they needed to bury them, but Saint told them not to worry. The earth was better off.

After a sheriff captured a white runaway prisoner alive just a mile away from Ours, near enough for death to have occurred earlier in the year, the St. Louisans realized that the plague had gone away on its own. They lifted the ban on Negroes but the fearful attitude toward them, as well as their absence from certain parts of St. Louis, remained the same from then on.

Eventually, Saint wanted better protection from the stones that didn't attract as much attention from outsiders. She created a new pattern that would hide Ours. She went to the east and south stones and replaced them while her companion replaced the west and north stones. From then on, Ours was marked on maps but impossible to find. People who wanted to visit to either cause trouble or interview citizens there about the plague found themselves standing in an open field where they expected Ours to be.

Everyone living in Ours had to be marked with a small scratch somewhere on their bodies in order to return to Ours if they left for any reason.

"But when we leave, won't it look like we came from nothing?" someone asked.

Saint shook her head and said, "You will always look like you are approaching from the visible horizon. People not walking over Ours or even through it. They're going around it and not knowing so."

This confused most of the residents, but a few understood and those few understanding it seemed to satisfy the rest. Some pretended to understand and that, too, gave comfort.

[2]

During the summer of 1846, a reporter from Delacroix attempted to follow a wagon full of Ouhmey home, hoping to discover where Ours lay hidden. He trailed them on horseback and marked any interesting landscape. To the west, a large mound afire with daylilies appeared after fifteen minutes of travel. After thirty minutes, bladed sycamore leaves suddenly sliced the sky above the shoulder of a hill, the increasing verdancy filling out the dull blue horizon. Oblivious, caught gaping at the sharp-white sky, the reporter realized he no longer saw the wagon. Thinking he had accidentally slowed down, he quickened the horse's pace into full gallop. Passing through a mist, he cursed when he noticed a rickety wooden sign explaining he had entered St. Louis, meaning he had somehow passed Ours.

He made several attempts and each time he lost the wagon, distracted by a bird swarm or his own mental ramblings coming to him with the dual rhythm of the walking horses and the wagon's squeaking wheels. Then the squeaking stopped. And there the hypnosis of atmosphere overpowered the reporter and put him to sleep. Lethargy overcame him at the same location each time: the mist, the near-ceaseless galloping, and, at the end of it all, the rickety sign taunting him.

Huffing, he decided to ride his horse beside the Ours wagon, ignoring the people's horrified expressions as he tried to make conversation with the horseman. When he gathered that all he could get from him was a disinterested "No, suh" or "I can't say I know, suh," he rode in silence and took brief notes without looking down at his notebook. They passed the mound that appeared to burn brighter beneath the red tongues of daylilies, then made their way through the thickening woods that threw down bough-shadow, sycamore leaves waving their shaded arrowheads above the reporter. He realized he had fallen asleep on his horse after his own snoring woke him and the shock of it sent him falling off his horse and into the tall, bladed grass. By then, the wagon was completely gone and the rickety sign reading "St. Louis ahead" mocked him for the last time.

When he returned to Delacroix, no one believed his ghost story and didn't care to investigate for themselves. He took out his notes to read over the descriptions of the landscape. Much of his writing consisted of illegible lines drawn down the page, signaling where he had dozed off. Single words floated vaguely on the page. Page after page of frantic scribbles until he came to an intricate portrait drawn in pen that startled him. It depicted a woman, Negro, and was drawn with incredible skill as though he had been a trained portraitist all his life. He rubbed his fingers across the page to feel the grooves the pen made with each line because it made her more real. 'Maybe this woman was on the wagon,' he thought, and dedicated the rest of his day to finding her while forgetting that he had no artistic ability in the least with which to sketch.

The reporter stopped every Negro in his path and asked, abrupt and cross, if they knew the woman depicted in the drawing. Everyone said no.

"What is this woman's name?" he asked, forcing the page into their faces. Still, whomever he asked politely feigned ignorance. He tried to threaten them, but even though he was white, his authority reached less there than anywhere else in the nation, as Delacroix had no laws banning Negroes from rejecting any level of advance from white folks.

He considered using intimidation, but his diminutive stature and own pallid complexion, much more intense than any others around him of his own race, ghosted him even out of his own imagination, such that he couldn't empower himself to raise his voice or puff out his rib cage where a chest of any sort should've been.

The reporter searched the busy streets, bumping into patrons and tightly packed vendors. Down the bustling road, past the butcher whose assistant he had already bothered for information, he found the assistant's son who shined shoes. The boy was no more than five years old, a seemingly easy-to-frighten child with big brown eyes and a tearful gaze of perpetual anxiety. When the reporter demanded the boy tell him the name of the woman in the drawing, the boy looked back to get his father's attention, but his father was busy quartering chickens. The boy looked again at the drawing and started to cry.

"This is not the time for your tears," the reporter said, kneeling and far too close to the boy's face. "Tell me who this woman is."

The boy moved his mouth to speak but something behind the reporter caught his attention. He pointed behind the reporter, who turned, prompting the boy to run off into the crowd.

Saint's blue dress and eventually her stern and stone-smooth face snatched the reporter's attention. He yipped in shock and turned red after hearing the ping of his bright voice. Saint smiled, her high cheekbones carved malevolent, and leaned a little on her snakehead staff.

"Little dog," she said.

"You" is all the reporter managed to say, his tongue fear-clumsy. He stood, tugged at his limp shirt collar, and, feeling more confident, showed her the sketch. Haughtily, the reporter shut the notebook with one hand close to Saint's face, the breeze from the notebook's closing causing her to blink. The reporter continued, "I must get into Ours."

Saint smiled and examined the activity around them. Vendors pushed carts of assorted crops, carpenters sawed planks of wood, while within the crowd each Ouhmey face froze in place, watching.

"What business do you have there?" she asked.

"There is word that your town is the center of a scandal. Death. It is imperative that I get—"

"You do not have my permission."

"The deaths of dozens of white men give me permit."

"That was long ago," Saint said. "And it had nothing to do with Ours; rather it was a coincidence of location."

"You will take me to Ours." He raised his voice and spat as he spoke.

Saint flipped her wrist and an ivory lace fan blossomed from her hands. She covered her mouth and yawned. The reporter jumped when she snapped the fan shut. "It was a pleasure meeting you . . ." She tilted her head.

"Marcellus Addington," the reporter said. "I will have your audience."

"Mr. Addington," Saint said. "A pleasure, indeed." She turned to leave but Marcellus grabbed her shoulder and spun her around. Wind picked up, then a burst of thunder shook the ground. At the sight of her eyes—both pupils and irises milk white, blue veins marbling—he released her and stumbled back. "That sketch was a warning. This, Mr. Addington, is a promise." She blinked, her eyes gone back brown as her eyelids opened. Saint rubbed her thumb against her staff, massaging the carving of a snake's jaw that, to Marcellus's witness, whipped out a split tongue.

Before Marcellus could gather himself, Saint departed. Quick as she had appeared she disappeared, into the throng, taking the sudden winds with her. Marcellus flipped through his notebook to reference the sketch once more, but the sketch had disappeared.

THE FINAL TIME Marcellus tried to get into Ours, he succeeded. Marcellus had jumped into the evening wagon heading to Ours. All went according to plan, which was no plan at all, simply him riding with the baffled workers who seemingly had no interest or energy in rejecting him.

As usual, he fell into a stupor once they reached the more wooded area, but this time when he came to, he found himself sitting on a chair inside a beautiful room. Fabrics of many colors made rivers along the floor and walls. Curtains hid what little sunlight remained of the approaching evening and dozens of candles lit throughout the room turned the fabric into frozen undulations scattered about the floor. As if he were underwater and on fire all at once. He tried to stand but couldn't. He wanted to scratch his face, but his arms wouldn't obey. Only his head was free to survey the rest of the room. When he saw the off-white chair in front of the wall of books, he thought nothing of its strange style, much more intricate than anything familiar to him, but the longer he looked, the more frightened he became. The chair, more like a throne, was made entirely out of bones.

It took a few days for people in Delacroix to realize Marcellus was missing. They assumed he went crazy chasing after the ghost town and just ended up in trouble, possibly eaten by a pack of coyotes. Eventually, all of Delacroix carried on as though Marcellus had never been part of their community. To do so was easier than wild speculation that what happened to him could also happen to anyone else there. When he finally reappeared, his hair was white along the side of his scalp and completely gone in the center. His eyes were both heavy and wide with alertness. When he spoke, gibberish tainted his tongue.

[3]

In autumn of 1846, Saint began to have vicious afternoon headaches. Nothing eased them, no combination of boiled herb and flower and no stones laid across her body. She would lie on her back while sunlight shrank and expanded around her, whistling as it did so. One throb caused the light to widen, and the whistle's pitch and volume went shrill and high. The next throb caused the light to shrink to the width of a coin and the whistle's pitch and volume fell hum-like and low.

When the light beamed its widest and the whistle's timbre shrieked, she saw through the blur of her pain a shadowy figure standing at the foot of her bed. He didn't seem menacing so she didn't fear him. He felt familiar, and though she couldn't see his face, she knew he watched her with unbreakable urgency. An hour passed before she could move without her companion's help, and once the headache stopped, she felt terribly hungry but otherwise well. The shadowy figure disappeared forever after the first appearance.

The headaches, however, repeated every Monday afternoon from 3:00 p.m. till just before 4:00 p.m. Then out of the blue, on the first day of 1847, the headaches stopped and never returned. She documented this in a leather-bound journal where she kept many happenings in her life as well as recipes, lists of conjures and when they were made, dreams and their interpretations, predictions, and enemies. In one note she had written about a man coming to her wanting to save his already-dead wife. "He will come to me in the evening, years from now. There will be eight of us in the room. A light will come and breath to the dead." She considered what she had written. The prediction was short and a bit elusive. Some people who visited her for conjure knew clearly what they wanted without shame. Others who sought her help arrived at her doorstep with despair clouding their judgment, just enough to make devastation into curiosity. Saint hoped that the man wouldn't come to her with hope, for she didn't have the gift of raising the dead and her awareness of this sat heavy in her heart.

Perhaps the journal's most important task was to keep Saint's memory in line. She couldn't recall anything before the moment she found herself lying facedown on a beach in Florida almost a century ago and the times between then and now were so fragmented she could barely remember the day, month, or year. Conjures slipped from her memory as soon as she put them to paper. She wrote, "Cannot remember root for ease of mind. Conjure for protection against evil eye didn't work last time I tried." What conjures she retained lost potency or backfired in shocking ways.

She had written the details of her headaches: dates, day, time, duration of pain. The pattern unfolded consistently but its meaning, if there was meaning, escaped her. Yes, she had once seen a shadow, a figure clad in dark, made of the dark, she remembered and wrote that down as well as "familiar," "not friendly but not evil," "watching me." She closed her journal. Her companion stood beside her the entire time, facing away as if to give her privacy, though he couldn't read or write or understand without her permission.

[4]

By the time he was six years old, Luther-Philip read with the ten-year-olds. Every day before and after school, Mrs. Wife went over the letters and sentences with him.

In the evenings, they closed the bakery and retired in a room in the back with two beds, one for the couple and the other for the son. Until sunlight ran out, Luther-Philip read. Then Mr. Wife would light a lantern so Luther-Philip could read some more over dinner. Mrs. Wife tickled Luther-Philip if he got a word wrong and fed him some brown cream bread if he got a word right.

After Luther-Philip fell asleep, Mrs. and Mr. Wife went back into the front of their home and prepared for next day's bakery rush. Mrs. Wife coughed and covered her mouth with her arm so as not to wake their son. She saw drops of blood in the nook of her elbow.

Luther-Philip woke the next morning smelling the usual fresh baked bread and hearing his father's footsteps enter the room to help him get ready for school. They walked the half mile together, Mr. Wife squeezing the top of his son's head and Luther-Philip giggling and squirming to get away. Luther-Philip practiced spelling words he learned the day before: p-a-p-e-r, paper; f-r-i-e-n-d-s-h-i-p, friendship; s-i-g-n, sign.

"How you remember all these words so well, son?" Mr. Wife asked.

"Sometimes, you have to see a thing to remember it, Papa," Luther-Philip said, and at the sight of his friend Justice waving from the school door, ran off without Mr. Wife. He turned briefly to see his father and grinned. Mr. Wife smiled back, considering his son's words.

The bakery still hurried with activity when Mr. Wife returned home, and he immediately got to work. Mrs. Wife was finishing up a cake when he got in. She coughed and shook her head. Mr. Wife brought her a cup of water. She drank it down and seemed all right until the coughs knelt her over.

"Been coughing all since you been gone. I tasted a piece of bread and choked. Haven't been right since," she said. Mr. Wife remembered the coughing had started the night before but said nothing. They pushed through the day and by the time the sun split purple on the horizon, Mrs. Wife had a fever and, knowing a fever could kill, Mr. Wife asked a neighbor to watch Luther-Philip while he ran to Saint's for help.

When he returned with Saint, Mrs. Wife had gotten much worse. Neighbors couldn't keep her cool with fans and water they dripped onto her face. She refused to drink anything and had grown pale. Within minutes, her fever became the death sentence Mr. Wife feared and his eyes clouded with tears.

Saint glared at Mrs. Wife. She stunk like an aged man, boozy with rum. When she blinked, Mrs. Wife was facing her. When Saint blinked again, Mrs. Wife's face had become that of a coal-skinned man with red eyes. Saint flinched and the man-face winked and grinned. A gold tooth flashed from the top row of his teeth. He rolled his face away from Saint and when his head rolled back, it was Mrs. Wife's again.

"Everyone out," Saint spat. "Everyone out of this damned house!"

"Saint—" Mr. Wife started but decided to gather everyone there and lead them out after he saw the impossible emotion chiseled across Saint's face.

Saint stood motionless in the stuffy room. A chair waited for her at the bedside, but she knew better than to go anywhere near Mrs. Wife's sick body. She stood and she waited. The lantern light tossed soft shadows on the walls that groaned and let in all the chatter and hisses of tree branches outside. Mrs. Wife moaned. Saint waited. Mrs. Wife laughed and the stench of cigar smoke filled the air. Her head dropped to the side, facing Saint. When Mrs. Wife opened her eyes, they were the sick red of a fresh wound.

Saint had only a marginal sense of familiarity for the possession she witnessed, as though a vacancy in her memory kept trying to refill with some truth. Never had she been possessed in this way, but she felt perhaps she had witnessed such a thing long ago and been less fearful. And with this present fear came a need to bow. She couldn't help herself and knelt before Mrs. Wife's bed on both knees and lowered her head like a devoted priest.

In a man's voice, Mrs. Wife said, "Why did the rooster cross the crossroad?" and laughed. The man's voice boomed and stuffed the room until the walls creaked. Finished, the spirit in Mrs. Wife went quiet, then scowled at Saint. "You never welcomed me," he said. "You never asked my permission to bring your shit into my home." He spat on the floor with Mrs. Wife's mouth. "Who you think you is? Throwing filth into my home. Leaving The Gate open." He spat again. "I should level this whole town. Arrogant filth. Amnesiac sphynx. Go close The Gate, fool, or more than water bring you down." Mrs. Wife went silent. It was over. The possessor's rage had expired and with it the smell of smoke dissipated until stale air floated throughout the room with nowhere to escape but through the chinkless roof. Mrs. Wife's body stopped moving and Saint didn't try to heal it. There was no one left inside the body to heal.

"There was nothing I could do," Saint said, storming by Mr. Wife and his neighbors. She continued speaking as she walked away. "Bury her immediately. Pour sea salt over the grave. I'll have the salt brought to you within the hour." With a quick stop, Saint looked off to the side and said, "I'm sorry," then marched on.

Mr. Wife said nothing, for it seemed Saint had apologized to the world, and who was he to respond for the world?

He took Luther-Philip by the shoulders and told him that his mother had died. He asked Luther-Philip if he understood and the boy nodded, astounded into calm. The boy would stay with Franklin and Thylias for the night. Mr. Wife and a few men from town wrapped Mrs. Wife's body in fresh linen and carried her to what was to become the cemetery: the only open land in town that stretched south by the easternmost road, Third Street, and south of Bank. Mr. Wife unwrapped his wife's face, touched her cheek, then rewrapped her.

After digging all night, Mr. Wife and the men poured the sea salt over her wrapped body before covering her with dirt, then covered the dirt with the remaining salt. In the lantern light, Mr. Wife caught a glimpse of the men's faces: confusion touched by anger. "I thought Saint—" one man began to say, then stopped. When Mr. Wife asked him to repeat himself, the man shook his head and said, "Naw, that's all right." But Mr. Wife had already heard the growing distrust in the grunts of the dirt-shoveling men, the question as to why Saint couldn't, didn't save Mrs. Wife. If she could free them all unscathed, why not this, too?

Back at the small house that doubled as a bakery, Mr. Wife swept the bedroom floor. He removed the damp, tobacco-smelling sheets and blankets from the bed he and his wife shared. Without questioning the pungent smell that rose from the linen's dull creases, he set the sheets and blankets on fire behind the house along with the dust he swept from the floor. Saint's companion had delivered the sea salt in a tied-up woolen satchel with a note of instructions hanging from the closed mouth of the bag. Tucked just under the string that held everything together was a small bottle of oil. He poured the oil into a bucket of water and cleaned the entire floor, back to front. When he finished, the room smelled sweet like a pine forest, and in that forest he laid himself down and wept.

[5]

Saint had put her own in danger and therefore become dangerous. While her companion delivered sea salt and oil to Mr. Wife, she visited Creek's Bridge. By the water, she undressed and asked for forgiveness. The creek fell silent for a moment, then sang again against the rocks its acceptance. She stepped into the cold water and, kneeling, hand-washed her entire body. It was late March and thirteen years had passed since she opened The Gate at the creek to throw in all the traumas her newly freed followers had experienced: lashing after rape after stolen spouse after sold-off child after starvation, all thrown into The Gate to free their spirits from enslavement, to give even the soul a second chance, but because she didn't close The Gate, anything could stomp from the other side and freely ride the back of anyone in town.

Spirits always live near water, this Saint knew, but some spirits require an invitation and instructions, neither of which she knew to give. She was rash, then, in her execution, and working with half a memory only made her more reckless.

While in the creek to close The Gate, she tried to remember beyond Florida's swamp water, but lightning cut jagged scars of light across the darkness of her own blank mind. Then came bizarre fruits and birds more colorful than a garden, and a brilliant storm catastrophized the sky above her while a subtle sadness stretched beneath the front of her skull until it popped and the living memory dissolved.

After she bathed, she cut open her palm and let blood drip into the creek. Because she had not closed The Gate properly and for years its now insatiable mouth had been open, she gave of herself to it. There were other, less painful methods, but she couldn't remember them. She only remembered that she had known them before. Still, Ours was lucky that the spirit that crossed over the water warned Saint with a single death instead of vanquishing everything she had built, one citizen at a time. One casualty was an immeasurable gift.

Familiar, the face of the spirit that possessed Mrs. Wife wouldn't leave her. It appeared when she wrapped her hand to stop her palm from bleeding. It lingered when she rubbed olive oil on her skin and tied several matches to her hair. On her way home, the face followed her like a neighbor sharing late-night gossip. It stayed with her when she refused to look at the bakery from which still emanated cigar stink that her protection wash pushed from the inside out. The face watched as she removed her shoes, covered them in sulfur, and burned one shoe on the front porch and one out back. The face grinned at her when she drew a hot bath with seven drops of geranium oil, seven pinches of sage, a pinch of saltpeter, seven cloves of garlic, a splash of lavender petals, and seven basil leaves. After she dried off, the face grinned beside her own in the mirror. It was an uncle's face or a father who didn't take his fatherly duties too seriously but knew how his praise alone could feel like all the love in the world. Hairless face, wide nose gold-ringed twice on one side. Beautiful onyx skin and the gaunt cheek grin he flashed her way, both reassuring, though the grin carried multiple meanings: a severe joy, the calm before the storm, an intricate expression of rage. The face's red eyes carried no desire to harm; rather they embodied harm itself. A single gold tooth would've, on any other occasion, made Saint laugh to herself, but all she could do was avoid its reproachful shine. And upon seeing this countenance in Mrs. Wife's room, her knees folded beneath her into a bow.

She did know this man, had to have known him. Why else did her fear soften into longing when his face disappeared, delicate as fog, after she peered into the mirror, as though the woman staring back at her was no longer enough?

She felt a similar kinship during her migraines when she had seen the man shrouded in complete darkness stand at the foot of her bed.

'Had to have been the same man,' she thought. At the snap of her fingers, Saint's companion closed the bedroom door. 'Had to have been the same spirit warning me as gently as he could, but I paid no mind, so he warned me less gently. He had been warning me all that time. Now look at this life.'

She invited her companion to where she sat and made him stand beside her facing the mirror. His height impressive, the mirror's wooden frame cut off his reflection. Eyes full of harm, his face no longer sweet, he gazed vacantly ahead without blinking. Saint grabbed his hand, then let go, his lukewarm skin a map to nowhere. She unwrapped her hair and let the long twisted locs drop past her shoulders, down her long neck. She sighed, and her companion rubbed her hair, attention fixed on nothing specific. In the mirror, Saint watched herself cut a sneer, upper lip curling like a page on fire. She sighed once more, and her companion lowered his arm. 'Death all around,' she thought. 'Death all around. For how long?'

Ours resided in Saint's shadow, its own shadow melting in her umbra's hold. She had freed the slaves and promised them a safe home, promised them freedom, something she always remembered having in some capacity for she could read whatever books she wanted, smell a cut of lavender fallen into the bowl of her upturned palms, split a gleaming trout and fry it in cackling oil without permission, and make love whenever and however she wanted. She wore what fitted her desire, whetted her anger when it felt best to do so—often, remorselessly.

Freedom didn't mean safety. Saint wanted to supply both. But soon she felt herself falling in love with those she had saved, and if there's anything more shockingly unpredictable than freedom, it's love. If there is an unhealed wound, love takes the shape of the wound. She knew, from the moment Ours became real, that the shadow of her love was cast not by her but by her broad-shouldered, insatiable hurt. It would only widen if she stayed close, if she decided to love them all anyway. Accordingly, she stepped to the side, taking not only her wound but her love with her.

That night, while lying in bed, Saint heard "Why won't he stop howling inside his self?" and shot up, intemperate with ire. That voice, belonging to a woman named Aurora whom she had abandoned years ago in a small town of shacks just outside of Ours before Ours was founded, followed ghost-quick to her bedside. Aurora, at the end of her teenage years or the beginning of her twenties; Aurora, sold from a New Orleans plantation to an Arkansas one as punishment for beheading a rooster without permission, the so-called master in New Orleans dead the day after she was sold; Aurora, severely bowlegged and slow-walking, witty and verbose, had somehow heard a voice coming from Saint's companion who hadn't spoken a lick. Saint knew, already, that Aurora had a gift that involved listening in on the feelings of others. She made it clear to Aurora never to use her gift on people without their permission, and Aurora agreed, but Saint's companion bellowed on the inside. The harder Aurora tried to ignore, the more compelled she grew to listen. Got to be so intense her nose started bleeding. "Why won't he stop howling on the inside?" she had asked, crossing the most explicit boundary. Saint nearly assaulted the woman, but instead, she left the shoddy shacks thrown up too quickly to be considered safe, left behind those who had grown to love the first plot of land they had made their own. Saint left that intrusive woman on her own beat-up porch, went so fast she burned up her lungs with heavy breathing, distraught because a stranger heard a voice that she hadn't heard in months, no matter how hard she listened in the quiet of that dismal house. Behind her, Aurora apologized, screaming that she didn't mean to and that something truly was wrong with the man Saint traveled with.

Now, Saint made her companion sit outside her bedroom door in a chair pulled up to the wall adjacent her room. His gaze struck the opposite wall without anticipation or curiosity, eyes staring bloodshot, shown by lamplight hanging from a tilted wall hook. If he blinked, she missed it.

She closed her door and returned to bed, lowering her open window to only a crack as if that would keep the kindling of Aurora's voice from burning her ears. Still, she would be lying if she said she wasn't curious about Aurora's well-being out there in the wilderness, surrounded by raggedy shacks. "Aurora," Saint said, "at least you heard some life in him." Her snake staff caught her eye in the moonlight. She left her bed and grabbed the staff, bringing it back to bed and laying it beside her. "At least you heard a life in there."

· CHAPTER 4 ·

The Climb

[1]

Wanting to be nearer to death, Mr. Wife wrapped himself in his own filth. He became industrious for death, pumping out sweat and snot and tears, and rising only to relieve himself out back.

In the outhouse, the dark engulfed him and he decided that the sunlight angling toward him through the cracks in the roof and walls succeeded only in giving dust a way to be seen. It had already been made obvious to Mr. Wife that nothing left worth seeing endured after Mrs. Wife's death, and the reminder of such worthlessness hurt him into spite. He squatted, wiped clean with some leaves, and went back inside with a steeling hatred against the light.

When he visited the outhouse at night, moonlight carried the weight of his disdain, and because the darkness had more strength to it, the dust coalescing with the darkness, the moon's rays were too weak to carry the debris of the living (his grief) or the dead (his wife). A subtle glow fell through the roof of the outhouse and he thought of the lantern light that glided toward him the morning he and Mrs. Wife reconciled. In this way, the moon had won him over where the sun had failed him, and despite the cold, Mr. Wife sat in the reeking outhouse until daybreak.

Boredom shook Mr. Wife from trying to summon death through inactivity. Waiting for death in stillness made little sense anyway. It was when one least expected it that the heart popped behind the rib cage, the brain hemorrhaged inside the skull, or the veins themselves fell victim to a violent torpor that shut down the body while death scooped out what remained. A horse kick to the chest, the crash onto the stony ground from a fast-moving wagon, an overturned surrey floating down a river, a bullet nesting in the bag of a lung, or in the middle of laughter so sweet that when the dead finally realized they were dead, it was too late to get angry—those were ways death came, and Mr. Wife had to live in order to make room for the scythe. 'Mrs. Wife must have done some living before she died,' he thought. 'She must have had some living done to die that way.'

Luther-Philip had been staying with neighbors from all over town while his father rotted in the dim cell of the back room. They would see one another for a couple hours during the day, catching up on details and working on vocabulary words until, on cue with the setting sun, Mr. Wife stopped talking, stopped responding, and fell into a daze so toxic Luther-Philip could feel it enter him. "Heartbreak spread like pox," one woman had told Franklin, who ended up being the first neighbor to take in Luther-Philip. Franklin reluctantly spent the most time with the boy and therefore spent the most time in Mr. Wife's company. For this reason, he was the one to break the bad news.

Mr. Wife eventually reopened the bakery. He smelled bad standing up there taking morning bread orders and rolling dough, a little fecal around the waist and pungent under the arms. He stopped bathing after Mrs. Wife's passing but reopened the bakery as though he vowed to her that he would. Business stopped immediately after the first ripe whiff moved from behind the makeshift counter and toward the front door. Mr. Wife remained baffled by this until Franklin told him in the flattest voice available to him, "You do not smell nice."

Three and a half weeks after Mrs. Wife was buried in the new cemetery without ceremony, because no one organized for there to be one, Mr. Wife took a bucket of water, boiled it, and asked a neighbor for some soap. The neighbor, excited to hear what she described to her neighbors as "the good news," damn near threw the soap at him. It took four days for people to trust that he had cleaned himself well enough before visiting the bakery.

Because Franklin was first to care for Luther-Philip—the smallest six-year-old Franklin had ever seen and also the smartest—when Mr. Wife needed help, he began to care as would family. After a while, Luther-Philip called Franklin uncle and Franklin's heart burst wide open. Even still, he made sure not to get too close to the boy.

Bonding with Franklin also meant bonding with Thylias, Franklin's adopted daughter who people believed had sped past being a child because of her parentlessness. Thylias taught Luther-Philip how to clean a gun. His small hands could barely hold the thing, and though guns terrified him, he did it anyway because he enjoyed spending time with her. She was impatient but not cruel, which meant she moved fast and gave short answers with the expectation that because they were short they were memorable. She always wore her hair in a bun sitting at the top of her head. 'Bird's egg,' Luther-Philip thought, 'she wears a bird's egg ready to crack open.' After Luther-Philip cleaned the gun, she polished it to give him an example to follow, and the next day he had to polish it without her assistance. If he did something wrong, Thylias made the sound of a hungry sheep "at! at! at!" leaving Luther-Philip to guess where he had made the mistake. He often figured it out and Thylias did all her grinning on the inside.

After they cleaned and polished the gun, Franklin taught him how to load it and hunt. They started small with rabbits. After the first shot, Luther-Philip couldn't write in school for a week. The recoil nearly dislocated his shoulder. The teacher at the school lit into Franklin, calling him everything God willed her tongue to call him. No one respectable would repeat those words, but those who heard about the incident understood and let it pass. Mr. Wife laughed it all off. He couldn't hunt if he needed to and wanted Franklin to teach his son "but maybe just let him watch until he get a little older," he said to Franklin.

[2]

When Justice's mother, Honor, walks down the road, she is mineral, a block of obsidian chiseled into human shape with a tawdry dress thrown on for further convincing. Before Saint freed her, the question "What is she?" was her second name, or a third if you count her slave name, Mary, and her birth name that she never knew, Aminata, meaning trustworthy. But now she called herself Honor, showing the tricky nature of names and their power to circle back through time even when memory or the mouth fails. And that she chose this name for herself in a circle of faces she would call friends and enemies, though there would be only one true enemy, made her name more important to her. There were witnesses to her becoming.

"What is she?" she remembered being asked indirectly, it being asked about her to her once so-called master by his children, who were so pale that sunlight devoured their skin. The impeccable blisters. The intricate rashes. Children allergic to God Himself. They took to staying in the house most days or beneath the shelter of large hats that made them sweat so much it was embarrassing. That Honor could withstand the sunlight, absorb it even, and deepen the luster of her skin, frightened the children, their hats shading their peeling faces but not hiding their looks of derision.

"What is she?" asked because she was darker than their imagination could comprehend, her skin making necessary and tangible their doubt that she existed at all. She couldn't remember the answer the children were given by their father, only that they saw her and thought it impossible that the answer to the question asked of her would be the same had they asked it of themselves.

One thing was certain: Honor was stunningly beautiful and mysterious inasmuch as she had a name that meant integrity though she lied like a weary dog, everything from saying she didn't love King when she did, from lying on Saint that Saint's conjures were faulty and that she conned people into uneven barters for her services. And King, Justice's father, stood right there with her, spineless and needy, always up under the woman and chasing her shadow because she didn't allow him to chase her body. Whatever she said, he agreed with and eagerly challenged all opposition. Honor could've said a pig spoke French out its ass one morning and King would confirm the nonsense while growing irritable with anyone who said otherwise.

They had both gone to Saint to get rid of and keep closer the other. King had fallen in love with Honor the moment he laid eyes on her when they met during one of Saint's plantation raids. In the wilderness, while waiting on Saint to procure houses for them in what was then Graysville, he attempted to strike up a conversation with her but found he had nothing interesting to say. He instead complained about his foot, which had been hurting him since leaving the plantation, mentioning the sharp pain in the arches, his toes cramping in his too-little shoes.

Honor nodded politely, but after a few minutes of listening to him complain, her patience waned and in a flash of annoyance she said, "Would you be quiet about your feet? We all got pains." King quieted and turned away, only to moments later talk about what felt good on him. He shared how he breathed more easily, saw more clearly, and felt enough strength in his arms to split a tree. Honor's eyes glazed over until King mentioned her "pretty hands."

All her life, Honor had protected herself with deceit, knowing that telling the truth made her vulnerable because it made obvious her fears. She lied about everything to keep everything safe in her life, but when this man with a name too big for him said that she had pretty hands, complimented her when she had never been complimented, she reconsidered, briefly, the healing power of truth, for wasn't she smiling like a fool after hearing his embarrassingly earnest words? She said, "Thank you," and the two sat in tenseless silence.

When they finally arrived at Ours, they were given houses next door to one another. Encouraged to speak by this closeness, King greeted her each morning with a smile, wave, and quick nod that carried discomforting eagerness. Honor waved back half-heartedly and proceeded out her door to take care of her business. Later that afternoon, walking back arm in arm with her girlfriends wreathed in laughter, Honor spotted him sitting on his porch with his feet propped on the wood railing, asleep in his seat. She quieted her friends so that they could sneak into her house. Inside, the women asked her, "You not sweet on King? He sweet on you. Mighty sweet. He talk about you all the time. Says you the purtiest he done ever since seen." They all laughed, Honor included, sipping on cider.

They were good and drunk when Honor stopped laughing and said, "I miss Henry," prompting the women to roll their eyes because she had gotten started again talking about a man who, after six years of relations with Honor and a promise to escape the plantation together, decided to slide on to another woman on the same plantation.

And it wasn't as if Honor could go anywhere to get away from the sight of them together, stuck on land that didn't belong to her while watching a man that used to be hers kiss up on a woman neither she nor Henry had paid much attention to before. In the grip of enslavement, even simple acts of retreat were denied.

"But Henry don't miss me, wherever he is," Honor said to her friends, for both he and the woman had run off before Saint arrived. Run off with the plans Honor and Henry had once shared.

The women sipped their cider in quiet. One friend held her cup above her lap, contemplative. "You don't have to worry about that with King. Wherever you are is where he will be," she said.

Honor nodded and smiled into her cup. "I believe you," she lied.

King woke from his nap on the porch to both of his legs asleep. He pulled them down and the discomfort shot through his skin and reverberated like sound leaving a struck bell. He wanted a woman to rub them back to life, then for him to be allowed to return the favor. He wanted future love and knew he needed a present love to make that happen.

Nothing from before Ours interested him any longer, nor did he experience much during his time of enslavement. He wasn't strong enough to wrestle for sport and pride with the men on the plantation, wasn't considered handsome enough to be offered devotion without question, wasn't considered smart enough to strike up idle conversation during the rare gift of idle time. The entirety of his past remained unremarkable in his mind. In Ours, he could start new, reconsider himself without the shadow of his past looming over him.

Inspired, he named himself King to establish a kingdom, the hair on his head the only crown he needed, coarse hair that grew from his scalp in uneven spikes. He often puckered his taut lips when catching a glimpse of his reflection in a pool of water, admiring his face because it was a new face, not the one he had in that old place. He touched his new wide nose with his new bony hands and rubbed the corners of his new beady eyes. Everything about him had been refreshed, and in this new form triumphed a powerful yet lonely imagination.

'Who I'm gone share my new self with?' he thought on his first day of freedom and that's when Honor ambled into view, two fat braids down either side of her head that she decorated with wildflower petals. He liked that she seemed so sure of herself, stood two heads shorter than him, and spoke in a soft soprano a few words at a time, reserving language for future use. To him this meant she believed in tomorrow and that alone encouraged him to want to build a tomorrow with her.

And she did believe in tomorrow, but only enough to tiptoe into it with the weight of yesterday on her head. King didn't care, too wrapped up in her high voice and the crooked top front tooth he noticed when she finally smiled wide after hearing a joke of his and, catching herself, shutting her mouth and turning away. Eventually, he started to court her, visiting her home in the morning and right before sunset. She didn't allow him past her porch for several months until, without notice, she invited him in after sweeping dust from her front door. She appeared at her threshold wearing purple beads around her right wrist and neck. They talked well into the night, then Honor excused herself and King took off.

Every day they met twice a day, Honor telling her lies and King loving every moment because a lie meant a truth lived somewhere inside the liar, and though he knew she lied often, could see it in the tremble of her lips, he felt good in her dishonesty. The fact that she lied to him also meant she paid him attention.

After making love to King, Honor woke in the middle of the night to an empty bed. Sweat dripped from her forehead into her eyes. She felt her heart's rhythm in her head. Frightened and disoriented in a familiar fear, she threw off her sheets and ran out the front door.

King, drinking cider on the porch, turned to face her, her heaving shocking him more than the sound of the door flying open. He couldn't see her face in the dark but heard in her breathing a fantastic dread that unnerved him. After that night, she stopped allowing him inside and soon didn't allow him to sit on her porch, her purple beads off and the absence of their soft clanking broke King's heart.

That's how it began, Honor kneeling to her desire to be held and panicking when what she desired went absent for only a moment; and King opening his heart, hoping his crown-shaped hair would symbolize to Honor his trustworthiness and ability to lead her safely wherever she wanted to go. She grew distant. He grew persistent. Honor, embarrassed by an abandonment yet to happen, visited Saint to keep King out of her face. King, with a freshly washed head, visited Saint so that she could solidify the destiny he knew belonged to him.

Neither knew the extent of the other's feelings and what more easily would've been solved with words was instead tried with conjure, and when they both won, they both lost and publicly blamed Saint's integrity for the stalemate, using this shared animosity to return to each other in the name of anger.

Saint retaliated with conjure, striding away from Aba while carrying a watermelon that could kill a town. "The largest you have," she said, and Aba reluctantly found one that seemed to carry in it the possibility of other watermelons. Everybody stopped and stared, could smell the freshness of the rind as she swaggered by with a sly smile. Her companion carried it over to the kitchen table and cut a wide hole out the side. Into this hole, Saint put three snake eggs and some of King's hair left over from Honor's conjure. She resealed the hole with the cutout part of the watermelon. Afterward, she buried the melon in the woods. This is how she would get her new price: they would never have a child.

Honor and King knew what Saint had done to them when no baby would come. Honor called it betrayal. King called it cruel. And whenever they thought their future promised a child—blood come late, nausea warping Honor's insides—Honor's cycle proved otherwise.

Saint only ended the conjure because it backfired. First, her lips cracked and bled incessantly. Days later, a back tooth wiggled, then another, both near falling out. When she noticed a loose loc of her hair on her pillow, she ran to the forest to dig up the earth where she had buried the watermelon. But when she arrived, she saw three full-grown snakes swell beneath, then writhe from the earth. She stood by and watched them slide up from the ground, glistening and sticky, and slither in three separate directions. Singing in their wake were their rattles shaking dry their threats. The desire to end the conjure had ended it. Afterward, Saint's body healed, and Honor was able to conceive. Eventually, the couple gave birth to their son, Justice, November 1, 1842.

Clouds gathered like a range of inverted mountains overhead, then parted for a moment to let a bit of light splay through the window beneath which baby Justice slept, sunlight burnishing his face. They took this show of beauty as sign that they needed to change their lives. Honor and King decided to live up to their names.

Navigating a self-imposed morality, the couple realized the biggest truth of their shared lives arrived right along with Justice. They were horrified of losing him. Saint made it clear that anything, including a future, could be taken before it was conceived. Honor knew from slavery that what is loved is always in constant danger of being abducted: somebody's child sold off without warning, somebody's husband, an aunt, a best friend. Gone, gone, gone. Sold off or killed. Lynched or tortured until their mind became something without a top. Thieves stealing enslaved Africans mid-errand from the first thief, who called himself "master." King took on her fear, and they came to the same thought and told no one about what they had decided to do. And this new secret carried the power of a lie, made them keep to themselves and move with solemnity at the fruit market, avoiding eye contact while fondling the tomatoes for a way out. They let no one hold the baby for too long. They didn't allow anyone to watch him while they busied themselves with important or mundane tasks. Justice slept, wrapped on Honor's back or strapped to King's chest, and by the time he turned four years old, they explained to him the necessity of the pain they prepared to give him.

[3]

Justice Jackson, son of self-named King and Honor Jackson, the former who worked as a surrey driver in Delacroix and the latter who tended a small garden in Ours and occasionally did laundering for hardly anything at all, sat next to Luther-Philip in school every day after Mrs. Wife's passing. Justice had heard what happened to Luther-Philip's mother and felt it a shame that someone could lose a mother like that. "Cough-death be the worse death, I hear," he said, and Luther-Philip nodded.

Weeks later, Justice saw Luther-Philip holding his shoulder as though it would fall off if he let it go. Justice shook his head. "Why you holding yourself?" he asked, and poked Luther-Philip in the arm.

Justice, the bigger boy, seemed even bigger in Luther-Philip's smallness. This intensified the startling lack of force behind Justice's poke. Never had Luther-Philip been touched that tenderly and he teared up because he knew no other way to react.

"I'm sorry. I wasn't—" Justice said, but Luther-Philip smiled and said that after school they should go to Creek's Bridge. This began a ritual between the two boys that would last them well into their teenage years.

The first time they went, an awkwardness nested between them, punctuated by a fear of being themselves of which they hardly had an awareness. They spent most of their time together in school under the authority of a teacher. That watchful eye stunted their personalities despite a sense of love flowing through the discipline they received during their lessons. But a sense of love is not actual love, and being told not to speak when they wanted to speak, to sit when they wanted to stand, and to read when they wanted to sing did nothing for the possibilities within and between them, for how could they express themselves honestly when their honest selves were viewed as disruptive?

In the presence of budding flowers and chipmunks darting from bush to stone, spoken language no longer satisfied, words too small for the big world unfolding lushly before them in the soft cries of birds too high up to see and from the grass so green it made them hate the dirt roads of their town. Learning to speak for the first time, they closed their mouths. They took turns following each other in silence, observing from poorly covered hiding places the deer chew on plants and stare out and scatter when startled. They pointed at what they found beautiful and looked at one another for confirmation.

Justice found a branch on the ground covered in ants that he shook off before walking with the stick like he saw some of the elders do in town. He arched his back, soft as a cashew, and squinted identical to the oldest man in town, who did so not because he had difficulty seeing but because he saw everything as questionable behavior. Luther-Philip placed his hands in front of his belly and rocked heel to toe. He nodded fast and repeatedly, turning his head to survey the land around him and giving a tight smile like their teacher did when she greeted them every morning. Still looking for themselves, they could be whoever they wanted to be in the woods. Only laughter left their mouths and even that they kept as quiet as they could.

THERE HAD BEEN a tornado and the boys wanted to see the damage left in its wake. In the distraction of the calamity it left behind—roofs peeled back, farm animals needing calming, flattened vegetables and upturned plants scattered all over the roads, an entire wagon rolled and tipped a half mile out needing to be turned right side up again and returned to its owner—the boys made their escape.

Needing desperately to play farther from town, they decided to hike north toward Delacroix. In the distance, a tree taller than all the others fanned its full-leaf expanse and blocked out everything behind it. They had wanted to journey farther, but what this walk lost in distance it made up for in inscrutability. The tree, a master of silhouettes, cast shadows that haunted and pierced the earth beneath it. The lower branches never had many leaves to begin with, the bottom half sharp with death, but the branches higher up were thick with green and activity.

Justice thought he heard a voice coming from the tree, but the sound had a pinprick to it, small enough that it had to have come from a specific spot in the boughs. He stood a good distance away from the tree and listened to the voice while watching Luther-Philip climb up and away from him. Seeing the lack of hesitation in Luther-Philip's climb sparked envy in Justice and he didn't know why. Climbing trees came easy to Justice. Nothing to it if you could get on that first branch. But fear stopped him from following, and the voice he feared in the tree had no effect on Luther-Philip, who touched the rough bark and pulled himself up without mentioning the whispers peeling from the trunk.

"Come on up," Luther-Philip called, but Justice stayed speechless on the ground.

Finally, he asked, "You don't hear that? Luthe, you don't hear that?"

Luther-Philip kept climbing. The boy didn't hear the whispers or his friend shouting up to him, and if there ever existed a loneliness so unique that it required another name, Justice had found it.

Justice looked up. Luther-Philip appeared to levitate in the tree. He had perfected his stillness such that he blended in with his surroundings and Justice lost him in the leaves. The tree and Luther-Philip became the only two things in the world and now they had become one, leaving Justice to watch on the outside, a spectator in his own friendship.

Walking around the tree, peering through the leaves to find Luther-Philip, Justice called up to him but heard no response and saw no movement. Justice crept closer to the tree and the tree-voice sighed. Bad enough that Luther-Philip left Justice alone with some ghost in the leaves but now Luther-Philip hid from his friend, tainting the beauty their silence once carried. This new silence carried betrayal, abandonment, and a haunting that with its unwanted privacy frightened Justice into rage.

"You can stay your coon ass up there if you like. You can stay up there and die."

Still no response. And as quick as his rage had built, fear had taken over. He stepped closer to the tree and the tree-voice he heard fell away. As he began to climb up, he strained to hear it again, to make out the tree's words smothered by the wind. Was it male or female? Somewhere in between or a wholly new kind of being? Did he hear smoke in the voice? A bit of honey? He started to miss the voice as a kind of accompaniment to his sudden loneliness, which told him that being afraid of the unknown felt a little better than fearing having no one to share the unknown with.

Justice climbed the other side of the tree, bark scratching against the bark-like skin on his play-rough knees. He made it to where Luther-Philip stood frozen in the branches and crossed over several more branches to get closer. Luther-Philip was staring at something caught in the corner of two limbs meeting at the trunk. Justice tried to find the source of his friend's distraction. Eye-level between them sat a nest, wiry and black, with rocks spread out in the dark strands. Tears dripped down Luther-Philip's face like rainwater from a shattered window. He breathed short, quick breaths and Justice didn't understand.

"Why you crying?" Justice asked. He stood a bit farther from the nest than Luther-Philip. A foul smell caught his nose.

Luther-Philip didn't answer, his attention unbroken.

Justice leaned in and finally understood what he had gotten wrong. The nest was made of hair with pieces of scalp still attached, and the tiny rocks were human teeth, some with just-dried blood still at the root. A few maggots squirmed throughout, making the teeth dance faintly in place. Just above the hair nest, impaled into the tree, were more teeth, the tornado having whipped them into the trunk. A breeze jostled the side of the nest and the stench rose up like fire.

"We need to get down," Justice said. "You hear me? We need to get down."

Luther-Philip cried to himself. Tears trailed down his open mouth. He had become absent in his own body.

Justice reached over to Luther-Philip as far as he could, desperately avoiding the nest made of hair and the teeth in it. He slipped and his elbow dipped into the nest, grazing over a tooth. Justice gasped and snatched himself back to his spot. He tried to reach again and, stretched to his fullest, touched Luther-Philip on the cheek with the tips of his fingers. "Luthe?" Justice said, and Luther-Philip blinked once and screamed.

[4]

Aba knew the place. He knew the place where perfect berries in the woods grew, perfect enough to tease the young with their dark gloss and arouse the attention of adults who wanted to get an early start on preserves and tomorrow evening's pie. He walked just north and over east past the tree soon-to-be-called God's Place and high-stepped into the bramble-stuffed woods to find his blackcap raspberries, blueberries, and blackberries.

Aba hoped to stumble on a pear tree like he did last year, the one he could never find again in the maze of green. He believed his lack of singing during the time he had found the pear tree kept him from finding it ever again, because singing helped him to remember, a little melody on his tongue as he confidently strode between trees and weeds. Because he didn't sing a song upon his arrival, or while his thighs tightened around a bough for the climb up to the second-lowest branch, or while his hand cupped the first soft hips of a ripe pear, light green as if inside the misshapen globe burned a verdant heart—with no song, he believed he lost the opportunity ever to find that tree again. But autumn hadn't yet arrived and he had already passed that tree several times while picking the darker berries from the green ones, a green like the color of a good pear in his rough hands.

The perfect berries grew on the way to the old gathering of shacks just northeast of town, a town Aba visited often after he had reluctantly left it behind for Ours. He decided to collect as many berries as he could and drop them off to his friends, particularly a woman named Aurora whom Saint hated enough to abandon one town and make another one while keeping Aurora and those who loved her out. Aba, who did love Aurora, felt indebted to Saint, but he never forgot Aurora's pale fingers and how they dripped bloody from berry juice.

He wiped the white dust of the raspberry vines from his fingers. The vine, the source tendon from which the bitter grew and on which the bitter grew into the sweet, a time-touched sweetness, told what fruit it held. White the chosen color of the blackcap raspberry. White on its vine and beneath its leaves that held winter close to its veins. It hid the color of winter on its undersides like a treasure. 'Winter in July,' Aba thought as he pulled raspberries from their white-coated vines and dropped them into his bucket. Their percussion began the song. 'The rhythm come first,' he thought, 'the rhythm then the melody.'

Everything had a heart in the woods. Ant to serpent to fox, everything had a heart and in the woods his songs had a heart, too. He wiped stray notes of berry juice from his bottom lip with a forearm. Plunk. Sweat pooled in his collarbone and his firm gut rubbed against the brambles before his hands could. Plunk. Gentle, he took only the darkest raspberries between pointer finger and thumb, each berry letting go their branches and exposing their hollows to mouth the air. Plunk. Plunk. And with his own raspberry-dark mouth, Aba began to sing a wordless song. It rang out all heart, all bellow. And the raspberry cavities opened as though to sing their own song alongside his, their sweet bruises staining Aba's fingertips, his palms sticky from the overripe fruit smashed by his tender plucks.

Over fifteen years ago, he walked into Ours, then named Graysville, astounded by his contact with white folks. They weren't friendly, but they sold their houses to Negroes and left their relatively new furniture behind. Some even left tools, clothes, an animal or two. No handshake. No eye contact. Saint stood nearby when the purchases were made, always within sight and smelling intensely of flowers.

By the time the last white man-woman-child packed up and went wherever they had gone, Aba had prepared himself for a sheriff, accompanied by several patrollers, to ride up and slaughter them all. He had heard about the Purchase and knew Missouri had become a slave state. 'How a whole state a slave?' he wondered, and never sat still for fear of the answer. He thought it peculiar that a state could become a slave, or slavery itself a state, though enslaving the land was nothing new. And if the sound of a rifle went off, he would go off, too, off into the enslaved woods until he found himself so far north that he found himself south again. But it never happened. Not a burnt building. Not an assault. Not a lynching. No arrests or confiscation of property. All contact with the white world ceased. He wasn't sure if they could even get letters because the post office had become a home. Besides, who would deliver the mail? Eventually, he found a chair and sat in it. Found his bed inside and slept in it instead of outside at the front door. He could rest if he wanted to. He could invest in stillness and be done with it.

But a few observations made him uneasy. First: the lack of contact from anyone white. That no violence had occurred against them solidified his second observation: finding work in Delacroix came too easily. Originally founded as a French trading post for fur, the French had long abandoned the location by the time Ours came about. Everyone there called themselves American now, of the ex-British variety, and had been doing so for nearing a century. Whatever sentiments they had about slavery would be purely American. Pro or against. But even abolitionists had their limits, and Aba imagined no abolitionists lived anywhere in Delacroix, let alone Missouri. This led him to his third observation, and this one uneased him the most: Saint hardly let anyone leave town without seeing her first and she often cunningly persuaded them that Ours contained everything they needed. "You don't even have to work if you don't want to," she had said. But to feel useful, to rebuke idleness, was important to them, and it takes leaving a place every so often to learn how to appreciate that place without resenting it. He could already sense the first bubble of resentment in himself and knew it would find its way into others. If they were so free, why on earth did it feel so small?

Eventually, while lost in his song, he found the boys sitting in their secret place, faces in their palms that could've been another world, lost as they were in them. Aba's song had no chance of reaching them where they were: in that tree, still. In the gyration of a maggot's hunger.

"What you boys doing out in the woods with no buckets?" he asked, and popped a berry into his mouth. He had them all mixed up now, the blue with the black and the rasp. All mixed up how he liked them.

Justice took his time acknowledging Aba, and Luther-Philip didn't move at all. They looked to Aba like they had been in great danger, were maybe still in it.

"Want some berries?" he asked.

"No, Aba, sir," Justice responded.

"Why not?" Aba liked that at least one of the boys knew his name. He knew Luther-Philip because he knew Mr. Wife and felt sadness over Mrs. Wife's death. He knew about Justice because he knew where all his fruit went. It always surprised him that the boy was ever born.

"We not hungry," Justice said.

"You talk for both of you?"

"I just know he don't, just like I don't, sir."

"Even if he don't want none, his 'don't want' not ever gone be like yours. He gone not want how only he can." Aba rolled the bucket around and the berries purred against each other. Getting no response from the boys, Aba turned away. "I'll leave you two to your not wanting," he said.

"We seen something. In the tree," Luther-Philip said, his head snapping up.

Justice smiled but a knife gleamed behind his eyes.

Aba didn't like the sound of Luther-Philip's sentence, the way the boy broke it in half like two separate thoughts he couldn't finish thinking. "In the tree, what?" he asked. "What you see, boy?" He sounded angry. He just wanted to pick berries, yet here he stood with children he remembered only because they were always together. Had he seen them apart, he might not have recognized either of them.

Aba had some tree memories of his own. 'Not a Negro alive,' he thought, 'with no tree memory.' But that they thought theirs was a special horror irritated Aba.

"Hair," Justice said.

"And teeth," Luther-Philip added.

Hearing "teeth" made Aba straighten his back. "What tree this?" Aba asked.

"The biggest one. We climbed up . . . well, Luthe climbed up and got scared, then I—"

"I wasn't scared!" Luther-Philip shouted without meaning to. It was Justice who nearly carried him on his shoulder one branch at a time as they descended the tree. And now Justice carried Luther-Philip's feelings in his mouth and that was enough carrying for the day. "You shut your stupid mouth, Justice."

And with that, Justice leapt on Luther-Philip and struck him in the chest. They rolled as much as they could, hitting each other everywhere but on the face, not out of love but out of hope that they left no obvious bruises. Justice kept shouting that he wasn't stupid, the repetition in rhythm to his punches. He overpowered Luther-Philip, but the boy didn't yield. Aba let them do it. They needed to get it out, but he miscalculated. Justice unintentionally didn't pull a punch and landed a hit on his friend's jaw. Luther-Philip's teeth clicking together shocked them both. Justice, embarrassed by the heat of his own body, removed himself from the fight and returned to squat on the log. Luther-Philip lied on his back, panting. After a while, Luther-Philip spoke, his back still planted onto the dirt.

"I wasn't scared. I was . . ." Luther-Philip looked at the sky, but the sky offered no help.

Aba waited for Luther-Philip to come up with a word, but it never came. "There's nothing wrong with being scared of something," Aba said. "How you think we want to make things right that's wrong? The scare of a thing be scary at first, then it be something else that make you want to change it. Everything begin with fear." Aba paused, tossed a blackberry into his mouth, and looked over at Justice. "You was scared, too. You both was trembling when I found you."

"Never said I wasn't, sir," Justice said.

"But the way you not saying is saying it. You got more saying for your friend than you do for yourself. What sense that make?" Aba said.

He reached into the bucket and grabbed two berries. "Which of these the raspberry and which the blackberry?"

"They both blackberries, sir," Justice said.

"Nope. I wouldn't have asked which is which if they both only one. Guess again."

Luther-Philip turned onto his stomach. "That one is a raspberry," he said, pointing to Aba's right hand.

"You guessing or you knowing?"

"You told us to guess," Luther-Philip said.

"But you can guess with knowing behind it," Aba said. "So, you guessing or you knowing?"

Luther-Philip rubbed his chin where Justice's fist landed. "I'm guessing, like you told me to."

"You guessed wrong."

"How was I supposed to know? They look the same from here."

"That's the problem with the way you looking. Look another way." Aba tipped the berries to reveal their tops. "Get in close, now. You won't see it sitting where you are. You gotta get close to know a thing. There." He described the differences to the boys, the hollow of one versus the closed top of the other. "Not everything that look like something you know is a thing you know."

Justice frowned. "Why not tell them apart by the outside? One shinier than the other," he said.

Aba grabbed some dirt from the ground and rolled the blackberry in it. "Now can you tell the difference?"

Justice shook his head.

"You can look for the shine but the shine not gone shine always. What you do? You look for the difference that always be there no matter what the outside tell. You know a thing by how it is itself on the inside." Aba blew off the berry and ate it. "You only saw that difference when you got up close. I had to tell you to do that. No sense enough to do it on your own." Aba lifted his bucket. The boys were tired, but they needed to get back, as did he. If something human found its way into the trees, then what Aba had always assumed had become reality.

Saint had given them safety, not freedom, but now safety had become questionable. Yes, of course, wind had blown hair and teeth and maggots into a tree. He had seen that much himself, only the hair had a body beneath it and the teeth were in some mayor's jar by the end of the day. What the boys had described was evidence that the world around them hadn't changed, and this unchanged world resided close enough to ride the wind into town. And if a scalp could ride the wind and get in undetected, then Ours was soon to find the scalpers riding in as well.

"Boys," Aba said, "I must make my way away from you. Or come with me?" He was gentle, then, mostly for Luther-Philip. Justice seemed to have about him some sense of the world, even if it wasn't firsthand. A dark lack of curiosity had made a home in him. Luther-Philip, though, was fragile as a mouse skull. The danger that put him in made Aba feel nothing but pity.

The boys followed Aba back into town. When they passed the tree, Aba sang another wordless song.

Justice disliked Aba's song. It carried too much of the same note and rang like a "getting by" song, not a song for pleasure. A work song with no words. Justice kicked up grass and dirt still wet from the previous day's storm into little cliffs as they leisurely made their way. Aba and Luther-Philip conversed with one another, friendly and animated, a few paces in front of Justice. He overheard Luther-Philip say something about the nest of hair and maggots and stopped listening altogether. The knife had returned to his eyes. Before Aba arrived, he and Luther-Philip had sat in silence for over an hour, neither speaking to the other. One waited to be spoken to while the other had become impenetrable. That is, until the fruit man arrived. Justice simmered. To realize that the heavy quiet he endured was a choice on Luther-Philip's part and not a necessity? Insufferable.

The wind had long ago died down and they were close enough to the tree where maybe that soft voice could be heard again without the interruption of windblown leaves or the distraction of Luther-Philip's fearful demeanor. Justice decided he would sneak back to the tree that night and find if he could hear that voice again. Fearing the voice without even knowing what it said seemed silly, so he would decide whether he should be afraid after he heard what it had to say. He wouldn't tell anyone of his plan, especially not Luther-Philip, who had hurt Justice's feelings by calling him stupid and talking to Aba before talking to him. What Justice didn't understand he read as duplicity. He needed the voice badly, now. He felt lonely for the first time in his life and the unease it caused stifled him.

By the time they returned to Ours, smells of supper rode on the breeze. The scent of baked bread filled the air and people finished their errands with patient walks home, laughing as they ended conversations or shaking their heads at the finale of almost-gentle arguments. Scents of family dinners dueled for attention on the road. Justice's stomach growled.

"You want some berries?" Aba asked.

"No, sir," Justice said, and before he knew it, he took off running the rest of the way home.

"Bye, Justice!" Luther-Philip shouted and waved. Justice didn't say goodbye back. He didn't wave.

[5]

Aba visited Saint before sunset. What he carried in his mind refused to wait and interrupted his appetite such that the open desire he had earlier for food, prompted by the smell of stew and pies his own fruit made possible, left no traces after he put distance between himself and the other households. If Saint had prepared dinner, no evidence showed. Sitting on the porch as expected, she nodded at Aba by candlelight, her porch table catching the end of sunlight and the dim moving flame of the burning wick. Her porch smelled like citrus. A stack of lemon rinds cupped each other in front of her next to a small jar of honey. Two cups of water waited on the table.

Saint didn't allow anyone into her home. Aba knew this and wasn't offended, after all these years, to be forced to sit outside as mosquito fodder, though the scent of citrus appeared to deter the insects.

The one candle made a dance of everything, including Saint's face that without warning transformed behind the flames, neither frowning nor smiling, between grimace and mercy. Gradually, Aba got used to the contours created by the flame's light, and Saint, regardless of how candlelight carved into her, remained her usual readable self.

Aba knew she expected him. Saint appeared cheerful though cautious in her own quiet way. Her staff lay across her lap, its snakeheads gulping the approaching dark. Saint's companion stood in the doorway that opened behind where Aba would sit.

"That woman never comfortable," Aba said to himself, then ascended the porch stairs.

Their friendship had been in limbo for some time now, ever since Aba asked Saint once if she had gone too far with clearing out the plantations. He smelled the sky break open with light after he finished his question, and Saint examined him as if he were a boil blemishing the beauty of God.

"You like them so bad, you can stay here and burn with them," Saint had said at the last plantation they raided. She then adjusted her companion's collar, touched his face, and shook her head. When she walked away in the wake of Aba's silence, he watched her hard, wondering if what she did to that man who followed her she could also do to him. Now, he stood on the top step of Saint's porch, half smiling and avoiding her companion's dark figure blocking her doorway.

"I saw you making your way to me a mile away," Saint said. She motioned for Aba to take a seat and he did.

"Two miles," Aba said.

"That's closer to the truth. What brings you?"

"Banter and a warning."

"Is the warning in the banter?"

"Maybe so. Maybe so."

Saint motioned to the cup of water closer to Aba. She took a sip from her own cup. He indulged and proceeded:

"Found two boys in the woods today while picking berries."

"Dead or alive?"

"Between the two."

"Justice and Luther-Philip?"

"Justice and Luther-Philip."

"Strange boys."

"No stranger than you. No stranger than me."

"But strange, nonetheless. What is the warning, Aba?" Saint's patience dropped like the temperature.

"The boys say they found scalp with hair, teeth, and maggots in the big tree. I imagine the storm winds tossed it up there. That's what I imagine. Unless—" Aba looked up at Saint and she smirked, then dropped all emotion.

"I do not use human scalp, Aba."

"That's what I thought. I thought that. So"—Aba clapped once, joyfully—"the wind it is." He watched Saint for a reaction and when she denied him one, he continued. "The wind had a warning in it and I'm telling the warning to you."

"The wind is all warning. Not much else but heartbreaking news ride the wind."

"But it rode it into Ours."

"Wind goes where it chooses."

"What else can ride into Ours, then?" Aba said. Saint took a sip of water, her eyes stayed on Aba. He had insulted her, and he had meant to.

"What danger has ever knocked on your door?"

"None. For me."

"Come again?"

Aba leaned in. When he spoke, his breath made the candle's flame wobble. "What you do with that watermelon, Saint?" he asked. "That you bought from me. What you do with it?"

"Used it."

"How?" Aba smiled when he asked. It mattered, *used* but not *ate.* The distinction delighted him.

"If you have something to say to me—"

"You not the only one who know root work, Saint. You brought with you a bunch of no-longer-slaves stolen from places that birthed root into the world. We not all at the end of our forgetting. Some of us still got African remembrance. You the one to do it best. Best not what's being argued. The wind is what's being argued. What the wind carry and what a watermelon carry often the same thing."

Saint yawned. "You talk like a riddle."

"And you live like one."

"Aba, you come to insult me all night?"

"No insult. Just wandering in my wonder." Aba finished his water. "I worry bout you."

"You worry about yourself."

"Are you not powerful over my self? If you brought us here to protect us, fine. You can't hurt us, though. You left the hurt with the slavers. You can't hurt us. I was surprised out my face to see Justice when he was born. And that he lived this long? Everybody in town knew what that watermelon was for. Ten years old, though. You must had changed your mind ten years ago."

Saint laughed, pulsed with ire but not toward Aba. "My mind was changed for me."

"Saint, I worry bout you."

"I worry about me, too, Aba. I do." Saint paused, her mouth parted, but the words sat on her teeth.

"I was one of the first you freed. We known each other a long time."

"Decades," Saint said.

"I just hope you realize why you brought us all here so we can realize it with you. Don't seem like you know."

Saint hummed one good time and that was that.

"That's all I came to say," Aba said, standing. "Should've said it when the saying was first needed. Maybe the saying was most needed now. Got so bad I didn't want to sell you fruit no more."

"Seemed that way."

Aba sniffed his upper lip. "You bitter toward me?" he asked.

"A little."

"You got any more melons back there?"

"Get off my porch, Aba, before I put you in a jar," Saint said, and blew out the candle. Smoke curled in the hug of Aba's laughter.

[6]

Keeping his self-made promise, Justice crept barefoot out of the front door and headed toward the tree, where he hoped the whisper waited for him. His parents slept hard, snoring into each other's mouths a sharing of dreams. In their hard dreaming, they didn't hear Justice leave into the darkness that rolled over the roads and hid what chewed and ranted in the gardens. His eyes adjusted to starlight being the most reliable light, the moon a snake-curve crescent overhead.

Ours felt abandoned. Empty windows stared back at Justice, stared out with an apathy night inscribed against the glass. But mostly softness embraced the houses, a muddling of particulars that left roof slants dull and doorways blurring into their walls. Justice noticed the rounding of the edges first, that the world felt smooth beneath the element of shadow. Pacing himself past washed-out facades and past the night's deep blue making indistinguishable stone from grass, Justice made short work of his journey.

Leaf rustle from the upper branches welcomed Justice, the incessant clamor calming as a mother's shush. Justice found in himself some form of bravery to speak with what surely had been the dead calling to him earlier that day. The voice didn't belong to a body. No one living had vocalized what he had heard. The tree's branches, giant bones under moonlight, bobbed in the breeze.

Justice went to where he thought he had first heard the whisper, away from the trunk of the tree and closer to where its lower branches leaned leafless toward the earth. He closed his eyes and listened. The wind went calm for a moment and the voice washed over his ear. Justice stilled himself in the grass. He shut his mouth and slowed his breathing through his nose. A long sigh unraveled nearby, easily mistaken for leaf song. He heard the voice a few steps to the left of him and leaned toward it through the dark as though the dark would support his weight.

"What you say?" he asked, and stepped closer. The voice sounded more human now, but the words were muddled beyond recognition. Then a different sound, the swish of someone sliding in the grass to the rhythm of a shekere. He ran away and tripped on upturned dirt he had kicked earlier that day, its small cliff catching him by the toe and throwing him forward. Before he could manage to stop himself from falling, a sharp sting ignited his calf. He screamed and, in the distance, a floating light loomed. Pain in his legs coursed throughout his body, and when he fell, his head smashed into the ground. His teeth punctured the side of his jaw and slit open the tip of his tongue. Something cold circled his ankles in a wreath, the shekere rhythm making his blood dance in his body. Then a floating light moving faster in his direction. *He here!* The light hovering overhead now. A blast tearing through the air. Fire pushing up into his flesh, then moving back down in reverse. Justice glanced at his leg. A head swathed in light pulled the fire out from his calf with its mouth. Pulled and pulled, then spat, then looked up toward Justice with a fearful gaze.

Curly. His hair curly. Justice watched as dark spirals twisted in light to free his leg of venom. The shekere gone. His blood stopped dancing.

In the sky, stars pulsed in the blue-black blanket. The snake-curve moon must have bit each star into the fabric stretched above him with a clarity so sublime it made his eyes water. Overwhelmed, he considered what it meant to be faced with two skies at once; one beckoning him from above with its hundred glowing wounds and sickled moon, the other a mix of storm clouds swirled together on the top of his friend's head.

· CHAPTER 5 ·

Venom

[1]

Saint was strangely oblivious the morning she found a large tan sack leaning against the railing of her bottom step. Flies buzzed and spiraled near the sack's mouth and settled where several lumps bulged the sack's sides. With the tip of her staff, she poked the lumps and nagged at the sack's opening that flared like a pair of blistered lips. A wild smell emanated from the bag mouth. When she untied the top, brown and dark green scales, drenched in condensation, threw back sunlight into her face.

Saint cut her eyes at her companion and he stepped heavily down the porch steps and lifted the sack. They walked to the backyard, where he dumped the insides onto the lawn. What she mistook for one large snake were three large snakes and all three tumbled dead and heavy to the grass: one snake's sequence of scale after scale interrupted by a gunshot wound that would've halved it if it were a normal size, the other two snakes had been decapitated. Their heads tumbled out last, thumping hard at Saint's feet when they landed and rocked a little, maw-wide with fangs sharp and slender.

Saint tapped her staff against one of the rattles and it sang. These, she decided, are the three snakes that crawled from the gutted watermelon conjure. They weren't supposed to come back and whatever summoned them, her revoked vengeance reinstated without her consent, made confusion of a conjure that should've been foolproof.

Saint pointed at the snakes and opened her fingers as though shooing them away. Her companion stuffed the rattlesnake corpses back into the sack. Pulling a pouch from a hip pocket, Saint poured a bit of black powder into her hand and blew it at the sack, which burst into flames.

'All three must be dead,' she thought. 'All three.' She entered her house and the breeze made from the door opening sent the various streams of fabric on the floor into motion. Waves of fabric writhed and bunched together toward the corners of the room. Sunlight crept against the room's innards, but Saint felt a chill that belied the stream of luminosity entering her home. Summer had been relentless. Many gardens suffered through heat stampeding from the sky and singeing holes into the collards while drying out the bell peppers. But a stagnant cold settled into Saint's house and she knew something headed her way; this time, she knew.

Saint grabbed a shawl from the back of a wooden chair her companion used when watching the front window. She looked around. She kept her home impeccably sparse, adding little to what the white folks who once lived in her home had left behind. Fireplace. In the center of the room stood a short table covered with loose pages and unlit candles. There were even candles in glass holders on the floor near the walls. Two large and plush chairs to the left of the room in either corner. The beautiful fabrics—red, yellow, black, baby blue, white, and sea green. A staircase off to the left rolled down dimly from the second floor to the first. There were also a wide archway and a door on the first floor other than the one leading outside. The archway led to a kitchen that would have been outdoors if not for the harsh St. Louis winters.

Saint sighed, shook her head, and made her way to the door that stood at the right of the archway. No place safe now. She closed the door behind her and sat in her chair of bones, candlelight dancing around her, more fabric beneath her bare feet.

She hadn't built the chair herself. Bones began to appear as a disordered pile on the floor a few days after she made herself at home in Ours. Surprised her when she saw it, so much so she winced when she noticed them, then had her companion sweep up what looked like a collection of finger bones and a skull fragment and take them into the woods to leave them there. She would've had him bury them, but not knowing to whom the bones belonged lessened any sense of obligation on her part. Not all the dead deserved ceremony.

The next day, the bones returned. Same spot, same position. Having seen strange things all her memory, which at this time had become reliable in recalling everything from her time in Florida to present day, she allowed the bones their space in the small room next to the kitchen. Days later, the bones amassed into a larger pile, dominating the wall's edge with their increasing number.

She understood the predicament when she saw a recognizable ring on a stray fingertip bone. Every single bone had once been part of someone she had ended on the plantations. The silver ring and its embedded aquamarine belonged to that so-called master's son who dropped dead the moment he stepped out of his surrey and touched foot to ground. She remembered it because she thought it pilferable but decided against taking it when its cheap gleam failed to keep her attention. It didn't protect him because he didn't understand its powers. It wouldn't work for Saint because she doubted it had power to begin with.

When enough bones piled as high as her hip, she told her companion to make for her a chair. The chair's design became more outlandish when bones from the dead bodies around Ours, reaped from her earlier and mistaken conjure with the stones, appeared beside the chair. Over a dozen skulls and twice as many femurs, kneecaps, and pairs of ankle bones. The small bows of clavicles, the butterfly silhouettes of sacrum and ilium pairs flanking spine bones stacked like ivory cups against the floor. Her companion added every bone that appeared in the room to the chair until, indeed, it had become a throne.

'Three of them dead,' Saint thought once more, meaning Justice and his parents. Who took care of the details? Who managed to kill the snakes with a shotgun wound and a good knife's work? Preparations had been made prior. The snakes had to have been expected or at the very least hunted after someone discovered their existence. Perhaps, they were spotted slithering from Honor and King's house, three incredible bodies sliding from the ajar front door and onto the road. Surely, that caused a public disturbance in town, unless it all happened late at night while everyone slept. Most people. And to know to bring them to Saint. 'To my bottom step,' she thought, 'on my property, without me noticing. No knock. Just left them there for me to see in the morning like a warning. No. This is a threat. A show of power. That even I can be taken aback, swindled into security.' And with that, the only person knowledgeable and audacious enough to do such a thing was Aba. She should've known. She always had known. She didn't want to know.

Saint sat in the dark room on the chair made from the skeletons of her enemies. The dark touched thick as molasses, while candlelight from dozens of glassed-in and open-flame candles bulged from mantels built into the walls. She sat and tried to remember. Her memory reached as far back as Florida, always Florida. She had awakened in a sand-caked dress barely on her, its white forever stained by her own sweat and the salt from the water that had also eaten away at her skin. Her mouth stung at the corners and her lips cracked to bleeding. She was thirsty, dizzy, and lost in breathtaking humidity.

A small girl in the prettiest little dress had approached Saint with a leather bag of water. She poured the water into Saint's mouth then disappeared into the bushes, the flower pattern of her dress eaten by squat plants and the darkness behind them. An hour later, a band of Negroes with hair like storm clouds or vines or with both sides shaved low, and bodies glowing as though polished by the salt air, gathered around her and kneeled. One man dabbed her bleeding forehead with a towel that smelled like roses. Two women rolled her onto her back, the men looking away just in case her clothing tore from her.

The women carried her on their two shoulders while the men closely followed, machetes in their waistbands, guns in their hands. Saint could hardly understand a word they spoke, a sprinkling of English dispersed within sentences constructed of beautiful if unfamiliar words, like rain falling on tin and through even that a bird calling for its mate. They walked for many miles, took intermittent rests for water, forehead dabbing, surveying the humid land, which became muddier as they went along, until finally they were surrounded by swamp, a landscape Saint had not seen before, where even trees bowed to the sodden ground that birthed them.

"Naket cehocefkvte?" a woman said, and Saint stared at her mouth. "Nombre? Your name?" the same woman asked, and Saint replied that she didn't know. "Call you Saint, then," the woman said. Saint didn't ask why and was too tired to imagine a reason for herself.

Sunlight dripped through cedar leaves and onto the thickets below. And within this memory of reclining trees, the sweet smell of rotting plant life and roasting deer meat from a nearby set of houses, the bird-rain language pouring from the dark mouths of her saviors—within this memory another memory bloomed. Lightning. Sugarcane burned to the ground. Winds strong enough to bevel the heavens. Hooved animals capsized, floating off, then sinking, their dead eyes staring, staring.

Saint tried to hold on to this storm in her head that occasionally and without notice punctured the easier recollections, though the speed by which it punctured always surprised her. As sudden as the Negroes who saved her from some coast in Florida appeared to her, they were eradicated from her thoughts by a storm that eradicated everything beneath it, a storm not in Florida, but before there, a time of deliberate oblivion; had to have been. Why else remember the destruction without the pain it delivered?

Breaking herself from that memory, Saint left the dark room of bones and stepped outside. She sniffed the air, grimaced, and looked for a sign of what approached. Just up the road appeared Mr. Wife, whom she hadn't seen in quite some time. He strolled toward her home. Where else could he be going, her house the last house on the northernmost road heading west toward some mangy woods that marked the end of town? Upon seeing him, she remembered the spirit's face that took Mrs. Wife's life to teach Saint a lesson. One life for one lesson, a cry-worthy price.

Two boys, Luther-Philip to the right and Justice to the left, flanked Mr. Wife. Recognizing them, Saint wished the day would end. Justice had survived. Fine by her. But what of his parents? She watched as the three stopped just beyond her house. Then Justice looked up at Mr. Wife—who nodded in return—and walked the rest of the way alone, right up Saint's stairs, and onto her porch. Saint smirked because Justice eyed her as though regarding a stranger whom he wanted to pass.

"They dead, Ms. Saint. I know it was me you wanted, but . . ." Justice paused. Up to that point they were face-to-face, but suddenly he lowered his eyes, scanned her porch, picked at his fingers. And for the first time, Saint saw the boy in all his details. His hair dense like the men's hair in Florida. He had grown into a solid boy, not much taller than the other children but vaguely more mature, expressed through a face that with little effort appeared bored and solitudinous. He favored Honor more than he did King, but he had the lighter brown skin of his father. His thin eyes secretive, expressionless. "I still got venom in my leg," he continued, and Saint realized why Justice stopped looking at her. He wasn't afraid, or shy, or even sad in such a way that it overtook him. Justice needed something from her and was too proud to ask for it, too fractured in his understanding that he needed help from the woman who everyone in town had said tried to stop him from being born. They never told him directly, but gossip has wings and whispering fails near the heightened listening of children. They murmured and he heard, clear as glass shattering across a floor.

Saint kneeled and reached out with both arms for Justice, who looked back at Luther-Philip and Mr. Wife, but they were already gone back to town.

Justice finally approached, and Saint pulled him in for a hug. When Justice slipped the knife from his back pocket, Saint's companion swooped down and grabbed his arm on its way down toward Saint's neck. Saint finished her hug with a squeeze, then stood. She liked how Justice kept looking at her even while her companion restrained his arm midair, Justice's hand clenching the knife so hard veins protruded from his small fist. He looked at her with blank rage.

"Let it go," Saint said, as kindly as possible.

Hot wind slipped between them. Justice dropped the knife. It clanged against the porch. Sunlight vaulted from the metal blade into a blade of light that lit Justice across his right cheek. Saint picked up the knife and stuck it in her head wrap. Other than the departed slit of sunlight, Justice's face didn't change, though tears slid onto his lips.

"I'll give this back when I'm finished. Sit on the porch. I'll brew what you need," Saint said, and, before she entered her house, added, "We will talk when I return. Don't run away, now." She closed the door, leaving her companion outside to stand in front of the door and block Justice from getting in if he decided to try his luck once more.

By this time, after Luther-Philip tried and somehow managed to suck some of the poison from Justice's leg, Justice felt a sharpening numbness beneath the knee. It started as a tingle, the firing of nerves until the fire burnt out into a cool melt that erased all feeling. The conjure snake's venom, Saint knew and Aba, too, needed more than a mouth and some bandage. It needed conjure for full removal; otherwise the venom leftover would spread and mummify a person alive or, least of it, require amputation of a limb. Better than the death that would've resulted had Luther-Philip not been there to do something stupid out of desperation. Saint didn't know Luther-Philip's mouth had saved Justice and would've wondered how his teeth hadn't rotted out in the process, but she assumed someone had helped him, always thinking first of Aba as the culprit of heroics useful or otherwise.

Even with a numbing leg, Justice marched on up that woman's porch, looked her square in the eye, and, when he believed the moment best for it, whipped out his knife so fast the hot air chilled around him and Saint. 'He won't run away,' Saint thought, 'but he might have some maroon in him, yet.'

IN THE 1700S, Florida was under the control of the Spanish, who allowed Indigenous Americans and enslaved Africans to experience a kind of war-tied freedom that rivaled the non-freedom of chattel slavery and rejected American settler interference in all its boldness. The catch was that the Indigenous Americans, called Seminoles because they had escaped from various oppressions in the newly established Georgia and South Carolina, and the maroons, Black Seminoles consisting of both escaped enslaved Africans and Negroes who had never been slaves, had to defend Spanish land against the American colonizers. Freedom always had its price: substantial, horrific, a currency of blood. But some maroon groups broke off from both the Seminoles and the Spanish, wanting to remain untethered, unbothered, and unbeatable on their own terms. This is the group that had found Saint.

Saint eventually discovered she had washed up near the Apalachicola River, right at the bottom of the thin strip of land that ran beneath Alabama. A woman who had offered her shoulder for Saint to lean on as they left the shore took Saint to her home to rest. There, Saint found the living arrangements more than suitable and the hospitality eased her pounding head and stinging, dehydrated lips.

The woman, who called herself Essence, made Saint lie down on a pallet on the floor of a house in a settlement hidden amidst water tupelo reflected so clearly in the endless lake that the trees appeared to grow from themselves. With all this water, the mosquitos flew their hunger into her legs and arms. Itchy bumps covered her skin already patterned with throbbing bruises, and it took everything in her not to scratch herself worse. Her stomach itched. She lifted her shirt just enough to show a thin but noticeable dent in the side of her belly. Fingering it, she knew it meant something important, but gave up on trying to know what.

Essence stepped out of the cabin and returned with some cooked deer meat, rice, and dandelion greens. "From friends," she said. Saint wondered if this woman and any of the others living there knew languages beside rain-on-tin, birdsong, and English. What she heard: a creole of French, Gullah, Spanish, Mikasuki, and Muskogee she would never learn.

Saint had been found off the Gulf of Mexico on May 3, 1758. By two weeks' passing, she had become mostly herself, memory not included. When she looked at her hands, she knew they were hands, that they could build, sweep, cook, wash, sew, fold, open, harm, and humiliate; but she couldn't remember a time when she did any of those things before waking up with sand and seashells in her hair. Occasional headaches pestered her. Déjà vu delivered her into deep melancholy, inspiring her sometimes to punch her lap or the ground in frustration when the simplest tasks reminded her of a past her mind could no longer touch.

Essence was pregnant and Saint hadn't noticed when she arrived, too busy healing her tattered body and forcing herself into unsuccessful bouts of reminiscence. But now, able to move and smile without pain, no longer distracted by her own bruised state and faulty mind, she saw every detail she had missed during her stagnation.

One day, while watching Essence prepare supper, Saint thought of Essence's firm belly as an egg where not only a child but also the beginning of a new world approached. Sometimes, she imagined being part of the world soon to come. Other times, she spiraled into sorrow when she saw Essence rub her belly. Essence's pregnancy seemed most familiar of all occasions of déjà vu, and because Essence would be pregnant for a long time, Saint expected her sorrow to continue for just as long.

By July, Saint had completely merged with Essence's household. There was Essence, of course, and her husband, Hu, who was part of the group that found Saint. He stood several inches taller than Essence with reddish brown skin. When he spoke, Saint understood him the least, but she learned his ways around words much like she had to learn her way around the land. He had shaven the sides of his head, leaving a single thick long braid of hair traveling down the center of his scalp and just past his shoulders. He kissed Essence frequently on her cheek, forehead, small pecks whenever he could, though Saint paid attention to the machete tucked to his left hip and the gun holstered on the right. He carried them everywhere, kissing on Essence while at any moment ready to sabotage a passing boat of colonists or assist with raiding some poorly defended plantation a day or two north in Alabama.

Sometimes, Essence threw metal bits she received from Hu's pillaging into a large black pot that sat near the wall by a small table they used for eating meals together. An iron chain wrapped around the pot's waist and sticks of cedar jutted from its mouth. Tucked amongst the sticks were tools: knives handle-down, hoes, hooks, and a few nails. Saint saw that a few planks of wood had several nails jutting from them. Essence must've pulled them off a ransacked boat or from a ruined house, Saint thought. She looked at the pot, a cauldron really, questioning its purpose and why Essence kept wasting good firewood and tools by leaving it all inside.

Essence and Hu treated Saint like a daughter. She appeared younger than they were, naive and a bit docile. Her soft skin confused them the most, dark and scarless. Even her head wound healed into newborn clarity. Her only scar marked her stomach, but they figured she was born with that one. Saint had a strong face, high cheekbones and brown eyes that seemed gentle at first but on second look contained a dangerous light. Essence was naturally tall, slender and long-limbed. Saint being a head shorter than her and a few heads shorter than Hu only made it easier to call Saint "girl."

Despite Hu's infrequent presence, the work he accomplished assisted not only Essence but the rest of the village. Whenever he returned, he came with sacks of hand tools, weapons, and rations to last them for a few more weeks, sometimes months. With these, Essence divvied out to her neighbors what she knew she didn't need. Then Saint delivered it all to everyone in the village. She became known as the Bag Girl and they were always excited to see her.

Essence noticed Saint's emotions went together with the weather. Coincidental at first, a downhearted glance matched an overcast sky. Shortly after, Saint laughed at one of the village cats assaulting a hen, and the clouds parted, revealing a sky that carried none of the animosity it held moments ago. Essence watched it happen for weeks until the second sign. Saint drew symbols into the mud and strange things would happen around the village. Some people became ill at random. Others were healed of an illness that had bothered them for years. Essence noticed that Saint used the same symbol, but the effect depended on if the base of the triangle faced toward or away from Saint. She also noticed how each symbol connected with a particular person depending on whoever upset or pleased her that day. Mama Sarah's bad hip went limber as a newborn after she thanked Saint with a hug and a basket of fruit. Saint came home and idly drew a triangular shape with the point arrowing toward herself. Jon Jon, flirtatious and never keeping his hands to himself, got a strange bout of stomach cramps after slapping Saint on the behind and saying she needed to come to his house for more. She drew her triangle with the base facing her, and Jon Jon shat his guts out for two days straight.

"You got, in you, energy, girl. You been told that?" Essence asked, then shook her head to reject any answer. Saint would have no memory of being told that she had bad breath, let alone something as vague as energy. "Somebody told you. You wouldn't remember them telling but somebody in life has told you. I tell you again." Essence rubbed Saint's locking hair with both hands and smiled. "Come with me tonight."

Saint nodded. A light in Essence's smile, some shimmer behind her lips that hinted at resolution, comforted Saint. That night, she followed Essence, who had packed enough supplies, food, and water for a few days, into the muddy wilderness. With the mirroring water around and beneath them, the night sky lit up like lanterns from their feet. Even pregnant—by how many months, Saint never asked—Essence moved quickly, the splashes beneath her nearly inaudible. 'It would be a couple months more before the baby comes, three at the most,' Saint thought, and tried to walk without shifting the water and soft earth too much beneath her. The ground pulled at her ankles such that when she lifted her feet, a sucking sound rang out. Why the earth wanted her more than it wanted Essence, she didn't know.

They stopped in the most luminescent part of the wilderness. Stars and the moon at capacity. Such violence in the sky: the shaking iridescence; the distant vibrations of heat; the fall, fall, falling of light.

They had reached drier land but remained near a large pond. Water lapped at the water tupelo and cedar trunks lain down in the wet that strangled their reflections. The sound of water disturbed by water veiled Saint in the shawl of its replete sadness. She barely saw her moonlit silhouette burst into circles after something unseen fell into the pool and was swallowed. It happened again. Drop, then swallow. Then again in other places. Rain. Gentle. Not a cloud in the sky but raining. Saint turned to Essence and saw her own face where Essence's should've been, only it was bloated, water pouring from her mouth, nose, and eyes.

She backed away from Essence and knelt in the mud. She shook her head to get the vision out. She shook fast and her head filled with pain, the feeling of violent water crashing behind her skull. She would've passed out if Essence had not touched her shoulder. The throbbing ache in her head turned barbaric. Rain poured heavily from the cloudless sky.

"Where you go? Where you go just now?" Essence asked. She shook Saint. "Where? Where you go?"

Saint wanted to cry. Tears gathered but remained in her eyes. She hid her face from Essence, behind her hands, and leaned closer to the ground on her knees, forced into a position of prayer, of begging though to whom? 'Anyone, anyone take this pain away,' she thought, because she couldn't say. Her eyes' wide appraisal mutilated her face. Her mouth stretched wide till her cheeks burned. She felt her countenance distort and it horrified her. Saint froze in a ghastly smile.

Before it could go on any longer, Essence touched Saint on the head. The pain left Saint, seemed pulled out from the top of her scalp. The rain stopped as well. Essence had seen enough. "Stand," she said. "Stand up."

Saint stood and uncovered her face. It hurt. A burst of lightning struck a tree nearby and Essence backhanded Saint across the face.

"Don't make me kill you, girl," Essence said. "You before me. You my girl. But you before me."

MUCH LIKE THE raindrops entering an endless lake near a maroon village hidden so well Saint swore even its citizens had trouble finding it, like raindrops entering and punching circles within circles from the surface of water, the reverberations of history echoed into the present. Had Justice waited a few more years, he might've tried to slap Saint first, his backhand made tender by bone meeting bone. Saint felt it as she imagined it. Justice in his thirties, a few heads taller than her, stretching his arm across his chest and releasing the built-up tension across her face. You before me. Since she knew that choreography, had experienced it once before and remembered the swing of Essence's arm every so often in the hastiness she called her memory, shock would be overwhelmed by precedent, precedent making easier to swallow the threat against her life because it was cushioned by a softer violence.

She rummaged through the heap of her knowledge and, yes, a death threat made familiar is a death threat made easy. Eager with nostalgia, Saint might've hugged Justice even harder had he slapped her first, then said her life meant nothing to him over his own, his own sun-splashed-skin-sheened-with-sweat life. But, no, he had hardly lived at all but was in a rush to kill. Haphazard and enraged to the point of unrivaled stoicism, Justice failed himself because he failed to plan with an imagination. Children, after all, think the cruelest things when angered and the specificity of their cruelty sharpens the aftermath. But instead of sharpness, Justice chose to throw a tantrum, chose to kindle the white flame of his anger too soon and was noticed, read like a primer, and stopped before he could even break skin. Saint wouldn't have a child with a child's mind enact unpracticed anger against her. Not in this lifetime.

Conjure venom had torturous ways. Saint made Justice wait for her, his leg and an arm or two stinging by now but still the envenoming reversable. She made him wait outside under the dull eyes of her companion.

Justice rubbed his leg, and winced at the worsening pain. Saint had rubbed her face the same way after Essence popped her so hard she saw daylight at night. Eventually night's darkness returned and with it the sky-bound bodies of light. Her ear had rang a bit after, yet through that bell of pain she still heard Essence's every word: "Don't make me kill you, girl."

Saint remembered nodding. She thought about that as she brewed tea for Justice, adding finely ground charcoal to the boiling water. Ground glass is what the conjure required, but she didn't trust herself to grind it as finely as the recipe required, lest she cause more harm and got the Ouhmey talking more than they already were. Going into town, what would everyone else think about Honor and King? They already knew about the conjure to stop Justice's birth, had picked the story's seed out of the summer air ten years ago and planted it into their own hearts. What would they think of her now that the flowers had bloomed?

"Guess I'll find out eventually," Saint said, speaking to her reflection in the tea.

Essence pulled several items from her bag: wood, coal, kerosene, two glittering rocks, dried moss, and four wide ceramic bowls. Already leaning against the trees were four wooden posts, waist-high, each topped with four small, angled spokes to hold the bowls aloft. She put the coal inside three of the elevated bowls then added kerosene. She then built a small fire in the remaining bowl with a spark from the two glittering stones and the dried moss. Finally, a reliable ember appeared, which she blew into a flame. To each bowl, Essence used the wood to transfer the fire made with the moss and stones. To the last bowl, she added coal and kerosene to enliven the original flame. Essence made a circle around them with the posts, each now carrying a vessel of fire. She and Saint were in the center. Saint saw her inky reflection in a puddle of water, looking for the handprint on her face. But she had been backhanded. No evidence of having been struck by a person she loved. The redness, the swelling, could've been a hornet's sting, not at all caused by a human.

Essence sat on the ground and Saint followed.

"You got energy. So much. You can kill with your ignorance," Essence said. "I thought I could help you. That's why I brought you out here. I unlock people. You all locked up, girl. I think somebody locked you up good. For reasons."

Essence reached for her bag and pulled out a knife. Saint flinched.

"Not for you. For this," Essence said, and pulled out an apple. "Half?"

"Yes, please," Saint said. She scoffed her half. Essence cut slivers off one at a time.

"I might can unlock you. Let out that big energy for you to use the right way. But the small you reach now you can't control." Essence sliced and ate a sliver of apple. She did this twice more before continuing. "But you here. This a thing I can do. I suppose I'm supposed to do it for you, my girl."

"You helping me remember who I am?"

"I can't do. I die. You die. What you don't remember come back and claw us off the world, girl. Clean off. You forget for a reason. Let it be buried so it don't bury we? If you supposed to have it," Essence looked to the sky and reached for something only she could see, "come back, come back." She laughed, then looked at Saint. "I will unlock you now. Is this what you want?"

"I don't know about energy. I don't want what it is. You say I can't control it. You slap me and make me feel bad when I did nothing to—"

"Rain. Yours. Lightning. Yours. You flood or flash us to death. You did that," Essence said, carving faster. She didn't look at Saint when she spoke and didn't stop carving until she ate the rest of the apple. "What if you flood and flash yourself here. Where will you take me? Hmmm? Back to Africa? To Spain, with these beasts in this fly-whored land. Spaniards use us as shields for their enemies. Believe that? Yes, Saint. Take me back. Take me home, girl. Into the earth and back again. Flood me to paradise."

"I didn't make rain," Saint said.

"Stupid. You saw something that frighten you, then you made rain. You move your hands from your face and look at me. Boom! Lightning cut a tree. What cloud you ever see? Hotter than bear cunt outside and it rain cold rain with no clouds."

Saint laughed.

Essence laughed, too, a hard laugh, then waved it all away. "I will unlock you this moment. Before my mind change directions."

"Crazy. Yes. Crazy," Saint said. "Unlock all of me, then. Do not spare a key."

Essence pulled a glass jar from her bag and stood. Tossing a white powder from the jar, she drew four lines moving from Saint to the circle of burning pikes. At the end of the lines, she drew arrowheads pointing away from Saint. When Essence finished, there were four slices drawn into the ground with Saint in the center.

"What you pouring?" Saint asked. When Essence didn't respond, she asked again.

Essence's voice moved around Saint as she walked counterclockwise outside the circle. "Close your eyes. Listen to my voice, girl. No drums. No singing. My voice all there is. This may take long. Everybody can't be here. You dangerous. You don't believe me but why no one else come? I say, 'No. Stay where you are.' So, I do alone what take a village. You close your eyes. Breathe slow from your belly. Sit up straight. Get your breathing whole. Yes. That's right. Now on your back. Lay down slow. Yes. Keep breathing slow. You the living thing in the circle, Saint. The arrows point to the path of your living. Drawn with ashes, girl. Your people. African ancestors called witches here. Stake-burnt. They with you now. Don't fear. They guide you. You the only living thing can be in there. I can't enter with you. Into your future. You gone move into the future, but you must die to get there. You have to die to get to what come after. Let the ancestors lead you there, girl. Saint! You hear me? You fear your people? Nonsense. You fear yourself. Your past. Dance into what come next, girl. My girl. Reborn, you. You feel them pulling you, Saint? Pulling you from midday into evening? The sun setting on your life, Saint. What will you do? Will you scream? Or let the dead have you?"

Wind picked up and blew leftover rain from the leaves to the ground. The wind-touched boughs sang out like rushing water. Essence stopped circling Saint. "Your feet pointing south where your head should be. Why your feet with the dead but your mind ain't? Turn. Turn yourself around, Saint. South where the dead live. You living a living life. That's not where the dead need you to be. Not if you going into what's to come. Keep your eyes shut. You can't look at the dead do their work. Turn, Saint. Be turned."

Saint felt her body spin on the ground. Wet dirt licked across her elbows, and the slurred gulp beneath her was the earth permitting her to enter its cool domain. The sound of her own body spinning against the sparse grass and mud fought with the declaration of wind in the tupelos. When she stopped spinning, she smelled a familiar scent. Sweet like fruit. Behind her closed eyes, a burst of light corrupted the darkness, and the sweet smell departed, replaced by the smell of the ocean.

Essence had made a mistake. Saint remained calm but the weather around her cascaded into violence. The storm she saw behind her closed eyes spun out into the weather of the open world. A blade of lightning leveled a tree nearby. Then lightning halved another tree closer to Essence. Feathers glided down first, then the birds they belonged to followed stiffly to the ground. Saint wasn't moving into the future; rather she spun into the past. The sugarcane, the dead goats, the salt air, and, for the first time in her splintered memory, a capsized ship, beside which floated many bodies. Essence hadn't considered that the past meant death for Saint and that the past was the only future Saint owned. The ancestors, in their confusion or ultimate wisdom, turned Saint right back to what she couldn't remember, what she had blocked out from herself. Realizing something was wrong, all wrong, Essence stepped into the circle.

WHEN SAINT FINALLY finished steeping Justice's tea, he had dozed off on the porch, facing the door. Saint poked the boy hard with her staff, a wooden snake head pressing right in his neck. He coughed and grabbed at his throat, moaned, and rocked a bit.

"Tea ready," Saint said, and sat the cup on the porch table and herself in the chair farthest from the stairs.

Justice limped back to the table and sat with his back to the front door. Saint's companion stood watch. Hardly any feeling remained in Justice's leg.

"You just gone look at it?" Saint asked.

Justice said nothing. The table, its woodgrain swirl, caught his looking, entrapped it in its endless brown maze.

"I let it cool while inside, but it works best if you drink it while heat's still on it," Saint said. "You do want to walk regular, right?"

Justice, with his head lowered toward the table, lifted his gaze only, away from the maze that had so entranced him, and glared at Saint. 'I know that look,' Saint thought. 'Know it well.' She allowed quiet to freeze over them. What's the use breaking silence with idle chatter when only one side had it in them to talk? What mercy in one-sided noise? Justice lowered his looking and slid the cup closer to himself. He sniffed the steam. He sipped.

"Plenty of honey in there," Saint said.

Justice took a larger sip. "Eat shit," he said.

Saint howled with laughter.

"I hate you."

"You do. You do," Saint said. Quiet again, then, "It will take an hour before the tea starts to work. You might as well get comfortable."

"I'll sleep in the woods before I sit here."

"Crawl to them, then. They just up yonder."

"Sphynx!" Justice hissed.

Saint shot up from her chair. "What you just call me, boy?"

Justice returned to his maze in the table.

It wasn't the word itself or that a child had called her something so awful. Had he called her a whore or a bitch, he would be just as uncreative as any boy attempting manhood. But now, she was fearful. Last time she was called a sphynx, a woman reeking of cigar smoke and booze spat out the word in a voice not her own. Saint hadn't tried to kill anyone, but Mrs. Wife left the world soon after. No one was supposed to die over an old watermelon conjure, either. Death and not being conceived were different, and that difference mattered. How those snakes returned, why they returned, she didn't quite understand herself. Though she hadn't forgiven Honor and King, she held no hatred toward them. So, how did an animosity she no longer carried resurrect an annulled conjure, and with such potency?

"I never tried to kill you, Justice," Saint said.

Justice put a finger in his tea and stirred it around. Saint sat back down. She wished Essence were with her then and the wish made little sense. That woman never popped into her head after that night in the circle made of burning pikes and ashes from dead Negroes. What a horrendous practice, in hindsight. Did Essence ask the dead for permission to use their ashes that way? Who first collected what once belonged to those burned at the stake? Saint hoped it was all a farce, though she understood by now that she had caused the storm, the lightning making kindling of several innocent trees. She closed her eyes while Justice drank, losing herself in thought.

WHEN SAINT HAD opened her eyes, still lying on her back, she saw Essence standing over her. Saint sat up and realized her body rested where it had always been. She hadn't turned at all. That the ashes showed no sign of having been dragged was further proof.

Essence dropped the bag of food and tools beside Saint. "This for you," she said.

"For me?"

"I can't let you come back, Saint," Essence said. She rubbed her belly when she said it. Saint saw the gun in her other hand.

"Essence . . ."

"This hard enough as it is. Don't harden it, Saint."

WHY NOT GET lost in the woodgrain's maze along with Justice? Maybe better thoughts waited at the maze's end. At the center of it all shines the single, unspoiled moment Saint could latch on to and that would latch on to her in return. It would stay, unlike the rest of her, right? There is a field in her mind. No, a marsh. Even better. Her toes slipping into the sopping mess of it all, just like they had in Florida, the Apalachicola murmuring its old song across her feet. And the women sharpening knives outside for butchering deer while the men cut umbilical cords with thread so thin it could slice a thought. There was singing in a language more complex than ancient Egyptians pulling brain matter from a dead pharaoh's nose. That was 1758, was it? And now, 1851, in a slave state, hidden like raccoons in a hollowed-out log, the Mississippi River thick as pig entrails and the weather fickle as a newborn, Saint sat in front of a boy who wanted her dead and the rest of the town must have agreed because no one visited her as though she were a living thing. They summoned her when they needed something, but to visit? To say hello? To ask, "Why you don't let nobody in your house?" instead of assuming she was uppity, playing royalty, as opposed to keeping them all safe from even what she didn't understand: bones growing from the floor, visions and migraines and signs of ruination. Why bring that upon anyone? It's best she kept her distance lest the entire town come with knives to hug her with because she accidentally killed somebody mama and daddy.

Perhaps, belatedly, those living in Ours saw what Essence saw in her immediately: danger. Pure, unbridled danger. Predictable inasmuch as, sure, you knew it would hurt when it came knocking down trees and singeing birds from their nests. Essence had wanted to protect her people and her unborn child, the most difficult life to protect. If danger takes shape, visits, then lingers around grown folks who have the power to stop it but do nothing, an adult may suffer from its presence, may fall victim despite warning signs and weapons galore. That would be personal; a pity, but personal. However, a child amidst danger meant something must be done about what was dangerous because the child knew nothing of power, not yet, and needed protection from every intrusion that takes shape in whatever shape it takes, including that of an amnesiac woman. So, get rid of her, the source and the burden, though you know she has nowhere else to go and no map to return to the door that never proved return was possible; get rid of the danger even when you once lovingly called that danger "girl."

Poor Justice, a child sent straight to Saint, the origin of his own suffering, in order to fix himself. By now, folks in town were probably wondering if he would ever come back, if good ole pernicious Saint finally did him in. But there, at the table, he waited unharmed, seething across from her. Saint, just as quiet herself, let him be. To sit like that, if only for a moment in a mimicry of peace, even though its illusion provided comfort Saint had no clue she needed. She wanted to try again. She tried again.

"Justice," she began. He looked at her. He was tired and so was she.

"I didn't kill your people and I never tried to kill you. You don't have to believe me." 'You weren't you. That's got to mean something,' she thought but wanted to say it to Justice. She felt his heat from across the table. Rage like that needed some place to go. Someone, not her—this Saint knew—was going to have to deal with it. And it ending well? Doubtful. "How your leg?"

Justice shrugged.

"You want more tea?"

"No, ma'am," he said to the table.

When the table received more respect than she did, Saint decided she was finished. She stood, grabbed her staff leaning on the porch banister, and headed back inside. "You can leave the cup on the table." Her companion followed her, leaving Justice inside the marbled district of the tabletop.

[2]

Justice couldn't find his way to the center of the table. Near the end of one tunnel marbled in the woodgrain began another path that led to a death drop off the side. Eventually, he realized he had all that time been following the lighter spaces in the wood's pattern, which had no way of leading to the center. He began tracing the darker routes with his eyes and found moving around the table's patterns more achievable, but with the center being part of the lighter spaces, a territory he left for momentum, for fluidity, his only option was to keep circling around his aspiration.

When he had gone home the evening he and Luther-Philip found the scalp, teeth, and maggots in the tree soon-to-be-called God's Place, he told Honor not of what he found but of what he heard. She went into the kitchen, wetted her hands, and rubbed them with salt. Honor grabbed Justice by the tips of his ears and twisted. He screamed out and backed away from her. She stared at the boy, with a look belying anything had happened at all.

"Sound like the dead want to speak to you. They don't never got a thing to say worth hearing. I pulled out what you had sitting in your ears. Don't look at me like that, like you never known hurt. Don't waste that look on me when you got a presence on you."

Honor told Justice how she once wanted to protect a friend who had later been killed for stealing a tomato. She called them presences, what remained after the flesh was gone, the *who* thereafter replaced by a *what*.

The story goes that one Saturday, after spotting a neighbor's shirt stuck in a tree, Honor fell into a dizzy spell as the scenery slid by, as though the planet sped its turning but left her behind. The hollow shirt billowed, filled up with nothing, and in its nothingness, Honor rushed back through time, rose up inside the hollow of the bodiless shirt and into a memory of a boy she once saw as a child, a boy she loved like her own brother. He had been shot in the head on a morning so lavish with green and birdsong that for a moment Honor thought he grew from the ground he lied on, as natural as a budding flower. "Why you never tell me you was a flower," she asked Justice while thinking of her childhood friend. Justice felt the need to answer because in him something warm like an answer welled up.

Honor's memory was unnervingly pleasant: she, maybe ten years old, could've been eight or nine, staring into the fingertips of dusk that faded into a solemn hush of maroon. Only a river yonder felt free to move away from the plantation despite being part of it. It trickled past, an escape that never stopped escaping. She heard what she thought was just a breeze licking at the inside of her ears but realized later that the wind had wrapped around a word. When she plucked the word from the air, she heard whispered, "Help me." Eight, or nine, or ten years old and damaged by a plea riding the wind like a witch.

So, when Justice came in talking about having heard a voice up in a tree, she damn near snatched his ears from the side of his head to get the voice out. Salt to burn the spirit. A painful twist to shock Justice out of listening to the voice at all. No need for a boy who had never seen a dead body to suddenly hear from one. No matter what once rotted up in that tree, it wasn't there now, and the presence wouldn't have her boy. Or Hell be her grave.

If Justice had paid closer attention to the voice and if his mother hadn't overshadowed his experience with her own long-ago memory, he would've heard what the voice wanted him to hear the entire time: "Unsafe. Unsafe." Perhaps, he wouldn't have felt so lonely then if he had known the presence was on his side and that its source was the nest of hair and teeth and scalp torn from a grown man killed not so far from Ours. "Unsafe," the dead man spoke so only Justice could hear. This is for you, it meant. A warning from someone who had no one to warn him when it was his time to be saved. Afterward, Justice never again heard another voice.

LAST NIGHT, after Aba shot the snake and Luther-Philip sucked venom from Justice's leg, the three made it back into town, Aba's first instinct to return Justice home. When they opened the door, Aba called out to King and Honor. No one responded, so Aba opened the door further, shouted a bit louder. When all three entered, Aba led the way to the one bedroom in the back of the house. All three found King and Honor wrapped up in scales with the rattlesnakes pumping venom into their necks like a second heart. Without any other purpose, the large snakes died locked on to the bodies of their victims. The venom pumped involuntarily from the dead snakes into Justice's dead parents. Aba cut off the snakes' heads, returned to the tree soon-to-be-called God's Place and collected the snake body just to bring it back with the other two, and stuffed the dead rattlesnakes into a bag—the heads first, then the bodies of the decapitated, and finally the one he shot. He told the boys to go to Luther-Philip's house. "I'll mourn later," he had said, speaking out of anger he regretted the following day. "I'll mourn later."

Now, stuck in the table's woodgrain maze, Justice rubbed his ears hoping he could put back inside what Honor desperately tried to remove. Perhaps, Honor's own voice could come to him from the dead. Maybe his father's. But after he removed his hands from the crescents of his ears, all he felt was a raw heat, all he heard was wind and leaf on leaf on terrible leaf.

[3]

Saint knew when Justice's leg healed because she heard, from her bedroom upstairs, a shattering outside. "I liked that cup," she said to the emptiness in her room, then closed her eyes.

· CHAPTER 6 ·

Expose

[1]

Justice placed himself as the first child and survivor in a long heritage of those who had tried to take Saint's life and failed. Before him, many people had made attempts but suffered, instead, from their own morbid and inexplicable deaths.

Often these deaths mirrored how perpetrators desired to kill Saint, but in the twisted reversals of the perpetrators' fatalities a sinister fog of dual elements—suicide and accident—draped over any hint that Saint had a hand in their ends. In her life after Florida but before Ours, one Negro overseer fell victim to a lightning bolt while sprinting to introduce Saint's stomach to a knife. Witnesses said the white-purple bolt dropped onto the pinprick end of the blade as he carried it in his mouth full of rotten teeth and the electric burst illuminated everything wet in his body until his skeleton flashed beneath his skin. The shock was gossiped to have been so fierce that it whitened each dead tooth and scraped the black off his gums.

Another attempt, this time by a white woman trying to hide her enslaved Africans, ended when the woman shot herself in the neck after tripping on something in the road while plodding to Saint for a closer shot. Weeks later, a brave soul, recently freed by Saint and Aba, finally revealed to a friend what he had seen and had been keeping secret, that "a little doll with a leg sticking out tripped the woman. Saw it clear as the face on your head," the man said, then left the same night to presumed safety in Canada. Aba had been with Saint during that incident and beheld other, even stranger fatalities, each clarifying his own fear and awe of her as they moved from plantation to plantation, freeing the slaves and killing the so-called masters quite on purpose. Each trip reminded him of his own experiences in the grip of enslavement, sometimes with far too vivid force.

[2]

Aba was a gift of sorts, estimated to be four years old at an auction in South Carolina and meant to be given to an Edward Eccles by Edward's half sister, Gertrude Towns, who had lucked up in marrying a no-talent journalism student, Ralph Towns, who stumbled his way through Yale Law School and stumbled out just as clumsily. Their inconsistent wealth came from selling two things: poorly written pamphlets about ill-understood political issues and what they called Native African art, the irony being that everything natively African had been destroyed before boarding the ships. When Edward rejected the gift, detesting slavery and Gertrude for her participation, she kept Aba for herself.

When Aba got older, Gertrude found a grotesque use for him in the evenings. Ralph had been warned about leaving his wife alone with a "young, strong slave" but found the warnings more humorous and paranoid than worth heeding. Why, exactly, would he need to show concern for his wife, a human, fending off a beast with her own sharp wits and a gun tucked beneath her pillow? But the warnings didn't consider Gertrude fending off anyone as part of the issue. Ralph never cultivated a distrust of women like his male peers and more to the point never perceived in Gertrude her full complexity and ability to wreak havoc. Therefore, he remained dedicated to kindling the flames of Gertrude's nonexistent naivete while unimagining her longings for Aba, which, if he had imagined with any precision, would've nauseated him as if she were to lay with an ape.

In Gertrude's mind, she had indeed committed an act of bestiality and it shamed her, though not enough to discontinue forcing Aba, then nineteen years old, to enter her and suffer her disgustful wrath after she had her fill and refused to look at him any longer, making him the culprit of her own yearning. Not even for the sake of her sanity could she make temporary her embargo on Aba's personhood, such that her looking upon him before, during, and especially after she raped him was indeed her looking at assorted monsters from her imagination come to life. For the sake of her human marriage, however, she had to get rid of Aba because she couldn't get rid of her imponderable cruelty.

Gertrude sold Aba, sending him to Kentucky from North Carolina on a buggy filled with other enslaved Africans restrained by chained manacles and ankle braces that slinked across body to body. With the two horses' unsteady verve, a white driver and his partner who whistled songs he picked up from the slaves working the fields, rode via a path poorly carved through but mostly etched by feet around the Appalachian Mountains. The trip almost killed Aba and did kill seven others, including a five-year-old and a sixty-three-year-old, all heading to their new so-called masters in Mississippi and Kentucky.

Then death came—barely at the middle of their journey—for the driver who had driven the buggy since the signing of the Declaration of Independence. With one cough he fell off the side and landed on the ground. His partner's death soon followed.

Abandoned at an elevation wholly unfamiliar to them, the enslaved Africans beheld with awe the mountains clawing the sky with slanted facets covered in sugar maples and yellow birches. The fat-hipped and poisonous fruit of yellow buckeye swung temptingly from their rank branches, but their height luckily prolonged the chained ones' hunger. The only means of navigation lay dead at the hooves of the seemingly confused horses that stomped, wanting to take off but instead lowering their heads in a way easily confused with mourning. For what seemed like an eternity, this horse dance swung intermittently between the two, one horse mourning, the other stomping, until both fell into a peaceful weariness.

A rustle, then the sound of a branch cracking, Saint appeared before Aba and the death-close group of Negroes, peering from behind a tree and smiling. She reached into the old driver's pockets for the keys and kicked him square in the nose as she walked by. Unsatisfied, she kicked him again and once more in some undesignated place on his face. She wore a dingy off-white dress familiar to Aba for it had once belonged to Gertrude. A splatter of blood blossomed on the bottom right hem. The year was 1810.

Saint said she found them by following the voices. She described it as calls for help pouring out of the surfaces of bark, houses, even the ground itself, that pointed her in the right direction. The agenda formed in her mind as she trailed the ghostly signs: free the enslaved, undo traps laid out by patrollers, be still. The others thought she was some wild woman who happened upon them coincidentally and with flawless timing, but Aba believed every word of her story. Nowhere else to go and without any means by which to go, he began traveling with Saint all over the south, acting as a lookout and helping the just-freed escape north. They had a system, fast but not traceless. Abolitionists sometimes helped, but Saint didn't like the assistance of white folks and frequently threatened their lives if they spoke to her carelessly. She avoided them as much as possible and suffered no casualties in her party for doing so. She inspired Aba in ways that reduced his previous enslaved life to dust. They plotted their raids to the finest detail and laughed in the wilderness when the plots sounded too good to be true.

Aba had his first taste of freedom with Saint, punctuated by her restlessness to free as many people as she could, as many as there were voices calling out to her for help. Had he believed in God, he would've thought He spoke directly into her ear. He believed more in Saint, and in the embrace of her intense smile he found comfort where others would've seen utter madness. Knowing that freedom could be given and obtained by following Saint, Aba could almost forget what his so-called mistress had done to him. Almost.

AFTER SIX YEARS of freedom work, Saint wanted to retire. All the traveling had worn on her and by 1816 rest settled on her mind. During their retirement, Aba made his way to Pennsylvania while Saint went her separate way without offering any details as to where or for how long.

There, he found squalor and invisibility. His first job and payment came in Pennsylvania, and the first time someone cheated him out of his money was in Pennsylvania, charged an unsightly price to live with people from all over the world who in keen desperation stole from each other with such zeal that they ended up stealing back what had been stolen from them without even noticing. Pairs of shoes went missing, a coin stolen from here, a piece of fruit taken from there. Then there were the rats swarming the streets and copulating in the walls, singing with their tiny childlike voices. Half the time he had no soap and the other half he had no water. Wasn't anyone to complain to and though he wasn't considered a slave, he had heard tell of free Negroes disappearing in broad daylight. He knew exactly where they reappeared so kept his head low and his mouth shut, having no freedom papers of his own. Winter come and the heatless room ate him up with cold. Summer come and the bugs ate him up just the same.

Almost twenty years later, Saint knocked on his door. When Aba saw her, he nearly fell over in fear, thinking he saw a specter of the woman because she looked exactly as she had when they parted. She may have looked younger, her hair cut scalp-close, a style Aba hadn't seen on a woman since he was a small child, right before he was taken on a ship whose name he was beginning to remember more than his own parents' names. Her brown eyes shined in the dull, dreary room and Aba felt shame having her there with his leaky ceiling and vermin scrambling toward various hideaways.

By this time, Saint brought her companion with her everywhere she went. He didn't speak and didn't make eye contact. He smelled like he lived outside, pungent as moldy earth and unwashed musk. When Aba reached to introduce himself to her companion, Saint intercepted Aba's hand and pulled him into his own room. The not-speaking man waited outside.

Saint wanted Aba to live in a new town she would make possible through conjure. "Just for our people," she told him. Safety like he had never known. So nobody can come in and take what's yours. So nobody can just walk into your home and steal everything you worked so hard to achieve, everything you ever loved. Her passion inspired Aba. He agreed and became part of her traveling band of the once-enslaved.

Aba knew Saint had changed but not right away. At first, he thought she had merely honed her skills. That they didn't have to hide anymore startled him the most, that they could travel in daylight with a barrage of Negroes and not be seen, let alone touched. But her torture of the so-called masters when she could kill them immediately frightened him. Illnesses potent as plagues, child-killing madness, her desire to pick them off one at a time so that they suffered bearing witness to the relentless pain of their loved ones. What should've taken minutes with her new skills took several days. Aba watched in the shadows as Saint and her companion rotated stones and made a dungeon of the plantations. One night, she set fire to the main house and stayed to watch until it fizzled out, the smoke finally propelled in shrinking braids from the wood and glass that held no more heat to feed it. That the so-called masters suffered held no space in his conscience. But Saint's willingness to keep her own people enslaved longer than necessary, just to inflict what he believed to be unquenchable vengeance, frightened Aba to no end.

What had Saint told him she wanted to do to slavery? Kill it, he remembered. She wanted to kill it. He had been cutting across a natural path where a blackberry bush used to grow but there now, posing as a cluster of lightning bolts frozen to the earth, ached branches with all the leaves and berries gone. They were returning to the woods just outside of what wasn't yet Ours after a successful plantation raid when she said it. Aba thought then that she had lost her mind. Slavery was just an idea that used people to pretend it, too, was a living thing, "big enough that you can't stop it," he had said to her, and she shook her head, repeating she wanted to kill the enterprise but said nothing about how to kill what slavery had done to their people. 'You kill slavery, you still got to kill the slave raised up inside the person,' he thought. 'How you do that without killing them is on you.'

Frustrated by how long it took to clear out a plantation, he asked her why she tortured the white folks and Saint became livid, telling him he can burn with them. He wondered if it would be so easy for her to kill him, knowing that rage as unbridled as hers could abruptly turn on friend and family. 'Maybe that's what happened to that man that's always with Saint,' Aba wondered, and kept close all he observed and all he felt.

In the early days of Ours, Saint often chose absence but would show up when needed and afterward seclude herself in her house that stood farthest northwest in the town. When Aba visited her, she wouldn't let him inside her home, and after years of feeling offended he finally let her have that in peace. She spoke in a direct manner with everyone, never loving, never caring, and never careful. Even the celebration at Creek's Bridge became a catalogue of commands: Do this. Come to this spot. Come at this time. Bring this. Go over there. Move. Don't move.

Move over that way. When she didn't use words, Saint's body language, charged with what all the others had witnessed her do, directed what came next, when, how, and for what duration.

She stayed away otherwise, standing off to the side while Ours operated as best as it could. Schools ran smoothly with three teachers and three classrooms that split the children ages three to five, six to nine, and ten to fourteen. Journeys to and from Delacroix had two backup drivers and always left on time. There was food, yarn for blankets, and a gun in every household.

She had once told Aba, "If you let people figure things out on their own without doing everything for them, they remember it longer." Other than occasional doula work or conjure, Saint made herself scarce.

But Aba thought she kept her distance for another reason, one dealing more with love or fear, because why else would she persuade people to stay in Ours if she also wanted them at arm's length? 'Somebody like that would be all up under you,' he thought, which led to other thoughts, other possibilities.

Then she bought the watermelon, and Aba knew Saint had planned something terrible. He had tried to kill his so-called masters that way. One of the enslaved elders told him how to do it, unable to do it herself because of her hands, her hands that could hold nothing, not even a knife, Lord, "so why won't they let me die free," the elder had asked aloud and Aba held his tongue out of respect for the unanswerable.

Many years later, here come Saint, more powerful than he remembered, asking for a fruit with no softness in her voice, a fruit he knew only for its ability to kill.

Everyone knew she had it out for Honor and King, who had gone around calling her a cheat after she did exactly what they paid her to do. Some people in town wanted them to get what they deserved, but no one in their right mind believed Saint needed a watermelon.

"Pardon?" he remembered asking her. "A what?"

"A watermelon. The biggest you have," Saint said.

Had anyone else asked, he would've done it without question. Even other patrons touched their clavicles in shock that Saint would be that way just over some gossip. They watched their step when she passed by, still greeting her but more quickly, heads returning front and center as soon as they felt their smile lingered a little too long. 'For someone not around much,' they thought, 'she sure do be around.' But they held their concerns close. None dared speak their minds lest they, too, wanted to find themselves at the tail end of a nasty conjure.

So, when Aba saw the rattlesnake wet-scaled beneath the lantern light, he shot it immediately, its size miraculous. And, if that snake wanted to, it could've killed Justice with its fangs alone. 'Saint, Saint, Saint,' Aba thought. 'What horrors you seen to bring that into the world?'

He felt anger when he cut off the snakes' heads, when he stuffed them into a sack, and when he put the snake he had shot in there with the others. But he felt absolute fear when he took the bag to Saint's, expecting her to be there waiting for him, but her porch was empty and the door empty of her silhouette. He knew she would realize he had done it. He didn't know how far she would go to show him that she knew.

[3]

With three dreams in one night, Saint punished Aba for leaving three dead snakes by her stairs. She kept her promise not to harm anyone, including Aba, but while Aba meant harm in all forms, she only meant of the flesh.

> The first dream: Aba goes out into the woods to pick fruit but finds the branches barren. He searches for miles without any luck. He is tired. His legs burn from endless walking. He stops to relieve the pain, but it only intensifies. He looks down and sees that from the knees down he has rooted into the ground. His knees crack and widen from the kneecap into a bulbous

knot of spiraling bark. His skin flakes then flares, revealing for a moment the marbling of blood, fat, and muscle that lies beneath before crusting over into scab, then bark. The bark begins to rise and cover his entire body. When it reaches his chest, his lungs seize up, his vocal cords warp into concentric circles of wood. He reaches for the sky and his uplifted arms stiffen above him and become branches. His fingers stretch out grotesquely and split from their tips into separate rays of wood and green itching out of him. He feels as though his suffocation has no end, just layers of immobility and the sensations of choking, of passing out, of ceaseless dying. His face twists outside of human recognition and brown chips emerge from beneath like bone rejecting its cage of fibers and skin. A tooth, pushed out from his deformation, falls from where his face used to be.

The second dream: Justice and Luther-Philip sit on high branches growing on opposite sides of the tree soon-to-be-called God's Place. They both fall at the same time. Aba can only catch one. He must choose. He puts the corpse of whoever he doesn't save into a sack and sits it in front of Saint's porch. The sack catches fire.

The third and final dream: Aba is lying on his back in a dimly lit room. He hears his own labored breathing, familiar as running water, rhythmic as though he's running through a tangle of harsh weather and vine, becoming a drum of lung and heave. His chest feels heavy, so he reaches to touch it and feels breasts. When he lowers his gaze from the ceiling, he sees himself staring down at himself. He is on his back looking up at himself grinding into himself. His own sweat falls onto his face. He hears his own breathing because he is breathing over himself. He goes to touch the face that is his and sees that his hand is small, white, and has immovable fingers like a porcelain doll. He screams and it is in Gertrude's voice.

Aba woke from the third dream not sure he had awakened. He touched his face and felt that he had one. Cold. Damp. Touched his chest and a heart replied. He looked at his hands though the dark kept them hidden. Flexing his fingers, he knew he had fingers. He reached between his legs and felt his thighs were wet and sticky. He snatched his hand away.

He cleared his throat and exhaled into the nothingness of his bedroom and heard the nothingness congeal in his own voice. He blinked and what had shown there moments ago shown there still, and though he felt a sensation akin to horror chill him in the summer heat, his belief that he had flesh that could feel the world around him began to waver. Yes, he had a body, but the nightmares desecrated what having a body allowed. He no longer believed in breath. He stopped believing in feet and kneecaps. He stopped believing in arms, in blood, in the hardheaded determinations of his brain and his will. If he ever had a chance to believe in the high heavens and his potential to be included, those days were over.

He had no idea that Saint, who went out of her way to free and house the once-enslaved, would use the horrors experienced during enslavement to hurt him. She hadn't killed his body, yet his belief in his own flesh and blood and mucus and tendon slipped away in the fallen tooth of his dream, in the burning bag carrying one or the other of his dead young friends, into the arms of a white woman doll pinned beneath whom he thought he was but could no longer be. Not again. Never.

Now that his dreams had become ammunition against him, he decided to visit Saint carrying only a pouch and his lantern. He dressed by moonlight in his best shirt, the one with all its buttons still sewed on and the ruffled collar, stolen perhaps from a so-called master or one of his petulant sons.

It took him a long time to put on his pants as he regarded each leg individually with the intensity of prayer. Raising the pant leg up to his knee, he touched his knee. Feeling it, he shook his head and raised the pant leg higher to the center of his thigh. Thick and hairless, his thigh trembled its fatty strength as he rubbed his palm against it with the motion of covering himself in lard for a winter months away. He did the same to the other leg with the other pant leg, regarded his knee, rubbed his thigh, and when he secured both legs into his pants, he noticed his flaccidity and looked at it for a bit, waiting for it to deform as an extension of his nightmares. When it did nothing, he raised and buttoned his pants, then headed out the door.

Saint's house caught fire with ease. Aba watched, neither amused nor vindicated. He watched with the energy of someone who had nothing left but stillness and time. He kept hold of the pouch just emptied of kerosene and wiped his hands on his pants. The lamp he broke for the flame lay cracked and smoldering against the porch. Fire gathered around the railings like morning glory and spun up, then out from where would've been blossoms. It nibbled at the stairs and caressed the veranda. Having made appetizer of the porch, it devoured the facade, which caved in first before fire reached the roof and the rest of the house. By morning, blackened strips of wood simmered, emitting small hisses and smoke ribbons from still-glowing cinders.

Aba, covered in ash, gazed into the void where once a house existed. He watched until Franklin led him away and when Aba turned, he saw that all of Ours stood behind him, observing him inscrutably. The light of the sun warped their faces as though they, too, were burning. He looked away, but the image remained with him. They didn't know what he knew, that Saint had threatened to burn him years ago and seemed closer to doing it now that she had sent those terrible dreams his way. Choosing life, he would burn her before she burned him.

They didn't find Saint's body in the rubble, her companion's body missing, too. Without a corpse, the Ouhmey's anger against Aba simmered low. Saint had to be alive, and when she returned, Aba better beware.

Thereafter, Aba never said another word and would die having been dedicated to his silence. Even after a month or so passed and, along with the coming of the most beautiful August day, the twins arrived like a pair of demons, Aba remained speechless. In this way, neither Saint nor anyone else in town could use his spoken life against him.

[4]

August, cool as a spring day and every flower gave its widest hips to the breeze-laden weather carrying fragrance from lilac that appeared where Saint's house had burned down and been cleared away. The scent roiled all over town, even to the farthest edges heading toward Creek's Bridge in the east and the tree soon-to-be-called God's Place to the north.

Franklin had just finished visiting the lilac bushes to pay his respects to Saint when he saw her sauntering down the path that led to Creek's Bridge. She held a bundle to her chest. She wore her hair unwrapped for the first time he had ever seen, and the long locs shook him. That she had decided to grow her hair into snakes made him want to laugh and curse her. She wore a long gardening dress and a white button-down shirt, modest enough that a teacher could wear, cool enough to survive the summers. As she got closer to Franklin, he saw that the bundle was two bundles, one covering each breast and wrapped in linen that embraced her back and waist.

"I'll be good Goddamned," Franklin said, and removed his hat. He said it again, "I'll be good Goddamned," and put his hat back on.

Tied around her were two babies, girl children, with the same face. Twins old enough to be aware of Saint's locs and grab on to them as they swung in their faces. Six months? Franklin wondered, then said it a third time, "Good Goddamned."

"Good morning to you, too," Saint said, and smiled. "This here Selah and Naima. Come. Don't be shy." Franklin looked closely at the same-faced babies, then back at Saint, then again at the twins and once again at Saint, who smiled long and hard as he gazed in a soft delirium caused by lilac scent and a month-long disappearance reversed and with company. "This one on your left is Selah. The one on your right is Naima."

Franklin squinted. "Now . . ." he started but couldn't think of what words should come after.

Saint beamed. "These my twins," she said. "See you around." She rubbed Selah across the forehead with her thumb to remove a bit of sweat and marched past Franklin and on into town.

"Twins," Franklin said, and decided not to follow Saint lest everyone think he had something to do with it.

[5]

A parade,' they thought. 'She parading these babies around like they the president. And where she get them from? What jollification she deserve holding some stolen babies? The nerve. The audacity. Just like her to have her house burned down and she turn up alive and with babies on her breasts, at that!' However, Saint's face belied their trivial disdain. She glowed like a just-made mother and that newfound light warmed everyone in Ours to her having twin infants, quiet as a pair of feathers, bound to her.

No one remembered seeing Saint this free after the Creek's Bridge washing. She skipped around town barefoot in all white with her hair draping down her shoulders instead of hiding it all under some elaborate wrap. Her locs' tight, dark-brown twists draped over her shoulder and tickled the babies' faces, which made her neighbors smile along with her and reach in to tickle the twins' fat cheeks. When Saint grinned, her own cheeks nearly kissed the bottoms of her eyes. And even though those babies didn't need the support of her hands on their perfectly wrapped bottoms, she held them anyway with a firm softness that could've been love.

She would never share with them where she found twins outside her own womb. Most assumed she had saved them from a plantation, their parents passing them to Saint before they could experience the full brunt of enslavement. But why not save them all? Had to have been a good reason, unless she stole them, the idea of which brought about nervous laughter.

All speculation aside, most folks were happy to see Saint enjoying herself, let alone alive. She never mentioned how Aba burned down her house, and no one else mentioned it for her. Even better, Aba made it easy to deal with his crime because folks read his silence as shame and not what it truly was. Aba had been broken, and Ours's righteousness stood where concern was better suited.

They hoped this meant Saint would take better care of everyone there. Getting rid of her never crossed their minds, but fearing her had begun to take its toll, and Saint needed to prove that she was done with those days of cursing her own. It felt even worse to hold anger against a woman with two fresh babies in her arms, a woman who smiled as though she read her own future and found unparalleled favor, enough to share with everyone in Ours.

Saint approached Aba's house, saw him sitting on the porch, and waved. When she caught Aba's eyes, her grin became a smirk. "Hey, Aba. Haven't seen you since we was friends. Heard you ran up on death and lived to talk about it. Right here in front of me to talk about it, yet . . ." Saint said, leaving space for Aba to talk about it, about anything. She leaned into his silence, on it, and when it continued to be reliable, she walked on, saying, "These my twins," in her wake. Aba looked straight ahead where Saint had intercepted his vision. He sat that way for a long time.

[6]

By the time the twins could walk and talk, Saint had taught them their letters, numbers, and tested their potential for learning conjure. Adjacent to small words and beginning arithmetic, the sisters studied the ingredients to basic cures. By the age of five, Selah could heal anyone in town of infected cuts and colic. Naima, though, had devilment in her. Without meaning to, she made every cure into a curse, worsening the symptoms the Ouhmey needed her to remove. She nearly killed a man when instead of relieving him of his toothache, she spread the infection throughout his mouth. Had Saint not intervened, the sickness would've attacked his brain and Saint refused to add another town death to her personal ledger.

To show there were no hard feelings about her old house burning down, Saint invited everyone to her new home that she and her companion built on the other side of Creek's Bridge. "Just walk through the field, cross over the water, and keep on walking for a bit and you'll see it."

There, painted dark blue, sat a beautiful house with a flower garden in full bloom on either side of the veranda and a lush vegetable garden farther out in the front. Vines climbed up the house and curled around the eaves. There were two stories and its facade faced west so that the sunset's violet interrogation of the land shone through her windows.

She told the Ouhmey that they could come in but should be prepared to see visions of what they love and what they fear. No one wanted to enter, unable to decide if they wanted their true fears to be known by Saint or their true loves to be revealed to them. Both could become a weapon in her hands, but only one could betray them, make them turn on themselves if its expression defied their expectations.

No one noticed Justice approaching the crowd despite how large the boy was. Fourteen years old and built well-fed, he stepped toward Saint, who stood on her porch's top step unamused by his presence.

"Can I come in?" he asked.

Saint looked at the twins, who looked back at her. Selah shook her head no while Naima nodded with much glee.

Saint motioned for the boy to follow her and as he ascended the porch steps, Saint's companion emerged from the door and stepped to the side so that they could enter. A warning or a reminder.

Not long after he had entered, Justice came running out shouting "No!" repeatedly. He stormed down the stairs and passed Selah and

Naima, Mr. Wife, Luther-Philip, and the crowd that had somewhat dissipated by the time he got there just moments before. The few lingerers talked among themselves, noting how strange Justice had become over the years and how, ever since his parents died, he had to live with Mr. Wife and Luther-Philip, which surely made things no better. Five years in that ghost house with the boy who sucked the venom out his leg and stopped gaining weight ever since, got taller but that ghost and venom must be eating Luther-Philip's insides cause he ain't nothing or nobody, sweet mercy. Nothing and no body.

Naima shouted "Yes," cajoling a response from Justice, and he delivered. He looked over his shoulder at the girl. Naima backed up a little and pursed her lips.

"Be a good girl, Naima," Justice said, his glare unbreakable, and in its intensity Naima saw daylight shrink around her until only she and Justice remained surrounded by black. He didn't stop glaring and Naima lost control of her eyes, looking every which way to keep from crying until, without any space around her that her eyes hadn't seen, she hid her face in her hands.

Saint slammed the tip of her staff onto her porch and Naima, caught in Justice's prodigious anger—so dense it hummed through the air—saw daylight again.

What Justice had seen in Saint's house lingered behind her as she stood in front of the doorway. It crept from the open entrance and Justice turned away from the sight of a clawed and bloody hand wrapping around Saint's door from behind.

"Evil," Justice said, meaning to point at Saint but his finger pointed to the monstrous fist holding what looked like Luther-Philip's decapitated head and pushing open the door to reveal more of the monster's impeccable horror. Saint merely cut her eyes to the left and the claw and fist crept back into the house.

"Indeed," Saint responded, and called to the twins to come inside. "That belongs to you, Justice."

Justice felt gravity flatten him and heat rise all around him. He shook. He sweated in his overalls, shirtless underneath. He swallowed hard but nothing went down. He stormed off, passing everyone and not looking back when Mr. Wife called to him or when the sound of Saint's door slamming shut resounded with a shotgun-boom behind him.

[7]

Later that day, Luther-Philip suggested they go to the lake for a swim. Naked, Luther-Philip tackled Justice as best he could in the water. Justice chose gentleness, always, toward Luther-Philip, greater than he had ever shown another person. When Justice splashed his friend, he arced the water too high so that the water split into jewels in the air before landing. He faked like Luther-Philip had strength enough to dunk him beneath the lake and rolled with his friend's lunges and swings. The cold water held them in its fist, so their skin felt each slap with a resonant, near-numb sting. Daylight caused the water to shimmer in their tight hair, lightning bugs at dusk. Sensing his feigned weakness would be discovered, Justice grabbed Luther-Philip by the face with the big pad of his hand and dunked him backward into the water.

"Don't drown, boy," he said.

Luther-Philip escaped, and his silhouette disappeared into the depths of the lake, breaking through largemouth bass spiraling their spawning beds. He swam more graceful than any fish, quick in the motionless water. He wrapped his legs around Justice's so that neither could kick to stay afloat, and they both went down. A pit of darkness opened at the bottom of the lake where light couldn't penetrate, as though a sinkhole in the center of the lake sucked in what remained of the shallow parts that edged closer to the shore. They sank deeper toward the bottom and the bottom unwrapped beneath them like the inside of an ear. They were entering their own minds, feeling the skin of the other, then feeling it no more until they couldn't even feel the water. From their building numbness came a strange unity that made one their bodies but not their minds, both boys experiencing the sublime the only way they could: Luther-Philip swimming faster into the unseeable; Justice neither struggling to get away from Luther-Philip's clasping legs nor working to push further into the dark, dropped frozen into the void.

Lightless, the bottom drank them in. Space and time halted. Direction became a fiction. They were now inside and to be inside, re-wombed and made to reimagine themselves in the darkness, created the ultimate possibility. Whatever they weren't they could become in the bottom. Others couldn't put meaning on them down there, nor could they take meaning away. Their bodies, without the ability of being seen, no longer existed in the way they knew them to. If they couldn't see their arms, then they could imagine any shape for them. If they couldn't see their faces, they could draw in their minds the face they most wanted.

Justice, incapable of understanding this freedom, this vision without sight, began to kick and fight away Luther-Philip's grip, believing his friend led him some place that offered an unlikely return. He reached down and pushed his friend's legs until they slid from him like an oversize belt. When he broke through the lake's surface, he was surprised by how rapidly he made it to the top. The lake had felt deeper while inside, but the bottom wasn't as far from the top as he had imagined.

Justice swam toward where his clothes lay spread against the grass, waiting to be filled by him. He stood naked in the water, his waist still submerged so that his legs seemed replaced by a reflected version of himself looking up at him from the water. Luther-Philip followed soon after and poked Justice in the rib as he passed by. Justice leaned forward in laughter and jogged to land. That's when Luther-Philip saw it, inside Justice's left thigh and a little to the back, the meat so soft there that Luther-Philip had trouble understanding why they put it there of all places. Yes, but who were *they* and why did they do that to him?

Luther-Philip focused on the bubbled skin in the shape of the letter *E*, something he saw once on a cow during a visit in Delacroix. Right on the thickest part of the left hind leg. When he had asked Mr. Wife if he thought the cow still felt pain from the brand, Mr. Wife told him that memory could be a kind of pain on the inside. He couldn't ask the cow, but he could ask his friend with a letter singed into his inner-upper thigh who did that to him and if it still hurt.

"Justice," he said. "How you get that?" He pointed.

"Get what?" Justice asked, not looking back. He stretched and the wingspan of his arms embraced the woods ahead.

"That *E* on your leg. Where you get it from?"

Justice sat naked in the grass. The heels of his feet touched where the water and land met. "Papa did it. Mama asked him to. She told me it means 'everywhere.' So people could know me if they find me."

Luther-Philip laughed an unfriendly laugh, disbelief in the cadence. He was calling Justice's parents stupid. "Justice, you have a face."

"Faces burn away," Justice said, and started to put on his shirt. Luther-Philip sat next to Justice, his thigh touching his friend's. Above water, their skin felt less like the water itself and more like something attached to a single feeling and thinking body. Warmth traveled from one to the other until the chill from their swim melted away. Justice laid his shirt back on the grass. Both boys stared at the trees across the water.

After a moment, Luther Philip asked, "Does it hurt, still?"

Justice rubbed it, which made it appear as though it did. "It used to feel. Not no more. Can't even feel my finger on it."

Luther-Philip looked at Justice and said, "I'd recognize you without that."

"You wouldn't," Justice responded, gazing across the water as if wanting to be there instead.

"How you know?"

"Wouldn't be nothing left, Luthe."

"Your brand would burn away."

"The brand for before, not after."

"That don't make no sense."

His thin eyes pearlescent, Justice said, "People would say 'They burned a boy over at Wilson's place. Not a thing left. They took his prick, too. But he had a letter *E* up inside his thigh.' Or, 'That boy they beat in the woods? Whole face up in his face. Can't tell his nose from his eye hole. But was a "E" between his legs.' It make sense."

Luther-Philip said, "Let me know it."

Justice took a deep breath and seemed to consider for a long while the meaning of the phrase. After some time, he turned out his leg against Luther-Philip's. Three prongs of raised skin, the three arms of the *E*, rolled into view. The rest of the burnt-on letter remained hidden.

Luther-Philip touched each prong. No telling whether Justice felt him touch against the three arms of the *E* that didn't feel like skin at all, rather something attempting to burst loose from underneath warm leather. Something hard and maybe dangerous, the stone possibilities of a family's fear.

After grazing the brand with his fingertips, Luther-Philip stared at his fingers, wrinkled from having been submerged in water. He couldn't feel Justice's skin because of his own numbness. He placed his hand on his own thigh. He rubbed between his smooth legs and bit the inside of his lip till it bled.

JUSTICE RECALLED the pain of his branding while Luther-Philip traced what the branding left behind. Elevated, a bulbous relief of skin marked an ugly detour from his own body that began early in his life. One morning, King had taken the hot iron to Justice's inner thigh and told him to bite into a rag doused in rum. King had ordered him to swallow as he bit, the alcohol glossing his mind and burning his throat. The brand had rusted over the years. Rainwater and the air itself ate at the surface, leaving on it the color of fire and dried blood along the handle and shaft. The letter the iron stretched into remained pure, but even a young Justice knew that something about the process would taint him. He was a child, and the smell of cooked flesh and the taste of sweet rum had become an irremovable fact. His parents' command that he remain silent about the branding solidified his suspicion that it shouldn't have happened. The rust bore the color and smell of dried blood. He would forever smell erosion between his legs.

Luther-Philip may have been right about his ability to know Justice no matter what happened to him. Before the brand, Justice's parents experienced no difficulty recognizing him. They called his name and when he appeared before them, they reacted as if the face and body presented to them were the ones they expected. But Honor and King were unconvinced it would last and scolded themselves for being so foolishly comfortable in a world that taught them that the dangers of coziness lie in oblivion, that what once took effort to cause harm would now find ease in the defenselessness that a sentimental remembrance allowed. To take for granted the presence of their own son was to saunter into ruin.

Justice didn't want to be ruined, and having so long touched himself there where the *E* pushed out from him, where blood and skin rotted solid, and feeling nothing, he had begun to believe life didn't exist there at all, and if he couldn't feel life where once he could, then his entire body ran the risk of escaping him into death.

But Luther-Philip's fingers proved Justice wrong. He did feel his friend's touch, like a subtle chill wiped across flesh he had thought was a grave. He reached over to Luther-Philip and grabbed his withdrawn hand, moving it back to where the brand's three-pronged hint of an *E* showed itself to the world. He held Luther-Philip's hand down on his thigh with just the weight of his own hand and stared across the water, glossed by sunlight broken into golden flakes across wavelets, at a consort of trees walling off the other side. The water tread sucked at the boys' feet, futilely pulling at them despite there being no destination for either boy to disclose.

[8]

Walking home from the lake, Luther-Philip turned over in his mind the image of Justice running out of Saint's house. He had to know what Justice saw that made him turn the way he did from that porch, his departure carrying with it a heaviness even Luther-Philip could feel. Did Justice drag his leg a little? Were his shoulders lower than usual, pushed down by what Saint's house had revealed to him? They were halfway to Ours's mainland, having crossed Creek's Bridge already. He took their crossing the water as a sign to ask.

"Justice," he started.

"Hmm?" Justice replied, looking ahead.

"What you see in Saint's house?"

Justice slowed to a stop and looked at the ground with such intensity that he may have been seeing through it, for all Luther-Philip knew, into the miasma of melted rock replicating its amorphousness on Justice's face that shifted patiently through countenance after countenance until stiffening into the phantasmal mask that, lifting his head with a snap, held such ire it made Luther-Philip stop breathing. The air swiped malevolent now, lilac scent pursuant no more. An overcast fell over the boys, then the sun returned, then overcast again more relentless, denser, and colder. They were nearly the same height, so why did it feel as though Justice blocked the sun? Instinct told Luther-Philip to back away and with similar reflexes Justice pursued. Then he pushed up on Luther-Philip, in his face, not snarling but with the power of a beast simpleminded in its needs. Before Luther-Philip could tumble backward, Justice grabbed him by the shoulders and embraced him, wrapping one arm around his back and with his free hand he held the back of Luther-Philip's head, resting the boy's chin on his shoulder. They were ear to ear and Luther-Philip didn't understand how his first fear had been replaced by another, less scrutable one.

"Don't leave me," Justice said.

"Leave where? What you leaning into, Justice?" Luther-Philip asked.

"Don't leave me alone."

"But I'm standing right here, Justice."

"Don't leave me, Luthe. I mean it."

"Where would I go?"

"Out. Out of here," Justice said, tapping hard the center of Luther-Philip's upper back.

Luther-Philip believed Justice meant to signal toward his own heart through Luther-Philip's body. With them embracing, with him being embraced by Justice, they were united even in gesture.

"That's up to you, Justice."

"Please stay there," Justice begged.

Luther-Philip repeated, "That's up to you," and broke the embrace, holding his friend by the shoulders and looking square into his eyes bloodshot with sadness and other feelings not yet expressed because not yet understood and not yet understood because not yet realized.

Justice dipped his head so that his forehead touched Luther-Philip's nose. He was crying now and because it had been five years since last he cried, it came out all wrong. Out of practice, his sobs scraped out from his throat, bringing with them the thick amber of calcified emotion amassed because he hadn't properly mourned King and Honor. His last memory of them: their lifeless bodies wrapped in enormous rattlesnakes. He didn't witness his neighbors carry their bodies outside of town to be buried, outside of Ours just in case an in-town burial would keep the conjure alive. Justice wished they had been buried right next to Mrs. Wife's salted grave over which no flora grew and no insect or mammal traversed. His large arms dangled at his sides and what tears wet his face also wet the small stones and flared weeds beneath them with brackish clarity.

"That's up to you," Justice heard Luther-Philip say, and a large black lake unveiled in his mind. He peered across the stretch of water and heard a ghastly roaring. At that moment, he made the connection between the roar and what he saw in Saint's house. He sensed the lake was his heart and that across that dark water lived what would be released if his heart were to break.

With Justice's brow still resting on his nose, Luther-Philip suggested they go back home. Justice nodded, thanked Luther-Philip without knowing why, and straightened. Justice saw in Luther-Philip's face the color of the darkest shade of woodgrain. He looked away so as not to get lost again, circling what he could never reach.

· CHAPTER 7 ·

Inside

[1]

In September 1858, a stranger entered Ours, and upon his entry the air cooled, deepening the early autumn chill. Saint and the twins believed they imagined the unexpected cold together. Saint rested on her porch, watching Naima and Selah pull carrots and rutabagas from the earth. Then a stillness as with the coming of evil and a sudden, small vortex spun between them in the yard, unwinding its yarn of wind thread by thread so that wisps of frost touched and disappeared across their cheeks. They felt the break in the weather but didn't know what it meant. Saint stood, yawned, and made her way into town just a half mile west, over Creek's Bridge, and right onto Tanager, the northernmost road, where no one noticed that ten degrees had been stolen from the early afternoon. The twins waited for her to return, embracing each other to keep warm.

Saint closed her eyes to see if she could better sense the occasion, and sure enough, south of town, someone had entered through a tear in the barrier. It would take a while for whoever entered to make it to the mainland, so she took her time, waving and smiling at neighbors while children raced and wrestled in the grass. It was the end of an overly long grasshopper season and the most playful of the youth stalked the brown leapers, falling to the ground giddy after having caught one of the hard insects. The children were in good spirits even after a nervous grasshopper spat its dark and sticky fluid onto their hands. They would let it go, watch it jump and glide elsewhere, only to hunt it down again.

Summer had been mild, and the approaching autumn introduced itself with the remaining heat the prior season hadn't used. Saint ambled as she was wont to do. Her deep red dress with onyx buttons from clavicle to waist interrupted the pale landscape with its own fire. But the cold that began in her garden stayed with her. She wore her hair wrapped in a large black linen scarf and her locs peeked from the top of the tower, which bobbed as she walked. Trembling, she unraveled her hair and wrapped the linen around her shoulders as a makeshift shawl.

Ours had only one entrance from the south, the rest of the border blocked off by dense woods. Saint stood at the crossway where the first east-west road connected to the entrance path and patiently watched for a figure to emerge. She looked to the sky, then nodded as though receiving instructions from deep within herself. A few paces ahead, Saint drew a circle in the path's dust, then drew another circle inside that one and one more in the center, the concentric circles so perfect they nearly hummed from the ground. She waited again in the commotion of the trees that lined the path and created a green and golden hall through which the unwelcome visitor would walk. Branches swayed in the breeze and the applause they fed to the wind grew endless.

Saint had every intention of being a wall. She stood stalwart, unfazed by the flies drawing arcs near her face and the boughs clapping for a stranger she wanted dead for disturbing her nap. A biting wind cut around her. She crossed her arms against the pleasure of the trees, but they kept cheering above her. When the shape of a horse appeared on the path, she sighed. When it became clear her visitor consisted of a rider and a cart holding numerous books and a large mound covered in a sheet, a small fire lit inside her. A horse she could handle. A man with a cart full of books and a sheet-covered surprise was out of the question.

Wheels cracked along the pebbles and dry grass as the horse slow-dragged the ragged cart behind it. The man didn't tug on the rein so much as he snapped both it and the horse into motionlessness and hopped out, sweat-drenched, just short of where Saint stood. He smelled of smoke and urine.

The man approached Saint and smiled. She nodded and killed a fly between her palms and flicked the dead thing off to the side. The moment he stepped inside the concentric circles, one foot went ahead of him and the other stepped behind, then he turned on his heels and his eyes rolled to the back of his head before closing. He hit the ground soon after. Hours later, the man woke and realized he was no longer in front of the woman in red. Every landmark that he remembered seeing before entering town—a leant-over maple tree, three large bushes to the right and two smaller ones to the left—remained, but the path he took that led him to that woman with the brilliant dress and impenetrable countenance had disappeared, somehow, in the void of a flat plain.

Saint returned to her porch, sweat dripping down the sides of her face, the cold air brought in by the intruder no more. Selah and Naima looked up for a moment, then returned to gathering vegetables from the garden. Naima chewed on a stick as she worked. Selah hummed to herself.

When Saint began to snore, Naima asked Selah, "What you see?"

"A man with a horse and a cart full of books come up on the path. There was something big in the cart under a sheet, too. He had on awful clothes. They looked burnt up. He was very handsome, though, brown like the bottom of a pot."

"How she get rid of him?"

"I don't know."

Naima frowned. "You was watching, wasn't you?"

"Saint killed the fly I was using to look," she said, bored with the conversation.

"She knew you was looking," Naima said, and put the stick back in her mouth and returned to work.

Selah hummed a bit more of her song, then responded as though the song helped her to get the words right. "Saint always know the looking of folks."

SAINT NEVER TAUGHT Selah how to look into things. The girl woke up one morning thinking she was flying over a river and her shock became panic when she couldn't land. She screamed and Saint entered the girls' room. Naima was lying down, wrapped in a sheet with her back turned to them.

"I'm flying but I don't want to. I don't want to," Selah whimpered into Saint's shoulder.

Saint saw that the girl's eyes were glazed over as though baby-blue milk had been dripped into them. She covered the girl's eyes with a hand and told Selah to lengthen her breathing. "Deep, deep breaths," Saint said. "Just think about being in my arms." She embraced the child and counted to ten. "Open your eyes." When she opened her eyes, Selah saw the fabric of Saint's dress and thought she was underwater, so kept on whimpering. It took seeing Saint's face for her to realize she had returned to the bedroom. Saint kept an eye on the girl but had difficulties figuring out what exactly had happened. She watched, but Naima made that unnecessary.

One day, Selah saw herself from overhead on the porch. Naima looked up and noticed a spider sat in its web over Selah's head. Naima grabbed the spider and flung it across the yard.

"Did you see me? See my hand?" Naima asked. Selah said yes and that now she saw grass. Naima screamed with glee and clapped. "You inside a spider."

"I want to be back inside myself."

"Do you feel like you got more legs?" Naima squirmed and waved her arms at her side.

"I want to be back. I do not want to be in a spider."

"Can you make it move?"

Selah held her breath and squinted. "No. It doesn't seem like it. Naima, I do not want to be in the spider anymore."

"Do that thing Saint told you to do last time," Naima said.

"I thought you were sleeping," Selah said, staring blankly ahead. No matter where she turned her head, she only saw what the spider saw.

"I was playacting."

"That's sneaky, Naima."

"Just do what she told you."

"That's sneaky and I do not like it," Selah said, her voice trembling.

Naima embraced Selah and said, "I won't do it no more, Selah. I won't do it no more." She meant it, but because Selah couldn't see her sister's face, she didn't respond to what she would've recognized as sincerity. "Close your eyes. I'll count to ten. You in my arms. Think about me."

When her sight returned, Selah didn't speak to Naima for days, and for days Naima refused to eat. It took Saint scolding Selah for Selah to finally speak to her sister and for Naima, hungry and thin as the horizon, to begin eating again.

[2]

The next day, the man with the horse and cart returned the same way he had come before. Naima felt him first, then Saint, then Selah. All three stopped what they were doing—Naima poking around an anthill, Saint making soup for supper, and Selah napping in a large, upholstered chair in the main room. All three faced the direction of Ours's mainland. Saint heard too much gurgling coming from the pot and investigated her soup. Black feathers bubbled up from the bottom where once were no feathers at all. She blinked and they were gone. Selah yawned and smelled smoke, sweet as a cookie, escape from her mouth. Naima felt water drip from her ears and down the side of her face, but when she wiped away the wet, she saw that blood, not water, stained her fingers. The three met outside and shared their conditions. Saint noted that each of their senses were under attack. She ran back inside. The girls waited, Naima covering her sister's mouth and Selah covering Naima's ears, and when Saint returned carrying her staff and a pistol, the girls' eyes widened with fear. She handed the pistol to Naima and said, "Anybody come this way, you do what you have to do." Naima nodded. Saint rushed off toward the woods. Her companion was nowhere to be found.

[3]

In Ours, the man with the whistling horse and the creaking cart full of Bibles and a sheet-covered mystery rolled on up Third Street past Bank, with the tiny cemetery on the east, and then Freedom Street, where Franklin and Thylias lived in a squat house on the northeastern corner. Franklin always sat on his porch with a shotgun between his legs and Thylias always sat on the opposite end of the porch with a shotgun between her legs. Franklin had made a habit of keeping his gun close by, something that rubbed off on Thylias. He watched the man and, not recognizing him, began to massage the butt of his gun. Thylias, bun tight as ever on top of her head, placed her fingers lightly on her gun as if placing her hands on her knees.

Over the years in Ours, the two sat in rapt silence on the porch, or orbited each other in the small house like two moons in perfect accord. They hardly spoke to each other but were not dismissive, merely thinned out by what they had lived and wanting now only to delight in the peace once absent in their lives. When hunger gripped one, the other cooked. If one felt sore, the other would rub a minty salve where it hurt. They kept to themselves out of obligation to this peace. They didn't fear their neighbors but were exhausted by a past that lacked privacy and were inspired, now, by selves they suddenly had time to get to learn. In the castle of their own company, they nurtured this newfound safety with parental fervor. Many thought them laughless, but together they laughed. Many thought them strange, and perhaps they were, lying on the floor of their house, looking up at the meeting of ceiling and wall against which night's vague illumination portraited itself with branch and moonbeam. And though not lovers, they found in privacy a platonic romance their otherwise history had vowed but failed to destroy.

It made sense, then, that they embraced their shotguns at the same time when the horseback stranger rolled in. What became learned mimicry for Thylias was instinct for Franklin, for as the man with the cart came closer, he and Franklin met eyes for a moment, seaming between the two men a rift in time no bigger than a thumbnail. The past rushed up through Franklin as he recognized in that cart-driving man's eyes a pair of eyes he had seen before on the plantation that Saint and her companion annihilated over the course of a few days.

Neither his so-called master's eyes nor the eyes of one of the overseers came to his memory; rather Franklin saw the eyes of another boy, older, familiar to him though not a friend. Franklin was a boy again, and both Thylias and the cart-driving man fell to the wayside as the older boy from his past came into view.

The older boy had shown Franklin a wounded fox he had found hiding in a dirt hole half-covered by a log. It was pregnant at the time but missing one of its hind legs from the shin down. The older boy regularly fed the fox scraps of fat and organ meat meant for himself and brought it water in a tin bowl. The older boy told Franklin not to tell anyone and Franklin promised he wouldn't.

The following Sunday, the older boy went to the fox without telling Franklin. Franklin headed to where the boys usually snuck off, making sure no one saw him. He found the older boy standing over the fox that had just given birth to four kits. The older boy took the kits up from the hole and kissed each one, placing them beside him. Franklin smiled but remained hidden and quiet behind a thicket. The older boy looked at the kits for a moment, shook his head, then slit the throats of each small animal with a peasant knife. After the boy killed the last kit, Franklin yelped as though he were next for the blade. The older boy turned to face him. His eyes were joyless and unoccupied. Franklin ran away and told his father what he had seen.

After a brief discussion, a few men, rallied by Franklin's father, understood: this trip had been the older boy's second that day to see the fox, which had died while giving birth. The older boy killed the kits as a merciful act. This is why he went alone: to keep Franklin from having to witness what had to be done.

The men agreed with the decision and tried to explain it to Franklin, but he heard nothing they said. During the rush back to the plantation, before their so-called master discovered their absence, the older boy, betrayed but redeemed by the other men, looked at Franklin for a good while before turning his gaze back toward their destination, right in time for one of the most respected men in the group to place his large hand on the older boy's head. Franklin couldn't hear what the man said to the older boy, but he did hear laughter.

The same look Franklin received from the older boy way back when now warped the cart-driving man's eyes. The reeking horse and the Bibles masked nothing of the undecipherable but darkly tinted gaze. All Franklin knew was that this look required a shotgun to keep at bay. It had something to do with death, that it follows, that it lingers wherever it lands.

Thylias spoke first, "Where you heading?"

"I'se looking for God here," the man said.

"Sir, you looking in the wrong place," Thylias responded.

The softness of her voice encouraged the man, despite the shotguns, to jump off his horse, reach into his cart, and pull out two Bibles. Thylias tensed up. Franklin held his breath. The man approached the two on the porch and before Franklin could shoot, Thylias stuck her hand out toward him.

"I'se got the Word of God to share with the people. These words set a sick soul free. God's Word the only word," the man said, and extended both arms. The Bibles' gold lettering threw back sunlight into his face. Instead of lowering the books, he squinted.

"I can't read a word in there, I'm afraid," Franklin said.

"I can but don't want to. Move along," Thylias said. Her fingers tickled the shotgun's side.

"The Word of God is final," the man said.

Without raising her voice, Thylias replied, "God watched my friends get whipped to the bone. Tarry no more."

The man lowered the Bibles and placed them back into the cart with much care. He leapt onto his horse, gave the pair on the porch one last look, nodded, then moved along.

Franklin's hand trembled over the shotgun handle. He hadn't stopped looking at the man since he arrived and watched him and his horse and cart mosey down the road with a stricken look.

He thought he had forgotten it, the test of manhood, the trial to put manhood in him so that it may stop all resonance of anything else: cowardice, fear, betrayal, the "womanly ways" of gossip, as the men called it, though their own gossip had brought them there to the hole. His father hadn't even led the pack of men that took young Franklin back to where the foxes were killed. His father allowed someone else's father to do that.

The men dropped Franklin into a just-dug hole and tossed the tiny dead kits in one at a time after him, their small, stiff bodies landing at his bare feet. The men shouted into the mud-mouth that he shouldn't fear the dead and egged him on to touch the lifeless bodies because "They won't bite. Can't bite. You never had nothing to be scared of." They ignored his screams—high-pitched, a birdsong, which only angered the men and humiliated his father, for even then, in a test of manhood, his son decided to sing.

Perhaps, this same birdsong attracted the young men to him while he played alone in the field because no other children would play with him. He sang alone to himself quietly, a wooden horse in hand that he made hop along the dirt road unlike a real horse and more like a bird, and the boys wanted to end the song, end everything bird once and for all. They pummeled him. Punched him in the face. Kicked him in the arms. The other men watched, yes, even his father, and Franklin understood this as yet another test that he didn't know the answers to.

The boys punched harder, kicked his legs, and teased him. He lay huddled into himself, crying. "Fight back, boy," he heard his father shout. Then a gunshot rang out and the boys scattered. All but one, who lay beside Franklin. It was the older boy who had cared for the foxes, bleeding out from the mouth, looking straight at him. When the boy's parents ran toward their dead son, the so-called master raised his gun at them. They stopped. The so-called master stepped over the dead boy and looked down at Franklin.

"You're safe now, son," his so-called master said, the man's smile full of tobacco. "Let this be a lesson to you all about property. You don't own nothing, so you don't care about nothing. I takes good care of what's mine. And I can break whatever belongs to me just as well. Keep your hands off what don't belong to you." The so-called master looked at the dead boy's father. "I'm expecting a new one from you soon. This debt yours."

Flies landed on the dead boy's face. Franklin looked for his father, but he had already disappeared behind a heap of unshucked corn.

Thylias touched Franklin on the shoulder and he jumped, returning from his childhood memories. "Let's go inside," she said. He nodded, watching where the man with the cart full of Bibles would've been had he, too, stood watch in the distance, looking back at a history-wounded man who clenched a gun he was too shaky to use. If the dead that Franklin thought he had escaped had, instead, followed him through bramble, he hoped the ability to protect himself and others in Ours lived within him. Instead, possessing every bone in his right hand and threatening to spread throughout the rest of his body, a drop of fear tainted his will. The southern entrance to Ours opened interminably before his shrinking courage.

BUT THE MAN with the cart had moved on, and he met hostility everywhere he rode. A father and his sons singing and playing banjos on their porch damn near threw their instruments at him when he tried to hand them each a Bible. A woman hanging wet sheets on a line vanished behind the fabric when she recognized the gilded word pressed into the cover.

Children screamed and ran home, not because of the Bibles but because the man yelled, smelled bad, and they didn't know him at all to offer him grace. He had made the biggest mistake by choosing Ours to peddle God in. For some of the Ouhmey, this was the first time they laid eyes on a Bible. For those who knew what it was, they nearly turned to stone from their memories.

The residents there had themselves been or were children of those who were overworked, unpaid, hobbled, starved, raped, beaten, tortured, sold off, experimented on, molested, and nearly hanged, all beneath the auspice of God's watchful eye. They prayed and a family was separated by a bill of sale. They went to tawdry outdoor churches where a white preacher tried to tell them their fate had been given to them by the very God they were supposed to worship, though he gave no reasons as to why God thought it plausible that a slave could serve two masters when no one else on earth was allowed to. And if their so-called masters were chosen by God, then why the hell would they want to serve a

God who may find benevolence enough in their abuse such that He would keep the abuse going on in Heaven as on earth?

They assumed Saint knew him because that was the only way he could have entered in the first place, and they secretly hoped she was coming to get him before someone shot him dead. Anyone else entering town as a stranger would've been offered a meal and a place to bathe, some clothes to borrow, assistance of some sort before Saint arrived to explain the phenomenon of an unmarked Negro entering town. But the Bibles made it hard and, too, the fact that he had entered their town without introducing himself while trying to give them his version of the Lord. Might as well trail mud into their just-cleaned homes.

Frustrated, the man slammed his fist into the sheeted object. It bellowed. He shouted, "The Word of God be the alpha and omega. None like Him and won't be none like Him till the final days. If you not letting God lead your lamb-ways from the wolves, the teeth of the Devil gone run through you. I'se seent it for myself, the Devil's work, and I knows it to be a job for God. Job had to lose it all to gain his understanding. Don't go on living like Job when you don't got to."

People began to approach him. Children who earlier had snarled and ran away now went to him with begging hands. Too young to understand (or old enough to understand but too ignorant to read the words properly), the children asked for Bibles plaintively, an unsteadiness in their voices the man mistook as the abrupt onset of the fear of God. Soon the adults followed, hands out, mouths gnawing the air in the way a soon-to-be-dead fish puckers one useless breath after another.

The man passed out the Bibles, thirty-three in all, and saw that a few more were needed. He made sure to tell them to share the Word of God though none listened, and their faces, sheened over with a glimmer of desperation, became one horrific mask that they all wore at once. The man found a bit of fear in him and when the Bibles were gone but the empty hands kept reaching, their mouths mouthing soft and slow Os with no sound other than the smack of saliva churning in saliva, he backed away. The people tugged at his singed clothes, so he climbed into the cart, next to the covered object, hoping to get away. Hands kept reaching and the man began to shout: "I'se got no more to give! You got to do the rest for yourself."

But their hands flared insatiable, clawing now. One man began to climb into the cart, affectless, no telling where his eyes were looking, but his extended fingers flexed to grab hold of something, anything in front of him, his hands scratching at the air, desperate, hungry.

The visitor in the cart leaned hard against the object under the sheet and soft thunder rang from the hollow. Everyone who had been reaching and slobbering stopped and looked around. When the lot of them saw Bibles in their hands, they made puzzled looks as though they were holding the ultimate riddle. They held on to them for a short time before returning the books to the cart, dropping them in one by one.

"What's wrong with you? My God, what's wrong with all them in the world?" the man asked, and when the road cleared of Ouhmey, he hopped out of the cart and headed east, thinking it would get him out of town.

He guided the horse and cart on foot. When he finally arrived at the pretty blue house with the garden in front and two girls with the same face, one covering her mouth and the other girl standing on the porch and holding a pistol aimed right at him, he knelt to the ground and bent forward till his forehead kissed the earth. By the looks of it, he threw words into the grass and laughed. His shoulders heaved and dropped, heaved and dropped.

"That's the man I saw," Selah said. Smoke eased from her mouth as she spoke.

"Speak more words to me," Naima said, her aim steady.

"When Saint went into Ours after the weather changed. That's the man who come into town uninvited."

"I can smell him from here."

"How'd he get back in?"

"I can smell him from here, Selah."

"I heard you the first time."

"I'm shooting him."

"Cause he smell bad?"

"Cause I can," Naima said, and shot at the man but missed. Dirt exploded in front of him. The man jumped up and tried to climb onto his panicking horse that bucked and pivoted, frightened by the sound. "Cause I'm bored." A trickle of red slid from her left ear.

"I won't stop you," Selah said. "Saint won't be happy, though. Saint won't be happy at all."

Naima put the pistol on the ground. "You right. Let's find something else to do."

"You can cover my mouth and I can cover your ears again."

"All right," Naima said, and the girls touched each other where they were both afflicted.

Seeing this, the man stood still. His horse calmed down, too, and let out a sharp whistle from its nose. The man said, "Free niggers a dangerous thing."

Naima released Selah's mouth and a stream of smoke poured out. "What you say?" Naima asked.

"I didn't say anything," Selah replied.

"Not you. You," Naima said, and pointed to the man. "You call us 'nigger'? You saying our head not on straight?" Naima picked up the pistol and descended the porch steps. Selah's palms were covered in her sister's blood.

"I don't want no trouble," the man said.

"Coming here and ain't even said what your name is. You here saying who a nigger but ain't said shit bout your name," she said, waving the gun around like it was a stick. Naima had no idea what "nigger" really meant, just that Saint abhorred the word and told her and her sister to never call another or be called that. "What it mean?" Naima asked, and Saint said, "It means somebody telling you your head on backwards and you believe them."

"Young ladies shouldn't say them kinds of words." The man fumbled his own words and fondled the hair on his horse's neck. He wanted to ride away but his shaky legs kept him from getting on the horse.

"And piss-funk men shouldn't come no place not saying who they is." Naima trained the gun on the man. "So who is you?"

The man stuttered, then stopped trying altogether. Wind taunted the stink from his body. He was young and felt it most then. Up to that point he hadn't lived much of a life. These people—free and playful and angry and taciturn and owning guns and using them—exasperated him not because of something innate in their personalities but because it revealed to him his own lack of personality. Sure, it was dangerous being free, but he wasn't dangerous to anyone but himself. And he saw what white folks, all their life free, did to each other and, after thinking about it, felt shame for what he said to Naima. These people were Godless and the only danger in that was a fire-paved road to hell.

He was born into slavery and sold early in his life to Pastor Sykes, a Christian who believed that slaves were his birthright to own because God had said so in the Good Book. When sold, the auctioneer called him The Boy, because there was no name for him in the registry.

So, when Naima asked him for his name, he had no answer. He was ordered to do things by Sykes but was never called a name, only Boy, You, My Slave, The Slave, Him, It, and Hey. He dug deep into his mind and came up with Reverend, something he heard a parishioner call Sykes mistakenly.

"My name Reverend," he said to Naima.

"Reverend a type of person," she responded.

"Reverend be my name," he said.

"'Reverend be my name,'" Naima mocked, then lowered the gun. "Don't move, *Reverend*. You hear me?"

"Naima, you so old and mean," Selah said, and started to laugh then cough up smoke. Naima laughed but kept her eyes on Reverend.

"I hears you," Reverend said, and sat cross-leg in the grass by the cart.

[4]

Saint found her companion in the woods close to the house. Her sense of sight was still under attack. Trees leaned in and knitted into each other. She squinted, and the trees unwound, standing back straight.

Her companion was standing with his back to her in a small clearing not even an eighth of a mile north. His head dipped to his right shoulder as though trying to get water to drip out. He did it a few times, then stopped. Then did it many more times with a violence and speed Saint had never seen a human accomplish. She approached him from behind. When she determined how far she wanted to be, she repeatedly pounded the tip of her staff into the ground. Her companion stopped beating his head against his shoulder. When he turned to face her, he moved more fluidly and, on his face, though subtle, an expression broke through. Even more to Saint's surprise, his mouth moved.

Her companion twitched and flinched. His brow trembled and his lips quivered. Speech wanted to erupt from his mouth, but Saint shook her head. Absolutely not.

"Return to me." She kept an even tone and gripped her staff till it hurt.

"Re–" her companion started. Saint shook her head again.

"I don't know what has happened, but you will return to me."

"Re . . . lease . . . m . . . mmm—"

"This is not the way. Return to me."

"Release . . . mmm—"

"You will submit," Saint said, and slammed her staff into the ground.

"For . . ." Her companion smiled, then frowned, near weeping, then found anger in his brow. Finally, he decided on a face of beseeching gracelessness. He stepped forward. Saint slammed the tip of her staff into the ground. A bolt of lightning coursed through the sky. He kept lurching forward, stumbling, moving his lips, but the words slipped around his mouth before falling out. "For . . . give muh," he said.

"Submit," Saint said.

Her companion moan-shouted. A line of drool dropped and dangled from his bottom lip. He stopped moving, lowered his head, and released a long, sad note. He did it once more, then looked up at Saint, pleading with his eyes though she showed no sign of caring. He stepped forward. Another bolt of lightning split the sky. He stepped again and stumbled off to the side but kept moving closer to Saint. Small bits of blood seeped through his shirt from his stomach. Saint's eyes flew open.

"Submit." Saint slammed down her staff again and a bolt of lightning cracked into a tree behind her companion. He took another step and another bolt of lightning fell from the sky, dividing a tree. With every step he took, lightning assaulted the trees and the ground, setting small blue fires in the leaves and circles of black char in the grass. Eventually, her companion had come close enough to touch her. He was taller than her, but she refused to look up to meet his eyes. With what little control he had, he lowered himself to his knees and touched the toes of her shoes.

"Re . . . me," he said. "Release . . . love . . ."

'Was that rain that landed on the back of his head?' Saint wondered. 'I didn't want rain.' She looked up and didn't see rainfall and thought it another illusion, like the trees twisting into each other. She looked down at her companion's head and sure enough water dripped down into his hair. She touched her face. It was wet. Her nose started to run. Her sight blurred. A warmth poured into her skull. 'I am raining on the inside,' she thought, 'and it's coming out.'

Her companion repeated his request into the ground, his fingers never leaving her feet. "Release me," into the grass. "Release me," over a trail of ants carrying a dead wasp. "Release me," slipping past circles of burnt flowers perfuming the air. "Release me," pulsing through the crab apples till they fell one at a time from their singed branches. "Release me," floating up to Saint's resistant but listening ears.

Saint wiped her eyes, sniffed, and was done with it. "There is no releasing you," she began, talking to the top of her companion's head. "There is only returning. And if you don't return, then what will I do with this anger?" She paused, then said, "There is only the way things were. I will have that. You will have that."

Her companion lifted himself from his bow. On his knees, he looked up at Saint's waist and said, clear as day, "Please don't do this."

"Submit."

"Please. Saint—"

"Submit."

"Saint!"

"There are worse things than this. Submit or I might show you."

Her companion stared up and Saint saw reflected in his grayed-over brown eyes what he must have seen: sky blistered white and purple, erased of all birds, clouds dissipating along with Saint's wrath; fingertips of branches etching into the sky an insignia for no language involving humans; and, perhaps, himself up there where, if allowed, he could join the dissipating clouds, the absence of birds, the sharp ends of branches carving, carving. But Saint didn't know that her companion was looking at her hair, then her forehead, and he stayed there because he didn't want to look her in the eyes and didn't want to risk doing so while attempting to move to her nose and, finally, to her mouth as she said, "Submit." Saint didn't know this and didn't care to know. She watched him close his eyes from which fell cloudy tears. When he opened them, all expression was gone. He had given himself up once more to Saint. She motioned for him to stand, and he stood, gazing straight ahead. She slapped his face, and he didn't respond. She slapped him again. Again. And again. Satisfied, she pointed to the direction of the house, and he led the way. She didn't follow. He waited some feet away for her. Around them, every tree had lost every leaf and the clearing smoked beneath her feet. Black circles of cooked dirt and burnt grass smoldered where lightning connected with the earth. Her original thought was true: she hadn't wanted rain, but she also hadn't wanted lightning. Standing in the aftermath of her emotions, she tapped her staff to the ground meaning to summon a bolt this time, at least a flash. Nothing came, not even the illusion of warping trees. She caught up with her companion and left the nothing behind.

· CHAPTER 8 ·

Instructions

[1]

After finding her companion in the woods, Saint peered at Reverend, who slept in the cart just feet from her front door. He had dozed off with his head resting on the wood railing of the cart, his horse statuesque and rank in waiting. She noticed an open book on his lap, pages turning in the wind, the sound of birds escaping. She hit her staff hard against the railing, waking Reverend with a quick jolt that tossed the book from his thighs. He beheld the fallen book and his lost page mournfully.

Early in Reverend's enslavement, Pastor Sykes had taught him how to read, just enough to get by with some of the simpler excerpted scriptures (a nugget from Psalms, a touch of Genesis). Sykes never whipped Reverend because he believed in the idea of a benevolent master. In this way, he considered both himself and Reverend to be closer to God than the others whose acts of violence against their slaves delivered them swiftly into the arms of perdition. And wherever the master went, his property followed.

The Third Great Awakening had impressed Sykes and he wanted to make a caravan of sorts where newly converted and old-time lovers of Christ would march across the country to spread the gospel, believing that the Second Coming waited right around the corner if they could just touch the four corners of the world with the knowledge of Christ's crucifixion and inevitable resurrection.

Traveling from Arkansas into northern Texas, Sykes gathered only twenty worshippers for his Christ parade and all twenty died of heatstroke, dehydration, infection from wounds come about during travel, fever, and various other ailments wholly avoidable had they been better prepared or not left at all. Sykes, having never traveled before and putting all his faith in a God whose miracles melted in the obscene heat, discovered faith wasn't enough to protect the body and watched as small groups of devotees spurted blood from every orifice imaginable or fell knee-bent to the ground while cupping a maggot-infested side, hand, or thigh that throbbed like a second heart. Delirious, one man held his swollen gut and whispered to it, "You be born soon," before dying right there. God had either abandoned Sykes and his followers or was teaching them a vicious lesson. The worst deaths, though, were the least vulgar. Those who died of fever, of depleted liquids, of sun devouring them pore to organ, for miles they rode their horses slumped over, and Sykes thought they were merely resting. At a water stop, he discovered that he and Reverend were the only two alive. The rest that followed had not ridden with them so much as silently haunted them from the graves of their saddles.

When the two returned to Arkansas, Sykes decided to build a small church. With his savings, he contacted a publisher to buy a large set of the cheapest leather Bibles available. Gold letters engraved on the covers and on the binding read: "Bible." It took a month to finish building the tiny church, which opened its doors October 3, 1857, just outside a town called Ferris that had a population of 175. Sykes named the church Second Coming of Christ Church. No one visited.

One day, a stranger arrived in Ferris with a wagon carrying a large silver bell. Engraved into it were hundreds of petals layered against the curvature of the bell. The stranger said he brought it with him from a trip to what he called Middle-Africa, taken from an abandoned village made up of tiny houses. He believed a "pygmy tribe" lived there, small as ten-year-olds though full adults. The bell hung in the center of the village beneath which lay human and animal bones.

Sykes needed a bell for his church and the asking price was inexpensive. However, the stranger warned that though the bell had brought him good luck, riches beyond his wildest fantasies, several of his spouses spiraled into madness because of it. He had removed the clapper to save himself.

His brief warning to Sykes before departing: "Ring it without speaking and all will be fine."

Being a Christian, Sykes dismissed the warning as superstition. The first time he rang the bell, he shouted as if anyone could hear him, "You must come to the Lord for the Lord to do work in your life. Nothing else matters but the Lord." Minutes later, everyone in Ferris, including the pastor of their one other church, came to service. Reverend, not allowed to hear the white Word, was always sent on some distant errand until Sykes had finished giving his sermon.

After several successful services, the congregation's behavior deteriorated. Sykes noticed that what was once eagerness became drowsy obedience. They didn't worship. They repeated what he said, dull-eyed, and every service their appearance declined. They looked emaciated, their faces and arms covered in fresh sores. They smelled worse than usual, many of them, and had untidy beards and unclean, lice-infested hair. Days later, laden with fearful curiosity, Sykes told Reverend to visit Ferris and report back any discovery, giving him a pass and an apple.

That Tuesday, upon arrival in Ferris, Reverend was terrified by the calamity taking authority over the town. People copulated in the streets. A woman had carved into her face nearly a dozen crosses. Dogs tore at a living mule's legs and stomach, maddened with hunger. Reverend turned his mule away but, before he could retreat, a man wearing a white robe tied at his waist lurched toward him. Light emanated from the center of his forehead. Reverend thought the Messiah had come to save everyone in Ferris, but the man stumbled closer to Reverend until he fell face-first in the road. A bullet hole the width of a nickel tunneled straight through his head. Madness had puppeted him through the chaos and straight to Reverend, and the light Reverend had seen was merely sunlight reflecting off a metal surface and beaming through the hole in the dead man's head. Reverend kicked his mule, and above his escape lightning carved crooked veins into the dark sky.

When he returned to the church, he saw Sykes standing outside with a lantern. A stormy overcast disfigured sunlight into a sullen pantomime of its former self and a strong wind rocked the bell without warning in the direction of the wood post that held it up. It began to resonate. Sykes went pale. Before Sykes could warn against it, Reverend spoke a word of encouragement: "They need God more than ever now. Y'all be fighting for God's love real soon." Sykes instantly felt an insatiable desire to pray in collaboration with shedding blood, and not long after his own feelings came to fruition did dust in the distance lift its skirt while, from under the hem, a horde of degenerates ravaged the hilly ground beneath their stampede. All rushed to the church and began violently praying, stomping over those who had fallen to the ground. A woman somehow set herself on fire and called out for God to see the might of her devotion. The fire caught on and soon enough the wooden benches and Bibles began to burn.

And like an angel that has accomplished its task, Reverend disappeared. In what remained of Sykes's mind he heard the rolling cart and his horse outside. The last thing he saw was Reverend saving Bibles from the flames and leaving him behind. The last thing he heard, that wasn't the curses and screams of a parishioner burning alive or praying in an unrecognizable language, was the bell's close keening, then not so close, then not at all.

Reverend took off from Arkansas and arrived at Ours, allowed to make it that far by nature of him constantly praying and the Bibles ringing the bell as they fell into it or the bell singing on its own when the cart bumped about on the uneven landscape. White folks brought him food instead of harassing him. They fed and watered his horse instead of taking it from him. He asked about the north and they pointed him in the right direction instead of robbing him. And each person who helped him collapsed into madness the moment he left. He fell asleep just a few hours away from Ours, waking not even an hour after a bad dream that horrified him to wetting his pants.

None of this explained how he found Ours, why Ours revealed itself to him, but it did explain how he made it there unscathed, safe up until he reached the blue house with the lush garden guarded by sable-eyed twins and thirteen snakes frozen in a woman's relentless grip.

[2]

You that lady I saw back over that way," he said, yawning and pointing toward some indiscernible location. Gnats orbited his ripening stink. Before he could say another word, Saint flashed him a look of disgust. A sudden overcast veiled the world gray. His silence followed.

She observed the cart's contents, scoffing at the Bibles and surveying the bell intensely once she snatched the sheet from its frame. She recognized the bell's origin right away, though she held no memory of having seen anything like it before. The word "biloko" entered her mind and a wave of heat coursed through her from her skull to the curve of her toenails. The bell was about as tall as a six-year-old, wide as a full-grown man, and surprisingly light. She stood stiff before the intricate metalwork of leaf patterns engraved on the bell's surface. When a bush rustled, the heat in Saint's body rushed to her head as she faced the bush with murderous determination. Danger. Danger all around.

Not knowing how she knew what she knew but not questioning her knowledge, she demanded Reverend keep his mouth shut for the duration of his stay until she decided her next move. She ordered him to bathe in her backyard and gave him oversize clothes from a collection of suits worn by her companion.

Saint wanted to test the bell without harming anyone. She gave Reverend permission to speak and asked him about his journey, his history, how he got to Ours, to discover through anecdote what otherwise would need example. She figured out the following:

1. If the bell rings once without anyone speaking, nothing happens.
2. If it rings once and an order is given (or something that could be mistaken as an order), those within hearing distance of the bell are compelled to follow the order.
3. If it rings again with the same order or a new order, those within hearing distance of the bell would have their need to serve the order, old or new, intensified.
4. The order itself does not need to be heard, only the bell's ring.
5. If an order is given but it can't be completed, madness ensues.
6. If the bell rings and an order is given but the one who rang the bell leaves, madness ensues.
7. If the bell rings because of outside forces, such as a strong wind, anyone can give an order.
8. Ringing the bell once without giving a new order, but after an order had been given during a prior ring, breaks the spell. The spell is not broken this way if an outside force rings the bell.
9. For some reason, the bell opens the barrier, ruins Saint and her daughters' senses, and confounds her companion into clarity if it rings within at least a half mile, even if unheard. Senses return after an hour or so. Her companion's clarity wasn't tested to see if it dispels on its own.

Saint speculated that the bell being brought to Ours made it more vicious, its new home not fit for its particular defense. She assumed the biloko must've been protected from the bell's effects by some other artifact, maybe a ring they each wore on their hairy fingers, or a gris-gris worn like a waistband. Without anything of the sort, its purpose to protect made it a weapon against anyone nearby.

As a small test, Saint lightly rang the bell and demanded Reverend and the twins jump. She had already given her companion the command to ignore all sound except her own voice. To reinforce her command, she filled her companion's ears with water-soaked cotton, then wrapped a thick band of wool around his head with the hopes that he would remain unaffected. He didn't move, and she was thankful, but Naima, Selah, and Reverend began to jump continuously. She rang the bell once more without speaking at all and the spell was broken, but Selah started coughing up smoke again and Naima's ears began to bleed. Saint rolled her eyes. When she suffered no illusions, she assumed it was because she had been the one to ring the bell. Knowing this information, she decided to destroy the instrument, but she heard her own voice in her head say that it was an impossible deed.

She decided to hide the bell in her home, locked in the back room where she practiced conjure. She sat it on a table beside her throne of bones, which had been rebuilt by her companion, piece by piece, inside a room she kept locked next to the kitchen. She called this room the divining room. The bones had followed her underground like worms from her burned-down house to the new house that she kept secret from her own people with engraving stones. She and her companion built, furnished, and hid the evidence of the new house until preparations were secure.

Saint had seen her original home burn down in a vision some years ago though she had no idea who the culprit would be, just when they would strike. So, she built a second home, better than the first because made by her own devices, and she laid a hard curse over it to protect herself.

Originally, the visions of love and fear that Justice saw when he entered her home were meant to be a trap for intruders because she had lost the ability to sense when someone approached, as evidenced by Aba's unannounced visit. If anyone unwelcome stepped past the front door, they would have to deal with what they could handle the least in life. Saint didn't know for herself which was worse: to be confronted by what you loved the most or by what you feared most deeply.

Love has a way of making old hurt and new joys share space, because hope makes a naive shepherd of you. You rear the two together and wonder why the joy gets gobbled up so fast while old hurt licks its fangs in the shadows. Saint expected the worst when she made love and fear share space, something they do naturally; she just offered a little assistance. With her own fears locked close and what she loved destroyed a long time ago, Saint had no trouble experiencing her own curse; everyone living in that house had to go through it as the curse didn't discriminate.

It seemed Selah and Naima had no fears, nothing rich enough to be reflected back at them, but when they both shared with Saint that it was she whom they saw as their love, she didn't know what to do with the information. And the confessions were different. Selah said she saw Saint as her love, but Naima said she saw both Saint and Selah. For this reason, Saint pulled Selah aside, spoke words for which she had no evidence, only a confident inkling. "Your sister's younger than you even though she born first. She come out the womb first to make sure everything was safe for you to come into the light and dark of this world. You sent her out into possible danger and because of her devotion to you she went on and did it. You are the elder sister. Now it is your turn to watch over Naima." Saint's words had nothing to do with love, but love wasn't the objective. She wanted Selah to feel a sense of duty that if absent could put them all in jeopardy. "Do you understand what I'm saying to you?" Saint held Selah's gaze in her own. Selah nodded, then ran off outside. 'Girl will kill us all with her indifference,' Saint thought, and prepared a meal for the three to eat.

[3]

Earlier that day, when she saw blood seep through her companion's shirt, she knew the fearful bell needed to be kept hidden. But now a new fear tapped her on the shoulder. She had been feeling it for some time, its approach draping itself over everything she did with a thick syrup that slowed down her very thinking. Its shape was limitless, more a pulsing that grew stronger each day. She felt tired more than usual. Her future visions weren't as frequent. So, she went off and got her some twins to protect herself, knowing that twins, especially girls, are the strongest gris-gris there is. Still, the lingering ennui, the trepidation soiling the air.

Saint closed her eyes to sense it with unrivaled focus, but whenever she tried, a pain in her stomach struck her to bending forward. She blamed her weakening conjure on the approaching omen's influence over her, and if her conjure couldn't stand up to whatever approached, then she and the entire town were in trouble. The dread had neither name nor face, arrived as pure feeling. Whatever it promised, it advanced with great speed and if she had been asked to look into her own life, she still would've had no way to predict the most terrifying thing in her house was a bell and eventually, after that, another woman's touch.

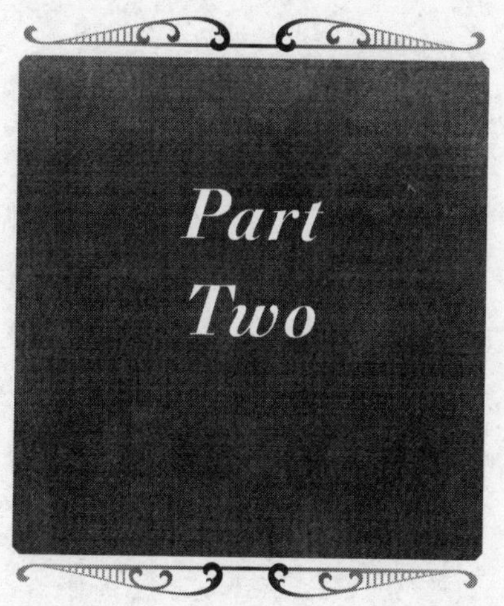

Part Two

· CHAPTER 9 ·

Monsters

[1]

Joyelle Arceneaux was born February 18, 1835, to a mother of mixed descent, Rita, and a French father, Henri. She grew up in Desmarais, a town southeast of New Orleans, right off the Mississippi River, that was officially part of the city but had been relegated to nearly mythological existence because of the region's poverty as documented by the 1840 census. If a place could be so shameful that its presence was wiped from history, memory, maps, and tongue, then Desmarais would be that place.

Joyelle, called Joy, grew up understanding that she was what people called a quadroon, which held an importance to others around her that she never understood and rebuked as a child and for the rest of her life. She was much darker than her mother, which stunned Rita and humiliated her father more than the substantial gambling debt he accrued over the years since marrying Rita. Believing Rita unfaithful, he beat and verbally abused her until Joy, age eight and with a blank face, stabbed him several times in the gut and side.

Amelia Chandonnet and Eloise St. Denis ran a boardinghouse in New Orleans on Orleans and Dauphine Streets, where Rita and Joy escaped to after Joy stabbed Henri a final time, killing him. Eventually, Rita would return to Desmarais to bury her husband's body and never return, leaving Joy with the two women as a daughter they were forced to adopt by a shared sense of moral obligation.

"Tell us the story again," Eloise would say, combing her hair with an ivory comb hand-carved by her late husband. Eloise was the older of the two women, dark-skinned and regal. She bitingly joked that she was mulatto and to her entertainment many believed her because of what they claimed was the red undertone of her skin.

"Please don't make the girl tell us again how she murdered her father," Amelia would say, severe and white as ivory. She was a self-proclaimed quadroon, tremendously aware of it, and relatively wealthy because of it, though she hid her small fortune—obtained through sex work, assisting Eloise with the boardinghouse, and miscellaneous accountancy contracts she managed for women who concealed their money from their husbands—from the world with great precision.

Amelia taught Joy every word under the sun, including "egalitarian" and "impudent," and how to read and write. She demanded the girl avoid considering a future in sex work and, instead, take to cleaning houses to build humility alongside her natural pride. Eloise taught Joy how to cook, clean, and calculate large numbers very quickly. She also taught Joy how to paint, mainly in the still-life genre. Joy relished the time spent with them and soon forgot about Rita altogether.

The *Picayune* newspaper reported a string of murders. At least once every other week a man was found killed, unmolested except for the wound that delineated the death blow. Blunt force to a skull. Gunshot to the head. Throat slashings. Extra watchmen were placed around the city at night to catch what they believed was a serial killer because three things linked them all: they were all men, they were never robbed, and all damage had been inflicted above the shoulders.

That the murders happened at all, let alone with such frequency, baffled journalists. Much of the attention these killings spawned was because many of the men were well known and white. The few coloreds who were found dead were also of high repute, most of whom owned slaves. When Joy learned that there were people as dark as her who owned others as dark as them, she laughed, thinking it a lie. How could anyone who could easily be a slave also enslave? She was a precocious eleven-year-old at the time of hearing this news and Amelia, the news breaker, grew livid at Joy's reaction. She cursed Joy out more violently than Joy ever remembered Henri doing and sent the girl to her room without supper. Eloise knocked and, with a plate of warm food, entered Joy's room, finding her weeping into her pillow. She sat near Joy and brushed the girl's hair with her hand.

Eloise told Joy of how Amelia's father had owned Amelia, Amelia's mother, and Amelia's mother's mother, and how he was grotesquely the reason she was called quadroon. When Amelia ran away, she tried to bring her younger brother with her. "Being promised land and slaves of his own," Eloise said, "her brother decided to partake in their father's trade instead of leaving with Amelia. After what her brother knew their father had done to the women in their family, he decided to join him. Do you understand"—Eloise touched Joy on the cheek—"how your laughter was in her brother's voice?"

The murders died down for a couple of months and so did the watchmen's attention. The very first day of lax patrolling ended with three men dead: slit throat, blunt force to the head, and strangulation. The women of the boardinghouse spoke about it with each of their boarders, assuring them they would be safe there. "Nothing like that has ever occurred near the premises," Eloise said. It was an unsustainable lie, as the strangulation happened near St. Philip and Chartres Streets, walking distance from the house. But the boarders, themselves vagabonds and thieves and immigrants laying low from whatever crime they were forced to commit by nature of survival, drifted into the lullaby of the lie.

Eloise kept a tight ship. She handled the meals, the collection of monies, and the schedule of reservations. Any late departures ensured a steep fee of two dollars, and a pistol guaranteed the strength of her word. Amelia handled the legal and financial paperwork, the officers who visited under the pretense that the two women harbored suspects of various degrees of crime, and the officers who visited for an ulterior service only a few knew were available. Amelia kept the boardinghouse out of trouble with the law while Eloise kept them from going out of business.

They kept the curtains' lace dustless and the flowers in the parlor fresh. The parlor itself was a room on the right side of the foyer opposite the kitchen. A small, mostly unused piano stood by a window in the parlor, its black top covered in plants and flowers. The Chesterfields stood opposite a long central coffee table, their tufts cinched as tight as mouths. A tall grandfather clock kept time in the center of the room.

Of the four rooms (not including the beds in the converted dining room) that they rented out on a day-to-day, weekly, or month-to-month schedule, only one was on the second floor where the women and Joy kept their rooms, and that was for any woman boarder, which they rarely received. The men they kept were private, clean, respectfully depressed, drunk but not violently so, and despite their misgivings they had their money on time because Eloise both frightened and inspired them to do so. Amelia, who they rarely saw, appeared to haunt the place whenever she was around, carrying a ledger full of inscrutable figures and wearing a magnifying glass around her neck like a charm.

The women, simultaneously aged and ageless, stayed in motion until quiet hours at 8:00 p.m. when no one was allowed to leave (except for financial or medical reasons), to enter (except for financial or medical reasons), and surely no one was allowed company except, of course, Eloise or Amelia, the latter letting down her pinned-up hair so that it reached her waist in light brown waves. When she was available, she sat on the balcony and let her hair dangle over the railing like a flag.

Joy started exploring her body in the beginning of her teenage years. She found her clitoris and nearly lost her mind in the throes of her discovery. Amelia taught her how to manage her cycle, how to pamper herself with sweets and perfume as she bathed away the blood, and how to rest when the pain became too much. Meanwhile, Eloise explained that she could have a child. But how was the child supposed to get inside of her, Joy always wondered.

Some nights, Amelia's suitors screamed so loud from ecstasy that it woke the whole boardinghouse. Those nights, she opened her door to let out the man she taught her name to, and the steamy scent of sex, red wine, and Florida water filled the hallway.

Once, a suitor exited and Amelia stood by her bedroom door, hair all over her head energized by some goddess of her own pantheon. She found Eloise standing in the hall, too, oil lamp steady in hand as she shook her head.

"You always look most Negro after," Eloise said, and Amelia smiled, then closed the door behind her.

But the one night Joy, not Eloise, met Amelia in the hall, Amelia felt a fear that shocked her sober. She saw clearly how Joy's silhouette displaced the light against the dimly candlelit wall. Candle flames waved behind their glass jars and barely illuminated the iron sconces. In Amelia's mind, refreshed by humiliation, the flames had made her vulnerable by nature of making her visible—and, yes, in that hall the high passion once enflaming within her and spilling from her bedroom did become a knuckle's worth of ash in the presence of this girl-child, not yet ten years old at the time, who rubbed her eyes and asked if Amelia was in pain or had lost her hearing because the man in her room kept screaming her name like she couldn't hear him. From then on, Amelia had been ruined from explaining the unique pleasures of sex, but she didn't know why, and *that* is what caused the most agony. She didn't know why something she loved doing couldn't be explained to another who, too, should love it when the time came.

Eloise described sex too plainly, then made it too abstract, "When you get older, you will meet a man with whom you'll want to start a family. He will kiss you if you are lucky, will rub your body if you are blessed. And when he puts himself inside you, it will hurt at first. Then, if you are one of God's chosen, you will feel as though a small orb of light is bursting inside you and it will keep bursting well after he has finished if he knows you as well as he should. Knows your pleasures. Then, you will no longer be God's, but his. Only his. And to get back to God, you'll have to go through your paramour first." None of it made sense to Joy, but when years later she discovered the small button at the top of her "organ," as Eloise called it, she wondered if she had found the orb of light on her own and if she should tell Eloise that she figured out how to find God without the intercession of a man.

[2]

Joy, thirteen and bored, wanted to go to school. The women allowed it, sending her to one of the most prestigious academies in the area. She outperformed everyone there, got into bloody fights, and was reluctantly expelled after a year. Her brilliance magnetized her instructors. Her temper horrified her peers. It was Amelia who decided to homeschool the girl, and Eloise taught her how to shoot in the marshes and paint on weekends. That neither woman seemed disappointed in her expulsion seemed strange to Joy, but she carried on as best she could to prove she was no burden.

One morning, Joy heard from the hallway upstairs a knock at the front door. She made her way toward the top of the staircase but, hearing a woman sob, she decided to stay hidden behind the wall. She stole a peek and saw a woman wearing a mourner's veil over her face. Amelia welcomed the sobbing woman into the foyer, offered her a cup of tea that was rejected, then offered her a glass of wine that the woman gulped down. Amelia poured another glass for the woman without asking and escorted her into the kitchen. Joy heard the door lock from the inside.

Soon, the conversation ended, and the woman headed to the front door with Amelia following behind and gently touching the small of the visiting woman's back. Joy caught a glimpse of the woman's face when she hugged Amelia without her veil. Her right eye and cheek were swollen and bruised dark purple. Amelia closed the door behind the woman and quickly turned around as though she overheard wicked gossip about her down the corridor. Joy hid more intently behind the wall when she saw Amelia's acidic gaze dissolve the room around her. Amelia left the foyer and reentered the kitchen, locking the door behind her once more, unaware that she imprinted in Joy the most important expression she would ever see.

That evening, Eloise fixed supper for the two of them, saying that Amelia had a late-night business errand to run. Joy played in her food and made no eye contact.

"What concerns you?" Eloise said.

"A woman visited today," Joy said.

Eloise nodded and unfolded her napkin onto her lap. She wore a corona of braids with a small purple flower in the front. The flower's color reminded Joy of the visitor's face.

"She looked beaten on. I saw her eye and her cheek when she exited the kitchen. I was on my way down but turned away when I saw her bruises. She wore a veil at first. I thought someone had died."

"Someone almost died," Eloise said. "We should extend your shooting lessons."

"I would like that very much," Joy said, then added, "Do I matter? I would like to matter in this world."

"Do you *matter*?" Eloise repeated this a few times, each time adding emphasis to a different word, looking for the appropriate flavor, the right lilt. "Do you matter in *this* world?" She sliced her veal into bite-size pieces, added butter to her bread, and rocked her wineglass until the dark red liquid tinted the bowl. She took a bite of meat, of bread, of mustard greens, and of roasted carrots and potatoes sprinkled with rosemary. She took one bite of each fragrant ingredient and chewed carefully. Joy watched and waited. With nearly half of her meal gone, Eloise said, "You don't mean a thing to this world. No woman does. No recognizable Negro does. We'd be much better off if this world . . ." Eloise took a sip of wine. "Their world must end, Joy. Never forget that.

The end of their world would allow us to begin." She took a gulp of wine and said, "Eat," then spoke nothing else for the rest of the night, ignoring Joy's final question: "But what about the animals?"

[3]

When she was fourteen years old, Joy came home from housecleaning at the Thompson's, a semi-wealthy British family, with bruises on her leg and arm. She rolled up her sleeves and dress to show Eloise, who was sitting outside on the porch reading a book. Joy explained how the family son, Roland, caught her alone in the shed and tried to take advantage of her. She had fought back. He had snatched her up by the arm and twisted, said he would get her eventually and that, more than money, he had patience. He had sniffed her long hair, moving his nose up and down the arcs of its wavy texture, then pushed her away. Eloise rubbed her wrists raw while listening.

She brought the girl inside and found Amelia sitting at the piano in the parlor, sipping tea and poking the out-of-tune keys. Amelia looked up from her playing and saw the dark purple oval on Joy's arm, Eloise's radiant anger in the dimming sunlight that slinked through the curtains, and then Joy's expression of bewilderment brushed with shame.

In the glints of their bladed stares, beneath the plum bruise she imagined would spread across her entire body, Joy wondered if boys (and the men they would become) ever learned how not to harm. Between her father and now Roland, a future in desire appeared dangerous. All she knew from the few men in her life was open hostility. The lace-gloved hands of women held and gently guided by men whose adoring stares unlocked bouquets from their wives' love-blushed cheeks—wasn't that the story shown to her daily along the bustling streets, chivalry as common as apples? Not bruises, but skin alive with love? When, if ever, would she be shown such softness?

"Who?" Amelia asked, squinting. She stood and cocked her head to the side. "Who?"

"Roland," Joy said, and lifted her dress to reveal the second bruise, which held Amelia's attention, a bull entranced by a veronica. And the expression Joy saw when the woman with the battered face left their home, the expression Amelia threw into the world without warning, was thrown in Joy's direction. Up close, it comforted her. The hell-struck circumference of Amelia's eyes, the texture of her small nostrils as they flared to the rhythm of the burning war drum percussing inside her that only Amelia could hear but, no, Joy could hear it now as well, rising inside her own body, and her fluency in its fact, in the war drum's time signature unlocking from her the memory of her father's blood warming her hands, didn't upset her. It woke her. She was that child again, knife in hand, her father's body unable to resist the thick blade from entering him and she unable to stop introducing the blade to his softest part. What once frightened Joy about Amelia became confirmation and, like a pristine mirror, demanded that she look back.

"Joy," Amelia said, "what do you want to do?"

Joy didn't know why she expected to be held. Amelia didn't embrace the battered woman when she left the boardinghouse and reentered the world that harmed her, and Eloise imagined there being no world at all in which anyone received an embrace. Joy's intuition said that crying was out of the question and though the women were patient, she felt the air in the room tighten every second she forced them to endure her silence.

"She's not ready," Amelia said to Eloise while looking at Joy, and Joy began to think that she must not be ready. What her unpreparedness disallowed mattered little.

"Then I'll show her what being unprepared does to a woman," Eloise said, and Amelia shook her head, then looked at the floor. Eloise stood haloed by the wide face of the grandfather clock behind her. She turned so that her back faced Joy. She unbuttoned the front of her dress and let drop the silhouette from her shoulders. Indentations in her skin covered her back as though each were ready to take in a slip of paper on which every cruel thing that ever happened in history was written.

Joy covered her mouth. There were too many to count through the blur of tears in her eyes. Her bones filled up with an unfamiliar chill, and the new element spread from her bones to her skin as goose bumps lifted from her thin arms. Amelia stood watch, taking deep breaths and holding her hand to her chest. Eloise told a story, but as she spoke, her voice crept from the shut mouths in her back:

"Eighteen years ago, after my husband died and before I met Amelia, I courted a man who stabbed me in my back twelve times because I refused him. In my own home. When I woke, I had been washed, bandaged, and my cuts were sewn shut. I was in my bed. My floor had been washed of blood. No one saw anyone enter or leave my house, neither my attempted murderer nor my savior.

"The men being murdered in the streets," Eloise said, buttoning up her dress, "were killed by either Amelia or myself." She placed her hand on Joy's cheek. It was warm and Joy wanted to feel that warmth forever. "The woman you saw with the bruised face, we helped her. Men who harm women for their own pleasure, they think they own the world, think they are it. If that is so,"—Eloise paused and smiled—"then I'll, without question, turn this world into ash."

"I'll ask you again. What do you want to do?" Amelia said.

[4]

It was cold the night Joy decided to and did kill Roland. Eloise and Amelia had taken her upstairs to Eloise's room to reveal the most powerful and dangerous secret kept hidden from her, what made it so easy for them to get away with the killings without leaving an inch of evidence.

Eloise had come across an old leather journal at an outdoor market.

Inside, in barely legible handwriting, were undated notes, recipes, musings, and memories from someone who signed their name as "Mine Own." When Eloise went to buy the journal, the merchant told her it wasn't an item of his to sell; he had never seen it before and would feel bad pricing something that someone else had lost. She took it with her, intrigued by the ramblings written inside.

She came across a recipe for a "Goodbye Stone," promising invisibility. Interested, she decided to make the object as described in the journal. What started off as a joke, as a woman's unquenchable boredom with her lonely life, became an obsession. Her near-death still plagued her with nightmares, her loving husband was dead, and Amelia's arrival had not yet occurred. Becoming invisible was the next best thing to becoming dead, though she didn't want to die, just wanted something close enough to death that she could forget herself in peace.

Eloise spent months looking for the ingredients necessary to create the stone and nearly had a heart attack when, while carrying the conjured-upon stone from the kitchen to her bedroom, she couldn't see her face in a circular mirror in the hallway. Her dress floated on its own in her reflection. A week later, naked in the late-night streets of New Orleans with the stone in her mouth, she found the man who had opened her back twelve times and followed him home. He was found dead by slit throat a little over a week later, discovered only because of the stench his corpse left behind. The news of his belated discovery pleased Eloise, for this let her know not a person in the world cared about him to miss him in a week's absence.

When Amelia first arrived, mind-broken and tormented by slavery, Eloise handed her the stone and told her to "make it right with yourself." Amelia returned three days later, and news had already gotten around that Monsieur Chandonnet was found dead by blunt force at ninety years old.

Roland, in his own bedroom, was shot in the head by his father's gun. It was deemed a suicide.

The women were ruthless and gave no gentler death to the Negro and gens de couleur libres than they did the white men who abused women. All met hammer, blade, or bullet with equal fervor. They usually left the bodies untouched and went for the heads, not because it was agreed upon, but because it was the way Eloise did it and so Amelia and Joy followed suit. Eventually, Joy, young and quick, became the best killer and most sadistic, deciding to injure more than just the head whenever possible. She adjusted to her duties, but arrogance swept her up and sent her crashing after her last victim's horse, startled by the sound of her concealed movement, kicked her square in the shoulder when she brushed past its hind legs without thinking. She flew and her head landed against the road. All she could remember before passing out was someone asking her if she needed help.

Amelia opened the door and there stood a man, long-legged and bright-eyed, gloved hands, and arms held out as if holding a wet blanket, but nothing was there.

"Excuse me. I believe she belongs to you?" he asked.

"What are you asking?" Amelia said.

"This girl, she mumbled this address before passing out."

"What gi—" Amelia began, then realized what was happening. "Joy? Joy . . ." She touched the empty space above the man's arms. When she felt cold skin against her fingertips, she pressed more deeply into the space that was no longer just space. "Sir, please come in."

"Please, call me Frances."

[5]

Joy fancied herself a curator of calamities. She had predicted that some doom would befall them because the entire household carried with it the weight of endless rain. Their sleeping had become relentless and eating patterns erratic. One could get away with murder only so often, and she was positive the three of them were sure to run out of luck before gaining more.

"It's as natural as breathing," Eloise had said once about killing, and Frances, having lived with the women for four years and having learned their atypical and ferocious ways, kept quiet her disgust by disappearing into her room on the first floor with the male boarders. She took no issues with being thought of as a man because often she saw herself that way or in no way at all. Just being alive and present was enough such that neither "he" nor "she" made her much difference.

Eloise carried no opinion of Frances's being man or woman and switched between "he" and "she" without care, but Amelia made it clear where she stood with her use of "he" when referring to Frances. She was suspicious of him, didn't like how he saw through the stone's invisibility, and didn't like how he managed to slip in and out of the house without anyone noticing.

Joy, on the other hand, determined Frances was what she would call "a lady" when she walked in on Frances bathing. Bringing clean linen to Frances and noticing that the door was slightly ajar, she didn't knock or announce herself and nudged the door open with her forehead. Frances, whistling to herself, had her back to the door. Joy admired the soft slope of Frances's shoulders, the impossible smoothness of her skin, the graceful paths drawn by her arms as she wiped down the wide curve of her left hip. 'Man or woman,' Joy thought, 'that is a lady,' and she silently stepped away from the door without being noticed.

Joy learned from Frances an array of conjures and their distinct purposes. One for helping others fall out of love or in love, one for protecting a house from evil spirits and any intentions misaligned with those of the household, one to make a sick man well and another to make a well man sick. Bury this jar—filled with lemon juice, goat heart, licorice root, chalk, and a strip of paper with the victim's name written on it—in the yard of your enemy and they will suffer each day with a new set of bad events. Toss this mix of dried roots behind you as you walk, and watch your enemies scatter from their hiding places. Frances said she gathered all these remedies, root workings, and conjures from her travels while following the tether that she hadn't felt tug at her chest since arriving in New Orleans.

"Been meeting people who were willing to teach me a thing or two. I hardly use it myself, but I can sense root work when it's close and know when someone is good or bad at it," Frances said, laughing. Neither Frances nor Joy had much skill with conjure but Frances could sniff it out like a bloodhound, locating the source and the intent just by the ingredients. Joy sensed it more than she could pinpoint it, but the feeling she had that something awful was soon to pass had nothing to do with conjure.

[6]

Joy had a dream that she was in a sugarcane field, stabbing her fingers into the darkness. When she awoke, her jaw hurt, her feet were covered in mud, and she had a bandaged cut on her side. Frances sat napping in the chair by her bedside. Joy stirred her awake by noisily inspecting and questioning the state of her feet and side.

"You walked in your sleep last night. Out to the garden," Frances said. "Eloise heard you when you opened the door."

Joy's skepticism flooded her face. She was still stuck in the world of the dark field of sugarcane and seeing Frances jarred her senses more than her filthy feet.

Frances continued. "I sat watch over you to make sure you stayed put. We tried to wash your feet, but you fought us off like a damn fool, so that's why your feet look like you been chasing hogs." Frances yawned and scratched her inner thigh near the crotch. "I hope this not a new habit cause I'm not playing warden every night. You hit me square in the jaw. I could see my thoughts for an hour."

Joy apologized and thanked Frances, who examined the room before settling her eyes on a spot beneath the bed. The words trembled from her mouth. "The night I found you in the road, when I carried you back here, I took a risk. I don't go around putting my hands on nobody cause it's not all the time right. So, I don't want you to think I did it on purpose, because I didn't. You were in danger, and I wanted to help. I didn't know what else to do. I want to get that out of the way." Frances's trembling spread from her voice to her body. "That's not what I wanted to tell you. I just wanted that out the way. I see with all the happening in this house that what I have to tell you won't seem so strange. So, I'm just gone say it." Sweat dripped into her eyes as she spoke. She wiped her face and cleared her throat. Barbs of heat pricked her back. "When I touch people, I can see what they been through. I don't know how far back I'll go when it happens or what I'll see, but I see a lot and I remember a lot. Not everything. Just most of what I see."

Frances waited for Joy to respond and when she didn't, she continued. "You was carrying a ice pick last night. I guess you so used to going out and . . ." Frances stopped speaking when Joy lifted her shirt and rubbed the bandage, though Joy looked at the wall across from the foot of the bed with a blank expression. Frances felt for the first time a sense of shame that required no incidental sacrifice. This shame, blood-heavy in her head, more personal and therefore more dangerous, flickered with potential and familiar loneliness. So many had lost their lives by trying to take Frances's without discussion. Thinking about the piles of bodies left in her wake, the impeccable care each potential murderer took to make sure she knew how unwanted she was, made Frances's eyes well up. Now, for the first time, her loneliness would be decided with words and for that she felt gratitude. She felt frail. She wanted to run away.

"I cut myself because I had no one else to kill?" Joy said toward the wall. She lowered her shirt but kept her gaze steady where it landed on an unnaturally dark spot staining the wallpaper.

"No. You cut me."

"I don't—"

"You cut me but it happened to you."

Joy didn't have to speak through her confusion because at that moment Eloise knocked on the already open door. "I saw for myself what he's saying," she said, standing in the doorway of Joy's bedroom. She entered and sat on the bed. "I asked that Frances leave you wounded so that he can show you what else he can do." She smiled toward Frances.

"Remember what I told you about me touching folks?" Frances said. "I have to touch you to show you what Eloise means."

"My convictions are clear. I have no secrets," Joy said.

Frances carefully unbandaged Joy's wound, letting the soiled material drop to the floor. She then put her hands over the open cut. After a few seconds, the wound was completely healed, the pain gone entirely.

"Is this like the stone Eloise and Amelia use?" Joy asked.

Frances shook her head. She reminded Joy of her lack of skill with conjure. "I don't know why I can do this. I just know that I can. I didn't mean to hurt you."

"If it's out of your control," Joy said, "then why should I blame you for this harm?"

[7]

A Virginia-born salesman, Yves Whitehead, whose product was the promise of a nonexistent device that would sort through clothes according to their size, visited New Orleans on his way to California. His sell pitch "I will sell you a promise that this device will assist you immeasurably, comparable to the invention of cast iron," after which he wove a seductive description of the device, showing patents and detailed illustrations depicting every sprocket and screw entering their mechanical and otherwise unseeable places. And he absolutely sold promises, for on the following day a mail carrier would deliver a receipt for "One promise." For this scheme, he had been chased out of Georgia, Alabama, and Kentucky. After spending months in jail, the time spread across each state, he decided he wanted a new life in California: fresher air, milder temperatures, and hardly any Negroes.

On his way to California, he stopped in New Orleans, having expended all resources to travel any farther. He had few friends and no relationship with his family, no teachers or well-traveled business mentors, so no one warned him about New Orleans. In that city, Yves's disgust materialized into a silence so formidable it rewrote him.

The Negroes were mixed among the whites and the whites with the Negroes; but the Negroes, whose various complexions perplexed him, were both slave and not slave, free to do what they wanted and free to go to hell in iron anklets. To his dismay, a white man's fingers brushed the brow of a Negro woman the color of milk, though her lips and nose told all her business, which was none of his business nor was it any business at all. Witnessing the kiss sent a shock through Yves's organ that stiffened him like the cross he might as well have been crucified on, guilty of a lust for the Negro pandemic to his kind.

"I can't tell the slaves from the merchants," he wrote in his journal one afternoon, "and the damned French," he continued, "speaking French and aimlessly sauntering with British spouses who had just shaken hands with some mulattress whose tainted child waved across the street to a white American man who in Virginia would have smacked the young creature clean across the mouth for such audacity. It is not that slavery does not exist; it does in full and authentic glory. It is that slavery does not exist alone. There is an 'other,' incalculable energy present," of which he couldn't find the source.

He believed that this was some other country far away from America, untouched by the Constitution, misbehaving outrightly against mores that separated the men from the beasts, the sophisticated from the fleeceable. Never this place that sickened him and aroused him with its savage Bacchanalia.

Imagine: a white man precumming like a dog to the sounds of

percussion and images of dark-skinned men and women dancing from the cave of his memory. It was this passion misunderstood as curse that perhaps gave Yves, in his heightened paranoia, a heightened sense of observation and contempt, because he caught Amelia wearing men's clothes and covered in blood as she returned to the boardinghouse late one night, her stone lost completely after the man she had gone to kill got in a lucky hit and sent the stone flying out of her hand, though it was not enough to keep his neck protected from the blade. She had been careless, wiping clean her hands but forgetting her face, which she had touched with a bloody hand while wiping away sweat. She threw on whatever clothes she could find and snuck out of the cottage shoeless and without hat or parasol to hide her face, avoiding patrollers, almost getting away unseen until Yves bumped into her as he turned a corner like a rabid dog, trying desperately to walk off his violent erection, his lantern leading the way toward no way and his mind believing Amelia was a vagrant until he looked up and saw her face that to him revealed a pampered life.

Amelia was shaken. She screamed when her shoulder met his, and ran lanternless into the dark, her face illuminated long enough to glue itself to Yves's mind: blood across her forehead, no shoes on her feet, eyes as frightful as his own, and as white as him if not whiter. The following day he learned that a string of murders had plagued New Orleans for years. The culprit remained at large with no evidence ever left behind and no witnesses ever to come forth. It took a week for him to discover where Amelia lived and upon learning she owned a boardinghouse with a dark-skinned Negro woman, both of whom were extraordinarily successful, he knew for sure that before he left New Orleans, he had to rid the world of them.

He needed no evidence, just what he saw and how it connected. He told a group of men who told a group of men until a swell of men arrived at the women's door, no neighbor coming to their defense because the neighbors had joined the group. These men, all believing they were next in line for murder, felt vindicated of crimes not yet committed and were easily convinced that a boardinghouse with two women of "confused blood," one Negro woman, and a tall Negro man would be their downfall. If either Eloise or Amelia expected a jury and judge to clear their names, the thought abandoned them because those who would make up the jury were in the crowd as well, looking on not with curiosity but with finality.

"Are we monsters?" Amelia asked.

Eloise counted the men, and with the curtains open and their visages fully exposed, the two women held hands.

· CHAPTER 10 ·

Frances and Joy

[1]

Joy was inconsolable, and at any moment she could kill someone. As was her way. Late autumn brought with it sharp winds burdened with ice that sliced where bare skin dared show itself. Frances kept quiet though she, too, suffered through the cold, having lost her gloves during the journey. Her laughable coat; her hardly there hat over her low-shaved head; her stolen boots—she had given all the warmest clothes to Joy and not even that stopped the woman's whimpering. Despite the freezing weather, Frances's wide smile dropped its half-moon over Joy's agitation.

This was the longest they had been without shelter, and they were both grateful that the snowfall had become lighter. But the Illinois wind carried knives, the cold's frenzy unfamiliar. Traveling through Mississippi, deranged with swamps and red dirt that the pounding rain made slide like blood down hillsides, had nothing on this desolation: Tree branches blanched with snow, weighted by it, so much so the boughs cracked and dangled from the trunk. The sky, a confusion of gray, showed more like a painting depicting a sky. The motionlessness above instilled below the same impression of stillness. Frances, tall and gangly, squeezed Joy's thin shoulder, and they kept moving.

The Revolutionary War had ended almost eighty years ago, yet about fifty feet ahead of them paced a soldier in a near-perfect uniform of the Continental Army, white buttons so clean they tossed back the brightness of the November snow. The soldier was about sixty years old and had a mule with him that rested under a shelter made of wooden planks stacked above two large stones. Frances and Joy nearly marched toward him, Joy wanting the mule and Frances wanting the single-shot she spotted lying at the man's feet. Joy stood behind Frances. The man spotted them and picked up the gun. His mind was racked. His teeth were rotten. He looked in Frances's direction but was unable to keep his eyes steady. The mule's ear flicked, touched by a snowflake. Crueler cold loomed.

The man shouted something incoherent and aimed the gun at Frances, who approached him. Her wide-brimmed hat shadowed the top half of her face, her cheekbones sharp as though carved by the icy wind. The man shot directly at Frances's chest but fell to the ground, a wound the size of the bullet in his own chest. Frances picked up the gun and wrapped it in a piece of cloth. She handed it to Joy, who put it inside a bag she had hidden beneath her thick shawl. Frances lifted the man's hat from his head and tossed it to Joy, who, smelling it and wincing, reluctantly put it on her head. Frances looked up into the sky as though listening to good advice. Joy coaxed the mule from his dwelling with a bit of pear. It must've been very hungry because when it walked to Joy she saw the beast had a limp. She shook her head and licked a flake of snow from her frown.

"It won't do as is," she said to Frances.

Frances touched the mule's front left leg. She held it there for a moment, then said, "Should be fine now." And it was, walking like a new man. Joy rode bareback in circles on the mule while Frances looked for more ammunition. Finding none, she told Joy to drop the gun, but Joy refused.

"There's bound to be shooting folks where we're going," Joy said. "We can at least look like shooting folks."

Frances watched carefully as Joy hid the gun within the myriad folds of fabric she wore.

"Leave it," Frances said. Her voice broke through the frost-flecked air. Joy's lips shook. She unhid the gun and tossed it behind her.

The two headed northwest to where Frances said she felt pulled, a tether cinched to her chest and leading to an unknown destination. Snow fell in large flakes from the pale sky and collected in Joy's hair that draped down in waves just below her shoulders. She looked like a bride who abandoned her groom and a few other lives all at once: decked out in several gorgeous shawls still carrying the perfume of their prior owner, a patchy fur cape, and the dead man's hat, every piece of her improvised wear taken from someone else. Her honey-colored eyes cut through the snow like a cat's mid-hunt and she squinted more from unhappiness than discomfort.

"We go this way we'll be close," Frances said, pointing.

"Close but not there."

"Close, still."

"And still not there."

Frances ignored Joy, who sighed and scratched her sinuses, mumbled something ornery under her thin voice, or curled up the corners of her mouth, which Frances couldn't see but assumed Joy was doing anyway, as it was her way.

When they reached the Mississippi River, they looked for a dull light said to be floating over the water. They had snuck onto plantations as resting points as they made their escape, staying with enslaved Africans whom they offered to bring with them but were told "not this time," which meant please come back when we are ready. An elderly enslaved cobbler told them the story about a woman who freed all the enslaved Africans in several plantations and led them into the river, "each and every one, child," so the water could take them back to Africa. The cobbler told them the light they needed to look for belonged to the spirit of the woman waiting for anyone who wanted to join with their people.

But an enslaved cook said she heard the woman was an enslaved African who killed everybody on the plantation because she lost her good mind and only had the bad one left. She killed others who were slaves and their so-called master before escaping on her own into a thick delirium that drove her straight into the muddy waters. As a thank-you to the cook, Frances barged into the big house. Gunshots rang. When she came out, she told the enslaved cook, "Well, looks like massa dead. Wife too. Shot her then himself." She then went to each overseer and taunted them to shoot at her, and they did, and each died right there with a bullet wound where they had aimed at Frances. "You should bury the overseers but leave the man and wife in that house just as they are. If somebody come looking for them, the story'll speak for itself. Hopefully, by then, y'all be gone."

At the tip of Illinois, a freedman Frances and Joy stayed with during their journey relayed a story about a witch woman come to free all these slaves across the river and set up a town in Missouri. He told them to look for the River Rider to take them across. In this weather, Frances and Joy knew the River Rider wouldn't be out for long if at all. They had nothing else to do but wait for the Rider's light or their deaths in the cold.

The mule bayed. Joy sneezed. Frances grabbed on to Joy's leg and lay her head on her thigh. Their faces stiffened as though beneath the skin an inner rage hooked the fat of their cheeks and pulled back, pulled back. Frances had not eaten anything for several days other than stale bread, old cheese, and fruit, which half the time gave her gut-splitting cramps. With the weather this bad they feared the water might freeze over before they reached it, but they heard the river's slurred speech summon them from down the way.

Looking out, white flecks of snow descended nearly straight down until a wind angled them into blinding slopes. Seeing far ahead, far across the river, became unfeasible even for Frances, who searched for the light she assumed easily mistaken for a hallucination, its small glow floating over all that soon-to-freeze water.

When the orb of light finally appeared, Joy and Frances waved their frostbitten hands in unison, right arms up and moving back and forth like small trees manipulated by an indecisive gust. They rocked that way for a while, hoping to attract the River Rider. The orb of light grew brighter and the sound of something moving in the water grew louder. When they looked out, squinted a bit, they saw a small figure with a lantern tied around its neck. It paddled on one side, then swooped the oar through the water on the other. Once the raft reached them, they saw the figure was child-size and wrapped in a thick, dark-red fabric from head to waist, only his eyes exposed. He wore black trousers that seemed so thin as to offer no warmth at all and wrapped around his shoes was the same red fabric tied at a knot around the ankles. A black bead necklace looped around his neck down to his navel.

"Two?" the River Rider asked without uncovering his mouth though it sounded as clear as if he had spoken into their ears. Frances nodded. The River Rider counted a second time. "No babies?"

Frances shook her head.

"Mule can't come," the River Rider said, and prepared the raft to disembark.

Joy, in a dense silence forced upon her by the cold, stared at the River Rider, who, swathed in the color of blood and tar and oaring across water that could kill a horse within minutes, could've been no more than eleven years old. She hopped off the mule, gave it one more pear, and kissed it on the nose.

The River Rider nodded and the three traveled across the stiffening river. In the raft's wake, ice forced apart by the oar and the raft's flat body gradually reformed until it seemed nothing had passed through at all. Frances heard ice cracking in the water's darkness as miniature floes caked in close behind them, ice that had been sundered reuniting in the drift while the oar that dipped and pushed through the freezing water bore no lasting consequence.

Their journey across a split in the earth called the Mississippi River was a kind of merging of the land itself that slushed in the silted and muddy waters as though to keep a promise that it would, indeed, reunite those two sides of the United States where, like a plague, colonizers ravaged the nation in utter disregard of those who had been there prior, those who in the wake of Europeans vanishing before their eyes to become this new thing altogether called "white" found themselves diseased with smallpox and scriptures, over-hunting and a greed made manifest, a living haunting that reshaped and voided out forests more ancient than them all and possibly older than the river—wide-hipped and unenchanted—which is all to say, save the three of them, there was no life there.

The river promised to become a solid mirror as its luminescent spectra crystallized over the water. Crossing over the upper slush, Joy's silence melted into a warm hostility. She sat cross-legged in the center of the raft and emoted. If they hit a rough patch of ice, she cut her eyes at Frances. If Frances sneezed, she sucked the roof of her mouth. When Frances unsuccessfully tried to talk to the River Rider, who responded with one word to her questions or not at all, Joy flared her nostrils and exhaled hard. She needed a place for her grief that she had been rushed through the motion of. No time to mourn or to say goodbye to her old life and old self. They simply packed up and escaped before all the spilled blood could cool.

The Mississippi River continued to harden. Undisturbed by the cold and the jagged motions of the raft, the River Rider stood close to the front edge as he oared the small party to where ice appeared like a fortress ahead, engulfing earth and sky in dizzying white. His red wrap interrupted the snowy landscape, and when the River Rider pushed the oar, stray fabric rose from his shoulders, licking the air with its flame. With a scrape, the raft slid onto the land and the jolt pulled Joy away from thinking about the end of the world in Eloise's mouth.

Much of the landscape on the Missouri side of the river lay identical to that of Illinois and Joy thought they had made no progress at all.

But Frances already took to the forest, her chest pulled forward to keep pressing on.

Joy stood with a moan, dusted snow from her lap, and thanked the River Rider. She tried to leave her final pear with him. He shook his head and pulled down his scarf. His mouth held mostly gums with a few teeth lining the top in the front and to the side, and three teeth on the bottom center with a couple on the left side in the back. Joy pulled a bowl from her bag and sliced the pear inside it with a small knife. The boy watched her work as she then pounded the pear into a wet paste with her fist. When she finished, her knuckles throbbed. The River Rider snatched up the bowl and eagerly tipped the slurry into his mouth. When he finished, he wiped his lips and handed Joy back her bowl with a grin. He veiled the bottom half of his face and trudged far enough down the river's frozen coast that he disappeared into the landscape.

Frances and Joy headed deeper west, Frances wrapping an arm around Joy's shoulder and pulling her in for heat. Every so often she paused and held Joy's hands inside her own hands to warm them both. After an hour of walking, Joy dragged her feet, and her eyes struggled to stay open. Frances let Joy rest near a tree while she checked their rations. All five of the pears were gone and she had no recollection of Joy having eaten any of them. The salted meat remained untouched. One apple, three pecans, more stale bread, and a carrot remained. They were running out of water.

In an uproar, the frigid air bit Frances's skin. Joy had stopped talking and her eyes were half-closed. The wet from her tears glistened in the thin of her squint, glossing her eyelashes. Frances lifted Joy from the ground and carried her through the storm.

Off to the side on a narrow clearing, tucked within a cage of wintering trees, stood a shack, utterly overpowered by nature until it became itself a part of nature, its wood walls splintered, the chinking—if ever any—gone after the logs warped through phases of wet to dry, hot to cold, moldy to inhospitable to any life.

Frances peered into the windows but only darkness looked back.

She tried the door while carrying Joy and it creaked opened into a single room. It stank the salty waft of rotting flesh, and had it been any warmer, no living thing would withstand it. Frances saw the bodies first when light from outside entered through the door, then the two beds carrying them, then the dead fireplace between them that she didn't trust because the house leaned on a weakened foundation, meaning smoke trapped in the crooked chimney may have suffocated the now-corpses. Extra blankets, still folded, lie at the foot of both beds and wood for kindling had been stacked in a corner. A small table covered in inedible food haunted the wall, right beneath the facade windows. A mess bucket, its human waste frozen, sat between both beds but nearer to the one with the smaller corpse. A hole in the ceiling let enter the dismal light of winter, wide enough for a few snowflakes to fall through and make a pillow on the dirt floor. Frances slid a chair from beneath the table with her foot, sat Joy up in it, and got to work.

By the time Joy came to, Frances had started a fire in the middle of the shack. Smoke exited the rooftop hole and canceled out the snow. The waste bucket and useless frozen food were now outside. Joy found herself covered in two blankets that had been beaten dustless and flat. Her chair had been dragged closer to the fire where she could see the beds and their captives. The rot smell remained though it softened in the smell of burning maple wood. Frances stood over the fire. The two bodies in their snow-corrupted beds brought peace to Joy, her breath's vapor hiding the gaunt shell of their faces. When it became clear to her that they were dead, her bottom lip quivered and the dead smell, made less prevalent by the smoke, grew in strength because of her new knowledge. She was thirsty and hungry, her tongue the texture of a poorly woven scarf. She thought maybe this was the end of the world Eloise had spoken of and closed her eyes to avoid seeing it coming.

When Joy came to in the shed a second time, she saw that Frances had fallen asleep by the fire. A cup of water sat on the table beside Joy and she drank till she choked. She was so parched that the water tasted sweet. A bit of salted pork and bread were placed on the table next to the cup of water. She wolfed them and examined the fire and the faces of the dead still tucked in their beds. She had known death intimately but never witnessed what happened to the body when death was over, only what happened as death was initiated. The bodies, observable without prohibition, were obscene. If they couldn't be honored with burial other than this stuffy cabin and the snow over it, then what? Watching the fire's light dance on their pale skin hinted at a better future for the corpses.

Without curiosity as to whose dead body held her attention from its worn bed, without knowing anything about the corpse's living past and the sins therein, and without much awareness at all projecting from her eyes any sign of consciousness, Joy moved across the shack with the deliberateness of a puppet to the smaller body and lifted what had to have been the corpse of a child out of its bed. The sheets clung to the corpse's body, making a smacking sound when separated from the skin, like lips that had not opened in years gradually opening. Cradling the dead child in her arms, she stepped to the thinning fire to kill what had already died.

Frances woke after hearing something crash into the middling flames. Cinders flew across the floor and the various hisses broke the sleep-keeping silence. Frances saw thin legs hanging from the pyre, arms splayed open and back arched as though the body were being smitten from behind. She cried out, "No!" rushed to her feet, and pushed Joy to the floor. She tossed water from a bucket into the fire, putting it out and soaking the dead body. Thin light illuminated Frances as she stood beneath the hole in the roof. She let out quick clouds of breath, gawking at the wet corpse over the wet wood beneath the cold air pouring in from above. "I'm sorry," she said. She repeated it until she made no sound at all. She mouthed the words as steam mingled with her breath. The house creaked and Frances pummeled Joy with her resentment.

"We already desecrating the tomb by being here. Why you go and desecrate the bodies?" she said. Joy looked up at the tall woman standing beneath that sorrowful radiance and wanted to stand with her. But she was unwelcome, more putrid in Frances's eyes than the corpse she had sent burning in a sleep-veiled daze. "Get out."

"This is not your house, Frances," Joy said.

"And these not your dead. Get out. I won't say it again."

Joy stumbled to her feet, grabbed her belongings, and stepped outside.

~

WHEN FRANCES LEFT THE SHACK, Joy had already settled beneath a tree. Frances passed her and returned to the path that ended with a stand of pine trees. Joy followed. Frances lifted her head, took a deep breath, and pushed on faster. Joy kept up without complaining. The incident in the shack wasn't the first time she had taken it upon herself to do whatever she wanted with someone else's body, but it was the first time she enacted violence against the already dead. Several times Frances had been around to stop her in the act of unconscious cruelty. If Frances ever decided to leave her side, who knew what Joy would do in the cold grip of memory. At that moment, she was reminded that Frances had told her to leave behind the gun. Even without ammunition, it held brutal possibility.

After an hour or so of travel, Frances stopped. "We here," Frances said.

Joy frowned at the ceramic landscape. "What is *here*?"

"Hold my hand," Frances said, and reached out to Joy without looking at her. Joy couldn't tell if she was still angry or just focused. Reluctantly, she grabbed Frances's hand and when they took a step forward, Joy's eyes burned. When she opened them, a long path in a hall of trees appeared before them. At the end of the path stood several houses with more in the distance. Before they could walk any closer to the smells of food and the sounds of music summoning them, they saw a woman wearing a black dress and a red shawl, and thought for a moment that the River Rider had returned. Two same-faced girls wearing sky-blue dresses stood on either side of the woman, one holding on to the black dress and the other standing a little ahead, arms folded beneath her own red shawl.

Frances couldn't take her eyes off the woman, who felt like a long-lost family member. 'We the same complexion. Got the same cheeks. Her eyes look dangerous,' she thought. 'Like mine.' She smiled wide.

"You made it," Saint said, more verification than relief.

'Made it where?' Joy wanted to ask but knew no answer would come. Frances, tearful and all-teeth, shined.

· CHAPTER 11 ·

Unravel

[1]

Two months prior to Frances and Joy's arrival, Saint and her companion went away for a few weeks without telling anyone, except Selah and Naima. When they returned, they brought with them a new set of Negroes whose so-called masters had met their ends beneath Saint's staff. This group was much smaller than the last, made up of only twenty-two Negroes from three small plantations scattered across the South and Southwest.

The new Ouhmey were given houses that had become empty after years of people moving out west on their own, to Saint's chagrin and against her warnings. Ours's seclusion became too much for some, and Saint didn't want a revolt from anyone thinking she was forcing them to stay. But each time someone packed up and departed, she told those who remained, "There may be worse things than slavery in the west. I can't rightfully say." That succeeded in keeping the rest from leaving town.

A few new smaller houses were built on every street for new residents taken in after future plantation sweeps. Reverend received a new house, which he turned into a living space and a church that no one attended. Thylias rejected a house, opting to stay with Franklin until he died, saying, "I'm staying here till he die or I die. Whichever firstly come." Franklin didn't protest, though he had wanted to.

The twenty-two new residents joined the community and brought much-needed life into town. When they arrived, they basked in the smell of lilac and held their breath to keep both it and the sweet scent of baking cakes in their nostrils. The roads were rough with pebbles but wide, and between each house stretched space enough for two or more houses. They imagined building work sheds, maintaining lush gardens, and playing with their children in the fields between and all around.

Then there were the children of Ours, of all sizes and running around, kicking up nimbuses of dust and filling the town with laughter. When not in school, they spilled into the roads, played wherever they wanted, dirtied their dresses and giggled at the games they made up on the spot. They ran around one man whose name they learned was Reverend, teasing him, hugging his legs so he couldn't move, and asking him to talk about Jesus. He swatted them away and the new Ouhmey swore they saw the flash of a grin on Reverend's face.

One woman from the new group decided that all the women should formally meet twice a month to talk about what it meant to be free women. She went by the name Glory Jenkins, but everyone called her Madame Jenkins because of the hoity-toity way she carried herself. It was no compliment, though she took it as one and everyone poked fun at her behind her back. How a once-enslaved woman got these ways, some Ouhmey thought, was either from being up under a so-called master's womenfolk or up under the so-called master who, ambushed by his own proclivities, had to at least train the Negress of the house regardless of him hiding her when white company arrived. Others thought Madame Jenkins an immense pleasure and wanted her company because they, too, felt highly of themselves, and why not?

As time passed, Madame Jenkins's ways infiltrated the ways and thinking of some of the other residents. She suggested they get together and talk amongst themselves about their specific issues as Negro women in the somewhat south. Why not share recipes and remedies ("Just sit some pennies in vinegar and your money come rolling in")? Why not think freely, complexly, and share those thoughts to see how life could be made easier for them all?

It took little time for her to slide into the rhythm of woman-life, and they welcomed her enthusiastically, helping her clean her tiny home, sweeping from the back of the house to the front and tossing the dirt at the foot of a tree, while commenting on how she should just take the bigger house next door, "cause it's been empty for some time," and Madame Jenkins smiled and said, "No. I'm tired of places where things can be hidden from me," and when the women all looked up at her, she almost cried from embarrassment until they looked down at the same time and returned to sweeping in the quiet of their mutual understanding that, yes, there is danger in a house with too many rooms.

At the first meeting, three women came. They each brought something to eat and a question they desperately needed answers to. They were fine with keeping the group small until one woman had problems with hitting her husband and the women in town gathered her up and sat in a circle fifty-deep in the grass behind the tiny house. They put the woman in the center and each of those forty-nine other women, Madame Jenkins included, said something beautiful about her: "You send your babies to school clean and straight-backed," "Your smile make me jealous of your lips," "I wish we was sisters cause you be knowing the good in things," and they laughed until Madame Jenkins entered the circle with the woman and asked her as loud as she could, "Ruth, who you when you hit Mathias?" and the woman sat alone in her head for a moment, then answered, "Can't be nobody but me," and Madame Jenkins asked the woman to stand and gave her a hug. "The you I know wouldn't hurt a bug." Then the rest of the women left from their part of the circle and one by one whispered both their disappointment and encouragement to Ruth, hugged her fiercely after they finished. By the final hug, Ruth was a crying mess, promising to do better. At the end of the meeting, she tearfully asked, "When we meeting again?"

Madame Jenkins invited Saint to one of the meetings, but Saint declined, impressed by the idea. "I appreciate you considering, Miss Saint," Madame Jenkins said, thinking Saint a much younger woman than she was, and carried on with the thirty-plus women who wanted to.

One of the aftermaths of Madame Jenkins's intervention was that her own relentlessly eager disposition toward romantic partnership infected the younger women. The older women warned the young ladies against Madame Jenkins's desire for male affection, but the idea of romance, its possibility, burned new and irresistible. Soon, they sought out young men for regular and public one-on-one rendezvous around town. This did two things: First, it made it obvious that there were more women than men in the town. Second, it created a need for new businesses to entertain the new couples ambling about with nothing to do but garden work, animal work, Delacroix work, and learning their letters. Mr. Wife's bakery became more popular than ever and with added visitation meant added visibility for Justice and Luther-Philip. But both boys rejected all suitors, Justice with a heavier lean into the darker edge of his personality. So awkward he was impolite, Justice scrunched his face and looked at the floor when a young woman waved at him. If she flirted, he flared his nostrils and turned away. Luther-Philip blushed but still said no. His kind rejections made the women swoon even more and eventually he had a line of potential suitors lapping up sweet bread just to be near him. Some brought him gifts of new clothes sewn just for him or a small basket of fried fish. They giggled and he darkened two shades, grinning all the while.

[2]

Though neither Selah nor Naima could tell, their living in seclusion had made them strange and more like the ghosts of children than living children. Where once their visible youth protected them from scrutiny, their blossoming into nine-year-olds made what were once considered petulant phases into worrisome futures.

They were juveniles but not toddlers, young but not incapable, such that their distinct vulgarities—Selah's overly polite manner while disregarding what had been communicated to her, even walking away in the middle of being spoken to; and Naima's ghastly and relentless rudeness that only deepened as she aged—were no longer adorable oddities.

They mostly interacted with others while running errands for Saint, but their presence, off-putting as two headless dolls, made it difficult for the Ouhmey to welcome them. After all, they were Saint's kin of sorts and isolation had warped the twins into foxes: skeptical of their surroundings and in constant search of an escape route.

The Ouhmey did think it a shame that Naima and Selah should be as cooped up as they were. The girls didn't attend school, which made them unfamiliar to the rest of the children in town. But it also never occurred to the Ouhmey to welcome the twins beyond their given tasks. No invitations to play with their young'uns, no thank-you gifts, no just-baked cookies wrapped in fabric. They were simply "Saint's girls," and though the Ouhmey believed Saint had grown warmer, she kept herself even farther from them than when Ours was first created. Half the time they forgot about her, the other half they missed her with an intensity that bordered resentment. And because the twins sensed hostility in indifference, they armored themselves without apology.

Then Selah, upon seeing Frances step long-legged from the hall of trees, felt for the first time a human-sourced fear that delighted her so much that she hid her face in Saint's dress. Naima, seeing Joy's long hair drape over her shoulders and mix in with shawls that were almost as colorful as Saint's floor fabrics, stood a bit in front of Saint and Selah in a defensive pose as though welcoming a messenger of war. She paid no attention to Frances until Frances got up close, her towering figure making her difficult to ignore. Naima thought, 'Who this man with all this leg,' and returned her attention to the woman with the shawls, the too-much hair, and sad mouth, who up close had the most frightening aura and eyes to match: an aura of death and eyes the color of honey throwing back candlelight.

Saint welcomed the two visitors and told them to follow her to Franklin's wagon. Thylias sat on the porch, shotgun between her thighs, hair bun a frozen demigod atop her head. She laid the gun across her lap and smiled when Frances smiled at her and shouted from the road, "My name Frances. This Joy."

Franklin drove them all to Creek's Bridge in a quilt-covered wagon, so shoddily made it was deviant. No one spoke the duration of the trip. Franklin kept his gaze ahead and Joy, still bitten by Frances's chastisement at the cabin, took to throwing her anxiety at Naima, who had nerve enough to stare her down. They walked the rest of the way from Creek's Bridge.

Frances, followed by Saint, entered Saint's house first while Joy waited cautiously outside with the twins. The moment the door closed behind them, the fireplace blazed up and a book on the table flipped through all its pages, front cover to back, then slammed shut before sliding across the table, stopping right at the edge. Then the orange fire in the fireplace became blue and the light turned the room into an underwater scene. Children's laughter filled the room, followed by the sounds of chains and crying. When hands reached out from the floor and grabbed Frances by the ankles, Saint thought to interrupt the vision somehow, but the hands weren't pulling Frances in, rather pulling themselves up through the floor as full-bodied children. Where should've been legs were fish tails belted by chains. Manacles braced their wrists and chain links dangled down from the metal rings, ending with clipped links from where they had been broken from the rest of their length. The children swam through the room unburdened by the metal they wore, laughing and spinning around Frances, who reached up and danced with them. Saint regarded Frances's walnut-colored skin stained blue by the blue flame. The color engulfed even the whites of Frances's eyes.

The room filled with swimming, filled with the blue percussion of iron on iron, of restraints clanging into song. Blue fire wavered and its light painted a sea on the walls. Leaving the circle, one child swam toward Saint. Eye to eye, the child leaned in, squinted, and jolted back. Saint didn't recoil when the child reached cautiously for her cheek and shook their head as though disbelieving what they saw. Satisfied with the feel of her skin on their own, they said, tearfully, "Us." Then, the entire scene ended as though it had never begun: The fire burned orange again in the fireplace. The swimming, fish-tailed children disappeared, replaced by the dull flamelight entering and mingling with the darkness it couldn't conquer.

By the fireplace, Saint stood holding herself, disturbed by what she had seen and even more by what she felt. Children's laughter echoed in her mind and a grave homesickness tore through her.

"You haunted?" Saint asked.

Frances laughed. "If I'm haunted, then you just as much a ghost as they are."

The circumference of her suspicion widened, and Saint felt both validated and regretful that she had decided to let Joy and Frances stay with her just so she could observe them.

Frances had already gone back outside, cool air racing in from the door she left ajar. Saint closed the door. Salt stink had filled the room, like the Apalachicola had crept through the crack of the open door and steered into her front room. Disregarding the cold, she opened the windows to relieve her home of the smell of the sea—foam frothing the water's surface, fish stink, brackish smell of decay. Sea for sure, not coming in from the once-open door but pouring from the mouth of the fireplace whose flame now softly asserted its heat, casting low shadows that shook like frightened animals beneath the chairs.

[3]

Joy refused to greet anyone in Ours on the rare occasion that she did go to town, and she resisted going for as long as she could. She refused to help at the school as a teacher, brilliant as she was, and refused to get to know the other women over tea. When men acknowledged her, she turned away. When women appraised her, she faked a cough to avoid looking into their eyes and seeing her own face fade away in a tear-mirrored reflection.

Folks thought she had "the consumption" and, instead of staying away, offered her even more help: noxious teas, sleep remedies, more soups than she could stand, herb-scented compresses, spice-laden berry cobblers, mint-soaked rags from which to inhale—it wore her down, this frequent and unrequested generosity of others, until what drove her off became a craving.

It took her passing the abandoned-looking, one-story house for her fearful concentration to return. Most of the plants had died in the cold, leaving the boney remnants of burgeoning thick-stemmed weeds and invasive trees to claw their skeleton remains against the house and sky. Smoke unspooled from the chimney and filthy windows shut out what little sunlight touched the panes. Standing in the doorway, a shirtless and withered man with a round belly looked out to the road, his solemnity infecting the air. Joy stopped and nodded at the man, who nodded back, then went inside, closing the door behind him. The creak of the door sounded like a frog saying "need" and, back at Saint's house, Joy asked Saint who the man with the frog door was.

"Aba," Saint said. "Door talk more than he do."

"Why doesn't he speak?" Joy asked.

Saint wandered toward a task she didn't have to do.

Joy visited Aba's house every day to nod and hear what his door had to say. One day the hinges creaked and she heard from the metal "please." She went to the market, bought a few apples, and left the basket at the front door. The next day, the hinges said "leave," and Joy made sure not to stick around any longer. The following day, the hinges said "Saint," and the next day, the hinges ached out another word: "now." From then on, the creaking was just creaking and eventually Aba stopped waiting at the door. It took Joy a week more to realize that the words weren't meant to be heard alone but together, and Aba telling her through the throat of his rusty hinges to leave Saint's house worried Joy enough to end what she read as the still-standing silence between herself and Frances.

When she mentioned the tension between them, Frances looked offended. "I was done with it after I said what I had to say. You the one moping around for a month and a half," Frances said, and offered her a spoonful of apple cobbler. Joy sighed and let Frances feed her. They were sitting on Frances's bed and the snow-bright day entered through the window. "Saint made it."

A bolt of lightning entered Joy's mind. "It's been a month and a half, already," she said. "How could that be? What have we been doing all this time?" She licked her lips and shook her head when Frances offered another bite of cobbler. How did so much time get away from them? And Frances, oblivious or unconcerned, said nothing about it; Frances, whose obsession with the past made her suspicious of the present and in sublime awe of the future.

Joy wondered what, in the first place, made her stay. This was Frances's adventure after all, and the tether that tugged Frances from New Orleans to Ours had no interest in tugging Joy as well. She had wanted to leave this place of unpeaceful quiet but to go where, and upon going, how would she survive the two wildernesses that awaited her: the unfamiliar Missouri hills and the dense hunger of her need to kill?

With her only family dead, Frances, her only friend, was all she had left and suddenly to the point of abuse: shepherded off, haunted by the image of her once-guardians propped up like puppets on the couch, not only did she not get the chance to bury Eloise and Amelia, she also never got the chance to mourn. So, the two dead women sat in limbo, waiting on her to call their names, to cry out, so that her heart could finally attend to their absence.

It didn't frighten her that a month and a half had passed so quickly. It frightened her that all that time had passed without her having broken down. When the floodwaters would come, she knew that after all this time they would nearly drown her. It was because Joy hadn't mourned that she felt fastened to this pilgrimage, as though knowing eventually the dam of her grief would rupture, requiring someone to sit close by and make sure she didn't rupture with it. She feared being alone, not knowing when the time would come, so remained near to her only living anchor to the world: Frances.

"We'll stay for two weeks. No longer. It shouldn't take no longer than that," Frances had said when they first arrived. But now Frances had fallen into impenetrable distraction. Joy knew how long Frances had been following the tether's pull all over the South and some of the North, too. Resistant though understanding, Joy didn't pressure Frances to abandon discovering the point of her journey, seeing that it had something to do with the woman downstairs whose welcome felt to Joy more like spying. She looked over Frances with skepticism. She saw Frances, but it seemed Frances had left her body.

"You all right?" Joy asked. Frances yawned and nodded. "What do you think of Saint?"

"I think there's a lot to know that we don't know. Not sure when she gone tell us, but for now I'm grateful that she's taking care of us."

"Why here? Why we stop here?"

"Where else?"

"Was she the one pulling at your heart all this time? Did she pull you into this place that only you could see?"

Frances shook her head. "Spirits guided me here. That pulling could be her needing me and our ancestors helping me get to her." She paused, then said, "Could be me pulling myself where I'm supposed to be."

"You can't pull yourself when you're only on one side."

Frances laughed. "Spirit world can make anything happen."

"I'm asking why the spirits guided you here."

"That's what I've been trying to figure out. But I know this is where I need to be."

Joy watched her eat the cobbler like a child and wanted to pop her in the eye. Frances's movements were slothful. Her thinking not as sharp. She seemed giddy but not happy. And the more Joy thought about it, the more she realized that Frances hadn't gone into town with her the entire time. She had thought it was because Frances was angry, but with that revealed as untrue, why had the person who carried her exhausted body into a lifeless cabin—making a fire, leaving her food and water—and who feared Joy would take anything as a weapon and kill without thinking, not walk with her in an unknown place full of unknown people? It was all too uncharacteristic, a mind tampered with, or something worse. She left for town and Frances retreated into sleep.

Joy passed Saint sweeping dust out the front door. The twins were in the kitchen banging on pots for only God knows why. Joy used the noise to ignore Saint and pretend she didn't hear her asking if she were heading to Ours. Joy shouted goodbye over the cacophony and with her basket hanging from the hinge of her bent elbow, she went straight to Aba's, knocked on his door, and waited. It took a long time for him to come out and when he opened the door, it creaked "what" in a long, trebly whine.

She needed help with something out at Saint's, she said. The moment the words left her lips, Aba attempted to close the door in her face, but she placed her arm in the opening. The door closed hard on her forearm. Aba snatched open the door, eye to eye with Joy. The hinges cried out "why," as the door opened, and Joy showed no signs of pain.

"You want to help me. Do not act unkindly. You might as well help." Truth was, Joy thought the man, in his decrepit state, looked just as magical and ornery as Saint and that look alone led her to believe that he also carried as much knowledge about conjure as anyone in town.

He didn't let Joy inside, so she stood out in the cold on the other side of the threshold while she described the emanations from the house when Frances entered and Frances's stupefaction and isolation. Aba's face creased with panic while she talked.

"No help," he creaked when she finished, "but to leave." She asked why he couldn't speak. Aba looked at the floor as he closed the door between them. The hinges replied, "Guess."

[4]

Usually discerning to a fault, Joy was so distracted by figuring out what was wrong with Frances that she didn't notice people watching her. Each time she stopped by Aba's, the town went stationary around her, its clockwork habits jammed by her visiting the man who had no more words after burning down Saint's house. Did she know he had done that? Surely, Saint had told her. She must have. They also noticed how the naked branches of the large weeds in front of his house leant in a little toward Joy when she visited. 'Both must have surely lost they mind,' some thought, while others believed the leaning branches and the squeaking door were both a token for something. For what, who could tell so soon? But a token for sure.

Their odd behavior caught Franklin's attention as he made his way to Mr. Wife's. He remembered dropping off Joy and the man she accompanied over a month ago at Creek's Bridge and thought it nice to see her visiting town to get to know folks. But seemed like she only took interest in Aba, who had stopped picking berries years ago and let his porch that once doubled as a fruit market fall prey to spiderwebs. How could he haggle over fruit with no voice to negotiate and charm his way into the best sell?

Mr. Wife used to sit with him on the porch, but that, too, stopped soon after Saint reappeared carrying all-of-a-sudden twins on her bosom. Mr. Wife would come knocking on Aba's door while Aba sat somewhere in the house ignoring him. After a week of being disregarded, Mr. Wife stopped trying.

"All it took was a week?" Franklin had asked, but Mr. Wife wasn't about to take another loss in stride. "Lost my woman, almost lost my son; it seems that way to me with all these snakes crawling about. Lost my friend. Who else want to make me mayor of losses? You?" Mr. Wife said, and Franklin shook his head and changed the subject. This was when the boys were still boys. Now, eight years later, Franklin wondered again if Mr. Wife had given up too soon while he himself never took to Aba's porch to keep the man company. Though he didn't think of himself as a hypocrite, he did feel a gnawing in his gut for which he had no name when he walked by Joy as she stood in the cold, speaking to a no-talking man.

Franklin wanted peers. Restless for male energy, he took to the roads to find folks to play a little bid whist for a sip of whiskey, but most of the men had grown as old as or older than him and were nestled up with the remainder of their lives, while the married men raised families, distracted by small feet and cries for milk.

Some of the older boys were off in the woods looking for winter game or up in Delacroix finishing last-minute work before the weather got too bad for travel. Franklin reminisced on days when the younger men stopped by his porch to talk and wondered when it was that they had all decided he was too old to drink with. As years passed, his life wisdom bored those who had been discovering their own adulthood: learning the scent of a lover intoxicated more than whiskey and learning how to let the burn of whiskey train them into pleasure. Franklin wanted to impart values of manhood and play games, something denied him in his own childhood, but the young men of Ours lived a life without much wonder or wander, and their restlessness demanded quenching. Ours's isolation had intensified their longing, and though sometimes the young men would come seeking advice or just to check in on Franklin, never did they stay long, which left room for the dead fox boy of his past to roll from the depths of his memory and stare at him from a near distance. He would blink and the ghastly image would roll into itself like a curl of smoke and vanish.

Franklin avoided the young boys completely, swallowed lumps in his throat when he heard their bright voices. He kept his head low and waved without proper acknowledgment, his heart pounding, his mind cloudy with a fear that made his eyes throb. No, he would be play uncle no more, Luther-Philip the first and last of that improvisational family that, had it lasted beyond its time, would've flattened beneath the weight of his history as the image of the dead fox boy slowly and eventually took over the faces of the boys that came near him.

He thought of the company of one man he had met in the forest and mistook for a deer. Had he been hunting, he might've killed him, the man's naked skin brown and shiny as a wet doe's. But that meeting happened over a year ago, and the shame of returning to those piercing eyes, those hands hard from carpentry, and that mouth that he decided to abandon because in it he found no future, kept him immured in Ours.

The one man in Ours he could've been close to, Aba, he never really spoke to and had no idea why. They weren't close in age, Aba either in or nearing his sixties, and Franklin believing he was somewhere in his late forties by now. But Aba reminded Franklin of the best parts of his father. This disarmed him, he who had accumulated much armor yet hid the hiding to make peace with himself and those around him. Truth was, men frightened Franklin, but over the years he had seen what brotherhood could look like by watching how the men in Ours handled each other. The longer he witnessed this, the more he wanted to take part, though his body quaked with fear. 'Maybe that's why they stopped coming by like they did,' Franklin thought, believing they saw his hands trembling and thought him strange.

What he had known of men was violence so careless it ruined a whole crop of boys. But Franklin's father, particularly after Franklin had seen a dead body up close, was kind to him till the end of his life. Franklin only wished that his father had stepped in and stopped what those men did to him, to stop the fight so the boy who cared for foxes wouldn't have been killed. Maybe then his yearning for and dread of those who should've been his brothers wouldn't overpower him.

Aba was kind to the boys, sweet to the women, and minded his business unless absolutely needed. Franklin had witnessed how he broke up fistfights, then fed the fighters on his porch while telling them cuss-filled stories that made no sense. Yes, Franklin should've gone to the man earlier on because now Aba had stopped speaking altogether. It seemed like such a waste. Heading to visit Mr. Wife, he began to feel angry and the new pain in his head swelled.

When he made it to Mr. Wife's, the place reeked of iron and musk. "Open the damn windows," he said to Mr. Wife, who begrudgingly did as he was told, then went back to work on a pound cake. "Nothing worse than a house full of menfolk," Franklin said, loud enough for Luther-Philip and Justice to hear, both sitting off to the side: Justice reading an old Delacroix newspaper while Luther-Philip scrubbed a pair of pants with soap in a tin tub. Franklin wanted them to know that they needed their own. Their own house, horse, business (to mind), and women. He believed more fiercely each day that Mr. Wife could move on and find for himself a new wife if he had no more children to raise. Justice and Luther-Philip, one seventeen and the other eighteen, should've been gone out the house years ago, married or making bed and working some job somewhere, perhaps for Franklin, who desperately needed repairs that he couldn't do alone and that Thylias wasn't interested in doing.

"Mind yours, Franklin, and I'll mind mine," Mr. Wife said. "If you had some your own, you wouldn't be so worried over this way." He laughed.

Franklin scowled, lingered a bit, said it smelled like menfolk who needed to get married, then headed on out, back to his unwanted solitude where the voices of snickering boys panicked him into a brisk escape.

Years ago, after Mr. Wife had started bathing again but before Justice moved in, the house had another smell that needed handling. The back room where Mr. Wife, Mrs. Wife, and Luther-Philip had slept still smelled like Mrs. Wife. Mr. Wife smelled it, too, and no matter how much he washed the floor with that tiny bottle of oil Saint had given him, the scent of his dead wife refused to leave.

He installed three windows in that room and painted over them so no one could look in or out while they were shut. He only wanted to release his dead wife completely from the house with a breeze, not remove his much-wanted privacy, but she insisted on staying and chased the wind out instead of leaving. It took Franklin to intervene yet again on behalf of the town and yet again over something not smelling quite right in the Wife home.

"You need to go to your woman's grave and cry. If you don't, she never find rest. Just watch. You wake up one morning and she cozy on your porch. Then how you gone get her back in the ground?" he said, and Mr. Wife, that very day, visited the small cemetery and noticed the smell strengthened the closer he got to the grave. What he found alarmed him. Mrs. Wife's hand reached straight up from the earth and perfumed the air with rot and a flowery sweetness. The salt had not stopped her from coming back and his unspoken grief for her broke the hold the afterlife had on her. Mr. Wife sat there all night, crying and reminiscing to Mrs. Wife's hand until it returned into the ground, taking the smell with it.

A decade after, Mr. Wife was mostly a man freed from his mourning but who, according to Franklin, had been kept hostage by two boymen who didn't have sense enough to go be full men. Franklin could see if they were daughters, him believing women were more subject to harm from the elements than any man. Hence him treating Thylias like he would a boy as if to inoculate her from what he believed were the weaknesses of her sex, though that didn't appease him completely and, in his eyes, had made her irrevocably unmarriable. Had he asked her, Thylias would've told him that she didn't ever want to marry, only to remain in their earned peace. Contrary to Franklin's belief, men had asked to court her, and she rejected them all to maintain mental clarity and retreat. Their stability together spoiled her for marriage more than anything else.

FRANKLIN RETURNED TO the bakery house a few days later and asked, "What you two do all day?" to Luther-Philip and Justice. Justice said reading and Luther-Philip said he had been cleaning everybody clothes, the same as they had been the last time he had visited. 'Dear Lord,' Franklin thought, 'they done made Luther-Philip the new wife.' He didn't know that they took turns cleaning each other's clothes and this just so happened to be Luther-Philip's week.

When Franklin pulled Mr. Wife into the back room, closed the door, and confronted him about the "boy-wife," Mr. Wife laughed in his face. "Nothing funny about it," Franklin said, and the gravity of his concern moved Mr. Wife from awkward humor to patient warning.

"Not in this house. I open the window when you say so. I listen to everything you had to say but not about my boys," Mr. Wife said. He spoke louder than he had wanted to. In the other room, Luther-Philip smiled. Justice folded the newspaper.

"You letting them run you, Mr."

"And you trying to run me. What sense you make? You want me ran or not?"

"We know each other, back-of-the-hand know. Skin close. We both men here."

"Which is why you know better than anybody not to tell a man about his house."

"Now listen—"

Mr. Wife placed his hand on Franklin's shoulders and said, "No. You said what you think needed saying and I respect you for that gift. But that's enough."

"You just gone let them sit around and live under you like pigs?"

"You watch your mouth, Franklin. Not long ago you was a pig on a plantation."

"Worked harder as a slave than these boys do as free."

"You better watch your damn mouth," Mr. Wife said, his finger in Franklin's face. "If they want to sit under a tree and pleasure they self all damn day, then that's just what the hell they gone do. They gone do with they freedom what they want."

Franklin smacked Mr. Wife's hand away. "They both gone play wife for you, Mr.?" he said.

Had there not been any air in the room, Mr. Wife wouldn't have noticed. He had been holding his breath. His body tightened. He was getting ready.

The dim light coming through the open windows hardly reached them. A draft coursed through the room, but Mr. Wife felt hot and when he finally unclenched his fists, he said, "I reckon Thylias mighty good, the way she hold that rifle." He smiled and Franklin hit Mr. Wife square in the jaw, knocking the man onto the floor. Mr. Wife laughed. "You the one want the company of men so bad," he said, holding his jaw. "Oowee! What make you so better being all your life married-like to your damn play-daughter but always looking for men to be up under." He held his chest and cackled when Franklin spat at his feet and kicked him in the shin, all while Franklin stormed out of the house and as Justice held a rag stuffed with packed snow on Mr. Wife's cheek.

Justice said he would kill Franklin, and Mr. Wife cackled once more.

"He a dollar there already," Mr. Wife said. "That punch had the last of his life in it."

A WEEK EARLIER, on an evening too warm for the season, Luther-Philip and Justice took one of their trips to the lake. They had fallen into the habit of not carrying lanterns, having learned the land so well they threaded through the bushes better than the dark itself.

Upon reaching the water, Luther-Philip undressed and jumped in. Justice took off his shoes and sat off to the side, letting the small waves chill the heels of his feet. He watched Luther-Philip take on the sunlight with the same shimmer as the lake water and nearly lost him when the sun halved low behind the bladed treetops across the way. The dipping sunlight carried with it all manner of sound, so a brief hush fell over the sunset-rusted water. Only the lake gulping down Luther-Philip's body sang in Justice's ears, until the night creatures burst into chorus.

The water was too cold for Justice, but Luther-Philip liked it just as he did during the warmer months. He swam up to Justice and splashed him. Justice tried to hide behind his arm, but Luther-Philip kept at it. His laughter cut through the dark, laughter nearly indistinguishable from the plashes, except for the blade-tipped apex of his voice when the laughter got good to him.

"Get in, Justice. Water's good as always," Luther-Philip said, and splashed Justice again, but Justice just observed what little he could make out of his friend, for the near-gone sun made Luther-Philip into a lean silhouette against the shadowy water. It took the moon's and stars' slow eruption for Luther-Philip's face to have its features returned to it just enough to reveal to Justice that his own face could also be seen, so he looked away, but Luther-Philip had already caught that last glimmer of sadness.

Luther-Philip waded out of the water and sat dripping wet next to Justice. It had been this way for a few nights, where an unnatural silence abused the curated silence between them. Justice tossed Luther-Philip a rag to dry off with, but Luther-Philip let the jewels of water slide down his taut skin illuminated beneath the bold full moon. At eighteen, Luther-Philip's leanness filled in with enough muscle to not think him unfed and the furious and sudden curves of his body made him appear hard to the touch, even in the dark that muted the edges of things, made errors of lines and soft cream of hard stones.

The night, too, had a way with Justice, who couldn't hide his bulk, which he carried with an ambling shame. He pivoted frequently to avoid colliding into others, paused, lifted himself up to get his chest and stomach out of the way of passersby, and treaded with a keen aptitude for invisibility. But with Luther-Philip, he spilled out of his body and allowed himself to fill in whatever space he wanted. He swiped cold sweat from his brow, he gnashed his teeth against short gusts of wind, he stretched his arms above his head and refused to carry his weight, which made him less agile but frighteningly fast. So fast that

Luther-Philip lost his breath when Justice pulled him into his lap and embraced him.

"You gone get sick," Justice said, and, grabbing the rag, began drying off Luther-Philip's head. He dug in his ears, twisting the rag inside the damp canals. He wiped behind the ears, then asked Luther-Philip to lean forward so that he could dry off his back. Justice wiped each spine knob individually before wiping under the shoulder blades. It was like polishing stone, only the shine went away too soon.

Justice passed Luther-Philip the rag and told him to dry off his legs. Luther-Philip turned around in Justice's lap and laid out. His back arched across Justice's thigh and his left arm dangled onto the muddy bay, making a living pietà of himself and Justice. Justice laughed and held Luther-Philip up with his arm and dried his legs for him.

Justice froze when he heard a rustle in the bushes behind them. Luther-Philip asked what was wrong and Justice covered Luther-Philip's mouth with his hand. They stayed that way for a while until Luther-Philip fell asleep and started to snore in Justice's arms. Justice turned toward the thick bushes behind them, but he couldn't decipher the darkness. He tightened his hold on Luther-Philip. He stared, listened, and waited.

Now, Justice watched Mr. Wife hold the snow-cold towel to his own face to relieve the swelling from Franklin's punch. Justice thought back to that night alone with Luther-Philip at the lake and how from then on, Mr. Wife made sure to keep the aspiring suitors at bay by asking the women to make their purchases so that others could get in. "Line getting long," Mr. Wife said, grinning though his eyes calcified against any compassion. Justice remembered and wanted to hide what to him was an unbearable vulnerability, to be seen without knowing one has seen you.

While Luther-Philip paced away his anger against Franklin outside, Justice asked, "How you keep people from leaving, sir?"

"Now where this come from? I'm bruised, not dying," Mr. Wife said.

"It come to me just now."

“You don’t keep nobody. Ain’t no masters left on this earth, boy. If somebody want to go, you can’t keep them from going,” Mr. Wife said.

“What if you end up with nobody else?”

“You always have yourself.”

“I can’t touch myself,” Justice said.

Mr. Wife dabbed his cheek. “Numb,” he said. “Can’t feel the left side of my face at all.”

“You held it there a mighty long time.”

“I did. Can’t hold nothing for too long,” Mr. Wife said, and looked at Justice.

“How long is too long, sir?”

“When it start hurting, the first sign. When you don’t feel nothing, the second,” Mr. Wife said, then asked, “Why you rubbing your thigh, son? Something bit you?”

Justice had been rubbing near the branded *E* without knowing it. He had no need to hold on to that letter; it did all the holding on needed. He hadn’t told Mr. Wife about what his parents put on him, and Luther-Philip only knew because they went swimming. The dark lake that was his heart trembled. He felt a bit of freezing wind rise from the black water’s surface and pour into his chest. Without thinking, he said “I got a *E* on me, sir.”

“What you say you got?” Mr. Wife said, shifting the wet towel on his face.

“A *E*. On my leg.”

Mr. Wife chuckled. “I don’t know your meaning, Justice.” Mr. Wife dipped himself and Justice some water from a nearby bucket. “Here.”

Justice drank the water and sat the cup on the floor. “Luther-Philip seen it. The *E*. He say I don’t need it but I got it. More like it need me.”

“What *E*, boy?”

Justice’s lips trembled. “It’s on my leg. It’s so my people could find me in the papers. That’s why I read the papers so much. To see if people do be finding people that way.”

“The papers?” Mr. Wife’s body slumped into itself. He kept his narrowing eyes trained on Justice, who didn't look away. "Show me," he said. "Show me what they did to you, son."

Justice pulled down his pants and hid his privates with his hand. He turned out his left leg and revealed the *E* burnt into his skin. Mr. Wife made a sound that carried all of history. Pain unfolding pain. A primordial echo of the first hurt finally crawling its way back. And each time Justice thought the pain had finished unfolding, more petals opened from Mr. Wife's mouth until the pain was in full bloom. After the sound ended, the tears began.

Mr. Wife studied Justice's face, then examined the brand. He tried harder to speak. Shook his head. He narrowed his eyes to push away the tears, incapable of seeing anything else, not even his own house, his own furniture in it, or the young man standing before him tagged like the slave he had never been, like cattle. The *E* branded on Justice's leg had branded Mr. Wife's mind. How had he missed that ugly scar for all these years? How did Justice hide it so well? And, of course, his damn parents burnt it inside his thigh and not on the outside where it would be most useful if ever needed. Even they knew to be ashamed of branding their boy, so hid it instead of simply not doing it.

Something inside Mr. Wife broke free, but this freedom he couldn't celebrate. This dead flesh rising up from a living body was too much, just too much.

As Mr. Wife cried and cussed, Justice knew that his all-along suspicions about his condition were right. What his family did to him shouldn't have been done. He raised his pants.

Mr. Wife stood and threw the chair he was sitting on against the wall. He smashed another chair into the table. He smashed the cake resting on another long table by the oven. He smashed it with his fists and threw the sweet ruin to the floor. Justice turned away. Another chair went flying. Justice shouted, "It don't hurt," and Mr. Wife, midswing of an iron poker toward the oven, stopped. "It don't hurt no more, sir," Justice said.

Mr. Wife dropped the poker. The smell of cake dazzled the air. Pieces of broken chairs, a splintered wooden bowl, dented tin cups, an upended bag of flour, a table cracked in the center, the old Delacroix newspaper ripped—everything unmade by his hostility, his grief for the living. And though he could no longer see Justice's gnarled *E* he remembered as though the image had been burned into his own mind and rested up against images of bags of rice, a stable of horses, fresh-carved bowls, flour waiting to be cupped and measured, loaves of bread handled more delicately than any body, butter, eggs, blocks of ice, a stream of satin, a page of silk, a hill of beans, and a shovel full of cow shit ready for the field. It became another object in the ledger of his memory, priced and allocated no importance more than its function: to feed, to keep warm, to get the job done, to make everything but itself prosper. 'No,' he thought. 'You wrong about it not hurting no more.' Mr. Wife could smell the smoke rising from that *E* from where he stood—feet away from the boy he called his own but knew nothing about, not even that he had an insignia branded into his left inner thigh, so what kind of parent was he to Justice if he knew and recalled the time of each bruise's conception on Luther-Philip's body but none belonging to Justice?

He closed the space between himself and Justice and embraced him. "You free," he said. Mr. Wife felt stirring in him another hit of grief, poignant to the point of sending him into a second tirade from which there could be no return. 'What is freedom?' he thought. 'What is this shit?' He rubbed Justice's head, just a bit higher than his own, and feeling the flesh of him—the meat and the fat and the warmth—against his own body made him feel sick.

When he released Justice, he looked into the boy's face, hoping that the meat would become a body again, some*one* returning from the some*thing* that he never had the mind to make the boy into, not before seeing the brand. Luckily, Justice's eyes brought his own selfhood back to Mr. Wife's mind. He squeezed the boy's shoulders and said, "You free," looking at his reflection in that big pool of Justice's dark brown eyes. Mr. Wife swam to the pool's bottom, got lost in the dark. 'If I can just look in his eyes,' Mr. Wife thought, 'if I can just see myself always in his eyes, I'll know that he seeing me back. We each other to each other. Let this be the freedom between us.'

· CHAPTER 12 ·

Dead-Time

[1]

Frances and Joy as a pair were the second and third strangers to enter Ours uninvited. Soon after they had broken through the barrier and moved in with Saint, a move meant to be for as long as it took her to observe their potential for danger, Saint lost track of time. Powerless against it, she decided to investigate the problem, but her memory also lost track of itself as her intentions tumbled about in her head. Hours passed without her having cooked a meal, reflected, read, washed her feet, or chastised the girls for dancing in each other's shadows. Hours melted into days, then the slow sloughing of weeks until finally a month disappeared in the calendar of her oblivion.

While time warped the house, Selah experienced a terrible headache. Tiny mallets beat the inside of her head, so she relied on Naima's help. She waited to expel her waste for when Naima bathed her, asking her sister to get a bucket and help her roll over. But Naima had started acting strangely. She sat in room corners most days and stared out into nothing. Then, with a sudden burst of awareness, Naima expelled her own waste in a bucket, bathed, made a quick meal of whatever was lying around, and fed Selah while rubbing her head. After completing those tasks, Naima sat on Selah's bed, trapped in the box of her mind.

In her short period of salience, Naima relayed that Saint had become the same way, disappearing for hours at a time only to return to accomplish tasks she meant for completion earlier in the day or that were already finished. Saint twisted her hair between tasks with a feverish look, leaving some locs of hair undone until the next day or longer. She cleaned the fireplace three times in two hours, made lunch at night and dinner at breakfast or cooked nothing at all for days at a time. She often went hungry without noticing until the next moment of clarity arrived. Naima had not seen Frances at all, and Joy, the most active, spent more time in Ours than she thought possible under this rapid malady that had infected everyone in the house.

Selah tested the limits of what she called the "lostness" and decided to try healing herself of her paralyzing headaches. It took three days for Naima to find what Selah needed and tie it up for her, so busy she was looking at nothing with her mouth open and collecting dust. Placing the healing gris-gris under her own pillow, much of Selah's headache dwindled. In a day, she regained the ability to walk and saw for herself the chaos of the house. With that same gris-gris and a tender touch, she raised Saint and Naima from their stupor.

Joy had just left for Ours. Frances had yet to appear, and Selah hadn't shared her healing gris-gris with her. But before Saint could climb the stairs and check on Frances, Frances came smooth down the stairs, fully dressed, eyes bright as wet coins, asking with an unaware smile what was for dinner.

'Is that so?' Saint said to herself. Seeing Frances completely unbothered and unaware of the shift in time took Saint back to when she got Naima and Selah and with them a striking collection of stories promising to haunt her in irrevocable ways.

[2]

After Aba burned down Saint's first house and thick clusters of lilac had grown in its place, Saint went looking for safety. Her second house, just east of Creek's Bridge, lodged her and her companion under the then-solid protection of her stones where the low field began to exclaim with woody-stem dewberry and black walnut trees until a full flourish of woods overtook the landscape. She knew that hiding amongst the trees like a fabled witch had to end and in preparation for the great reveal of both herself as not dead and of her second home, she went searching for a safeguard to assist her and her conjure that grew less reliable by the day. She took a three-hour stroll with her companion to the Mississippi River to find the one who could bring to her the strongest protection: a set of twins.

Intuition, a set of legends passed on through hearsay, and memories from once-enslaved Africans she had freed, all dictated to her the benefits of having twins and their natural gift for the otherworldly. Their single face repeating on two bodies could ruin a nation if allowed, and where some chose to kill them immediately after they were born, others chose to honor them. Saint would do neither. What she felt incapable of accomplishing on her own she would accomplish as three. The twins, neither demons nor gods, were still reliable.

Sometimes, Saint felt danger in the trees, in the sky regardless of the weather, regardless of which birds speckled the blue or gray above her. If anything, the birds were an augury awaiting consultation. With her limited time, she decided to assume there existed bad omens in all she experienced, making the desire for twins even stronger. They would be raised to call her Saint, not mother. Any inclination Saint had to coddle their beautiful selves would be resisted. Danger had a way of showing up where love resides, so she made it her duty to never love them. She would educate them in the ways of conjure and teach them everything about the world's ugly ways and striking possibilities.

Knowing exactly what she wanted, Saint found the strange man who wore the face of a boy and made her request. He had helped her countless times before, bringing enslaved Africans to freedom on his raft undetected in a way that not even Saint understood. Some called him the River Rider. She knew him as Husband and Son, for he said he was both married to the water and born from it. "My mama water," he said to Saint on more than one occasion, then once added somberly, "She give me my child then take her back." Politely, she had nodded when she heard the first part for the second, third, and fourth time. It was the other part, the part about giving and taking back, that gave her pause and pulled from her a soft look as though to corroborate his statement. He inspected the river then, maybe hoping for what was taken to be returned. Nothing bubbled forth and with no evidence of his being a spouse or a father, Saint referred to Husband and Son as just Son. When she called his name, she heard his near-toothless mouth smack open with spit as he grinned.

"Can get them for you. Don't ask where from," he told her and handed her a stack of papers tied together with twine. "As always."

'As always, indeed,' Saint thought, tracing the twine with a finger. Because Saint requested, Son collected newspaper clippings, pages torn from pamphlets about recent legends and ghost stories and wanted ads offering reward money for exceptionally dangerous Negroes. She didn't tell him why and he didn't ask.

Saint looked over the materials in her divining room. The clippings dated as far back as the 1740s, consisting of stories such as:

> "Legends along the Apalachicola River: The Rice African," December 2, 1740: Husband found shot in the head in the forest. He had been arguing with an African male about the amount of rice he had sold to the African.
>
> "Mysterious Negro Not Found after Death of Mr. Gerald Colfax," February 1, 1802: Witnesses say a

> well-loved Mississippi planter died mysteriously of a gunshot wound to the head after shooting a free colored in his head for allegedly sleeping with his daughter. The colored wasn't found.
>
> "Wanted for murder: tall, dark, unmuscular nigger male with unnaturally perfect teeth," February 3, 1802: Not liking the tone of an allegedly free nigger male who wouldn't move out of her way, a terrified South Carolinian white woman sent her brothers and husband after him. The four men she sent were found dead of various stab and gunshot wounds. Reward: $500.
>
> "Mysterious Failed Lynching. No Body to Bear the Rope," August 3, 1810: North Carolina, six men were found burned alive in the woods. The man who discovered the gruesome scene found near their bodies rope, a shotgun, and a knife. The scene resembled that of a lynching though no colored body, dead or alive, surfaced.
>
> From the pamphlet "Strange Deaths in American South, vol. VI," September 22, 1822: Man found in his Virginian home having choked to death on what appeared to be several issues of *The Liberator.*
>
> "Sense Killed along with Town," September 30, 1849: The entire town of Galley Brook, Florida (pop. 73) discovered dead by independent militia in search of a tall negro male who murdered three men and two women one town over. Several bodies bore gunshot wounds to the leg, torso, head, and through the back.

On October 3, 1858, Saint returned to Son and received a single article from a New Orleans paper about the slaughter of two women, described as a "negress and a thin quadroon," in their boardinghouse by the hands of a "tall Negro savage and his dark mulattress lover." Unimpressed, Saint nearly tossed the clipping into the fireplace until a phrase at the end caught her attention. "Thirty-five men dead in pursuit of couple." 'How on earth?' she wondered.

A month later, the barrier around Ours trembled so hard that books fell from their shelves in Saint's house. Pans hanging from the kitchen walls clattered like bells tolling an approaching storm. Galloping by, a family of deer, seven deep, heading away from Turney. Even then, the wisdom of animals.

Saint locked her companion away in a small shed about a quarter of a mile north, just in case this visitor had something as bad or worse than a cursed bell. It was then that a horde of white moths lifted from the sheet of November frost covering the ground and fluttered over her head, into the trees, and disappeared into the sky. Seconds later, it began to snow. What had once been a meager annoyance became an impertinent omen forcing Saint to gather the twins, wrap her hair, dust her face with sage ash, and rush into the freezing cold prepared for battle.

She saw Frances and Joy, the former shaking inexplicably with awe and the latter looking hungry. The wind blew snow into the air one good time and the once-shapeless foreboding of her fears manifested before her. She forgot about Joy altogether. 'This what's been coming to me all these years,' Saint thought, and saw that she had to welcome into her town what she never had the power to keep out.

Now, with Frances smiling at the bottom step all tall, lean, skin aglow, and oblivious as only a man could be, as though the entire household had not been in disarray for over a month, Saint realized her mistake. All this time it never occurred to her that Frances, a woman in her perception, could have been that "tall negro male" mentioned in the stack of clippings given to her by Son. All this time Saint was looking for someone who was looking for her, too. Successful in her search, what now did this untouchable person want?

[3]

While the twins washed the floor, they secretly watched Saint between scrubs. Naima noticed first the squelch orchestrating Saint's throat, a wet meant to hide a feeling but by hiding it too forcefully revealed it instead. Selah noticed a bit of candlelight in Saint's chest, an uncertainty burning away a wick's fragile length.

Joy, too busy noticing Frances's recovery to notice Saint's agitation, felt betrayed. Her conversation with Aba hadn't proven useful. It only supplied for her a journey at the end of which Frances returned to her senses without Joy's involvement. Not betrayal, then. She had become a burden. Might as well be invisible again. And if invisible, was she to kill again? The thought of blood stilled her. She poked her slice of hen's meat with a fork and in her mind heard a man's scream coming from the flesh.

The night Frances had found Joy after the horse kicked her back in Louisiana, she had just killed a man who had raped his own daughter. Invisible with Eloise's stone in her mouth, she tortured him before taking his life with a smile he couldn't see. She had knocked him clean out and when he woke, he found himself tied to a chair with his mouth rag-stuffed and secured by a thin piece of twine knotted hard at the back of his head. She indulged in his panic when he saw the sharp instruments floating like marionettes, his house suddenly haunted, the butcher knife finding all the ways to open him. The deeper she dug, the wider she grinned. She remembered what she did to that man's body with his own fork as she carved into the hen's breast at the dinner table, Saint asking questions, Joy and Frances answering around them.

"Strange," Saint said, pulling on a loc of hair. Lethal, the air and the moment. The twins stopped cleaning, the new silence like venom. Frances kept eating. Joy watched an iron gate emerge between the two.

Frances wiped her mouth. "What is?"

"My hair. It's gotten longer but I don't remember rolling it. Seems like time went on and did its own thing for a while. What do you think, Joy?"

Joy looked for direction from Frances, who kept her glare on Saint. "I suppose so. We hardly know each other and—"

"Yes," Saint said, with a razor-thin smile. "I agree. We know little about each other. We still strangers, really. Yet, it's been a month and a handful since y'all been here and not much knowing sits between us. How that be?"

Joy would've responded with more confidence if Saint had been looking at her, but all that time Frances had been Saint's focus. Joy cleared her throat. "Sometimes one can become busy—"

"With what?" Saint said to Joy. "What you two got keeping you busy? What you run away from expecting it to stay away?"

Night was soon to come. The twins turned their brushes bristle-up on the floor and left them there. Both girls folded into the growing shadows throughout the room. They were to light the candles, and their small frames emerged from the shadows after they lit their respective candles only to disappear again in the darkness they hadn't yet lit. When they finished, Naima and Selah went upstairs. At the sound of their bedroom door closing, Frances motioned to Joy that she should follow suit. Joy looked at Saint one last time before grabbing her plate of food and an extra drumstick off a hen. Saint told her to leave the bones of what she already ate behind. Joy placed them on the table, then headed upstairs.

"What's we got between us, Saint?" Frances said.

"That's what I'm wondering," Saint said.

"What else you wondering? Let's put it all on the table. What else on your mind?"

"Plenty of room on the table," Saint said. "I'll get us some tea." She cleared the table of chicken scraps, making sure she gathered all the bones. In the kitchen, she heated a kettle of water for the tea and scraped off the bones with a knife into a small pan of water waiting for her on the floor. The bones she would clean, bless, and then use for conjure. The water could be added to the slop for the two pigs she had out back. She sat cross-legged on the floor, pulling off leftover skin and fat from the carcass. Any uneaten meat from the hen, she tossed into a bowl for salting. 'Should keep for at least another day or two, especially in this cold,' she thought.

She returned from the kitchen with tea and newspaper clippings she received from Son. Pulling them one at a time, she showed them to Frances. "Something tells me you know about these," she said, honey-voiced.

"I almost found you here," Frances said, and handed her the North Carolina story from 1810, with the six men dead after what appeared to be a failed lynching. "I was heading into the mountains. I was closest then. To you. The tether tugged hardest then. I believed it. Then there these men come up to me saying I had no right acting like I had no master. I told them I had no master. They decided they would be the ones to change that." Frances took a sip of tea. "I'm not sorry to say they was mistaken."

Saint read the story over and thought hard as to whether she was ever near that place. When recollection arrived, she smiled. It was an accident, but she found herself acting as a child who had been caught doing something she was told not to do, grinning guiltily but for what? The year 1810 rang a hard bell; that's when she found Aba up in the Appalachian Mountains chained to other enslaved Africans. He was a teenager then and she had managed to give him some of his boyhood back. It seemed to Saint that his loyalty grew from a sense of purpose reignited by the simple act of no longer bearing iron. What manacles the body manacles the mind, she remembered hearing from an older woman who had lost all five of her children at an auction that sent them scattered in a star pattern across the South. Saint made it her duty to find this woman's children. "Every last one," she had told the woman. "I just need an article of clothing, a piece of hair, a baby tooth, a rag with their sweat on it. Anything."

The woman had something of the sort for only three of her children. For the other two, just the memory of them looking back over their shoulders, the eldest boy mute with outrage while his younger sister wiped tears from her eyes, her mouth atremble as though forming a string of curses. Saint found the other three children and devastated the plantations of two minor planters and the gaudy household of a sullen Negro woman who with her own freedom decided to enslave a child who favored her enough to be her son. "This slave boy is nothing like me!" the woman protested, and lost her life on that day to the sharp end of a hoe. It took Saint over a year to collect them, but she brought the three children back one at a time to the woman who had made a kind of home in Delaware. 'Frances might've followed me all that year,' she thought, and reached into her mind to find traces of a tall man's shadow, but the traces weren't there.

Before Saint could get her mouth set to ask a question, Frances handed her another article. And another. And another. For each one, Frances shared how the tether that guided her to Ours had also yanked her to the locations mentioned in the clippings. There was no telling where Saint would end up during those journeys to find the Delaware woman's children. But that was only a year's time. It was plausible that Frances had been following her for that long. But the idea that Frances may have been trailing her for over one hundred years without her knowledge unsettled her deeply.

"Then I lost you. Ended up in New Orleans. The spirits stopped pulling me to you," Frances said, then added, "I didn't mean for those folks to die that way."

Saint tilted her head and peered at Frances, whose face had softened after telling so many stories of failed attempt after failed attempt. "Who cares about you killing somebody?" Saint said, laughing. "I've killed plenty of people in my life, on purpose and on accident." She leaned forward, placing both elbows on the table, and sat her chin in the vase of her palms. "How? I want to know how."

"Do you know why you do what you do? Do you know what you do when you do it?"

"Not always, no."

"Neither do I." Frances emptied her teacup with a final slurp and sat it back on the tray.

"But you do know why you not walking around with bullets in your ribs, so tell me."

"No."

"What question did you hear me ask you?" Hearing her brusqueness, she smirked to soften the edge.

"I'm not saying I won't tell you. I'm saying I don't know why."

Saint straightened in her chair. Because her first mind told her to cut Frances down, she ignored it. In the kitchen she pictured the knife lying on the table and imagined aiming it at Frances's slim throat. The violence alone would've been worth it, though to gauge how Frances would respond (with what resolve, what power) interested her more. In lieu of the blade, she offered something that shocked even her.

"Allow me mentor you. Help you learn what it is you do so you can understand. I think that's why you been sent to me," Saint said.

Frances demurred. "That's not it, Saint. I ain't here to be helped. That much I know." She stood and pushed her chair under the table. "You got it turned around. I know you don't believe a thing I say, but I come all this way to help you. I feel it. And ain't leaving till it's time for me to. Today not that day." She went upstairs and closed the bedroom door behind her.

Saint sucked the top row of her teeth. Outside, a clawed creature scratched hungrily at the walls. Trying to get in and winning.

· CHAPTER 13 ·

Hell

[1]

December ended with a snowstorm, having begun in loneliness. Ours, soon to be devoured by snow, shut its doors and cleared out its fields of animals and firewood salvageable enough to burn in the by-and-by. Cows, horses, mules, goats, and chickens were locked tight in their pens and small backyard barns.

"Bring in all your beasts with a few days of food," Reverend shouted, and folks listened to this baffling moment of Bible-less clarity, though Noah with his ark winked from the bottom of Reverend's throat. Folks tucked away their cats and "sth sth sth" their dogs into the barns with the rest of the animals.

When the first flakes fell, they fell with grace. Crystal wingspans open, the frozen patterns pasted themselves against the tree trunks and ice-stiffened grass. They clung to the already iced-over pebbles in the road and whited-out windows like a mob of cobwebs. The large flakes besieged every corner and unhooked every shadow. Soon, porches and fields beamed white with snow. Fireplaces blazed in the snowed-in houses whose facades were powdered with flurries. Then came the wind . . .

[2]

. . . that made curtsy the eaves already heavy with hardened snow. A crack here, a crack there, and snapped branches conspired along the ground, a chain of Xs soon hidden by the snowstorm's onslaught. Houses leaned and their creaking seemed to be the source of the wind and quake that blew out the candles and shook down the porcelain cups and cast-iron skillets from the shelves and walls. Dogs barked at whining ceilings buckling beneath the weight of the coarsening season. Cats curled into themselves beneath people-heavy beds. In the fallow distance, the endless white light reflecting off the snow confused a rooster whose crows barely broke from the barn.

[3]

For two days it snowed, and snow blocked all the doors in Ours. It took two more days for it all to melt just enough for men to squeeze between the cracks of their barely opened doors with a shovel in hand. Every able-bodied man dug into the snow and tossed it away. They dug themselves out and then their neighbors. Dig, heave. Dig, heave. When a path around the doors and porches had been cleared, the women came out with their brooms and swept away stray mounds of snow. The men sweated hard under their coats as they took their time shoveling. When they came nearer to each other, they heard the disparate rhythms of metal crushing ice and began to match their digging to their neighbors'. When the rhythm had been established, the song began:

Call: Ain't no massa here to hold me down.

Response: Hit that shovel down. Take the hilt in your hand and split the land. Hit that shovel down.

Call: But all this snow like a massa on the ground.

Response: Hit that shovel down. Take the hilt in your hand and split the land. Hit that shovel down.

Call: Got children in the house with bellies to feed.

Response: Hit that shovel down. Take the hilt in your hand and split the land. Hit that shovel down.

Call: Got a woman in the house got some sweeter needs.

Response: Hit that shovel down. Take the hilt in your hand and split the land. Hit that shovel down.

Hit that shovel down. Take the hilt in your hand and split the land. Hit that shovel down.

And this begat the field holler without a proper field, snow having devoured the plants and stones, all vegetation wiped clean from visibility, all beasts tucked away beneath beds of ice and in the skeletons of trees. The field, then, became the weather itself, and the holler worked against such weather that overruled their land and their needs and their wants. The weather manipulated them all, giving them malaise when they wanted energy, impatience when they wanted endurance, rest when they wanted lust. It chilled them to nothing until on its own whim it returned everything it had taken as would any god. This, too, was lord and Lord, the very climate dictating their circumstance, and the shovel, the song, the field holler rejected that dictation. Once the call and response died down, a lone voice, Mr. Wife's, lifted into the quiet, and alone he sang against the unruly cold:

Mr. Wife: I love my woman even though she dead and gone.

Hear my soul climb up to my heavenly home!

And his voice took off from there in a wordless shout, a long note inflected with melisma and yodel, breaks and inversions, until the wordlessness became the world; and his sons, Luther-Philip and Justice, were the only two with nerve enough to shovel through the cascade of hope and blue notes bursting from the man who had kept his losses with him and counted only his gains, excepting Mrs. Wife, the one loss that took over for all the rest. And in that loss he lifted his voice and made a tremulous bounty of his pain—shovel down—until it resonated into faith—shovel up—and his sons hearing the letters of what couldn't be spelled pour out from their father's mouth understood just enough to make tears slip from their eyes—shovel down—and Justice dropped his shovel and fell knees to ground and howled at the winter-dull sun—shovel up—taking over the shout with his own interpretation of the weather, the thick gray overhead burdening, burdening—shovel down—and though he had never set foot on anybody's plantation, he shouted like he had, like he was at that moment in the presence of the cruelest so-called master—shovel up—dear mercy, this boy marching with his voice toward a freedom he already have—shovel down—and demanding more cause what he got, mercy, what he got not enough—shovel up—then Justice stood and, with a voice that not even he knew he had, sang out in a belting tenor:

Justice: Ain't nothing but love in my body.

Got no room for nothing else.

Ain't nothing but love in my body.

Won't stray from the love of myself.

And they got to shoveling hard then, as if beneath the snow awaited the love they all wanted. "Nothing but love, mercy. Somewhere in me is love that leaves room for nothing else," their shoveling sang. And Justice let out a shout that rang clear from the bell of his spirit and resonated across town, while at the same time, across Creek's Bridge, Joy dreamt she cut up a man with a pair of scissors and his wide-eyed scream woke her up from her nightmare.

[4]

Night after night, dream after dream, Joy killed again. The carpenter who assaulted his daughter, the apothecary who habitually battered his wife, the drunkard who denied his spouse meals and locked her in the attic against her will—each man and more visited her from the afterlife and took shelter in her dreams, only to lose their lives once more behind her closed eyes. One time, she woke outside in the cold carrying a wooden spoon after dreaming she bashed in a man's head with a hammer. Another night, she woke in the upholstered chair on the first floor of Saint's house, a skillet in her lap. Most mornings, though, she woke in her bed, no weapon anywhere near, with the screams of men from the dream still scratching in her ears.

How she felt after each dream depended on the dream itself. After killing the apothecary, her stuffy sinuses cleared. After killing the drunkard, she awoke with a fierce taste for liquor. On the off night that she killed her father again, she awoke in the middle of the night crying, and she continued to cry until sunrise. Frances had no remedy for her, and she didn't dare tell Saint. 'She might make the dreams worse,' Joy thought, and thereafter reminisced on the big sister guidance of both Eloise and Amelia, for after they nearly lost her the night the horse banished her into the air with a kick, the two women began to show more affection toward her. She was forbidden to kill, though Eloise allowed her to continue her shooting lessons, to Amelia's dismay. And Amelia took up the habit of brushing Joy's hair every morning, gifting the girl a hand mirror that Joy took with her as she escaped New Orleans with Frances.

[5]

Joy woke again in the morning, and the hand mirror that was Amelia's gift to her lay across her stomach. It had shattered during her travels from New Orleans and looking into it she saw herself split across the forehead and, because a smaller piece of the mirror had fallen out of the frame, missing her left eye and cheek. She kept that piece wrapped in a cloth in the bag she traveled with.

She noticed Frances missing from her bed. They had been sleeping off the snowstorm, eating fruit preserves and salted meat, rice and hot water corn bread fried in lard. Heavy foods to sit on the stomach for their entrapment in the snowed-in house showed no signs of relief. Spiders clung to the ceiling corners of every room, forced up there by the silence that had grown thick and unruly beneath them. Dust levitated in the chilled air. The adults kept to themselves when possible. The twins didn't speak to one another. The new visitors had occasioned new distance between them. Naima resented Selah's lack of solidarity in her anger toward the two interlopers. Selah languished in quiet, keeping her thoughts about the guests to herself.

It nearly ruined Naima's bond with Selah, for though she didn't challenge Naima, Selah believed her silence should've protected her from her sister's anger. She thought righteously of her innocence, and her young mind gripped the idea that to not speak at all, to not show behavior, meant that one was without blame. She didn't consider that a refusal to act was an act, therefore a behavior with consequences.

Selah sat in a chair to the right of the fireplace, pretending to read a book she pulled from some shelf. Naima sat to the left side of the fireplace, pretending to cough and clearing her throat of nonexistent phlegm. Selah protested that she was trying to read, and Naima said Selah read like a pig with shit in its eyes, and before Naima could clear her throat good, Selah leapt from her seat and launched the heavy book at Naima, the front cover smashing into the girl's face.

When the book hit the floor, Naima's head was still spun around from the impact. Without missing a beat, she cleared her throat, coughed, and cleared her throat again. When she finally turned her head to face Selah, she smiled and let bloody spit drip from her broken lip to stain her white dress.

Nothing hurt Naima more than Selah not loving her, and she was bound to spiraling into gratuitous desperation when even a hint of spite or distance came from Selah, enough to harm herself and possibly others if they stood in the way of her devotion. Selah, not loving anything completely except Saint, prided herself more on not causing harm, willing to smile during conversations she had completely stopped listening to. She chose ignoring what caused her dismay with such potency that it was questionable if anything at all had happened. So, when blood dripped from Naima's mouth, Selah's first thought was that she had broken a promise to herself that she doesn't make anything happen. When Naima said that her bleeding hurt, Selah knew she had broken a second promise, which she had made to Saint: that she would watch over Naima. Selah wiped her sister's mouth with a rag from the kitchen while Naima played idly in Selah's hair and sucked on her lip that she bit as hard as she could right after the book hit her face.

Saint descended the stairs and the girls shuffled to appear innocent. The woman passed on by, giving the floor all her attention and, therefore, not seeing the bloody mouth or the girls trembling just a few feet away from her. Naima and Selah watched the woman and speculated the issue in whispers.

"Maybe a witch riding her at night," Naima said.

"But Saint stronger than any witch," Selah said. "Maybe demons."

Naima looked shocked. "How a demon get in here?"

"How anything get in here? Where the man?" Selah asked, referring to Saint's companion around whom she and Naima were raised, though they weren't given a name to call him. "Don't he usually watch over her at night? Maybe because he gone from the door all manner of demon go in and out at night."

"'All manner of demon,'" Naima mocked. "Who you sound like?"

"I sound like myself. Who do you sound like, Naima?"

Naima thought for a moment and said, "The people," and left it at that. She liked Selah's point, though, and told her so, suggesting that after the snow melted, they go and find the man Saint hid. Selah agreed only if they made sure to keep Saint in ignorance. "She probably already know we thinking it."

Immaculate with anxiety, sweat collected in the dip of Selah's neck. Just thinking about Saint knowing what she was thinking from the beginning of day till its end chilled her over. She didn't want to have to consider curse or consequence in the aftermath of Saint's potential discovery of her young thoughts, thoughts she hardly kept up with as they briskly blew through her mind with the force of a flock of birds. It took only the sight of Saint to freeze Selah up inside herself with the hopes she couldn't be read from the inside out.

Where Naima, neglectful of all feelings not sourced from her sister and Saint, trounced through the day only wanting to please her twin and guardian until her own feelings compromised such devotion, Selah delved into the dusty books brought from the old house before Aba burned it down. She searched through the dusty shelves to live amongst the dusty people who dwelled inside.

Tucked between tomes of fiction were other books on medicine and philosophy. A compendium of analyses on anatomy and consciousness, spirit and the flesh, caught Selah's eye. In one book, she found a feather holding space between two pages, one page reading, "The spirit and the flesh, united not by God but by man, must be divided as intended once more in preservation of the flesh." She looked for the dictionary to define "preservation": the act of keeping from injury, destruction, or decay.

When books didn't suffice or their advancements were too complicated, she hoped to find some animal or insect whose sight she could borrow and journey wherever they journeyed, beyond Saint's constant demands and Naima's demanding attention. She braided her hair to make it easier to tell herself apart from Naima, though no one in Ours seemed to notice and continued to mistake the two.

Saint never sent the two girls on errands alone, calling on them both to take care of tasks that only required the labor of one. "Naima! Selah!" Saint belted from upstairs, followed by a tepid "Yes?" from Selah in contrast to Naima's counterbelt, "Yes, Saint?" To be alone with Don Quixote, wrapped in the myth of Medusa's temperamental and writhing hair, or in the field between Ours and her home, the soft limbo of wildflowers in which no one could find her, had to remain a fantasy because Naima's proclamation that Saint knew their thinking—said more so with pride than dread—left nothing secret to Selah, and no hiding place offered even a glitter of longevity.

"If she knows already, then why do anything at all?" Selah asked. The two sat with the question, because even if there was an answer, the two girls were incapable of finding it.

[6]

Saint's very living had become a prison. She had only herself, and on lonesome days when she sat locked in her room, she carried no special skill to mother her own entertainment. Though snow had stopped falling in the mainland of Ours, it continued falling over her house, gathering and rising past the first floor and well up to the bottom of the second-floor windows. "Look at that," she said to herself, and regretted speaking to her own transparent reflection in the window. As far as she could see, the heightened snow had frozen into a sheet of ice at the top and stretched into the woods. The world changed miraculously outside her window, and she watched with rigid admiration.

She sulked in her bedroom alone, taking her meals as far away from the rest of the household as she could. When she heard footsteps, she tensed up and hoped no one would knock on her door lest they endanger her fragile peace. She left her room only to prepare meals as a proper host but eventually stopped leaving at all, forcing the other four housemates to scrounge for food and cooperate for survival.

Astounded, Selah groaned at how poorly they performed in the kitchen: burning rice, making pudding or stone-hard tablets out of hot water corn bread, undercooking beans and overcooking grits. Each time she knocked on Saint's door to let her know she had brought her a plate, Selah felt a hot shame and began to sweat in the cold house. "She won't eat it," Selah said, and sure as water is wet, Saint left the plate of food unmolested by the door.

This happened for two days straight before Naima took a deep breath and entered Saint's room without welcome. She found the woman in bed, delirious with fever, mumbling inconsolably with a Candle of Unfixing half-melted and no longer burning. Minutes after telling the others what she discovered, Naima, too, became suddenly ill and passed out on the kitchen floor. Selah, unable to heal either Saint or Naima, fell next. Frances, with fabric wrapped around each palm, had to carry both girls to their beds. Joy refused to touch them. "Whatever they have, we are surely next in line to receive," she said. But minutes turned into hours and the two women were alone in their health, caring for people Joy considered their antagonists.

"Misuse of conjure make you sick," Frances said. "It has to pass like anything else." She opened all the windows upstairs to cool off the sickly and used the snow gathered on the sills to melt down for drinking water. Joy noted what food remained and rationed out the days they had left. She pulled out all the jars and sat them side by side on the table. She dragged out the large bag of rice and nagged at herself when she spilled cornmeal from its lopsided sack onto the floor.

Saint's winter preparation inspired and angered Joy. It appeared that the woman had stocked up on food with the idea that there would be more than just herself and the twins living there. She took this as a sign of care, which she then translated into a premeditation for her and Frances's torture. Surely, Saint wanted to make sure she risked nothing while involving herself with the two visitors, and to deter risks she had to get information. That is what Joy would've done and her own methods included everything from using a hammer and nails to inserting a makeshift speculum of two wooden spoons, the only difference being Joy, a mere teenager at the time, had tortured her victims not for information but for pleasure.

[7]

Frances kept busy. Joy kept her distance. While Frances wiped sweat from foreheads traveling between two rooms to administer care, Joy spilled beans onto the kitchen floor to count them and toss them back into their sack, only to begin the calculating enterprise again in an endless circle broken only after her shoulders and back tightened from leaning over the dry goods like a fortune-teller predicting a complicated and unlikely future.

It took two days for Selah's fever to break and five for Naima. Soon after their recovery, the two girls were back to a quiet chaos in the dominion of a small room corner, or in the kitchen where they preferred to have all their indoor play. But Joy had become a frequent dweller of the kitchen, documenting foodstuffs, counting grains of rice in the palm of her hand, anything to keep from having to deal with the two girls and their not-mama mama.

So, the girls took their play to their room, which made them close witnesses to Frances's trials with Saint's sickness. Saint remained stupefied with fever. She occasionally murmured unrelated phrases and the names of candles molded for protection: "Candle of Unfixing. Where did the feel-good moment go? Rooster's Blood. Full Moon Be Lit. My face has always had this look about it. Reveal Mine Enemies. Path of Wisdom. Forked Road Made Clear. Candle of Rigid Command. But you were supposed to take the bones into the yard. They can grow into shocking beasts." She sipped water under Frances's careful, guiding hand.

Eventually, Frances became obsessed with healing Saint. Weary, coaxing mashed vegetables into Saint's mouth, Frances wondered why she was pulled to Saint. She knew she needed to help her, but so much of Frances's life had been tied up in a limited memory, starting at the Mississippi River and snipped from the rest that came before. Daily, it seemed she lost a little remembrance here, a little there. If she could touch herself and be given the gift of back sight, she would never let herself go. But as it was, she could only read into others and the ability unsettled her as she maneuvered carefully around Saint's skin.

The twins watched from the doorway as Frances sat by Saint's bedside, dripping cold water onto the woman's feverish brow and opening and closing the window to keep the temperature even. Looking for a shawl for herself, Frances instead found a pair of gloves in a trunk beneath the window. She also found extra blankets folded at the bottom of the chest and added those to Saint's cocoon, then wrapped one around herself. What she couldn't cool off in Saint she would sweat out, keeping careful watch. She pulled the trunk from window to bed and sat on it.

Seeing Frances struggle to save Saint warmed the twins to her. Selah, the first to speak, reluctantly shared with Frances that maybe a demon snuck into Saint's room when no one was watching. Frances looked at the girl with soft eyes and thanked her for sharing. "Seems that way, don't it?" Frances asked.

Selah rocked on her heels and watched snow pile up outside. "We will be buried in this house," she said.

"We be all right," Frances said.

"We will be buried and nobody will come looking for us," Selah said. The lack of solemnity in her voice sealed her words in the air. "No one looks for what they don't miss."

"That's not true." Frances spoke without condescension. "The first part. The second thing you said might carry true."

Selah stepped into the room and stood by the bed. Naima watched from the doorway. They were truly identical and had enough hair on their heads for everybody. Thick and fluffy hair reaching out to God knows who. If Selah undid her plaits and wore her hair unrestricted like Naima, then telling them apart would rely on listening to and watching them closely. That's how Frances noticed their sudden discomfort. Though the twins kept quiet, the curl of their lips, the brilliance of their teeth, and the vicious intelligence in their eyes constellated their emotions without them knowing it.

"Naima," Frances said, "what you feeling?"

Naima frowned and looked away.

"She knows no one likes us in Ours. She knows we are in this snow forever," Selah said.

"Didn't Saint make Ours? Hell, seems to me they would love Saint," Frances said.

"She hurt people there. Sometimes on accident. Sometimes not." Selah played with her fingers as she spoke, interlacing them, then holding them firmly in either hand.

"They can't tell the difference," Naima said.

"We hurt people without meaning to, sometimes," Frances said.

"Sometimes we mean to," Selah said. She left the room, passing her sister in the doorway. Naima followed behind shortly after.

Frances kept her eyes on the empty space left by the twins' exit. "Naima," she said, finally. "You don't have to stand out there." Minutes passed, then Naima finally inched back into the doorway. "You can come in."

"I don't need permission," Naima said.

"You right. You right. I would like for you to come in. Please?"

"I'll stand where I want my body to be."

"I hear that," Frances said, and turned back to looking over Saint.

Naima waited a while before speaking again. "Where you come from anyway?"

"That's a good question. Wish I knew. Can only tell you I was found. I come from being found."

"Who found you where?"

"Some men in a small settlement off the Mississippi River. Had to been 1700-something. I was floating up the river in the wrong direction. I know it flow north to south, but I was floating south to north. They found me on the water naked as a tree branch and decided that's exactly what I was, so they tied me to a tree, knotted my wrists together in front of me, threw a blanket over my head . . ." Frances said, her voice softening as her mind got lost somewhere.

Naima had been leaning on the doorjamb and stood straight up. "You old," she said. "Maybe old as Saint."

"Been around a long time. I don't know why it's that way."

"How you get away from the men?" Naima asked.

"I didn't on my own. They fed me watery soup that gave me cramps and kept me weak. They spoke a round language. I didn't understand a breath of what they was saying. On the second day, they took the blanket from over me and started messing with my hair. I had it in plaits. Don't know who plaited it. I can't work hair that way worth a damn. Nobody ever taught me how, I believe. If they had, I don't remember."

"I can ask Selah to teach you," Naima said.

"That would be nice. Would like that very much. The men undid my hair and all this rice fell from my scalp. Just raining rice from my head. Remember looking down, thinking it was such a waste and that they could've added that rice to the damn water they was feeding me. Or planted it to make more rice. Just a waste.

"Well, they kept undoing my hair and rice kept falling all over my lap. Kept me chained up for three days, tied to a tree by the waist, hands was tied and kissing each other at the butt of my palms, and the only thing they thought to do was mess with my hair.

"After the rice stopped falling from me, they looked at me for a long while and one of the men whispered something to the other man that made him laugh. They had set up camp by the river. The rotten stink of the water made my head hurt. When I think back, I think the soup they fed me was just water from the river with whatever scraps they had left over. Every time they took the blanket from over my head, I kept my head down because I didn't like the way they looked at me, but I heard in their voice something sinister, something forthcoming. Then one of the men pulled out his prick and went all over me like a dog. The smell of his piss hugging the smell of the river was too much. His piss smelled like a dead animal. I couldn't hold myself in no longer.

"The man who watched his friend piss on me threw a bucket of water on me to rinse off my sick but there was still some sticking to me. My belly pushed out all that river water they fed me. I felt out of myself after that. Couldn't keep my eyes open. The smell of my own breath made me even sicker. They left me there to die, I believe. Then the Indians found me. They cut me loose, undid my hands, shook their heads at the rice around my feet and caught between my legs. They shook their heads, and I knew they agreed that it was wrong to do rice that way. To treat something useful in a bad way and abandon it. I saw a woman come up from behind a group of men and scoop up as much of the rice as she could, what didn't have my sick on it. The smell of the river didn't hurt so bad. I realized that all that time it was the men I was smelling, not the water. One of the Indians spoke to me, but I couldn't understand. He spoke something else next, and I couldn't understand that, either. Then he spoke English and, wouldn't you know, I didn't understand a lick of that at all. I didn't learn English until later. I just remember him asking, "Why?" Over and over again, "Why? Why?"

The man called out to someone behind me—I was still sitting with my back to the tree—and before I could turn my head right to see who all was there, I was being washed in sweet-smelling water. They fed me fruit and left a bundle for me by the tree. Some kind of berries. They left a long warm blanket, too, that I been lost. Breaks my heart. Most beautiful blanket I'd ever seen. Someone brought me a pair of pants and a shirt. The woman that gathered up the rice put it in a little leather bag and sat it on my lap with so much kindness. The last thing they left me was a pouch full of drinking water. Soon after that, they was gone."

"Who they was? Indians got names," Naima said.

"They ain't introduce themselves."

"I'm meaning who they belong to?"

Frances looked at the ceiling for the answer. "I told this story to a old runaway once who was living up in the woods round there, tucked away behind enough trees you could hide God in there with him. I used to travel around without resting and I met a lot of people that way. I know it was the walking that keep me living this long. Hell, something in me knew that if I stopped walking, I would fall dead wherever I was. Had to keep moving forward, but my mind was always behind me, trying to see what was, and I let it do what it had to do, but I decided to keep on moving forward to see what would be, to put more living behind me to look forward to. My body could be where it wanted to be, but my mind had to be in a different whenever. Been like that since those men found me on the river and tied me to the tree. I always kept moving with my mind anchored to what was.

"I told the runaway the story about the Indians saving me and he told me they was probably Choctaw. Said they was all up in Mississippi but stayed over east most times. He swore it was them. Years later, I saw a band of Choctaw moving real slow, heading west. It was fall 1831, the weather was getting cooler, and the president had told all the Indians who been on that land longer than some of the trees to get out and head west.

"Never seen anything like it. I was traveling in the other direction, following a pulling in my chest and knew that I best be on my way to going where it pulled. I'd been all over and didn't quite know where I was except that I was in Mississippi, dodging white folks and stealing food from plantations at night. The night before, an enslaved woman who cared for me and hid me well in a barn and sometimes her quarters told me we was by Pearl River. I wanted her to go east with me. I was liking her, and it would've been easy to bring one more along, but she said she had people to care for where she was, so couldn't go.

"The Choctaw was going west, I east. Hundreds. In a line. A quiet not like anything I ever heard. The weather, angry wind cutting through the trees—I couldn't hear it for the hush. The ground so stiff with their anger it shattered like glass at my feet. That's how crisp a day it was. The air carried knives. The land was corrupted. That's all it was. Hell. Corruption. Something that used to be one good way made into a bad way. A man cradled a child in his arms, and I could tell the child was awake and old enough to walk. It felt like he didn't want the young'un's feet touching the dirt. I was near Pearl River then when I saw the Choctaw leaving home.

"It got so cold to me. My hands stung on the inside. Everything I touched pricked me with needles that wasn't there. I couldn't feel my skin. Just the needles trying to get out my hands. I made a fire to warm them up. Wasn't even cold, just a chill in the air that day. But something in my body froze over.

"It was so many of them, thinking back. Hell. Not a wagon in sight, at first. And the quiet. The quiet wasn't peaceful at all. Like a death march. I sat back by the fire and watched them. The smoke made ghosts of their faces. They didn't pay me much mind at all. I knew it would be funny to them, seeing me out there keeping my hands warm over a fire when it wasn't even snow out. But they had terrible work to get done. Sunlight out but the distance before them was unknown. They had to focus.

"Then I thought I saw myself walking in a small group off to the side of a wagon, the first wagon I'd seen my whole time watching. I looked back into the fire and back up at them and squoze my eyes real tight cause every time I looked up, I kept seeing my face in the line of faces. I thought the smoke was tricking me, but more faces like mine broke through the smoke. Each face that was my own face looked at me from different shapes and sizes. Then I looked close at the wagon, covered with dingy canvas and pulled by two horses. The slaves, all eleven of them—all eleven walking, one a teamster leading the horses—belonged to whoever was inside. Had to be, cause whenever the wagon stopped, the slaves stopped, even if people ahead and behind kept going. One Choctaw boy walked by the wagon and kicked the wheel hard a few times before walking on. An older woman walked arm in arm with a younger woman and motioned that she wanted to stop. She stared a moment at the wagon and that's when I noticed the hole in the covering, a flap of canvas open like a piece of skin. The older woman stared straight into that hole, then motioned to the younger woman that she wanted to move on.

"A few days later, I got near Alabama and saw the charred remains of what looked like a camp. I said to myself, 'They burned down they own homes in protest,' but it was the white folks who did it. They rushed in and burned the whole thing down and stole what they thought was valuable. I looked around to see if I could find any supplies but wasn't nothing left except the remains of a building where one of the walls kept standing. Seemed like it chose to stay that way. Like it was still protecting something. Like it was a gateway to a knowing I knew I was walking into but wasn't ready for. Hell, I still smell the smoke climbing up from under my feet. I'm telling you. I can feel it now. The earth is on fire. My hands lose their cold. That was sorrow trying to creep into me, the cold. This heat, though—this here another thing. I go over to the wall and bones everywhere meet my feet. I feel that maybe I've come upon somebody's evil. But the bones have something mournful about them. A skull missing the bottom of its mouth stares up at me. And I hear a scream rise up from it, like heat, voices from the dead whose bones they belong to. I can't make out what they saying, but it hurt. My head. My body burning up by the words. The heartbroken. The rage of the Ancestors. Scattered across the burnt-up remains of they home. Hell. Not many bones left. I figure the folks I saw passing by took as many as they could before the white folks came and ran them out. How many families you think they was carrying on they backs? Either that or the white folks stomped the bones to dust when they saw them there. Nothing evil about the bones except what happened to them. It ain't like when animals go in and mess over a place cause they hungry or afraid. Instinct to blame for that. But I'm talking about human choice and the choice is to tear up a world. To smash folks' ancestors up like that. What it mean for somebody first thought to be to destroy somebody else? My chest on fire. The bones screaming in my head. The bones scream out and my skin flares up, screaming with them: 'Ruin. Desecration. Ruin. Desecration. Do you hear me? The bones and the earth are desecrated!' Hell. Hell."

Frances stopped speaking. She panted and clenched the blankets where they covered Saint's legs. When she finally looked up, she saw that Naima had crept into the room and sat on the opposite side of the bed, one hand on her tiny lap, the other on Frances's gloved hand.

"Deep, deep breaths," Naima said. She squeezed the top of Frances's gloved fingers. "Just think about my hand on yours." And Frances was grounded there, in the enclosure of Naima's hand over her own, not knowing that Naima had learned what to say from Saint. "You stay when you belong."

[8]

Saint's fever broke the following morning. She awoke to Frances asleep at the foot of her bed and wrapped in a blanket while sitting on the trunk. She had fallen asleep leant over Saint's legs. On the left side, tucked under the covers with an arm wrapped around Saint, slept Naima. The girl's tart breath warmed Saint's neck while Frances's breath warmed her feet.

The windows let go their frost. The red oaks, sugar maples, black tupelos, and sweetgums clanked their snow-struck branches against each other. Though the snow had stopped falling, the wind carried on, wild, howling, and harassing the trees. 'When's the last time I'd been touched,' Saint thought. The miraculous configuration of the three of them on her bed she could hardly believe. Exhausted, she rested there awhile, wondering what the rest of the day had in store, considering what it had already dropped into her lap at the spark of day. Naima nestled her head into Saint's armpit. 'That won't do,' Saint thought, and poked the girl in her side.

"What you doing in here?" she asked, then added, "This my room." Naima sulked and held on tighter. Saint had failed. The twins, at least this one, didn't understand what it meant to be a tool, and Saint had allowed it to be unclear that she didn't love them and that they shouldn't love her. And now everything fell into murky waters as she found herself stroking the girl's hair, Naima damn near purring as she did it. Surely, there could be no injury in this little thing, she wanted to believe, had believed it before. She knew better. 'Didn't it begin with this last time,' she thought. 'The last time I was held this tight was when—'

And like that, she shifted her legs from under Frances, stirring her awake. She told Naima to get up and wake her sister. It was time for breakfast. It was time to move on.

· CHAPTER 14 ·

Evergreen/Thaw

[1]

Days after Saint's fever broke, drenched in sweat and the stink from a dead man's breath, Joy woke up from a killing dream. She needed Frances, was unsurprised by this need, yet felt ashamed. Unable to bear the weight of her nightmares alone, she called out to Frances. Hearing no response, she crept over to her bed to shake her awake but found the bed empty.

Joy pulled back Frances's bedcovers and got in. The air above the bed took on the smell of the bed, which was Frances's smell lighting up that side of the room with an herbal flourish. When Joy woke the next morning, Frances was asleep in Joy's bed. Joy didn't like this switching of where they slept; though, night after night, killing dream after killing dream, she woke startled and smelling like the afterlife. Each night, she staggered to Frances's bed, discovered it empty, then got in it, falling asleep soon after. 'I'm making a habit of this,' she thought, and decided on the fifth night to stay in her own bed. But the killing dreams poured into her until she returned to where Frances had stopped sleeping, which just so happened to be where the dead wouldn't follow.

Those nights, Frances had a need of her own and she knocked on Saint's door to fulfill it. The first instance, Saint resisted.

"You want what with me?" Saint asked, blocking the door with her body.

"Your feet. I want to sleep at your feet. Like I did when you was sick."

'All leant over like that?' Saint thought, then said, "Looks like you like a painful sleep."

"It wasn't so bad. Best sleep I had in a long time."

"Are you a dog that you'd sleep at your master's feet?" Saint raised her eyebrows as though a point had been made. When Frances said no but that she could be, Saint's eyes flew open. "Absolutely not," she said. "Return to your room."

"I can't sleep in there."

"Then the chairs downstairs will suit you, or the floor since you've become a dog," Saint said, and shut her door.

Frances did lay herself on the floor downstairs after stoking the dying embers in the fireplace for heat. She returned upstairs to her room a few sleepless hours later to find Joy had switched beds. Frances took Joy's bed and blinked at the shadow-painted wall throughout the night. She turned her back to Joy and covered herself with the blanket, hoping that in the morning Joy would think she was asleep and leave her alone.

Insomnia ate Frances up, each night a replica of the voided-out rest from the night before. Desperate, Frances tried Saint again with the unshakable belief that her poor physical appearance and uncommon clumsiness throughout the day had convinced Saint that she needed to sleep by her feet.

"Just for tonight," Frances pleaded in a whisper in the hall. The wait at Saint's door lasted for a long time.

Saint said, "I will destroy you if you do anything unsightly." Frances smiled and Saint let her in. "Get something to cover yourself with from the trunk. Bathe and chew on a mint leaf first. Don't come to my bed with any smell upon you," Saint said, and Frances obeyed.

When Saint blew out the three candles at her bedside and extinguished the lamp, Frances sat on the trunk, then laid her head right beneath Saint's blanketed feet, forehead to foot bottom, herself cozy beneath two heavy quilts. Soon after, she fell asleep.

Saint felt the warmth of Frances's head engulf her feet. Through the blanket, heat rushed up from her soles, shot up through her shins, and pooled thick at her knees. Frances put her left arm over Saint's shins, using her right arm as a pillow. Her back arch seemed to lead somewhere intimate, somewhere known, as it curved up a tiny bit from Saint's toes then down into the shadow of the night against the floor. The sea of darkness congealed beneath the trunk, dimly lit by moonlight announcing itself through the window.

It appeared to Saint that they were floating on stranded flotsam after a shipwreck. 'Or maybe we were thrown overboard,' Saint wondered, as the bed began to wobble beneath her. She smelled salt water and heard coming through the ceiling the bright songs of seabirds in despair. A wave tilted the bed to the left and it creaked with a ship's voice. Saint clung to her sheets. Were they now the remnants of a sail? The mattress stuffed with cotton, wool, and horsehair now soaked through and sinking like a doom-struck mind. The wooden bedframe became a raft, every side jagged with splinters. Frances remained asleep, her torso resting on the bed raft while the trunk beneath her bobbed above the water's surface until it disappeared completely beneath the water, leaving Frances floating on her back.

A sudden sense of regret overpowered Saint. How did she and Frances get here? Had she not been clinging to the sheet-sail with all her strength, she would have slid into the sea's inky pool. It was the sea, right? The ceiling opened up and, yes, she could see bird silhouettes interrupt the stars and ashen moon. The birds spiraled overhead, screaming, agitated. A wave took its frothy hand and upended the bed-raft, tossing Saint into the water. Its cold undid her quiet. Another wave pushed her and the sorrowful wood with its deranged sheet-sail out, out into the wide course of the sea. She looked for Frances in the night's hazy glow and found that the water had carried her many feet away. It was Frances's soft snoring that returned Saint to the bedroom. The bed again a bed. The trunk, a trunk. The floor still as a gravestone beneath them.

[2]

From then on, Saint allowed Frances to sleep at her feet so long as she left before sunrise. Saint neglected to return her trunk to the window, keeping it at her bedside as a perpetual sign of welcome. Immediately, as though sensing that at any moment Saint would renege on her invitation, Frances promised, without argument, that she would leave when told. She kept that promise for a week until one night, when the east-facing window filled with the blue just-born light of morning, Saint heard Frances creeping to the door and called out to her. "My feet cold," Saint said.

A few moons after, Frances found herself not in her usual place at the edge of the bed, with her forehead resting beside the two hidden mounds of Saint's feet beneath the covers. Instead of her forehead resting, it was her nose sniffing. Next, her lips grazing. A few nights later, Frances woke to find that her chest touched Saint's feet while her head lay in the center at the foot of the bed. Before Saint woke, Frances carefully returned to her original position and remained there for another week until, early February, Frances had scooched her entire body onto the foot of the bed. Scandalized, she woke to Saint's near expressionless face frozen in observation. The bed creaked beneath them, shifting their weight as they considered each other. Without meaning to, Frances held her breath.

"Afraid of the floor?" Saint said, lowering her head as though she discovered pity for the first time in her life. "Is that how you will remain?"

"If I go any further, my head'll be off the other side," Frances said.

"I sleep at the edge and haven't fallen off yet. You'll live."

A month later, at Saint's request, Frances lay parallel to the conjurer, sleeping above the covers that kept Saint warm beneath them. Though on the same bed, their two bodies remained two separate grammars, two languages refusing to approach one another. They remained stiff in that unspoken awkwardness, not touching, not even grazing each other by the tips of their elbows or an occasional bump of the toes.

Eventually, the two did find themselves talking long into the night about mundane occurrences that held little consequence: *Joy and the twins getting along better. Naima still sour on her, though. That's cause she think Joy's beautiful and don't know what to do with herself. Is that it? I always wondered what that was about. And Selah just as quiet as ever. She think nobody know what she thinking, but we know. She just as sick of us as Naima is. Joy ever going to settle in? Seem like she spend all her time by the fireplace. Naima ever going to treat Joy like a person? I believe she will. Give her time.* They reminisced about what wasn't yet distant enough to matter while stars poked holes in the sky's dark argument, until the sun, engorged with the force of spring's slow approach, annihilated all difference.

WELL INTO FEBRUARY, Joy, Naima, and Selah had finally gotten used to knowing where Frances slept at night. It was never a secret, just an unawareness, some disruption in the days' pattern signaling that a new pattern was soon to take its place. Bedtime, Frances passed the room she shared with Joy; entered the twins' room to hug them good night, horrifying Naima and making Selah giggle; and went straight into Saint's like she had been sleeping there since the day she arrived.

Selah and Naima, in their own mischievous way, enjoyed the change. Joy, however, resolved her bitter feelings by nagging at Frances over the tiniest offenses, refusing to reveal how Frances's distancing herself from her, while simultaneously bringing herself closer to Saint, had introduced to Joy a spectacular loneliness. She turned twenty-four years old, and no one said a word. 'Not even you, Frances,' Joy thought while complaining to Frances about her scratching her sinuses. "You sound like a rabid wolf chewing itself on the inside," she said with her mouth, but with her eyes, long having taken on the wet shine of someone recklessly in need of attention, she asked, 'How could you miss my only birthday?' She left the table abruptly without offering to help clean.

From then on, she bathed infrequently, locking herself in her room to ripen in peace and hunger, demoting her eating privileges to sneaking very small meals in during absurd nightly hours while everyone slept.

Joy had become accustomed to Frances being the only one in her life after they left New Orleans, the only one who would ever care about her, despite her ways. After the two women who mothered her for many years were killed, she allowed herself one measly day to mourn, to scream and punch the ground, to curse, to feel guilt, and Frances watched her immense grief unfold in the blank embrace of the woods. Now that her last friend found comfort in Saint's bed, who would kiss her forehead the number of times that equaled her age? Twenty-four kisses gone to dust and she gone to dust right along with them.

One night, lying side by side, one above the covers and the other beneath them, Saint brought Joy's behavior to Frances's attention, and they agreed that she needed to get out of the house. Fast. They all did.

"Frances." Saint spoke facing the ceiling.

"I'm here. I'm awake."

The sound of Saint preparing to speak crackled in the dark. The wet of her lips parting, then closing, her tongue washing over words not yet ready to exit her mouth, her slow inhales, and heavy exhales. She hummed one nearly inaudible note.

"There's a forest between us," Saint said.

"A forest?" Frances said. She laughed at the description—sudden, verdant, and full of restless shadows—but felt wholly intrigued by the notion. A forest carried familiarity. She knew trees, the feel of grass sharp against her ankles. She could name a bird or two and had spent much time hiding in the wilderness to keep safe from other humans who frightened her more than if she had happened upon a pack of wolves. A forest wasn't all bad. But this forest between them had gnarly roots, its mysteries not a safekeeping for the hider but an absolute weapon against any who imposed. This element—not the earth, or the sky, or fire—was an insatiable father and tyrannical mother.

"Sprout up generations ago without us knowing," Saint continued. "It's here, now, fully grown, thick and angry. We've been here before. Maybe, in another life, you were my sister."

"No. Your protector."

"What's the difference?"

"There's a sea between us," Frances said. "Not a forest. A sea. And it's not violent at all. It's sad. It's got a crying sadness."

A sea. Saint could smell the salt water again, hear the birds screeching their parables overhead. What lesson was she to learn from their late-night wooing of the moon, their irresolvable terror? No. Not a sad sea. There was no such thing. The sea was the source of sadness, not a reflection of it.

"How'd you know to wait for us when we came into town?" Frances asked.

"I felt you enter the moment you stepped foot inside. Only one person ever did that, and he didn't mean to. I get the feeling you did it on purpose."

"Joy didn't see the way, but I saw it."

"How's that?" Saint said. She yawned. The house insisted on groaning as a gust rushed around it, trying to get in. A draft leapt across the room. "You under your covers?"

"Am," Frances said. "I see things as they are. Always been that way with me."

"How long is always?"

"However long my memory is."

"Can't say I have much of a memory. I don't recollect much these days."

"I got enough memory for the both of us." Frances laughed.

"What else can you see, then, with that memory?"

"The children in the water."

"What?"

"Children in the water," Frances said. Saint became aggressively still. She had all that time been lying on her back. When the house braced itself against the weather outside, the ceiling sang as though the cold air entering the room had entered a lung and shocked it into troublesome life. Now her own memory of the children in the water entered her and she fell prey to the anvil of its presence.

Star-quiet. Window glass shook beneath coats of frost. "I see them like they happening now," Frances continued. "I close my eyes sometimes and they there swimming around behind my eyelids. Sometimes they a memory and sometimes they right there. When we saw them together, they felt like both memory and the present. There're grown folks, too, but the children come more easily."

Saint turned toward Frances, whose face took on the shallow glow of night. "Who were those children with the fish tails?" she asked. It had been months since the vision had occurred.

"Them your people. Our people. From the ships."

"We had legs on those ships, Frances. And barely that, for some of us."

"And we grew tails in the water."

"And we grew tails," Saint said, sure that the dead in those waters would never want to live again with the memory of those ships still in them. "In the water." Her voice fell flat as a windowpane.

The room made an aching sound. Frances sat up on her elbow, resting her head in her hand. "I'm sitting here telling you that you got people waiting for you, loving on you in the water that would've brought them here, and you look at me like I tried to change your name without asking."

"You can't see me in the dark."

"I see things as they are and I can see by the sound of your voice that you looking at me like I stole your name."

Saint stretched beneath the covers and the sound of her legs against the bed was the sea coming forth again. "I've seen stranger happenings in my own reflection." She readjusted her hips and a wave of cold crept into a gap in the covers and crashed against her waist. "Make no mistake about who I am."

"I don't know a thing about you."

"Not a thing. Be sure of that, always. But keep listening. I have words for you yet."

"I'm listening. What are they?"

Saint rolled from her side onto her back. It felt better this way. When she spoke, it might as well had been to someone floating overhead. "Why would anyone who jumped or was thrown overboard make the grave of that water their home?" she asked.

What Saint believed to be a wound, Frances believed to be a door, and Saint didn't understand how Frances could step through all that blood and come out thinking she was clean.

"Why would anyone who could jump stay on board, knowing they was headed to a death they didn't ask for?" Frances asked.

"Are we dead?" Saint asked. She nearly fell asleep waiting for Frances to answer. A dream lifted its shell and crawled toward her. She felt its approach and wondered what, this time, needed her as witness. Before she fell fully into the dream's mouth, she heard a voice.

"We here," Frances said.

"Then let that be enough," Saint said, then the two—separated by layers of covers, a body of water expanding between them, and a forest of silver-leaf trees clustered wider than the world—closed their eyes.

[3]

The weather had aspired to kill everyone in town. Selah felt it in the air, sniffed it seeping through the cracks of her bedroom window. Though it had not snowed much since January, the aftermath of the snow had fangs for the Ouhmey. Houses had been damaged, animals frozen to death, fences made to bow to the ground. The Delacroix wagon had a broken wheel that needed fixing quick. The pain of those in need in Ours resonated throughout her body.

Selah had to go to where the hurt leaked to her. She bundled up warm in her favorite dress that she kept folded and hidden under a loose floorboard downstairs so Naima wouldn't steal it. She wrapped herself in every one of Saint's fabrics she could force herself to use, for they were beautiful. Soiling the beautiful didn't interest Selah. As a final preparation, she gathered as many herbs as she could from the kitchen and folded them into her borrowed fabric.

In the pit of night, Selah snuck out the house, following the compass of her own throbbing head and burning body straight into a town she couldn't care less about. She didn't want to be there in Ours where she and her sister were hated, but the call of the people gave her such an incessant hurt through the window that she couldn't resist.

When she arrived in Ours, everyone's frantic pace surprised her this late at night. She learned that for days it had been this way, and by sunset little had gotten better. People shuffled around house to house carrying boiled water, torn linen, quick meals of corn and peas and grits, extra blankets, whiskey, and an assortment of other items people needed. Lanterns hovered firefly-slow over the injured, the air dense with emergency.

Ours's frigid landscape promised early graves. Every other season had spoiled them: summer sun's white tongue elongated across verdant scenery, coaxing corn from their perfect rows; autumn's gold and burgundy leaves mimicking sunsets pinned to boughs waiting to undress; spring's rain stippling windows with wet beads, the town covered in the jewelry of storms.

But winters brought impenetrable ice, limb-threatening frostbite, and an enviable determination to live through it all. This, too, was part of freedom: fending for oneself, no so-called master to blame when rations depleted. In these moments, they remembered the best of themselves, though this winter had snapped so many bones and stifled every lung caught in the frozen air. Freedom was hard, this they knew and showed themselves grace. However, this time, they needed help, and when Selah stumbled toward them, they didn't know whether to laugh or cry.

Though the town had their feelings about the twins, everyone knew that Saint had a healer girl and a sickness girl and hoped the healing one, hair braided neatly in a corona on her head, was the one who had come to them in the most desperate night of their lives. One house contained a little girl with an unbreakable fever. Selah dug around in her fold for the right ingredients in the right amount. She asked for boiling water, told them to let the herbs steep and to remove them before drinking. "Don't let her drink the leaves," she said before running off to the next house, leaving in her wake shocked yet grateful whispers about what she had done.

A man just wanted something for the pain. He had fallen off an icy slope looking for firewood not far from town, breaking his leg. Three men who traveled with him carried him back. All evening he suffered and fell in and out of consciousness. He, too, had a fever, but he just wanted to die without all the hurt in the world beating on his leg. A pyramid had replaced his shin, with a bone steeple borne from miscalculation—did he jump too soon or too late on the ice-choked ground? Selah had never seen bone press against skin that way, wanting to escape the flesh it was meant to keep in shape. The foot and shin had rolled over inhumanly while the knee stayed in place. A break and a dislocation. Selah burped and tasted bile in her mouth as she rushed from the house to stand by the doorway.

Closing her eyes was her only protection. But instead of finding peace, her imagination crushed her as it replayed the leg's breakage as though she had been there to witness it, the pop and resound of bone leaving bone clucking behind her eyelids. Then providence came without warning. Reassurance. Ability. Stoic confidence. A grown woman taking the reins in a child's mind and saying, impatiently, "It's not something for you. It's for me." Selah opened her eyes. She breathed cold air through her mouth, and her lungs burned.

When she returned to the man, she hardly had control over herself. She told everyone to move out of the way, firmly grabbed the leg, pulled down, slid it over, and locked it back in. "Sweet mercy," she heard from the crowd, but the leg was set. She did the same with the knee, sliding, jiggling, measuring, acting. Selah asked for whiskey and a woman poured her a glass. She asked for a knife, and someone handed her one. She drained the loose blood from the leg, poured some of the whiskey over the cut, and drank the rest. She made the same tea for this man that she had made for the feverish girl. "Who know how to make a strap to keep his leg still?" she asked. Someone offered to do it. Selah nodded and left.

All night, she mixed herbs, bandaged wounds, reset what was broken two more times, made poultices, and held hands until she ran out of supplies and energy. She did all of this without complaint and with the feeling that she was halfway out her body. By that time, Ours's gratitude set in and the piercing agony that broke her sleep disappeared. Satisfied, she trekked back, snuck inside, made herself some tea, and went to sleep in the chair by the fireplace.

For now, this would do. Raising her fingers to unhook the fabrics that Saint once let own the floor, Selah knew something about her had changed. There existed no inkling of love in her for those who lived in Ours, not even a speck-of-pepper worth. But she couldn't resist the pull to help them.

She returned to Ours twice more, had even started carrying a basket just so she could bring more herbs and supplies with her. When she reset a boy's arm, she used the situation as a lesson. "Put your hand here," she told a group of onlookers, then called one over to her so that they could do it themselves. "This is how you put him back together."

By the end of the third night, Selah could hardly move her legs, and her arms burned with exhaustion. Her face twitched. Her eyes darted around in their sockets. She felt a loss of control over her body and her mind fogged over with heavy decisions she needed to make while having zero wisdom with which to make them. When she spoke, the words leaving her mouth felt hard to say, the rhythm not hers, the direct tone an inaccuracy of her own coyness. Even her voice left her mouth in a cadence foreign to her. She moaned while leaning on a woman's kitchen table after helping a niece with a persistent phlegmy cough. With her herbs depleted, and her own small body shaking, Selah returned home. And on the third night, when she opened the front door of her home with the hopes of sleeping away her fogginess, she found Naima waiting for her by an already blazing fireplace.

"You not only yours," Naima said.

Selah closed the door behind her and sat the basket down. Naima's striking gaze opened her, a knife to a fish.

"This your third time leaving," Naima said.

"You are being sneaky again," Selah said.

"Next time you leave without me, don't sneak back."

"You don't tell me what to do."

"And you don't do like you only yours. You don't belong to just you."

"I don't belong to anybody. Not Saint and not you."

"I was careful this time," Naima said, looking down.

Selah looked down, too, and saw the hammer in Naima's hand. Its metal prongs teethed the air. "You'd hit me?" Selah asked. The sudden rage of her sister frightened her. She didn't know where it came from, but she knew it had to have always been there.

Naima looked into the fire. The light bronzed her face into an artifact. "I don't know what I would do. There's no telling who," she said. Selah went to her sister, who looked up fiercely. A warning sat on Naima's brow. Selah stopped. The orange and yellow light lit up Naima's left hand. Three swollen fingers. One for each day Selah had snuck away. Naima planted seeds in them, Selah believed. 'Fruit will come out. Would there be petals,' she wondered, 'from my sister's pain? Would she cut off her whole hand, too? Would she do that to herself just cause I left a few times?' The sound of burning wood popped, and Selah knew Naima's fingers sounded that way beneath the hammer.

The sisters beheld one another. A kind of peace overcame the room.

Abruptly, stuck time came unstuck; Naima went upstairs without saying another word while Selah took her usual seat in the upholstered chair and watched wood crumble to ash in the fire. This was the final day of February. Both she and Naima would turn nine years old at the end of March.

[4]

The second day of March, Saint's household went to Ours to break the spell of malaise winter had cast on them. She introduced Joy and Frances to everyone as though introducing old friends from one life to old friends from another. It had come to be that way between Frances and Saint, at least, the two giggling and whispering to each other as they walked close.

While they joked, Joy trembled. She gave a thin smile, said, "A pleasure to meet you," speaking softly. Nothing with a hint of possible friendship came from her greeting. She had figured out long ago how to remove kindness from her honey-brown eyes without adding menace. A few of the folks already knew of her, having months ago speculated on her relationship with silent Aba ever since she stood in his doorway. They flashed a half-hearted smile and kept going.

Frances, charming and ready to laugh, had everybody thawing in her hands. Her jokes unbuttoned their coats, tickled their ribs, and brought tears to their eyes that they thanked her for.

"Man, you gone make me pee," someone said. "That woman with the legs nearly had me early to my grave," someone else said. Word got around that there were two funny Negroes making their rounds, a man and a woman, both with long legs and a childlike grin that forgave them for sins yet committed. "She" smelled like corn bread or "he" smelled like they all had more work to do cause he done outworked them all. Frances winked at Saint and nudged her tenderly with her elbow, and folks said it was like a bullying big brother or a younger sister trying to loosen up her spinster kin. One woman whispered to her closest girlfriend, "I wonder . . ." while biting her bottom lip. A man hammered a little louder just to get Frances to face him, her lips making him hard as a goat. The children said mister and miss and Frances said, "Huh?" to both, smiling a strong, toothy gate.

Not quite spring but warmth laced the air. Melting snow revealed how many animals had died during the storm, their corpses the next step to pestilence. Saint prepared herself to give orders and keep folks calm if needed. But she wasn't needed. With a sense of prior preparation, everyone got to work in carrying off and burying every chicken, stray baby goat, old mule, cat, and dog they found.

"Damn it! Not Kindred," a voice said behind Saint, Kindred being the oldest dog in town, belonging to no one and therefore everyone. But unowned with specificity, he held no space in anyone's mind to be cared for; therefore, he remained without a home throughout the duration of the terrible weather. Kindred's death just so happened to fit into the rhythm of the town, a rhythm that Saint found herself outside of as she watched this community grow more unfamiliar to her. Startling as a revolting adolescent. If she hadn't known better, she would've sworn they all hummed and marched in unison as they cleared the roads and yards of animal corpses.

Ever since Mr. Wife lost Mrs. Wife to what the town thought was a fever, no one thought of Saint as much of a healer anymore. Selah had recently taken up that mantle, so they assumed Saint knew her own limitations and sent the one daughter who could do what she couldn't, which was fine but peculiar to send a child into the night woods alone. If they wanted to live, they had to do so on their own, as Saint's chance appearances were unreliable because too seldom. Some assumed she moved so far out to get away from Aba's house-burning ways, while others believed Saint wanted solitude more than to lead. Either way, with a handle on things thanks to Selah, their thin grudge remained gossamer and eventually dissipated altogether.

A man with a splinted leg called out to Selah from a wheel barrel pushed by a teenage boy. He thanked her but looked at Naima when he did it. The boy wheeled him away before anyone had the chance to correct him. This happened again when the once-feverish little girl from three nights ago stopped the group and thanked Naima as though she were Selah. Then another, this time looking at Selah when he thanked her, then two more who couldn't decide who was whom, so they looked between Selah and Naima, then directly at Saint. "Your daughter really helped us these past few nights. Thank you for sending her down," one man said, then took off to catch his hat that a sudden wind snatched from his head.

Saint swallowed hard, cocked her head to the side and eyed Selah, who sighed, exhausted by the direct and misguided attention.

"You been here helping people?" Saint asked.

"Yes," Selah said.

"Who went with you? Nai—"

Before Saint could get the name out right, Selah said, "I came alone. Something in me said I had to, so I listened. I heard them crying through the window."

"From way back there?" Frances said, pointing in the direction of the house.

Selah told everyone what she had been up to the previous three nights. The insufferable cold. The blood. Broken bones building tents in the body. Naima listened on, expressionless though inside she felt the sensation of water boiling over. After Selah finished her story, Frances hugged Joy around the shoulder. For the first time in Naima's memory, Saint smiled with all her teeth. Her smile shined and the light entered Naima's eyes, striking her into an impenetrable dark.

Naima heard their voices, though a black stain layered over her seeing, an every-color that erased the people speaking in front of her, around her, people who misnamed her without apology, people who ignored her because of her sister's selfish heroics. She looked ahead because she had no need to face whoever spoke. They weren't speaking to or of her anyway. What it matter? Nothing called her from the sky, so she didn't look up. The ground, whelmed with melting ice, the water from which would have otherwise shown her reflection, showed to her instead a bottom-of-well black.

"What you looking at, Naima?" Frances asked. When the girl said that she was looking at black, Frances hollered, "Best thing I heard all my damn life!" Had she listened with her whole self, Frances might have caught the vacant tint to Naima's voice, the awkward rhythm of her speech, and her uncharacteristic lack of venom. Too busy with looking through the unfamiliar fullness of bottom-of-a-well black, Naima lost herself, swept away in the dense distraction of her newfound darkness. Frances, overindulging in cheer, found humor in every movement and sound even as Naima stumbled forward, arms stretched out in front of her. Naima breathed in and out of her mouth with the fervor of a hapless dog. It only became clear that she needed help when she stepped closer and closer to Joy.

Everyone rushed back home to figure out the ailment, to no avail. Selah knew of no remedy for bottom-of-a-well black and no one else had ever heard of such a thing happening out the blue. Frances asked Naima what she saw just before she only saw black, and she said Saint's smile. Instinctively, Joy lowered her head to avoid the gleam of Saint's teeth while Selah covered her own eyes to retain full color in her vision. Saint closed her mouth, covering her incisors with her tongue.

To get rid of bottom-of-well black, Selah thought maybe they should cover Naima's eyes in white. She dipped a long strip of old bed linen into a doughy white flour and water mix, then laid the strip over Naima's eyes as she lay in bed. When Selah checked on her an hour later, nothing had changed, and Naima refused to speak to her. Selah left her alone for the rest of the day.

Naima's condition improved only after Saint took to sitting at the girl's bedside to feed her. Saint thought it was the soup she made. Frances thought it was the attention she paid. Saint protested that Naima didn't want anyone's attention, but Frances reminded her of the morning she found Naima snuggled up beside her. "When you were sick, she slept by your side. That's what a daughter does." Saint licked the bottom row of her teeth, then she licked the top.

It took over a week for Naima's sight to return, but it returned purple. Eventually, Naima got used to seeing the world this way, and by her and her sister's ninth birthday, a warm March 22, she dissolved her anger toward Selah into acquiescence that purple seeing wasn't much different than her purple fingers.

Back in February, after Naima had hammered her fingers in protest against Selah visiting the Ouhmey, Saint didn't ask what had happened to her, rather why she did it. Naima shrugged and Saint, for the first and final time, slapped Naima clean across the face. Naima decided to keep her tears to herself.

That was the second time someone she loved had struck her in the face. The first time, Selah had thrown a book so hard at her head Naima thought she had entered its pages. The third time, the town did it with their misnaming her. Repeatedly, they called her Selah. And no one, neither Selah nor Saint, protected her name by correcting anyone who had gotten it wrong. No one protected her measly three syllables.

So, of course, her eyesight went black after Saint smiled an incredible smile at Selah. Naima hardly believed it even happened. Turning nine years old recalibrated her feelings of having been betrayed. Though she shared this day with Selah, it was important to her that she make it her own by somehow impressing Saint. Before she could come up with an idea, someone knocked on her front door.

[5]

A man had come to see "Selah the Healer," as he called her. His wife had just given birth to a healthy baby. Moments after giving birth she passed out. Nothing the midwives or her husband did to revive her worked. She had not opened her eyes since looking at the baby and everyone began to worry as her breathing grew more faint. Soon, she barely breathed at all.

When he demanded the midwives help him find a wagon, they looked at each other for a while until one spoke up, "There's no need for that."

"A wagon," he repeated. "A wagon. Get me a wagon and horse for my wife."

Another midwife said as calmly as possible that there wasn't a reason for that because she had passed on. "You got to let the dead be dead, Jacob. You got your daughter here. She need you here in the now. She'll be needing you all her life," the second midwife said, but Jacob wouldn't listen.

He said for one of them to take the baby. Watch over her. "You won't help me save my wife, then help by watching my daughter." He handed the newborn off without seeing to whom and began wrapping his wife's body in every sheet he could find. He lifted her from the bed, cradling her in his arms, and walked out his front door. He made it almost a quarter of a mile to Saint's before a wagon caught up with him. "Let's get you to Saint's," Mr. Wife said.

MR. WIFE STOOD behind Jacob, avoiding the faces of those who lived in the house. He remembered what Saint told the town years ago about their love and their fear confronting them if they ever stepped foot inside her home, so he waited by the doorway for the vision to arrive and overpower him. Until then, he watched Jacob beg Selah to help his wife.

"She dead," Naima said.

"She not dead. She still breathing. Why can't you see? You got eyes just like me."

"Watch your mind, Mr. Jacob," Saint said. Jacob quieted down as Saint approached the woman he carried in his arms. She touched the woman's forehead, then her throat, then her heart. No sign of life. Saint returned to her place beside Selah. "He came here to see you. It's not for me to decide what you do with your gift," Saint said to Selah.

The pain returned to Selah's head. It traveled like a stream of hot iron throughout her body. When it touched Selah's knees, she grabbed hold of herself. "Put her on the floor," she said. She had lost control of her mouth again; her thoughts were muddled with another's. "I'll see to her when you lay her down."

Joy grabbed Frances's hand as they watched Selah lean over the woman's body and rub her hands back and forth, sliding her palms from the woman's clavicle down to her navel. "What's her name?" Selah asked.

"Georgia," Jacob said.

"Georgia. Georgia, if you hear me, it's Selah. I can feel a pain in my body that's telling me it's not time for you to go yet. You are still needed here. Bring yourself back. Follow my voice, Georgia. I know you can hear me. I feel it. I feel you hearing me, Georgia. Come back now. Come home." When Selah placed her hands on Georgia's heart, it started to beat. Soon after, Georgia took a short quick breath. Saint opened her mouth, awestruck. Joy clenched Frances's hand till it hurt. Frances held on. Naima stared, an inscrutable emotion cutting into her face. Mr. Wife felt a strong wind fill him up, belly first, then his chest. He watched as though watching himself be born, as though watching his own wife—

Georgia's chest rose and fell as her lungs filled with air, then emptied. Selah kept her hands over the woman's heart. She shook her head no. Sweat poured from her. She rocked on her knees as she tried to steady herself on Georgia's chest. The room turned into wet paint. It spun around Selah. When she looked up, she saw Jacob's face and felt tremendous pain in her body. His hope slashed into her. All this time it was hope that had hurt. Not a sense of duty. Not the need of others to be healed. It was their hope, their faith, dragging a hot spoke down her skin. The longer the woman breathed, the more pain Selah felt. And as if sensing her pain, Georgia stopped breathing. Her heart stopped beating. Georgia's head rolled to the side, exposing her neck as if asking to be kissed there. Selah, exhausted by agony, fainted to the floor.

Jacob dropped to his knees, lost in the disarray of his broken faith.

Joy released Frances's hand.

Saint kneeled and rested Selah's head in her lap, saying, "I see you," over and over again.

Naima ran upstairs and slammed the bedroom door behind her.

And Mr. Wife smiled, realizing a vision of his fears and what he loved wasn't coming for him like it had for Justice, whatever the boy had seen causing him to storm from Saint's home in a rage. What he loved—Mrs. Wife. What he feared—reliving her death. They both played out before him in the shape of another's living then dead-again body. He put on his hat. It was time to go.

[6]

The following morning, Selah woke in tremendous pain, a burning on the inside of her body that leaked all over her, pulling from her a ferocious heat. The pinpricks of it escaped each individual pore and it woke her to screaming. For a while, she hadn't experienced pain since she finished her three-day escapade into Ours to heal the sick and broken. Since then, her body felt as though it belonged to her and all seemed as normal as possible, considering Naima slept across the room with a hammer under her pillow.

Then Jacob visited, and Selah lost herself again, pain reentering her through an unexpected path. His eyes when he stared back at her, eyes heavy with want, singed through her. She realized then that there was something in other people's want that hurt her hard. It had nothing to do with the body of his wife or even the reviving of her, though she understood later: what appeared to be a revival was Selah giving the corpse her own life.

Saint had stayed by her side the evening Jacob visited. From when Selah passed out to when she came to, begging for water, Saint waited at her bedside ready to bring comfort to her. Naima pretended sleep, as was her way, but Saint and Selah paid no mind to her pretending and whispered to each other well into the night, never even mentioning Naima. That is what Naima waited for and for hours she held in her pee so she wouldn't miss hearing the song of her name.

House quiet as the moon. Naima got up, pissed in her bucket, and watched Selah sleep. The girl murmured in bed, rocking to and fro in what Naima assumed was the grips of a dark dream. 'That's what you get,' she thought, 'for showing off, trying to bring the dead back. Nobody bring the dead back to life. Not even Saint. So why'd she let you do that?'

Naima felt dizzy as she crept to go downstairs. In the hall, she heard Saint and Frances arguing in Saint's room. Sometimes she could tell who was speaking by their voice, but most of her eavesdropping relied on what was being said to tell whose words belonged to whom: *What you let her do it for? She has to make decisions on her own with her own gift. You supposed to guide her to be more responsible. It's her gift. She just a child. It's her gift and she has to learn the consequences of using her talents for the wrong reason. That's just it, Saint, cause when did you ever tell her that raising the dead ain't something we do? She knew. Woman, she could've died. And she knew she could have. And Naima? What about her? She know, too?* A hush fell over Saint so dense that Naima felt it prod at her in the hallway. 'What about me?' she thought. *Naima don't raise nothing from the dead. She don't make the sick better. She don't fix bones. She make the sick sicker. Lower your voice, Saint. She make a broken leg swell up around the break. Saint. She don't so much raise the dead as she make the living die. What has gotten into you? What on earth has gotten into you? She has to learn for herself what her worth is, too. I've heard all I need to hear. Selah covers the living and Naima covers the dead. Nobody has power over life and death. Killing people the easiest thing to do, Frances, but giving life? Bringing a life back completely? It's not our place. Maybe so, Frances, not ours but it might be Selah's.*

Naima stood in the doorway so long that she peed a second time, on herself in the hallway. So long that an azure light entered the bedroom window behind her, a blue that hardly gave nuance to the purple in her eyes. Humiliated and hurt numb, she stood in her cold pee for hours, the sun rising at her back. Before everyone woke, she removed her night clothes and wiped up the pee with them. Selah slept hard in her bed, not stirring as Naima moved about, putting on a new dress, sliding the thickest socks she could find all the way up to her knees. She tossed the pissy dress into a pile of other soiled clothes for Saint to wash. Her coat waited downstairs in a tiny closet under the staircase. She put it on, then her shoes, and headed out the door.

DAYBREAK AND SELAH screaming at the top of her voice, heat tearing her up inside. She screamed "Fire!" and Frances entered the room first, then Saint who, without thinking, threw herself on top of Selah's thrashing body. Joy stood in the hallway and looked down toward the commotion. Frances checked the room for the fire but only saw that Naima wasn't there. Selah cried that the fire blazed inside of her.

"Watch her," Saint told Frances.

"I'm coming with you," Frances said.

"I got to figure out the problem. Selah in there fitting about."

"You ain't notice," Frances said. Her face awash with disbelief.

"Notice what?"

"Naima not in the room."

Saint went pale. 'How the twins just up and leave the house without me sensing a thing?' She rushed past Joy, down the stairs, grabbed her shoes, and ran out the door. Frances asked Joy to watch over Selah and, without waiting for an answer, sprinted after Saint.

[7]

A plague. Sores. Rashes. Vomiting. Swelling around the neck. Yellow tongues. Eyes jaundiced into unsightly fruit. Fingernails discolored. Toenails falling off. Hair loss. The moaning, moaning, moaning. Ours covered in moaning. The animals were fine. Limbs still attached.

Moths here and there, out of season, fluttered on the rooftops, on the fenceposts, on the crooked horn of a goat. The people suffered. Severely. Frances entered one house and a man assaulted her, begging for water. His breath reeked. An unalive stench weighted the air. Frances found water for him and demanded that he lie down. The man grabbed on to her, his yellow eyes darting around like hummingbirds. "Lay down, you not well," Frances said. When the man clung even harder to her, moaning in pain, Frances removed a glove and wiped a finger across his forehead. He released Frances and slid to the ground. His forehead, once covered in lesions, became clear as a baby's.

Frances put on her glove, sat the man up against a wall, and turned to leave the house. In the doorway, stiff with rage, stood Saint, her closed mouth tight and trembling. Frances looked away and Saint stormed out into the sickened road.

Folks crawled out from their doorways into the warmish morning. Saint heard Frances close the door behind her and walked away, toward anywhere, just away from her, from—is that why?

A woman called out for help, leaning out her window, and Saint rushed to her, comforted her and said she would see what she could do but please go back inside please. A moth landed on the sick woman's head.

Is that why—? Saint sat a boy upright who had fallen over on his porch in a chair right under the veranda. He had left his room to look for help for his uncle but felt an illness overtake him the moment he opened the front door. She wiped the boy's brow and was reminded of Frances's naked finger healing a man with touch alone. 'Is that why she don't take off those gloves? Every day. Every night. I hardly noticed but—' Saint thought as Frances caught up with her and Saint ignored her turned away hurried off until Frances's gloved hand grabbed her shoulder. Saint spun around and a bolt of lightning severed a tree behind her. Frances released her.

"Don't you ever touch me!"

"Saint, please."

"Don't you ever," Saint said, as though the words eroded her mouth.

She marched north toward the tallest tree that the children would one day call God's Place and found Naima there, sitting high enough up that she had to have flown. Dozens of gray pieces of silk fluttered around her. A piece fell low enough to where Saint saw its details: a gray moth. When it landed on Saint, it popped into a cloud. Saint covered her face and stepped back. Naima had plagued the entire town with her gift.

"Naima," Saint called up to her. "Naima, can you hear me up there?"

The girl looked down, turning her head as if searching for the voice's source. 'She can't even see us,' Saint thought as she waved real slow. Naima stood on the branch and walked down the trunk of the tree as if walking down a road. When she got close enough to the ground, she stepped onto the earth like stepping onto somebody's porch. Saint and Frances looked on in amazement. Naima smiled. Streaks of purple fell from each eye down her completely white face.

"Naima," Saint said.

"Yes," Naima replied, walking toward Saint's voice.

"You did all this?"

Naima nodded. She held out a finger and a silver diurnal moth landed there. It popped into a purple cloud of plague that floated to the ground. "You proud of me, Saint?" Naima asked. A child's voice, cream-soft, left the death mask of Naima's face.

Heavy want weighted Naima's words. Even then, with a need to be seen and an innocence that belied her transformation, both her need and her innocence had awakened in her this disturbing force. Saint recognized all this death coming out of Naima was partially her fault. There's a thin line between strictness and neglect. Though she had no understanding for where either twin received their gifts—asking Son their origins was out of the question per their agreement—whatever awakened in them both required her attention and control. They were her responsibility, regardless if she loved them or not, or if she cared about their feelings or not. Because they lived, had life in them, she had to recognize their every breath and achievement with balance.

Saint knelt in front of Naima and reached out her arms. "Come," she said. Naima ran to her and they hugged each other with a squeeze and rock. The moths faded. The dust flew off somewhere with the wind. Naima's face became its deep brown again. When Naima opened her eyes, she saw in all the colors. "Am I your daughter now, too?" Naima asked.

"My daughter? Too?"

"People was saying Selah your daughter, but you don't call us that. You ain't say they was wrong, so they must be right. But am I your daughter now, too?"

'Daughter?' Saint thought and smiled through it. Everyone had become eager and dangerous all around her. "Yes," Saint said. She didn't see it but felt somehow the plague clouds leaving town just south of them. Heard, maybe, a cheer of celebration burst from Ours as they all discovered themselves healed, not yet dead. They also belonged to her, in sickness and in health. Each and every one. "Yes," Saint repeated. "You are both mine forever."

· CHAPTER 15 ·

Understanding

[1]

Saint held Naima's hand, now cold after summoning moth after moth of plague into the town to prove a point. That she, too, was worth it, that if Selah could bring the dead back to life, then Naima could deliver the living to their deaths just the same. Forced to pay attention, Saint acknowledged the arrival of a world terribly nimble at undoing itself, shuddering in the complication of envy and pride.

The three—Saint, Naima, and behind them Frances—left Ours without making sure everyone had survived, letting the handful of citizens they saw creeping out of their houses be evidence enough that the worst had passed. Feeling as though they were sneaking off, Frances asked solemnly if they should make sure everyone had indeed healed. Saint's back was the only answer she received.

With Naima's hand in hers, Saint stomped away from the ghoulish faces awakening into life again in Ours and away from Frances, who she couldn't get rid of and who wouldn't leave on her own. She stomped with the force of someone abandoning a hard past, having finally found respite and a way to defend it in the future. But Saint had no defense, not one that came to mind immediately, and as she took in the cool morning air, she remembered Joy, who, like a boorish child, had taken a plate of food upstairs to her room, a plate she had loaded up with an extra chicken thigh before hoarding it and herself in that borrowed bedroom as though biding her time.

If anyone knew about Frances's touch, it would be Joy. Fickle Joy. Morose Joy. Don't-speak-when-she-enters-the-room Joy. Secretive Joy, so much so Saint decided she herself had been betrayed by Joy's silence because wasn't she owed the truth after offering them lodging and food for free? To be up front expressed a true sign of character. Instead, she discovers the person she had been living with could heal a grown man in seconds with just a touch. When thoughts of being touched that way entered Saint's mind, her breath shortened and she clenched her teeth, accidentally biting the tip of her tongue.

She listened to Frances pant some feet behind her and Naima and said to hell with trust, too. Never did her any good anyway. What good it do Jesus, on then off the cross, in and out the tomb, His Father looking on having known already what his creations would do to his Creation, Jesus done in by a kiss. What sense that make? And right when Saint thought she could take no more of her own anger, at the entry of Creek's Bridge sat a man Saint thought looked familiar. That he looked up and smiled when he saw her told Saint he had been waiting to be found. "Franklin," Saint said under her breath. Franklin tried but failed to whistle through his swollen lips. He stood and wobbled a bit when a fierce breeze rushed past him. Because he was coming from the east, Saint knew he had visited his old lover in the shack town a few miles northeast of Ours. Franklin and the lover hadn't spoken in a year. Saint didn't know a dumber man.

With nothing joyous to make it make sense, Franklin tried to smile, but his swollen bottom lip trembled, throwing out a grimace. Bruises covered his skin. And was that a tooth missing from the bottom row, its vacancy irritating Saint to the highest degree? She wanted to be alone with Naima. She wanted to wreak havoc upon Frances, though she hadn't yet imagined how. But Franklin's broken mouth and mottled body distracted her from her wants. Mostly, she wished he would stop trying to smile.

Franklin stood when he saw Saint because he respected her. Not even his battered legs were going to stop that. He clenched his left side, a fractured rib harassing him, and rubbed wherever the blade-edged brambles that intercepted his escape had cut his arms. Thin lines of blood soaked through his torn shirt and where stray threads tickled the open skin they, too, had begun to stick to the adhesive of his bleeding. He couldn't lift his arm, so it bumped aimlessly against his leg when he walked.

"Howdy," he said, coughing soon after. "I'b so, so, so, so, so habby to see you."

[2]

Just northeast of Ours lived a small band of outsiders, living not so much in a town but in a gathering of shacks folks called Turney. How they got the land to begin with remained a mystery to most who encountered them; however, those who knew the truth kept it tucked close.

Several shacks, spread throughout the dense woods, made up most of the town, appearing more as a repeated mistake that a single person kept making while attempting to build a decent home. Ten sturdy shacks with lopsided roofs circled a clearing that acted as a meeting ground. Franklin had met up with his lover Foster there once a week, listening to Foster's people play clapping games while they roasted wild game caught the same day.

It had been over a year since Franklin last saw Foster, and this was part of the reason for his current state.

He first met Foster by accident, May of 1857. During a walk to the lake to fish, Franklin made a wrong turn and kept on going. Foster found him pacing in circles, mumbling to himself, then to the tops of trees as he looked up through the sun-laced boughs for direction. Foster stepped into where he knew he would be seen, wanting to be seen, smelling Franklin's craving for a hunt in the air.

Franklin thought he had found a deer when he spotted Foster's naked figure leant over, picking berries from a bush. But when the deer started to hum, Franklin saw what his heart had always desired, what his mind thought all along it had feared.

Without missing a beat, Foster told Franklin, who gawked adoringly at the man cupping berries in a single palm, "Come on. You might as well just come on and have a taste."

By August, meeting after meeting by that raspberry bush, kiss after kiss, Foster refused to move into Ours with Franklin and Thylias, whom Franklin described as trustworthy. "I'm needed in Turney," Foster said. Seeing the torment in Franklin's face, he led him by the hand to the scattered homes, to wet clothes drying on low-hanging branches, to a joyful man with large white blotches on his otherwise brown skin, standing in a doorway and waving enthusiastically at Foster, to a bright-skinned woman who squinted at them as they neared her.

"Hello, Aurora," Foster said to the light-skin woman, and she stopped squinting and spoke back. The sound of a crying infant filled Turney, but other than that youthful sound, there was little evidence that more children lived there.

Franklin recognized with ease Foster's importance to Turney, and it made him spiral deeper into desire. What originated in the woods as stunned lust evolved into perilous love. With every chimney Foster helped build, every mud siding he added to a wind-racked shack to prepare for winter's fist, and every coal-scented poultice he mixed to dress wounds, Franklin's resentment toward Turney grew.

He went so far as to ask Saint to visit Turney to scratch into Foster the symbol that would allow him to see and enter Ours. She refused to step foot into that ramshackle town, was angry to have been asked, but said she would meet this person in the in-between lands.

Foster treated Saint with remarkable respect, so much that Saint agreed to mark him just on principle alone, giving Franklin credit for sharing with her Foster's interest in leaving Turney for good. But when she mentioned it to Foster, he had no idea what she was referring to, having decided long ago that he wasn't so much smitten with Turney as he was indebted to the Turnians for keeping him safe and hidden from every law and enforcers of the law that tried to kill him.

Armed to the teeth with her own irritation, her grip on her staff tense in preparation to flog, Saint leveled Franklin's optimism with a sharp-worded rant, warning him never again to waste her time, then striding back to Ours.

Franklin and Foster argued then, well into the night beneath the shoddy wood planks of Foster's roof. Soon after, they laid into each other, rolling on the humid floor, licking the salt from each other's necks, biting into a shoulder to leave teeth marks trailing in the skin, digging into the back of whoever muscled their way to the top, lips meeting, then parting, tongue tasting tongue and drinking in the curses from moments before when anxiety like a venom dripped from their mouths, Foster taking in Franklin's gentle strokes, Franklin taking in Foster's relentless length, until the morning birds uproared at the first sign of daylight, the trees a dense cascade of chirps and whistles, pulses of music and clashing caws reverberating invisibly from the treetops, somebody's cat crying a few feet away, then the sound of a door squealing open then clapping shut and the cat cries no more, Franklin's heavy breathing into Foster's mouth, Foster exchanging breath in return, and with the force of a gale tearing through a village, Franklin opened his eyes and every musician of bird, insect, and human hushed as he took in the devastation from the night before, which was his own realization of what they had done for the first time—made rooms of each other where the single room of the shack had not been enough, where the mouth had not been enough, the gleaming globes of each other's eyes not enough planet to traverse, so they had to go inside, into the dark infinite, where afterward the lightless room of the other required them to find each other by calling of the name, Foster panting Franklin's name while Franklin disappeared inside of him, Franklin facedown in the dirt spitting Foster's name into it like a seed he had desperate faith in. Yet, having lost Foster for so long inside of himself, which, too, became a type of location, a kind of seeing anew, it made no sense that he now observed Foster lying there next to him, mouth open into an uninteresting, foul-smelling cave that was too shallow to get lost inside of. And just like that, the memory of dead baby foxes bounded back, his boyhood trapped beneath a rain of corpses plopping into the hole with him in it, the dead boy on the ground facing Franklin with rigid condemnation. He put on his clothes and went back to Ours.

For months Franklin refused to see Foster and avoided going near Turney, and because Ours was invisible to Foster, Foster had no way of finding Franklin. Without a lover but burdened by loving memories, Foster waited by the berry bush where he first laid eyes on Franklin, every day for several hours until by November the weather made it impossible to wait.

'There used to be a field,' Foster thought, walking back the final day of his waiting by the berry bush that by then had lost every berry. 'There used to be a field and now isn't no field.' He thought about what it meant for a thing to transform and discovered within himself the first myth of his mind. A beautiful land, a fruitful land, flat, undifficult, known because knowable. Then without warning, the topography loses its consistency, the inexpressive arithmetic of a pasture drops into a cliff, and the last appraisal of the land no longer holds.

The worst memory for Foster was waking up that morning and seeing Franklin had gone. No letter left to find (with what pen? what parchment?) and nothing scratched into any tree or the walls of the shack for that matter. Franklin had left no message with a neighbor, had left nothing of importance to him such that he would have to return to get it. Just absence. Had Foster a raring imagination, perhaps he could've considered the emptiness that Franklin had replaced himself with as Franklin's new form, but how many others had taken this form before him? Be it by choice or force, how many men had, overnight, turned into the very air he breathed?

It wasn't Foster who beat the shit out of Franklin, rather a new lover, one who appeared to Foster in November, and assisted with the tasks that were once all his own. This man endured the winter months and had prepared for the harsh, wet spring. He slept where Franklin once slept, emptying the shack of Franklin's presence with a sage brushing and prayer. So, when Franklin, at his wit's end with yearning for the company of men, decided to mosey on into Turney and grab Foster from behind—hoping Foster felt the same, needing him to—a man who called himself Rain grabbed Franklin by the neck and whupped his ass.

"I'b so, so, so, so, so habby to see you," Franklin said to Saint, and Saint looked off to the side as though hoping the answer to her secret prayer would soon step forward and smite Franklin clean from the earth.

"You went back to Turney, didn't you?" she asked, and Franklin nodded, grinning, then burst into tears. He reeked of whiskey. He had gone to Turney drunk. He had gotten whupped drunk. He sickened Saint. "Stupid," Saint said. "Stupid. Cruel. Stupid." She let him sob a little more before saying, "Move out of my way."

Franklin looked hurt, his feelings this time, and asked her to help him. "Maybe the healing girl could hel—?" Before he could finish, Saint put the tip of her staff against his forehead and pushed, sending Franklin stumbling backward and falling onto the bridge, the pain dull and enormous.

Saint said, "'Healing girl'? Selah, is her name. What right you have to see somebody whose name is of little importance to you? Cruel. Stupid. Get out of our way!" But he couldn't move. The fall had further sored a rib and the pain, so all-encompassing it rang, made it impossible for him to hear a thing, let alone see. Looking up to the sky, Saint took a deep breath, then looked over her shoulder. "You," she said to

Frances. "Come do what you did to that sick man in Ours to Franklin. Let me see for myself what you been hiding. What you had the nerve, the damn nerve to keep hidden from me while living with me. The audacity of men. You, too, may be cruel, but don't be stupid."

Frances removed her gloves and placed her hands right above Franklin's forehead. She tried not to touch him, to remain just close enough that she could feel the heat from his body in her palms. But she had to touch him and discover all his past life with it. She closed her eyes against the dead foxes, the untrustworthiness of men, and the relentless fear of a little boy Franklin. Every bone, bruise, cut, swelling, and abrasion healed. Franklin sat up, judged his health, and sat in disbelief.

"If you can move, I strongly suggest you do so," Saint said. Franklin nodded speechlessly and scuttled off to the side. Saint cut him a look and he ran fully across the bridge, apologizing. "If you say a word to anybody anywhere at any time about what happened here on this bridge, not even a god would be enough to stop me. Not even a god, Franklin. You understand?" Franklin said yes and thanked Frances, then Saint. Clear-eyed, frightened, he watched them cross the bridge.

'THAT WASN'T HEALING,' Saint thought. 'That wasn't healing. Wounds don't just close. Bones don't just unbreak. Skin don't just unbruise. There is blood loose in the body. Broken vessels. Torn muscles. Time. It all takes time. Even if Selah had brought Georgia back from the dead, the woman would have still been tired from having had a baby. One don't just skip across one moment to the next over some healing. Oh—' Saint smiled then. One moment to the next. Because, not only did Frances "heal" Franklin, she had also made him sober. Not a lick of drink on his breath when he thanked them.

'Frances ain't a healer,' Saint thought, and instead of heading toward the house, she headed toward the small shed where she had abandoned her companion during the winter to keep him safe from Frances and Joy, not knowing then what they were all about. Now that she had figured out a thing or two about Frances, she held no fear that Frances posed a threat to him.

Frances, now walking at Saint's side, didn't dare ask where they were going. She observed Naima, who seemed completely undisturbed while holding Saint's hand. Had Frances had the nerve to look at Saint, she would've seen a haughty smirk. Instead, she looked ahead as they approached a small shed grown over with dead vines.

"I'd like you to meet someone," Saint said, opening the door.

From within emerged the tall man whose eyes focused ahead of him. He wore the blank expression of someone lost in the void of thought. Frances thought he smelled like moldy earth.

[3]

Back at the house, Joy blinked twice. Slow, hard blinks, and the kill-heavy glaze that a second ago had covered her eyes dropped its cloudy veil. Selah's stoic face came into focus, already bored with the event, already calculating a way to return to her rest.

Joy would've done worse than nick Selah on the clavicle if the young girl hadn't, in a mother's tone, asked, "What I do to you?" right as Joy completed the knife's downward arc. Selah had opened her eyes just in time to see Joy standing over her with the biggest knife from the kitchen in her closed hands, held just above Selah's already-hurting body. Too exhausted to fight, too annoyed to raise her voice, Selah raised her tone instead. Before the blade had a chance to enter Selah, Joy blinked twice and stared down at her almost-victim with the agonized expression of a child caught digging in her nose.

She lifted the knife from the small cut it made in Selah's collarbone and let it drop to the floor. It's metallic thump annoyed Selah, who wondered why she dropped it when all she had to do was get it up off her. It had become obvious to Selah that Joy had come to, but come to what? If Joy ever had a self to return to, Selah never noticed; she only wanted to sleep, and once the sound of the knife meeting the floor left her ears, she rolled her back to Joy and returned to her rest.

Stupefied, then embarrassed, Joy picked up the knife from the cold floor and left in tears.

She thought the need to kill had gone out of her, leaving only remnants of its past in the form of night terrors. Suppressed in her sleeping mind, the need to kill had no way of making her into a sleepwalker witlessly searching for prey behind closed eyes. Sleeping in Frances's bed, however, stopped the dreams. Stopped them completely. But what had been refused a home in dreams returned to the old home of her physical body.

Her last moment of walking murder was mere anecdote. Before reaching Ours, Frances had told Joy how she slaughtered a rabbit in the woods during their journey from New Orleans. "Woke up and you was covered in blood and cuddled up with the damn rabbit like a baby doll."

Deranged with a sudden surge of melancholy, Joy closed her bedroom door and rushed to her bed, knife still in hand. Her vague reflection in the blade showed her half of her face, the other half cut off by the sharp slope where the cutting happens.

She wanted Frances back. All to herself. That time in the woods, the split-open rabbit at her ear like a seashell. Frances had removed the bloody corpse before Joy woke. They never slept far from water, so washing Joy's face and hands was easy. Her clothes were the only bloody evidence of the kill.

Soon after, Frances lit a bonfire, skinned the rabbit, beheaded it, emptied its bladder, removed the guts and organs, rubbed the last bit of whiskey all over its body, then left it hovering over the short flames on a stick held up by two uneven yet sturdy towers of stacked stones. By the time Joy woke, she had a fresh face, clean hands, and a dress pasted on to her with rabbit's blood. She thought it was the sudden coming of the month, but Frances shook her head and laughed. "You know better," Frances said. "You know your body better than that. You blame all the blood, all over you, on the moon? Moon ain't do it to you."

Without the enticing smell of iron on her face, without the brownish-red crusting over her fingers (Frances even cleaned out her fingernails), and without the corpse itself there as an icon of her destruction, Joy felt relief almost instantly. It seemed to her that it had never happened at all. They ate well that afternoon. Her killing had been useful, though Frances kept herself from making eye contact for the rest of the day. That hurt Joy, enough to ask Frances to tie her to a tree every night. Frances exploded.

"That don't make no got-damn sense, Joy. Not one bit of that make sense. You want to be whipped at the tree, too? You want somebody to wet all over you? I'm not tying you to no damn tree. Might as well hang . . ." Frances said, stopping herself, but it was too late. She swallowed hard before she finished. "We don't use trees that way. We don't volunteer ourselves to nastiness, Joy. Don't ever offer yourself over to madness." Shaking her head, she whispered, "How you got so much hate in you?" but she said it not to Joy, but to the no place in front of her.

"It's to keep us safe. To keep you safe," Joy said. "How is that hate?"

"What danger you ever be against me you be against yourself," Frances said.

Joy had seen for herself bullets flying at Frances's back, head, shoulders, arms, neck, hands, thighs, shins, and each time the person who shot at her ended up carrying the injury they had meant for her. A man shot off his pistol and his own kneecap exploded. Another shot at her chest, and a hole burned through his heart. Joy knew this, had witnessed it all.

She and Frances had returned to the boardinghouse after shooting practice and found Eloise's and Amelia's dead bodies posed on the couch, surrounded by men who waited all day for Frances and Joy to return.

The first man shot Frances square in the head. The second, insensible with malice such that he didn't see his own friend die beside him, shot Frances in the chest. His miraculous aim put lead in his own lung. The third man aimed at Frances, and Joy wished they had aimed at her as well because she sensed why they avoided harming her at all; they were saving her for something else.

Six men, one of them Yves, in the parlor, shooting at Frances just to shoot themselves. Joy never got the chance to grieve Eloise and Amelia, whose bodies had slumped into each other after the commotion, their foreheads touching in mock nap. Frances made her go upstairs and grab whatever she could fit and carry into a hand-stitched leather bag that Amelia had bought her for her birthday. Without delay, they were off, patrollers on their asses because the gunshots from the house caught their attention. Luckily, they found a horse in front of a bar to steal, which brought more gun-toting men after them. Joy rode in the front, leaning forward like Frances instructed her to, and Frances sat behind and leaned over Joy, a shield, while immediately healing the horse whenever it was shot. Had it not been for everyone who tried to kill them ending up dead themselves, they would've been caught, easily, before leaving town.

Only after Frances stopped looking Joy in the eye did Joy find some hallow ground within herself under which she buried her urge to kill. She refused to be further isolated, having lost already two women she had called family. 'Somebody will see the future with me,' she thought to herself, as she suppressed the want to kill so deeply inside of herself that it manifested only as dreams.

Joy remembered all of this while peering at herself in the knife's facet. No one had held her ever in her life. Not her tepid mother, abusive father, or Amelia and Eloise. She had been hugged, but briefly. She had been shoved, and once her father slapped snot so hard from her nose that it landed several feet away. That form of touch was brief and sharp as the knife she held in her hand that she turned to make her halved reflection disappear and reappear in the metal. What she wanted was to be engulfed by a lover who wanted nothing more than to wake up and find her still asleep next to him. Without that, how was she any different than the knife in her hand: sharp, hard, cold, and indifferent?

Frances was right about her not being an animal, but the implication that because she wasn't animal then she must be human wasn't right, either. Perhaps, she was a weapon, and what else is a weapon to do except harm others? She considered stabbing herself in the heart to get her weapon-life over with, but she wanted to live even if that meant others may die. Did that desire to live, despite her murderous urges, make her less human, too? Before she could take seriously her own question, she heard crying coming from downstairs. She put her knife beneath her pillow and followed the sorrowful sound.

At first, it seemed the crying came from the room itself. Joy stood alone downstairs, but the soft sniffles and low moans persisted. She soon realized that the crying was coming up from the floor, from the space where Georgia had lived then died. The sound brought up in Joy a maudlin sympathy not for herself but for the world and the world's hard ways. She knelt near the spot where Georgia had once been and touched where she remembered seeing her legs. She then spoke into the space, saying to Georgia, who wasn't there but was, that she would be fine. Comfort, the need to give and receive it, overpowered Joy. She laid herself down next to where Georgia lived again and died again and wrapped her arms around the no-body. Soon, the crying stopped.

[4]

Boredom forced Selah out of bed. Feeling the slowness of the world, she ignored her pain, which was dulling by the second, and made her way downstairs. Distracted with purpose, she had forgotten about Joy almost killing her and sat her attention on cleansing the front room of Georgia's spiritual energy. Saint taught the twins years ago that wherever a person dies a hard death is where a spirit rests its tortured head. 'House is crowded enough as is,' Selah thought, 'without dead Georgia moaning about.'

Downstairs, Selah scrubbed the floor where Georgia had lived then died a second time. The strong smell of lemongrass, clove, lavender, and sea salt eased her labor. She had boiled the water with a bluestone inside like Saint showed her, then took the water off heat before adding the other ingredients for steeping. The process soothed her. The brushing anchored her. She brushed in six tight circles where Georgia's head had lain, six where the torso had been, and six wider circles where the legs were. She did these three times each before letting the dampness air-dry and sprinkling ground rosemary over the floor. She did this around Joy, who slept on the floor through it all.

After she woke, Joy considered the rosemary'd floor beside her head. She sat up, acknowledging Georgia's life-death spot. It glistened where the morning light touched the damp wood, and Joy got the sense that Georgia's spirit had finally found its true resting place.

Selah had seated herself at the table in the center of the room, laying her head on the hard, flat surface that hadn't been cleared of dust that in her laying outlined her throbbing head. Nevertheless, the cool wood comforted her. When she saw Joy surveying where she had cleaned, she closed her eyes and wished the woman would go back upstairs to play with her one good knife.

For months, Selah observed Joy do nothing but whine and coerce Frances into feeling fault for living her own life, a long-occurring activity Joy had difficulty accomplishing on her own. Not like Frances was much better, sleeping in that impersonal bedroom with a woman she was too stupid to see only wanted her close for safety. That's how Selah saw it, but at least Frances got pleasure lying up under Saint, no better than a piece of lint between the toes. What did Joy get with her lingering? Then quick as a sneeze, the image of the knife entered Selah's mind, leading her to touch her clavicle as if searching for a forgotten locket. Still not angry, Selah opened her eyes. She felt woozy and out of her body as she had the days when she visited Ours at night, resetting bones and steeping tea. Joy stood by the window, looking out into the sunny cold day.

"It is nice out," Selah said. "You should leave."

Joy didn't respond. She idly fingered the curtains as daylight engulfed her face.

"You should leave," Selah repeated.

"I'm sorry," Joy said. "I can't go."

"You can do whatever you want."

"I'm not leaving Frances."

"Frances already left you."

Joy cut her eyes at Selah. "What did you say?"

"Frances left this morning. Why are you still here? My head hurts. That's why I am here. I would be outside playing if my head felt good."

"I'm waiting on her to get back."

"He will get back when he do. You could be looking at flowers right now while he's away."

"I don't want to look at flowers right now, Selah."

"Why not? What a flower ever do to you?"

Joy sat at the table, adjacent to Selah. "Do you want breakfast?"

"Saint say if you don't clean where the dead died, they never leave that spot." Selah moved her eyes from Joy to the space behind Joy where Georgia's body had been. "If you're fixing breakfast, I can wash your sheets." Selah's eyes returned to Joy's.

"I can wash my own damn sheets," Joy said, and headed to the kitchen. She stopped when Selah started speaking again with a voice that sounded different: deeper, a tuning fork ringing out in pure disgust. Turning around, she saw Selah's hair had turned ash white.

"You won't ever have a past, not one you respect, not one you can lean on or learn from. I know what's ahead for you and it's the same as what's behind you. This means you have no future, either. Might as well do something real with this sad life you living in the now. Instead of sleepwalking in your own dirt, waiting on a man who never waited on you, who dragged you from one murder to the next. Now you want to spread your nastiness all over the house. Talking bout 'Do you want breakfast?' You have not bathed. Do not touch any food in there until you have bathed. Keep your shit to yourself," Selah said in an older woman's voice, then her hair darkened back to black and her voice returned to its child's timbre. "No thank you."

It wasn't fear that made Joy stop and listen to the grown woman speech and sound coming from the young girl Selah, or that made her watch the gray return to black in Selah's thick hair. Every syllable rolled out carefully, tinged with what reminded Joy of Eloise's cadence, the forceful know-it-all-cause-I-seen-it-all husk over the smooth golden kernel of each word. Yes, Joy stopped and listened because Selah was talking like a grown woman, one she missed. But Selah wasn't Eloise. Never could be. She was no longer sure what Selah was.

Joy celebrated privately that she kept her hands to herself because, surely, her eyes were playing tricks on her, and her ears had locked on to a flash of nostalgia. 'Maybe there's too much dust in the room,' Joy wondered, double-checking if indeed she couldn't put hands on Selah because, yes, the gray hair she thought she saw was all a figment of her imagination. Must've been. Curiosity got to feeling so good to her that she found herself standing in front of Selah, who still rested her head on the table, looking pitiful and giftless toward the west-facing windows.

No, not a grown woman, but "You better watch your mouth if you want to make it to grown," Joy said to the downed head on the table, not even seeing that Selah herself, though exhausted, still in pain, and dizzy with hunger, wore the face of someone who carried little if any understanding as to why Joy raised her voice. Joy tasted only audacity in the air around Selah, saw only ambivalence in the child's slumped shoulder, and wanted to fistfight the girl. "Cause you not grown," Joy continued. She grabbed a bar of soap from a shelf in the kitchen and came back into the front room, still talking, "Cause you think Saint running things around here that you got some of that running, too. But let me tell you a thing about running things . . ." Joy was halfway up the stairs and Selah couldn't hear the rest of the sentence, just hard-edged mumblings upstairs until Joy slammed the door behind her.

But Selah was too shook from also hearing that voice not her own—older, near-breathless with irritation—leave her body to care what Joy felt. Licking the roof of her mouth, she touched her neck and swallowed hard, staring into the space before her. Only after she had calmed herself did she wonder how long it would take for Joy to realize that she went through all that trouble just to go upstairs without a bucket of water to make the soap count.

· CHAPTER 16 ·

The Outsiders

[1]

Mornings in Ours were built for humiliation. Spring unlocked a powerful yearning from young flowers eager for bees, while the young adults sweated into strange beauty with the fervor of saints. Dogwood blooms overtook lush yards, wagons moseyed on by bearing whatever fruit and vegetables that arrived early that year. Children just out of school counted one to one hundred as they passed Reverend, who in peak voice belted a homemade hymn to the children's rhythmic counting, followed by ecstatic damnations everyone expected in the way foul breath is expected from a known and recurring culprit, though no less offensive.

A few weeks before, in a flash of something unlike God but God enough for the desperate, Reverend thought he had been blessed with the song that would have congregants fighting to get into his church. He stayed up all night humming it, for it had woke him at an hour when songs are easy to forget. But when it came time for him to share it, he couldn't compete with daily life. Roof repairs and door replacements, nails hammered into wood adzed flat for a tabletop, work was to be done in the crisp mid-May air. Doing his part, Reverend lifted his chin to open his throat for a full bellow, and the sound of metal hitting wood drowned him out.

Walking past Reverend's frantic pleas, Thylias carried a bouquet of flowers she bartered for with a bowl and several cups she no longer wanted. The vendor's garden had come in early and strong, and winter frost had given his flowers an unpredictable shock of colors, colors for which Thylias knew no names. The thought of calling the beyond-red of the roses "red" dug a chasm in Thylias's chest. She clenched her jaw to hide feeling overwhelmed. Her bun sat high on her head as she walked past Reverend, catching the part of his rant where his frustration had become unbearable to him. "God don't like ugly," he said, nearly into the woman's ear. Before she could react, he hurried away shouting scriptures at the backs of people's heads as they briskly rushed away. Without knowing why, Thylias started to tear up and walked the rest of the way home with her face buried in blue hyacinths with a touch of lily and a single beyond-red rose pushed off to the side.

She sat the bouquet in a thin vase she had purchased in Delacroix the day before. Its maker had painted white-tipped waves of blue water all over the surface, decorating the waves with small black marks he said were sticks in a rushing river. Thylias liked to think the marks were people instead, floating belly up in the water, only in a hurry if the river hurried.

Franklin searched the room to see where the sweet smell emanated from, and upon seeing the flowers, the blue waves, and the sticks or people drawn in, he acknowledged them with the disinterest of seeing a leaf fall from a tree and continued to creep about the house. On the floor, he noticed a curl of hyacinth curve toward his feet. The small blue figure triggered in him the ability to see the rest of the beauty in the house, curated by Thylias, whom he mostly ignored as he aged, and thus had for years ignored her turning the house into a conversation between herself and the emptiness she longed to fill. The maroon rug with gold and dark-blue insignia spiraling throughout that stretched beneath the table where he and Thylias ate meals together. Dustless, the doorframes and floors, windows and chairs all shined. The air, pristine, also dustless, carried the scent of flowers and the natural world that entered from an open window that framed Thylias's own small lily garden a few feet away from the front door. One painting of an overabundant landscape hung from a wall adjacent to the fireplace. All around Franklin a curated life in which he had no say burst forth, awakening the sense that he had somehow been left behind by the rest of the world, trapped in a dialogue between a woman and space itself.

In Ours, the grass that grows is sharp. It gleams at its edges, such that when the buttery light of spring falls into it, the light cries out and yellow pours slowly over the earth. Without saying where he was going, Franklin stepped into the spring day, his suspenders molded over the curve of his back as he looked down in shame. He appeared to be crying into the grass along with the buttery light. Greetings from neighbors didn't reach his busy mind as he moved hurriedly up Third toward Tanager. He made a left at the corner and, passing Reverend's church home, knocked on Aba's door. When it opened, the hinges spoke to Franklin, but he only heard them creak. He asked Aba if he could come in, but Aba stood in the doorway, blocking his path.

Aba hadn't had company since Joy visited him last winter. He had slept through Naima's plague, waking only to a headache and sour mouth. And on the day Naima lost her vision, when Saint, Joy, Frances, and the twins stood not too far from his house, he was drunk down to his socks.

Days spun by and he let them, enamored with his own voice screeching from the furniture. When not awake, he slept and inoculated himself from nightmares with a remedy he learned from Saint, the very person who had made his dreams into a torture chamber. He shut his door against them all and retired to his bedroom hoping against dreaming. Then Franklin knocked.

Aba pointed to the top stair of his porch, and Franklin took a seat right there. He left Franklin outside for a moment and returned carrying two warm cups of water. Franklin, Aba was certain, was at least twenty years younger than him but had aged like spoiled milk in just a few years, with the worst of it happening in recent months. He wondered what the man wanted with him now after all this time living in Ours and paying him no mind. He stopped himself from lowering his eyes to meet Franklin's, allowing the bent-over man some dignity despite it being clear none remained.

Tree shadow found the dirty corners of Aba's porch in the advent of spring's soft light. To him, it seemed the dirt from inside his house rolled to the outside, leaving a thick grime over the porch and at the base of columns holding up his veranda. Where Thylias had beaten away the look of filth in her and Franklin's home with flowers, Aba had no one, himself included, to brighten the hue of solitude lingering at the edges of everything he owned. If he had ever wanted a wife, the opportunity had hurried on past, and despite his corroded desire to speak, he found recently that uninvited guests came to him anyway with unknown intentions that irritated him more than inspired him to talk.

"How long you gone not speak to anybody?" Franklin asked. A breeze slicked down the untrimmed grass of Aba's lawn. When it passed, the grass stood blade by blade.

Aba rocked on the porch and it creaked, "For as long as I need," but Franklin didn't understand. 'Only Joy can understand me,' Aba thought, and fought against missing the woman he had met six months prior.

Soon after Saint returned to town with infants Selah and Naima, Aba started hearing a voice in the air. At first, he mistook it as his brain's rowdy thinking, but the utterance wasn't inside his head. His ears trembled with the force of having been spoken into, intruded upon. He heard the voice, so much like his own, as he paced his once-quiet house, opened cabinet doors, sat in a chair, and rolled over in bed. When he stopped moving, the voice went away. He learned then that the house had taken on the responsibility of speaking for him without his permission. Joy, the first and only person to translate his house's noise into speech, shocked him when she gave signs that she understood what he was saying. It made sense that it was Joy. Spending that much time with Saint must have carried severe consequences.

"We losing this town, Aba." Franklin spoke into his knees, ignoring people who passed by waving at him and Aba. Aba nodded at the passersby. "We losing the town."

Aba thought Franklin was the one losing: his mind and his body right with it. In an old memory, Aba recalled a story of an enslaved man who had climbed up a tree because he claimed the ground was on fire. "Hell on earth," the man screamed down, and his enslaved brethren and so-called master gazed up, blocking the sun that peeked between the thin leaves with their hands. The so-called master demanded the man get down from that tree before he shot him down with his pepperbox, but the man shouted, "How? How y'all standing in the fire like that way?"

"I know you can talk but don't want to. Your business. Just know we need a man like you present in the ways of this town. We losing Ours," Franklin said. Aba thought he heard a sob caught in the man's throat and looked away across the road at a neighbor boy dragging a mule by the reins.

"We never had Ours, fool," Aba creaked against the stairs.

Franklin went on saying that he had seen things in town, but for the life of him couldn't articulate what he had seen. He stammered on about men being men, rubbing his hands together, and paying little mind to himself as he trailed off lost in his mind's dungeon where what he really wanted to say rotted away.

Aba scratched his balls, still watching the boy tug at the mule. He found himself dozing off, half listening to Franklin and half watching the tug-of-war between child and animal. He caught himself nodding when he heard Franklin say something about Mr. Wife's boys sitting in the house like wives. Just this past fall. Luther-Philip doing laundry and Justice moping about, ignoring the young women who came to see him. "Not good for young men to be under each other like that . . ." Franklin trailed off and Aba looked at the man with the shameful arch in his back and a neck that hated its head so much that it refused to hold it up, and laughed.

"Them boys minding their business. Where yours?" Aba creaked into the stairs, but his laugh drowned out all sound. People running errands nearby stopped and watched Aba crack up, startled by the man who hadn't made a peep in almost a decade suddenly bursting into guttural music.

Franklin took refuge in his anger. "There's nothing funny to what I'm saying to you," he said. Readying to go, Franklin leaned forward to stand. Aba had become the second man to reject him and his warnings, the last of any men with whom he felt he could bond. After Foster's new man beat the daylight out of him, he wondered why he had returned to Turney in the first place, to kiss on a man whose empty mouth reminded him of dead foxes and the vacant stare of a killed boy. 'You call yourself a man?' Franklin thought, not sure of whom he was directing it to, and images of Foster and the dead boy filled his mind in a barrage of desire and blood.

When Franklin's ass lifted off the step, Aba snatched him down by the arm. Franklin tried to get free, but Aba only tightened his grip and eyed Franklin like he wanted to set him on fire. He let him go after a while and the withered man stumbled to his feet and off the porch, hasting down the road toward Third.

Aba closed the door behind him and started back laughing again. He laughed till he cried, then stopped himself, thinking about his old friends Luther-Philip and Justice. 'Been years,' he thought in stillness. 'Been years and the years ain't been kind.' He settled in a dusty chair facing the window and looked across the road for the boy with the mule. They had managed to get on and had moved away from Aba's view.

Aba remembered the end of the story the enslaved man told him. When the so-called master couldn't get his own slave out of the tree with commands, he told his white overseer to go and get his pepperbox.

"You all on fire," the man shouted from the tree. "Hell got you by the feet and you got nowhere to run to. I'se flying home. I'se flying back home on away from here."

Gun in hand, the so-called master aimed one good time and shot into the tree. What fell was the man's shoes, while a storm cloud of blackbirds lifted from the leaves. They flew up and away as one. Dozens of blackbirds, well over a hundred, up into the air like a fist. The enslaved African man, living or dead, was never seen again.

[2]

Franklin rushed home, upset that he couldn't hold up his head as a flag, signaling to all that the militancy of his anger required them to move out of his way. But there was, of course, no military, only anger without power. His frailty, and the fact that he was one of the first ever to be in Ours and therefore well known, his hunched-over back, his chin bumping into his sternum, humiliation having taken from him all spine and pride—it all inspired pity in the Ouhmey, which encouraged conversation from everyone who may have otherwise allowed him peaceful passage. They met his anger with humor, which only angered him more.

By the time he made it through the door, breathless and hurting all over, all he wanted to do was destroy each vase, decapitate every perfumed flower, break the plates, shred the painting, set fire to the rug, and piss on what remained. Thylias looked up from her newly upholstered chair, the fabric softer than rose petals, and softly said, "Hello."

After leaving Foster the first time, Franklin began to see the dead boy who cared for the foxes everywhere. At first, he appeared in Franklin's mind bound to moments spent alone with harrowing insecurity. Eventually, Franklin saw the dead boy's image in stains across a table, in wind-drawn patterns in the dust outside. Then during the worst of it, the dead boy's face overtook the faces of the other boys in town. At night,

Franklin saw him behind closed eyes and in the gray film of a morning's first blink. This went on for a day, then a week, then daily for a month. Every second took the shape of the dead. History had become a haunting.

One early morning, Franklin went to the back of the house and closed the door behind him as he entered the back room that he and Thylias used for storage. He grabbed a gun from a drawer full of tools and medical supplies. Mice dashed from the dried goods left over from winter. The gun glistened blackly in his palm. It was cold to the touch. He held it until it felt as warm as his steady hand.

Franklin took a deep breath and closed his eyes, behind which grass swayed against wind rubbing its belly across the blade tips of green, rubbing cologne from animals and wildflowers in the woods where Foster had stood and stared doe-naked and lean, rubbing its chilly swell across Franklin's back as Foster once had conversed his fingers with Franklin's back. Wind bewildering green, green bewildered beneath Franklin's bare feet approaching Foster for the first time, hands bewildering time—fingers against a nipple nimble as a finger setting the minute hand back, such turning. And the gun he held became Foster's hand warming his cold palm for the last time. Then the gun became the hand of Franklin's younger self reaching out from that dark pit filling with fox corpses. And in a final flash of curiosity, Franklin beheld the mouth of the gun as he had the dark pits of the eyes belonging to the young man who had been shot dead by their so-called master, the bullet keeping warm in some terminated organ. Franklin closed his own eyes in the storage room. He smiled, then shot himself between the eyes.

[3]

Before comprehending that her only friend and companion ended his life in the storage room, now promoted to a golden shrine by soft-fingered sunlight glazing over broken tools and Franklin's thoughts glistening pink and wet against the wall—before she could even start mourning good, could in her disorganized trunk of effects find the one dress capable of depicting her grief, Thylias heard the gossip.

She learned that her neighbors only spoke her name when talking bad about her, and that they cared even less about Franklin, alive or dead, razing what Thylias had grown to know and love about the man she spent most of her life with: mostly that he was beloved by more than just her. Meanwhile, they treated Thylias like she was a snake hatched from the blood of Franklin's suicide and not the young girl who was one of the first to occupy Ours all those years ago. How could they not know her, she who was an original?

What Thylias thought to herself after seeing Franklin's limp body, after running to the nearest person walking the streets and drooling the words out with her screams of "He dead! He shot hisself dead!" was that outsiders had no business making more outsiders from the inside.

After a week of mourning, Thylias returned to her home, having spent the day of Franklin's suicide and the seven days thereafter staying with a neighbor, Nathan Goodlove called Goodlove, who, during Thylias's long visit in which she found not only the power of silence but of tears, washed Thylias's body toe-tip to head-top because she couldn't stop crying long enough to do it herself.

Goodlove warned her that if too many of her tears mixed in with her bathwater, she would bathe in her own sadness, allowing grief to follow her for the rest of her life. Hearing this, she cried into the soapy water. Her body glistened in the large wood tub as Goodlove washed her back from which, by the fourth day, bones began to show. She hadn't eaten a crumb.

Inarticulate with sorrow, Thylias decided to live in lack, starving herself and ridding her once thick body of all fluid by crying and sweating beneath covers she didn't need. She wanted to speak the language of bone, because flesh—Franklin's and her own—had failed her, her noticeable rib cage seeming to her its own alphabet her fingers could touch and her eyes could read as though looking upon a newspaper. She soaked in the broth sourced from her own weariness, and like a vicious acid, sadness corroded her body into an angelic form. Goodlove referred to her pronounced shoulder blades as "Thylias's wings," always washing those first before washing the rest of her body, the whole of which felt light and brittle beneath the weight of his patient hands. If an angel, not the angel of death, whose bones reflected the loss he aimed to spread around the world. She became the fragile angel of *here*, devoid of any interest in or imaginative power to confirm an elsewhere in another time, discovered only by living another way.

While Thylias stayed with Goodlove during her period of deep mourning, Saint, the twins, and her companion entered her house to retrieve Franklin's body for burial and get rid of Franklin's spirit that had taken root in the corner of the storage room where most of the blood from his head splattered against the wall.

Saint and her companion stepped into the house first, leaving the twins outside. Upon entering, Thylias's flowers began to wilt in their vases, and an invisible entity spat twice on her companion. She wiped the viscous fluid from his face and from his lapel with a dark red kerchief, unable to determine from where it fell, though she knew it came from somewhere in another realm, from an unfleshed source, having heard the *p-tuh* before seeing the hot spit land on his cheek.

Fine. It made sense that the dead wouldn't welcome her companion, he who embodied the liminal, and how would Franklin feel now, with his ever-knowledgeable eyes that only the dead have, after seeing the true nature of her companion? How would Franklin feel while trying to anchor himself to the one place he felt welcome? 'How an anchor gone move an anchor,' Saint imagined Franklin's spirit saying as she entered the storage room, pointed to Franklin's corpse, and watched her companion carry it outside like lumber.

After Saint's companion removed Franklin's body, the twins entered the house. Naima heard the moaning first and pointed to a family of shovels leant up against the bloody wall. Franklin's cry poured from behind them, his sad wailing thick and buffoonish. Saint lit a bushel of cedar and juniper and smudged out the corner of the room, sprinkling muddy water from the Mississippi over the place where shadows seemed their densest though nothing intercepted the light to cast them.

For three days, they smudged and doused the corner until on the fourth day, Franklin's pathetic moaning migrated from the storage room to the thin neck of one of Thylias's vases, echoing out among the white folds of dying lilies. Naima guided them to the correct vase and Saint smudged its small glass mouth. The wailing moved once again into a thin crack in a windowsill. Naima pointed, Saint smudged and poured muddy water into the space, and Selah waited in case the angry spirit harmed either of them. Naima cursed, Selah yawned, and Saint cracked her knuckles with her thumbs when the spirit locked itself in place in the ceiling. It started up its moan again and a light mist fell over Saint and the twins.

"Perhaps the first few times were unclear," Saint said, looking at the ceiling. "Therefore, I will make this final time the clearest. Get out of this house, Franklin, before I do something forever more convincing." The house creaked once. One soft sob rang out into the room. Naima said the sad voice had gone away. They assumed this meant his complete exorcism succeeded.

However, the first day Thylias returned from Goodlove's, she saw Franklin sitting outside on the porch in his chair, balancing the pistol he killed himself with on his lap. He faded soon after she saw him. So realistic was Franklin's embodiment that Thylias found herself thinking that perhaps he survived the shooting and unburied himself from his grave—his grave, she thought, and dropped to her knees in front of her porch. She wondered if she had missed the funeral, if that was why he sat there, refusing to move on because she didn't say goodbye.

When she brought this to Saint's attention one day during a thank-you visit to Saint's home, Saint scowled and said, "Wasn't no funeral. Funerals for the living, not the dead." Thylias tried to protest, saying that the dead need funerals, too. Surely the dead want to see who loved them and how sad everybody is that they gone. But Saint waved her hand in front of her to show she was done listening. "You want to remember him, do it on your own time. The dead know all things in death. How else you think they come to guide us as our ancestors? All knowledge of what was and is belongs to them. Funerals for the living. He not haunting you cause wasn't a funeral. He only up under you because he is a selfish man and saying goodbye don't make any kind of sense to him. Becoming an ancestor isn't easy. It's a service, and Franklin, helpful as he was alive, never learned to love properly, so his death is mutilated by his hollow living. Now,"— here she smiled—"I can get rid of him by force if he's bothering you still," Saint said, but the edge of how she said "force" made Thylias tremble. How could Saint think that Franklin had no love in him? 'Didn't he keep me without anybody asking? Didn't he show the young'uns how to be in the world? Didn't he do whatever favor asked of him? Whatever you asked of him, Saint? What is love if it can't be any of those things?' And as though hearing Thylias's thoughts, Saint said, "Obligation and love not the same thing. There's a difference between doing something because you feel it's your duty and doing something because your heart would die otherwise."

Thylias argued that her heart, already in the grips of despair, would sooner die from there not being a funeral than it would if her own death walked up on her. It was settled. Saint encouraged her to carry out the ceremony on her own if she believed it would cure what Saint thought was a double haunting: Franklin's ghost and Thylias's own broken heart. Before Thylias passed the threshold, Saint remarked, "Show him he was loved in this world so he can leave it." With that, Thylias carried out the funeral by herself on a beautiful morning. Franklin's spirit appeared by his burial spot while Thylias shared a few words. But her own pain endured.

[4]

An idea: Saint had to get Joy out of the house. Away from Frances. Something about the girl's clinginess made it difficult for Saint to watch Frances and make a final decision as to how she would handle her. She needed Joy outside, farther away, in Ours's mainland maybe, but certainly out of her home. She had hoped bringing her companion out of the shed and into the house would frighten her. However, Joy seemed impressed and at peace with his work ethic, which was merely his following Saint's commands given to him by subtle, near-lazy gestures. And when the twins celebrated his return, cheering and dancing when he stepped through the front door, Joy assumed he was the strange father returning from a long journey.

Every menial and laborious task in the house, Saint's companion did without rest or complaint. The two small rooms on the second floor that faced west and hovered over the living room were utterly empty and had attracted spiders and squirrels chasing each other in the space between the ceiling and the roof. He removed most of the pests, leaving only a handful of adult spiders for their useful hunger but removing all egg sacs plump to bursting in their webs. The squirrels he chased out with a broom after undoing the roof one plank at a time and silently sweeping clean the crevices. He washed all clothes, not judging the piss-damp pile of garments stacked in the corner of the twins' room. Because he got in no one's way and managed to keep the house intact and vermin free, even Joy, anxious and eager to leave though not without Frances, found comfort in his sturdy and remarkably quiet presence.

So be it. Days later, Saint entered her divining room with an oil lamp and lit every candle along the wall. She decided to give Luther-Philip a charm. She wouldn't tell him what it was for, just that he needed to wear it and follow her instructions to the letter. She closed her eyes, tapped a finger against the eye socket of a skull that headed her armrest, and called to Luther-Philip through a dream.

[5]

Twice, death had slid its veil over Luther-Philip's life.

That first veil of death occurred when he was a child, after his mother died suddenly in their only bedroom. For three days, bereavement greeted him as a curtain set against the edges of the day. Sunrise, and his eyes opened to an obscene gauze blanketing over his seeing, a sorrowful cloak that wasn't there before his mother passed away and that refused to fade beneath his patient blinks. It took hearing his mother's name for the gauze to completely leave his sight.

Those days, his father went without speaking much and when he did speak, it wasn't Mrs. Wife's name. So, Luther-Philip took to saying it to himself, "Miss," and the paradox of her name in that moment confused his young heart, for indeed his mother carried with her the word of his captivity. He had missed his mother's dying, had missed her burial, and because there was no proper funeral with boisterous singing and shared memories, he ended up missing the opportunity to free himself from his bond with death that mourning otherwise would've broken.

Once, carrying a heavy sack of flour into the house, Luther-Philip's father stubbed his toe on a loose floorboard and sent the bag flying ahead of him in a clean arc that tossed white flour into the air. Though most of the flour hadn't spilled out, enough escaped overhead like a burst of snow stuck in the miasma of its own slow flight. Luther-Philip entered the house behind his father and saw his dead mother break through the airborne dust and kneel over Mr. Wife's fallen body. She stared up at her son with an expression of having been caught naked in a field. Soon after, she faded along with the last falling clouds of flour.

When he told his father what he had seen, a quick smile flashed across Mr. Wife's face before morphing into astonished fright that Luther-Philip mistook as suspicion. From then on, Luther-Philip hid his feelings for fear of being mistrusted.

Now, a man still living in his father's house, he hardly remembered seeing his mother in a storm of flour. He hadn't experienced the gauze that disappeared at the sound of his mother's name since he was a child, and she never again appeared in the fickle element of dust or at all, ever again. Eventually, her absence became an abandonment burrowed in him. He grew impatient with his father, who openly shared stories with Justice about Mrs. Wife, annoyed that those memories weren't his own and secretly angry when a memory that included him didn't return to him for his own remembrance. It seemed a part of himself he hadn't met or had forgotten died right along with his mother.

Once, absentmindedly yet with a trace of malice, Luther-Philip wondered aloud if his father fabricated memories out of grief until one of Luther-Philip's doubtful outbursts sent Mr. Wife rushing into the back room. When he returned, he was carrying a doll made of twisted twine with a dried-up rose petal pinned to its chest and a letter *M* written on the rose petal. "You don't remember her making this for you, boy? It's of her," Mr. Wife said, and handed the doll over. "Here." But Luther-Philip refused to take it, embarrassed into anger that he had forgotten something so precious. Though, as the day proceeded, he directed his ill feelings at his father, because why was the doll hidden from him in the first place? He let out another outburst, quieting down only after his father took the doll out of his back pocket and threw it at Luther-Philip. "Get your mind back right," Mr. Wife said. "You left it behind then just like you left it behind earlier today. If you want the damn thing, then keep up with it. If not, shut your mouth." Luther-Philip grabbed the doll from the floor and left the house, his father shouting behind him, "You ain't the only one who lost somebody!"

At any moment, anyone Luther-Philip loved could die and disappear from the earth, drift out of his memories, and leave him more a husk than he already was. All that work put into getting to know them and loving them gone to waste. He carried the doll to Creek's Bridge and sent it floating on its belly down the rocks, watching as it got stuck between sets of jagged stones only for the water to unsettle it again and carry it away.

After that, Luther-Philip smiled more, laughed louder, oiled his hands to shining and fragranced the back of his neck so that his leaving left a trace of romance. He flirted with the young women, yet refused to court them. He looked them in the eyes and felt nothing for them. He indulged in good times but refused to give those times room to sit in his mind for too long, allowing more room for future good times, more oiled hands, more batting eyes that carried no future in them.

Eventually, he came to like the attention, and to his suitors' vexation, they couldn't stop themselves from trying to get the handsome bony boy to pay attention to them. He accepted their gifts without giving any of his own. He kissed a few foreheads, then smiled coldly when no longer interested. He was omnipresent, then vanished like a well-fed god.

Mr. Wife laughed a knowing laugh; however, watching from the corners of the room or outside at a distance where he remained unnoticed, Justice seethed.

While on an errand to help an older neighbor rebuild the roof of her caved-in shed, Justice confronted Luther-Philip. It had been quiet between them for the duration of the job. They had just finished placing and hammering down the second-to-last plank of wood when Justice asked if Luther-Philip ever smiled at him without meaning it.

Luther-Philip laughed. "What kind of question is that? How you smile and don't mean to? If I smile, I mean it." They were standing inside the barn's dark, splintered here and there with light from the yet-filled cracks between the slats of wood and the open space ready for the last wooden plank. Luther-Philip considered the work they had just completed. Justice considered the back of Luther-Philip's head.

"It ain't right how you do the women who like you when you don't like them back," Justice said.

"How I do them?" Luther-Philip smirked at Justice without knowing it.

Justice's face was mostly shadow-hidden, except where a blade of radiance cut angular down his face. "Don't look at me like that," he said.

"Like what?"

“Like that. I’ll break your nose.”

For the first time, Luther-Philip stopped smiling. “You won’t break a damn thing,” he said. “The hell’s wrong with you? You won’t break no part of me. I’ll look at you how I want.”

“I’ll break your face if you smile at me like you don’t care,” Justice said.

Luther-Philip tensed up, prepared to fight, but Justice remained standing where he was. In that stillness, Luther-Philip found himself noticing what the shed contained: nearby, a shovel leaned against the wall; several nails jutted from the same wall and hooked on their heads were hand tools sharp enough to break through skin. He left that shed breathing hard and trailed by thoughts of murder. In a small place, ways to kill another came quickly. He promised himself to never be caught in a position like that again, in the tight dark with the anger of his only friend banging against him until every item became a reckoning in waiting.

After two days of mean mugging and silence, Mr. Wife told them that they needed to figure out their issues like brothers or “like enemies. If you gone fight then fight.” But the rift between the two didn’t allow for either intimacy. Luther-Philip wanted freedom, so offered freedom in return. Justice wanted loyalty, so offered his entire self to another. But they were unevolved in love, so with clumsy steps they toed the thin line between generosity and selfishness, selfishness and resentfulness. Too easy to be cruel, the laziest choice, and hypocritical by default, for what animal destroys the home it wants to live in? Yes, the heart of another is the first home one chooses. To harm that heart is to say, “I rather be homeless.” Cruelty makes a liar out of the cruel.

Maybe, intuitively they knew this and chose rolling out dough in the bakery several feet apart instead of elbow to elbow close as they once would’ve been. Mr. Wife said nothing else, kneading his portion of dough a little harder than days before.

This is why when Luther-Philip felt an unexpected urge to stop by Saint’s, he told no one. Simply put on his shoes, dusted them off, and went on his way without looking back. He was most of the way there when he realized in the clearing just before Creek's Bridge that nothing good ever come from Saint. All he knew was that she kept her voice soft with him. He hoped she would keep that same softness this time around.

[6]

Like startled fawns, Saint, sitting in a chair under the veranda, and the twins, playing a handclap game on the stairs, looked up at once when Luther-Philip stepped through the small tribe of trees that led to the house. Their three unbroken stares clung to him like wolves in the apex of hunger, something in them having eaten the fawns they once were. He slowed his pace to a halt. Before he thought to run away, the cold assembly of woman and girls shattered as Joy, on her way to the garden, disregarded their tight silence and, too, Luther-Philip standing dumbstruck just feet away. It took her looking up a third time—the first to wipe her brow, the second to gander at the twins, whose beauty she had allowed to soften her stance against them—to see Luther-Philip frozen in place.

"Who's that?" Joy asked, and Saint responded that their visitor was a man late in his boyhood. If Joy heard her, she gave no evidence and nodded in Luther-Philip's direction. With that, he pressed onward.

"If you here to see your dead mama again, you might as well go home," Naima said, starting up the clapping game again with her sister. Selah giggled and quickened the pace of the game.

"Mind yourself. He here to see me. Stay where you are. I'll bring it to you," Saint said.

While Saint was away, Luther-Philip stole glances of Joy. She caught him once and shook her head. He felt a pain in his chest and realized it was his heart learning a new language.

"They making love right in front of us, Selah. Like we not even here," Naima said, much to Selah's pleasure.

"Saint say love not a thing to put trust in," Selah said.

"What's her meaning?"

"I don't know. I kind of know love and I kind of know trust. But they hard to know together." Selah flicked a bug off Naima's shoulder. "I don't know how to carry two things at once yet," she said.

Saint returned with a leather necklace that held a small glass vial from which herbs, soil, and various spices emanated a sweet balm. She lifted the necklace and instinctually Luther-Philip lowered his head to accept it. She instructed him to return to her every Monday for three months.

"Never take this off. Sleep in it. Bathe in it. End of August the last time you need to come back," she said, "the beginning being the first Monday of June." He asked what the necklace was for, and she made it clear that telling him would only make him behave stupidly so "just mind what I say with your whole mind. Return the first Monday of June, yes?" She swatted him away, returning to the garden.

Before leaving, he made sure to get one last look at Joy and promised himself he would learn everything he could about her each Monday he was to visit Saint or die from heartbreak.

The first Monday Luther-Philip returned, Saint had prepared for him a spot in the garden marked by a set of shears and gloves. She told him to trim any rot he spotted on the leaves. "Leave the rest of the leaf. Just cut out the rot."

He knelt and began removing yellow, brown, and black spots from the leaves. Blight. He learned the word in school back when his mother was alive. He let the rotten trimmings drop to the ground before deciding to collect the discolored scraps and put them in his pocket because he thought they would make the ground sick. Joy stepped from the house wearing a gardening hat that hid her face. Luther-Philip kept working even after hearing the door swing back.

"You're doing it wrong," Joy said, and knelt beside Luther-Philip.

She pointed to a leaf on the ground bruised in its center by a circle of rot. "You didn't have to remove the whole leaf. Just cut out where the spot is. Hand me the shears. Like this." Joy found a leaf that had a central blight. Grabbing the tip of the leaf, she opened the shears and stuck the sharp point of one of the blades on the outside of the bruise. While pulling the leaf taut, she drew a circle around the rotten area and the yellow part dropped out from the leaf. "That's how she wants it to be done." Joy stood and went back into the house. Luther-Philip sat for a long time staring at the door, waiting for her to return.

[7]

The second Monday, June 13, Saint sent Luther-Philip to gather plants from the woods. She didn't tell him what anything looked like, just that she needed as much of everything as he could find: wild ginger, mullein, wrinkle rose, dandelion, goldenrod, big mint, and Queen Anne's lace. When he tried to ask for descriptions, she smiled and shut the door in his face.

After almost an hour of looking, Luther-Philip had only found the dandelion and Queen Anne's lace, having ignorantly passed everything else in large supply. Saint sent Joy out to help him and, reluctantly, Joy put on her gardening hat and went to the woods. She pointed out everything he needed, chastising him for not knowing how to identify the herbs, roots, and plants that save lives. To herself, she mumbled how useless an adult he was. To Luther-Philip, it sounded like prayer.

Joy's beauty blossomed intolerably in her early adulthood. Filled to the brim with angst, she used her long fingers to almost summon the plants from the ground, hardly struggling with the wild ginger that she uprooted as an example to Luther-Philip, who paid more attention to the sweaty portrait of her face than to what her hands accomplished. Her tawny skin shown darkly beneath the shade of the gardening hat.

She snipped, tugged, and plucked Saint's ingredients once for each plant and made Luther-Philip do the rest. As he joked and told mindless stories, she remained impenetrable, focusing on how clumsily he uprooted the ginger and how milky resin dripped down his fingers as he broke stem after stem of dandelion.

"Not so rough," she scolded, looking down on his kneeling body. "It won't be any good if you do it that rough."

"How you know so much about plants?" Luther-Philip asked, wiping his forehead.

"Frances," Joy said.

"I want to learn, too." Luther-Philip smiled at Joy. "Thank you for showing me."

Joy's mouth trembled. She looked away.

THE TWO WALKED back to the house beneath the punishing summer sun. Luther-Philip's fingers itched. He rubbed them across his pants, then scratched one hand with the other, switching back and forth until both hands became raw. Joy told him it was because he had been too rough with the plants, bruising them till they released their creams, and that all the juices mixing can sometimes eat up the skin. They took a detour to Creek's Bridge. Luther-Philip unbuttoned then rolled up the sleeves to his shirt and rinsed his hands. He was the slimmest man Joy had ever seen, and the tautness of his body, that she could see each small but firm muscle in his forearms flex as he massaged his fingers in the cool creek water, interrupted her seriousness as she imagined his hands becoming dark and sleek fish wrestling underwater.

The two began to find in each other affinity among the plants, hastily folding one flirtatious half and the other caringly judgmental half into a whole neither knew what to do with. Monday visits no longer sufficed, and the two started seeing each other during the week, meeting halfway between Ours and Saint's home only to decide to linger in that middle unoccupied territory, studying plants and each other, their appetites for each other growing little by little as they bypassed boredom, suspicion, and curiosity, to embrace knowledge, knowing that they could never know everything about the other. No, never everything.

While the two engaged with each other in shy and, in Joy's case, sharp banter, Saint took time to observe Frances in peace.

[8]

By mid-June, Frances had taken to sleeping in one of the empty rooms on the second floor at the front of the house, making a pallet for herself opposite the window to watch dust float in the air and count each speck. It was clear to Frances that she had overstayed her welcome, her abuses pushing forward the clock of Saint's patience to its sharp end.

The night after Saint forced Frances to heal Franklin, Saint moved the trunk, which had acted as a sign of welcome for Frances, from the side of her bed and back against the wall beneath the window. She then put a chair outside her bedroom in which her companion sat guard overnight with haunting quiet.

"You explain to me your gifts or you sleep elsewhere," Saint had told Frances.

Afterward, Frances sat cross-legged in the empty room upstairs to clear her thoughts. She had hoped to find answers in the isolation, because she felt an unspoken contract had been signed between herself and Saint, the terms of which mystified her. In her thoughts, blue and gray smoke snaked in a field of white, swirling together, then dispersing at the command of an unseen wind. Then the smoke pulled taut, stretched, and curved into ligament and signature. First, the four leanings of the letter *W*, then the straight-back-to-buttock arch of a lowercase *h*. Frances watched her intangible thoughts spell themselves out to her, and at the end of the inscription, what remained floated before her as a ghostly phrase, "Who knows her," at once an inquiry and a statement, a fragment and undisputable completion.

Who could know Saint? She had built no altars to her ancestors or to any spirits at all. Not even a dusty side table with cold coffee and stale toast for the dead. And if the dead did visit, which Frances doubted, how did they find her without candle smoke to follow, no mementos glowing into the ether to lead the way, no glass of water for their parched throats, and nothing to tempt them to return in the first place? Prayer. Supplication. A fragmented ego, the dust with which to softly pave the way.

This epiphany instigated others: that Saint's conjure seemed nothing like the conjure Frances knew and involved more direct action from Saint's own will than any interjection from the spirit world. Frances could count the number of times Saint used herbs, and oftentimes she used the wrong ones or ones different from what Frances had seen many other gris-gris kings, houngans, hex workers, conjurers, root workers, and devil catchers use in their own distinct practices. Saint didn't visit the surrounding natural world to fix up dying trees or mold-infested plants. Other than her own garden, she wasn't a caretaker of the world in any way, and when gathering herbs from the woods, she didn't heal the earth of the damage she had caused it.

With each revelation, Frances involuntarily moved farther from Saint's bedroom. First, she wondered if Saint was telling the truth about herself. Then she wondered if she was something more menacing, like a devil playing in her face. When she thought, perhaps, Saint was a god, she laughed bitterly at herself. What god she knew had this much fear?

A few nights later, Frances found herself sleeping in the musty shed where Saint's companion had been hidden and rendered unknown all those winter months. She slept on the hay bed, at peace in the sealed-off room through which no light from moon or stars could invade.

Finally, after a week of being unable to share her secret with Saint, Frances had begun camping out by Creek's Bridge. She would've remained in the wilderness if Saint's companion, lantern in hand and mouth sealed into an inconsequential line, hadn't been sent to get Frances on the second day of the second week of her being outdoors.

On the third night of the second week, avoiding sleeping in chairs downstairs or in the private and airless room at the face of the house upstairs, and having completely abandoned the room she once shared with Joy because that was the first space to exile her, Frances settled to sleeping in the hallway by Saint's door. It was then she decided to take heed of how Saint's companion sat all night outside her bedroom, his gaunt face illumined by a single lamp hanging in front of him from an iron hook on the opposite wall. Without blinking, Saint's companion seemed to suck in with his eyes both the immense shadows of the hall and the solitudinous light that touched like fog across his face. The light's weakness only intensified the power of the dark that molded a shell like a closing mouth around the sitting man.

Up close, Saint's companion was almost art, a statue chiseled into a strong-faced lover whose thick lips carried the weight of incredible intelligence. In the protruding globes of his eyes, Frances swore she saw the origin of sorrow, before it had a name and could only be recognized and measured by the wisest of priests. Seeing all things as they were, Frances knew something was off about him on the inside, beyond the mind and in the core of the spirit, but she couldn't tell how. It was clear Saint was the reason why, and Frances believed Saint went this far to protect herself. A shudder of grief caught Frances off guard.

The hallway, cradle of stillness and darkness, had become a prison, and though Saint, locked in her room, seemed the prisoner, she was the warden, and the long purgatorial hall laid claim to Frances. She reached to knock on Saint's bedroom door. The man, without leaving his chair, snatched up Frances's arm before her knuckles could tap. The man lowered her arm back to her sides, then let her go, his strength remarkable. The whole time, he did this while looking straight ahead. She tried a couple more times to knock, reaching faster each time, and both times Saint's companion snatched up her arm and firmly readjusted it to

Frances's side. Saint didn't want to be bothered. 'Morning, then,' she thought, and returned to sleep at the other end of the hall.

Saint's companion had no aura at all, no sign of struggle within radiating out. The map of his spirit, unnavigable, offered no leads as Frances carefully studied his body. An empty shell? No such thing. All light in him had been forced into submission, and within this stark obedience a spark of what remained fizzled into hibernation. With great care, Frances reached for the man's face, unpolished by sweat though the corridor's length seemed to bend from the heat. She felt the man's forehead with the back of her hand. He was lukewarm, his skin a cooling bowl of water. Wanting to touch him with her palm, to open his past without his permission, for who in this state (whatever this state was) could give such a thing, she pulled back instead. When she returned to the other end of the hall, she was happy with her wisdom and disappointed in her cowardice.

[9]

Frances was ready to share everything and stopped Saint one night before she closed her bedroom door. She babbled uncontrollably that she could try, had wanted to try, but couldn't for the life of her get the words right because "the words don't rightly exist. They just don't. I don't know everything, but I can tell you about my past. All of it. In the order I remember." This satisfied Saint. She dragged the chest from wall to bedside.

As Saint expected, Frances knew nothing about her gift or her origins, but she shook her head when she learned how Amelia and Eloise truly died, though not surprised by the brutality they suffered. This also further proved that Frances had been following Saint, Eloise a name familiar to her but she would never tell Frances why. No, never.

Frances made it clear that she couldn't raise the dead and so left them there. Wouldn't have brought them back if she could. Explaining how every bullet meant to hit Frances ended up hitting the shooter instead, Frances's voice went light and shaky, her eyes flitting about the candlelit room where even shadows seemed to avoid falling on her for fear of their own eradication. She had been untouchable from physical harm, but not from being treated like a monster, the one threshold of violence her talent couldn't decipher as violence. She could be pissed on, locked up, spat on, starved, and abandoned to die without anything happening to the culprit. If her heart was broken, then the heartbreaker continued to live in ignorant peace. But let somebody try to stab her, shoot her, knock her upside her head with a hammer, burn her alive, run her over with a horse, forcibly remove a tooth, decapitate her, or drown her, and the moment of incredible hostility is met with its mirror, and the aggressor is stabbed, shot, knocked out, burned, stomped clean into the earth, made toothless, beheaded, or asphyxiated by nonexistent water.

Had she remembered, Saint would've counted the times that people had tried to kill her only to have strange deaths befall them. Not mirrors of their violence, necessarily, but inexplicable events that if ever told would hardly be believable. As untouchable as Frances was, she at least had a consistent law that protected her: hurt me and the hurt goes back to you. Saint, however, had no such consistency, and the many who dropped dead while trying to kill her never crossed her mind because most times she had no idea she was even being pursued.

She remained detached while Frances revealed this twist, one that limited Saint's ability to defend herself if ever she needed to but excited her thoroughly as she imagined all the ways to take a life without taking it. 'Wouldn't even make a scratch,' she thought, blinking slowly and nodding here and there like the stories Frances told really touched her.

But that, unbeknownst to Saint, was the real issue, for when Frances fell asleep after revealing whatever she could—not knowing why her attackers suffered their attacks on her or why when she touched people she healed them and saw their pasts (this made Saint sit up in her seat)—

Saint stood at the foot of the bed and watched as the dim firelight made yellow undulations over Frances's body, snakes of light rippling up and down her frame, yes, revealing beauty in flickering moments, like this moment where Saint watched what candlelight does to a person she thought she had grown to hate, but instead she discovered what truly brought her down was that she *wanted*, which meant Frances had something to be desired, which meant Frances had power over her, which explained why those winter nights when they shared the bed together she, too, felt beautiful under the curatorial conversations that molded inside of her something she had grown to believe she could never feel again; Frances, long-legged and woman and man and both and neither (so everything, everything) moved Saint. But when she saw Frances touch that sick man at Ours and *heal* him, she realized that with movement comes eventual stillness. "Is that why—" Saint had asked herself then and asked herself now, looking with a mix of adoration and contempt at Frances's sleeping body, long as a cool night. "Is that why—" as Frances curled into herself over the bedsheets, made herself into a comma where Saint, bereft, undone, breathless, had wanted no pause, no stillness, no wait . . .

"Is that why you never touch me?" Saint asked into the night, and the night responded by blowing out the one candle left burning. She remembered telling Frances never to touch her, back when Naima had sickened all of Ours, but she didn't mean it, or she did, but only for that gloved touch, that touch hidden beneath a veil. Saint wanted skin. So she stood in the darkness, believing in Frances because she had kept herself from barging into Saint's past, and hating Frances because she kept the possibility of healing Saint from Saint.

'But no, no, no she does not heal,' Saint remembered. 'And she does not know this, or she does but can't find the words for it, but I have the words for you, Frances. You send things back. You make what was done come undone. You unweave the world around you. You do it when you're frightened. You do it when you touch people. You do it when you're near people. You play with time, Frances. You send things back.'

But Saint didn't want to go back. Unwavering, she believed that all she had was now. Frances's bare feet pointed up, and had there been more light, Saint would've seen the subtle lines in her sole. But night allowed her to see only the shape of the feet and their direction upward. Their nakedness put her on guard, then enticed her. She didn't know if touching them had the same effect as touching Frances's bare hands. She swallowed hard and reached. Her index finger touched Frances's heel. Nothing happened. No flash, no weakness in the knees. She didn't feel younger or particularly healthier. She held it there for a while, then pulled away.

Ashamed then angry, she stood. A dingy blue light touched Frances's foot where Saint's finger had touched, then, shadow-tickled by a branch's silhouette, Frances turned on her side and closed her knees, pulling beneath the blankets the feet that had enthralled Saint. In this diaphanous light, Saint wanted to touch, to be touched, and her heart clamored at the thought of what she would lose by doing so, and what in that loss she would inevitably gain.

· CHAPTER 17 ·

Kwame's Crown

[1]

Flowers offered no scent to evening's altar, and the musk of neighbors' horses fell into the ruts of shadows. Stagnant air filled with folklore as each house in Ours bore whispers of the dead, their murmurs in chorus with leaf rustle and the subtle scratch of mice squeezing their heads under a front door for a taste of rice deserted in a bowl on the floor, the one who forgot the bowl listening closely to ghost stories as though somewhere in the eerie narrative their own name approached, while in the cemetery, lying above his own grave, a man opened his eyes to sunset rusting the windowpanes. He lifted himself from the dirt and stood in the grass that entered his translucent feet.

[2]

Franklin stared at the grass that entered his translucent feet. Then, he began to levitate, indiscernible from clouds, as evening air rushed through him. He looked down from his growing height, his burial shrinking in the distance his floating created between himself and the ground.

The house he had lived in for almost thirty years became a building block in a crowd of toys portraying a town. Then the toy trees shrank, their leaves hissing in the wind that billowed Franklin above all he had known.

[3]

Billowed above all he had known, he saw, from the windy sky, roads crisscross each other into an unfamiliar board game. Lantern lights moved in concert like a conspiracy of fireflies beneath him, their carriers unaware of Franklin's spirit rising above them, observing them take their time. The tree soon-to-be-called God's Place towered dutifully over all things living and dead in Ours. Shaking the day in its clutch, its knotted branches waved at Franklin.

[4]

He saw the lake and its attending trees whose gnarled branches waved at Luther-Philip and Justice as they swam and clutched each other against solitude. The lake glistened back, a sprinkling of small fires under sunset's surrendered light. Even from high up, he saw with the eyes of the dead the hundreds of fish fin their hunger through the dim water. When he turned his head, he saw the spare and somber cabins of Turney scattered across the woods, the crooked brown heads of their roofs sloped into quiet confession.

[5]

He saw Foster's crooked and quiet house and lowered his ghost form into the woods just outside of Turney to walk the nostalgic walk in his new invisibility, past where he mistook his once-lover for a deer that would soon learn and speak his name with an animal hunger. He was shocked to see the forest populated by other transparent figures of human and uncanny forms communing beneath oak shade. The forest spirits climbed out of bark and bush, some out of the leaves themselves. It was then that Franklin heard the drum playing, and the human and uncanny figures flew on small wings, floated on footless legs, paced on four paws—turned in the wrong direction from the pelvis to confuse its predators—toward the music. Through these haunted woods, he stepped without stepping to Turney, soundless though beneath where his feet would've made sound were the scatterings of nature broken by weather and beast.

[6]

Nature, weather and beast, scattered about him, through him as he made his way to the fire-lit drum circle with the forest spirits and listened with the living Turnians to Rain, Foster, and Aurora feverishly play their drums. He and the forest spirits watched outside the circle, but Franklin wanted to enter the circle and dance to the rapid rhythms that pulsed from the hollow wooden hearts of the instruments. Some of the living humans entered the circle and danced. Then, as though always there, a gathering of powerful spirits not from the forest but from, it seemed to Franklin, the music itself danced alongside them, some so close and synchronized that it appeared they saw the gossamer forms pull out their hair and bawl, blow fire from their mouths, and stomp barefoot in cyclonic flourishes, until one at a time the spirits climbed onto the backs of the living humans and rode them horselike inside the circle.

[7]

As the more powerful spirits climbed onto the backs of the living, Foster's trance broke. He looked up and stared Franklin square in the eyes, never stopping his hands from licking the taut leather top of his drum. Then Foster played harder, faster, which quickened Rain's and Aurora's pace, the latter who threw her head back and ululated, the sudden birds in her throat flocking into the night sky, and the drumming ceased, and every spirit released their mounts and disappeared, leaving the living they had ridden sweating and spasming on the dirt floor of the circle. Foster screamed Franklin's name, which made Rain and Aurora look up and out into the night, searching for him. Rain didn't see anyone who resembled Franklin, but Aurora saw a silhouette of light in the shape of a man standing right where Foster looked. Foster screamed Franklin's name once more. His voice cracked. Again, he screamed, and where Aurora's bird voice had filled the cool air now screeched the bladed throats of bats from Foster, who lowered his head onto the top of his drum and wept.

[8]

Franklin lowered his head and wept as he left the circle and reentered the woods, following behind the forest spirits. Soon, all the other spirits were gone, having climbed back into their leaf-covered sleep. Franklin made it to Creek Bridge, then to the tree soon-to-be-called God's Place and placed his hand on the titan's bark. Laughter. He had begun to laugh and the echo of it shocked him into realization of what he was doing. His laugh reached Ours, and the children listening to ghost stories and the adults telling them froze in the quick and deep cadence like a maelstrom in their ears. It reached the grave of his former so-called master whose skull sucked in the laughter through a bullet hole and shattered. It reached the top of the tree soon-to-be-called God's Place, weaving its thread into the branches for the wind to catch hold of. He rose to the sky, buoyed by his laughter. He felt no heat and no chill. A small flock of lost birds flapped into and out of his translucent body.

[9]

He felt no heat and no chill, and a small flock of birds flapped into and out of his translucent body. And though time meant little to him in this state of newly dead, he still perceived speed and noticed its rapid increase as he brushed past another set of denser, darker clouds that smelled of rain and into where nested the stars that he knew in his death-knowledge were other suns. There, forming as a constellation, was the face of his mother, whom he had never known except now in the all-knowledge of death. It came to him that she was still alive, just hundreds of miles away from Ours, married, and free. She was free. The higher he went, the more he came to know, and with a spark's quickness, his true name came to him: Kwame Annan.

[10]

"My name Kwame Annan," Kwame said repeatedly, until what felt like crying came upon him, though it was simply the overwhelming sensation of being filled by the purple-black haze of the cosmos.

[11]

From the cosmos, he looked down onto the earth and into the purple-black haze of Ours's collective memory. The death-knowledge the dead have gifted to them swept through him, and the answer to a question he had not yet asked—"Forgiveness for whom?"—came fast in a flux of visions.

[12]

In a flux of visions, Kwame remembered what he once couldn't remember because he had been so long with it, like someone losing a pair of glasses that all morning rested at the top of his head. So long with it and it so long with him, until every rejection, every instance of loneliness, crept him closer to his immaculate suicide. He watched as the universe showed him Thylias scrubbing the walls and floor with a wash Saint gave her. She scrubbed, deadpan, so quiet it was vulgar, even after Kwame's old, dried blood browned the suds. 'Forgiveness,' he thought, 'for everyone and myself for all I did."

[13]

The moment he forgave himself for all he had done, he began to dissipate. Uniting with the endlessness, a vision fell upon him: war. Somehow, he had to send a warning to Ours that visitors with cruel intentions were heading their way. Time was limited, so he had to get it all in one try.

[14]

With limited time, he tried to get the message out all at once. He first gave the approaching war a name, because "war" alone carried the weight of all wars. He called it Feardom. He then had to tell them when to be ready. His feet started to fade, then his shins, his knees, the roundness of his belly. Right when erasure gripped his neck, he called out to the first person that came to mind: Aba. By the time his mouth and nose faded, he realized the horrendous mistake he had made. Back in Ours, flowers offered no scent to evening's altar, and the musk of neighbors' horses fell into the ruts of shadows.

Part Three

· CHAPTER 18 ·

White Sheets

[1]

Frances had questions for which Saint wasn't prepared. They spoke near-whisper, each word articulated carefully because they wanted to be careful with each other, finally, this time.

Frances wanted to know where Selah and Naima came from, and why they could do what they could do. Saint said she promised not to ask the man who brought her the twins where they came from, given only their birthday and names. She told Frances that Son arrived with the twins on his raft "just like you and Joy. Son been around a long time. He is both child of and husband to that river. I never see him far into land, but I know he gets there on his own time."

Frances nodded. "So, he asked you to take the girls?" She waited with rapt earnestness.

Saint stirred her tea with a fingertip. 'Still hot,' she thought, 'we just sat at this table and already she's asking me the stone questions.' She had been demanding that Frances share everything with her, no matter the sting, no matter the blood. And here they were, open finally, in the pleasantries of afternoon tea, the twins outside playing, and Joy somewhere not-there to interrupt them with sulk and sigh. Saint felt more secretive than ever.

It seemed to her that Frances wanted a kinship. She knew little about sisterhood. Essence those years ago came the closest, and the many women Saint met throughout her adult life disregarded her, revered her too intensely, or hated her.

"What you willing to lose, girl?" Saint asked herself aloud, not meaning to, and Frances didn't move. If she heard, she didn't let Saint know, and Saint couldn't tell if this made Frances more or less trustworthy. There still existed a hint of suspicion: a gap sat in the story of how Frances and Joy escaped from New Orleans. She knew the men had come to kill them all. But why?

"I will tell you if you finish your story."

"Which one? Told so many by now," Frances said.

"About the white men who came to the boardinghouse. What they want?"

"Wasn't just white men."

"What you mean? You said they came into the house and kill—"

"Was all kinds of men. A few was white. Was a couple Africans and a Indian. All kinds came to the party."

"What tribe?"

"India. From over the ocean."

"What he doing over here?"

"Killing women, looked to me. Wasn't just cause the women had African in them, either. Was that the women was women."

Saint tilted her head. "I'm sure them having African blood didn't help."

"Didn't."

"And is that what you call it where you from? A party?"

"Where I'm from I don't know nothing about, except that the water hold me. What I'm calling it is what it was. They raided our home with a smile, Saint. What you want me to call it?"

"Something with more blood in it," Saint said. "Party sounds jubilant."

"There's blood enough for me in my mind. What you need to see it for?"

"To know it was there. To know it was there," Saint said, her back straight against the chair.

"I'm telling you it was there and I'm telling you it's in here, too," Frances said, pointing to her head.

Saint blew air hard from her nose. "All right."

"You don't believe me," Frances said. "You never have. Feel like I'm locked up in my own mind until I say one truth you willing to believe because I say it how you want to hear it."

"Don't put your words where they don't belong. I believe you."

"And I don't know why the men killed them. Because they wanted to? What reason folks have chopping off a man's length and saving it in a jar?"

Saint grimaced. "The folks doing that are white folks. And we know why they do it. You said there were others there. Not every hurt have the same reason behind it, Frances."

Frances leaned back and cocked her head, an invitation, a challenge. "So, what make a man who look like me want to hurt me?"

"Envy, of course," Saint said.

"You think a white man cutting off a Negro's prick ain't about envy?"

Saint smiled with one side of her mouth. "We may all do violence, but we don't do it the same way. You do violence with the same heart you love with. The way that brings you closer to yourself." Wind blew hard. The house creaked, then settled into itself. Outside, the twins screamed and laughed.

Frances pushed an index finger down on the table. "Does lynching work for you? Is that a better word? Would that make a thing that ain't happen to you more believable?"

"I believe you," Saint said once more. "I have nothing more to say."

Frances lowered her head as though thinking, then nodded once, her eyes down in her lap. "You better than these lies you tell," Frances said in a low voice that acknowledged there would be no apology from Saint, no reconsideration of tone or phrasing. That wasn't Saint's way. What she offered was, perhaps, bigger than niceties, than social graces that so often proved to be insincere, but it didn't do the work of embracing who sat on the other side. Saint saved time, going straight to what could be done and doing it. She was neither sorry nor a liar. So she began:

"I asked Son for twins. Years before you got here. I sensed something was coming. Someone. There was danger in the coming and I needed to prepare. My gifts fail more and more. Some days I can hardly see what's before my own eyes, let alone what's to come. A man come up to my house and left a bag of dead snakes by the stairs. I should've seen him coming. Luckily, I saw him burn my house down in a vision before he did it; I just didn't know when he was leaning to do it. Not really. It just came to me, and I knew I had to leave that old place and come here to this open land, to build this house just for the occasion of losing the other.

"Aba left the dead snakes. Burned my house down, too. He seem to think the snakes belonged to me. He'd be right in some ways. Wrong in others. Who knows what he think now. He won't speak." She continued, telling Frances of how a watermelon conjure that went on for too long turned against her and killed Honor and King without her wanting it to. "Almost took Justice, too."

Frances's finger anchored her to the table. The whole time she kept quiet, and Saint kept talking faster, the stories hardened in her made butter-soft in Frances's company.

"Before that, when Ours was new, I had everyone go to the creek over yonder. They danced, naked as birds. Had to learn how to use their bodies again. Had to learn they *could* use their bodies again. Had to sweat out all the filth that didn't belong to them. Get it out their veins, their skin, and put it in the water. Send that slavery sickness someplace else and be new. Then years passed and Mrs. Wife fell ill. I was sent for to help her get back right. They said she had a fever. A fever? That's all you called me for? I thought it was something too little for me. I wanted to say, 'Make her some tea and get up off my porch.' But when I went to see her for myself, I smelled more than sickness and saw a man's face with red eyes where Mrs. Wife's face should've been. After I got everybody out the house, the spirit inside Mrs. Wife lit me up. Told me to close the gate. Called me a whore. Spat on the floor. Took Mrs. Wife's soul right along with it. Cigar smoke poured out that woman's mouth. You hear me? When she was alive, she wouldn't put nothing past her lips unless it was on a spoon.

"I've seen the insides of folks' skulls splatter the heel of my boot. I know the warmth of that same splatter on my face. I know more ways to take a life than to save one, and I hesitate none-at-all when I need to make a choice that would break anybody else. I know the color of a throat opened from here"—Saint slid a fingernail from the left side of her neck—"to here"—to the right—"because I did the cutting.

"That spirit taking Mrs. Wife's whole life with it just to spite me gave me deep fright and told me all I needed to know about myself; I was small; I couldn't help the people I was meant to help; I needed help; and that's why I asked for twins to protect me from you. Then you come and show me you hardly even know yourself, who or what you are. We a house full of fools."

Saint heard herself getting louder but couldn't stop talking. She said, "How would you know what I am when you don't know yourself? Don't tell me what I'm better than, Frances. You don't know a thing about my qualities. You don't know my talents. Don't even know your own. Not well enough to tell the truth about them. Not well enough that your own life don't become a lie before your eyes and mine." 'That's enough,' Saint thought. "Don't you ever." That's enough. That's enough.

Frances lifted her finger from the table and cleared her throat. "I—" she started. She looked over to the stove. Steam lifted from the teakettle. She went to it and poured the hot water into a large bowl, grabbed a rag that hung from a hook on the wall, and sat the bowl of steaming water in front of Saint's feet. She untied the thin strings of

Saint's boots and slid them off. She touched the thin fabric of her dark stockings, the color of coffee, and pulled down on the stubborn streams from the sides of Saint's calves, down past the ankles, and off from her toes. There wasn't much water, but it carried enough heat for ten feet. Saint looked on with a perplexed glare, still stuck in the molasses of her anger and too confused by Frances's quick hands, gloves and all, changing the world with her nimble fingers.

"You've known places," Frances said. "We all know somewhere inside ourselves we never thought we'd know. Dusky places. Places more ancient than God." She lifted Saint's right leg just above the bowl of water and began to wash her feet. "But your feet ain't been nowhere my feet would be 'shamed to walk." There was something regal to Saint about Frances wearing those gloves while getting between the crevices of her toes.

Frances buffed Saint's toenails with a rag till they shined and squeaked. Water dripped down Saint's heel, and circles radiated where the drops fell into the bowl. Sisterhood made more sense to Saint: Essence, over one hundred years ago, had washed Saint's entire body like this the day she was found off the Apalachicola. If that wasn't friendship, sisterhood, and love, then nothing else in the world had definition. Nothing else had a name to behold.

Frances began humming a melody-less tune in a feathery alto burnished by all she had come to know. It came out crooked, full of sad notes that curved in and out of happier ones. Saint thought she felt the vibrations of Frances's humming travel up from the soles of her feet to her belly, then to her chest, and up through her neck until she, too, started humming along with Frances, who took her time washing Saint's feet toe to sole and back again. What began as a tickle that made Saint wonder what her childhood was like became a life-fortifying balm. That she had feeling down there, after all these years of walking, standing, running, and kicking skulls like acorns surprised her.

Even while wearing gloves, Frances's touch carried energy. No need to return to the past—not all the way—but a little past could be beneficial, to bring back from the depths of the disreputable an ounce of light. Saint bore no calluses on the bottoms of her feet; rather time itself sucked away all sensation. Feet were for travel, nothing more. Now, Frances showed her there was more life yet to be reminded of, more once-upon-a-time to embrace with a girlhood's care for novelty and possibility.

Frances stood behind Saint and unwrapped the fabric from around her hair. She took the loose root of a loc and began to twist.

"Who taught you how?" Saint asked.

"You teaching me," Frances said, moving on to another loc. "You got beeswax? Honey?"

"Honey would make a mess. Beeswax. Jar on the floor by the cornmeal. No. Under the window."

"How you get the wax to stay soft?"

"Sunlight." Saint waited a while before asking, "What did you mean saying I'm teaching you?"

Frances rubbed beeswax on Saint's new growth, tugging then twisting the hair between her fingers until it rolled tight like a thin cigar. "I feel you in my heart, like a rhythm telling me how you want me to do it."

Outside, behind the house where Saint allowed plants to grow wild though not uncultivated, for she had planted most of what grew back there, the twins listened to Saint and Frances hum while they harvested the fecund plants of red and white clover and milk thistle, the latter of which pricked their fingers and clung to their dresses. Sweet smells from the flowers filled the air. Bees landed on the anthers of violets until their legs took on the bright dust of pollen, which they carried from plant to plant, one carrying what it fetched from a flower to Naima's hair, then away it went.

The girls listened until the singing stopped, and one person started to cry. Naima said she heard Frances crying. Selah believed Saint had begun to cry. They bickered for a while until Selah suggested that they both cried in unison, and that it was just part of the song. Naima frowned, saying that it was "unpossible" to cry the same way at the same time as somebody else. "Can't no sadness be sad the same as somebody else's," she said. Then the crying stopped and the girls were left with the sound of flies buzzing in their ears, the sweet smell displaced by the powerful stench of a dead rodent nearby. They had been distracted, had missed the rot stench and the flies signaling the dead's presence amid song and tears. Now, between Selah and Naima, the two worlds refused to merge.

[2]

A nap glued Saint to her seat in the kitchen, day-warm. Her bare feet, renewed by Frances's touch, tingled with a new life and the new life stirred her awake. She heard movement in the other room, human sounds of throat clearing and page turning, and carefully brought herself to standing. Abandoning her chair, she found Frances sitting by an open window, attempting to read torn-out pages from a medicine journal, *Atalanta Journal of Medicine and Psychology*, vol. XVI, South Carolina, 1852:

Affidavit toward a Theory of Necromania Temporalis Aethiopica

by Dr. Malachi R. Brown

> I propose and duly support present and future study of a theory of "dead-time" more appropriately documented under the variation "necromania temporalis aethiopica" the black obsession with the death of time . . . Following the erudition of Dr. Samuel Cartwright's invaluable location of drapetomania and dysaethesia . . . the negro's mental incapability of comprehending time and learning how to process and document time's passing persuade him to move at an erratic pace while working, to sleep during disallowed hours . . . to run away . . . to suffer from uncontrollable gluttony, and to show difficulty in learning

> commands and skills otherwise simple for domesticated animals . . . They show a fear of waking up at proper times, as their minds are incapable of understanding the linear principles of civilized temporality. To "kill time" is a negro pastime because to appreciate time is to understand how it engenders life. Thus, it can be argued that to understand time is as principled and ethical a knowledge as understanding the difference between life and death. Therefore, the negro can be subsumed in a category between the living and the dead . . .

Frances hadn't looked up from the page when Saint entered the room. She remained entranced by the words there, many of which were new to her, no more readable than a sequence of black crumbs. Saint watched Frances slide her finger beneath each sentence and wherever she paused, Saint said the word aloud and gave a quick definition: "Theory, an unproven idea . . . plethora, that means an amount more than needed . . . drapetomania, that is something that does not exist anywhere else outside of the white mind." Saint assisted this way, standing over Frances until they both finished reading the entire article. Waiting for some reaction, Saint placed her hand on the chair back and shifted her weight off her renewed feet. Not long after, Frances returned to the beginning of the article and said she didn't understand.

Saint explained that she found the journal in Delacroix and purchased it on a whim. After reading through its pages, she came across Dr. Malachi R. Brown's article and found it so dimwitted it was humorous, so offensive it rivaled unreality. In fact, her meeting Frances and experiencing those inexplicable shifts in time helped her to realize time was a fallacy that protected those for whom obedience to imaginary limits reigned supreme, organizing chaos without undoing it.

"Protection from whom?" was the question that for Saint bore the same answer regardless of the day, hour, minute, or second. Fear of the Negro knew no bounds because time knelt at the feet of the Negro who had no end, only an unencumbered and endless beginning. For Dr. Brown, his followers, and silent detractors, the ongoing preoccupation with the Negro gave no hint of breaking because the Negro gave no hint of breaking. 'Who, then,' Saint thought, 'was the true slave?'

As if on cue, Saint heard the clop of a horse outside as Reverend rode up to her house.

[3]

No one had come to Reverend's church, and no one listened to his outdoor preaching on doom and inferno. He shouted as though on fire, and most passed by his burning. Some nodded politely while others snickered and shook their heads, amused and pitying. Off to this errand. Off to that one. They were a busy bunch, Reverend noticed. Not much for noticeable sins. Ever since he made Ours home, he had seen only a couple scuffles. One over a pig invading a neighbor's garden and another between two men over a woman who wanted nothing to do with either. Mostly, the Ouhmey kept the peace, kept working, and tended to their own affairs. Folks invited him to dinner or out fishing, and he bored his hosts. No one asked how his day was because his conversation remained frozen in religious persecution. The young women who found him physically attractive turned heels when he complimented them then raucously announced their lack of love for God. He spoke passionately, which they loved, but about one thing. There was nothing else he knew, and he didn't yet know that there was more to know.

Folks had always known the children in town loved to tease him, and he let them, sometimes played along with them, and that alone proved his heart. If he saw someone holding an infant, his cheeks swelled into smile and he would stop mid-ramble and ask if he could "just hold him for a little while," and they had let him. Sometimes he cried a little at the soft weight of a new life. But then he had to give the infant back to the parents, back into the vacuum of their adult silence. Without somebody's baby in his arms, he was no longer of interest.

Reverend felt trapped, closed off from all the other adults in town, so it became more important to him as the days surged on that he deliver his community into the waiting arms of the Lord.

Knowing they needed a shepherd was one thing, but he knew they couldn't see in the Lord the shepherd of their needs because already in place stood a false prophet. He was convinced Saint had become for them the Alpha and Omega, discouraging interest from the Good Book with a wave of her serpent-wrapped staff. Eventually, after months of being intimidated and shunned, Reverend built up the nerve to see the false prophet herself. He put on his good overalls, grass stains be damned, watered and saddled his horse, and headed out toward Saint's house.

"AFTERNOON," Reverend said, and smiled big. He stopped his horse and grabbed two Bibles from a sack tied to the saddle. Saint waited just short of the bottom step. Her companion looked straight ahead from the top of the stairs, flies landing on his emotionless face. "I got God's word for you and your husband," Reverend said, and held out the two Bibles to Saint, who turned her head away from him but kept her eyes steady on him. Though Reverend saw the blade in her look, he savored more his own confidence in the Lord. He read her outrage as shame surfacing from her sins and felt encouraged to press on.

"Husband?" Saint asked.

"Yes, ma'am," Reverend said, just smiling away while Saint looked at the books, then looked back at Reverend with steely indignation. "Your husband right up there." It was silly to think that a woman wouldn't know which of her only-husband was referred to, let alone where he was standing, yet Reverend pointed to her companion, believing Saint had a husband to point to.

"I beg your pardon?" Saint looked full on at Reverend, who lowered his smile and cleared his throat, hoping that alone would clarify. As he spoke about the man on her porch, how he was happy that so many people in Ours had found themselves with God-sent love, Saint stared at him as though an elephant's trunk grew from his forehead, until she finally touched her chest, squinted, and said again, "I. Beg. Your pardon?"

Reverend's horse stomped impatiently in the dirt. The heat was nearing unbearable.

"Well," Reverend said. He realized his arm burned from exhaustion. He had been holding the Bibles up to Saint the entire time. Saint didn't touch them.

"You can keep your Bibles. I have my own. Several, heartier versions," she said, and turned to head back upstairs to the front door.

"What about your husband?"

Saint stopped. There was rain in her voice as she spoke with her back facing Reverend. "You should be on your way." When she reached the top of the stairs, she wished Reverend a pleasant day and her companion stepped to the side to follow her into the house. He shut the door behind them.

Reverend sat the Bibles at the bottom of the stairs. He turned away from them, and Saint's door flew open. "You forgot something on the stairs," Saint shouted down to him. She didn't step outside. She didn't blink.

Reverend nodded in her direction, took his Bibles, and headed away into the blazing afternoon. Saint stood in her doorway until the man and his cart were a speck down the road.

"You not gone tell him the Bible he got a slave's Bible?" Frances asked. She had made a plate of toast and marmalade, enough to feed a nation. Saint grabbed a slice.

"What Bible's not a slave's Bible? If a slave hold it, then it's a slave's Bible," Saint said.

"But he missing most of the books and don't even know it." Frances chuckled and took a bite. "Bible so thin he can slide it down his ass crack."

"That's what he should do with it. Get off my porch and out my way. Talking about 'your husband.'"

Frances said, "Well, why can't he be your husband. He fit to it. He clean up after everybody, hammer the crooked straight and the straight crooked. Sound like a husband to me."

"Fit to it? You more fit to be my husband than he is."

"Where he come from, then, Saint?" Frances had gotten serious again, and her body stiffened in the chair, anxious to hear a response, so rabbitlike she froze in waiting for the answer to come with the fangs she knew it would have.

Saint licked the top row of her teeth. "You tell me." She smirked, then grabbed another piece of toast on her way back out the front door. "Or if it suit you," she added, nodding toward her companion, "ask him. Let me know what he say when he say it."

Back when she was alive, Eloise had taken to Frances with ease, trusting her to take over Joy's shooting lessons and escort her to the French Market during free time. She shared, too, with Frances where she hid the journal that contained the invisibility conjure. The only other person who knew the journal's location was Amelia, and with them both dead, while Joy packed her belongings, Frances opened the upper door to the grandfather clock in the parlor and retrieved the small journal. Everywhere she went, she kept it with her, buried in a pant pocket or tucked inside her winter coat. Its pages no wider than her hand and the handwriting tiny and close to unreadable.

During the night, back in the frozen cabin with the dead bodies, Frances read what she could of it by firelight while Joy slept away her fatigue. She came across a word she didn't know. It had been written as a folktale, all "once there was a . . ." and "moral o' the story is . . ." as if transcribed from somebody talking it out. A children's tall tale to keep them from being naughty.

Before Saint reached the front door, Frances said, "Quiet as he is. Most of the time he just doing what you tell him to do, but . . ." Frances looked for the right words. "Seem like he waiting on something."

Without pausing, Saint looked over her shoulder. "For the beginning of one world after the first world stop belonging," she said.

Frances fingered the notebook in her pocket, searching for a page in the dark to explain the dark.

[4]

Back in Ours, a dejected Reverend had made it home, and just after he had tied up his horse, someone tapped him in the middle of his back. Out of breath, a young boy, no older than six or seven, stood before him holding a dirty red rag in his hand. The boy dabbed his face of sweat with the rag and shared that something was wrong with Aba.

"Mr. Reverend! Mr. Reverend," the boy repeated, punctuating the ends of his sentences with the man's name. Hearing it renewed Reverend's energy. "Mr. Aba acting out of his way, Mr. Reverend."

When Reverend asked, "What way?" the boy grabbed his hand and pulled him to Aba's house. "Who boy is you? This my first time seeing you round here," Reverend asked the boy.

"I'm everybody's boy," the boy said, and pointed to Aba's house. "But my mama name Zerlinda Anastacia Dawn but everybody call her Mama Dawn."

The name sounded complicated and unfamiliar, yet it impressed Reverend, so he thought about little else. They stopped right outside Aba's yard. "And what's your name?"

The boy pointed to Reverend's house and looking in that direction said, "Chi my name."

"Chi? What kind of name is that?"

"Will you help, Mr. Reverend?"

"What's wrong with him?"

The weed-trees had grown into green, jagged monstrosities in front of Aba's house, blocking the facade entirely from view. Only the bottom few steps came into view, the first step protruding like a swollen lip from the austere carapace of leaves and branches drawing an arc over the short walkway. The boy wiped his face with the red rag, his sweat darkening it near-black, and said that he went to drop off a lunch plate and when Aba didn't open the door, he opened it himself and found the man on his back, mouthing at the ceiling, pulling his finger this way and that as if painting in the space above. "That was a long time ago and my mama told me to come back and see if he better. If what I saw didn't look right I was to tell her, but I'm telling you, Mr. Reverend."

Reverend told the boy to run along to his "mama with the pretty name," and to tell her that he was there to see to the issue. The boy thanked him and said goodbye. When he disappeared down the road, Reverend prayed before stepping into the dark shoal that was Aba's porch.

Inside, Aba was lying on his back, the house hot and dense with the scent of cooked onions and cabbage coming from the plate of food he hadn't touched. He moved an index finger like a paintbrush against the dark canvas of the distant ceiling. Sparse light broke through the curtain of leaves blocking the windows.

Reverend whisper-shouted the man's name, "Aba!" but Aba kept scribbling in the air. Reverend went over to him, knelt, and was about to pray but no words came. When he opened his mouth, instead of "Jesus please!" he shouted, "God damn it!" and covered his mouth. He apologized to God for briefly losing his way.

Aba continued scribbling in the air with his right hand and tapped rhythmically on the floor with his left. The rhythm quickened and became more intricate as he dropped his right hand, slapping it into the floor, too. The sound frightened Reverend until at the final beat, a fire of inspiration rose up in him. Before it could fill him completely, Aba stopped, blinked twice, and faced Reverend.

"What was all that banging about? What was the feeling you put up in me?" Reverend asked.

Aba rolled a bit on the floor. Reverend heard it creak. Aba scratched his sinuses and flared his nostrils.

"Forgot you can't talk. Food here for you but you need to let God work on you first, yes sir. I felt something was in you when you was moving your hand in the air like a sword of a righteous angel battle-ready for the Lord yes God but I wasn't verily able to see the power that was the Lord's handling of you and mis-saw your writing in the air as bedeviled but that angel went from your finger to your hand to your body-all-of-it and I ain't never felt a thing like that take me over in my whole of living. Your gift God-given just like Jesus was given to us on that cross on Calvary or any of our cousins hanging from a tree Jesus done come and gone day to day in many forms month after month in the field head full of cotton Lord and you whipped in the field and your blood spilled scripture in the wake of our labor Jesus Jesus Jesus . . ."

Reverend went on like this while helping Aba sit up against the wall. He placed the plate of cold food in his own lap and fed Aba bits at a time with a misshapen spoon the boy Chi had brought with the plate. Aba ate without complaint.

Inspired to talk by Aba's hands slapping music from the floor, Reverend spiraled into a rapid, labyrinthine testimony that only God knew the path of, all while spilling food on the floor in the distraction of his ecstasy. Eventually, Reverend stopped feeding Aba altogether and fed himself the cold meal during brief moments of reflection.

"You lit up something in me Aba I can't get Jesus off my mind you got Jesus in your hands," Reverend said. A breeze swept through the window across the room, swelling the sheer curtains and pushing branches into the window. Nature wanted in, it seemed to Aba as he tried to get his mind back right. He barely remembered waking up from a drunken afternoon nap to the night sky surrounding him and words falling into his ear, then the stars hissed down toward him, then the smoky swirls of light, the hard planets and their moons and rings of glowing dust—all thinned-out and rushed toward him as a line of pure energy. A message sat in the light, but he only remembered a part of it, "fear," so he found himself on the floor connecting the sundry dots of the stars that remained in the galaxy, wondering if connecting them would complete the message that he couldn't recall. The stars began to pulse and the pulse became a pattern. Aba patted the floor to get it right, to keep it in his body memory.

Then Reverend came in loud and wrong and broke the spell with all that "Loud talk," Aba creaked beneath himself but only he heard his complaint, "nonsense rambling about nonsense." Reverend broke the spell, then ate the man's food. Didn't matter that it was cold. It was Aba's. If Reverend had paid more attention to what was going on around him, to making sure Aba was in his right mind, to minding his own damn business in the first place, maybe, maybe—

But nature wanted in. The wind picked up and Aba smelled rain on its way. It took him too long to get Reverend out his house, and by the time he got privacy, it started pouring. Had Reverend left just a few minutes earlier, he could've beaten the downpour, but he insisted on staying, on hearing more of that "Jesus drumming," nearly begged Aba for it, but Aba wanted no part.

Instead, Aba took off his clothes and went out the back door. In the field that awaited him there, he strode into the fast-falling rain and tilted his head up, letting the rain blur his eyesight and fall into his nostrils. If the stars could tell him what he needed to know, then maybe the rain could deliver the rest of the message, too. He took a deep breath. He peed for a good while, releasing all the liquor that had dizzied him into a series of fantastic and grueling slumbers.

With a not so sober mind but a deeply sober heart, he listened to raindrops *shush* up the leaves and patter on a sheet of abandoned tin. He listened to how wind quickened the rhythm the rain made against everything it fell upon. The wind was the will of the beat, the rain and what the rain fell on the method.

Aba slammed an open palm to his wet chest and the bass-heavy slap burst through the hiss of the rain. He stomped his bare feet on the ground and drummed on his chest with his fists, then clapped. Thunder shouted back at him with a challenging roar, and he drummed his body in return. Back and forth the sky roared and hissed and Aba drummed and stomped. The sky spoke to him and he learned how to speak back. He opened his mouth wide, making the face of a man mid-scream, but the only sound that left him came from his hands and feet striking his body and the ground. The wingspan of his joy about took him to the treetops as he ran farther out into the field and dance-talked, interpreting the drums in the sky, the ancient and restless cymbals of rain crashing down all around him. For so long he had become a mere object in his own house, allowing the soulless nothings to speak for him. The squeaky chair, the door hinge that needed oil, the rickety steps all spoke in his stead. He had become no different than an assembly of wooden figures. Now he had another way. What Reverend felt in Aba's rhythmic floor slaps bridged Reverend to the cosmos, to a cosmology past his understanding. This is what the pulsating stars wanted to show him, that if he listened to the sky, he could speak with its voice.

[5]

June crept into July, which crept into August, and it was time for Saint to retrieve the protection charm from Luther-Philip. She summoned him on his final day of labor and wordlessly held out her hand. They didn't need to speak, and the boy took off the necklace and placed it in the center of her palm. Overcast, the hot day turning humid, the smell of rain teased the air. She told him to hurry home to beat the storm. He asked where Joy was and if he could see her, but Joy overheard from her seat in the front room, off to the side where she couldn't be seen, and didn't make herself known.

"Not today," Saint said. "Come back next week." Saint closed the door and turned to Joy. "You sure?" Joy nodded, looking straight ahead where no one stood.

Days before, Joy had laid her head on Luther-Philip's chest and listened while the grass beneath them took the shape of their lazing figures. The listening got to her, or she had already been taken in by the holding of hands, and in that state of rapture she longed to put the soft shell of her ear to his bony chest. Even her heart went dumb, matching its pace with what Joy heard coiling through her ear's tight spiral. Should've known then it was a storm, the way it spun into her and tore her up inside. Their backs to the grass, holding hands like children, until she rolled over and listened deeper than deep.

Luther-Philip never tried to do more than hold hands. She liked him more because of this. He never even touched her waist, let alone her breasts, though she turned herself toward him during the hand holding in the grass just to see how he would respond. When he only kissed her forehead, she took it as his way of being a gentleman. Her body—made utterly foreign to her by means of invisibility, only later to become uncontrollable as she sleepwalked with an unbreakable intent to kill—became knowable against Luther-Philip's warm body. She felt a liquid heat rise in her whenever he asked her a question about her interests, about what was medicinal and what was poisonous. By the time August rolled around, it was too late to return to the uninterrupted solitude she had longed to keep weeks before.

But the night before Luther-Philip was to return the necklace, a night terror of Joy killing him in his sleep rode her till the blood on her hands, so warm in the dream, woke her. She saw that her sweaty palms cupped sunlight that entered from the bedroom window. That morning, she decided to keep away from Luther-Philip from then on. He never did return to visit Joy on his own accord, which hurt her even more.

With Luther-Philip gone back down to Ours's mainland, Saint entered her divining room with an oil lamp and lit every candle. She poured out the contents of the charm's vial onto the table and looked for the stone. It was missing, and the wax seal she used to close the charm hadn't been previously broken. She couldn't remember what the stone's absence meant. Flipping through her journal, she found the page for the conjure that came to her in a flash of inspiration, then left her mind just as quickly. The meaning: "If the stone goes missing, then protection has failed."

For years, at a distance, Saint had watched Justice, fully aware of his anger that she assumed came from thinking she wanted to kill him. When he had asked if he could enter her house, nearly as wide as the door and strangely soft-spoken, it didn't shock her that a monster would bare its fangs and claws as it crawled down her fireplace and crept bipedal toward Justice. What shocked her is that the monster held Luther-Philip's decapitated head, presenting it to Justice like a trophy. His fear destroyed whom he loved. Justice had bolted out the door, unable to face himself as he truly was. Saint knew then to make the charm for Luther-Philip to protect him, but since it failed, she decided to visit Justice in person.

[6]

Joy recalled the order of events. Luther-Philip hadn't returned a week later as Saint suggested. Joy looked up and it was September. Her sorrow became suspicion. The timing of Luther-Philip's disappearance: first Saint gives him a necklace charm, then the closeness between her and Luther-Philip builds, then the charm's removal, and now where he gone to?

Joy took her broken heart and ghastly desperation to Saint by first snatching up a shovel from behind the house. When she entered the front door, she let the shovel's blade drop and scrape against the floor as she skulked from the threshold to the right side of the sunlit room, where Saint had made a small flower-filled sitting area. By the end of September, every flower would be dead.

With limited patience, Saint closed her journal, stoppered the inkwell, and faced Joy, who stood over her, heaving with implacable fury.

She expected an attack and wanted nothing more than for Joy to put her hands on her so that she may return the favor, but Joy let drop the shovel's handle near Saint's foot and said, "You have made me a dead woman." She searched Saint's face, heavy-breathing, her mouth trembling with the rest of the words she could hardly get out. "You have made me a dead woman before I could even become a woman."

Joy grabbed the shovel's handle, her gaze steady on Saint, and went to her room. The scraping sound of the blade against wood followed her as she dragged the tool to and up the stairs. It banged on each step, making the shovel's metal mouth chime, the toll of a rusted funeral bell.

What held Saint in place seemed to hold the light where it was, coming in from the window at the house's facade. "She never had a friend in her life," Saint said to herself. Anger, yes, would've made sense to Saint, but whatever *this* was that Joy expressed baffled her. Thinking she should tell Joy that Luther-Philip's distance was his own decision, Saint knew it wouldn't have made any difference. A broken heart builds broken thoughts. In her bafflement, Saint sat motionless until daylight turned orange with approaching evening.

[7]

Saint and Frances were amiable the rest of that summer. They avoided talking about their pasts and thus avoided the pain of hardly remembering them, though curiosity remained. Saint breathed easily around Frances, which allowed more room for laughter. Frances found herself calmed by the softer presence of the woman who had just a week or so ago locked her out of her bedroom.

Out of curiosity, one morning Frances left with the Delacroix wagon to see the town for the first time. With Franklin dead, Justice had taken up the task of driving the wagon. She didn't remember if she had met the young man before, but seeing him now brought a chill over her that belied the early-September heat. She climbed into the wagon with the others and Justice looked back at her over his shoulder, a threat in his eyes. Frances nodded hello to him. Justice glared, then turned away.

When they reached Delacroix, Frances cringed at the gas lampposts lining the streets, blank as dead trees. Large single-family houses occupied one block while on the next block merchants, bankers, insurers, lawyers, and various custodians of the earth and state scrambled into and out of two-story buildings hooded by entablatures supported with capitals that squared off at the top, leaving way for smooth columns to drop down to the base. Every place was built to appear more important than it really was, but the columns gave the look of self-righteous prison cells more than anything else. Even the slaughterhouse, an out-of-place barnlike structure with a gaping hole in the front as its workstation, carried the air of haughty importance.

She stepped off the wagon onto the cobblestone road and nearly twisted her ankle on its unevenness. Before she could look back to see if Justice glared at her clumsiness, he had already signaled to the horse to move along.

Frances came all this way to see what the fuss was about, wondering why Negroes who didn't have to work a day in their lives would choose to in a town not their own. She had asked a few Ouhmey on the ride up why they labored in Delacroix, and the answers were similar: "To keep busy," "To make saving money," "It's just good sometimes to get out of Ours. Not a nearer place that would have us with our living breath." Someone added to that "Or our dead breath," and the wagon broke into laughter and "You sho' right. Not then especially!" They wanted a good life and believed preparing for it outside of Ours gave them a better chance. Frances disagreed.

Frances believed Delacroix's issues distracted the Ouhmey from what needed to be done in Ours. Why was Mr. Edwards tampering with gas streetlamps up in Delacroix when he could help get started a road of lights in Ours? Why did Ms. Glory make shoes just for them to be sold under a white man's name? If they want to keep busy, Frances thought, they got plenty to do in Ours.

Frances returned to Delacroix the following day to deepen her investigation. The streets clamored with noise, and the putrid smell of slaughtered pigs, human piss, and dog shit assaulted her nose. A man whipped his horse across the side of its face because it wouldn't move from the water trough. A sick woman lay out in the middle of the road while grown men and women called her names from the other side of the street. When the children mimicked their behavior, the adults chastised them and chased them away with kicks and curses.

Before she could take it all in, she saw someone from Ours carrying a load of dirty sheets. It was a young girl Frances had seen escorting an elder from the women's meeting in Ours. Madame Jenkins had invited Frances to the meeting, and she accepted graciously. When she arrived, dressed in a pant suit with a white shirt unbuttoned at the first button, she sat amongst the other women, who wore their best dresses to the occasion. They were mostly welcoming. Some giggled. Others hid their smirks behind cups of tea. The topic was "medicine," but what the women discussed had little to do with chemistry, ointments, or home remedies. They spoke of the heart, the mind, and the spirit. Frances listened all night to these women, some who were born into freedom, others who were brought into it by Saint. Maman Cosi was the oldest woman there, sharing that she was eighty-seven years old and remembered the day she stepped foot on American soil as a six-year-old girl: "Soon as my naked feet touched down on the harbor, I forgot my language, you know. Just like that. My name, my home name, my word for 'love,' gone. And I knew then, at six years old, was lot more loss heading my way.

"When we talk bout medicine, we first got to talk bout what the body need, what the body want, and what the body had taken away. When we come here as slaved peoples, from all over Africa, we come here with Africa in us. The air we breathed there. The food we grow from dirt there. The sounds we heard from the sky to a baby's cry. Everything we made up of is Africa. I know some people 'fraid of the Bible, but I say this to you, young people. How Adam was made from clay and God's 'magination, God made us the same way. We all got African water coursing through us and African dirt packed up in our muscles. Even our bones full of dark, dark earth of where we come from. And can you believe what the dirt here in this new land did to my remembrance? Here, our bodies was made of the land itself. Land not our land. Land that don't know or love us. The plantation covered our flesh, and everything we did belonged to the one who held us like he would a tomato, a tobacca plant, a piece of cotton. I know of a time when I was picking potatoes from the ground and looked like I was taking my own head off and satting it in my basket, over and over again. Was the madness of the land burrowing in me.

"And they treated our bodies like they treated the land. Explored us! They explored us cause we was no different to them than the unknown west. It took me becoming free again—cause I was born that way and made to forget—to gain back my remembrance. All my Africa-self came back to me in 1834. I was old then and older now. Freedom was the medicine that give me back to myself, you know. I was born free, and I'll be buried in my good grave free."

The evening neared its end, and Frances felt compelled to share. "All I know of my people is that they in the water." A couple women snapped open their fans and cooled themselves with tilted heads and suspicious eyes. Others were outwardly confused, lips pursed to conceal questions they didn't know how to ask. A handful of women nodded politely, while a handful more openly revealed a complex, heavy-lidded anger. Madame Jenkins ended the night on Frances's words.

It was a long walk back to Saint's and Frances felt shamed away from that place. She would've become embittered against those women if not for Maman Cosi, who called to her before she made it too far. "They all our people, even down there," the woman said, then nodded to the teenage girl whose arm was linked up with hers at the elbow.

They made their way deeper into town, blending in with the late-evening crowd of oil lamps.

When Frances saw this same girl who nights before helped Maman Cosi through the crowd but now carried sheets so soiled that she could see the filth thirty feet away, a door slammed in her head, then another, and another. Frances observed the girl until the girl entered the back of a building and didn't return. Frances waited the time it took for the girl to wash the sheets and watched her hang them on a line outside. And she watched a man who had just left the bank sneeze into his hand, walk out of his way to the glistening white sheets—still wet from wash, the perfumed scent of which carried over to where Frances stood—and wipe his grimy hands on one of the corners. Frances watched the girl watch him do it, the girl then shocked into soundlessness, into a posture of humiliation her body would remember till the day she died. Frances sat silent on the ride back to Ours, her own shoulders slumped, her face buried in the dark between her knees.

Frances spoke with Saint later that evening at the dinner table with an air of growing agitation. Joy and the twins looked on as the two women debated. Saint nodded and chewed as Frances made her point. But the words came too fast and before she could stop herself, Frances had begun to raise her voice.

"They could be doing good work here for themselves and each other, Saint. They go up there and them white folks turn they noses down on them. If your conjure wasn't on them, they'd have lynched them clean from the earth by now. And what happens when your conjure wear off? You said so yourself your gift be here one day and gone the next. Who's to say when that day come for Delacroix? It's not safe up there for them."

"They decide where they want to go, Frances. I force no one to stay here. You know that. They decided they wanted to work and make a living. They decided they wanted to get out of Ours every so often and see a place different from this one. You want them to go crazy staying cooped up in this small town?" Saint said. "They need more than just here."

"I want them to believe in what they got here. There's a world here. You can show them that."

"Every day they wake up and teach the children their letters and numbers, bake bread and shuck corn, repair what's broken and heal who's sick. What on earth you think they do with their lives? Suckle white babies all damn day?"

"Might as well."

"You watch yourself, Frances. These people you call 'your' people have the right to move in this world how they want. They want to go up to Delacroix and make money and feel a part of something, so be it. I don't like it. But I decided to make it easier for them to—"

Frances stood. "These my people just as much as anybody else."

"These my people long 'fore you got here. You better keep it clean. That's the end of that. Have a seat or take yourself out of the air's way. Can't nobody eat with you breathing over them."

"You can't just leave people behind, Saint. You can't just leave them to die!" Frances said, surprised that she had said it, despite the hurt coming from a place hidden and burning her, a torturer's torch against the face of a traitor.

As the two argued, the twins faced whoever spoke, their heads turning at the sound of the other's voice. Joy played with her food.

"So we not on the same side?" Frances asked.

"You imagined the sides," Saint said. "You imagined the war. Now sit down or leave. Pick what side of *that* you want to be on."

Frances chose the front door, leaving Saint to consider how nothing was ever purely sudden. Every feeling had a history that could unbury the dead and still find some life.

· CHAPTER 19 ·

Deluge

[1]

Weeks before Luther-Philip returned Saint's necklace, Justice closed his eyes and entered his heart without meaning to. He never aimed to visit that dark realm, but it rarely alarmed him when he opened his eyes and its familiar darkness overtook what was once a verdant landscape, his quiet bedroom, or his own dirty palms.

Inside his heart, the black sand, black water lake, and black sky were only distinguishable by how the white moon reflected off the water, showing the surface's ripples in white lines. White flowers grew from the black sand, their six petals in tight clusters giving off their own light, which was the whiteness itself. He heard the water sweep the shore and from the other side of the lake a mighty growl reached him. He wasn't afraid of the growling, though he had never seen the animal within him that made the sound. His heart drummed, black water trembled, and the light upon it receded farther from the shore. As the water receded, the growling grew louder, meaning its source drew nearer.

Justice noticed his heart's lake shrink the first night Luther-Philip didn't beat the sun home after working at Saint's. Luther-Philip came back smelling like grass, hands swollen purple, yellowjacket stings bulging from his arms. And a smile. All that pain and a smile. When Justice asked where he had been, he just smiled harder, rubbed Justice on the top of his head, and said, "In the Garden of Eden." Justice knew there was an Eve in that story, and he wondered for a hard, long time who she was in Luther-Philip's life.

From then on, Luther-Philip came home late at night and every night that Justice asked where he was, he responded with something cunning, until finally he asked his father about Joy. The tide receded then, and the growling pierced through Justice with a clarion's power. Not only was Luther-Philip working for Saint, but he was also building a friendship there, getting comfortable, like a second home.

The more time Luther-Philip spent away with Joy, the worse Justice acted around the house. Temperamental outbursts, cracking eggshells into the batter, dragging and slamming furniture around as if the very legs and surfaces of the chairs and tables had been chained to him and only a feral shaking could rid him of their restraints. Until Mr. Wife grabbed him by the arm and told him he had to get his own house if he wanted to abuse what little they had.

"We don't got much as is. Why take away more from the little we got?" Mr. Wife said.

Justice would be fine for a day, a day and a half, until he again couldn't take seeing a grinning Luther-Philip enter the door at night. Justice's anger stretched itself all over the house. That's how he ended up a block south in his own place, which everyone in Ours thought was long overdue and hoped next that Luther-Philip, too, would find his own house just to give Mr. Wife the rest he deserved.

In Justice's new home, the furniture was sprawled across the floor, left behind in disarray after the last resident's hasty leave, the fabric musty and filth-ridden with under-use. Sunlight revealed clouds of dust climbing the air. A damp smell of rotten wood haunted the room farthest back. In the bedroom stood a bed mounted on a torso-less beast with bronze feet carved into leopard claws and over which a sheer veil hid the bed. On sight, the dismal mattress seemed to Justice an elevated and occupied grave.

Dead leaves imprinted onto the glass their veiny patterns. From a broken front window, breeze entered like breath.

It took Justice three weeks to clean up the house because he refused any help offered to him. He tore down the back wall where mold had taken its toll and rebuilt it with his own stubborn labor, bound by pride to his work. He fortified the new wall with clay at the base and insulated it with hay, mud, and more clay packed densely against the wall. In front of the new wall, he built another wall, sandwiching the earthly materials between. The idea came to him to keep animals from chewing and sneaking into the house with ease, but it would also make this room the coolest in the summer and warmest in the winter. By the middle of September, he had finished rebuilding the entire backroom's walls, keeping the black water lake in his heart steady as he forgot about Luther-Philip in his labor.

Until he led a trip to Delacroix and saw Frances climb into the wagon for the first time. He recognized Frances by description only, having never formally met the man, but knew immediately who he was when he stepped one long leg onto the wagon and helped the others get in after him. Justice knew Frances as Joy's caretaker, both of whom lived with Saint in her ghost house on the outskirts of town. The black water lake in Justice's heart trembled at the sight of hearsay becoming flesh, as the much-gossiped-about man looked Justice in the eye and gave what appeared to be the most dishonest expression Justice had ever seen. A smile, unwarranted, unasked for, and from a friend of the woman whom he had never forgiven. The waters of his heart shrank from the shore. Justice, with uncontrollable resentment, scowled back at Frances and returned to face the dull path ahead.

Ever since Justice moved to his new home, he hadn't seen Luther-Philip, so he didn't know how to feel when after returning the wagon and horse to their post, he saw his old friend sitting in a rocking chair on Justice's porch, drinking a glass of water he must have carried with him from his own home, for Justice recognized the glass and swore, too, that he recognized the water as being Mr. Wife's water: special with a familiar glint caused by the sun striking the glass just right. Justice, suddenly a ten-year-old boy again, grinned, though he wanted to shout his friend to hell and back. Instead, he hugged him fiercely and, with a small voice, asked where he had been.

They spoke for hours—"Joy went away," Luther-Philip said disinterestedly; "This house almost rode me to early death," Justice said—until it was early afternoon and hunger struck them both. Luther-Philip asked if he could come inside.

Justice's house was immaculate. Spotless. Fresh-smelling. Plants hung from hooks on the ceiling and from hooks on the walls. Pots and pans shined from where they hung above the wood-burning oven, the cast-iron skillet just oiled the night before. The furniture the white folks had left behind was gorgeous and soft. He had scrubbed the upholstery of the two large chairs and one sofa with lavender soap for nearly an hour. The table, holding on its dense back a wooden bust of a Negro woman, stood atop a bright red rug spiraled with the insignia of fleur-de-lis surrounded by a blue-and-gold spiral motif. When he showed Luther-Philip the bedroom, he pointed out the leopard paws, calling them wolf claws, and said how sometimes at night he felt the bed move around the room, then right out the front door into the woods. He didn't share that last night when this happened, the bed carried him over to the lake where he and Luther-Philip hadn't been in some time. He had dipped his toes into the water and when he felt the water's chill, he was back in his room, feet cold and wet at the tips.

Luther-Philip kept visiting Justice the following days, telling Justice that he wanted a house of his own, too. There were a few still unoccupied that would need cleaning up or he could build himself a new one, Justice told him. "Up to you," he said. "You decide what you want in life." And just as he said it, his heart shook.

Justice considered this as he poured stew into a bowl for Luther-Philip, as he watched the young man eat out the carrots one by one, and as he said goodbye and waved to his friend heading down the road and out of sight. He waved even after it stopped making sense to.

AUTUMN SNAPPED GREEN quick from the trees, leaving behind gasps of gold and red on the branches. In the morning, limbs from an overgrown bush tapped on the glass as if to wake Justice. Flat red leaves brushed against the windowpane, then pulled away. He imagined red leaves as bloody fists that left red smears against the window. The thought kept him awake all night.

By September's end, Justice took a sharp knife to the knocking branches, sawing away what beckoned at sunrise and moonglow for entrance. Then Justice's bedroom fireplace gave to the room a sound that the knocking branches had distracted him from: cinders hissing like a stern whisper.

His shotgun house consisted of a front room where he read and cooked, connected to his bedroom with the sleeping cat of a bed, and ended with the back room that he had turned into a workplace for carving wood and building furniture, which is where he had carved the bust of the woman that sat on the dustless table in the front room. Her image had come to him on a night when the combined sounds of window tap and fire crack drew in his mind a scene: Honor looking to the sky, her neck craned in such a way that sunrays painted her pensive face in victory.

But when the fireplace hissed and he heard in its hissing the retelling of his family's murder, he left his bedside and headed to the chilly front room by lamplight to gaze at the carving of the beautiful woman shown from her clavicle up. At night, beneath the dismal glow from Justice's oil lamp, his mother's sculpted head didn't capture her looking up into the dawning or setting sun; rather it mocked her face the moment Aba's lantern light revealed its swollen and frozen contours almost a decade ago, her countenance death-stuck in the grip of snake venom, neck not craned in glory but contorted at an agonized angle.

By putting eyes on his own creation this way, to him it seemed he had brought her not back to life but back to a living death, permanently frozen in the moment that demanded from him the most terror.

AT THAT MOMENT, Luther-Philip woke in the lonesome back room he shared with his father. He fiercely missed his mother. After she died, the pallet that was replaced by a bed became a pallet again, Mr. Wife refusing to sleep in the deathbed any longer. Luther-Philip slept in the lone bed. His father had long ago replaced the painted-over windows with new glass, and night showed visibly through the windows.

Luther-Philip stared out through the glass at the moon's diffused light nesting in the treetops. Inspired, he took a walk to the cemetery and found his mother's grave covered in red and yellow leaves. Mid-autumn chill made more noticeable his own body's warmth, and the revelation of blood moving through and heating him felt as though he were being hugged from behind.

No gravestone marked his mother's burial, rather a pyramid of stone globes. He touched the top stone, leaving three fingers there until their heat and the cold of the stone became indiscernible, his flesh melding with the very grave that over the years had fallen into a disdainful state. He felt increasing shame as the distance between his younger self and his older self grew in concord with the distance between his memories of his mother and the current unease that he missed someone he no longer remembered.

Luther-Philip heard the crunch of dead leaves beneath him. His fingers stung with frostbite, and his knees stiffened in their kneeling at the grave. Where he had hoped to feel sadness, he felt instead discomfort and impatience. He took a deep breath of the cold air. He wanted it to hurt, but it refreshed him. Whatever sorrow he needed refused to come and this frightened him. He pulled his numb fingers from his mother's grave.

A SUDDEN KNOCKING. Justice opened the door. Luther-Philip tried to smile, but his face had grown as numb as his hands. Justice offered nothing to eat or drink. Luther-Philip wanted neither. They sat on the couch together, one's damp lantern and the other's lamp offering unsteady but reliable light. The two devices stood like ancient pillars throwing their torchlight into the open threshold between them, inside of which the wooden woman both familiar and unknown looked away from her voyeurs.

Luther-Philip saw in the bust his own mother turning away from him because her grave had been abandoned, so what now was the reason he had disturbed her slumber? That it was Justice's mother never crossed his mind. He didn't see the small happiness in her expression, the cheekbones too high for bitterness. He didn't see the two braids starting from the center of her head and meeting at the back to create a tiara, a style his own mother never wore. He didn't see the intimate care Justice took in digging small holes to make her pupils, the lift of her eyebrows as she took in some grand view. He saw what he wanted to see, which had nothing to do with what was there.

Justice, sitting on that same couch in arrested silence, eyed the sculpture's head tilt he himself had hewed with the fury of carving his own unforeseen hatred into the quick-coming future. He snatched up the bust and his lamp and stormed to his bedroom.

Luther-Philip jumped from his seat and followed, saying nothing when Justice gazed into the fireplace, holding the bust of Honor by the head between two fingers. He said nothing when Justice tossed the semblance of his mother into the fire. He made only a sound rattled with sad epiphany, an infant's ignorance becoming a toddler's awareness. He watched the fire darken the woman's face that had become in his mind the face of his own mother. He ran up to the fire, reached in, pulled his mother from the fire, cradled her charred face to his chest, and retreated into himself.

That was enough. Justice gawked at Luther-Philip cradling the bust and let out a single laugh from his humorless face. "Put it back," he said. Luther-Philip ignored him, and the black water lake inside him receded. Roars from the beast stirred Justice's anger.

"Put it back." He repeated with urgency, with a crack of desperation.

Luther-Philip rested in his silence.

"That's my sadness you got in your hands. You got no right." He had closed the distance between himself and Luther-Philip without noticing. His heart pained him. Firelight painted his face into ghastly contour. "Luthe . . ." and sprouting before him, God's Place and a ten-year-old Luther-Philip in the tree, silenced and stilled by the nest of hair, teeth, and maggots. Gruesome smell rising from the scalp meat. Scent of smoke woven in the thick wafts of hair. This the earliest memory when their beautiful silence lost its beauty. Now, again, before the smell of burning, their silence had been corrupted and Justice's heart shunned from any attention.

And the black water lake inside his shunned heart had nearly disappeared. The beast on the other side crept toward him on the land the receding lake revealed. This was the first time Justice had seen its form and after the water had completely disappeared, he saw that the beast's full body was the creature that had come to him as his fear during his visit to Saint's house. He stumbled backward and fell to his behind on the soft black sand. The beast tilted its head and leered, its facial features, body, and clothes limned in white light. It wore what Justice wore, had Justice's face and thick hair with two horns like a bull's curving from its head, and two blazing holes of white light for eyes. Its feet were hooves, the knees bent in the wrong direction. It reached out to Justice a large, clawed hand. A soft growl poured from its mouth, its smile smug and convincing. Justice reached up to grab the hand of the beast that was himself.

The floor creaked just outside his bedroom door, a long moan with some weight to it. Darkness veiled the source. Then the flash of a familiar face in the shadows. Deadly. Dead-serious.

The black water lake in Justice's heart flooded the space between himself and his inner beast, washing the creature back to the other side in an eruption of roars. Rushing back into view was Luther-Philip holding the sculpture to his chest, gazing into the fireplace. Justice held his raised fist over Luther-Philip's head while Luther-Philip, oblivious, cried and clung to the charred idol. Justice lowered his hand to his chest and looked toward the doorway where Saint stood, had been standing for some time without being noticed, noticed now because she wanted to be. Creak as a warning. Staff bottom firm to the floor. Her companion right behind her, stalwart, his expressionless eyes intruding. Justice couldn't tell if she had come to his home or sent him a powerful vision, one that kept him from breathing. Eventually, Saint and her companion slinked back into the darkness and were gone.

HE HAD TO go see her. This he knew and regretted knowing, had trembled the moment he woke to the thought on the couch. He left Luther-Philip, who had fallen asleep in Justice's bed with the bust still in his arms like a doll. Cold crept about, so Justice lit a small fire in the bedroom fireplace before leaving out, dressed casket-sharp.

Saint's house remained as unwelcoming as before. Selah was sweeping the porch when he got there, and she stopped sweeping as he approached. By the time he made it to the bottom step, she had gone inside while Saint and her companion greeted Justice at the threshold. Saint nodded, then returned inside, leaving a trail of stinging cold for Justice to follow.

Never had Saint allowed someone entry to her divining room. She wanted to see his face up close, to hear his voice as clearly as possible. The monstrous vision from Justice's last visit had not left her. Last night he proved his potential for danger.

Justice sat in a rickety chair opposite Saint's by the small table. Dozens of candles burned all over. The throne of bones cackled from its skull mouths, Justice believed, when Saint's weight hit the chair. If he wanted to turn around and leave to his home where a friend sadder than a stormy Sunday waited, her companion blocking the door made that impossible.

"You knew to come," Saint said. A threat lingered where should've been the mere sharing of an observation. "And now you're here. Any blood on your hands?"

"No," he said. The candles frightened him. Every flame waved, a testifying witness around him. "But blood still on yours."

"You know what you planned on doing to your friend? I bet you do. I bet you know, just like you knew why you pulled that knife on me the first time we met. 'Member that?" Saint smiled with half her mouth.

Justice looked at the table and its woodgrain only deepened the memory. "I don't forgive you, Saint."

"I saw your demon. You saw it, too." The room filled with quiet, reflecting the utter quiet of the rest of the house, which made Justice's recollection of the roaring inside him more powerful. His legs shook. Without thinking, he rubbed the top of his right hand. Felt the thin bone.

"I have no medicine for what's in you. No conjure for the monster you are. Only advice." Saint spoke softly. "That little scar of yours don't own you. Own your damn self."

Justice slammed both fists into the table. "Who owned you when you killed my family? Who had you on a chain?"

"And if you ever show up in my visions again how you did last night, Justice . . ." Saint tapped her fingers on the skulls of her armrests.

"You love talking about slavery, but you not talking about how you just as bad as the masters."

"Justice—"

"Who you still chained to? I bet he know. Don't you?" Justice called over his shoulder to Saint's companion. "You chain him up to you, don't you? What give you a right to own him?" He stood, knocking his chair to the floor. "What animal is you, dragging him around like a dog? Who dog you still is, Saint?"

Saint was about to speak until Justice took a deep breath and, with all his might, barked at her.

Every candle in the room blew out except one on the table that lit Saint's face. Her eyes were completely white with spinning clouds of blue. It seemed to Justice she had stopped breathing. "Out," Saint said with her throat. "Out!" like a bloody cough.

Saint's companion stepped to the side and opened the door. Justice blew out the final candle, kicking the floored chair out of his way.

Like she God. Like she Jesus fresh off the cross. Bring people to Ours and act like she the queen. I heard about what they do in kingdoms. Kill anybody who don't do what the king and queen want. She think she run somebody. She don't run nobody. She kill any and everybody all she want and nobody raise a brow. Now she in my face talking about blood on my hands—then he imagines his hand around Luther-Philip's neck, punching him.

When he returned home, Justice lit lamps throughout the house. The gloomy day made his home feel less alive. In that gloom, the house appeared carved from stone. Everything with a name had lost its name in the stark savagery of the gloom's undoing. In the bedroom, Luther-Philip continued to sleep.

Justice pulled the bust of his mother from between his friend's arms, placing it back on the table. He returned to the room and got in bed with Luther-Philip, still dressed for a funeral. Warm, stiff clothing made it hard to wrap his arm around his friend. 'What made him take it out the fire,' Justice thought, and dozed off in the complete malaise of a day.

When he awoke, Luther-Philip was no longer in the bed. The fire had gone out and the room's lamp had been snuffed.

"You burn your house down leaving your lamps on," Luther-Philip said as he entered the room with two cups of tea. "You need food." Justice agreed. After they ate, they sat in the front room and silently beheld the sculpture once more before Luther-Philip headed home.

EARLY EVENING, Luther-Philip returned. The bust was gone from the table. He called out to Justice and heard a wordless response toward the back of the house. When he entered the back room, he froze, said, "Why?"

Justice was sitting on the floor, pants off, blood on his hands. "I'm not nobody's animal," Justice said. "I'm not a animal. I'm not a animal. I'm not a animal. I'm not a animal, Luthe." He mewed.

With the sharpest knife he could find—"I'm not"—witnessed by the bust of his mother positioned to face him though she was carved to look up and away, Justice had begun slicing off the brand on his leg—"a animal"—not cutting much, not getting far.

JUSTICE CLEANED AND wrapped his leg. Luther-Philip watched. It took forever to boil the water, even longer for it to cool down enough to safely pour over the wound. Then witch hazel followed by what little alcohol Luther-Philip could find. A flap of skin slightly folding up from the *E*'s top arm stopped midwave and folded back onto the leg beneath the pressure Justice applied under the watchful, horrified gaze of his friend.

The following day, Luther-Philip didn't return to check on Justice. Nor the day after or the day after that. Limping around Ours, Justice was asked about his well-being while he looked for Luther-Philip. He lied, something about a sleeping leg that wouldn't wake up, and nodded when offered an unwanted remedy. Luther-Philip was nowhere, gone from the world, it seemed. Not at Mr. Wife's, where Justice left him a letter, not by the tree soon-to-be-called God's Place, and not by the lake which took all day to get to and all day to return from. All the while,

Justice grunted as he hobbled about without cane or long stick, without a shoulder to hold on to.

[2]

One day, Joy went missing, evidenced by the absence of the scraping of the shovel against Saint's floors. The grating noise had morphed from frightening, to irritating, to angering, to useful as Joy announced herself with violence against the house, giving anyone who wanted to avoid her misery a chance to escape.

When Frances asked for help to look for her, Saint outright refused. The twins agreed but looked in unlikely places, such as beneath a stack of wood, behind the teakettle, and in each other's mouths. They feigned disappointment each time she didn't appear and would've been convincing if not for Naima's recorded fantastic hatred of the woman and Selah's notorious disinterest in anyone not Saint or Naima.

Frances asked around Ours if anyone had seen her. It took a while, but eventually someone told him that he should ask Aba. "Not like he say much."

But Frances didn't try Aba because she didn't need to. Come to find out, Joy had taken her new best friend, the shovel, and dug herself a five-foot grave just southeast of Creek's Bridge. Without meaning to, Naima stumbled upon her lying on her back in the hole, open to the elements, the shovel laid on her chest to feet. Naima took her time getting to Ours, but eventually she caught up to Frances to let her know. "Her crazy ass in a hole she dug down by the bridge. I told her she need to get up out from there but her ass crazy so she stayed in there."

Naima said it loud enough for folks in Ours to hear. By the time Frances made it to where Joy had dug herself the grave, a large group of people had followed behind to come see for themselves. "Girl, get up from out there," someone chided, as if the hole took Joy farther outside than she was. "If you die, then what you gone say?" someone else chimed in, to great agreement. Ignoring the chorus, Joy remained where she lay with her arms crossed, the shovel tucked underneath their firm embrace.

When asked if she needed anything while down there, Joy blew air from her nose. When asked why she was in that cold dark hole, she sneezed. It became a game, the children asking one question to hear her petty snorts, the adults asking the other to hear her infant-like release of snot. Frances shooed most of the game players away and jumped into the grave, after which Joy let out a piercing scream that chased Frances back to the surface.

Someone offered to float her out by pouring buckets of creek water into the grave until she rose to the top, dead or alive. The Ouhmey shrugged off that idea, mostly because it would've taken forever. A woman told Frances to jump in there again and just snatch her back to the surface, but another made the point that she could just hop right back in there whenever she felt like it or dig another hole when no one was paying attention. "You got to fix the ailing that got her in there in the first place," an older man said, barely audible over the autumn wind. Soon enough, people returned to Ours to avoid the chill and to avoid catching whatever Joy had. However, before the spectators fully dispersed, Frances overheard someone mention that no-talking Aba could probably get her out. Hearing his name a second time, Frances went to him at once.

Upon seeing her, Aba slammed the door in Frances's face so fast the wind of its closure billowed her open coat. Frances knocked again. No response. She was about to give up when both Selah and Naima ran up to the door and began knocking. First Naima. Then Selah. Then Naima. Then Selah. They took turns that way, making a counting game of it: Naima knocking once, Selah knocking twice, the next girl adding one knock until the beat fell relentlessly upon the door, accompanied by their high-pitched giggles. Naima fussed when Aba opened the door on what was to be her thirteenth knock. "You messed up my count," she said. "You must be ready to go."

"He look ready," Selah said. "You ready, Mr. Aba?"

Aba blew air hard out his nose and Selah said that he acted just like Joy. She rocked on her feet, ball to heel. Naima dug in her ear, then sniffed her finger.

"What it smell like?" Selah asked.

"Something God don't touch," Naima said, then said to Aba, "Joy need your help. You slammed the door on Joy, not Saint." Aba's face softened then, to both Selah's and Naima's chagrin. They had both expected chaos, a little battle to ensue, which is why they came in the first place.

Instead, Aba, shirtless, grabbed his coat, put on his boots, and followed Frances and the girls back to the hole that Joy had dug for herself. Aba understood as soon as he saw her. He looked down and Joy look up. Her eyes grew brighter, and she bent her knees. Aba jumped down to the newly opened space she made for him.

'This not a grave,' Aba thought, 'this a beginning.' Silence, a need for it, a hunger for isolation to keep one's inner clarity intact—in her grave he saw his own refusal to speak.

He patted the dirt wall and Joy responded yes. He patted it again and she asked if a week was long enough. Aba nodded and climbed out of the hole, bringing Joy's shovel with him. It took a while but with various gestures and pantomimes he somehow managed to get Frances to understand that Joy would remain in that hole for a week, lying down, covered in dirt up to her neck like she was under a blanket. Frances was to bring her water throughout the day. No food. If it rained, she had to use common sense to know to check on Joy in case the dirt caved in. Aba finished his gestural speech and went home.

The following days, Frances brought Joy water. On the fourth day, she started speaking to Frances again, asking for more dirt to cover her body. On the sixth day, she wanted to be buried completely, dirt over her head and the hole she was in filled to the top. Frances resisted, arguing with her until she lost her voice. Joy, firm and with much volume, requested that she be buried completely. "I will not be able to leave unless you do this for me. Just for a day," she said. Frances covered her head and passed on all food and drink for herself until it was time to retrieve Joy from the ground.

When Frances returned on the seventh day, she searched for Joy's grave. She found the small linen dress that Joy had been wearing draped over the burial. Frances nearly tore Saint's house up looking for Joy, and looked up and around every tree that caught her eye. It would take hours for Frances to learn that the once-buried woman had sauntered over Creek's Bridge and through the small field that stretched between Saint's house and Ours, her bare body exposed and caked with dirt. What happened when Joy reached the intersection of Tanager and First became a disputed story:

JOY WASN'T NAKED but wore thin golden armor covered in intricate engravings of playing children. The moment her feet touched the cold stones of the road, a prolific garden sprang up all around her and followed her as she walked Tanager to Second then First, making a left on First and summoning lilies from the turn of her heel as she headed south toward Oriole. Hyacinths, roses of every color, bougainvillea climbing the fences, melons breaking from the ground while their rinds split overripe in the lush spring-summer of Joy's passing.

OR, Joy wasn't naked but wore black, roiling storm clouds as a dress. The moment her feet touched the cold stones of the road, a curtain of ravens lifted from the earth in an endless torrent that could only be explained as every pebble, grain of sand, and dust fleck cracked open and released shadow after shadow of wingspan unto the heavens.

OR, Joy was naked, but no one could see her except the Ouhmey's houses. The moment her feet touched the cold stones of the road, every window and door to every home in Ours flew open, a harmonic chorus of continuous notes streaming from the open mouths of the doors until she passed and, as though offended, the windows and doors slammed shut at the sight of her naked ass.

WITHOUT LORE, THOUGH, Joy walked naked and straight-backed to Aba's house, opened the door without knocking, and didn't leave. When Frances discovered this, she protested on Aba's porch, yelling as loud as she could that she needed to come on out and put something warm on her body. Joy, with much cheer and not a lick of clothing, opened the door to her new home and asked Frances to bring her belongings with a kindness that frustrated Frances even more. After a few days of her protesting and Joy asking Frances to bring her her things, Joy got her way and woke up one morning to a well-packed sack of her belongings, including her broken mirror, though the loose shard was missing.

Frances returned a couple weeks later to speak with Joy. Joy asked Aba if it was all right for a visitor close to Saint to enter his home. Hesitantly welcomed, Frances sat in a chair by the window and across from Joy.

"When you coming home?" Frances asked.

"I am home," Joy responded.

"Your home with me."

"My home is wherever I decide to lay my head. Didn't you decide to change where your head lay without needing my approval?"

Aba chuckled once in the background. He went into the bedroom and closed the door when both Frances and Joy cut eyes his way.

"You leaning heavy on something that can't hold you, Joy."

"You missed the hard time I had watching Selah while y'all went looking for that other one. You missed the times I needed you when the dreams got bad. You—"

"I'm here now trying to get you to come back with me. Don't that count for anything? Don't it?"

"Nothing different will come of it. Not a thing." Joy was indifferent.

This delayed visit fit the pattern she had escaped by coming to Aba's. Had Frances come earlier, she may have been more receptive. Because Frances didn't come begging the next day, Joy knew it was because Frances had lost track of time with Saint.

"This not the place where you supposed to be."

"Why do you want me back? You can visit me here when you want to see me. Can't you do that? Can't I have my own thing without being your shadow?"

"My shadow?" Frances was hurt.

"I followed you from New Orleans to the wilderness, through Mississippi, back across the river to this place. I stayed with Saint for you. I never left your side. The nightmares get bad, you nowhere to be found. Saint get sick and you by her side for days. We hardly share words in that house. But when I come to do a thing that's for me, you don't want me to do it." Joy's voice became lighter. "Do you know I almost killed Selah?"

"You what?"

Joy nodded. "I woke up because she spoke to me. The knife point had already broke skin a little."

"Damn it, Joy!"

Joy shook her head. "Nuh-uh. Don't chastise me now. Too late for your concern now."

"What if you do that to Aba? Then what you gone do?"

"You rather me in the house with Saint? I'm sure I can find a way to cut her down in my sleep."

"Joy—"

"Or you want me to stab myself from stabbing you? You want to watch me while I—" Joy stopped and tilted her head. "You trying to watch me to keep me from hunting somebody? You can't watch me and Saint's feet at the same time."

"That's not what I'm saying to you."

"Let me have something for me. That's what I'm saying to you."

Aba stood in the doorway. Frances took the hint.

Before descending the porch steps, Frances tilted her hat to Aba, then said to Joy, "I just came to say I miss you. That's all."

"I miss me, too," Joy said.

Frances stood on the porch for what felt like hours. It took time for her to understand that she didn't understand a thing, didn't know at all what the offense had been. What she did know was that if she kept talking, kept missing the point, even this cold farewell could get colder. Instead of pushing the situation, she pushed herself on back to Saint's, her goodbye stuck in her throat.

[3]

It took some time for the gossip to cease, but winter's violent backhand smacked crooked the houses, covering windows and sealing doorframes with ice that couldn't be broken with shovels. The Ouhmey exhausted their stored supplies and food. It didn't snow much that season, but frost grew like mold on every surface. Boulder-size porcupines of dense ice decorated Ours in a scattershot. The icicles at the tips of those monuments were so sharp and thin that when wind blew past, it split into separate gales.

Some blamed the cruel winter on Joy's naked march into Ours and Aba's welcoming her without protest. Unbeknownst to the outside world, both had refashioned for each other the other's life. Just before the first shock of hoarfrost, Aba stopped drinking, brushed his floors spotless, and wiped down the inside of his windows and the filthy walls. Joy laundered their clothes and inventoried their food to make sure they had enough to survive winter. Though Aba refused to speak, he and Joy had thrilling conversations throughout the day, she going star-eyed when he described how he learned hambone from the universe and he practically melting with sympathy as she told stories about the men she killed in her adolescence, the blood, the night terrors. She kept the use of the invisibility stone to herself because Aba had shown a staggering hatred toward anything that reminded him of Saint's conjure.

Aba didn't know he was sixty-seven years old but let him tell it, he was older than sin. He looked as young as any laboring man and was stronger than most, his belly round and solid, his face aged yet taut. As day slid into night, his muscles seized up in a tight and dull pain. He misunderstood that pain to mean death had its hands on him. He didn't let Joy know this, but it became more difficult to hide his nighttime discomfort. Eventually, she took to rubbing his neck before bed, which alleviated enough stress as to send him dozing in her arms.

On her birthday, Joy told him it was her twenty-fifth time around the sun, and he wrapped her in a climate of shame with his shocked gaze. They did touch and sleep naked together beneath a generous supply of blankets and ways to make love. He enjoyed her company and that she understood him without words. She enjoyed being taken seriously. When he came to her at her makeshift grave with a look of understanding about him, she knew instinctively that he was a man her dreams wouldn't force her to kill. So, when he tried to drop his heavy and unasked-for shame on her, arguing that he was old enough to be her granddaddy, she raised her palm to quiet him and said, "Had I wanted a father in any form, I wouldn't have killed the one I had." Joy's candor often confounded Aba into furious blinking. Coaxing him to calm, she would rub his round belly and remind him of what she called his genius: that he could speak without uttering a sound.

During the first winter they shared, Aba would go outside wearing as many articles of clothing as he could and return somehow with fresh kill, wood for the hearth and fireplace, or buckets of ice to melt for drinking and bathing water. Joy never went with him on these trips, but she knew he was the only one capable of such resourcefulness in Ours.

One day, she asked to go with him, and he obliged because two sets of carrying arms were better than one. What she discovered was that he stomp-danced in the woods with enough power that the animals ran from their burrows in deep horror: rabbits, ground hogs, the rare mole. Ice fell from the trees and cracked from beneath his pounding feet, the force from which reverberated back up through her body until it shook into higher frequency the beating of her heart. The trees, disrobed of their ice, gave up their wood easily and soon after, the smallest of the trees was felled to the ground.

It took the entire day to chop enough wood worth bringing back and once they returned, Joy, for the first time, beheld Ours in its frozen attire, with its streets absent of life, the fences glossy with dense spiky flumes of ice. She realized with growing distress that she and Aba may have been the only ones left alive. She asked him to do his stomp dance to shake some of the ice free from the houses. At first, he resisted, grimacing soon after she asked and crunching the ice beneath him to say, "May cause trouble." Joy became relentless with asking, and he eventually gave in and stomped. The earth shook and the sky with it. Ice crashed down from the eaves of every house.

Folks rushed out and ran to their sheds or to the woods for more firewood and meat. This eased up any petty feelings Ours held against Joy and Aba for the spectacle that past autumn. And as with any old frivolous nonsense, all was soon forgiven and forgotten.

[4]

Then the March flood came, as torrents of rain swept through Missouri, lifting the Mississippi River from its muddy prison and swelling it through St. Louis neighborhoods closest to the bank. Brown, miasmic water crept through the city, slurping at building foundations and emancipating smaller trees from their roots. The smell of rotten vegetation wafted along whelmed streets while tethered boats crashed over the docks.

The melting ice mixed with the endless rainfall, pushing the tides farther west in crests tall enough to sweep a wagon from the road. Deeper into the city, horsecars swayed, then rocked to their sides, buoyed by the putrid water that carried all it held captive like a swollen vein down several streets, until a small dam of horsecars blocked off a road's end. In three days, St. Louis lay in sludge and desperation, while north, Ours found itself beneath several inches of muddy water. Animal and human shit from flooded barns and outhouses that were never dug deep enough thickened the deluge into rotten catastrophe. The earth reeked and became indistinguishable from the waste carried and abandoned by the racing downpour.

One clap of thunder and it ended.

The sky opened its monochrome to reveal the clearest sky that year. Blue, icy still with remnants of winter. Everything had been put asunder in Ours, and before Saint or anyone else in town realized it, the stones that protected the town with unfindability, too, had been overturned and washed away.

In St. Louis, a band of enslaved Africans took it upon themselves to escape during the flood. It took no time for the runaways to find the impossible-to-locate town of Ours, so well hidden it had risen to mythical status.

[5]

By April, the thirty-seven refugees from St. Louis—twenty-two children and fifteen adults ranging from ages four to a guess of fifty years old—had filled the rest of the houses, one house becoming an orphanage of sorts for the various children to be taught the ways of Ours and freedom.

Joy, one of the first to spot them entering town, assisted with managing the children's well-being. When she asked them to give their names and ages, the youngest one had to introduce them all. The other children seemed openly embarrassed by the request and shrank themselves to go unnoticed. All the newly arrived young had been slaves and forced hourly to sing. The youngest's voice was hoarse as he explained.

Twenty-two children of different ages but their sizes relatively the same. Small. Febrile. Twenty-two versions of the same person. Even the eldest boy at seventeen years old stood no taller than five feet five, his femur nearly visible through the delicate skin on his legs. Several had jaundice. Each who could have adult teeth had at least one adult tooth missing. When checked for bruises, some were found to have had broken bones that weren't properly reset. Burn marks. Contusions about the ankles and wrists. None of them could read. It took everything in Aba's arsenal to stop Joy from going to St. Louis and killing the woman who had done this to them.

"I'll just be gone for a few hours," she said.

"Those days gone," Aba said, tapping his chest. "Don't lose yourself in what's gone."

JOY GREETED EACH CHILD with her biggest smile, rubbed their heads, kissed their foreheads, made them laugh for those whose laughter had not left them, and made the ones smile whose voices had abandoned them. 'They will feel happiness today,' she thought, and spent many hours with them in the orphanage that would be run by three of the adults who entered Ours after the flood.

At the end of the day, Joy found Aba practicing his letters at the table. He looked up and smiled. He tapped his shoulder, then his chest, "How your heart?" 'My heart?' she wondered, because even after finding some semblance of care in Aba's presence, she still maintained that her heart was a thing of swords. But in the company of the orphaned children, it seemed her heart wanted to study war no more.

"We are taking in a child," she said.

Aba scooted the chair from under the table in a flash of dread. "What?"

he asked through hard claps. Unwilling to repeat herself, Joy spoke aloud as though to a grander audience. "We must get this place ready." Immediately she set to cleaning their already immaculate home.

Aside from his apprehension, Aba carried fear of children, not because there was anything particularly wrong with the fact of a child except that a child could be taken so easily, and enough had been taken from him in his lifetime. But avoiding loss is not a power given to the living; regardless of his protests, of which there were many, a child would come.

· CHAPTER 20 ·

A Show of Force

[1]

Ours fell into a funereal overcast the first week of April 1860. It didn't rain that week, but sunlight's absence skeletonized once-blooming flowers. Each house was limned in gloomlight breaking from the dark and bulbous clouds overhead, a swollen dusty sunlight, compassionless as it thinned out whatever and whomever it touched in its own soft swelling. Eventually, the scent of lilac would wash over Ours again, swiping the small square blocks, a perfumed finger across a collarbone. But for now, from the quiet of Saint's home, a distended sadness lifted past the rooftop and petrified the sky.

The trinity had finally broken her: Joy, Frances, and Justice. Joy desecrating her house, Frances talking loud at the dinner table, and Justice a mere visitor knocking over her furniture, and worst of all—standing over her while they spoke, infantilizing, rude, domineering, their emotions snappish, cyclones with no trajectory and with endless fuel.

She almost killed Justice that day he barked at her, felt the itch in her left knuckles and the soreness in her right knee. If she had any less care for Justice, whom she liked very much, for he reminded her of Essence (calculated, determined, overly protective), she would've dropped a bolt of lightning through his skull without even meaning to. However, sorrow took over where murder fell away. Because he reminded Saint of Essence, he also reminded her of why Essence had to get rid of her. Unable to fully control her "energy," as Essence had called it, Saint posed a threat to everything Essence loved. Wasn't it the same for Justice? After purest contemplation in the cold dark room, Saint felt a feeling she no longer had words to describe. And because language failed to designate a proper space for the feeling, the weather had to take the brunt of her uncontrollable, unnamed emotions.

Hence the merciless conditions —icy winter freezing over the houses, sudden flood ripping through the roads—that only ended once she recalled the name of the emotion she had been feeling and laughed herself into clarity, astonished that she had gone so deeply into herself to pull out "shame." Shame for what, exactly? Because there were no hooks in Saint's heart on which to hang anything less than pride, shame had no place to put its coat.

Word that orphans entered Ours without her intervention reached Saint by Selah, Selah seeing through a squirrel's eyes the short procession of refugees lurch through reeking mud, one handheld lantern dully painting the ground before them with frail light. The ghost canopy of the winter-stripped branches allowed the squirrel's vision to break through. Then the rain picked up once more and the squirrel dove into the wet boughs' rudimentary mesh. Selah left the animal's eyes for her own.

When the rain finally settled, Saint sensed the stones had washed some feet away from their original spaces and overturned. She returned them to their posts, their cold flat backs impressed into the softened earth, their abstract symbols faceup and stark against the unmarked rocks' crude geology. She was glad that those who entered were whom she would've allowed entry anyway. The nearly two dozen children. The handful of adults. Perishing was the only option available to them no matter where they went, Saint guessed. And by the time summer arrived, half of the orphaned children had indeed died from various illnesses.

[2]

Because of their seclusion, what Ours knew of the rest of America was limited to whatever news reached Delacroix. A shoddy line of telegraph connected Delacroix to St. Louis, with the former often receiving messages much later. Still, the town's paper printed what it could with as little space as possible, since few people seemed to read the paper.

Years prior, news of the Compromise of 1850 and the Fugitive Slave Act had been shoved into the smallest columns of the paper while more local affairs became the centerpiece for the day. The longest article on the Fugitive Slave Act mentioned President Millard Fillmore as a necessary spokesperson for the South and spoke more to the violence enacted against white abolitionists and those sympathetic to the "Colored cause" than to the Negroes found dead or dying all over the nation.

One white man who lived in Newcrest, Virginia, and spent twenty-three years helping runaways escape north, received twenty-three lashings while forced to watch his captors shoot his horses in the head. A white girl, no older than twelve years of age, was shaved bald and paraded around town wearing a sign that read "Nigger Friend" for feeding a runaway down in Kentucky. One story about an abolitionist couple from Decatur County, Georgia, was so violent that the journalist described the scene as if he had stumbled upon a secret love affair: "May no others follow in their passions."

Less still to receive any attention were the ravages against the Apache, stamped out by dragoons sent to annihilate their villages. Slaughter after slaughter had gone without mention in any article, genocide unrolling like daylight from a hell-dark horizon. Scalpers carried their terrible bounties no different than carrying coins, gloating from village to village with viscera of all the once-living glistening from their boot bottoms. Not a word from the press. America was being born, after all, in the east, while the west remained a grim canvas for an imperial art form. It wasn't yet America over that way. No. Not until every Indigenous

American had been extinguished. Otherwise, it was still Mexico, the "savage unknown becoming known" as one lonely article put it, and who in their right mind had time to worry about a place not yet mature for slavery?

Eventually, the folks in Delacroix found in themselves the budding hostility Frances had seen all along. She had been wrong about Delacroix having a growing hatred specifically against Ouhmey because their hatred grew against everyone, including themselves, enhancing the squalor where squalor laid its head and digging ever-deepening trenches between the poor and the rich, the latter whose numbers declined by the year. The whole town suffered from financial woes, expressed by filthy streets that crept into the people and became filthy ways. The mayor of Delacroix pilfered tax money at first in negligible pinches until year after year they became more noticeable. Eventually, a rat infestation manifested, starting in the stables where animal shit usually collected by the city and made into fertilizer remained in the stables to fester. For a few months, the gas lamps along the street remained off because there was no gas and without money to pay the night patrol, patrol numbers dwindled. Hungry and with family, those who were meant to protect the town turned to criminality in the unlit streets that were once their patrol routes.

A year later, the Civil War began, and news of its unparalleled destruction made its way to the telegraph. Most of Delacroix cared so little about what happened east of the Mississippi River that they remained mostly untouched and uninspired by the calamity. Some went off to fight for the Union. Fewer for the Confederacy. Most carried on as their private angst left little room for a war they couldn't see. Years passed without worry or wonder. Though they lived in a slave state, there were no slaves in Delacroix to lose. Those who would've owned a slave had no means, and those who could afford one had no interest. Toward the Ouhmey, a veil of neutrality covered their eyes. But soon, the veil would grow more transparent, and those living in Delacroix would begin to question their and Missouri's neutrality in the approaching years.

[3]

A misleading telegraph from a St. Louis operator arrived Wednesday, July 22: "Monday, July 13, 1863, New York City: Black Joke destroys Lexington Ave during draft week." The operator, requested by the commissioner, asked for clarification and received a telegraph stating that riots in New York emerged after Congress passed the Enrollment Act for conscription to the Union Army. "Several Irish laborers have paved the streets with the blood of coloreds and statesmen alike, all in an attempt of eradicating both and humiliating Congress into reversal and rejection of the act." When news broke early that morning, a line of Delacroix militiamen blocked the Ours wagon from entering the town to keep anyone with ideas of rioting from executing those ideas.

Seeing that his path was blocked by gun-carrying men, anger and fear touched Justice's voice. "We got a right to work," he shouted from his seat. Some of the men had their guns raised and pointed.

"As do we," one of the militiamen said, without malevolence, which angered Justice more. "Safer for you if you turn around. This is for your protection as well."

Exile in the name of justice was a coward's exile, a justice that Justice couldn't stand by because to him it had no bearing. When he returned to Ours, he visited Mr. Wife and asked for a rifle.

"This no time to hunt," Mr. Wife said.

"This no time to be hunted," Justice said.

"Boy, what's hurt you?"

"Nothing yet. Might change if I don't get that rifle."

"Rifle don't keep away hurt, Justice. It cause it."

"If deer had a rifle, would we hunt it the way we do?"

Mr. Wife smirked, but he didn't budge. "You want a rifle, you prove you man enough not to use it."

"I rather prove I'm man enough to use it."

"You need to tell me what's happened to you right now."

Justice explained the turning away, the guns resting at the militiamen's sides, the hands steady, the few who aimed at his people. He didn't share how one of the gunmen aimed directly at him and how from the black hole of the gun's mouth he heard emanate the endless disclosure of hatred. Hatred pure enough to fall asleep to, so reliable it was, so unfettered and dustless. It whispered to Justice, and he wanted to hear more, was tempted to ride on up to the gun mouth not yet hot and lend it his ear.

'I dare you and your soul to pull that trigger,' he said in his mind but no, no he didn't tell Mr. Wife this. He left it at "I'll come back tomorrow after you've thought it through. I'll come back tomorrow cause tomorrow waiting on me. That I know. Nobody taking tomorrow from me."

The following day, Mr. Wife gave Justice the gun without ammunition. "I want you to walk around for a couple days with this on you," he said, and Justice heard in the man's tone a refusal to negotiate.

The walk around Ours felt like a stroll through paradise. Strapped around his shoulders, resting between his shoulder blades, the rifle's weight calmed him.

He strode all over Ours with the rifle strapped to his back, the town quiet as late afternoon breezes and a lack of errands sent most of the Ouhmey dozing, fed up with having been ejected from Delacroix. Such is the inebriation of boredom. The children were in school with the older youth while some of the elders cussed and played chess at a table set out in somebody's yard. The few others who remained awake tilted their heads a bit when they saw the makeshift militiaman strolling around like a sheriff, something Ours never needed. So "What he doing?" someone snickered to their girlfriend, then shrugged off Justice's proud ambling with a smooth "chiiiiile" before returning to her conversation.

Some birds flew nearby, and Justice aimed the rifle at them. A man at the chess table shouted for him to put the damn thing down "'fore you kill somebody. Damn nuisance." Justice heard him say it but he didn't care, imagining his pretend bullets snatched a bird from the air.

He returned the rifle to his back and ambled a circle around Ours. When he made it to Bank and First, he heard hammering coming from Thylias's house. No one had really seen or spoken to her since Franklin's death, but they knew she was alive because she had taken up the habit of hammering throughout the day and sometimes at night. What she was building for herself in there remained a mystery as no one felt brave or eager enough to knock and ask. Had they checked in on her from time to time, maybe she would've invited them in, cried on their shoulder a bit as she explained her carpentry. But Justice shared his neighbors' disinterest and walked right past Thylias's house until he made it to the corner where he turned left, heading home.

'That's a good idea,' he thought, 'home for a bit then back at it after I rest my feet.' Under this desire for comfort, Justice grew eager to return to what belonged to him: a home that had become like a companion and that had introduced him to patience and gratitude during crushing isolation. The dark, after Luther-Philip left without returning, intimidated him at first, seeming to move as his friend's shadow had moved while he was there. Now, on his walk back, it appeared the shadows in his home had found their way outside and were waiting for him on the top step.

He saw their shapes on the porch before he heard their laughter. One voice he didn't recognize while the other's familiarity brought up in him feelings of abandonment. The tap of the gun against his body became a second heart, the pulse of which propelled him more quickly toward the voices whose bodies filled in with details as he got closer.

Luther-Philip waved at Justice from Justice's porch and beamed. Beside him stood Joy, now radiant even beneath the shade of the porch canopy. Justice didn't know how long it had been since Luther-Philip stopped coming by.

By the time he made it to his own steps, he was full-on angry, sun eating him up. Sweat glossed his forehead and dripped into his eyes.

Luther-Philip paid no attention to Justice's frown and kept on smiling bigger until his cheeks made him squint.

"Let's go on in," Luther-Philip said. "It's hot," and he took Joy by the hand and led her into Justice's home without greeting Justice with anything but a smile.

Inside, Luther-Philip dipped three cups of water from a bucket on the floor and handed one to Joy and one to Justice, who stood baffled in his own doorway.

"Where you been?" Justice asked.

"This here is my friend Joy," Luther-Philip said, posing his hands toward Joy with the carelessness of presenting an unasked-for gift.

"I asked where you been, not who she is."

"What you mean where I been?" Luther-Philip chuckled.

And that was it for Justice, whose leg still stung from the memory of what he had done to himself with a knife. And beyond that, he recalled his conversation with Saint, where she might as well had mooed in his face and called it his language. In her candlelit room warped by a condescension he never knew possible, she called him everything but a child of God. Before he could leave with a clear mind, he barked at her without meaning to. It felt good when he did it and the only thing that kept him from doing it again was Saint's uncanny anger. Justice had stormed from her home back to his house that, from the moment he entered, became a barn beneath his hoof-hard steps and heavy breathing, the water in the bucket suddenly in a trough, his own musky scent offending him as would any rank horse.

Shame sent Justice hiding in his own home. Then, in the lightless hold of the back room, amongst his cutting tools and splinters of wood, he decided, with the figure of his mother as witness, to cut himself free of his animal marking. And of course, his only friend came looking for him as a true friend would, and discovered blood stained both flesh and the mind, only it was nearly impossible to wipe clean from the mind.

Luther-Philip had wondered in that back room, gazing with disgust at the flap of skin Justice cut loose from his leg, how Justice had found the speech of other beasts beneath his skin. What was meant to be Justice's cries came out as a bird's mating call, wolf's whimper in a bear trap, a goat obscene with innumerable confessions. Perhaps, Justice deciphered an owl hoot as answer to "Where is God?" or could translate the calligraphy of worms. As if a test, a dog barked outside but Justice neither yipped nor howled in return as he slid the knife a little deeper into his leg before releasing it to clank to the ground. Instead, when Justice moaned, he sounded like a heifer to Luther-Philip, who heard between him and Justice the sudden slamming of many doors.

Thereafter, Luther-Philip stayed away, leaving Justice to fend for himself in the nothing of seclusion. 'At least,' Justice thought, 'be missing me while you're away. Why ever you're away, be missing me.' Summer slipped in and out of sunlit days. Flesh stink rose from his leg as it drained pus. Justice cleaned it better after that. Kept it wrapped tighter until the infection ended. Yet distance strained the friendship between himself and Luther-Philip. The longer he went without seeing him, the more the wound of Luther-Philip's absence festered. Eventually, how Saint treated him couldn't hold a torch to what his so-called friend continued to do to him.

Justice had written a letter and handed it to Mr. Wife to give to Luther-Philip. In it, he asked for a response to his grievances, a visit to hash things out, but after weeks had gone by without a visit or a letter in response, Justice wanted to fight.

"What you mean where I been, Justice? I live in Ours just like you do." There it was again, that chuckle that told Justice that he might be stupid, and that there was someone in the world who wanted him to know.

"I wrote you," Justice said, poising his lips over the words to follow, but no other words came.

"Your letter. I read it. That's why I'm here now." Luther-Philip pulled out the letter from his pants pocket. The paper had thinned, become darker around the creases of its four-square fold, creases so deep that the letter began to tear while a corner had curled into a dog-ear at the top.

'With her,' Justice thought, and glared at Joy, who had all this time been silent. What else was she to do, poorly introduced and forgotten by the man who had brought her on a whim.

Luther-Philip had popped up at Aba's after hearing the news Joy had moved into town. He visited with a basket of freshly baked bread under his arms. He attempted something like an apology for not seeing her sooner, even back when she still lived with Saint. Some excuse fell from his mouth, some unconvincing reason for his distance. Joy nodded politely, eyeing the bread, not caring about what Luther-Philip had to say. He began appearing more frequently, never staying for long, almost as though he only meant to pass the time while with her. Then out of nowhere, "Let me introduce you to my friend, Justice. Makes no sense you two haven't met." And he grabbed her by the hand and dragged her to his friend's home. On the way, he spoke with more energy about Justice than he had ever given her.

Now, on Justice's porch, Luther-Philip said, "Brought Joy over so you could finally meet her. She said she never met you all this time she been here." Luther-Philip kept talking, hadn't stopped talking. Joy's smile faded. Justice wondered what took so damn long for his friend to visit him.

He didn't hear what Luther-Philip said to him. In a town that small, a person had to run off past the woods, up to Delacroix or down to St. Louis to go unseen. It had to be a purposeful unseeing, one that required looking for the person who you knew was looking for you just to keep tabs on how to avoid them. The thought of being watched the whole time he was looking for his friend, his brother, was unforgivable.

Luther-Philip laughed one more time and the black lake in Justice's heart shook. Justice spun the rifle strap and aimed the rifle at Joy. It shocked him when he saw who stood on the other side of his aim, but he held steady there, marveling at how satisfying it felt to possibly shoot her because it would hurt too much to shoot his friend.

It took Luther-Philip stepping in front of Joy for Justice to lower the gun, which he did, and as Joy's face disappeared behind Luther-Philip's, Luther-Philip's contemptuous glare took over. "What you doing? What you doing aiming that at her for? You lost your mind? Put that thing down. Put it on down, now." At the nadir of Justice lowering the rifle, Luther-Philip grabbed Joy's hand and pulled her past Justice and right down the stairs. Justice kept his eye on the woman, frightened, for as Joy allowed Luther-Philip to drag her out the door, she, too, kept her eyes trained on Justice with incalculable menace.

The next day, Mr. Wife came to collect his rifle from Justice. Justice pointed to where he had hung it on the wall. Mr. Wife didn't move. After several still minutes, Justice went over to the wall, grabbed the rifle, and handed it to Mr. Wife, who snatched it from him.

It took everything in Justice to keep looking at the man who took on the responsibility of raising him after his parents had died, but he kept his head level with Mr. Wife's out of respect for him and for himself. And he lifted his head back up after Mr. Wife, in a blink, slapped him across the mouth. Light went flying from his sight at incredible speed. Justice expected tears, not from himself but from Mr. Wife. He was faced, instead, with Mr. Wife loading the rifle, and became stricken, tearing up in the warmth of humiliation, and seeing through his tears the tearless man stand before him with his chest heaving and a cold stare. Justice stepped forward. Mr. Wife lifted the rifle and aimed it at Justice.

"Justice," Mr. Wife said. His mouth trembled. "What this feel like to you? Huh? Tell me. What it feel like?" Mr. Wife shouted, and Justice held his breath. "What it feel like? You want to be hunted? Hmm? Speak up!"

Justice just shook his head, his slob-filled mouth open and mute. Without words, he made a bleating noise.

Mr. Wife lowered the rifle and said, "You not ready for this; never will be." He sniffed hard one good time, took three steps back, then turned and headed out the door.

Neither the snatching of the gun nor the slap broke Justice's heart. Not the rifle being loaded, then turned on him. He already knew what that felt like, and though it stung more to see Mr. Wife behind the weapon, it didn't sting him the most. It was Mr. Wife walking backward out the door that hurt the most. Those three steps back were no different than a man pressing his lips together when asked if he knew someone. They were strangers now. Justice stood alone in the center of the room.

[4]

The same day Justice lost his rifle, Selah collapsed in the field between Saint's home and Ours. She and her sister had been playing when Selah stopped laughing and dropped to the grass. Naima knelt by her and noticed all of Selah's hair had turned gray. When Selah lifted her head from the grass, crow's-feet stepped from her eyes, and her cheeks were sunken in.

"Selah?" Naima said.

Selah nodded. "I remember you. You look as you did when we were children."

Naima lifted Selah onto her back and ran home, Selah's body lighter than the clothes Naima wore. In the house, she lowered her wizened sister in front of the fireplace in the big, upholstered chair, Selah's favorite, and appraised her sister's well-being. Overwhelmed, Naima thought of Frances, who years ago had found herself lingering in the past, getting stuck there in its foul influence and dragging outbursts of pain from long ago into the present. Frances, having a memory like a never-closing door, would know what to do.

But Frances wasn't around. Neither was Saint, the house empty but for Naima and Selah. A chilly breeze entered through an open window. Selah wrapped her thin arms around her body, skin loose and thin.

Though she hadn't said anything, Naima had witnessed this transformation before, but not for this long and not to this extent. Before, only a few tufts of gray had appeared in Selah's hair while soft exhaustion glazed over her eyes. It happened almost in an instant. Two blinks and Naima saw her sister how she had always been, an exact echo of herself. Naima concluded that her imagination caught her during a perilous state of boredom and didn't mention what she saw to anyone.

The second time it happened, it lasted longer, and the older Selah spoke for the first time, "Sister, how have you returned to how you once were all those years ago?" Naima had been standing at the bedroom window, speaking terribly of Joy, when she heard Selah's soft snickers collapse into the dark-hued inquiry from a strange woman calling her sister with a voice thick enough to eat. When she turned around, Selah was still aged and smiled with amazement at Naima. "How do you look that way?" Then Selah closed her eyes, her hair darkened youthful again, her eyes' corners smoothed as the injustices she would perceive in the future faded.

It happened a few more times after that, and Naima finally told her sister about the aging when it took almost twenty minutes for the Selah she knew to return. Selah swore her to secrecy, but when at the next occurrence it took an hour for Selah to revert to her younger self, Naima protested.

"You stayed old longer this time," Naima said. "You need to tell Saint."

Selah groaned.

"Where you go when you go?"

"I don't know," Selah said. "Please don't tell Saint."

"Why not?"

Selah pulled at her fingers and gazed at her dress. "I don't know. It don't feel like the right thing to do."

"Not right for you to turn old, either."

"Naima,"—Selah sounded as though she were about to cry—"why can we do what we do?"

"How you mean?"

But Selah seemed to have forgotten she asked a question and shook her head, saying, "You can't tell Saint," then with anger, "I will never forgive you if you do."

"You just want to leave me. You just want another way to leave."

"I will never forgive you. She tells us what to do enough as is. If you tell her this, she'll find a way to use me getting old for herself. She will. So don't tell her."

Naima agreed to keep her sister's secret then, but regretted doing so now, now that the old woman Selah had aged more than previous times and showed no intention of leaving. She brought a quilt to the woman Selah had become and wrapped it around her. The woman coughed. Naima boiled water for tea, the scent of mint adorning her fingers as she prepared the herbs. The woman Selah shook as she drank. Naima closed the window and tossed a log into the fireplace, but the woman grabbed Naima by the sleeve of her dress and shook her head.

"No fire," Selah said. The woman sipped the steaming tea and beheld Naima.

Late morning raised its head into a warm afternoon, forcing Naima to reopen the window and let out some of the woman's dying smell from the house. She had never liked the smell of dying things even though she, born with influence over death, knew when someone was sick, was about to be sick, or was near the end. Though the idea of death carried no menace for Naima, how the body decayed into various and obdurate stinks, and how flesh appeared to dissipate from the bone disappointed her. What she wanted—anarchy of the body, the unpredictable music of the sickly's resistance to rot—oftentimes rallied, instead, toward peaceful acceptance of the end. The aged Selah settled into her dying, causing Naima to purse her lips with unflagging determination. "I will never forgive you if you do," Naima heard her sister say as she remembered their conversation and wondered why Selah seemed frightened of Saint. She pondered by the open window though it offered her no way out.

Sigh. Would it be so bad for Selah to end this way? Twelve years old, the twins had a good life on earth. Dutiful, without complaint, the two worked for Saint and found their play and refuge anywhere they pleased. Children and therefore experts of the imagination, every burning thought came to life at their whim. What didn't belong to them? If they wanted to ride a flying boat in the middle of winter, they took a deep breath and at their feet the sky rolled out before them in a swath of pale blue while a tree carved itself into paddles and a vessel large enough for the two of them.

However, this womanhood, this "getting old and on with it," as Naima remembered Saint saying about a woman she disliked ("she need to just get old and get on with it"), was supposed to be better measured, no? Though she had no memories of it, instinctually Naima knew that someone or something held the responsibility of taking a person step-by-step through life's stages. Who transitioned the infants into young'uns, the young'uns into young adults, the young adults into full adults, and the full adults into elders? Who, after such wisdom, transitioned the elders to become ancestors?

"Sister," Selah called from the chair. "Sister, you still there?"

Naima liked the way old woman Selah called her "sister." It was urgent, hot but loving, as though each time she said it, she had to convince Naima of its truth.

"Sister, you still with me?"

"I'm here. By the window," Naima said.

"It's almost time for me to go. Watch me go as I go? With your still-young face. How you stay young like that? Huh, sister?" Selah laughed. "How sister-death stay young like that? Tell me your ways."

Naima knelt beside the chair and held woman Selah's cold, thin hand. She tried to rest her head against her sister's bony thigh, but her ear landed on the seat cushion instead.

"I know you not really my sister," Selah said. "I know all this is in my dying mind."

"No, no, it's me," Naima said. "It's me and you here like always."

"Like always."

"Remember when we . . ." Naima began but couldn't come up with a memory. In the moment she most needed to remember any story she shared with Selah, the only thing she could recall was hammering her own fingers in retribution for Selah's secret night excursions to help the people in Ours. Not the game they played on Aba's door, or when Selah first entered the body of an animal. Her fingers throbbed now in recollection. The pain nothing like what she felt during Selah's unshared departures or what she felt now waiting for her sister to die. She held woman Selah's hand while thinking of her own swollen fingers and smiled just to pass on from one side of sorrow to the other.

Selah coughed. "I don't remember much nohow. Don't worry. I don't remember, either."

"Why won't you come back? Why are you staying old?"

"No choice, girl. Why didn't you get old and stay old with me? You the one run off with that man . . ." and here Selah trailed off, leaving Naima alone in her thoughts about a man and leaving her sister.

"I would never leave you. Not for nobody."

"Even 'fore you left, you gave that man so little. You gave him so little of you, Naima. Why don't you give him a little more?" Selah nodded off. "Just a little more of your heart, is all I'm saying." And she fell quiet.

Naima squeezed Selah's hand. She buried her face into her sister's knuckles. Not a lick of warmth left in them. That soon? "I would never leave you, Selah," she said.

"Leave me where?" Selah said. Girlhood had returned to her voice and when Naima looked up tearfully, she saw Frances pressing an ungloved hand over Selah's wrinkleless forehead. Selah smiled, weak.

"You have a fever," Frances said. She lowered her hand from Selah's brow and headed upstairs. Halfway up, she called down, "If you see Saint, tell her it's important we talk. You do that for me?"

The twins nodded.

Frances collapsed on the bed, clenched her sides, and pressed her teeth together in agony. Centuries unfolded within her in sweltering waves, the heat of which made her sweat out her clothes until she began to feel she was underwater.

She felt her blood quicken to the rush of the waves, the recognizable pulse of ocean summoning her. 'It was all in the water,' Frances thought, 'and all in the blood, held by the body.' Over and over again, the blood in the body spoke to any presence of water it neared, rushed through the heart while trying to go on home to the splatter, the puddle, the lake, the waterfall, the river, the inlet, the sea, the ocean, the rain that fell and the humidity that floated and distorted the horizon, the liberation of water evaporating in an urge of sunlight, back to the sky just to defy its transcendence and return to the ocean, the salty ingestion of blood in the ocean meant to last billions of years, billions of years the inconceivable, unaccounted-for enslaved thrown from ships with names more beautiful and personable than they deserved—*La Amistad, Antelope, Aurore, Duc du Maine, Elizabeth, Esmeralda, Fredensborg, Guerrero, Hannibal, Hebe, Henrietta Marie, Hermosa, Isabella, Madre de Deus, Manuelita, Meermin, Midas, La Negrita, Trouvadore, Wanderer, Zong*... the bell of a wave's crest dropping into the water, tolling the blood of enslaved Africans that chose the ocean or had the ocean chosen for them, blood that would go back to its kin calmly or in engulfing rages of flood and hurricane, or a hymn only hearable by the slaves, enthralling them, fixing their attention to the water, which was another home anointed by the blood of kin, made acceptable by their god, the water into which they marched and married, yes, Frances felt that tug at her chest, her own blood pulling her where she needed to go as she laid on her side, arms clenching around her, her knees tucked, her gaze blank and infantile, her mind frightened but triumphant in fear, yes, because there was a home in the top, middle, and bottom of the ocean, something to return to calling from

Selah's own blood, the heat of it, traveled from that young girl's skin into Frances's body and sent the woman corkscrewing into profound madness and memory. Seaworthy? No. No body is. But making do. And much was due.

BUCKLED AND MIND-TRAPPED, Frances knew Saint needed to hear this revelation, but Saint hadn't been around all day. Looking for her without rushing, Frances took her time unclenching her jaw and staggered dizzily down the hall toward Saint's room. There, she was met with an empty wall where the bedroom door used to be and behind which no sound emanated. She closed her eyes, focusing on the area where she was sure the door should've been had it been there. In her quick trance, she realized that Saint had blocked view of her bedroom by the use of stones. The door was open, Frances sensed, and she discontinued her focus so as not to see into the room that Saint put so much effort into hiding.

Frances's face flushed of color as she considered what Selah's past revealed to her. She had never seen someone move into the future, their body aging by the second, and for Selah to do it without any control only deepened the already deep suspicion Frances carried when it came to all three of the dwellers of Saint's place. Conjure had rules, took time, required intervention from the spirit world. But Saint and the twins had built no altars, prayed at no tree's base or basin of rock, didn't watch the moon and didn't care about the sun, and sickened and healed without asking any spirit for direction. 'Ain't right,' Frances thought.

To harbor any resentment toward these three would be hypocritical, Frances knew, since she also had a way of being in the world that required no intercession from the spirit realm. Mystery held the moment by its tail. There existed more for Frances to learn about Saint and her twins, but also about herself. She changed her mind and returned to Saint's disappeared bedroom door.

Focusing on the space where the energy of the stones felt strongest, she saw, through the hidden open door, Saint embracing her companion from behind as they lie on their sides in bed, Saint's curved back to the door, arms wrapped around that quiet man with a tenderness Frances hadn't seen from Saint. And seeing it made tears whelm her eyes, ashamed to witness something she had no business seeing. But the soft of it, the warmth.

She turned away from what wasn't for her to see and walked downstairs. The twins shouted in the backyard among the butterflies and milk thistle. Frances watched them on occasion as they wreathed their heads in wildflowers and made stories to act out together. Their eternal possibility. Edgeless curiosity. She laughed hearing the twins laugh, shook her head when she couldn't summon a memory of her own childhood. Was she humorous growing up? Somber? Did she have a high-pitched laugh? When she cried, for how long and how deep the feeling?

Perhaps Frances had more to herself than she had imagined, her mind fluid as a poem. 'Of course. Where you been all this time?' Frances thought. And where had she been? She started to consider, for the first time, getting angry and not knowing why.

· CHAPTER 21 ·

Communal

[1]

Tangled in hard thoughts, Joy said to Aba, "He wanted to blow my voice back into my head."

Aba heard her speaking, a trace of a human voice as he went to the bedroom to retrieve his pistol from beneath a pile of clothes folded over a slave Bible gifted from Reverend. Then, gun in hand, he stopped hearing her at all, and instead of her near-whisper testimony he heard a sharp, relentless whistle that had no whistler, starting at the back of his head and careening forward ear to ear until it filled both ears with a teakettle's ready pitch.

Just moments before Joy told him this story, he had been rubbing her feet on the porch stairs, morning light inching over them as early wakers tended to their daily chores, blushing at the scene the two made of their delight to touch and be touched. He rubbed her calves like some secret to living a good life would squeeze out. Joy tilted her head back and hummed. Then she went stiff, quiet, and Aba thought maybe she suddenly felt ashamed of what they were doing and so stopped the rubbing. She said she wanted to go inside and tell him something important.

Inside, she told him how she had meant to tell him about Justice, but Aba had made such a beautiful dinner that night, then asked permission to be inside her for the rest of the night. And he did just that. So, when morning came and he wanted to rub on her legs, the thought of Justice pulling a gun on her had been buried beneath rabbit meat and lovemaking. 'With all that rubbing, must've come unburied,' Aba thought, and then he heard nothing else but the teakettle sound, bright and without break.

He heard the whistle when he put the gun in his pocket. He heard it when he pushed Joy from in front of the door, her arms stretched out beside her.

"I'm not gone kill him," Aba said, already on the porch and the boards moaning beneath him. Looking back as he walked on, he saw Joy standing in the doorway, shaking her head slow with a wary smile, all peace vacated from her.

EVERYBODY STARED AT ABA, as though during his rush to Justice's they, too, heard seeping from him the thin, bright sound. Word traveled about what Justice had done, and they knew Aba was on his way to see the man who tried to kill his live-in woman.

"You heading there now?" someone hollered from their mess of a yard and "Took you long enough!" another said, his laughter knife-bright and pitying. Even the stones crunching beneath Aba's boots said to him in his own voice, "Even you could be taught a lesson. Even you, my friend, can be knocked down from on high."

The closer he got to Justice's, the more potent his anger became. It wanted him, and he wanted it. The whistle grew its loudest when he crossed into the yard; past the perfectly built fence; up the stairs that held his weight better than his own; and up to the porch that had been painted, beam and banister, a white whiter than possible.

Gladly, Aba wrapped his thick hand around the gun handle and turned the knob to Justice's door, screaming "Boy!" with the bang of the door hitting the wall as it flew back like an eagle wing, revealing

Justice lying on his back in the middle of the floor. Justice was weeping, covering his face with his massive hands, one hand barely muffling his booming cries. Aba put the gun back in his pocket and rubbed his slack jaw. Unable to compete with a dirge, the rageful whistling ended swiftly.

Justice cried so hard he must not have heard Aba storming into his house, a ruckus no bigger than the tip of a hen's nail in comparison to heartbreak. And he didn't stop crying until Aba kicked him gently in his side. When he looked up, Aba reached out a hand.

Eventually, they found themselves sitting on the porch, Aba in a whiny chair that Justice offered to oil but Aba didn't let him. He had hoped to translate the noise into his own speech and leaning forward said, "You hear?" Justice looked at the wood slats of the porch and Aba knew it didn't work.

"You not gone shoot me?" Justice asked and Aba's brow furrowed in surprise. The gun sat deep in his pocket. He had forgotten it. "Papa"—Justice paused—"Mr. Wife put a rifle to my face. I figured you'd do the same."

'Pistol, not a rifle,' Aba thought. He shook his head *no* before clenching his hands in his lap. They both waved at gawkers strolling by beneath the sun's punishing heat. They waved and Aba's irritation with being watched grew. He stood and motioned for Justice to follow him. Side by side, they headed east then north and kept going right past the tree soon-to-be-called God's Place, turning east again until they were at the small clearing where Aba first found Luther-Philip and Justice. This time, Aba punched Justice square in the face, making his jaw lurch.

Justice touched his left cheek, his eyes packed with venom. Aba pulled out his gun and laid it off to the side. He leaned forward and smacked his chest, rocking rhythmically on his feet. With two quick flicks of his fingers, he motioned for Justice to come at him, a dangerous smirk on his face. Justice hunched over and mimicked Aba's rock.

They fought hard, fist to face, tackle and pin, tasting blood and not knowing whose it was. They growled, snarled, and huffed. They spat crimson from their mouths and blessed the grass. Air burned their lungs. Insects ate at them as they rushed forward one last time, arms linking, elbows popping, shoulders taut in their hidden striations against the opposing force of the other. They smelled each other and grew furious. They looked into each other's eyes and wanted to destroy. Violence became a haven. Aba dug a heel into the ground and pushed off with the ball of the other foot and with a twist managed to get Justice's arm under his armpit. He went for the slam until a sharp pain took out his weight-bearing knee and the two men crashed to the ground. Aba lay there gripping his leg, unable to stand. When he turned on his back, he saw Justice stand before him with his pistol, the one bullet still in it.

Justice eclipsed the sun behind him. He held the pistol flat in his palm, handle facing Aba.

They sat on a log and caught their breath beneath a leaf canopy. Leaf shadow bobbed across their bodies with haunting movement. Soon, in uninterrupted peace, Justice put his face in his hands and started up his weeping again. Aba winced and watched wide-eyed as Justice embraced every tear that fell into his hands.

Aba had never seen a grown man cry this much in his life, let alone a single day. He playfully pushed Justice on the shoulder, and when Justice looked up, Aba opened his mouth and fanned Justice's hands away from his face. He then made his own hands into bird mouths, opening and shutting them.

"Talk?" Justice asked.

Aba nodded.

"You don't talk. Why should I?"

Aba jabbed himself with his thumb and twisted his fists beneath his eyes while exaggerating a frown. He then clapped his hands and swiped them away from each other in front of him. He jabbed himself again with his thumb, then sat up straight and lifted his chin. He had no idea if what he wanted to communicate was clear, but Justice sat up straight and began to speak.

"I believe I got evil in me that I can't get out. Saint thinks so. Thinks I'm a monster," Justice said.

Aba glared in bewilderment. 'The monster of monsters,' he thought, 'thinking you the monster. That's what a monster would do.' He softened his countenance, which offered to Justice permission to continue.

"She not wrong. There's something in me that wants everybody to hurt like it do. It look like the devil when I see it. It's in me and it wants to come out. I don't want to hurt nobody else but it do. It even wants to hurt Luthe . . ." Justice trailed off.

'This was the price of love,' Aba considered. 'Love a burden and if you wear it too long the wrong way you be done wore yourself thin. You got to give it right to get it right. And when you don't give it right, then the getting get all wrong. You be wanting it how you give it when nobody in their right mind want to give it to you like that: stone-hard, heavy-handed, unfairness getting unfairer by the minute. Cruelly. Love that try to hurt you cause the hurt feel more real that way. But it ain't.' Aba, light-headed with regret, sighed hard. It wasn't totally his fault. Just partially. He was but one person who could've told Justice the truth about love. 'You can take it anywhere with you, but it has got to be the right size, the right kind. Just because you can carry love don't mean it's light.'

Aba only knew so much about love himself. But there were people who could teach Justice what Aba was slowly learning with Joy. It had been about a month since Aba's last visit, yet he knew they could help Justice unblock whatever stood in the way between him and himself.

"We gone go somewhere Saint hate," Aba said with a shuffle of his feet against the grass as he stood, but Justice couldn't understand. He nodded for Justice to follow, and they hiked through the woods just outside of where Saint's stones blocked out the rest of the world.

[2]

About a mile or so northeast, a collection of shanties blistered the woods with their delinquent architecture. Dogs barked, tied to laundry posts and narrow trees that snagged their necks as they hopped in an eager dance to the tempo of their hunger. The town appeared empty except for that sprinkling of dogs, a dozen or so loose chickens, and a menagerie of hoofed beasts fenced in a tight square just north of the last few lopsided shacks before the woods overwhelmed.

Justice heard singing crescendo from a nearby window, and when he looked at Aba for confirmation, Aba pointed in the direction of the modest baritone coming from a shack off to the right of them. Aba signaled for Justice to wait, then approached the shack. Aba knocked on the door before entering without a welcome. The singing stopped. The breeze died.

Justice waited outside, sore from fighting earlier and confused by his surroundings. He didn't know another town existed this close to Ours. As children, he and Luther-Philip ran through, climbed over, pissed in, and wrestled on what he thought was every patch of woods around Ours, only to realize as an adult that they hadn't gone that far from their homes when they explored all those years ago. The world only felt more known to them back then, and that more waited on the fringe of what he knew chastened him.

The scent of ash wood burning from the outdoor kitchens at the center of town added some coziness. In the pots dangling from hooks hammered into small scaffolds built over the stone-enclosed fires boiled stews from which emanated the scent of cinnamon, mint, and rosemary. Wind carried the musty odors from some of the shacks' old wooden frames mossed and ivied-over in complex trellises. The shacks' frontages gawked at each other in strange dispatches of dust and humor, competing across the laneless scramble and scattering over the land. Some shacks faced west like the one Aba entered and therefore faced Justice with their perturbed welcoming.

Out from one, a frantically moving woman, big-lipped and pale as a foot bottom, exited carrying a large and handleless wicker basket under her arm. She marched behind her house to the laundry lines from which hung sheets and articles of clothing. The laundry smelled like linden flowers.

Aba stepped out and waved at Justice to come in. When Justice entered, he saw two men sitting cross-legged on thick, colorful quilts on the floor in the center of the one spacious room that made up the shack. The larger of the two wore an open white shirt and white pants. The smaller man, who introduced himself as Foster, was wrapped from the waist down in a light blue fabric, underneath which he wore white pants. Cowrie shells strung across his waist like a belt. He didn't smile when he saw Justice, though he had gentle eyes.

Foster motioned for Justice to join them on the floor, and Justice sat across from the bigger man who Foster introduced as Rain. Rain, smileless, nodded.

Aba joined them on the floor and immediately began rocking around, rubbing his hands on the quilt. The hiss of his palms swiping the floor drew nods and looks of concern from both Foster and Rain, the former who asked, "How long?" which sent Aba into a frenzy of swipes, chest thumps, and floor rocks where the wooden planks buckled beneath his weight.

Foster looked at Justice, then Rain. Rain nodded once, his posture long and in line with the wall behind him that was decorated with blue and white beads and cowrie shells, bones, and a large tapestry of a tall green rectangle in the center of two large rectangles that made the backdrop of the tapestry. The bottom half stretched red and the top half spread blue. At the very top of the green rectangle sprung an intricate symbol of loops, curves, arrows, dots, and flourishes resembling flower petals. On the floor beneath the tapestry were a half-full glass of what looked like water, a few uneaten slices of corn bread, and piles of coins. The display mesmerized Justice.

Foster said to Aba, "It will be done, friend."

Aba patted Justice on the shoulder, then stepped outside. Justice heard his footsteps dampen in the distance till he heard only his own breathing in the silent presence of the two strangers observing him.

"He will return, Justice," Foster said. "He's told us a lot about you."

"How when he don't talk?" Justice asked.

"He was just talking then. Didn't you hear him?" Foster made a sympathetic face. "Or you heard but didn't understand what you were hearing?"

Justice knew one thing for sure: he didn't like Foster's tone.

Foster stood and poured a clear liquid from bottle to cup. Rain followed behind and spooned steaming rice from a basket into a bowl and poured a gamey soup over the top. Justice watched them sit the bowls on the floor near where they sat. They repeated the process, sitting cups and bowls down again. Justice could hardly pay attention to their dance in his frustration. Their intimacy, thick and relentless, made the room hum.

"I was sitting right next to him, and he didn't say a word."

"He spoke with his body and with his surroundings. How else would I know your name? You never told me."

In the wide country of his thinking, Justice found no answers. Warmth came over him and he wanted to leave. "You don't talk, either?" he asked Rain. When Rain's eyes connected with his, he felt he had given the silver-haired man many kinds of permission, including continued silence. Rain's hair draped and shined against his skin like a silver shawl over wet earth.

"How your week been?" Foster said.

"Tell me who you are first, sir."

Foster nodded. "Just an old friend of Aba's. We go back a ways. He helped me build some of these houses you see here. This Turney. Folks from everywhere who never been welcomed anywhere come here to live or to hide. Or both. Nobody else wanted us, so we wanted ourselves."

Foster showed no emotion, his serenity a comfort that uneased Justice as much as it soothed. Rain's gaze sailed through the room without menace.

A rooster crowed outside, followed by a choir of dogs meeting up with the crowing. A high-pitched voice fussed at the howling dogs, and they quieted. Justice wondered if the voice belonged to the pale woman he saw.

The voice shouted something else outside, this time to the roosters, and Justice went to the window, spellbound by the woman at the laundry line and his precise memory of her. He saw her pull down the shirts like they were people she had grown, people who folded at her touch and fainted into her arms. She started speaking again, audibly, to herself it seemed, then to someone unseen, out of the frame of the window, then even farther out, beyond the frame of the world.

It took Rain calling Justice for his attention to return. Justice took his seat on the floor, mystified now by Rain's voice, bass of which turned the room into liquid.

"That's Aurora," Foster said. "She just be talking and sometimes somebody there and sometimes it's not. She's one of many reasons we don't live in Ours. Saint's not fond of some of our people. Few of us have permission to live with you all. But we do not abandon each other in Turney." Rain rested a hand on Foster's knee. "You ready to answer my question now?" Foster asked. His knee touched Rain's in return. "You were telling us how your week been."

Where to begin? Saint already called him a monster and if he had a monster in him, it shouldn't lead in introductions. He felt himself sweating, then tasted it as the bitter salt dripped onto then past his open lips. He panted and the room tightened around him. Colors in the tapestry swirled first, then the rectangles contorted with the spinning of the room. His own life frightened him into anger.

"Don't you have weeks of your own to worry about? How your damn week been? You touch each other every day of it? You tell me that much," Justice said. Even though he wanted to stop punishing everyone around him, he couldn't. His chest tightened beneath an invisible pressure, sinking in deeper with each breath.

"Our week wasn't a good one. We lost an elder, Maman Gi. We lost a mountain in our community, and everyone has spent most of their days inside. Other than me and Rain, only Aurora, who's been washing Maman Gi's clothes and linen, has seen what the day truly looks like beyond the walls of a window. She meant everything to us and now we have nothing. We celebrated her three days ago, but we can barely stand the sight of one another without her."

Justice felt more alone in his heavy breathing, cross-legged like the men sitting across from him who were more like stone guardians long abandoned by their makers.

Rain cleared his throat, tying his hair back as he spoke. "If by asking us questions you mean to not answer what we have asked, then you have exhausted that notion. We have been kind."

"Aba brought me here, then left. I didn't ask to be brought here. Don't know why I'm here," Justice spat as he spoke.

"Yet, you have not left. You have stayed. We know why you are here. We know you are not ready to know why you are here. You know you are not ready to tell us your anger. You decided to stay. You have not left." Rain gestured toward Justice and said, "We even gave you food and drink, but you didn't notice. You didn't notice that all this time we have waited for you to join us and have allowed our own food to get cold in our waiting."

Where Rain pointed, sure enough the same food and drink he and Foster had prepared earlier for themselves sat in front of Justice, too. If he was going to leave, if leaving had ever been possible, he had lost all hope to do so now and remained in their house until ready to speak.

THEY LIVED IN RELATIVE PEACE, riding an agreement Justice hadn't agreed to except for what grief held him there. Neither Foster nor Rain complained, and Justice helped with the chores around the house and throughout town. Each day, Foster asked how his week was. Justice just shook his head. Foster would put a hand on his shoulder and nod, then carry on with whatever his own chores were for the day. Rain only spoke when needed, mainly to warn Justice when he had gotten out of line. For those few days, the man with the silver hair and wet-earth skin didn't find it useful to talk otherwise, not even to Foster. Still, he was kind if distant, and he left Justice mostly to Foster's care. Aba didn't come back to retrieve Justice, and Justice didn't leave on his own accord.

Since the first day of his arrival, he paid begrudging attention to Foster and Rain's affection for one another. The two prayed together at the altar, cooked with each other, stole kisses and quick touches on the waist and face. Some afternoons, Rain, on one side of the shack, played a gourd covered in a net of colorful beads while on the opposite end Foster played a thin drum with a stick in his left hand and his right hand striking bare on the drum top. The shack vibrated with the heart of their music.

Once, during one of these musical interludes, a throng of emotions overwhelmed Justice. In the presence of their constant love and percussion crisscrossing over his head, he felt empty. He became mean, hostile. He fed his portion of food to the dogs, aimlessly wandered Turney instead of helping, and snapped at Foster when he asked if Justice needed anything. Foster's gentle voice sent him over the edge. Rain kept to himself, not even cutting an eye at Justice, and loved on Foster more. Justice thought it unfair that a love like that existed. He wanted nothing more to do with them.

[3]

Later that night, Justice heard drums peal from the center of Turney. Standing, his body went loose. His thoughts warped into a shape he didn't recognize. His feet moved on their own out the door to the source of the sounds that had possessed him, leashed him, and dragged him toward the courtyard.

Many folks sat and stood in a circle, dancing in and out of the flesh-hot ring to the rapid playing of three drums. The dancers approached the drummers until the rhythm changed and the dancers turned away, moving back to the circle's edge. The drummers sat together playing their parts, sweat wetting impact upon impact of stick to goat's skin, palm to drum top, the thin ropes sealing the skin to the wooden instruments like a promise.

Justice approached the torchlit ensemble to the rhythm of the playing, curiosity bending into fear, then warping back to curiosity. A very small boy sitting in the grass hit a stick against an empty rum bottle. Each clink pushed Justice ahead with a finger point of sound nudging him in the back while the drums ungently summoned his feet. The rest of his body leaned back at an angle so violent his lower back ached at the torqued hinge of his hip, for his legs were being taken in one direction and his torso's unwillingness to be led forced it to curve away in the force of his feet's ghastly momentum as the drums sped up, until he broke through the circle and made his way toward the drummers, his feet now marching, his torso tugged by the rope of sound before him that he saw came from Rain, Foster, and Aurora playing thin-bottomed drums, Foster's larger than Aurora's and Aurora's larger than Rain's, until Rain abruptly played a rhythm out of sync with Foster and Aurora that became the new rhythm, faster, full of screaming through which Rain made his exit, leaving Foster and Aurora to devastate the air around them with sound, Justice's body aching all over, a collection of voices singing off to the side but the blood-filled rhythm overtook him, pushed him to his knees. He wanted to scream "Stop!" against the betrayal of his body no longer listening to him, that had not listened to him since the first percussive lick wrapped those ropes to his feet and tugged him step-by-step through this circle of people wearing their whitest attire, one woman with a face fitted for wrath gripping her knees with her nails till she pulled blood while tears leaked from her tightly closed eyes and dripped onto her open lips, teeth clenched against a blistering scream-moan that issued past the stone wall of those teeth, while a set of three women wearing blue dresses spun in place in unison like a sisterhood of weathers, and a man barely standing, cradled from behind in the arms of two others, slithered feverishly in their grip, each in their own ceremony until Aurora changed the rhythm once more and rubbed her pale index finger across the drum, making it moan, and Justice's body stood tall, his muscles flexing, his eyes weeping, and his spirit dropping into his heart where his beast-monster-self resided, and the beast-monster-self roared like a temperamental bull because a man of great power rode its back, the man's ruddy skin breaking through the black-white monochrome of Justice's heart as though the red of the man's body had become his new heart and Justice's beast-monster-self bucked and roared beneath the massive weight of the man until exhausted it collapsed heaving and crying under the heavy man and the man motioned for Justice to join him but Justice refused and the ruddy man shook his head sucked his teeth and rushed toward Justice. Justice's eyes flashed open, and he witnessed the slaughter of a black pig. Soon after, he passed out.

Under a rooster's rough caw, he woke the next day sore and with swollen muscles that throbbed to the beat of his heart. His whole body a drum. He smelled like rum all over. 'A drunken dream,' he thought, until he noticed the cuts on the bottoms of his feet and recalled how the black pig didn't even squeal when the dark blood poured from its open throat.

Turning from his pallet, he saw Foster and Rain observing him from the center of the room, offering no relief from the weight of their shared gaze. He had fallen asleep in Aurora's lap, her arms wrapped across his chest, his head resting on the pillow of her left thigh. She slept above him. 'We been this way the entire night?' Justice wondered, and wrapped his own arms around his chest to embrace Aurora's embrace.

"You up?" Aurora asked. The scratch of her voice scratched Justice's ear into better hearing. He cleared his throat and asked her what happened last night. "You was rid," Aurora answered. "You for moving? Let's join our brothers." So they did.

"Tell us what you saw last night," Foster said.

Sitting with the others, his body ached all over, throbbing inside to out, whole body giving birth to itself, but he felt well. More aware than ever and at peace. He shared that last night wasn't the first time he had visited his heart and that the beast with his face waited there every time he did. He explained the monochrome of his heart, black and white, the white illumination giving shape to the black that was the source and surface of all things. Water that he knew was water by how the white ripples drew waves against the flat blackness separating him from the beast, unless Justice was angry, which made the water recede and allowed the beast to close in on him across the nothing sand. "Bad things happen when it did," he said, "things I'm ashamed of." But last night, a muscular man who seemed more than a man, with skin the color of dried blood, visited him, riding and wrestling the beast into submission.

"Careful," Justice heard Aurora say, but she had crushed the *R* into a cough, and the end of the word sounded like "fool," which is exactly what he felt like listening to her speak. "Visit your heart now?" she asked.

Justice took heed of what he heard as a warning. Careful. He had to be careful going back into himself. He remembered the man inside him, his immense body, his anger that Justice didn't come to him when called.

"Just touch your heart and feel it beat. Drums sent you there. Drums'll send you back," Aurora said.

Justice shook his head.

Aurora tilted her ear toward him. "Got a boy burning in you. I hear him. I hear the fire."

A fire. Justice hadn't told anyone there about the *E* branded into his leg and Aba didn't know about it to tell. So how did Aurora know about a boy burning and that the boy was still in him burning alive?

Justice felt hot all over. He removed his shirt and pants almost without thinking, the *E* an epitaph emerging from his thigh. Anger whelmed him as heat overpowered him.

"Go back into your heart. Find what you afraid of. That man you saw in you only quieted the beast. You go deal with it."

Justice closed his eyes. The muscular man the color of blood was gone. The subdued beast still lay on the black ground, huffing, growling. It looked at Justice with its white-light eyes and roared. Its horns scratched against the ground, leaving jagged white lines in the black space. Justice approached the beast that shared his face, pacing himself, trembling. The closer he got, the more the beast snarled, livid at its own exhaustion.

It didn't surprise him when the beast clawed at him as he got closer. It also didn't surprise him when the beast bared its teeth at him. What surprised Justice, enough to make him kneel and touch the beast on its face that was his face, is that the beast began to cry. It was on its back now and opened its hairy legs to reveal an *E* in the same spot Justice had his *E*.

"Let me know it?" Justice said, and touched the beast's brand. It burned his fingers, still hot, yet he kept them there, gently rubbing circles against the painful letter.

"I got you," Justice cried out, which brought him back to the room with Aurora, Foster, and Rain. "I got you. I got you." He didn't resist Aurora wrapping him in a white sheet. He didn't resist the three of them finding their spots around him and holding him. "I got you." He said it again. "I got you."

[4]

Two weeks later, Aba returned to collect Justice. He smiled when the young man understood his claps and body pats. 'Must've worked,' he thought, and knew for sure it worked when Justice said he was staying in Turney. Already a glint in Justice's eyes, a penny-shine worthy of all the joy in the world.

"To keep learning," Justice explained. Everyone agreed he would stay with Aurora on some days and Foster and Rain on others so as not to wear out his welcome with either household as they trained him up in spirit. If he wanted, he would get his own house there after successful training. "Please tell everybody back there—" Justice started to say, then smiled the words away. "Be well, Aba. Thank you."

Aba gave Justice a knife and told him by rubbing together his hands, "This the only tool you need, now. Go. Work." He nodded, waved at his friends, then headed back to Ours.

An old story came to Aba as he trekked home, one he heard from Saint when they were first becoming friends. It went: There were once two friends, Here and There, chatting on opposite sides of a road that split into a crossroad. They had been friends for as long as the sun and moon chased each other in the sky and the ocean tasted of tears. They laughed at joke after joke and discussed important family matters with each other with the trust of siblings.

"My wife is pregnant but can't keep down her food," Here said. There told him to give her banana in the morning to soothe her stomach.

"My children do not listen to me when I give them instructions," There said. In return, Here replied that he should tell them bedtime stories that do not end, saying that he will not finish the story unless they behave the following day.

All was well between the two friends.

Then one Monday, a mysterious man who had never been seen in the village before walked down the path heading toward the crossroad. Here looked up from his pulling of yams and saw the man from the side. How beautifully dressed was this man in a coat of bright scarlet! Before the mysterious man could fully pass, the friend returned to his work remembering he was on a tight deadline for the market and couldn't be distracted.

On the other side of the road, There saw the man as he walked by and couldn't believe how sharp he looked in his black coat. Before the mysterious man could fully pass, the friend ran into his house because his wife needed his help with something and had called him to come inside.

At the end of the day, Here and There met as usual and discussed the mysterious man with the beautiful coat.

"That man's scarlet coat was astounding, no? Like blood on fire," Here said.

"You mean his black coat was cleaner than a raven's," There said.

"I beg your pardon, but I think you are mistaken. It was obviously scarlet."

"Do not joke so poorly. It was black. Where were you looking?"

"Are you calling me a liar?"

"Are you saying I do not know my colors?"

The two men went on like this for a while, eventually revealing that their friendship itself had been at a crossroads the entire time.

"And your children are poorly behaved and always have been. I never liked them," one shouted.

"Well, your wife is the most obnoxious woman in the village," the other shouted.

Unknown to them, the mysterious man watched them argue right above their heads, grinning at their discontent, which was their honesty finally set free. He darted his head as each friend took his turn cursing the other until both went inside of their homes in a fury. The following day, the men gathered supporters from the village to defend their honor and within hours the entire village was laid to waste. The two friends, bloody and out of breath, looked at the damage they had caused and sobbed. Something fell from the sky and landed between them. It was the coat: scarlet on one side and black on the other.

The two men apologized. Having lost everything but each other, they promised that from then on, they would never let anything trivial come between them ever again. There would be no hatred, for hatred was neither Here nor There.

"My, my, my, my, my!" Aba said, his feet rustling in the grass, then chuckled at the scenery before him, which was the tree soon-to-be-called God's Place sitting its big self in a town of free Negroes. 'We had been good friends,' Aba thought of Saint, then shook his head I'll-be-goddamned at the tree and thought, 'All this time. All this time. Come to find out, slavery the slickest trickster I ever knowed.'

· CHAPTER 22 ·

Reunion

[1]

Every dusk, before the blank witness of Thylias's back to the window as she worked up a sweat in the front room, the sun rested in the west, varnishing her wet skin until the moon took its place, which became for Thylias the only sign that she should either rest or set up her own lamp to keep working into evening.

The pattern of celestial bodies as they appeared and disappeared crept into Thylias and ordered not only her steps as she briskly skipped from nail to nail throughout her house, hammer in one hand and nails jangling like loose keys in the other, but also ordered how she hammered. The pattern she once pounded into the walls surrounding Franklin's old bedroom had been an arc mimicking the sun dipping into the horizon. The new pattern she hammered was an upward arc mimicking the moon rising counter to the falling light. Soon, the sky stretched as dark as the bruised insides of Thylias's hands.

When she slept, the hammer rested beneath her pillow, and the nails rocked then settled on a shoddy table next to a pot of dying lilies bowing from the pot's rim. She slept hard and peaceless because the sparks of dreams fell upon her and kept her working even in sleep. She had no recollection of the nature of her dreams, just that she had dreamt and felt a refreshing tiredness of someone knee-deep in good living.

While awake, hammering nails into the wall in arches that interrupted each other, that grew from the humped backs of other arches and mirrored in curved parallels their nearest neighbor, her focus steeled, piercing every wall in the front room until she ran out of nails and had to use blades: hunter's knives, butcher knives, the stake end of a hook, lengths and sharpnesses of varying degrees smashed into the wood. She knew she neared finishing not when she ran out of nails or sharp replacements but when she stopped looking for any and everything to hammer into the wall. She sat in wonder of what she had wrought, curious and suspicious of the pleasure curiosity made possible because she knew how quickly curiosity could bend toward risk.

Had she been successful? During her hammering, she hadn't discovered why she felt compelled to impale the wall in the first place; but now, exhausted, heaving in the front room and engulfed in lamplight while night's visitation tried but failed to intrude on her, she thought two things: 'I been all this time fighting myself,' then 'No, I been heavy with loss and the poor wall had to take it on.' But both sentiments felt superficial as she cautiously approached the wall. She wiped her forehead with the back of her hand and illuminated the nails in the wall with the lantern hanging from her tight grip as though traversing a cave over which was written, in a distant yet familiar script, the prayer of some ancient peoples who had inscribed power in its purest form into the surface, into the dwelling itself, agitating something on the other side . . . and there it was—on the opposite side of the nail-wounded wall was Franklin's old bedroom whose door she hadn't opened since she closed it after Franklin's death. She imagined his lone pair of brown leather shoes, the folded knitted blankets, assorted coins and rings in a silver lockbox—she imagined it all shrieking inside the room as nails broke through to the other side and closed in like an iron maiden. 'If this anger,' she thought, 'it don't feel like any I've known.'

She hung the lamp from a hook overhead. She grabbed the hammer and started to hit the nails deeper, saying aloud this time, “I am angry,” wanting to feel it, because she deserved to feel it, had earned it. She hammered. “I am angry.” Hammered. “I’m angry.” Hammered. “I’m angry!” louder this time. It had taken so many nails because it took that long for her to figure out that she wanted to harm something, to cause hurt, make it suffer, damn it all if it didn’t deserve it; something needed to be broken.

“Wake up,” she yelled at herself. “Wake up, woman.” And she hammered one last nail to wake up inside of her a growing hatred of the town for not properly mourning her friend, of her friend for shooting himself in the head like he was a hobbled horse, of herself for not feeling it any sooner. Forty-four years old and for the first time she leaned into it: This anger. This disgust. This contempt. This coldness. This detestation. This power.

SHE SLEPT FOR days straight. And for days straight, she simmered.

[2]

Loneliness knocked on Luther-Philip’s heart like a desperate suitor as he sat in Justice’s abandoned home, listening to rain patter against the roof and windows. The unrivaled neatness of the house saddened him even more. He sat on Justice’s couch and waited for him to return so he could apologize for telling Mr. Wife that Justice had pulled a gun on Joy when he could’ve spoken to Justice as a friend, gotten to the bottom of his ache and seen for himself what the issue was. But anger has a way of quickening time, and he had fallen so suddenly and deeply into anger that no thought of grace touched him. ‘Wasn’t it clear he wasn’t going to shoot her?’ he thought, then just as fast felt silly for thinking such a thing. Grace? Sure. But trust?

Anger snatched him up again: with Justice and with himself. The fantastically neat home Justice had curated in his short time there seemed a sparseness in competition with Luther-Philip's own vacated happiness. The table refused to collect dust. The rug's colors shone brilliantly despite only cloudy light entering through the window. The couch smelled like flowers.

The bust of the woman stood on the table. Smoke stench still wreathed the wooden face staring at him with an expression of pleasure-touched shock, some delight exposed just above her head. Luther-Philip looked up, too, hoping to see some sign of Justice etched into the ceiling.

After Justice had been gone for two weeks, Luther-Philip visited the schoolhouse he hadn't visited since he was a child. Sunset arrived in a rush, and the roads emptied early while folks retired on their porches and in their yards for a nightcap and stories. He entered the schoolhouse and found everything much smaller than he remembered. He found his old chair, the one with the carved symbol of an abstract blossom at the headrest. Next to it, what would have been Justice's chair sat as empty as his house.

Luther-Philip unlatched the collection of feelings that he kept to himself and tucked the image of the empty chair inside his mind, where he could trace the abstract blossom with his fingers all he wanted without being caught. A barrage of birds flashed past the window and startled him, their caws shaking him to look about the schoolhouse that had become as small as a thimble in the night's hold. No room for him and his friend. No more room for childish things and the pleasures therein. Being grown frightened him. He became more uncertain every day of his life. After the birds passed and his heart settled, he walked to his father's home with a question on his mind.

"What does it mean to be a man?" Luther-Philip asked Mr. Wife, who had been sweeping his porch before his son arrived with a question harder than he had energy for. "Hell, I just learned," he wanted to say, but that wasn't true. Though once a slave, he knew even then that to be a man meant to be unoccupied with things that had nothing to do with him unless he chose to make those things his business. It was the right and ability to make a choice. A choice about anything at all and to do so with wisdom. And to stand by those choices and all that comes with them. He knew that much enslaved, and he knew it free, so he shared that with Luther-Philip, that first part about choices. He kept the part about enslavement to himself.

On the way back to Justice's house, his father's words rang in his head in a hard way. Did I choose Joy over Justice? Hell, didn't Justice choose to aim a rifle at a woman who offered him a smile? What could he have possibly felt he needed to defend? He sat on Justice's bed, window open, hardly any air getting through, and asked himself question after question in the sweltering heat.

Chest pain woke him in the middle of the night. Sweat dripped into his eyes. He dipped himself some water from a bucket in the back room and with his bare feet stepped on something sharp. He went to put on some shoes and grabbed an oil lamp to see the floor. It was covered in splinters of wood and a small piece had stabbed him good. He swept up the mess Justice had left behind and it wasn't until he finished cleaning that he looked at the table in the center of the room and saw a silhouette in the lamp's dim light. Bringing the lamp closer to the figure, he swayed its creaky handle like a pendulum before a wood carving of two people. The small carved figures, two boys, held hands, one of them laughing. The other's face had eyes and a nose, but no mouth. He carried the figurine of the two boys to the front room, sat it on the table next to the bust of the smoke-scented woman and clenched his teeth. His lips trembled. His eyes burned.

With his mind too full to hold anything more, he had to handle the whelming right there. The world before him had become stuck and he didn't know how to get it going again.

The next morning, he wrote a note to Aba and left it on his porch beneath a rock. Aba found it, read the words that Joy had taught him and stumbled across the ones he didn't recognize. After an hour or so with the letter, he figured out what Luther-Philip wanted, folded the letter, and placed it into his shirt pocket, delicate as a square of silk.

A month later, Aba knocked on Justice's door knowing Luther-Philip would answer. Before the door fully opened, Aba pointed north at an angle and nodded reassuringly at Luther-Philip, hoping that was enough. It was enough.

[3]

Justice was sitting with his feet at the lake's edge. Luther-Philip didn't want to disturb him. It seemed a stranger and not his old friend waited at the water of their youth, intricately wrapped in white fabric for a shirt and wearing loose gray trousers with the bottoms rolled above his ankles. Gray hair speckled his head though his blemish-less, hairless face shined in the sun with a youthful glow.

Justice didn't turn around when Luther-Philip sat beside him, and Luther-Philip believed it was because Justice was angry with him. But when he finally got the courage to look at the man sitting beside him, the peace across Justice's face, Justice looking not at him but across the water, offered Luther-Philip reprieve he didn't think he deserved.

The lake touched their feet with insistence that felt to Luther-Philip brazen and hungry. He had brought a rice sack with him and pulled from it a bowl Justice had carved and the many berries he found in preparation for this moment. He grabbed the loose fragrant orbs in fistfuls from the bottom of the bag and dropped them into the bowl. The two men ate together until none were left.

"I've been living in your home," Luther-Philip said, watching the water. "I've been missing you."

"It's your home now, Luthe," Justice said.

"That will always be your home."

They both spoke toward the lake, tossed their words into the water to wash them before sharing them with each other. Water sucked at their feet as they spoke.

A need for clarity overwhelmed Luther-Philip. There was much that he wanted to know, to say, but he had trouble beginning. The past carried too much weight and he believed the future was unnavigable. He wanted to shout it all out. Dizziness overcame him until he realized he had been holding his breath. Disappointment. Humiliation. Shame. Disappointment, again. Then an absence of definitive feeling no different from the water carrying the flat light on its back, light that could be a good or bad omen. He felt the countless possibilities rush through him, tingling through his fingers.

"When you coming back?" he asked. Justice didn't respond. "You got to come home some time. You don't have to live in Ours anymore. But won't you visit?"

"This a visit." Justice looked at Luther-Philip for the first time. The softness by which he looked, lake water gathering in his eyes, broke Luther-Philip's heart, and he decided in that moment that the light on the water, much like the light gathering in the beads of Justice's sweat, meant to point toward a new request that had never been made of either man, therefore it would take time for them to know what to do with themselves, let alone each other.

"Joy did nothing to me. I was feeling empty," Justice said. Something flopped in the water not too far off from where they sat. "I wasn't angry at her. I was angry at you."

Luther-Philip looked at his knees. His mind bubbled over with missing his friend, the sudden death of his mother, the sprawling limbs of the tree soon-to-be-called God's Place cradling scalp rot like it was a newborn. Joy was in there, too; how quickly he had stopped caring about her after she stopped wanting to see him. No question why. No checking in on her. No making sure. A shame. He didn't feel offended, nor did he feel concern. No grief. Not even a sneeze. The first time he spoke to Joy after he all but abandoned any thought of her was when he started missing Justice. Then he brought her to Justice's house like a cat bringing the head of a mouse to its owner. And here he was, lonely as a hangnail. For the first time, he wondered if maybe Justice and Joy had been lonely, too.

On his way to the lake that day, while collecting berries for his meeting with Justice, Luther-Philip walked past the tree soon-to-be-called God's Place and attempted to avoid looking at it. But the wind blowing hotly through those leaves helped him remember that Justice, all those years ago, carried him down that endless trunk when the headless scalp entrapped him. In that corpse stench, a breakthrough, respite. Sweet. Justice smelled sweet then, like fruit set out for too long.

"Was I a good friend to you?" Luther-Philip asked.

"Still are," Justice said.

Luther-Philip pulled out the carving of the two boys from the sack, one boy joyful and the other mouthless. "Can you finish this while we sit here?"

Justice gazed at the incomplete carving, then touched. His thumb, sticky from blueberry juice, rubbed the mouthless boy's face, leaving a trace of violet. His index finger cradled the back of the faceless boy's head. Justice offered a slow smile. "Forgot I started this." He pulled out the knife Aba had gifted him and got to work on the boy's mouth. "Won't be as nice. Don't have the right tools. Knife too big." He chiseled away under the round nose and into the oversize cheeks. "Which one you think you?"

Neither boy favored Luther-Philip, especially not the unfinished one without a mouth. Besides, he was more touched by Justice using his talents to remake him from a piece of wood. He wondered for the first time how his friend saw him: as a boy embracing happiness or as a boy standing with his arms at his side, palms facing up in surrender. Had he ever been that happy or that vulnerable he had no idea. More important than *which* emotion was *when*; when did Justice ever see in their time together something worth carving, worth remembering to carve into wood like a signpost to show where one has been?

Luther-Philip felt a tap on his chest. Opening his eyes, he woke lying on Justice's thigh where he had fallen asleep, facing up at Justice, who pointed just ahead where the finished carving stood close enough to block most of the view of the lake. The same calm smile Justice offered to Luther-Philip now belonged to the standing wooden boy. The jumping boy's left hand connected to the standing boy's right shoulder. The sculpture still needed a base, but for now Justice rested it on a rock. From Luther-Philip's perspective, the lake's water supported the two sculpted boys, allowing them to stand on and jump from the light-glazed dark of the water.

"This yours." Justice scratched the conch of Luther-Philip's inner ear. "I always meant to finish it and give it to you. Just didn't work out the way I wanted it to. You ended up with it anyway."

Luther-Philip looked at the gift and saw loss, saw goodbye in that wood. "You won't come home?"

"I'm home wherever I go." Justice paused. "But nothing in Ours for me."

Luther-Philip sniffed the air. He leaned into Justice. The nap he took on Justice's thigh was the best he had experienced in a long time. He decided to hold that nap as close as he would the gift of joyful boys carved into permanent joy . . . cloves. Justice smelled like cloves, a spice Mrs. Wife sometimes used when baking sweet potato pies. No wonder he slept so well and no wonder his mind burst, spilling every feeling he kept to himself in a hiding place no feeling ever belonged. He spoke aloud one of the hurts meant to be his most concealed. "I don't think I'm being free the right way."

"No right way to be free."

"Our mothers didn't know freedom longer than we did. My father wasn't born free. Neither was yours. Mine still finding out how to be free and he don't even leave the house none, let alone Ours. How we supposed to learn from them when they never been free long enough to tell us how to do it?"

"No right way to be free. That's why it's called *free.* You make all the right and wrong with it as you want. Just be mindful how much of each."

Need a mind to be mindful. Luther-Philip didn't think he had much of one. He was always a smart boy and turned out to be a decently thinking man. He could read, though he didn't read as much or as well as Justice, and he had a way with getting people to like him. Charm is what Mr. Wife called it. "People want to be around you. You can't allow everyone that closeness, so pick and choose, son," Mr. Wife had told him one day when an influx of potential suitors entered the bakery wanting a loaf of bread or a brown cream cake and leaving their hearts in Luther-Philip's hands. He paid the young women no mind then and would be hard-pressed to remember any of their names even though he grew up with most of them.

When his mother died, he was kept away from her body. As he got older, he took for granted that his mother even had a body to begin with. When she was buried, his memory of her followed, leaving him to look for what he needed elsewhere. A little attention here. A little affection there. A kind compliment. Someone to look at him lovingly. His mother couldn't do it? His father incapable? Get it from Justice. Women start to fawn over him, let them get a turn. Get something new from Joy, then when she cut herself off, don't even miss her. The only one he missed entirely was Justice, and this missing bordered grief. Not even his mother-grief was as strong, for when was the last time he had visited her grave with this much enthusiasm?

"Justice."

"Yes, Luthe."

"You ever miss your people?"

"Every day. You miss your ma?"

"I used to miss her all the time, then I just stopped."

They sat in silence for a while, waiting on each other. "Was she good to you?" Justice asked.

Luther-Philip sat up and rested his hands in his lap. "She was. We used to do all my lessons together after school and in the morning before school." He sniffed and wiped his eyes. "People leave too fast to love them. And it hurts"—Luther-Philip touched his chest—"right here."

"I got you," Justice said, and slid his hand under Luther-Philip's. They laid down and fell asleep that way, feeling the one heart break and re-form beneath their two hands.

[4]

Thylias woke one morning with a fever. Had been asleep for days and sweated through her sheets, window open, the warm breeze shaking her through to the marrow. Half-delirious, thirsty, angry all over again, she stepped out of her house carrying a Bible and looked over to her left where in plain sight spread the plain and sad burial grounds. She could see the plank of wood hammered into the earth from where she stood. 'Franklin is under there,' she thought, then blinking once she saw herself standing at his grave, shaking her head, then with another blink the image faded. Her fever climbed.

She floated in her outrage all the way to Reverend's house beside which she could see a few dozen chairs lined in the yard. The chairs were packed tight, leaving no elbow room or knee room for that matter, but the rows and columns were neat, showed much care in their placement and calmed Thylias a bit as she wobbled to a chair closest to a tall box of wood Reverend used as a pulpit. Her fever spiked and she felt heat steam behind her eyes before which the landscape blurred and warped, then returned to solidity. Reverend had left a little aisle in the center of the rows of chairs that all faced east toward daybreak. She sat in a pulpit-close chair while the sun laid into her and kept her trembling low.

She heard talking coming from inside the house, one voice going on about "Jesus" this and "the truth about it is" that, until the ramblings faded, and the front door opened, giving life to the voice again, Reverend stepping out the door and walking around the house to the side yard. He rambled ferociously. Then silence. Thylias knew then that he had seen her sitting there with her head rolled back over the headrest, the morning sun gaining heat each passing second. His pace quickened and the grass hissed beneath his bare feet and already Thylias was sick of him and regretting coming there. Unfortunately, he was the only one who could get done what she needed, despite her disgust about it.

He came up to her and shook her by the shoulders. She rolled her eyes from the back of her head to the front and Reverend rolled into view. "Sister Thylias!" Had she been any sicker, his shaking would've killed her.

"I should've let Franklin shoot you all those years ago," she said. When she heard her own voice, she rolled her eyes back to the back of her head and let out a terrible cackle. She moaned when the humor left her.

"When you get here?" Reverend asked, his hands still firm on Thylias's shoulders.

"Unhand me. I got a right to pray without you touching me."

Reverend did as she demanded and pulled a chair from beside Thylias to sit in front of her. She moaned louder.

"You sick," he said.

"Everybody somebody sick, doctor."

"What you want here?" Reverend asked. "You never come here. This the Lord's home and you don't like the Lord."

"I came for some medicine, doctor," Thylias said. Her head hurt. The fever hissed inside her. She tried to look at Reverend but her eyes hurt too much to move. "You got some medicine for me, Reverend? Some blood of Christ for the dead?" Reverend leaned back in his seat and Thylias let the fever keep talking. "I have been forsaken. Franklin been forsaken. His body. Underground. Did you come? Did you?"

"Come where?" Reverend squinted.

"So, you act that way, too. Like the rest of them. Like your ideas of Heaven too big for Franklin. Plenty room for him up there. The ground is full. It's shouting, 'No more room down here! Send him up! Send him up, God damn it!'" Thylias weakly tossed her hand up from her lap and let it slap down when she saw Reverend cringe at her curse. A dull pain bellowed throughout her body. "'Send him up!' But he still here. Still down here waiting on his own to come. Did you come while I was sleep? Did the dead call you while I was sleep? They have a strong voice behind our eyes." Reverend reached for her hands, but she snatched them away. A chill shot through her, and she cried out, holding herself, shaking. "You ever known a feeling like that, Reverend? A feeling so cold it make you hold on to yourself cause no one else will? Make you hug your grave cause no one visited you to tell you it's all right to move on?" She paused, took a few deep breaths, trembled, then continued. "Somebody stepping over my grave. Somebody stepped on my shadow. Get off my shadow, Reverend." She gave a weak laugh.

"Your shadow behind you," he said.

"Just be sure not to step on it."

"You sick."

"'Servants, be obedient to them that are your masters according to the flesh, with fear and trembling, in singleness of your heart, as unto Christ,'" Thylias said. "That's somewhere up in Ephesians. Why you not with old massa, you love the Bible so much? You came here smelling like piss and smoke. Your massa the one pee on you? He try to burn you up, up, up?" Thylias raised her hand in a slow arc, following the movement with her eyes before letting both hand and eyes linger at the apex. She dropped her arms and head with a hard moan, slumping forward in the chair. "Or did you burn him up?"

"You sick and nasty woman." Reverend's whole body shook.

"You want to know why nobody listen to you when you talk about God, Reverend? It's because you just like God. You don't listen. You go around doing whatever you want to do, stepping on people's shadows, charging the living with all the vice you can muster and abandoning the dead. Jesus took care of the dead, too, Reverend." She opened her eyes, sunlight filled her skull like a dam and her head felt good for bursting. "You not like Jesus at all. Ask the people." She rubbed her right eye hard. "God got one tooth and is digging it in my head right now. You don't even know where a lot of us came from. Do you?" She balled herself up on the chair seat and canopied her eyes with her right hand. With her left, she kept pulling down on her dress to hide her well-hidden behind. "I'll tell you where. But you got to listen. Will you listen?" Reverend looked on, unmoving. "Saint found a big number of us on the Grantwood plantation.

"I was a younger girl when I saw Hell on earth. Both my parents was sold off. Only company I had was Franklin and I was given to him to make babies with in a stable. Franklin said no and Grantwood was about to kill him until gunshots rang outside. Grantwood run out like he was big and bad. Me and Franklin dressed and looked out the door, saw for ourselves Grantwood aim to shoot at Saint and Saint swat the air in front of her and Grantwood, I will never forget this, grabbed at his throat like he was choking and fell to the ground dead, amen, amen, amen.

"But I was supposed to be talking about God. The light in your yard feels good. What God supposed to feel like." Thylias shook her head. Her bun, tight as ever, seemed to pull her head back straight as she shook it. "Grantwood used to have us out in the field with a preacher from the city. Middle of summer, hotter than a cow's hole, we sitting outside listening to this man talk about how we'll be slaves in heaven. I can see it now, heavy chains around our feet dragging through the clouds talking some 'Have mercy Je-sus! Praise your unsullied name! Got a cross burnt in my back just for you!' Tearing those clouds up. Rip heaven up right from its soggy floor. You ever wonder where thunder come from? Ask a dead slave. Storm in the blood, Reverend. Thunder at the tip of a finger, at the edge of a corn husk before it hit the bottom of the basket. Snap. Pop right off the stalk. We always made weather. Slave or free. Make it rain just by standing in the sun. On Grantwood's place they didn't care if we cooked out there listening to God come out a man's hell-mouth sideways. Some of us did cook. Fried like a egg and died right there. The preacher stood under the shade while we sat in the sun listening to him yell scriptures while the eldest of us slid into summery death. If any of us fell asleep in that heat, we'd get ten lashings. If we couldn't remember one sermon's lessons the next Sunday, we got whipped. Can't remember what Corinthians did? They'd spell it out on our backs. They made little Christs out of all of us but couldn't tell you our names. And don't let it be winter. Wasn't no better indoors, everybody cramming up close to get some skin heat while the preacher over by the hearth and you think he let any of us near him? Like to think he wanted all the slaves to go up to heaven in one swoop; he surely didn't want any of us surviving the cold. Then you"—Thylias sat up in her seat, feet flat in the grass—"came here with a wagon full of slave Bibles, smelling like hell itself and mighty mighty filth, and think you gone just come and pass them out to us? You can't throw slave God our way when slave God thrown us away."

"Don't blame what happened to you on God. Don't do that. I don't know what you came here for but this a holy place, Thylias, and I'm not gone let you blame God for your pain. That pain came from the preacher and your master."

"I have no master."

"Don't blame God for what your no-master did to you. You can leave here quick as you came. Ain't no slave Bibles here. The Bible is the Bible."

Thylias shook her head, then let out a loud, sharp "Yip!" and held herself. Chill crawled where warmth had hit her good and she stood up. "You don't listen and that's why your chairs empty. You don't care about the living and forgot about the dead."

"Get on away from here!" Reverend stood, too, and pointed in the direction of the road. Thylias followed his finger and imagined breaking it off.

"I'm not going anywhere until you say you gone give Franklin a homegoing."

"He killed hisself. Why would I play with God like that?"

"Because you owe him. You owe him. You owe him," Thylias screeched until it hurt. "You came here saying how you're a man of God, but slave

God didn't show you how to love your own. There's a ladder on your tongue you think folks climb to get to you but it's you who need to climb down and come speak to us. Climb down your ladder and test your words on the burial place. You owe us that much, Reverend. You owe the earth and the bones in it and the worms taking in the flesh your service. And you will give it to Franklin. Tell us what the God who love us say, not the one nobody got study for." Thylias rocked a bit, straightened herself up, and proceeded to the road. "I came here to tell you that, Reverend. Sick as I am. Long as you alive, anybody in Ours die you will send them to God and let Him sort us out. Not you." She threw the Bible she had brought with her at him. "That's the real Bible. That other book you carrying on about thin as sin. It is sin. You got less God in your mouth than the rest of us do!"

When she stepped onto the pebble road, the sunlight hit her face at an angle and threw rainbow circles across her eyes. She fainted, her last thought one of gratitude that Reverend didn't live on a hill.

For the first time in a long time, her neighbors from all over town came to see how she was doing. Somebody had taken her home and put her in bed. They spread the word, and everyone came with pails of water and soups for the fever. They saw the nails hammered into the wall and paused at the front door or staggered past, not breaking their gaze at the pretty arcs made of dangerous metal. In some places, there weren't arcs, just a wall stabbed with a blade of some sort. They weren't afraid of what they saw, just mad at themselves for not being there for her when she needed them, seeing the nails not for what they were but for what they needed them to be to make sense of it all. Where Thylias found power, they found insanity.

While recuperating in her bed, her window thrown open and for once cool air entering with the scent of flowers, she remembered telling somebody that had a pretty face how it was wrong, "just wrong that Franklin didn't get buried properly and don't you agree? Unbury him and look at his back. Some of us got the same scars, but not everybody can handle the scars on the inside."

Days later, her fever broke. Reverend, taking her living through the hell of severe illness as a sign, agreed to say some words over Franklin's grave. The whole town came to see what they believed would be a spectacle, after which they would need to comfort Thylias and to pay their respects the right way. Everyone except the Saint household attended, wearing their best clothes as demanded by Reverend, charged by the sound of his own voice as he took to the streets shouting through cupped hands his plan to send Franklin "on to glory."

They wore dresses and suits that they hadn't worn in years, colors and flourishes, frills and suspenders, coral buttons and high hats, shaved faces and dense braids and puffs of hair embroidered with laces and ribbon. They wore their best parfums and colognes taken from their once so-called masters—Eau Superbe by Rue Rancé, Fugue by Roger & Gallet, Murray and Lanman's Florida Water cologne. They brought with them their individual renditions of beauty as a gift to the dead and to Thylias, who watched her neighbors arrive on horse-drawn carts decorated with golden Alexanders, marigolds, and spikes of blue vervain, and followed by horn players, banjo music, an ecstatic dirge worthy of the dead it meant to honor.

Reverend waited for everyone to gather, his handkerchief in hand and already soaked in sweat. Most who came stood around the grave while others sat in the few seats scattered about. Sitting farthest from the cemetery, Joy and Aba held hands, Aba every ten minutes kissing her shaking hand because now the dead, after her self-internment, made her nervous with a newly gained awe.

After everyone settled in, Reverend stood before them petrified. He had the heavier Bible in his hand, leaving the slave Bible at home, and didn't know where to begin in its pages. Its weight frightened him, the God that had been absent all that time now pushing into him.

Thylias sat in the front row, and he heard her say, "Exodus 21:16."

He turned there, a place that didn't exist in the Bible he knew, and read, "And he that stealeth a man, and selleth him, or if he be found in his hand, he shall surely be put to death." He stared at the page for a long time, and everyone waited on him. Not knowing what he wanted to say, he opened his mouth and began.

AFTER THE FUNERAL, Thylias hugged Reverend and thanked him. He nodded, unsmiling, and looked at the ground. Soon after, someone shouted, "Aba!" Reverend scrunched his upper lip to his nose and headed toward the voice. "Joy, what's wrong? Goodness, someone bring a wagon," he heard. When he reached the commotion, Reverend saw Aba's fingers draw shapes into the white heat of the blank sky. Aba stomped into the soft dirt. Reverend grinned hard. The sound of the Lord had returned.

"He need some wood for his feet," Reverend said, and grabbed an empty chair. He laid it on its back so that Aba's feet could step on the headrest. The moment Aba's feet hit the wood, everyone hushed and, for the first time in years, they all understood him. "Feardom coming," Aba stomped. "Feardom on its way."

· CHAPTER 23 ·

Nothingness

[1]

Saint and Frances had a period of peace. It began with an apology that opened between them space enough to breathe, a small boat to share over the dark waters of their once-swelling egos. Frances woke in the dark of early morning, belligerently cold despite summer's heat climbing to the second floor. Against the floor she wore only her clothes and a thin quilt to cover her body and considered choices: those she made and those she didn't; those her neighbors made and those they didn't. The choice of whether they would work or sleep or fuck or cook or eat or clean or teach or learn or effervesce in the company of each other. Where to live and where to die. How to prepare themselves for a hard future, to muster enough fortitude to withstand what they expected: that someone would come and take everything they had gained from freedom. They were ushering themselves into a new life without Saint the best way they knew how.

Frances made her way to Saint's bedroom door. As expected, Saint's companion sat guard, disallowing a knock, so Frances called out, and the power of her voice broke the unnatural chill from her body.

Covered in dark and her deepest imaginings, Saint woke early that morning, too, but sweating. She had become too warm beneath her blankets and gone to open a window when she heard her name shouted outside her door. The voice's agility startled her, that it entered through the closed door, then curved through her room until entering her ears from behind, just over the shoulder. She didn't want another body in her space, so she lit a lamp and opened the door. Frances's long silhouette quivered against the wall.

"Let's go for a walk," Saint said.

WHEN THEY RETURNED, they rested on Saint's bed, laughing like old friends. Still dark out, sunrise hours away, the lamp extinguished. They held hands—one gloved, the other bare—while on their backs they looked at the ceiling, searching for stars.

"Why you let people call you him and her?" Saint said.

"Makes no difference," Frances said with a chuckle. "Neither mean that much to me."

"You see yourself as a woman?"

"Sometimes and all the time."

"Sometimes a man, too, then?"

"And all the time."

"What were you born as?"

"I was born as moving water," Frances said. After brief silence, their breathing in tandem, Frances continued. "I remember only being always grown. How the Mississippi brought me up. The men that fed me Mississippi water for food I learned, years later, were French after I heard those same sounds leave a man's mouth many miles from there. I remember staying with a woman named Freda on one of my journeys—I was always walking somewhere—and repeating what I thought the man sounded like to her. Ju-ju lu-lu shay-voo-vo, and what not. Freda told me it sounded like French, and I never forgot her telling me that. The men who tied me up spoke French. I will never forget that.

"Freda lived by herself in a house hidden so well she sometimes had trouble finding it. Deep in Mississippi, covered in leaves and vines. She called it Nzambi's Throne and I never asked who Nzambi was. She did that covering of her house with leaves and whatnot herself, then all the green grew on its own that way. Just took over. But somehow, I stumbled on it. Think it was the tether in my heart that got me there safe. Trying to keep me alive, so it pulled me over that way, and I saw through the leaves and whatnot. I knocked on the mossy door that gave a little, the wood damp, and she must have looked out her window first cause later she told me she don't mess with nobody but that when she first saw me she knew I was family. Maybe she saw me in her mind like I felt you in my heart.

"Freda had escaped a plantation ten years prior and made her home with the help of some folks who lived nearby. She built a little bit at a time, living with the others who had escaped their plantations and went for the swamps. I called them my swamp kin. They knew the thick waters like I knew the loose water. I had only met with them a few times and only to exchange goods and a kind word before I had to make my way toward wherever the tether pulled me. I never smelled great, cause I only had the clothes the Choctaw gave me when they found me tied to the tree, all my rice spilled to the ground. I had rice braided in my hair. Did I tell you that last time I told you this story?"

"You told me," Saint said. It had been a long time since she heard this story one quiet night by the fireplace while everyone slept upstairs. Joy still lived there. Saint remembered it was a cool night. Candlewicks fastened their trembling flames down to the nothing of burnout. Of all the details in Frances's story, Saint remembered the rice the most, because the moment Frances described how it spilled from her hair, it began to rain.

Frances nodded. "I don't know where the rice came from and haven't worn my hair that way since. Just chop my hair off whenever it get too long and keep it moving. I still have some of those grains to this day.

"Freda said I looked familiar every day I lived with her. First, she said I looked like an old lover, then the old lover's sister, then she laughed at the top of her voice and say real soft, 'I swear I know your people.' I asked if I could stay with her for a few days and ended up with her for a year. I saw how she did her root work and helped her with most of it. I never caught on to doing it myself. No matter how hard I tried, no root I worked did anything but make my hands rash up.

"She showed me how she kept her place protected with a burning pot of oil she sent floating down the Mississippi, her own name written with charcoal on a piece of paper and placed inside the pot. We woke up the plants, the rocks, the animal bones. She taught me about her altar after getting permission from the spirits for me to look at it. Most peaceful life I ever had. I learned how to rub feet from her. She let me practice on her feet, then she would do mine. She loved how soft mine were. Said it made no sense, all the walking I do. That's one thing I proud myself on. Soft feet. No matter where I go or how long I been going there, something about me staying soft.

"We ate good, talked sweet to each other. She taught me her body and mine too. I didn't know what to do with what I had but I remember her saying, 'You built well,' and that make me smile to this day, cause after the tether tugged at me to go, nobody else saw me like she did.

"One man came close. A free man in Philadelphia. He was well known and as beloved as one can be being a Negro in this country. You know, they say you free wherever they believe free to be, but they just keep you trapped in different ways. He didn't have to worry about much, though. He told me he loved me, but I don't know. It didn't feel like when Freda would say the same thing. Hers felt like she was freeing herself every time she said it. His felt like he was hitching a bag of rocks to my back. I can't even remember his name. I laugh cause my memory usually don't let me forget anything, but his name just as gone as it want to be."

"I'm sure it's for the better," Saint said.

"I'm sure. I left his company after three months. My itching to leave started when he wanted me to keep my hair long and wear dresses all the time. Now, I like a good dress. I do. Why you laughing? I just don't like to wear them all the time and I don't own a single one myself. I can't run in a dress and I do a lot of running. And when I stopped wanting to wear dresses all the time—'get me a good suit,' I told him once—he started saying mean things about my body, calling me mannish and saying because I was tall I needed to be softer. I wanted to yell at him, 'Look at my damn feet!' But I kept my mouth shut cause I needed a place to stay until I felt the pull again. I knew he really wanted me to dress like that because me not doing that made him feel uncertain about what he liked. Well, I told him he was a coward and maybe didn't know what he liked after all. I took him to bed that same night and made him call me sir all while we was rolling around that bed. By morning, I was gone. Just left and told myself to wait someplace else.

"I traveled all over this country for decades. Everywhere I ended up, folks attacked me. I been punched hundreds of times, kicked, stabbed once, shot at. Then one day I was surely going to die. Many women cornered me and started punching me at once. The men just watching, laughing, and encouraging them to aim at my 'balls.' When I said I ain't have no balls, they asked why I looked like I did, and the women kicked me down there anyway. Then I heard a woman cry out loud as murder. Then another. And another. And the punches kept coming but fewer and then I stopped feeling them. When I opened my eyes, all the women had bruised faces, eyes swelling big as eggs. And, Saint, my whole face felt better. The men ran to the women, this was in . . . damn, this had to been in South Carolina, or maybe Virginia. Don't ask me the year. Every year the same year to me.

"The men thought I had got some strength back and fought all those women off me. Had to think I was a demon to do that that fast. The men rolled up their sleeves to get at me next and one by one they fell back after their punches touched my face. I only felt a slight breeze and a nudge to the cheek. I knew I had to run when a man's chest exploded from the bullet he tried to put in me."

"Cause he shot you?" Saint asked. Frances nodded. "You didn't stop to think about what was happening?"

"No time to think."

Saint winced. "You never spent time with yourself to consider what was going on with you?"

"I spent a lot of time trying to protect people from harming me. I never got a chance to do anything to hurt nobody. I just was. Me being alive made them angry and I thought it was cause they thought I was a man. So, when they asked me if I was a man or woman, I said 'woman,' and they'd try to beat and violate me. So, I said to myself, 'Say you a man, Frances,' and when I started doing that, they tried to do the same. One man tried to cut off my manhood, and when he saw I ain't have none, he stabbed me and ended up stabbing himself. So, I stopped saying what I was cause in the end it didn't matter. They attacked me man, woman, and unknown and hurt they self." Frances, her hands gloved and sweaty, clenched one of Saint's hands and Saint squeezed back. Even after Frances loosened her grip, Saint kept a tight hold on her hand.

"Been attacked in every state after I left that man in Philadelphia. At first, I thought he had put a curse on me, until I went to New Orleans and things got much better. Few people cared what I looked like. Was a period where folks would openly glare and neglect my eyes. It took an older colored woman in a dress that surely cost more than all the slaves she had trailing behind her, to tell me that she found my clothes unsightly. 'Beautiful face; however, those clothes, those clothes cause an unbearable ache.' An unbearable ache. I'll never forget that. And they had a place down there where people who looked like us could play a drum and white folks didn't want to burn them up. Folks was down there speaking everything, too. French, Spanish, English, and mixing them all up. I couldn't half the time understand what nobody was saying to me even when they spoke English."

Saint said, "I remember you told me you didn't always know English."

"Not a lick of any language. But as I met with people, words started to come to me. It happened with English and Spanish. After a few weeks, I had learned English like it never left."

"You must have already known it and had forgotten it along the way."

"Could be. Same with the Spanish, though I can't speak a lick of it.

Not really. I can understand it well enough. Can't read it as well as I can English. You speak something else?"

Saint laughed. "I can do anything in English, French, Spanish, and can read German, Dutch, and Portuguese, though I don't speak or hear them too well. Spanish sometimes hurts to hear. My head gets foggy and aches. Sometimes I dream in languages I don't know the names to. When I speak them in my dreams, the ground opens beneath me, and I do not fear falling in. One sounds like boulders sliding slow down a muddy hill into warm water. I can't speak them at all when I wake, though I love those languages the most."

"Girl, you speak the whole world!" Frances laughed. "Mercy, mercy. How you know all them?"

"I don't know. I just heard people speaking, then realized I knew everything they were saying and could say it just like them. Hearing them opened a hidden door in my head. I didn't know I could read those other languages until I passed an announcement rallying against some trade tariff in six languages and I could read every word."

A blue and purple glow entered through the window. Leaf shadow interrupted where the newborn glow touched. Total darkness eased into shade. An eruption of birds warbled the coming of dawn.

"You must feel better about folks working in Delacroix. I meant to ask you on our walk, but we were too busy talking about nothing," Saint said.

"Not a thing. But silent walks be what's needed sometimes."

They fell asleep holding hands, the awaking sun only deepening their slumber. While they slept, they touched their own bodies, Saint with a hand on her face, rubbing her cheeks in her sleep, massaging her stomach, squeezing her shoulder; Frances arched her back, traced her collarbone with her fingertips, cupped her ears and tapped her fingers against her forehead. She hugged herself tight, covered in sweat, and rocked. Saint hugged herself tight, covered in sweat, and rocked. Morning light burst through the window and they rocked, holding their bodies, rocked in unison, in the same direction, motivated by the same force that inhabited them both and overwhelming the room, smell of salt, sting of salt across the lips, and the room lit up with the brackish motion that was sweat becoming ocean, and they moaned and rocked, wave crash ravaging their bodies, an expectation, a beckoning for them to join, Saint opening her eyes and there was the storm overhead. Birds broke from the lightning. Splintered wooden planks bobbed all around her. A barrel of wine spilled sweetly into the water, and a circle of bodies enclosed an array of bodies facedown in the storm-freaked ocean, waves the shape of mouths, and such hunger—

When Saint woke, afternoon light had stretched its fingers across her face like an eager lover. She sniffed her wrist, smelled her nightgown, her hair. As though expecting to be surrounded by water and corpses floating within, she looked down and saw the floor, the kicked-off sheet, and her staff. Had been a long time since she had that dream, and Frances was in bed with her the last time she had it, too. She ignored her anxious heart and headed downstairs and saw the mess Frances and the girls made of the kitchen.

The following day, Saint wanted to share the dream with Frances but decided not to. She wanted to figure it out on her own, its source, its relentlessness. A pang of guilt. A flash of resentment. From what? Toward whom?

Later that week, she washed dishes and swore she saw a smoking, disembodied hand floating in the basin. Another time, she washed her face in the creek and felt someone push her head face-first into the cold water. Lifting herself from the creek, ropes of water fell into her eyes and behind the liquid veil she saw an outline of a person. She frantically dried her eyes. She was alone.

Saint rushed home and spoke to no one until the next day, not even Frances, who carefully gloved her hands then rubbed Saint's head until she fell asleep, near tears.

By the second week, Saint had no sense of time and kept misreading the clock in the front room. She suspected Naima had played with the clock but no one else seemed to notice. Only Saint felt time congeal around her, walking around in the same hour all day regardless where the sun floated in the sky. 'Still three o'clock?' she thought, the day purpling into night unlike any three o'clock she had ever experienced.

One day, noon never happened, too many hours then too few. She didn't know the day, month, or year. 'Must be spring, then, if it feels like it,' she thought, though it had been spring for a long time it seemed. She carried on as best she could in the confusion of hours.

She finally asked Frances if she, too, felt the days melting by, the hours becoming mud in the back of her mind. Frances laughed and shrugged. "I never know what day or time it is," she said. "I only pay attention when other people make me." Saint asked the twins, and they shook their heads in unison.

With that, Saint let go of time. Birds sang because they wanted to, not because it was time for them to. She ate when she was hungry, not because it was breakfast or suppertime. Want to sit in the garden? Why wait till morning? Get out there now while the bees sleep and the moon watches nosily as dirt cakes beneath your fingernails.

Peace unlike any she had ever felt overcame her, then overpowered her. She laughed aloud from her belly and the twins were horrified. She hummed and the household petrified around her. Frances touched her own sternum and grinned warily at the sounds that continued to spill from Saint's joyful mouth. They mistook carefree for careless and wondered with strict despair if this woman hadn't lost her mind.

Even with that wariness, times were good for a while without measurements of or care for time. Even folks from Ours who visited Saint for conjure work left her porch not knowing the when-or-how-long of things. They left, instead, confident and wondering if the worries that had led them to get fixed were even worth the travel.

Peace lasted until what Saint had experienced only in dreams interrupted her awake life: the sound of creaking wood followed by that of water splashing around outside the house, the pungency of seawater, gull calls in a blaring chorus overhead, puddles found all over the house that wet only her feet, and a ravaging hunger she couldn't satiate. The twins did their best to comfort her while Frances dried Saint's already dry feet.

Saint asked if anyone smelled *that.* "Y'all don't smell that?" When asked what she smelled she said, "Mess," and became enraged. "Mess," she spat, then stormed off, checking the corners of every room, under every piece of furniture, sliding chairs about with a viciousness that seemed to implicate them in the crime of hiding the stink of shit that haunted only her.

Frances intervened directly when one afternoon Saint almost drowned in a daydream about drowning. She wasn't asleep, just resting, when the water started to rise in her bedroom. Her companion sat outside to make sure no one interrupted her time alone. When the water reached the top of the bed, she tried moving her arms and legs, but her body went coffin-stiff. When the water reached her ears, she screamed out.

She heard commotion outside her bedroom door, her name being called, the fear in the voices, but her companion wouldn't let anyone pass. Frances called for her to "get this man up from here, Saint," but Saint's mouth, eyes, and nose had filled with water. Then a burst through the door and Frances scooped her convulsing body from the dry bed. The twins looked on from outside the door, holding each other. Saint's companion lay shaking on the floor.

"Bad dream," Saint called it, but felt otherwise. If the water that wasn't there could drown her, take away her mind, and knock out her companion on the way, then what of the stones protecting Ours? She closed her eyes, finally, and just when she felt safe enough to stop holding her weight, Frances spoke.

"You need a altar. That little thing I made back when you was sick ain't hitting on nothing cause you not the one who made it."

"I don't have a god," Saint said, nearly a whisper.

"Make it to yourself. Make yours for you first."

The following morning, Saint made an altar on the small circular table in her room. Uncertain of what to put on it, she followed intuition, which led her to discoveries about her own interests that showed her she had been a stranger to herself for a long time. She didn't know that she preferred weeds over flowers—bird's-foot over daisy, red clover over tulip—until she had to decide what she wanted to bring to the altar as a reflection of her tastes. Dark rocks attracted her more than common gray stones. She didn't want a sheet over the table, just the bare wood, over which she also placed a full-length Bible open to the first page of Ecclesiastes where she had underlined a section of 1:7 that read, "All the rivers run into the sea; yet the sea is not full."

By the time she finished, she had added a domino from her onyx domino set, a plate carrying a spoonful of cooked rice, a pile of dirt from her garden, and shards from the cup Justice broke many years ago. The dreams ended in sleep and in wake. Thereafter, Frances and Saint seemed like old friends to Selah, like lovers to Naima.

The more Frances and Saint got along, the more the smell of the sea came roaring in, overpowering the house a few minutes at a time. Saint's head began to hurt. Nostalgia clouded her mind while ravishing her heart. A song, just the melody without words, came to her, but placing its origin escaped her. She sat for days contemplating its music, wondering why she wanted to cry as she hummed to herself.

Frances also grew more attached, trailing behind her with a puppy's intent, growing irritable when Saint wanted to be alone, and reminiscing about her own life every night in bed. Saint found that she liked hearing the stories, even when they saddened her, and waited for night to come just so Frances could tell another tale of everything she remembered.

[2]

The morning Delacroix turned away the Ours wagon by gunpoint, angering Justice and embarrassing the Ouhmey, Frances stepped outside, not saying good morning to the girls or Saint who all three sat at the table eating apple butter and toast, mouths too full to be first to speak so they took to staring at the back of Frances's hatted head and bony, boxy shoulders as she strode her tall self out the door with impressive speed and no good morning.

Going west toward Ours, Frances stopped to linger in the overgrown, wildflower-laden field that stretched between Ours and Saint's house. She had never gone north or south through the wildflowers and tall grass, the sweet scent of green alive all around her. She decided to go north, and when trees blocked her path a quarter mile out, she headed back to see what lay south. Another stretch of densely packed trees blocked her way, sending her back to what she discovered was the center of the field, a world all its own encircled by woods, which gave her the impression that something important had once been there in that field and had been erased, a small town maybe or a pass-through marketplace. With only two entrances and exits, the location worked to keep watch of who entered to better protect the center, and immediately Frances's curiosity turned into feeling trapped.

Soon after she entered Ours, she learned about Delacroix turning everyone away by gunpoint because "the Civil War made the white folks nervous," someone had said. No matter the labor they had all put into the town they didn't live in, pushing it closer to perfection than those living in Delacroix could've done alone. No matter that Saint's conjure was meant to soften the white folks to Negroes who just wanted to work and make an honest living, defiant against boredom and their own fears of having used up their best energy on a wretched plantation. Delacroix turned them away.

Frances sat on a porch with some of the men, listened in silence, nodded occasionally, shook her head when appropriate, and drank a little with them. They spoke brashly most days, laughing at the expense of each other and spitting when they talked. Humiliation appeared unexpectedly from an improvised story like punches in the arm, and they punched, too, playfully telling the storyteller to "lie to me some more." The men were never cruel, just bold and excitable as fire, except on the day Delacroix sent them home.

This time, they were agitated, jittery even. Unwanted disquiet coursed through them, and they vibrated with betrayal. They tapped their feet, shook their legs, scratched their throats, and sighed. They cussed some, then sighed some more. Debated on what they should've done and "Had I been closer to the front I would've—" The lies stung because they strayed too far from the truth. They wouldn't have done a thing differently because they had no resources that made anything else possible.

Frances heard how Justice carried the bulk of the outrage and went looking for him half-heartedly. She ended up at Madame Jenkins's home, hearing her side of things as she had heard it from several people, herself rarely one to visit Delacroix. Coffee in hand, black and full of sugar, she shared that there were, according to reports back, at least twenty men standing there just outside of town, far enough so that any gunshots would sound faintly in the distance. They had that much sense not to alarm their own people. It didn't take much strategy on Delacroix's part, because the only Negroes they ever had to deal with came from the same direction at the same time on that same road every day. The refusal was just twenty white men making double claims, as Madame Jenkins called it: that they were protecting the Ouhmey from Delacroix's citizens while the guns and stances said they were protecting their own from Ours.

"'It's for your own good we treat you this way,'" Madame Jenkins said, pantomiming the gunmen in Delacroix. "They treat us any old way and crown us with it. Who asked for that kingdom?"

Frances went looking for a horse to borrow. She remembered how to get to there. Previous trips had worn a pale path where flattened grass trailed beneath the ghost weight of past wagons. She found the horse first, then borrowed a sheet from Madame Jenkins, just washed and only given to her because she thought Frances mad for asking to take it. Frances draped the white sheet over her shoulder like a dead dog. Prepared, she rode toward Delacroix.

A good ways out, she tied the horse to an abandoned post. She walked the flat terrain northeast, the view ahead devastatingly plain. Cold wind cut across her skin, much colder than in Ours. The trees nearby had already begun losing their color. Flights of birds heading south punctuated the sky with an augur Frances was neither quick nor interested enough in to catch.

When she made it a thousand steps northeast, she pivoted and turned west toward Delacroix. As she walked, she made a large shawl with the sheet, wrapping it around her shoulders and face from the nose down, then wrapping it around herself twice more, leaving a loose hood of sheet over her head.

When she walked up on the Delacroix gunmen from the east, it took a while for them to notice her: a phantom in a suit of light, heading toward them at a glacial pace. The slow speed unnerved the men more than their inability to tell what they were seeing. Then the suit of light shown to be a garment of some kind and dark skin shown through the panel left open from the wrapping. "No coloreds allowed!" Then a warning shot lifted from the band of gunmen. Frances didn't stop or turn away, so they lifted their guns. She didn't slow. The first bullet unlatched a man's left ear. The second bullet drilled a hole into another man's neck. They were confused, not seeing the mysterious person shoot back, not even lift a hand, but they kept on shooting, the man who lost his left ear shooting again and opening his right lung. 'All of this,' Frances thought, 'and saying they protecting us.' She marked where the bullet wound appeared in the men who shot at her and knew by the lethal aim there existed rage, not protection. She marched toward them until their pain-warped faces became clear. They crawled bloody along the dry grass toward Delacroix, where a small crowd had gathered, attracted by the gunshots. Surely those watching waited for reinforcements to arrive, but Frances would get them, too, if they came for her. After all, this was to make sure no one came for her, for Saint, for the girls, for all of Ours. 'No more running,' Frances thought. 'We not gone die in the storm,' though the only storm was the barrage of bullets. Gunpowder, piss, smell of shit, armpit rank: close enough to smell it all. No reinforcements came. She turned her back to the men and returned east, hearing the final cowardly gunshot ring out behind her. Didn't even turn around to see the back of a man's neck burst open.

Saint woke later that afternoon to the shot-up sheet folded neatly on the front room table, unfamiliar, smelling like war. From it, a bad energy frothed up, something tapping on a memory of hers that she had almost forgotten despite her whole life being where it is now because of it. 'Aba, old friend,' she thought while dragging her index finger against the sheet's cool texture. She opened it till it covered the entire table, and through the holes in the sheet she saw the tabletop. Tracing the holes with her index finger, then fondling the gaps where the fabric frayed, she let slip her finger from the holes' rims onto the naked table. Fifteen holes, she counted, then counted again and came to thirty-seven when she found evidence of the holes doubling, tripling even, onto each other, the openings shaped like clovers.

Lifting the sheet to her face, she investigated each hole scattered throughout, looking through their small, singed windows. On the other side, her home split up into coin-size visions. Naima ran inside and went to the kitchen. Before she ran back out, biscuits in hand, Saint called to her and asked about the sheet.

"We found it balled up outside in the field. Me and Selah folded it and brought it inside to play with later." Naima, sensing Saint no longer needed her, ran back outside.

Saint folded the sheet, carried it upstairs, and waited for Frances to appear. 'Is there more to come?' she thought, her burning house flashing before her. She imagined a deranged Aba watching on and not even flinching when embers popped into the air and landed on his face.

They didn't argue that night. Saint unfolded the bullet-hole riddled sheet over herself and Frances and settled in. She sensed Frances held her breath beside her, the silence of someone who wanted to disappear, and waited for an explanation to corrupt the quiet. The stink of gunpowder funneled from the sheet's holes while moonlight struck the white fabric a ghostly phosphorescent such that the holes appeared to throb.

"Where'd you go this morning?" Saint asked. She waited to hear any sound from the other side of the bed but only breathless reticence and the deadweight Frances made of her body responded. Waiting for an answer irritated Saint and she found herself harassing the holes with her fingers that refused to remain idle in the smoke-smelling room where, as more time passed, she began to feel less safe.

She felt it the first day Frances and Joy came to Ours, snow on the ground muting their approaching footsteps as she and the twins looked on from a closing distance as the two strangers struggled toward them. Saint felt that something was off: a bit of omen in the air, too much remembrance without the moment to be remembered revealing itself, this act of remembering having with it neither anchor nor sail. It simply drifted in and spun about its bottom, a curved leaf over water.

To her chagrin, she had begun trusting Frances without believing she ever should. Out of her control. Every obstacle she built between them crumbled at her feet. She had wanted company other than the children and her voiceless companion, but she didn't know to what extent. When Frances asked to sleep at her feet like a pet, a fire rose in Saint's chest. She believed it to be anger. She believed many things.

Then, the desire to be touched had blazed erotic in Saint, and she clenched more closely the blankets over her body, wondering when the desire would end.

But it never ended. It grew as would any insatiable hunger. Each time she became suspicious of Frances, her every desire bloomed, her pulse quickened, and she wanted to be held in the garden of her yearning. When Frances had washed Saint's feet with her gloved hands, through the leather she felt a potent energy pour from Frances's fingertips and enter through the soft pads of her feet. She leaned back, closed her eyes, and let the warm feeling embrace her. Saint's breathing slowed, the flash of nostalgia congealing into a molasses of intimacy. She felt as though she were being cared for by a long-lost friend. Her head clouded in the impeccable high of kindness and touch when Frances twisted her hair. Dull scent of melted beeswax rolled into each loc. And the song they began to sing together, wordless, no melody but still holding together, rolled out her mouth and covered her until she had begun to cry.

"Where did you go?" Saint asked. The sheet's smoke scent nauseated her with its familiarity.

"Delacroix," Frances said.

"How many were there?" She listened to the sticky sound of Frances's lips part. Heavy breathing punctured the silence.

"About twenty," Frances said.

Saint closed her eyes with hope that her temper would cool by morning. She found herself not at peace but also not wanting to curse Frances when she woke hours later to sunlight sauntering up the sky that still held a dark grace. She turned toward where she would've seen Frances had there been proper light and barely saw Frances looking just over her, out the window.

"Why?" The question surprised even Saint who'd asked it. "What did they do for you to kill them so easily?"

"Didn't have a weapon on me. All I did was walk."

Saint heard the twins rush downstairs, giggling out the front door. "Do you know how many people in Delacroix?"

"Can't say I do or care to know."

"Over one thousand, Frances. You think the twenty or so men you killed the only ones with guns? You kill them, they have hundreds more with guns. What happens if you led them back to Ours?"

"They killed themselves trying to kill me."

"You knew that's what they would do. You knew it. No innocence in that. Now they will seek retribution."

"I came from the east."

"It doesn't matter what direction you came from. Your body a map leading right back to us. They will go wherever they know Negroes to be. You think people who tried to put thirty bullets in you gone think about you coming from the east or about you looking like the folks they kept out of town?"

"Your conjure ain't work. To get them to let us work up there. Must've wore off."

"You vex me, then blame me?"

"You messed up, Saint, and will keep messing up if you don't get serious."

"Keep your mouth off me, Frances. You put everyone in danger."

"We was in danger any damn way. From the beginning. I just made sure—"

"That you inspire a whole town to war and lead them back here? If the damn conjure ain't work to keep them nice, what if the stones stop working to keep them out?"

"You could've stopped them from intruding."

"I'm not a miracle worker, Frances."

"You could've kept the Ouhmey safe. Ain't you a conjure woman?"

"I can't keep everybody safe, Frances. If I could do that, then—" she stopped, catching herself. "Spit on me again. Spit on me again and see what conjure get to be between me and you."

Frances sighed and smelled her sour breath. What she wanted to say: *You freed slaves with a staff wave and a squint of the eye. How many you lose coming up here? Not a damn one. Not. One. I seen you take your ain't-right roots and heal sixteen people from the brink of death. Your pot rusted out and you got not a nail to your name but nobody threaten you, not even the weather. No salt at your threshold, no vinegar in your cabinet, and you only burn leaves when you desperate but not one ghost in this house even with the gates you open and leave open everywhere you go that you only close cause you remember last time you left the damn thing open a spirit killed somebody and you ain't got sense enough to know who was in her cause you don't know the spirits to say they name in the right order on the right day with the right sacrifice to keep them calm.* Instead, Frances said, "If your conjure was so strong, you wouldn't be afraid of some white folks doing to you what you could've been done to them. If you gone play God, play God. They always get us first while we sit and wonder what happened. You want to lose what you love that way?"

Saint stood and the oil lamps blazed up on their own. "You killed them over a tantrum. They separate themselves from us, like how you wanted us to do all along. But because you don't like the way they gave you what you wanted, you went and killed them. The closest town of free folks outside of our own is northwest, not east. And had you come from the west, you would've put them at risk, you selfish, walking damnation. What if we ever need to pass north for some reason? You made a hostile territory more hostile. You said nothing about if there were any survivors. If you left anyone alive, there's even more a chance to be invaded. Don't interrupt me.

"We can never go south and a whole river sliding down the map on the east. Nothing but slaughter out west. You let my stones, that you can freely pass, be a wall in your mind while you put Ours in true confinement.

"You want me to kill every white person I encounter, regardless of what they do? Stupid. It might not look like it to you, Frances, but I love Ours and everybody in it enough not to stand in their way. Now, what do you love enough to keep your mouth shut and your predictable hurt to yourself?" With nothing more said on either side, Saint asked Frances to pack her things and leave her home for one in Ours, "or wherever else in this world you may find more comfort than here."

"I made a promise to you," Frances said. "To help you."

"With what?"

"And I'm not leaving till I do what I said I would do."

"You don't even know what you supposed to help me with. Leave. Leave this house."

"I'm not leaving you."

"If you won't leave, you can be carried out," Saint said, and swatted in Frances's direction. Her companion entered the room and grabbed Frances from behind, picking her up from the floor and walking backward out the room. Frances kicked and shouted, trying to break free, spit flying from her mouth, tears in her eyes. Saint shook her head, believing she stupidly allowed a madman into her home. And for what? To be touched? 'Not a hand in the world worth that much,' she thought, and turned to open the window.

No shuffling or shouting behind her. No stomping feet. Why was it suddenly so quiet?

Saint peered over her shoulder. Frances's and her companion's eyes were closed. Then her companion's eyelids flapped violently, revealing the whites behind them. When she looked down, she saw Frances's gloves on the floor, her naked palms touching the back of Saint's companion's hands.

Her companion's skin grew a deeper brown, grew softer, full of life. His eyes watered. His mouth trembled, the beginnings of language, of thought, of will. When his grip loosened, Frances fell to the floor. She looked up at Saint. "I'm—"

But Saint's companion began coughing, holding his stomach where blood flooded his shirt. Saint fell to her knees at the presence of death.

"Saint," her companion said. He knelt to the ground. Saint rushed to him, past Frances, and walked him over to her bed. "Saint, you letting me go?" he asked.

Saint cried into his shoulders. Shook her head no. 'I had stopped it,' she thought, 'I had found a way to give us some time.' She laid his head onto her shoulders, resting her head on the top of his earthy hair. For decades she had waited, decades spent figuring out a way. Now this. Now this warmth she hadn't felt in so long. His full voice. Hot blood she tried hard to forget now staining her bed, the old wound opening to her as would any book to surrender its knowledge. But she already knew this death once and didn't want to be reminded again.

"You letting me go, Saint?"

"Sebastian" is all Saint said through the tears. "Bring him back." She turned to Frances. "Bring him back. Turn this back around."

Frances shook her head. "I can't."

"Bring him back. You did this. You did this."

"His body been dead a long time, Saint. That spirit was locked up in that dead body. What you been doing, Saint? What you been doing to people?" Frances repeated at first to Saint, then to herself until her voice faded off.

What had she been doing to people? 'Keeping them alive,' she thought. 'Best way I know how.'

Sebastian's voice cut through her thinking. "Thank you," he said. "I love you for this. You tried so hard. You always try so hard. Why you try so hard?"

Saint shushed him. Nose to his hair, she sniffed. She lifted his head from her shoulder and rubbed her nose inside Sebastian's ear. He let out a low laugh. She laid his head back on her shoulder, then smelled his hair again, rubbing a finger across his lips. "I love you, too," she said. Then his head felt heavy, his body a stone. Death leant on her shoulder like a best friend.

Saint didn't hear Frances speak or come near her. Saint screamed. And the house, in the vortex of her scream, left from the world into cold nothingness.

· CHAPTER 24 ·

War

[1]

Aba clapped and stomped well into evening and throughout the night until his palms went raw and his feet swelled up. Joy sat near him, still in her funeral attire. She applied lavender oil to Aba's neck in hopes the scent would anchor him back to the house.

At night, she heard bursting from his reckless applause "Feardom! Feardom!" in an alarum so abusive she thought to escort him outside. Rhythmic, the tempo became marching pace and the imagined war jostling Joy's mind slipped into a portent. If not an approaching army, then herself an army of one against his music.

The following morning, Aba continued to beat the floors, pausing only when Joy removed his pants to wash him from the waist down, him almost kicking over the tin basin full of hot water. Removing his shirt proved difficult, but she managed to get it off him despite his claps into oblivion. She washed him, dressed him in a new pair of pants, and left him shirtless and by himself in his tumult.

Once, Aba jostled so hard he kicked over a bedside table, sending Joy's broken mirror to the floor. She swept up the empty mirror frame and shards without even looking at her reflection. In a moment of peace, she buried it all in the backyard.

Later that night, Joy slept in a chair in the living room, but found no respite thereafter. She lit a lamp, and that's when she heard screaming coming from outside, then a banging on the front door. Madame Jenkins begged for entry.

[2]

The women sat across from each other not speaking. Joy had wrapped Madame Jenkins in a heavy quilt before seating her. Still, Madame Jenkins shivered across from Joy, barefoot as she had come. Joy and Aba weren't her closest neighbors, Mr. Wife living across the road from Madame Jenkins while Joy and Aba stayed several houses down with plenty of land between. Aba stirred in the next room and Joy closed the bedroom door.

Joy felt around for more matches in a small table's drawer over by the front door, but there were none. Extra matches were in the bedroom, but she dared not risk waking Aba. The women had to make do with the one light throwing its muted illumination onto the table for the pitiable séance of their shared company. Perhaps less light was for the best, as they now looked not at each other but at the flame.

"I saw the light through your window and ran right over," Madame Jenkins said.

"What made you scream?" Joy asked.

"The dark."

"There's nothing to fear about the dark."

"It's what's happened in the dark." Madame Jenkins leaned into Joy and Joy held her close, rocking her a bit and rubbing her arm with her two clenched hands. "I hadn't seen her in years. It had been years. Why now?"

"Seen who?"

"The cut-up girl."

Joy looked up sharply, thinking she saw a shadow dart in the lamp's dull light. "What cut-up girl? Don't bring nothing into my house."

Madame Jenkins shook her head. "The one Saint helped me bury when she freed me." Night noises crept into the sitting room.

"Tell me about her," Joy said, meaning this version of Saint who was kind enough to help somebody bury another, but Madame Jenkins started talking about herself. "Wait." Joy let go of the woman and grabbed two small glasses and a glass bottle of liquor. She poured the whiskey into the glasses halfway and slid one glass to Madame Jenkins, who eyed Joy, then slid the glass back, tapping the rim. Joy filled it to the top and slid it back to Madame Jenkins, who downed it, then slid the glass back before Joy could even taste from her own glass. Madame Jenkins made a small measurement with her fingers. Joy filled it a quarter of the way and when Madame Jenkins didn't take up the glass, Joy filled it a little more. The woman nodded, then sipped from the glass and began to speak:

"I was once beholden to a traveling doctor named Stoddard for two years by the time Saint found me. Before that, I was on Mistress Dreyfus's plantation in the field from childhood till the point Dreyfus sold me off to Stoddard. He was a traveling doctor who purchased me to be his medical assistant after Dreyfus caught her son eyeing me like the problem was me. So, she sold me off to Stoddard.

"People thought he had lost his mind for teaching me medicine, but he was greedy and refused to pay anyone to assist him, so he made a one-time purchase of a slave to never have to pay somebody ever again. He preferred to use that money to further fund his research and whores, of which there were many since he weren't an attractive man in any way, shape, form, or deviation.

"He taught me how to read, calculate, and measure. I learned how to draw blood, inject the balms, take temperatures, mix the poultices, and stitch easy wounds. Though he wasn't kind, he didn't beat me and always fed me regularly. I foolishly counted myself lucky, somedays grateful, even, to no longer be in the fields.

"Six months into my time with him we settled in Arkansas, and Stoddard started a clinic, paid for by the wealthy patrons of a local college, to do research on women with diseases special to their sex. I'd never seen anything like seeing such things these women borne.

"He became a doctor of renown, trusted with developing what the white folks called 'technologies of flesh' to assist with lesser-known ailments. I never did learn what that meant, but the work we did was on slave women who had similar hurting to the white women who came to see him." Madame Jenkins slid her glass over for more liquor and Joy poured. "Lithopedia," she continued. "Stone babies. Dead in the womb and turned into stone. There were many women. Maybe something poisoned the water and locked them babies up in themselves. Maybe something about the whip and endless labor can freeze a baby in place. Stoddard was trying to figure out not only why it kept happening but how to remove the stone baby from the one white woman without bleeding her out. That was the problem anyway with the doctors there and the Negro women. The doctors kept killing them off, so the white woman kept hold of her stone while Stoddard cut open Negro women every which way without regard of them living or dying. And every time I wish the women would die so that their suffering would end, they lived and their living made him more bold.

"Stuck in the womb like a little piece of history. You'll never see a thing like it. Stone babies be in there holding their head in their hands, feeling the weight of the world on them, worried so bad they said 'nope' and rejected the world that was just gone reject them anyway. It just curl up and make a little earth of its own inside of you. Imagine that.

"And then this one young girl come and she was supposed to have her baby but it never come and they'd had so many women who suffered from this that they knew what it was without asking questions. Stoddard took the girl into the room and got to work. He left out a hour later, speculum in one hand and some other sharp instrument I'd never seen in my life in the other hand, and he tells me he failed and to 'dispose of the body.' I was to wrap up anyone who died during the procedure and make sure they got buried in the Negro cemetery. If there weren't space, then I had to find a river for them to be thrown into. Imagine that. But when I went in the room, the curtains were shut tight and the room oil black—" Madame Jenkins landed her eyes someplace in Joy's home but she saw only the scene from the past unfolding before her as though the lightless room of memory tossed the blanket of itself over Joy's face, over the table, over the oil lamp's wavering light and the voice coming from the void of remembrance spilling from the blanket, "Missus? You sew me back up, missus?" and reaching for the thick closed curtains, Madame Jenkins untied the cinch and let sunlight in and the voice building around it a body of a young girl sitting up and holding her stomach, not dead, very much alive, very much breathing, holding her open stomach and asking politely, so politely it hurt to hear something that gentle with that much harm done to it, gentle voice asking for a missus to close her up and Madame Jenkins doesn't realize she had covered her own mouth until she cries out and the sound falls muffled, covering her mouth as though anything in that room was private, and the girl, the most polite girl asks again, not even crying, not crying, just patiently holding herself together, afternoon sun glistening in her eyes, and Madame Jenkins lays the girl back on the table and rubs her head before grabbing needle and thread and sewing that young girl back up, sunlight at Madame Jenkins's back and the girl breathing hard as she is sewn shut, dead minutes after the suture was completed, her plaits loose about her head, and Madame Jenkins unbraids the girl's hair and does the braids again into something as beautiful as she can manage, her fingers moving with incredible care through the girl's dense hair still warm from her scalp and the softness, the softness enough to make Madame Jenkins smile in forgetfulness that the girl was indeed dead but in this moment in her mind she lived and deserved to leave the world looking special so 'No, she not dead, not until I finish,' Madame Jenkins thought then as she thought now, sitting across from Joy speaking none of this—

"You can stop right there," Joy said, and Madame Jenkins blinked and the room reconstructed before her in patchworks of quilt, the doctor's room flaking off in squares revealing Joy's table, the oil lamp, and Joy reaching over and touching her, Joy doing this without even needing to hear what Madame Jenkins saw in the dark—she couldn't get it out, had sat there the whole time frozen in the past while Joy watched. Madame Jenkins nodded, mouth ajar, at Joy's words. She nodded and took another sip of heat.

The same day Madame Jenkins sewed that girl up, Saint had arrived with her companion and freed her and the women who had and hadn't yet been experimented on. When she asked Saint about Stoddard, worried he would see them leave, Saint smiled and said, "Got to have eyes to see," and pointed to a jar on the table looking back at them. "Bring the girl's body," Saint said, her hand on Madame Jenkins's shoulder. "Keep some tenderness for yourself." They buried the sewn-up girl just outside of Ours, for the dead couldn't be brought into town.

[3]

For seven nights, Joy left her lamp on. Each night, a different person knocked on her door. Sometimes three visited in one night, sometimes as many as ten. Some folks shared long stories, most had brief tales, explaining how the very night of their visit to Joy they had experienced their fears with a potency more voracious than its first instance.

The fears came as dreams, visions, premonitions, illusions, physical embodiments that could touch and affect. People had heard from Madame Jenkins of how good a listener Joy was, but she said nothing about the liquor, had instead told them to bring their own bottles if they thought they needed it and that is what they did. Eagerly, they came to Joy's door, sometimes standing in line, jars of liquor in hand, just to exorcise their fear into her ear and drink away what remained. Aba slept through every visitation, having stomped himself into complete exhaustion during the day.

Back when Saint first gave him the necklace, Luther-Philip had told Joy of the time everyone visited Saint at her new home in the woods and how Saint warned them that their fears and loves would appear before their eyes in every dustless, echoing room had they come in. A parlor trick, Joy had called it, but Luther-Philip swore it was real and explained how only Justice had gone in and soon after he entered he ran out screaming, "Evil!" Joy said he probably meant Saint was evil, but Luther-Philip said, "No, he saw something in there that belonged to him."

Now Joy sat remembering his story as though living a memory of her own. If it were true that fear and love appeared to visitors in Saint's house, then what had her visions been and why hadn't she recognized them? She thought for a while until irritated, then frightened that there wasn't a thing on earth she loved or feared.

She considered those nights she sat by the window waiting on her neighbors to deliver their frightening stories. It felt audacious that someone with no comprehension of their own fear assisted others with theirs.

After the last neighbor left her home for the night, she laughed hard to herself then shut down, unemotional. She remained stoic for two days straight, refusing to speak with anyone else about what frightened them.

Joy tended to Aba as her emotions reset. She managed her chores draped in lamentation and braided and unbraided her hair with the meticulousness of drawing and undoing a maze. On the third day, her tears came as a not-yet-known understanding made itself known. She grasped, finally, her fear and love and that both existed plainly before her in a way that made them seem invisible. "Me," she said. "Me."

Early morning, while Aba flapped his hands to talk at the ceiling, Joy asked Mr. Wife if he would take her to Saint's house so she could visit Frances. It had been far too long since they had seen each other, and the last time they spoke carried more hostility than she had liked. She was curious to know what Frances loved and feared, as revealed by the curse upon Saint's home. Mr. Wife obliged, having shared his fear with her for an hour two nights prior. "But I ain't going in there with you," he said.

Heading to Saint with Joy in tow, Mr. Wife didn't go far before coming across the twins standing in the field between Saint's house and Ours. Saint wasn't with them, which wasn't uncommon, but in this instance Mr. Wife found himself irritable and impatient, steering the horse through the grass over which clouds of insects floated and interrupted his view. Sharing a stick between them, the twins took turns poking at something in the grass. He smelled animal rot and guessed that the girls had something to do with it.

He thought he could, with an adult mind, hide his disdain, particularly of Naima, whose uncivility he would've exchanged for the company of the very corpse she poked. But when he saw their shared face putting perverted focus into a death he could smell feet away, his disdain not only lasted, it grew.

"Think you can bring it back to life?" he heard Naima say as he rode closer.

Selah shrugged. "Maybe what's dead should stay dead."

"You just scared you can't do it."

"*You* do it, then," Selah said, and Mr. Wife heard the venom from afar.

"What you gals doing in that grass there?" he called from his horse. When they didn't look up, he shouted, "Hey!" but didn't leave the saddle. He looked back at Joy, who sat in the wagon on a square of hay, pure exhaustion on her face.

Naima looked up, spat into the grass beside her, and returned to poking the animal corpse. Selah ignored Mr. Wife altogether. He didn't know what to do next, so he deboarded his horse and slow-stepped toward the girls as though toward a threshold he had encountered in a dream but never crossed because the dream itself wouldn't allow.

Mr. Wife noticed Selah tracked him with an empty stare from the moment he jumped off the horse to when he stood beside her. In the grass, he observed the emaciated ribs broken and clefted open by powerful jaws of some animal that, by the corpse's appearance, wasn't hungry at all. Just mean, for all the meat it left behind. Or frightened away from its own hunger by something more dangerous.

"A dead mole," he said to them and kneeled to get a closer look. He felt the girls watching him as he grabbed a nearby stick and explored the innards. "No telling what did this. Could've been a fox." He stood and asked the girls when they found it. "Just now?"

Selah shrugged. Naima scowled.

"Saint around?" he asked. The girls looked at each other and Selah looked away, wide-eyed and caught in the confines of a secret knowledge. Naima's face contorted angrily. "Did something happen?"

Naima's watering eyes told him to invite them into the cart and, as they boarded with shameful silence, Joy reached down to help them up, giving a surprised look to Mr. Wife when both girls took her hand.

They all arrived at Saint's house to find that it was no longer there. Not the garden. Not the weeds out back. No debris. Where Mr. Wife remembered there being a house was now a collection of toddler-tall weeds. The twins waited in the cart as he stepped into the absence of house, spun with his arms open to collect pieces of the house's hidden remains in his spread palms. A small flock of birds lifted from the grass nearby where surely the house had been and flew through where the front room's chimney no longer reached.

On the ride back to Ours, he heard crying coming from the wagon and "Shhh. Shhh," that was both the wind in the leaves of nearby trees and the voice of one of the girls comforting the other. After he crossed Creek's Bridge and reentered the field, he purposely rode past the dead mole to smell it one last time.

[4]

The twins spoke only to Madame Jenkins, who when they arrived said, "Awe, my babies," and meant it. She called all the children of Ours her babies and made no exception for Saint's twins. Selah hugged the woman and held on. Naima's glare softened. When was the last time, if ever, anyone called her baby? Then Madame Jenkins's big beating heart at her ear, soft breasts pushing into her face, and firm hands grabbing the back of her head while stroking her thick hair without contempt. When had anyone ever touched her this way? Fearlessly, like they wanted her around?

In Madame Jenkins's small home, where the horizon lowered into glowing pitch through a single pair of north-facing windows, the girls slept on a pallet, both rejecting Madame Jenkins's offer of her own bed, which she had set up near the sleeping fireplace. Stacked pots leaned in the corner of the dead hearth. Potato peelings freshly cut and dropped into a wicker basket gave the home an outdoors smell. "Gone fry those up later," Madame Jenkins said when she spotted the girls eyeing the slices.

With just a few candles, the modest home filled with light, allowing the three to see each other. With a clamor of pots and a resurrection of the fire, Madame Jenkins prepared dinner while the twins waited outside away from the heat. After dinner, the twins bathed in the sweetest-smelling soaps they had ever felt against their skin.

Selah noticed a few chairs side by side with their backs to the wall. She asked what they were for, and Madame Jenkins shared how they were for social meetings for the women in town. "Some things we need to share with each other to keep ourselves alive," she said, unfolding an extra quilt for the girls to lie on and throwing open the windows. She observed the dark, listened to how the silence outside sat different from the silence inside. Most times in the summer, the meetings were held outdoors, and when winter arrived, no woman dared complain about the tight fit of the no-longer-slave quarters.

"What ladies talk about?" Naima asked.

"How to be happy," Madame Jenkins said. When she turned her head from the window, she saw that the twins were asleep.

The twins slept hard on the floor, two girls growing up with just the company of Saint and that one woman, Frances, whom Madame Jenkins wished hadn't stopped coming to the social meetings after her first time. Surely, there wasn't enough love for the girls in that house, if any love at all, for what mother would leave her children outdoors like that?

"Hide the whole house? Not even leave them a piece of house to sleep in?" she said to herself. She doubted calling Saint a mother for she never heard the twins call Saint anything other than Saint, and Saint never called anyone anything but their name or out their name. So, what were these girls to Saint that she could discard them like so?

THE FOLLOWING MORNING, people who had heard of the twins' abandonment by Saint came to see them, bringing hand-me-down clothes, a basket of sweets, a kind eye that was so hard to come by. Naima looked at the gifts and squinted away her tears. Selah watched, rubbing Naima's back, then stopped, shooting a look at the door. She sighed and stood, dusting herself off.

"We'll be leaving soon," she said.

The door opened and they were swooped up by a panting Madame Jenkins, who escorted them to Aba's house. "He need your help with something important," she said in a rush of breath, and though the girls made faces (one intrigued, the other suspicious), she didn't notice, moving quickly out the door into the bright day with the air of emergency engulfing her.

As they walked, neighbors greeted them and each one had a story about fear that Madame Jenkins eagerly shared with the twins. They absorbed the stories with unharnessed curiosity, wondering if these were the same fears that would've appeared to them in Saint's house. By the time Madame Jenkins dropped them off, she had told them everybody's business in a breathless sweep of excitement that neither girl kept up with nor wanted to end.

The girls grinned when Aba opened his door, and he shot air out of his nose in response. He looked at Madame Jenkins, then back at the grinning girls, who started to giggle. Aba smiled softly at them as Madame Jenkins ushered them inside, adjusted their collars, then headed home.

Aba tapped his chest to clear his throat and the girls said, "I don't know," in unison. He popped his knuckles and Naima responded, "You know her better than we do." They understood Aba's sound talk, which relieved the man and encouraged him to speak more. "You understand me?" he asked, tapping his foot. The twins told him that Saint taught them how to interpret drums and that all he was doing was drumming with his body.

"Makes no difference to us," Selah said. The girls sat cross-legged on the floor and started playing a handclap game. Aba heard words spilling from their claps, two singing voices filling the room with rhyming nonsense the girls clapped into existence. Because he looked like he wanted to join, they invited him to play, teaching him the intricate rhythms and movements. This way, he told them what he needed.

The morning of Franklin's second funeral, the other half of the message that had fallen to Aba so long ago came in a sunray. He had looked up, bored and having just finished yawning, when a beam of light entered his eye with the rest of the message that he believed came to him from the stars themselves: "feardom" was the complete word and with it came flashes of a scene that unraveled to him for days on end, wrecking his body with endless motions as he translated everything he received. There would be visitors, on horses, strangers that enter the town from the south, and they will lay Ours to waste three days after the fear visions end. Why they would be able to pass Saint's stones he didn't know, but it had to have something to do with the fear visions plaguing them all. He figured with Saint's house gone, the conjure she put on it had nowhere else to go except into Ours, releasing the fears but keeping the love. Ours had little time to prepare for the visitors. "That we could all be killed," he said in a final round of claps, "is the true kingdom of fear."

The girls looked on, impressed with the story, and Naima asked him to tell it again but to do it with the song the stars gave him. After several protests of there being no time, Aba rubbed his hands dry of sweat to begin. He didn't remember the entire rhythm, having received it in a trance not even hunger and thirst could break. He clapped to them what he recalled and Selah's face paled.

"You heard wrong, Aba," she said.

"Heard what wrong?"

"Not three days. Two. They will kill us tomorrow."

"Nobody killing us," Naima shouted.

If the deadly visitors would be there tomorrow, then Ours needed to be ready today. The twins began to bicker, and he quieted them. "I know what we need to do. But you two have to help me. Will you?"

"Why should we?" Naima asked.

"Why should you what? Help?" Aba said.

"No reason's good enough."

"Girl, you want everybody here to die?"

Fireplace and hammer came to Selah's mind, vile desperation painting Naima's face the night she confronted Selah for leaving the house to help those in need in Ours. Naima hammered three of her own fingers in protest. She didn't want Selah to help then and didn't want either of them to help now.

It wasn't that many years ago when Ours's children taunted the girls with the adults' laughing approval. Not even after Selah spent three nights helping them survive a harsh winter did anyone attempt to tell the twins apart. Not until today did anyone other than Madame Jenkins show them care and consideration, but to Naima it resembled pity more than anything else.

Ours was as distant as any star Aba mindlessly clapped and stomped at, and if the twins wanted to, they could save the handful of people in Ours they had grown to like. In the silent stare-off between Aba and Naima, adult and child, Selah considered what had happened right before Saint's house disappeared.

Selah had been playing outside with Naima but went back in for a drink of water. She heard arguing upstairs in Saint's room. The shouting above brought her strange pleasure. The collaborative nature of arguments that didn't involve her thrilled her, so she sat in the big chair by the fireplace, listening to the raging altos lilt and boom from wall to wall. Not in her lifetime had she known Saint to sound this angry. Because of the intensity, the gravel scraping Saint's throat, Selah thought that Saint must've been enjoying herself, too.

The only reason she stepped out of the house was because Naima had called for her from outside. The sky shone white and hurt her eyes before they adjusted from the hold of the dark interior. She thought she had gone blind, signaled by the dull pain pounding through her head from the white luminescence the sun slipped over everything. A stray chicken's dingy, off-white feathers glowed in its strut. Even the smell of grass, ripened by the hard light, dizzied her. A bit of frost crusted strangely over the tulip petals. She couldn't tell what season it was. How long had she been in the house that, after taking those first steps into the garden, felt like emerging from the bottom of a vast body of water?

When she got her bearings in the sunlit world, she found Naima up the path leading to Creek's Bridge. "Come see," Naima had said, and took her to the dead mole. For Naima, seeing the bones with meat still on it interested her the most, and she said so to Selah, who observed the corpse in a teeth-parted stupor. For Selah, the idea that something had the power to make a strange beauty of another creature's death left her rapt in the purple of the intestine spiraling like yarn from the mole's corpse.

By the time their curiosity waned, leading them to return to the house, the house was gone, along with it the garden and its frosty tulips and the backyard succumbed to weeds, the small animal kennel that occasionally held chickens, a pig or two, and a goat, all of which would be slaughtered and eaten or salted by winter. Everything gone, including Saint, the most hurtful of all disappearances.

With nowhere to go, no one to feed them, no one to tell them what to do, and no roof beneath which they could hide from the rain and sun, Selah trembled. She touched Naima on the arm and said, "We have no home here," and like that, Selah resigned to the arrest of this new sensation: humility.

Naima didn't fight, to Selah's surprise. She didn't turn violent. She just stopped speaking, which is how Selah knew that the new sensation had risen in her sister, too, and taught Naima that a thing called *always* had no stamina and no reach.

"We should help, Naima," Selah said, returning from her memories with her mind made up.

Aba sat patiently on the floor. The girls returned his watchful eye. Naima snarled when she finally agreed.

[5]

Soon after, Aba told Ours about the danger approaching town and everyone prepared themselves according to his plan. They had to build a platform in the tree soon-to-be-called God's Place, gather all weapons and ammunition, see who could climb trees and who could kneel in the bushes without their knees locking up. The girls went trapping birds: Naima making them sick and stuffing dozens of them into several bags and Selah healing them for the next day's release. Aba told the remaining orphans to hide in the schoolhouse tomorrow morning and gave the oldest child a gun just in case. Showed him how to use it once, then left him to figure out the rest.

The final step: make sure everyone in town understood Aba's stomping and clapping. The children picked it up the quickest, heard his sentences as clear as a voice speaking into their ears. It took the adults time, time for the drum memories to come back, a collection of sounds that said when to move left, to move right, to dip, to pivot, to turn, to wait, to stop, to start, to hold each other, and to let each other go. Percussion patterned to say hello and goodbye, to say the enemy is afoot and help is on the way. It took Aba four hours to teach them his new voice, which ended up being the oldest voice they had ever known. Sounds from the past translated into spoken memories. Rainfall from the other day told someone to bring in the firewood. The old foot-stomp rhythm somebody taught themselves a year or so ago reminded them to hug their children because it had been too long. The racing heart, a warning to salt the thresholds before going to bed. The one time a rooster fell dead from a rooftop, landed so hard that the sound of its thump on the ground reached a mile away? A joke from the other side of life that if they didn't take their days slowly, the days would take them.

The Ouhmey practiced listening to Aba drum with his body and enacting what they interpreted. He moved farther away with each percussive series, and still they heard him even when he stood in the tree soon-to-be-called God's Place, stomping away on tin-covered planks of wood made into a platform in the branches near where the nest of hair had been.

The night before the invasion, Aba asked Joy if she could go to Saint's house first thing in the morning to see if the house had returned. If it had, she was to bring Saint and Frances back with her. Joy refused and demanded to remain by his side. He smiled, shook his head no, and kissed her hands. First the left. Then the right.

"Please," the wet of his lips spoke for him across her knuckles. "Please?"

The bed had a lot to say beneath their bodies, sweat slicking the sheets till they glided between them, the bed taking the shape of their lovemaking. Joy tasted sweat and whiskey on Aba's lips and her mouth watered for the salt and burn. In Aba's voice, the bed frame sang out, "Everything I got's yours." They undulated above and below one another, emerging from each other in waves. The bed frame sang out, "Be inside my heart, Joy," and she rode a new rhythm into him. The bed sang out, "Let me stay in until morning?" and elucidated their shapes becoming one. After they finished, she held him in her arms until he softened inside of her and, sliding out, rolled onto his back. He reached for her hand, and she fell asleep with her forehead tucked beneath his armpit. That night, Joy dreamt she had to choose between two destinations. She chose left and when she reached the path's end, a single skull lay in a barren field. In the dream, she was resolute, disappointed but not surprised. She said to herself in the dream, "I knew it would come, but not like this." She woke the morning of the invasion, promising that when the time came, she would know when to stop watching for Saint's house to reappear. She would know when to run back home.

[6]

When the horsemen entered Ours, it seemed to the one leading the militia that they had entered suspended time where only what appeared God-made remained animated against stiff and emblematic houses standing in for real ones, the entire scene before them a once-dwelling now relegated to an ordeal for ghosts.

The militia leader had a spectacular imagination wedded to cynicism. He heard the unruly wind mock the true wind of God's controlled authority, felt the earth beneath his horse give way, saw trees perform recalcitrant adieus that, too, were against the laws of God and His natural order. Everything blew too hard for too long; smelled too ripe, too sweet, too ready to be taken; looked too wild, too cared for by savagery, for even the grass had hips and the crab apples round as buttocks dropped to the ground, then bounced and rolled to his feet like lazy Eves.

The only man-made sound, that of ceaseless snoring, came from a house with a west-facing facade just west of the dismal cemetery where in lieu of tombstones stood rocks and wood to mark the graves.

He dismounted his horse, rubbed his long beard, removed his hat, and scratched his bald head with a long yellow pinky nail. He donned his hat and called out for someone to come outside. Anyone. He just wanted to talk. Was looking for someone, a few someones, and would be on his way once he retrieved whom he searched for. He spoke with great intention, wanting to be understood by whatever he would discover there that stole this land and the houses on it.

He arrived for two reasons. First, to follow up on a long-ago received telegraph sent to the Missouri governor, Hamilton Rowan Gamble, from Delacroix that stated a "genocide of its militia had occurred by the hands of renegade slaves, the only two towns with such a population being Salvation from the west, and Ours from the south, the latter having been part of a prior hostile interaction. We have all reason to believe the attack originated from Ours. Our resources to counter the assault are minimal." The second reason, as a clandestine favor to a wealthy and secret pro-Confederate who had years ago lost his child slaves during a flood, to find and remove said slaves from Ours, assumed to be there under the protection and discretion of other renegade slaves.

The militia leader asked Delacroix for more information about Ours. Their response offered little assistance as they couldn't pinpoint how far south, the current population, its terrain, or even if it still existed. They briefly described how for decades they allowed Negros who said they were from a town called Ours to work there, and after receiving an infuriated response from the militia leader asking why they would do such a nonsensical thing, they responded, "We can procure no record for further elucidation."

When confronted with the job by Gamble, an old friend who was overwhelmed by Missouri's neutrality being tested in the war and therefore unable to tend to Delacroix's request, the horseman questioned its validity, having been up that way for many years and never seeing evidence of a town. Gamble responded with indignance that the horseman—neither a sheriff nor an officer, just a hired ex-soldier who would be imprisoned for treason against the Union if not for the favors pulled for him by the governor—should be quiet and do what he was told. He then reminded the horseman about the White Plague back in the 1830s that seemed to come from Ours and killed dozens of folks within a mile's radius of the town. The town existed. He just had to keep looking.

And it shocked him so bad once he found an opening in a set of trees that didn't exist the last few times he had ridden by. Just appeared and outraged him into shooting the first tree he saw that hadn't been there during his first scans of the land. And now, with his motley of deranged, fanatical militiamen, he wanted nothing more than to unsee the unseeable, the truly not-thereness of the town that in its very presence belied the presence of any Negro involved for, surely, how could there be in the aloneness of the wilderness this place with houses larger than any he or his men could ever live in? That it existed caused great offense and that supposedly black faces populated the homes, surely there were some miscalculations, for how could any colored take up space and it not be underground?

Then the birds troubled him, far more than what made sense, appearing like unexpected rain, like fog tumbling down a hill. He felt they laughed and screeched with harpy glee, but they were birds being birds above a man who sensed danger in everything Negro. 'Truly,' he thought, 'truly this is a jungle unfastening before us.'

He scratched his sinuses, hawked up phlegm, and swallowed. The snoring from that cemetery-close house ended. A maudlin silence followed, then a door cracking open cracked open the silence and out walked Luther-Philip from the cemetery-close house. His stride long and without pause as he proceeded toward the large band of horsemen who outnumbered Selah's morning count of thirty-five by at least ten. The leading horseman appraised Luther-Philip and saw no threat, only haughtiness, and Luther-Philip's pleasant smell disgusted the horseman even more: cinnamon, was it? No. Clove? He had expected a musk more putrid than that of the men behind him whose rank sweat glistened them with the oil of filth and hard labor. 'Must be the end of the world,' he thought, then shot a line of snot from his nose onto the ground.

He asked Luther-Philip if any children had come to this place (he didn't ask for this place's name or the man's name before him; why would he and what "man"?) and Luther-Philip said every child there had been born there and born free. The horseman disbelieved him but nodded. He asked if he could see the children there and Luther-Philip said he couldn't.

"Yes, yes. Of course," the horseman said, and pulled from his pocket a piece of paper and read from it some decree of the law of the state of Missouri, a false warrant of search and seizure applicable to all places of residence within Missouri, and Luther-Philip blinked at the horseman.

"No paper not written here work here," Luther-Philip said, and the horseman felt himself turning red and could hear the restlessness of the riders behind him, some men he knew and some he didn't and the latter fidgeting, ready to fight, to shoot freely and ransack the town.

'Bout to be free any damn way,' the horseman thought, and the thought angered him even more that the Civil War seemed a promise already fulfilled on behalf of the coloreds. 'Make this easy for yourself,' he thought. Luther-Philip stood before him and blinked dimwittedly at the horseman, such that the horseman folded his paper and signaled for the men to spread throughout town and "Take them all unharmed. Ignore their papers if they present them to you."

Thunder. Sky sun-heavy, bluebird blue, yet thunder. The horsemen stopped and looked up, confused by its volume and pacing. Then the shots rang out and six horsemen fell from their horses. When the leading horseman turned to take up the man who had refused him the children, he caught sight of his back entering a door and the door closing shut behind him. Two of the six horsemen writhed on the ground, bullets where the blood poured. The other four lay dead: head shot, lung shot, heart shot, neck shot. The aims impeccable.

The horsemen unholstered their guns and took off into town, determined to knock down every door and kill every black face they saw. The leading horseman, having lost control of his militia, went looking for the sound of the thunder that rang all around them.

Another six from his cohort downed by gunfire, over a quarter of his men dead or severely wounded, his own horse stamping over the head of one of his fallen men, the skull crunch of which accentuated the thunder that now upon deeper hearing sounded like a metal drum and had interspersed throughout its percussion handclaps, a sacrilege African madness, the horsemen thought, encompassing them in a cypher of death. Six more men shot from their horses. Not a shooter in sight. Unweighted horses kicked up dust as they trampled the bodies of their shot-down riders.

One horseman kicked down a door to a house and was blasted into the air by shotgun, his back sailing over the stairs and landing hard onto the dirt and stone ground as the newborn hole in his chest gargled like a baby's mouth. Another man unlatching the bar to a barn door found himself at the end of a smoking barrel wielded by a young girl, no more than ten years of age. Because of her short height, the hole in the man's head slanted up such that upon receiving the bullet he felt in his final moments as though he had been picked up by his head and suspended midair.

Each door broken into became a portal to death. Some of the militiamen took to shooting up the houses from the outside only to run out of ammunition and be shot from the sky afterward. The leader looked up and finally saw the glints of metal from attic windows. He dropped his glare and caught a suspicious shadow bob behind a set of barrels awkwardly stacked in front of a fence. In the trees, should-be slaves with guns, their silhouettes phantasms with predilection for blending with the shadowed bark.

The leader swore he was hallucinating the whole thing, then four more horsemen introduced to their own blood spilling into the shocking bowl of their hands. Bone crunch. Dust in the air. Horses maddened by their sudden weightlessness and the sound of small explosions encircling them. The metal drum's thunder coming from the north scorned them to sudden graves.

The leader rushed his horse onward through a line of bullets, his shoulder clipped by hot lead and blood spurted forth as seven screams exploded behind him to the beat of the thunder-drum that intensified the farther north he went. Bullet in his thigh, no spigot to stopper the letting. Instead of revealing his pain with a scream, he clenched harder on the horse's rein past where the road became a dirt path leading to a giant tree. He kept going through the field as it elevated into a small hill, kept the horse going at apex speed until he came upon the tree where in its branches had been built a platform supporting two same-faced girls on either side while a man stomped and clapped in the center on a sheet of tin, from which a sound that shouldn't have been able to reach all the way back to where his men were being slaughtered had not only reached but communicated.

He slowed the horse to a soft amble and approached the tree, near delirious with pain. He stopped far enough away to see that the two girls and the stomping man paid him no attention, hadn't even noticed him, but he had gotten close enough that he could hear snatches of words. One twin stared up into the sky, giving what sounded to him like directions. "Left of Miss . . . house . . . horses. Tell Mr. Wife and . . . there . . . bake . . . one nor . . . front . . . south . . . and one hiding behi . . . should trim . . . the day . . ."

The tree-man's stomps and claps, chest pounds and thigh slaps, changed with each instruction. The leading horseman kept his eyes on the other girl who sat on the edge of the platform, legs dangling, one stocking up and one down, her mouth moving at incredible speeds, her eyes open wide but seeming to look nowhere at all, her face white with what he thought was dark paint drawn down from her eyes like tears. The man shook his head, thought witchcraft, thought godless interpreters of the weather, fools of the pharaoh, thought thoughts he had no idea he could think up, devil-sanctified thinking, he a feverish fabulist for his own downfall. He acknowledged everything but his awe for what he witnessed, awe he would never confess to himself or to anyone else, not even to God, who he believed had truly left this place and had abandoned him and his men the moment they left St. Louis and entered this hell town.

Twenty-two child servants to retrieve and surely all forty-seven of his men dead now, an outlandish number to begin with, a coward's gamble, for how could he fail with that much power against what he had heard was a town of no more than one hundred, was surely the town rumored to have disappeared from the map after a plague swiped through St. Louis County, a town full of slaves absent of even cobblestone roads, let alone a telegraph line.

Forced into the twilight of his own optimism, he watched the performance in the tree unfold before him with the eyes of a child. A white moth fluttered near his face and exploded. He vomited, leaned from his horse, and fell to the ground. His lungs burned. Puss-filled sores covered his skin. He looked up at the tree, and the three still paid him no mind while he coughed up thick, green phlegm marbled with thin streaks of blood. The stomping man had his eyes closed in deep concentration while the twins seemed to be blind. They couldn't see him if they wanted to. 'This,' he thought rapidly, 'is why they are this far away from town is why they weren't there with the others they needed to be here they are open to assault they are open my boy so do it!'

Blood dripped from his nose. He reached for his gun. It mattered not which one. He forced himself onto his knees. He aimed and shot in the blur of sickness. He heard the scream that wasn't from one of his men. It mattered not which one. Satisfied, he died in a position of prayer, his chin touching his chest, his arms limp at his sides, fingers still touching the top of the gun as it lay on the grass. Other than the birds' exodus from nearby trees, the last thing he heard was the name of the one he killed. It was a beautiful name.

· CHAPTER 25 ·

God's Place

[1]

The morning of the invasion, Joy thought she heard her name called from the woods behind her. She had been watching grass sway where Saint's house used to be to see if it would return when *Joy Joy Joy* fell from the sky and fluttered soft as a butterfly from one ear to the next. She couldn't distinguish the voice among her memories of voices, but it touched her with a hint of familiarity, and she found herself turning away from the open grassland and walking, then jogging, then sprinting back to Ours.

When she crossed Creek's Bridge and made it to the center of the open field that separated Saint from Ours's mainland, Joy found herself turned around in a space as familiar as the teeth in her mouth. She blinked and the world as she knew it spun on an unnavigable axis, making north become south and east become something else altogether unmeasurable. Retracing her steps back to center, she somehow made her way back east, close enough to Creek's Bridge that she could hear its water trickle. It took her calling Aba's name for her to find her way, Aba's voice returning to her from behind. She discerned her location in the field and believed she knew the tragic reason why her body, not the world, had turned against her.

Joy struggled through the patch of trees and past the worn fence that separated the town from a slight hill where the tree soon-to-be-called God's Place arrogantly stood. Distracted by the tree, magnetized to it such that she never took her eyes off its height, Joy didn't notice the dead bodies sprawled on the roads just south of where she had been, some of the dead tossed inside a wagon to be taken anywhere but there.

White-hot sky washed out the green and gave the outlines of objects a dusty aura. Everything haloed. Everything angel. Running breathless toward the tree, Joy saw two figures standing in an upper branch where there should've been three. She couldn't tell who was who from that distance, just that they all looked so small. As she closed the distance, *smallness* took on a new meaning: not a body bent in grief but hope, tiny as a mite.

Not too far off from the tree, a horse ran in a tight circle. Naima nodded her head toward the field, and Joy saw the dead militiaman on his knees, chin touching his collarbone, the horse drawing an invisible pen around him.

Joy climbed the tree and saw the gunshot wound bleed out from Aba's chest onto his shirt, all over Selah's hands, which she had stacked over the bloody opening. When Aba's dripping blood landed on the tin, Joy heard her name called as she had heard it in the field.

Wan light poured from Selah's palms into Aba. Naima watched on, rubbing her sister's back. Selah's eyes carried no light, and if any healing happened, it only kept Aba on the brink of life. Joy placed her hand over Aba's open mouth. He wasn't breathing on his own, rather the pulse of light entering intermittently lifted his chest to the rhythm of its entering him.

"Selah," Joy said, touching the girl's cheek. "Stop, please?" It was the kindest "please" Naima had ever heard, the question of it like sugar.

But Selah kept going, shaking her head no, rocking back and forth on her knees. Naima called out to her, and Selah said no, then shouted it and fell unconscious into her sister's arms. The light faded from her palms. Aba stopped breathing. The horse that circled the dead rider reared up on its hind legs before dashing off and disappearing into the wilderness.

Help arrived to carry Selah's and Aba's bodies from the tree. Someone had heaved the leading militiaman's corpse into the stinking wagon of corpses. The filth of their living habits smelled worse in death, and the Ouhmey shook their heads if a corpse started to roll out of the wagon, as if to say, "If that shit touch ground, it's staying there."

It took two trips for them to take all the dead to the outskirts of Ours where the western barrier would be. They buried them all in shallow graves, sometimes two or three in the same hole. Uninterrupted forest for miles.

[2]

The children shared their beliefs on death with one another. One child asked where dead people go. An older child responded that they heard the good ones go to Heaven. "Where Heaven at?" another child asked. And the older child said, "It's the highest place you can think of. God's Place." When they all gathered at the tree to witness Aba's burial, they looked up and saw that the tree had no end that they could see. Its upper limit never arrived in their eyes, and the few birds that flew by did so at what appeared to be the center of the tree. Some of the wiser children swore they remembered seeing the top of the tree from afar but standing beneath it they felt mistaken as awe erased all common sense. They looked at each other next, astounded, a little fearful. "This God's Place," a child said. The other children, even the oldest ones, agreed.

[3]

After the funeral, a few words from Reverend followed by a long ringing shout to send Aba home to his maker, Madame Jenkins and the women of town threw a feast in honor of Joy and in memory of Aba. Every elder in town kissed Naima on the forehead and held Selah's hand. The girl hadn't yet awoken, and Madame Jenkins let her rest in bed while festivities carried on outside. Eventually, the two sisters were left alone. Naima, sitting in a nearby chair, watched over Selah unblinkingly, losing herself in the face that was her face. Dozing off, she nodded, until she smelled smoke, sweet as a cookie. From Selah's open mouth, black smoke spiraled into the air. Naima remembered and touched her ear. She trembled when she saw the blood on her fingers.

[4]

As the funeral for Aba ended, a distortion of light and space appeared as a bubble where Saint's house used to be, then Saint's house reappeared in a burst of wind that set dust flying outward in a circle. The front door opened and out came Frances carrying a potato sack full of her belongings. A veil of fog covered her eyes. She descended the steps, made a right at the end of the front yard's path, then another right heading farther east. She trekked through thorned plants and disrupted the secret chattering of insects. Without blink or tear, stumble or fall, Frances stepped steady-paced, even-breathed, and affectless toward the outskirts of Ours. No paths cut through these woods, but the uncultivated land hardly impeded her. Steady-paced. Fog over her eyes. Countenance flat. When she stepped past the barrier stone, the daze lifted, and she found herself in the middle of the unfamiliar woods.

She turned straight east, past where Kwame met Foster for the first time. She continued for another half mile or so until she reached what appeared to be a small village. A light-skin woman with beady eyes stood watch. Justice's gaze darted up from his wood carving.

In Aurora's home, drums hung like fruit from cords hammered into the ceiling. Beneath them stood a set of stools carved into gawking humanlike figures mid-squat whose backs formed the seat of the stool and whose raised arms and palm-up hands made small armrests. Plants and dozens of brilliantly colored flowers took up most of the space. Everyone sat on blankets on the floor.

Frances had no memory of her walk there, and through her throbbing head she barely recalled what had happened while in Saint's house. When she saw Justice with Aurora, she believed she arrived at a potent mirage. It took Justice explaining to Frances where she was for her to accept that the reality in which she found herself was suddenly unlike the reality from which she had stumbled moments ago.

Aurora squinted as she handed Frances a bowl of thick rice. "I thought you was Saint when I first saw you. Confused me. Didn't I say that, Justice? 'Why Saint dressed like that?'"

"I look like her to you?" Frances asked, eating the rice with her fingers.

"You sound like her inside. I don't see too well. Ain't blind, just don't have the strongest eyes. But I can hear an ant piss in a thunderstorm," Aurora said.

"I didn't think anyone knew Saint like that outside of Ours."

"Wasn't always a Ours to be inside of," Aurora said. "We all come from some other where."

They spoke a bit more, eventually realizing that there was no telling what happened in Saint's house that got Frances into Turney, but since she made it in one piece, she might as well stay until she figured out where she wanted to be. Frances picked at the leftover rice grains in her bowl, eating them one at a time. "Y'all got an empty house here?"

"We can be sure soon," Aurora said, and that evening they situated Frances in a house just across the center of town and Aurora, as shoddy a place as any in Turney, with a single bed, a couple chairs, and small side table flanking the bed. Frances didn't need much, just a place to sleep and good folks to talk to until she figured out her next moves. But she couldn't sleep and the following morning at the sound of the breakfast bell, she spoke with Aurora.

"Something not right," she said, then looked around. Cold weather slinked through the town center and the leaves burned red, brown, and gold overhead. "Something not right."

Aurora smiled. "You just now figuring that out? Nothing right in the world, Frances," then pointing to a ready-made plate, she asked, "You hungry?"

For a week, every second felt deranged to Frances until she stopped leaving her home, afraid that time had gone broken. She looked out the windows occasionally, watching the children play and the dogs run around freely until roped to a post. She lit a fire every day at sunrise and again at sunset. Aurora took to bringing plates to Frances since she refused to step foot from the house. Eventually, Frances stopped eating the food and simply sat in the chair facing the westside window. Stuck there, she stared out vacantly at a vegetable garden visited frequently by gardener and pest alike.

One day, she watched a rabbit gnaw on a head of cabbage only to be shooed away. It returned, gnawed some more, then caught a bullet, becoming part of a stew that night. Frances smelled the rabbit cooking with the very cabbage it had chewed up. Hunger returned to her with incredible violence. Her stomach churned and sang. Her hands shook from weakness. She opened the door to get a bowl, but the house leaned to one side, then leaned back, creaking like an old knee. A putrid smell filled the room, getting in her clothes and sticking to her upper lip. She tried to open a window, but it wouldn't budge, as though hammered down with nails on the outside. It took the fireplace to burn blue for her to fully understand, and beneath the burden of full understanding, she acquiesced and made the chair facing the garden her permanent place in the house. Aurora began knocking on the door before opening it just enough to slide dishes of food and a jar of water inside. Sometimes Frances ate. Sometimes she didn't. However, she made sure that the window had her as an audience of one, afraid that if she turned her head, she might miss it. She just might miss her chance to make it right.

[5]

After Aba's funeral, Mr. Wife fell ill to the point of being unable to move. Luther-Philip helped his father into the front room and sat him at the table. Sick as a dog, Mr. Wife could only stomach a cup of water. Then a bowl of grits. A cup of tea with herbs Luther-Philip had left over from his time with Joy. He boiled some water for himself and bathed out back, then returned to setting his father right. Vegetables chopped up and boiled for soup. More herbs for fever added to the pot. He fed his father and held the man's hand throughout the meals. He told him everything he had kept to himself and from himself.

"I don't know how to love nobody right," he said.

"Then what you doing here?" He squeezed his son's hand.

Luther-Philip didn't know how long but he knew it wasn't long at all before he would also lose his father. He didn't want to be there to see it. For years he had collected his feelings and placed them inside himself as though hiding them from the scavengers of the world, not thinking that he may have also been hiding them from himself.

At the lake with Justice that last time, seeing such peace upon him, falling asleep then waking up to the sculpture of the two of them finally completed, while the water that lapped at both their feet lapped at the feet of the sculpture, teasing it into its cool water, summoning it beneath the surface—it all came rushing back in the red and wet eyes of his father sipping on the soup and chewing bits of overcooked potato and carrot, peas boiled pale and mushy. Even then when he thought he had learned something about himself he just ended up forgetting about someone else. How does one love in this world? Where is there enough room inside a self to love so many others?

Thoughts of being unable to love kept him up all night. He missed Aba, so gathered a handful of berries and lay them at the trunk of God's Place. Frustrated with the meagerness of his offering, he slammed his hand over them and mashed the fruit into the ground. "You got to get close to a thing to know it," he heard, as though spoken from the tree. Dark purple juice dripped from his hands.

After his father recovered, the two of them walked to God's Place. Luther-Philip told Mr. Wife what he had experienced as a boy there with Justice. Not just the snake, but the nest of hair, and how Aba had come to the woods to teach them how to see a thing for what it was. How to really look. He and Mr. Wife hung their oil lamps on a low-hanging branch of God's Place and counted the stars in that private sky. Mr. Wife said abruptly, "One of them Aba. Another is Franklin. Your mother surely up there. Honor. King." Luther-Philip wondered what other myths his father knew, and if knowing them made it easier to live.

The next day, morning sky not fully lit, Luther-Philip rode out of Ours from the northern entrance on a stolen horse. He had few belongings to begin with so brought everything he owned plus some of Justice's things, including the carving of himself and Justice. He tied three sacks to one side of the horse and two to the other. Not knowing if Justice would return to Ours, he left the bust of Honor behind just in case. A world he wanted to know waited for his arrival. He decided to get close to it, to try and maybe learn to love it. "West or East," he said to himself. Not wanting to deal immediately with a river, he chose west.

[6]

Later that morning, Mr. Wife woke with a racing heart. He rushed to Justice's old place, but Luther-Philip wasn't there. He thought nothing out of the ordinary until his son had been gone for a few days, then a week. He fell ill again soon after he realized that Luther-Philip had taken off and his goodbye was spending time with him one night under God's Place. It unnerved him that the last time he and his son spoke they spoke about death, so he pretended instead that they had spoken about new beginnings.

Ours got involved in getting Mr. Wife better, and mostly they succeeded. What lasted and would last until his dying day was a cough that left him perpetually hoarse. The sound of his own voice broke his fortitude because of its sadness. Had he the capacity to know that grief wasn't reserved only for the dead, he would've grieved both Luther-Philip and Justice. He missed them dearly. Had he a strong voice still, he would've called out his sons' names and grieved the lack of a response.

· CHAPTER 26 ·

Grief

[1]

The once-empty bottom branches of God's Place lit up with pinkish-white flowers. From a distance, their color reached the Ouhmey who witnessed the miracle that many believed was Aba's body giving life to the once half-dead tree. Naima hoped for Selah to wake up just like God's Place.

Bone-white moon and a star-freckled sky sloughed their light into Madame Jenkins's window and touched Naima's face. Where once sat a smile now sat instead an impatient taut line as she anticipated Saint coming into Ours to collect her and her sister. Wan light washed her face into a derisive mask.

The previous day, Naima's ears bled and smoke puffed from sleeping Selah's mouth. 'She must've used that bell,' Naima thought. 'If the bell reaching us, maybe the house back.' She waited for Saint's high-held head to break through the shadows and take them home.

Days later, grief became Naima's pet. She cradled it in her arms while watching Selah breathe in her endless sleep. She inhaled grief instead of the scent of food steaming in front of her. She ate it to the rhythm of her labored breathing, having lost her appetite for white beans and eggs, gamey goat meat and turnip greens, a slice of sweet potato pie. Bedtime, she cuddled grief to her chest, and it coldly held her in return.

Madame Jenkins noticed but couldn't break Naima's sorrow, not with gifts of good stories or a new dress she had sewn herself. Got so bad Naima seemed to float, grief taking the place of blood and muscle, leaving her with impressive emptiness. Naima haunted the one-room home, eyes low-lidded. One evening, Madame Jenkins swore she saw the girl glide on her toes across the grass behind the house.

Then one day, Madame Jenkins looked up and Naima was gone. She looked everywhere, behind every tree and up into their canopies for the girl as if she had become a bird trapped in the sky-reaping leaves. At the mercy of panic, she returned to her home to sit beside Selah's sleeping body before heading out to town to ask everyone if they had seen Naima. Then a knock at the front door. It was Thylias, who greeted with a slow and cheerless nod, bun exposed as always in perfect posture atop her head.

The night before, while Madame Jenkins slept heavy, snoring and pillow drooling, Naima stepped into the night toward Saint's. Wanting. Needing.

Lanternless through dense night, Naima made the left turn toward the road that led to the clearing that led to Creek's Bridge over which sat the only home she knew. Insect chittering rained down from foliage that moonlight stained into the look of waving hands. "Come here," whispered the night song of wind absconding from the woods whose darkness husbanded what little glow entered from above. Naima stood before the open gate the trees on either side made of the road, flattened by fright. Looking back, Madame Jenkins's home came into view as Naima's eyes adjusted to the dark. She saw to her right First Street lancing south toward the cemetery. No returning to Madame Jenkins's house, no going back to Selah trapped in the shackles of slumber, so she turned down First.

Houses of people she had never met pushed their dull porches toward her, their windowed masks made monstrous in the reckless lunar light that tossed illusions over Naima's seeing. She took off, running down the road, failing to escape her imagination fashioning restless monsters around her. Bone-crunch of pebbles below her flight. By the time she ran halfway down First, her ankle twanged beneath her weight, throwing her cheek-first to hard ground, her eardrum ringing, and around the ringing night closed in predatorial.

This much night shouldn't have been possible, but it molded around her as her head pained her in pulses, jaw to crown. Then, through the cocoon that darkness and hurt wrapped around her, the sound of a hammer bang shattered the frightening shell like a burst of cold air. Naima moved toward the hammering, was given confidence by it, as the moon's wan glow returned to clear the way before her. Then the hammering stopped. Orange light floated from an open door, then balanced on some invisible scale that waited for Naima's arrival.

Thylias was sitting on her porch, leaning forward as the approaching tumult of cry and curses drew closer. Insects spiraled around the lantern and landed on her. She let them. She leaned forward in her chair until she found herself standing, then walking to the road as the image of Naima came into view.

"Heard your foul mouth from the house," Thylias said, but Naima didn't remember saying anything at all as she stumbled her way there. Her face hurt. Her head throbbed. "Why you out at this hour and alone?"

Loose flap of Naima's bottom lip dropped. "I got lonely," she said.

"Loneliness not a thing you walk off. You get used to it. Come inside."

Naima rested in Thylias's room that held little other than a bed and a small table with a drawer in which Thylias kept petals from dead flowers for their lingering scent, replacing them whenever the collective scent of their shared deaths expired. The room had no window.

Naima was fine until she heard the door lock from the outside. Her thrashing could be heard on the other side of the door, and she made a furious fuss for hours, banging on the locked door, shouting awful things to the woman waiting outside, until she fell asleep with sore fists and a ragged throat.

She woke to the sound of a skeleton key unlocking the door. Thylias stood in the doorway, candle holder in hand and her bun unwrapped and draping thick wavy hair down her shoulders. She carried a stern look, her cheekbones high and the cheeks made hard from her clenched teeth. Without speaking, she left the door opened and walked barefoot away. As the woman left, the smell of food entered the once-locked room and Naima's anger settled into tolerating bitterness. She stepped into the short hall, looking at the floor as she skulked to the table that had a plate of food and a morose-looking Thylias waiting just for her.

"Why the hell you lock me in there?" Naima shouted.

"You said you was lonely. You thought you was gone stay in there when you left from wherever you was? Or did you want to find yourself in the woods?" Thylias said.

They ate in silence by candlelight, morning sun not yet risen. Thylias's house was noisier than Naima remembered it last time she was there with Saint and Selah. Iron cookware rocked on their ceiling hooks, clanging into each other, urgent as heavy bells. To Naima, it felt the house held an endless squall, creaking and moaning wood in chorus all around in sync with the iron bell-pots and bell-pans. Candlelight fought against the moving air whose source couldn't be determined. In the interior din, Naima hated Thylias's quiet and stillness. She looked at the woman's face expecting to hate it, too, but found herself warmed by what she saw, some kinship that tripped up her heart.

Embarrassed, she looked away, and that's when she saw the nails hammered into the wall on the other side of the room, opposite the wall that bore the entryway, and wrapping around the corner into the short hall leading to Thylias's room and what used to be Franklin's room. The nails stopped adjacent to Franklin's bedroom door. She hadn't noticed the nails when she first arrived or when she sat to eat, head down, wrapped in her own harsh feelings, not seeing the clear warning that she shouldn't be there. That no one should.

Despite her intuition telling her to stay seated, she scooted her chair from beneath the table and went to the nailed-up wall. From where she had been sitting, she didn't notice the patterns, but up close it was clear that something beautiful had been pounded into the wood. Arcs of nails repeatedly interrupted by other arcs of nails. Hills of nails rolling up and down the wall, broken up by a knife in some places or a shard of thick glass, and there was no telling how Thylias hammered that into the wall without cutting herself or breaking the glass into hundreds of pieces. Naima stepped backward and observed it all at once, then turned the corner to see what little the dark allowed.

Discerning about all things dead, she assumed correctly that the door belonged to Franklin's room and that the nails were there for him. "Thylias," Naima said.

Thylias shot her a look. "Ma'am. You will call me ma'am."

"Your name Thylias."

"Look at that wall full of nails and tell me my name again?"

The lilt of the question stung Naima and made her reconsider, gazing at the nails then back at Thylias. Still, she didn't relent. "Thylias your name. Why I got to call you ma'am?"

Thylias placed both hands on her lap. She hadn't moved an inch from the table since Naima left her sitting there. "You know what a bitch is?" Thylias asked.

The girl paled. Of course, she knew. It was the word of disappearance. It was her favorite word because it hurt people away from her when she wanted space. She couldn't remember where she first heard it, only when she first said it to someone, and the look they had given her, as though she had stopped time, thrilled her. "Bitch" made people freeze up, sometimes made them ask, "Girl, what did you just call me?" and stop speaking to her altogether. On days she wanted to be left alone, she said it to anyone who breathed near her as she ran errands for Saint. If they couldn't hurt her first, she would be all right for the rest of the day.

But it was a misunderstood power because people didn't come back when she most needed them, a need that shamed her each time she felt it. She knew the magic word to make folks disappear, but after they disappeared, it seemed that she, too, disappeared from them. They were already mean to her on their own, but what choice did she have to interact with them when Saint sent her to pick up or drop off a conjure? She thought it unfair to be beholden to the same effect of a decision she made that wasn't made on the other end. No one ever called her a bitch, though she did hear them whisper about her hair "standing on top of her head," about her being "one of them Saint girls" whose name they never tried to learn, and about her curt way of speaking though no one taught her any different. "Little rude girl." "Saint's terror." "The mean one." "The dirty one," as though she didn't spend more time washing her ass than Selah. They called her everything but her name and everything but a bitch, and she came back each time to collect their orders and their abuses that stacked so high they toppled over her, until she decided that was enough. Seven years old and full of spite, she called the first person who shook his head at her when she walked by a mangy bitch. "You mangy bitch. Shake your head at your mama." And from that day on, that man kept away from her. Simple. But she had only meant for him to stay away for a little while, not forever, and her confusion from watching how the other children could act out but be embraced after being corrected turned into a feeling so ugly it had no limits. She threw the nastiness at everybody and ended up throwing it at herself from time to time. She called herself ugly though she didn't think she was. How could she be ugly when she had her sister's remarkable face?

But now even that face wouldn't look back at her. Naima felt hints of this future back when Selah snuck off to Ours without her, hints that Selah had not only imagined a life of her own but had claimed it, could claim it only if Naima weren't involved. The first finger she hammered in retaliation to her sister abandoning her hurt the most. The pain of being left alone, when Selah was the closest person she had next to Saint, dwarfed the pain of the other fingers she hammered.

It would be years after she smashed her fingers when Naima realized that Selah had no space for anyone else or their feelings. Sure, love existed, enough for Selah to smile at her sister and make sure she didn't get too close to a snake or poison oak, but when quiet draped its cloth over Selah's eyes, Naima knew her sister had gone off to some other place, possibly in the freedom of a bird or fox. Naima believed she possessed no skills of freedom, no gifts of her own that would allow her to follow Selah to wherever she escaped. She made sure to speak with her loudest voice whenever the veil of freedom covered Selah's eyes, though eventually not even the bright blade of her voice cut loose the caul.

The night after Saint watched Selah try to resurrect that woman in the front room, Selah shared with Naima that she wanted to run away but didn't know where to. Naima's heart dropped.

"I don't want to be Saint's anymore," Selah had said. "I don't want to put my life in others' death anymore."

Naima promised to protect her so that Selah wouldn't want to leave her alone, and she made Selah promise that she would stay with her, not leave her behind in the house with Saint, who made it clear she had no intention of loving her, only protecting her and not even from Saint herself. If either of the girls hugged Saint for too long, she shooed them away. Their smiles went unreturned. Saint made sure they ate well and left the house clean and went to bed even cleaner, but she didn't kiss their foreheads or squeeze their slight shoulders or hold their hands unless they proved their usefulness to her. Young but not stupid, the empty value of Saint's attention grew more obvious to them, and where Naima wanted companionship through the storm, Selah wanted to do away with the storm altogether.

Now, Naima sat in the nailed-up house of a woman she hardly knew while thinking about her same-face sister who found a way to escape after all in the seduction of infinite dreaming. Selah got away, went inside herself and decided that was good enough, and because she never cared about formalities, or considered she meant something to the people in her life, she left without even saying goodbye. Even a dog deserved a goodbye.

"A bitch a girl dog," Naima said.

"This is true. And I been called a bitch all my child life until I came to Ours. I have the right to be called ma'am in my grown life. You may not think about other people's feelings, Naima, but that don't mean they gone go away. You a child and as a child you learn how to respect people older than you so you can know when you not getting it when you older."

"I don't get it now," Naima said.

"Then you already know better and don't need telling." She walked over to Naima and asked, "May I touch your face?" No one ever asked permission to touch her. They just reached out and touched her wherever and whenever they pleased.

"No, ma'am," Naima said.

Thylias smiled and wiped her fingers across the heads of the nails. "Thank you," she said.

[2]

On the third day of Naima's stay, Thylias told her she needed something to guide her grief. She explained how she woke up one day and wanted to hurt somebody. Anybody would do. Hurt them so they would know just how she felt sitting cooped up in that house with her most loyal friend in the dirt. But hurting people only gave them a hurt that was theirs, and she wanted them to feel her specific pain.

"Grief not giveable in that way. You can't give somebody what you feel to make them understand," Thylias said, and described how she came about a box of nails and went to hammering them into the walls. At first, the placements were random and not very healing to hammer in, but the violent banging distracted her from the banging happening inside of her. Then she noticed how without trying she had made a kind of pattern: arcs, one beneath the other to make a band of sorts, that stopped and started into each other. So, she kept that up and liked the way it looked, which made her like the sound even more. "Like thunder from a gesture," she said. "Had a sky of sound in my hands. Just like that."

Eventually, she imagined Franklin still slept in that room and not underground, that he just needed some waking up music. She hammered more fiercely, and when she ran out of nails, she used anything sharp that wood would take. "Found a piece of broken mirror in the road once. Don't know where it came from, but I put it here," she said, pointing to where she wedged the glass in an open space between the nails. "Cut myself terribly. Terribly.

"You have to find what turn your grief useful to you," Thylias continued, observing what little of her face the mirror shard between the nails showed her. "And you shouldn't leave here before you do. I can't keep you here if you want to go. I'm surprised you stayed this long." Thylias locked eyes with Naima. "I shouldn't have trapped you in my room. I apologize. I had no other way in my head to keep you from wandering off again. Do you forgive me?"

"Yes, ma'am," Naima said, though she didn't know if she knew how to forgive.

[3]

That night, Thylias woke to the sound of the front door closing. She had taken to sleeping in Franklin's room now that Naima slept in her room. Though Thylias slept well, it took a while for her to find comfort where her old friend had found no joy of his own.

She felt the pressure of the nails entering the walls, pushing in a little closer each night. Sometimes, in the middle of the night, she would hear a hammer knock scattered patterns against the wall, then one powerful bang followed, shaking her from the bed. She would then go to the living room where empty quiet greeted her.

When she heard the front door close, she grabbed up a shawl, an oil lantern, and her gun and checked Naima's room. She called her name before opening the door. The girl was gone. Outside, she saw a light not too far from the house, floating in the graveyard. Mrs. Wife and Franklin were the only two buried there after all these years who had grave markings. The other dead, the dozen or so orphans who died soon after arriving in Ours, had only flowers to mark their burial. That the flowers grew back every year meant a longer life for the orphans in death than they had in life.

Thylias approached Naima among the flowered graves and saw that her head was uncovered. "Put this on your head," Thylias said, passing her a long white scarf. "Don't sit with the dead with your head uncovered."

Naima wrapped her hair and Thylias left her alone without asking why she had taken company with ghosts.

When Naima returned, she blew out the lantern and left it on the floor of her room. She changed into bed clothes and went to Thylias's room, got in bed with her, rolled herself into Thylias, and fell asleep.

THE LAUGHTER OF water falling into a bucket woke Naima. Thylias was bathing outside, naked, joyfully immodest as she stood in the yard out back, lathering her body with a soapy rag. Naima watched from the doorway the suds caught in the woman's belly fat, rolls of flesh covered in soft white bubbles, and wondered if she would ever take up space that beautifully. Often, she wished she was invisible and often she was treated that way to her detriment. But here was Thylias in quiet nude, refashioning the space around her into a stage where she was both performer and part of the adoring audience, water the only sound other than her heavy breathing as she diligently washed herself. Sunlight washed her along with the water and spun rainbows inside the bubbles.

"Help me with my back?" Thylias asked. "I'll wash yours."

Thylias handed her a rag from the bottom of the basin, and they washed themselves, wetting the grass as they handled their bodies with care. Naima took Thylias's rag to wash her back but froze.

"What do you need?" Thylias asked.

"I never washed somebody else before," Naima said.

"You don't have to touch or be touched if you don't want to. Those days over, Naima. You understand?"

"Yes, ma'am," Naima said. With Thylias's rag, she washed the woman's back, marking where skin folds took in her hands, holding them as she cleaned skin smooth as porcelain. Thylias asked if Naima wanted her back washed and washed it when she said yes. They rinsed with a small bucket of soapless water poured over both their heads, laughing and screaming while the cool water cascaded over them.

They air dried, hidden from the rest of town by tall bushes that created a gallery from back door to the middle of the backyard, where a toolshed and outhouse stood on opposite sides, guards watching over their dancing in the lifting sunlight. Gnat clouds floated their lace over the scenery, and it seemed to Naima that they were trapped inside the body of a ghost. As she spun, grass prickling her feet, she wished Selah was there with her and began to fall back into her grief.

While Naima washed the floors, Thylias chopped onion, tomato, and leftover mint and added it to a cast-iron skillet glazed with lard. She added corn bread, a splash of water, and honey, making a makeshift grit. The two ate while a breeze touched their bodies through the open window, sweet potion of flower scent caught in the moving air.

"Ma'am."

"Yes, Naima."

"I want to cut my hair."

Thylias inspected Naima's hair. Thick, hateful of gravity. She tried to run her fingers through, but they got stuck, as if each finger had fallen in love with Naima's hair and didn't want to leave. "Cut it how?"

"Low as a boy's."

"I'll help you. You didn't ask, but your hair is pretty."

"I know. I want to grow it back this way. I just—" Naima started laughing hard. She didn't know why but something in her got to feeling good. "I just want to see it get like that with all my attention."

"Let me find some shears. Gone have to go bald so it grow out low like you asking. You ready to be that new?"

"Yes."

Thylias thought it a shame for all that pretty hair to drop to the floor like that. She grabbed a few fingers worth of hair and scissored it off. When it was low enough, she went looking for Franklin's razor, strop, shaving brush, and soap.

"Come look," Thylias said, and showed Naima how to strop a razor. She slid it up, blade side facing her, then turned it and slid it down. She lathered the brush with the soap in a little bowl of water, then handed it to Naima to lather her head. Then she handed her the razor. "You will cut yourself. That's just how it go. Go slow. Be gentle to yourself. I'll get the mirror."

Naima had hardly nicked herself while shaving, and Thylias's assistance lessened the bloodletting. They burned Naima's hair and buried the ashes out back. Restless, they took a walk about town.

'She crazified the girl with her own crazy,' someone thought, waving and smiling at the two as they passed by. Stares, whispers, dropped baskets, mouths covered, laughter, "I'll be damned," "My, my, my, my, my," porch sweeping paused, clavicles clutched, "That's how my mama used to have her hair," "Girl looking cute as a song," tears from reminiscence, nods of approval . . . they only headed west down Bank, then a right on First, then another right back down Freedom till they got to Third Street and headed south to Thylias's house.

Closing the door behind her, Thylias worried about what Naima thought, but the girl screamed with glee, "Did you see the look on that little girl's face back on First Street? She smiled and waved at me, and I heard her say to somebody, 'She so pretty!'" Thylias nodded, knowing that Naima would be on her way to her whole self soon.

[4]

"Ma'am," Naima started.

"Yes?" Thylias said. They were sitting on the porch in a night cool enough for a shawl.

"Why Franklin kill hisself?"

Thylias waited for a while before answering. "Maybe," she said, then stopped. She wanted to honor the gentleness she heard in Naima's voice. "I think it's cause he could choose to."

"Was he sad?"

"We all sad, Naima. Sadness the first feeling, the one on the bottom. It's what we put on top of it that helps us keep going. That's what I believe. One time I asked Franklin if the dead had dreams and he said the dead don't have nothing. Franklin couldn't put nothing but more sadness on top of the sadness he already had, and when it got too heavy, he had to say, 'Am I gone keep being sad or am I gone be something else?' And he chose to be something else." She paused. "He was better with being dead and having nothing, than being alive."

"I heard Saint say he shouldn't have never killed hisself."

"Maybe so. Maybe so. I'm of the mind that we can never know what someone needs unless they tell us"— Thylias tightened her shawl around her shoulders—"or show us. Naima . . ."

"Yes, ma'am."

"Many of us have had few occasions to make choices. I think Franklin choosing how he wanted to die was for him to be free his own way. I don't like his choice. It hurt me deep that he did that. What I know well enough, though, is that he did what he wanted with his life because it was finally his. Only his. You understand, don't you?'

"Yes, ma'am," Naima said.

"Good," Thylias responded, happy to know that someone understood, even if they were a child, because she herself still wondered what she knew, what she could know, and how much she had already gotten wrong.

[5]

Joy sat at her canvas and frowned after hearing a knock at the door. She had taken up painting again, landscapes, something she hadn't done since her days with Eloise, and the disturbance distracted her to bisecting a deer with a thin, dark green line of paint, belly to spine.

Paintbrush in hand, she opened the door to Thylias and Naima, the latter holding an apple cobbler they had made together as a gift to Joy, paying their respect. Seeing the cobbler, Thylias looking healthy, and Naima with no hair and an unknown light in her eyes, Joy held her breath.

"We made this for you, ma'am," Naima said, and the "ma'am" struck Joy across the ears. She scrutinized the two visitors, then invited them in with a soft "thank you." They quietly ate the cobbler together right from the dish, the half-finished painting with the split deer watching close by. When they finished, they looked at the empty dish and warped into softer versions of themselves, caused by full stomachs. A house creak made Joy laugh until she realized it wasn't Aba speaking. Embarrassed, she pushed away from the table and returned to her canvas, standing before it with growing focus.

"I started this painting after putting Aba in the ground. It's of the tree he's buried beneath," Joy said.

"You saw a deer there?" Naima asked.

"The deer . . ." Joy said, then waited. The deer represented Aba's spirit, or her grief, or an abstraction yet understood by the painter. Hope. Peace. Fear. The deer faced the viewer, perhaps startled by being perceived, perhaps welcoming whoever looked to enter the landscape with it, make of its world a new home. ". . . I saw once while out with Frances."

"It's very beautiful," Thylias said.

"Like you, Ms. Joy," Naima said.

Joy scowled. "Did somebody else die?" she asked. "Was there some other death I'm unaware of?"

Thylias laughed. "No. No one else died. Well,"—she paused—"unless by die you mean of an old self."

Joy had not turned away from her painting, distracted by the deer of her own rendering, the white of its tail waving with the brush strokes that made it. She was tired and Naima's sudden kindness landed clumsily. She decided to test the water. "How's Selah, Naima?" When Joy finally turned to face her company, she saw the girl looking at her hands in her lap. Naima didn't answer, just looked down and fiddled her fingers. Joy looked at Thylias for an answer, but Thylias just shook her head, pursing her lips. "I see," Joy said, though she saw nothing at all. "Naima, stand for me, please?"

Naima stood and Joy embraced her, holding the back of her smooth scalp and resting her cheek on the top of the girl's head. "I don't know what has happened to you," Joy said, "but I am so sorry it has happened to you." The girl nodded. She didn't know if this kind of attention hurt or helped. All she knew was Joy touched her and the warmth felt new.

· CHAPTER 27 ·

Conviction

[1]

The day of the invasion, Selah didn't see the horseman break through the volley of bullets and ride up just feet away from God's Place, for the birds she had entered to watch over Ours all amassed over the town in a vortex of fear. Selah jumped from bird sight to bird sight, telling Aba what horseman she saw and by whose house on what streets.

The Ouhmey swiftly killed all intruders and suffered few injuries. Birds settled in trees after bullets ceased tearing through the town, the streets clogged by living and dead horses and the corpses of men who had no business barging into Ours demanding their children. Audacity such as this required death, which is why Selah needed little convincing to climb into that tree and direct Aba's percussion to where the bullets needed to go. But when that one horseman rode up close, she missed him, and it took the sound of the bullet leaving his up-close gun to shock her out of the bird she had inhabited a half mile south and return to her own body, her own sight, and watch the horseman—bleeding from the eyes and nose, rotting on the inside—die slowly in Naima's wave of sickness.

Naima's intense focus broke at the sound of the bullet as well, and when she came to, she saw the sick, stubborn man with his gun still in hand. Outraged, Naima widened her eyes and he died in a rush of illness.

Selah listened. That bullet had entered a place important, Selah knew. 'It's in his breathing,' she thought, and put her hands to Aba's chest to keep him alive with her own life force. In the back of her mind, she saw Saint lording over her, that snake staff digging into the floor and her stern gaze digging into Selah. She shook her head to shake out the vision of Saint, but Saint's image soon took over her vision of Aba.

The image of Saint rhythmically pounded its staff into the floor of Selah's mind. Naima rubbed Selah's back, but Selah didn't feel it. Getting away from Saint and the demand that she raise the dead had erased the world.

The only time Saint had ever encouraged Selah had burned shame and fear into her memory. "We will try again some other time," Saint had told her, "when you get stronger." When Selah protested that it hurt too bad to pour that much into somebody to bring them back to life, that Saint's hope that she could do it hurt the worst, Saint said, "Pain gets easier. It has no other choice." She kissed Selah on the forehead, and what should've been a good feeling nauseated Selah instead.

While keeping Aba alive against his body's wishes, Selah dove into the dark beneath the vision of Saint, into the depths of what felt to her like oil that loosened into cool water, then opened into air. Weightless in the void. To get away from Saint's demands, she fell into the unknown and found that she knew it, at least a little, for this is where she went when under the pressure of healing those she couldn't heal. This is where she went when the older woman took over her body. But after Frances had touched Selah that one time, the older woman couldn't come back and no longer waited in the dark recesses of Selah's need.

Not too long after Frances's touch chased that woman away did Selah realize the older woman was herself but from a long time into the future. How her older self got inside her younger self she didn't know, so in secret she took to pretending she was asleep while contemplating how to reach her older self on her own. If that woman from an approaching time could come to Selah, maybe Selah could go to her. In this moment of Aba's dying, she needed the woman Frances had chased away, back into the after. So she dove.

She heard Joy's voice from the outside saying "please" so sweetly that she began to feel guilty for having held on to Aba's life in the first place. She was about to give up on finding her older self and just go on and let Aba pass away into his own peace. 'He deserve rest,' she thought. But the tap of Saint's ominous staff returned to her mind like the loud ticking of a mean clock, seconds shaved off as quick as Aba's breath sliced and seared by a bullet. If Aba died, Selah knew she would be forced to bring him back, to make the painful attempt while disregarding her own life. No. No. No. Never again. Selah released both Aba and herself from the tethers of the world, floating . . .

[2]

. . . in the great nothing, deeper than she had ever traversed, the surrounding darkness bursts open into a garden of light. Pulsing orbs of various colors speckle the canvas that had once been no different from an empty night sky. Inside the orbs, Selah sees people who look like her and Naima. Kinfolks living inside their bubbles of time. They wear bizarre clothes, enter colossal buildings carved from metal and carriages that move without horses. They carry weapons, wearing all black or suits or green and brown uniforms. Around her, their voices bleed out from their orbs, creating a cacophony from which she can't escape. Conversations pummel into her. Screams beckon for her. Laughter removes the pain she felt while putting hands on Aba. In one orb, she sees a woman who looks like her, rocking a baby in her arms. In an adjacent orb, another woman with her face, a bit older, sits in a crowd of people who watch young blacks in caps and gowns walk across a platform, grab a document, shake white folks' hands, then take a seat.

A dark orb depicts a ship sinking into the depths of a large body of water, the ship torn asunder by a storm. Beside it, an orb shows a town full of people celebrating a couple, a woman nearby pounding yam with a large pestle in a giant wooden bowl.

One orange orb attracts her so much that she touches it. A bright orange light overtakes her sight and when she comes to, she finds herself standing in line behind a stream of Negroes, backs straight, facing forward and focusing on the task at hand that waits beyond where she can see. She can't control her body, as though she had entered an animal, but she knows she is inside a person this time, one who smells like sweet perfume.

She catches a glimpse of the person she has entered in a window that reads "Gloria's Hair Emporium est 1925." Seeing the year, she understands that she has gone into the future but not how or why, and seeing that the woman looks so much like her makes the unfamiliar world more familiar.

She learns the woman she's inside of is named Naima, which makes her smile. "Get moving, chile. Folks is waiting. You hear me, Naima?" Hearing this, Naima turns away from herself in the mirroring shop window after giving her reflection a curious look, surprising Selah into believing this woman sees Selah resting inside of her.

When Selah sees Naima's mother, she can barely contain herself inside the young woman's head. She cackles at the resemblance, rubs her hands together greedily like a fly. It becomes clearer to her that this is her lineage as though the mind in which she sits has been hers all along.

The line of Negroes, all dressed in suits or skirts that hit the knee or just under, pushes forward, a slow river of people filed neatly, newspapers tucked under arms and brimmed hats blocking out the eager sun. It's hot outside and one man in line says, "This the hottest election of all my life. And this long line don't make it no better." Selah doesn't know what is happening, even after Naima enters a bank that is shut down for the day, selects several names on a ballot (one a Franklin Delano Roosevelt), and disappears the ballot into a box.

A young man calls out to Naima's mother, calls her Dr. Holiday, explains that the "liniment worked mighty fine, Dr. Holiday. My grandfather sends his regards." Children outside jump as a rope spins above and beneath them. Selah wants to join them. Naima passes them with her mother on the way down the street.

In a blink, Selah is back among the orbs, and without thinking touches another. In this future, she is inside an older woman in a candlelit room, white drawings of arrows curving and pointing in many directions all around her. The person she is inside of shakes small bones in her hand and throws them to the floor. A turned-over shoe shows its bottom to the woman and white arrows dart toward the toes' direction beneath the sole. A black rooster sneaks past the door and the woman begins to speak, "Thank you for visiting me, young ancestor," and Selah is thrown from the woman's body and back into the orb garden.

Each orb shows to her descendants from the future. 'These my kin,' she thinks, and reaches for a light blue orb that shows the face of a woman who looks only a little like her, and as she flashes into this world, she finds herself in a bed, charts and metal devices all around, a man telling the person she is inside of to push while a handsome man with big puffy hair stands at the foot of the bed watching on with extravagant worry.

Minutes later, the doctor's rolled-up sleeves reveal dark brown skin with curly hair covered in a wet sheen of sweat. There's crying, and the doctor passes the baby to "Mrs. Johnson. It's a boy. Congratulations," and the handsome man with the big puffy hair says, "Evie, a son. Baby, you gave me a son!"

Music plays in the background, "Betcha by golly woooow" crooning from a small box someone brought into the delivery room. Selah wants to see more of the mysterious music box, but Evie keeps turning her head to look at the baby that Selah thinks looks a fool and a mess.

"Thank you for letting me have music in here. I know it's not protocol,"

Evie says, then the box begins to speak "That was 'Betcha by Golly Wow,' brand-new from the Stylistics, Dionne Warwick's favorite male group." Selah wonders how the man's voice got inside the black box and what Stylistics meant and who Dena Warnick is.

She is thrown into the orb garden before she can learn more, and when she catches a glimmer of herself in another orb that appears to be filled with only water, she notices she has grown into a young woman.

She visits several more orbs, staying longer in each one, hours, days, weeks, months, years. She learns that her own age changes depending on whose orb she visits. She goes in as a thirty-six-year-old visiting a seventeen-year-old descendant and returns to the orb garden as a seventeen-year-old. That she remembers everything from the lives she eavesdrops on excites her, the puzzle of the future coming into stark clarity as she moves from Negro, to black, to African American, then to Black.

She learns what a radio is, a car, oil sheen, and Vernor's Ginger Ale. She sees people of all races holding hands and singing against a war that wilted the flowers woven into their hair. Luster's Pink Oil Moisturizer and disco. Aretha Franklin and Soul Train. Watching the Soul Train line in one life and dancing in the line in another. She watches the women she inhabits fall in love with men who love them fiercely, imperfectly, but never with fist or slap, though sometimes in the embrace of addiction that lights up their veins and delivers them to early graves. The bent spoon, the blunt syringe, the white rock of disaster a rocket ship, baby, to the moon and stars that burn the smoker to the bone.

In 1990, she learns what HIV and AIDS are, sees for herself what the invisible insurgencies do to a brother who dies in her descendant's arms in his own bed, twenty-five of his friends dead over the course of two years. Cancer and diabetes ravages one descendant in 1993, while in 1995 she learns how to bring somebody back from an overdose and how to lose them after bringing them back. The burnt spoons clink hypnotic in her brain. Blunt syringes unsew a vein. For the first time she sees poverty in Black towns and neighborhoods that knew of no such thing. But she also learns that the fighting spirit in the Ouhmey transfers into the time beyond, and that the desire to live confounds the forces that try to undo.

After living six years in the 1990s in a single descendant and the first ten years of the 2000s in another, she wants to leave the bodies in less time, but she stays longer each visit, living through years in mere moments, her own age in utter confusion, lost in the time jumps, both woman and girl, having gained hundreds of years of experience from the various women whose compiled lives welcomed her unknowingly and taught her phrases like "Keep on keeping on" while their children rolled into early graves.

Then she opens her eyes after touching the orb she thought was empty, the one that looks like a ball of water, and wakes up inside the body of a teenage boy. She has never been inside a boy before and immediately wants to go back to the orb garden. The room is dark. A small clock near the bed reads 11:47 in glowing red numerals. Selah knows she will be with Him for a long time and prepares herself for the worst.

What happens is much different from before. She can smell what He smells, taste what He tastes, and feel what He feels emotionally and sometimes physically: the fried whiting placed over a bowl of grits, His piss stinging dark yellow into the toilet, the sneakers with the worn-out insole soring His feet as He rushes through games of football. When He brushes His hair, waves take over His scalp and the feel of the hard bristles against His head are hard bristles against hers, delivering a satisfying chill down her back. When He sees a girl He likes and hardens, her stomach roils, and the sensation overwhelms. She isn't merely inhabiting His body. Selah has merged with Him and the luster of His life illuminates and challenges her own.

The boy somehow moves throughout the day without hearing His birth name. He is lovingly called Boy, Nigga, G, the homie, son, Deazy, which is the closest thing to His name she hears. When He brushes His teeth, He does not look at Himself in the mirror, focusing on parts of Himself that keep His face in disconnected fragments. It takes her days to see what this descendant looks like.

When He showers, she feels a nervousness when He washes His behind, a reticence to soap near His asshole, but He does it and she can't understand why this act of cleaning Himself brings the boy so much shame. He takes His time getting into the shower and rushes to get out. His own body seems to repulse Him. His big hands. The hair on his thighs. The dark of his elbows. He doesn't want to know them at all, and it disrupts her desire to see and know Him.

One morning, He goes downstairs before the rest of the family wakes, to look at the photos over a mantel in the living room. Selah's heart races, which is the boy's heart racing, as she sees through His eyes the same woman who voted decades ago, the photo in black and white and her mother beside her. The handsome man with the afro appears in another photo kissing the pregnant woman Selah had been in on the forehead. The woman holds the hand of a young boy, no older than five. The photo that He focuses on is one of an older woman holding a baby in her lap. He tears up and Selah's own eyes grow wet from their shared sorrow.

At the dining room table, His mother says, "Fix your face. I'm not gone tell you again. You too big for that soft shit," and the feeling inside of Selah is a new pain that doesn't sting but throws open every hidden window in the body. His body is soft, but strong, and Selah's confusion sits in the hurt because He sits in the hurt. She wants Him to look at His mother, to read her face and body language for clarity, but He keeps His head in His plate of food. She cannot stop looking at His beautiful hands.

His mother washes dishes and kisses Him on the forehead when she leaves the room. He looks up finally, letting Selah see her face. His mother looks nothing like Selah's people, and she frowns at the surprise of her freckled cheeks.

Later that day, when His father comes home from work after a security night shift, He is playing *Mortal Kombat 11* on the Xbox in the basement. His father grabs the second controller and plays along, smelling like Irish Spring soap. Selah sees that it's His father who is the earlier descendant and the sadness in his eyes angers her. He and His father play the game for almost two hours, Selah wondering how they don't speak but between them exists a bond that moves from them into her, one that makes Him smile on the inside as He decapitates His father's character with a bladed hat. His father rubs Him on the head, then climbs up the stairs and into bed. She does not know what His father's voice sounds like.

At night, He reads a short story in a *Playboy* He has stolen from His father. When He finishes, He stares at the nipples of one of the models, rubbing His balls, then slides the journal between His mattress and the bed frame, His imagination too stunted to get Him hard. Selah can't sense what He thinks but watches the streetlights paint the inside of the bedroom a dirty yellow as He looks at the one tree on the block until He dozes off.

He has a few friends. His mother likes none of them. His father doesn't care. They smell like cooking grease, onions at the armpits of their shirts, and cheap Avon cream. His mother knows they are clean of body, but their clothes are never clean, and she tells Him this with disdain, hateful of the boys' mothers, never mentioning the fathers. Selah wonders why. When He goes to his room, He mumbles under His breath, "Blessings don't come even." Selah agrees.

His friends are poor and underfed, and this makes Him love them harder, especially His friend Torrance. His mother shakes her head and sends Torrance home immediately after he's eaten at her house. "Wash your clothes, Torrance. If you need to do that hur, let me know. Use dish soap if you need to," she says. "You hur me, lil nigga?" she asks, and Torrance says, "Yes, ma'am, I hur you." "Aight, get going." "Thank you for the food." "You know I got you," she says, then disappears upstairs.

Soon after, He walks Torrance to the door and Torrance says, "My mama ain't gone let me wash my shit over hur. She'd cuss me the fuck out if I came home with clothes smelling better than urbody else's. She a goofy gal." They dap up and plan to meet the next day to play football. Selah thinks Torrance's voice sounds like fire.

He sits on the porch. A young woman named Candice walks up to Him and sits on the porch, her body heat adding to the hot summer. "What's the sitch, Deazy?" she asks, rubs His knee. He doesn't want her. He doesn't have language to say no to her because He doesn't want to be called funny. "You funny boy?" He's been asked a few times since Selah arrived. He shuts them up on the field, using His body to devastate the boys who try to talk shit about Him as He steamrolls into them. They call Him funny, and He lands His full weight onto them. He catches the football and folks don't even try to stop Him. Selah thinks this power is what makes them call Him funny, because she laughs when they can't stop Him. But today, she learns funny doesn't mean laughter. He shakes His head at Candice's advance. She says, "I knew you was funny," but Selah notices no one has laughed. She notices that she feels anger and her head fills up with blood.

"Sit yo stupid ass down," He says.

"Who you calling stupid? You tweakin," Candice says, but it's half-hearted.

"You. Who the fuck else hur?"

Candice pushes His head hard with the tips of her fingers. He grabs Her arm and forces her to the porch. Selah is breathing hard. She doesn't know why they are fighting. Why they hardly smile at each other. They tussle for a little bit more until He says, "Come on," and goes into the house.

Selah learns that she can stop feeling what He feels with his body if she closes her eyes and huddles into a ball inside her own mind. She does this whenever He touches Himself in ways that bring pleasure. The first time it happened, Selah didn't know boys did that and when the white, sticky fluid shot out from His dick she screamed and closed her eyes. Every feeling went away then, as though she had fallen asleep inside Him.

When she opens her eyes and unfolds her body, Candice is putting on her clothes. "You going to the party tomorrow?" she asks.

"I might. Ain't thought about it," He says. Selah has never felt this feeling He feels now and for the first time she tries to impart her will to Him. When Candice finally leaves, she kisses Him on the lips and proceeds down the street. The feeling fills Him up. He goes to the bathroom and looks into His eyes for the first time. The mirror is speckled with toothpaste and missing a piece of glass on the bottom right-hand corner, the black backing with old glue darkening the space where glass should've been.

He opens the medicine cabinet and takes out a bottle of Tylenol, pours half the bottle into His hands. He looks into His own eyes and steals Selah's heart. "O Deazy, you got Naima's eyes," she says, and the overwhelming, unnamable feeling in Him relaxes, as if He hears her for the first time. He doesn't hear her. She knows this. He has calmed down. He puts the pills back into the bottle. This is the fourth time He has done this, but the first time Selah felt as though He might go through with it. Selah knows what this would do to Him if He does it, had seen in 1974 the aftermath of a handful of pills on a lover. Her descendant was able to save her lover, but would this descendant always be able to stop Himself?

Then, that night, while He is asleep, she finds that she can see His memories in a similar way she can see the orbs of the future. His memories float about like fireflies, and she wonders how memory is connected to time since they both look the same when up close: orbs of light, the future orbs big as a head and frozen in place; memory orbs were insect-small and fleeting. She reaches for one and it moves away from her fingers. They mostly escape her, but she eventually finds one she can grab. Touching it does not send her into the memory; rather it puts the memory inside her. It is a memory of His grandmother holding Him in her lap. He is five years old. She is telling Him stories. Another memory is of an uncle teaching Him how to fish. And another of His father giving Him a piggyback ride. Memory after memory of love, intentional and effortless, care that she had seen from previous futures of her descendants. It challenges what she thought was His sad life. She searches through many of His memories but can't pinpoint the source of what He has become. She wonders if He even knows why He is so sad, or if He is under the hold of a conjure.

By the tenth day of her settling inside of Him, she learned to love the taste of hot chips and grape Vess. She recognizes that Torrance makes Him laugh the loudest of His friends and cheers Him up when he notices the lamp in His eyes has gone out. The two remind her of Luther-Philip and Justice, and this thought makes Selah miss her old life, until she hears a clock tick or a mouth pop or when He habitually knocks on the desk in His room, making beats—all of which brings back images of Saint and her staff.

Selah is shocked to hear His mother cracking up at a television show that she invites Him to sit next to her and watch. He does. On the television, a man dressed up as a woman rolls her eyes and pushes her long-nailed fingers into the other women's faces. He and His mother laugh. Selah worries she is missing something because she doesn't find this funny, but is happy that He is happy, feels His happiness fill her up. She wants more of this for Him. Tired, He leans on His mother, holding most of His imposing weight. She doesn't push Him off. She holds Him and they laugh for three episodes straight until time for dinner.

Something has changed. His father comes through the door from a morning shift, smells the meat loaf, and shouts, "Oh, we EATING eating tonight." This is the first time Selah has heard his voice. It is booming and edgeless, how she imagines smoke would sound if it had a voice. He is not a large man, but his voice takes over the space with its warm quality. And this, too, makes Him happy.

They eat together, tell stories, shit talk, gossip about ole dude at the corner store who was shot in the foot by Azrael for feeling on his sister booty. Shot in the foot and dared to say something. "'Make it worth my time, then, nigga, or shut the fuck up,'" His father quotes Azrael, and He shakes His head while His mother says, "He be doing too much."

In the basement, His mother decides she wants to learn how to play *Mortal Kombat.* She plays against His father and wins, pulling off a fatality. "Last time I play with you," His father says. Outside, a storm takes out the electricity. They light a few candles. His father tells a story about His's great-grandfather and how he used to salt the thresholds of his house.

"This was back when granddad lived in Gary, Indiana, and his sister stayed with him. She had stepped out, right, and my granddad, the night before, salted the thresholds of the house. I'm talking sea salt at every doorstep, in the windowsills and shit.

"So, this woman comes by to see my grandaunt for lunch. Granddad knew of her but wasn't friends with her, but he knew his sister got along with her well, so it was cool. He greeted her and she was like, 'Is Beetle in?' They used to call my grandaunt Beetle. And he tells her, 'Naw she stepped out but you can wait inside. Hot out there. Come on in.' So tell me why she look like she about to step in but then stop like it's a glass wall in front of her. Kid you not! She gone say, 'Naw, I'll wait out here.' He invite her in again, says, 'Beetle be back real soon. She just went down the road,' and the woman getting nervous, crinkling her dress in her hands. 'Naw, just tell her I came through,' and the chick walks off." His father laughs, "She don't ever visit again. My grandaunt got to go to her raggedy friend's house from then on cause the woman wouldn't step foot into my granddad house." The air is spiced with fear and anticipation. His mother laughs nervously while He sits stuck in the images He's created in His mind: a thin woman wearing a large, brimmed hat and a cream-colored dress with matching shoes and stockings, her eyes all blacked out and wide with spite when she turns her back to His great-grandfather, who smiles knowingly at what he's done and who he's done it to.

Selah listens to the story and recognizes Saint's ways in the great-grandfather; not the invitation, but the salt, its effectiveness against evil and unlikable Negroes, whatever that difference might've been. At least with this story, she knows that conjure has made it this far into the future, well respected and intimate. For the first time she feels protected inside of Him.

BUT SOMETHING IN the air clenches shut the following day. The summer sun drops onto everybody and angers them with its relentless heat. Selah feels His anger as He fixates on what happened moments ago. Torrance showed up for football in the park and halfway through the game he picked a fight with one of the other boys and all twelve of them ended up rumbling in the hard grass. Selah thinks back to how it was so easy to rile up Torrance by calling him a "musty nigga," when they all were musty as hell out there. But the temporary and changeable stink on some of the boys was assumed a permanent stink on Torrance, and because he knew they believed he was filthy and that his filth was an unchangeable reality, Torrance swung on dude, and He had to get involved to defend His homie from folks He thought was all homies.

Selah wants Him to stop fighting. Her heart breaks with each punch. Her fists throb with His. Someone screams, "Gun!" and they all scatter, not knowing who had the gun or if there even was one.

The two boys stop at a corner store. Torrance steals a honey bun while He distracts the cashier by buying an orange Fanta and some double-A batteries. Outside, He sees Torrance's honey bun and asks where His at. Torrance breaks far more than half of the honey bun off and hands the little bit left to Him, who shakes His head and walks off.

Selah feels His anger rise up in her as the boys walk home in the middle of the street, Torrance flipping out again, swearing on his mama grave he was "bout to beat that nigga ass. On my mama, he fucked with the wrong one. Come see me! Bitch ass niggas, P the fuck up," Torrance shouting at nobody nearby cause the boys back at the park are four blocks away. And He says nothing, moves faster, wanting to get away from Torrance, who is hopping up and down, his shirt pulled up over one shoulder as he punches his hand harder than he punched the dudes at the park, cappin like he hard, which only pisses Him off more. They live on a quiet set of blocks in a dangerous city. When the two realities meet, He gets nervous, wants to disappear.

"Dead it, T," He says. "F'you was gone do something, you woulda done it back thur."

"Drove as fuck," Torrance says.

"Say less. Say less." They are close to His house. He sees His father sitting on the bottom stair of the porch, drinking a glass of water. Quiet night. Torrance seems to notice the quiet and silences his rage. But His father has already heard.

"What was all the noise about?" His father asks. "I heard y'all all the way down the street."

Annoyed, He points to Torrance and shakes His head.

"Get on in the house, then. Food ready. Torrance, call your mama when you get inside and let her know where you are. I know you ain't told her."

After dinner, the two boys sit in the basement. Torrance was quiet throughout dinner. Afterward, he took a shower while His mother washed the boys' clothes. Torrance is wearing an old shirt and some shorts of His. Everything is too big, the shorts' drawstring tied as tight as it can go.

"Aight, so why you get so mad over dude calling you musty when we all was musty as fuck?"

"*We* ain't all shit. He said it to me cause he think that about me regardless," Torrance says. "And I'm sick of niggas thinking I'm dirty. I shower just like errbody else."

"It be your clothes, man."

"I know. Shit."

"Wash them hur."

"Naw my mom would be shamed."

"You already eat hur. She shamed about that?"

"Sometimes."

"Well, let her sometimes be shamed about you washing clothes hur. Y'all can split being shamed."

Torrance laughs and thanks Him. Selah wonders how often Torrance allows himself to have this soft look on his face like he does now. She likes it on him and likes how He brings this out of somebody who she thought only knew anger.

The mood shifts a bit after He asks about the gun, if Torrance had seen it himself and Torrance says no. Neither of the boys saw the gun but both ran, just like everyone else.

"It wasn't even that serious," He says. Torrance nods. "Folks ain't shot around hur since last summer after . . ." but He doesn't finish. Selah wants to know what happened last summer that has made it chilly inside Him. She holds herself, the cold coming on strong and the look on Torrance's face like he is being drained of blood. "I didn't mean to—"

"I didn't take it no way. It is what it is. My brother in Heaven," Torrance says.

"Facts. Rasheed was good people," He says. They sit in silence until it's time for Torrance to go. The chill inside Him gets worse.

THAT NIGHT, He wakes to a light glowing outside his closed eyelids. It's red and deep. Selah notices it, too, and screams when He opens His eyes. A man draped in red light is standing over His bed. The man has a gunshot wound in his head, off-center toward the left. The chill returns to Him and Selah wonders if this is Torrance's brother, Rasheed. The man reaches toward Him and His body seizes, turns onto its stomach, and is pressed down by the air itself. The man in red touches Him on the back of His body in several places before He is spun back onto his back. The man looks sad, shakes his head, and says, "Don't leave Him alone." He points now to Him, between the eyes, looking through Him and speaking to Selah, then is gone in a blink. He cries out with a sob-struck voice, "Rasheed," but the man is gone. "I'm never leaving

Torrance alone. You ain't got to worry about that. Why you keep coming to me? Go to your brother. Why you keep coming to me!"

The chills make sense to Selah now, as this isn't the first time Rasheed has come to pay Him a visit, which only solidifies for her that this is indeed her descendant, a seer of the dead, someone whom the dead feel obligated to communicate with for whatever reason. This instruction of "Don't leave Him alone" feels like it was for her, not Him. She doesn't know what to do with His body turning over on its own, the ghost touching Him, and what feels like an augury. Her descendant doesn't sleep for the rest of the night. She sits with her knees to her chest and wraps her arms around her legs, afraid but not knowing of what.

IT'S THE FOLLOWING afternoon when Candice visits again. Selah doesn't understand why she can't see that He doesn't want her company. 'No other boys for you?' she thinks. When Candice calls Him a punk for not taking the hint, Selah feels a new blaze light up in Him, but the front door opens and His mother steps onto the porch before He can react. Neither He nor Candice knew she was home. Her car is gone and so is His father's. Candice stands up when she sees His mother.

"Baby, who you calling a punk?" His mother asks.

"I was just messing around. Wasn't no thing, Mrs. Gaudry," Candice says.

His mother laughs. "Why you call my son a punk? Cause he won't sleep with you."

Selah wants to see Candice's eyes, but He will not look up from the steps. "Don't nobody want your son," Candice yells. "You tripping."

"I know what I heard. Been sitting in the window since you got hur. You ain't gotta to lie to me, Candice. Ain't trying to shame you. Just saying I see you and you can talk to me if you need somebody to listen to you."

"You don't know me!"

"But I know your daddy," His mother says. "I know him and his ways *very* well, Candice."

The air stiffens. He looks up and out into the street. Selah wants Him to turn around so that His mother's face is in view. She wants to know what shape her mouth has taken after saying those words.

Candice steps down from the bottom porch and steps backward toward the sidewalk. He glances up and catches her broken countenance. Selah has never seen that much hurt in one expression, not even when Naima felt betrayed and smashed three of her fingers. It was like looking at a sky grow overcast and forgetting there was ever a sun there to begin with. "Fuck both y'all," Candice says. He stands up, but when His mother speaks He gets real still.

"Relax, baby. She can cuss me," His mother says to Him, then to Candice, "I been thur, love. Witnessed a lot of shit in my life. Nothing can come out your mouth that'll wound me. Gone sit down, son. See, I'm proud of this one right hur. This my heart. He my whole heart. I protect what I love, Candice. If you not gone protect Him with me, then you can't come around hur," His mother says. "God bless you and I hope you take my invitation seriously."

Candice storms down the walkway, but when she gets to the sidewalk she stops and bends over, clutching her chest. She cries a leaning-into-it kind of cry.

His mother descends the porch steps to where Candice is and stands before her. She speaks assertively and quietly into the girl's ear so that He and Selah can't hear. "I love you. You understand me?" she says audibly, and Candice nods. They part ways, Candice walking down the street and His mother going back inside the house. He stares out toward the street. Selah wishes she had the language for the fullness she feels, whether it was a good full or a bad full.

AT THE CORNER STORE, people talking about the fight from the other day. Say one of the boys had a gun and was looking for some of the other boys who was there. No one uses names because no one really knows who all was there. Not really. He buys His orange Fanta and steps out, avoiding eye contact. More police cars around than ever. Folks had gotten used to not seeing them after Rasheed got shot and they said it was an accident. Was supposed to be a taser. Was supposed to be a regular traffic stop. Why didn't he just get out the car? Why didn't he cooperate? And the neighborhood, small and predominantly Black, put up blockades at every street for two weeks to keep the cops out. After that, they stopped patrolling the area. Neighbors got more invested in doing their part, nightly patrolling the streets in groups to make sure the young folks could safely get home. Chastising the dope boys with Bibles, Qurans, and photos of all the young folks they had killed: "Y'all remember Khalil? Was killed right here by some folks living right here. He was six years old. You listening to me? We need to figure something else out, cause this not us," and sat there in groups reading the holy texts out loud, which chastened the folks looking to buy a 20-piece for a quick high. Some of the dope boys threatened the neighbors but they didn't move from their foldable chairs. "You'd shoot your grandmother?" one of the women asked her grandson, who hadn't recognized her before pulling his pistol out against her. "I know you would. That's why I'm sitting here. So you can do it with your eyes open."

Eventually, they removed the barricades and kept up the neighborhood watch. It wasn't until the fight in the park that any mention of a gun had happened that summer. Hearing all this, He leaves the store with His soda and tries to get home as fast as possible, and Selah feels His heart drum Him along the way.

It doesn't take long, though. A police car rushes beside Him, turning the corner adjacent to the one He walked down. Then a *bloop* from the police siren, an infraction made that somehow only the police knows has been made and now He must bend to a knowledge not His own. Selah hates the sound of the siren, had experienced it in nearly every future she visited, and only twice in those timelines did the officer treat her descendant with dignity. The other times: a baton to the skull, pepper spray in the face, a dog sicced on them, a knee on the neck, a hand fondling and groping, fingers prodding and entering, some racial slur, several guns pulled for a missed stop sign, face slammed onto the car hood because "you shouldn't have sassed me," tear gas on a peaceful protest, rubber bullet to the eye, size intimidation as the officer leans into the car and refers to himself as "a godly specimen" and meaning he could use his body in perfectly ghastly ways, a plunger shoved up the ass of a cousin while her descendant was forced to watch. And with each case, a settlement, a resignation only to be reinstated elsewhere, character assassination of the victim, eternal bullying from the police force as they urinate on one descendant's property and shit outside the house of a neighbor, like vengeful children, a luciferous gang, like a military against the lone nation of another's body. Selah has seen enough to know that He should stop walking, should kneel, play dead, and even then He wouldn't ever be safe, even if He complied, He could still be harmed in some way; call it an accident, call it "what did He do to deserve it?" call it He should've stopped sooner and faster and laid flatter on the ground, call it Rasheed's legacy, call it a few "bad apples," God-fucking-damn it, the inconvenience of somehow getting the bad one every fucking time, the inconvenience of losing your life, the lack of luxury to test each apple for the gun-toting worm.

Selah needs Him to stop moving, she shouts it in His head but He doesn't stop.

Now, hearing the *bloop* of the police siren again, Selah's heart drops inside of Him whose heart drops, though He keeps going. The officer *bloops* his siren again and the boy moves to the sidewalk. But the officer, instead of driving on, follows Him as he walks on the sidewalk and tells Him to stop walking. "You hear the siren," the officer says and still He doesn't stop, even though this cop is Black and should be okay, right, but naw because He thinks the Black ones have something to prove and distrusts them more so He keeps going, remembering a year ago when Frosty, the only white boy on the block, complied and they shot him in the leg. A month after that, a five-year-old girl was shot dead by a SWAT team while she slept on the couch. The suspect in question lived with his girlfriend in the apartment two doors down the hall. Every moment is wrapped in a grave, so why not keep moving, get home, get to His mother and father, get to His porch where He, in life or death, can be fully known?

When the officer jumps out the car, Selah's dropped heart climbs up her throat. She notices His hands hurt. He has squeezed them into fists. He sees His house across the street.

"Get on the ground!"

But He can't stop. The narrative is inconsistent. He believes He will be killed regardless of what He does, and He wants to be killed where He is loved.

He crosses the street. His hands are in the air, but He doesn't lay in the street. He stumbles and the Fanta flies from His shallow shorts pocket. When it hits the ground, it makes a popping sound, and Selah feels a pull on her body as the orbs summon her back to the garden, and before a single bullet leaves the mouth of a gun, she is back in the orb garden with a hand on her shoulder. She turns, panicked, and sees an older woman wearing an old nurse's uniform. The woman watches her sternly and squeezes her shoulder hard, wanting it to hurt to snap the girl back to reality, the girl who now looks as she did back in Ours.

"You do not belong there, young Selah," and Selah knows immediately who this woman is; it is herself, older, from her future, wrinkled about the face, hair in immaculate curls, her eyes wild and spectral in their sockets. "You cannot be in that boy as he dies."

"He is mine. He is my bloodline," Selah says.

"He is not yours directly."

"His people my people."

"Selah." Future Selah kneels to meet her younger self eye to eye, but Selah is hysterical, fighting to get out of the woman's grip. The woman digs in with her nails. She doesn't let her go.

"You're hurting me."

"What you think bullets feel like?"

"I can save Him. I can keep Him alive till help comes."

"You will die in Him and kill me, Selah. And I will live the future you made for me."

"Don't you care about his life?"

"None of these people whose futures you stepped in are from you, Selah. This Naima's line. You don't have a line. You don't have children, Selah. Even if you did, you'd kill them all off by dying in this boy who ain't yours. I am yours. You needed help. You came looking for me and I helped you mend those folks, fix those bones, cut the blood loose. I helped you do that, Selah. You helped you do that. Don't get rid of yourself in the future."

Selah stops fussing and stills herself. "Naima's line . . ." She lowers her head. Future Selah pulls young Selah's face up to meet her own.

"This is His fate. If He dies with you in Him, Selah, you will not be able to come back. I cannot get back to you again. Look." Future Selah shows her arm to Selah. It is aged into near mummification. "I can't be in the future beyond my time. In His timeline, I would already have been dead by almost one hundred years. In your timeline, if Frances hadn't sent me back, you would've died the death I died but in your own time. We can only coexist here, Selah. But I know how to get you back to your time. Let's get you home."

Selah nods. She nods and nods. "This is Naima's child, not mine." She smiles. Future Selah releases the girl's shoulder and stands. She reaches for her anterior self, but Selah stands on her own. "I'm sorry. I didn't understand what I was doing. I do now." And with that she reaches back into the orb and is sucked into the future. "My home is with Him. I will turn His now into a future."

Future Selah screams into the orb, decays on the other side. Not even a speck of dust is left.

Back in the future, the Fanta bottle rolls, and spills. The sound of orange carbonation fizzing in the street is that of meat sizzling on a grill. A voice calls out to Him and Selah doesn't know that it's His mother because she has never heard her emote in this way, a strange weather spilling from her throat that can't settle into its thunder, into its downpour that is His name in sudden soprano falling, falling, falling.

Selah feels every bit of pain He feels as she holds herself to shake it off. But it won't fall off. The pain clings like someone in love. She reminds herself that love is the reason why she returned and places her hand on the ground of His mind and pushes life into Him.

She smells the saltiness of ocean water but doesn't know that's what she smells. It's delightful and briefly makes her homesick. The light from her hands brightens, then disappears right along with the smell of the sea. As quickly as the light diminishes, the pain is gone. He opens His eyes, and the room of His mind lights up with daylight, the street black and hard against His face and covered with Jordans and flip-flops with socked feet in them, an elder's Payless slip-ons sliding into view, all of them appearing sideways in His floored glance so that they look like they are standing on a wall.

Selah isn't sure what has happened, doesn't know why He is suddenly able to roll onto His stomach and push Himself to kneeling. Then He stands, the world going right side up again, His wounds closed. The bullets lying warm on the ground. The pain gone. The pain gone. The pain gone. The pain gone. The pain gone. The pain gone. For every bullet that had entered Him, the pain is gone. Cast-iron skillet burning in the oven. A pot of rice boils over on the stove. Televisions go unwatched. The dope boys unhide their hands.

Selah sits inside Him and touches herself. She feels her face, clenches her teeth, and laughs from the gut. When He sees His mother's baffled look as she considers His body from behind police tape, as she breaks through the tape and pushes away the officers who try to keep her from the raised-from-the-dead—when He sees her rush to Him and feels her touch His lips as though to pull from His mouth the secret of His return, He unclenches His fists. Then His mother asks, "Baby? Baby how? Is this you?"

He nods when Selah nods, smiles when she does, cries as she cries.

A car pulls up. His father runs from it, leaving the car door open, and for the first time, Selah hears His name. Born from the mouth of his father. "Dontrell-Elizah!" A memory floats by Selah. She grabs it and learns that Dontrell is His father's name and Elizah his mother's name. The two in union created him, and now Selah has joined. She presses her hands against the windows of His eyes, basking in His name that is now a part of her.

· CHAPTER 28 ·

Gone

[1]

A storm wrote its vicious epistle against earth still slick with morning dew. Of the dirt roads foot-and-cart-carved into rows, rain expanded their width, muddying wider the paths and burying the flattened grass while raindrops cackled against the fields it flattened. Rain escaped from the dark-gray sky and the branches were forced to bow.

From the east, a figure disturbed the solid sheet of rain, briefly interrupting the rain's onslaught against the earth, merging with the weather till the figure's shape was itself family with the storm. At the first door it came upon, the figure knocked, and when the door opened—a candelabra carried like a bouquet of horns by the occupant—Saint looked up from her downcast soaked stare and said as though speaking to a friend disappointed beyond forgiveness, "Excuse me. Are they with you?" They pointed her in the right direction. She noticed the bitterness in the occupant's eyes and drifted solemnly to Madame Jenkins's house. Saint knocked, Madame Jenkins opened the door and snatched Saint in from the cold.

Saint saw Selah lying in the one bed lit by a family of candles sitting on top of a chest. Before Saint could touch the girl, Madame Jenkins said, "You may get her wet and sick if you drip over her. Let's get you dry."

Saint undressed by the fireplace, then wrapped herself in a quilt in front of the fire, tea in one hand, a cigar in another, her first in years. Madame Jenkins offered her bedclothes but she refused. "I have no intention of staying the night," she said, tasting cigar smoke as it rolled against her tongue. It was delicious when placed beside her pain and the pain she knew was on its way.

Madame Jenkins wrung out Saint's dress and hung it near the mouth of the fireplace, giving Saint time to settle into what she thought was the hold of emptiness. She told Saint about Aba, where Naima was, and that Selah hadn't woken since the invasion.

"From Delacroix?" Saint said.

"No. They entered from the south, demanding we give them the children. We gave them something, all right."

"How many did we lose?"

"Just one."

"And them?"

"Not a single survivor."

"Aba the one we lost, then?"

Madame Jenkins nodded.

"The stones should be back hiding us. I wouldn't expect retaliation."

Dry and relaxed after her smoke, Saint touched Selah's forehead with the back of her hand. Warm, not feverish, with soft and even breathing. The girl slept peacefully. Seemed a shame to wake her to her own bad feelings. Even this rain, soothingly singing against the roof, may have been Saint's fault. No telling these days.

She had felt the last bit of hope in her shrivel up after she—'not now,' she thought, and pulled herself away from the bloody bedsheets Sebastian had bled on, the bloody man she caressed into his final death. But the image and the sticky warmth kept clouding her view, manipulating her thinking. She had to go through it again to get over it. Maybe that's why she failed the first time. Was too busy making sure the blood didn't bleed to realize it was too late anyway. She should've let the blood run the first time so that now she wouldn't be sitting in heavy recall, seeing Frances standing just over her shoulder as she held on to Sebastian's body, a body she laid on the floor with kindness and over which she laid a sheet she snatched from the bed in one swoop and let billow down over him; and her watching the hill of air trapped between the sheet and his body relax against the outline of his body, finally, at rest; and her taking her time standing barefoot in a puddle of his blood, the heat gone from it, the metallic smell rising up; and her staring at Frances, who stood stuck in fear, holding her breath maybe, rigid as the dead would be; and her leaving Frances frozen in her own feelings as she grabbed her staff from the wall by the door, exited her bedroom with her blood-wet feet smacking against the floor, headed down the hall and steps, unlocked the divining room's door with the key she kept hanging from her neck at all times, waved her hand over the room, which lit each candle into fierce burning, uncovered the bell, struck it with her staff, and said in a whisper that she barely believed she spoke at all, "Leave Ours and never return."

Saint had first listened to the floor upstairs groan beneath Frances's weight, then heard Frances descend the steps, sluggish as a sleepwalker. After Frances shut the door behind her, Saint returned to Sebastian's body and mourned.

Sitting in front of Madame Jenkins's fireplace, she tried to reach as far back into the past as she could. When only rotten fragments of remembrance returned after considering the name Essence, she knew, too, that she would lose the memory of Sebastian if she continued living. She had already lost most memories from before having met Aba in the Appalachian Mountains. Her past crumbled within her: no more Apalachicola River, no more living among the Muskogee for years before the Revolutionary War tipped everything into chaos, no more listening to the voices in her head lead her to freeing the enslaved, and no more knowledge of fear to guide her into a more careful living.

The one thing she did fear, possibly the final fear she carried with her from her life before Ours, had already happened and bled all over her bedroom floor. She wondered how long it would be before even the memory of him faded. She tipped her head back, closed her eyes, and allowed the firelight to penetrate behind her eyelids.

IN THAT WARM GLOW she remembered a tall, wide man had approached her on foot, whistling a mesmerizing tune, then smiling when he saw her sitting out front on the dirt porch of her home tucked away in Mississippi shadows, a home she had built after retiring from freeing slaves with Aba. He carried a staff that he tossed from hand to hand as he walked. The man seemed unaware of the sickness stones surrounding the small plot of land and the stones had no effect on him, despite her intentions to keep everyone away so that she could enjoy the sounds of birds without interruption. He smiled. Saint raised her eyebrows, preparing.

"I always wondered who lived here," he said.

"Perhaps you should keep wondering," Saint said.

"Now why would I do that with you, owner apparent, sitting beautiful before me. I don't usually travel this way, but must be serendipity that I decided to today and find you, today, sitting here."

"Who taught you that word?"

The man squinted and grinned, "Which one? Serendipity?"

"No," Saint said. "'Today.' Seems like you just learned it, the way you keep saying it like you need to remember the meaning."

"Not the meaning. The flavor."

Saint burst into laughter. She motioned for him to come closer to the porch, then stopped him just before he reached the shadow of her rickety awning. "Bluestone?" she asked, understanding why her own stones didn't work against this protection. The man nodded and the muscles in his neck drew her attention to the rest of him as she regarded the silver chain that held the silver casing which held the bluestone resting on his chest.

There's a certain gentleness in blue that's capable of deceiving whoever perceives it, shielding its wearer in a kind demeanor they may not fully embrace, let alone agree with. Blue was hard to come by in nature, anyhow. There's the sky when it cooperated, some bodies of water, and the rare bird. In the iridescent shell of a fly, blue may appear in a flash, then without warning turn green then red. Flower petals are tricky. The cornflower, iris, and delphinium carry more purple on their velvet than anything else. And when summer laid it on down to rest, autumn sucked the color out like marrow from a bone. In that way, blue never stuck around, not for long, so when Saint came upon the color and the color chose to stay, caution stuck close to her heart for, at any moment, blue—gentleness, kindness, tranquility—could burn red.

"May I join you beneath the shade? Today." He paused and smiled. Saint saw then that his top four teeth were flanked on either side with long pearly canines. He licked his lips before continuing. "It's hot."

"Nobody told you to wear all that black," Saint said. A chair waited just opposite of where she sat. She pointed to it and said, "All yours."

Beneath the shade, she offered him water and asked where he was headed. He told her that he only took this path when he wanted to go root gathering. As he spoke, Saint watched his hands placed neatly on his knees, rings polished into perfect luster. Amber, jasper, obsidian, and garnet: four stones on four fingers of the right hand placed on a sharp knee on a long leg. Those were stones for protection, stability, calmness. 'Like he off to war,' she thought. He asked if she knew she was surrounded by wealth in the woods, and she said she was aware, that's why she settled there. He had laid his staff on the ground. Saint peeked at the artistry of snake heads meeting at the top to make a small crown while their bodies made up the staff's length.

"You make that?" Saint asked, pointing to the staff.

"No. It was a gift from someone I healed," the man said. He gazed into the woods and tilted his head, then yawned. He was comfortable. Saint thought he was bored.

"I don't want to keep you," she said.

"You're not keeping me at all. I am keeping myself near you. However, I do have work to complete. I'll be much obliged if you would allow me another moment like this in the future?"

Overcast, the jewelry gleamed less so, but his teeth beckoned from his mouth their own pearlescence, the one dingy bottom tooth in the center making the others that much brighter. She agreed, and he returned the next day, asked to sit beside her again, and took his seat. If he noticed the cup of water sitting next to the front foot of his chair, he didn't mention it, and Saint felt minor disappointment in his lack of awareness. But when he reached down and took the cup in his bejeweled hand, he looked over at her as he drank the whole thing, stared at her the entire time his throat flexed down the water. "I appreciate this," he said. "Today, yesterday, and maybe tomorrow."

He hadn't returned for two days and on the third day, Saint found herself eager for his company. On the fifth day, just when Saint thought he was gone for good, near soundless and like an upright shadow defying its maker, he appeared from the woods wearing all black. He didn't come to the porch. He invited her down, instead, to take a stroll with him. Saint put on her shoes. "We never properly introduced ourselves," Saint said.

"Because I feel like I've known you all my life and some of my death, too," he said. His earnestness made Saint nervous. "My name is Sebastian."

"Saint," she said, and into the woods they went, returning only once more to Saint's house to retrieve her things the following week.

[2]

Window open. Scent of roses woven with rain blown in. Sebastian played in Saint's hair while she rested her head on his chest. From his open shirt spilled curls of hair that tickled the inner coil of her ear. Bass from his voice filled her head as he spoke:

"What your people like?"

All this time, Saint had been holding Sebastian's right hand in her left while he massaged his left fingers into her scalp, looking for answers Saint didn't have. Essence's people were her people, but that's not what he meant. Mother. Father. Kinfolk. Whose blood she got in her and how many are there? What they eat and how? What songs they taught her to help her during her pilgrimage? Instead of saying she didn't know, she said, "I only know who cared for me like family. But you're asking for something outside my memory."

"But did they love you?"

"Who?"

"The ones that cared for you like family. Did they care out of duty or out of love?"

"Both, I feel. Who can half the time tell the difference?"

She told him about Essence, about being found on the edge of sand and shells, seaweed snake-wrapped around her ankles, her yawn stinking of salt. She told him, focusing on one of his fingers in her hand as an aide-mémoire, that Essence exiled Saint to protect her people from Saint's unbridled abilities. Saint told him about those, too, of stonework and storm revising landscape in the upheaval of her emotions. She told him of her time wandering the swampland until she found a Muskogee-made road and followed it to civilization, a town of mostly Muskogee and a few Negroes that she settled into with unflappable privacy that both offended her hosts and demanded to be honored.

Then the voices came, a chorus of instructions telling her where to go and when, who to find and how to find them, a chorus of begging, circles of prayers pulling, pulling her toward the enslaved Africans who upon seeing her were either horrified or pacified: the aftermath of God giving them what they had asked for.

For decades, she disoriented her enemies, learned their paths, and laid stones to weaken then destroy them. Every instruction she received came from the chorus in her head and stopped as soon as she finished the job of freeing whoever waited on the receiving end of the appeal, the endless begging that she could no more resist than she could ignore. Afterward, without warning, the voices stopped altogether. Supplications ceased, her mind the clearest it had been in years. "Then I came this way. I needed time for myself to rest. I needed time to just stop so I could sit and breathe." She prepared herself to stand then, to pack up her things and return to the small shack she built. But Sebastian stayed playing in her hair.

"You've lived a life," he said, and laughed. Moments later, his fingers stopped their dancing about her head, his own breathing slowed. He had fallen asleep. A small wind gathered the scent of roses, their many open doors.

[3]

Mexican healers called Sebastian a curandero. Fools called him a houngan. The fearfully devoted called him a witch doctor. Whoever they were, they traveled for days, weeks, or months across the Southwest's impressive violence, up from the tip of Florida, and just around the way from the Carolinas to reach him for a chance to purge their lives of imagined and actual evil.

He was grateful whenever they found him in his cottage, his head tucked between countless loose pages of research and opened books, while jars of roots and leaves watched over him. Bottled liquids shined decoratively along the endless shelves built into the walls from which potted plants hung vine after vine from each ledge, thin emerald curtains.

Saint watched as he advised against mal de ojo and kijicho powerful enough to wipe out livestock with a blink. As Americans expanded west, so did their malefactions, and the curses brought about by these newfangled Americans carried more complicated spiritual disasters than Sebastian had ever encountered.

A curandero from Mérida, who said he was born of the last Mayans the Spaniards missed and the first Africans to ever touch Mexican soil, visited Sebastian late one night while he and Saint slept. A storm headed their way from the west, bringing with it not only the scent of rain but the metallic stink of lightning flaring up the cooling air. Thunder followed, masking the hard rap at the door made noticeable only by its rhythmic difference from the explosions above. When Sebastian let in the curandero, Saint had already started a kettle for hot water. The curandero introduced himself as Piya de Nuestros Dioses Zurdo, which, upon hearing, made Sebastian flare his nostrils in a short burst. The visitor refused to let them dry him off and asked that the hearth remain lit, the hot water to be used to soak his feet and not for tea. It was by the fireside, with his feet warming in a wide washbasin, that he began his story in Spanish:

"In the beginning, there were thirteen of us set out to visit you, brother. Your name had reached us weeks ago on the back of a one-legged crow caught in the wide-mouth embrace of the wind. The crow fell from its flight after lightning fell into its small body and delivered it to the ground. One of the thirteen of us found it during his morning patrol and carried it to us. Written on its back in the smallest print made possible by the blazing sword of the storm was your name and how to reach you." Piya de Nuestros Dioses Zurdo then pulled from his coat pocket the one feather from which still emanated the stink of a burning coin, and over which was written, in what he described as "irremovable ash," the word "Santiago" and intricate directions to "your home," he continued.

Thunder assaulted the sky. "These directions we decided to follow because in Mérida our traditions have been made forbidden by the conquistadores, such that the voice of my grandmother has stopped coming to me and my uncle's spirit no longer stands by the window to welcome sunrise. We have tried everything in our power to protect what remains of our spirits, but the Catholics have razed our altars in our homes and kill anyone who resists conversion." Piya de Nuestros Dioses Zurdo leaned forward and rested his elbows on his knees. "I believe you can help us."

Sebastian had been staring at the feather the entire time he listened to his visitor and passed it to Saint. "What do you bring in exchange?" he asked, and the visitor revealed a small bag knotted at the end with thin golden rope. From it, he retrieved a booklet and handed it to Sebastian, who, after turning several pages, froze for a moment before examining his visitor and saying, "She is the one you are looking for. I am not a saint."

Seeing her shocked face, Sebastian nodded at her, holding back a smile. He already knew she was special, and though he needed no extra proof the curandero's visit solidified his notion: she was someone the world knew already and desperately needed, though she had no idea of her influence.

Saint carved for him a set of stones, six total, meant to make severely ill anyone with intentions of harming ancestral spirits and their descendants. After giving him instructions on how to use them, their visitor left in a hurry, saying, "I am the sole survivor of this journey. In the name of my dead, I thank you." By the time he left, it was morning and the storm had been extinguished by the sun.

[4]

The booklet from the curandero became Sebastian's new obsession. He always kept it close to his person and made sure to hide it whenever Saint came in close for a kiss on the cheek or assisted with a root or conjure. Patrons came to him mostly for protection, his most-well-known and powerful skill being the haint jars that took the most time to make, which required more assistance from Saint and therefore more secrecy in hiding the booklet.

Sebastian taught Saint everything he knew, beginning with making her own altar, but she couldn't catch on to caring for it daily, watering it, leaving offerings, and conversing with her ancestors. She had no idea who her ancestors were, loved no gods of her own, and knew no spirits who knew her in return, so the altar bore gifts to no one at all.

Sebastian allowed her to help anyway, though he handled the blessing of all materials. Once the haint jars were sealed, he wrote the names of the patron's ancestors on the outside in black ink mixed with the patron's own blood taken the day the request for the jar was made. Together, he and Saint delivered them if the person who made the purchase didn't feel safe traveling with an enclosed container of an agitated spirit meant to protect them.

They delivered such a jar to a man named Perry who suffered from abuse from someone he kept secret. He shared only that someone punched him often, sometimes to the point at which Perry lost consciousness. Defending himself only worsened the duration and frequency of attacks. Afraid the next visit, the next punch, could be his last, he requested a jar from Sebastian via letter, explaining when to come, where to meet him, and how much he could pay. When they arrived, after the purchase had been completed and instructions on how to use the haint jar given, Saint asked Perry if he had nowhere else he could go, no family who wanted to watch over him with love and machete. The man said no, thanked them both, and left somberly into the dusk.

SAINT EMPATHIZED WITH PERRY, in some ways wanted to depart with him into the dense loneliness that waited for him on the other side of his journey. She knew what it felt like to not have family but thought it worse to have had family, then lost it. She hoped then, for Perry's sake, that he had never experienced love from a true family, that he had carried this solitude with him as a point of origin.

Saint knew the gist of Sebastian's origin story. Family memories he shared were few. His mother and father lived on somebody's plantation. They bought his and his maternal grandparents' freedom. He remembered a grandfather's grinning face clouded by cigar smoke, a gentle madness in his eyes from having been forced to live old and free without his entire family to enjoy it with. Sebastian's grandmother, who cherished Sebastian dearly, went missing one day after moseying into the woods and disappearing between a maple tree and a blueberry bush. He went to find her and found instead a second berry bush newly grown.

Grandfather died and Sebastian was alone in that house until he didn't want to be alone anymore. Coyotes bounding in the yard, skunks wreathing the house with their musk. He stepped out the door one morning, free and ignorant of the world, and decided to learn all he could in the aftermath of his grandparents' deaths.

He considered himself a lucky child when he thought back on it as an adult, the falling sick on the Mississippi roadside and being found not by someone wanting to enslave him, but by someone wanting to teach him how to speak with the earth and listen for what the earth had to say back to him.

For the rest of his childhood, he lived with a man who went by the name Moon, who wore thick socks and cork-bottom slip-ons as dense as the Bible he kept in every room. Moon had a slow gait, was tall, headstrong, and took nobody's mess, not even his own, back talking himself if he thought unkind ideas about himself: "Now, Moon, you know that's not of the Lord," or "God made you, Moon. Act like it."

He had four teenagers staying with him who had come from all over Mississippi, and he expected each one to be of, in, with, about, and for the Lord. Amen, amen. Sebastian came smelling like the outside and his grandfather's cigars and Moon wiped him down, nine years old when he found him, and he scrubbed every edge of his body until his skin shone bright and raw. The other orphans treated him well enough, neither too loving nor too bitter about his arrival. They were half-grown and fully tired of Moon's overbearing love, heavy as chains, heavy as the cross on Christ's back.

But Sebastian learned to love the discipline that reciting Bible verses built in him. Prayers kept his mind at ease and off thoughts of his dead grandparents or fruit. He gagged every time Moon made a fruit pie or tossed fistfuls of berries into his mouth. Got so bad Moon took to eating the damn things in his room, but he wasn't about to let a boy dictate much more than that in his home.

He loved Sebastian ever since he found him on that road. He babied him, fed him the edge of the pan of everything he made because Sebastian loved crust, and made sure Sebastian knew every day that he was important because chosen to be alive. But Moon had issues with his face. He didn't like his features and playfully called him a "nigger mask," though his eyes gleamed with an inner sorrow. How to be hugged by someone who, when they pull away, looks upon your face with disgust, a face much like their own? Sebastian never learned how.

Moon mixed his Christian living with other spiritual thinking. He salted his thresholds and read Psalms. He lit black candles and left sweets on a mantel in his bedroom, never saying for whom. He knew the New Testament like the back of his hand and the Old Testament like his own tongue, but heeded shadows darting in room corners not as evil spirits but something that needed tending to on the other side. He taught all his ways to Sebastian, who lived alone with the man after the teens he cared for became adults and took off one by one. Free Negro and poor, Moon prayed that they wouldn't be intercepted on their way to building a life, and when he passed away, Sebastian took over ownership of his home of seeming contradictions.

That's when he found hidden beneath a floppy wooden floorboard a collection of books, pamphlets, and letters about root work, Vodou, ancestral communication, the banishing of demons, feeding your protection spirits, and many un-Christian ideas that clarified for Sebastian nuances Moon embodied but for which he left no evidence of how he had learned. "He was a damn priest," he said to himself, studying every page he found and practicing each recipe and root working that made sense to him, leaving the more lethal-sounding ones in their hiding place. He documented it all in a journal of his own.

Soon, he found other objects hidden in the house: jars full of gemstones on a hard-to-reach shelf, a locked pantry full of dried herbs labeled and organized alphabetically, and vials of liquids labeled with horrific identifiers that were once fresh but needed to be disposed of (cow's blood, black rooster blood, "cat yurn"). What made sense to keep, like the clover honey and milk of dandelion, he kept.

Eventually, he started making roots for close friends in town and when they were proven to work, he began selling them clandestinely because he wanted no trouble with the church, even though members from the congregation visited him in cloaks at the peak of the night for some of his "magic plants." He protected himself by protecting their secrets and from then on everybody understood that there was nothing to understand.

It crossed his mind to look for his parents, but the plantation they had been on was seized by a bank and every enslaved African sold at auction. This was a common story, the incompetence of so-called masters, the impervious will of the state to maintain a system that allowed broken people to attempt breaking others.

Because much remained in place to maintain this system regardless of his free status, he had to be careful with his living. He was sure he lived in the only Negro town in all of Mississippi, and that it existed only because of a family of gens de couleur libres who never crossed the Mississippi River to see how their no-name town held up.

This family's money loosely protected the town. No one knew exactly why they had chosen this project, this experiment of Negro freedom, though it was speculated that their youngest daughter had guilted the patriarch into doing it to offset the sin of owning enslaved Africans. Money carried that kind of power, to relieve sin without prayer or pardon from a priest and without stopping the sinful behavior, but Sebastian knew one day that the money and its power would dry up and the covenant between Negroes and whites would dismantle in flames.

He traveled to Louisiana often, finding willing clients who understood the complexity of roots beyond the fear of what many considered witchcraft, though once during his travels a drifter had called him a "nasty Voodoo priest," figuring the stones Sebastian wore on his fingers and the staff of snake heads he carried were evidence he deserved such scorn.

A woman who happened to be passing by eyed down the drifter till he moved across the street, then proceeded to vanish into the crowd. "Don't mind him," she said. "A particular mind carries particular demons." Her name was Eloise St. Denis.

Their friendship blossomed necessarily and with good timing, her status in the city one of power and mixed feelings, for she was a woman with money and not of mixed ancestry. He liked her because she was opinionated, had been in love and didn't want to be in love ever again, and had a powerful mind that frightened him. She laughed at his jokes but didn't touch him, jokingly called him "my giant" for he was a tall and broad man, complimented his broad nose and full lips, and loved his dark skin that glistened just like hers. Everything he had ever questioned about himself she made him surer of. 'I need this nose,' he found himself thinking one morning, looking into a mirror. 'I need these lips. My God, I need these lips of mine.'

Loving his lips so, he decided to test them on Eloise, and she accepted. He moved his hands from her face to her waist, and she didn't move. When he moved his hands to her behind, she bit his bottom lip hard, drawing blood. They didn't speak for almost a month, until walking by her house, angry still but curious about her well-being, he heard from the open window the sound of an untuned piano. He leaned into the window and watched Eloise play around, tapping here and there, then playing chords into a titanic composition. She finished playing, her back turned to the window as she sat at the piano bench, and asked, "Would you like to apologize first, or shall I?"

"How did you know I was here?" Sebastian asked.

Eloise pointed to the grandfather clock facing the window, the glass case subtly reflecting him standing in the window as if he were a ghost trapped inside the clock itself.

He apologized from outside. She accepted and invited him in. He leaned his staff on the clock. They sat on the couch and watched the minute hand make its slow rotations, their arms touching, her hand in his. She didn't apologize. He didn't need her to.

[5]

Friendship is not what he wanted with Saint, and when he laid eyes on her he saw marriage right away. He assumed she was no older than thirty years old, but as they spoke, he discovered that she was far more knowledgeable than any thirty-year-old he had ever known. She spoke of the Revolution as though she had experienced it, had seen George Washington leave Philadelphia with his hat on crooked. "I've lived longer than even I know," she said, and he kissed her right away.

She shrugged her shoulders when asked about her past, but he kept asking, savoring each nugget of her lived life that she seldom shared. He learned that for decades she traveled around the states freeing the enslaved because voices in her head told her to. "Started after years of living with the Muskogee. I would be minding my business, resting or roasting fish, and out of the wind I'd pick up someone whispering in my ear everything I needed to know about how to free somebody miles away. And most of the time it felt out of my control. I'd find myself standing up, leaving my home, shotgun in hand, and instructions spilling into my mind, my body moving on its own until I returned to the Muskogee and was stirred awake by the sounds of their and the Negro children laughing. If not for that laughter, who knows if I would've returned to my senses."

"If those voices ever call you while with me, please let me follow?"

"Can you fight?" Saint asked. They laughed knowing the answer was yes.

After four months together, they married, and Saint was with child. But complications ensued. Cramping. Difficulty sleeping. Then after a month, she miscarried. Saint wouldn't allow Sebastian to touch her for a long time and cried every morning and every night for two months straight. In the void of her sorrow, it rained every day, ruining the garden and sickening the animals.

When her grief dried up, anger remained, and she flashed it about like a knife. Her demands to be left alone increased. Rainless thunder and lightning storms assaulted the town. A mighty drought desiccated crops. It took Sebastian grabbing her by the shoulders and saying with a force she didn't know he had, "We can try again, but I need to touch you to be able to do that, and you need to let the dead be dead. The baby is dead, Saint. Not you."

She didn't like the sure way he said who was and wasn't dead or how he looked her in the eyes like he wanted to fuck her. He was wearing the wrong eyes for words like that, lids a little too wide, not wet enough, irises like wheel spokes going and going in the wrong direction. But she got herself together, spiteful as a wasp, and for one week more made him sleep in the workshop before returning to her caring self. This time, being forced into his work helped, offering him priceless hours to delve into fertility research, and after they tried a second time with no pregnancy, he suggested he fix her.

"I'm not broken, Sebastian," Saint said, but she knew what he meant, that he wanted to root her down and get a baby out of her, and she wanted to be rooted down, too, but differently.

What he brought her to drink smelled like a forest and the salve he rubbed on her stomach cooled her skin. He rubbed her head at the temples and massaged her neck and shoulders daily until Saint, without warning, said, "We must try again right this minute."

She conceived twins, and Sebastian couldn't have been happier. They named them Maria and Nala. Two weeks later, Maria died and a day after that Nala followed. Saint cried every morning, daydreamed all afternoon, and cried again at night. Sebastian dove into his research with more depth, sleeping in the workshop without needing to be told, calculating, measuring, enduring. When he returned to bed, his hands were cold.

[6]

They both decided to throw themselves fully into root work, devoting energy better spent for lovemaking on developing serums and powders meant to make easier the lives of others. Saint took abundant notes, for her memory couldn't hold it all in and he tutored her through everything she needed to know.

"We must work on your emotions. You make weather with your feelings. You can feel however you want, but you can't go flooding the world with your heart," Sebastian said. And they managed an agreement that Saint made with the universe: she would learn to detach her gift from her feelings and how to bring rain whenever she pleased. She failed each time, and each time she feared Sebastian would leave her like Essence had. But he stayed, fascinated that she was "so close to God," he said. "Between your storm making and stonework, my love, my love . . ." He would shake his head, proud, amazed, and as her fear and shame lightened, so did her lack of control. No, she couldn't "do weather" at will like Sebastian wanted her to, but she could stop herself from doing it when her feelings overtook her.

Sebastian had to take a trip a few miles south and asked Saint to stay and watch the house. "Someone coming to pick up that order over there on the table. Could you make sure they get it? It's already paid for." He headed out, book of notes in hand, and waved goodbye as the horse ambled down the road.

Hungry for study, she returned to the workshop and ground rosemary and coal. Midway, she forgot the next step and opened her book of notes. Surprised that her handwriting was not her own, she squinted as if that would change the script, then realized Sebastian had taken her notes with him and left his own behind. She flipped through his writing to find the proper root and read a bit of something unfamiliar. Her lips trembled as she closed the book and returned it to where she had found it.

They argued that night about what she had seen: notes on the human body, intricate sketches of the main organs of the body (she had no idea he could draw), an estimate of how much blood the body holds, and the effects of sunlight and soil on the skin—these intrigued her, and she wondered why he never shared this with her.

He reached into his pocket for the notebook he hadn't used since leaving and noticed for the first time that he had Saint's notes and not his own. She watched his cheeks tighten. Wind stirred outside. 'We were doing well by each other,' she thought, 'how quickly the roses close.'

Saint then flipped hurriedly to a page where she found the word "sembie."

"What is a sembie, Sebastian?"

In the notes, the inked shapes had lifted from the page like bats and entered her mind: "resurrection," "revivification," "logic of Christ upon the cross and spirit of Christ beyond the veil of the tomb," "defiance of both heaven and hell," "interruption of the chronology of God." A drawing of a person lying in a circle reminded Saint of Essence's attempt to get her "energy" under control. Even the arrows drawn counterclockwise—a sun moving from east to west, life to death then back again through the underworld to begin once more—followed Essence's pattern. Sebastian added a drawing of a tree as the vertical dividing line of the top half of the circle and a wavy line representing water as the horizontal line halving the circle. Written across the chest of the drawing of the human figure was the word "sembie."

Human flesh symbolized as treetop and its vein-patterned roots; as the sky and underwater; as north, south, east, and west; as the rising and setting sun; as the blur between the living world and the Otherside: Saint tried to follow the complex patterning, the disregard for the laws of nature, laws that Sebastian himself had instilled in her, a betrayal beyond her understanding as she lifted the drawing up to Sebastian's face, forcing him to look upon what he had created and kept away from her. She shoved the drawing into his face. "The world don't spin slow enough for you so you gotta give it a second go round?" Saint asked.

Sebastian snatched the notes from her. "This is theory, Saint. Not a practice. Not something that should ever be done." He looked at the notes and his look melted into the pages. "And these notes are not my own. I copied and expanded on what belonged to Piya de Nuestros Dioses Zurdo and he got this knowledge from an African man in what they call Belize. The man didn't even share his name for fear of what may happen to him if discovered sharing this.

"I no more have the talent to accomplish this than I have the interest. I do not have the interest, Saint." Saint glared at him. When she saw him crying, the notes torn from the notebook and crumbled in his fist, she nodded.

"Yes," she said. "I believe you."

[7]

Sebastian wanted to introduce Saint to Eloise. He hadn't seen his friend since marrying Saint in 1828. Now it was 1830, and he thought it a shame that the two didn't know about each other. He told Saint all about how they met, about how she procured patrons for him in New Orleans, kept his name out of the mouths of those who would sully his reputation with superstitious ignorance.

When Saint asked if he had ever been romantic with Eloise, he said he tried once, and she bit him. Saint howled with laughter, imagining blood staining his mouth, and kissed him. "Then she can be a friend to me, too."

When they reached Eloise's home, the door was already partially open and blood tracked from just outside the doorway to inside the house, leading back to Eloise's bedroom upstairs. Sebastian rushed inside. Saint followed and stood petrified when she saw the body of a woman lying in a pool of blood. Sebastian opened his bag and pulled out strips of linen. "Please douse my instruments in alcohol," Sebastian said, and Saint went about cleaning his instruments. "We will need boiling water and towels next," he said, and Saint took on the new tasks without question.

Sebastian soaked a strip of linen in witch hazel, then used it as a towel to clean off the blood from Eloise's body. He immediately began to stitch Eloise's many wounds. As soon as he pulled the final stitch shut, he poured witch hazel over the stitches, following that with alcohol, then wrapped the woman's body with the bedsheet, after which he and Saint lifted her belly-up onto the bed.

Sebastian pulled a bottle of green liquid from his coat pocket, opened Eloise's mouth, and let three droplets fall in. He looked around frantically, opening drawers, and found a hand mirror. He placed it over Eloise's mouth and exhaled hard when the glass fogged up. Saint watched the woman's chest rise and fall, then looked away. They didn't think to clean up the blood on the floor first, so Saint stood in it as it cooled and dried to rust beneath her.

Hearing laughter of passersby outside snapped them back to their senses. They wiped the floor with a towel and rinsed it with the pot of hot water. They then cleaned off their shoes. Blood limned Saint's dress around the skirt's bottom but there was nothing they could do about it. They left immediately, just in case whoever tried to kill Eloise returned.

No opportunity to catch their breath as they proceeded out of the house, Sebastian holding tight Saint's hand and dragging her down the road, tilting his hat in greeting and, too, to hide his face. Saint remained exposed to witnesses, her dress sweeping blood across the cobblestone. They hurried past others, bumping into people, saying excuse me sometimes, saying nothing most times. Then they were running again, going in the opposite direction of the foot traffic. Someone shouted profanity at Saint. Looked her in the eye and nearly spat it in her face, and when she turned to see if Sebastian had heard, he was too busy looking ahead, running toward a future that didn't seem to matter if it had her in it.

By the time they made it to the colored boat, they were a sweaty mess, shaken out of their wits. Sebastian was sad to leave his friend in bandages, risking infection. He understood that she still may not make it without food and water. He was no studied doctor but once had to help Moon care for a friend's niece when she split open her head after falling from a tree. Seeing the blood then, how viscous and bright then dark it became, taught him to carry always not only his roots but his thread, needle, and anything to clean a wound.

While Saint thought about the soft openings in Eloise's back closing at the pull of his thread like the mouths of embarrassed lovers, she seethed. Blood hardened the body of her dress, and she was calmed by the fact that the material was dark, so the stains were mostly unnoticeable. Secrets kept piling up, little bones stacking into a fortress built between herself and Sebastian, for now she wondered about the green liquid that brought breath back into Eloise's dead body. She knew the woman was dead. Over ten stab wounds making red graves across that woman's back and Eloise didn't fall into any of them? Not likely. By the time she and Sebastian made it home, Saint had honed her anger.

"Woman, what's gotten into you this time? What is it now? My friend might be dead and you're biting my heels soon as we walk through the door."

But formulating full sentences proved difficult. She wanted to say clearly what she felt, that betrayal lingered over every moment they spent together, that her feet hurt from being dragged back to the dock, that seeing all that blood did something to her by which language wouldn't abide, that—

"She was already dead, Sebastian!" she finally said. She fell onto the dusty couch and unlaced her shoes. She rubbed her feet, cracked her toes, and undid her dress. Surprised by her own calmness as she spoke, she continued to speak. "You told me it was theory. That it wasn't real."

"That's not what theory mean, Saint. It means—"

"I know what it means. I know what it means. I know what it damn means. You told me it was a theory. Then you pour a green liquid into

Eloise's mouth and all of a sudden she's Lazarus. Didn't even have to call her name. You work faster than Jesus."

"Saint, please—"

"Why didn't you bring back our babies!"

That was it.

That was it.

All that time that's all she wanted to know.

Sebastian looked hard at Saint. Saint stared back until her eyes blurred with tears and everything began to drown. He retrieved his bag and pulled out the small bottle of green liquid, unstopped it, and let drip two droplets into his mouth. He embraced Saint and kissed her furiously on the lips. Spearmint. The burn of alcohol. It was mint oil. Not a root. Not magic. Not Jesus in a bottle. He explained how he couldn't think of a way to ease up Eloise's breathing, that he thought maybe her throat was tight, because she was breathing, just not the way he thought she should be. Maybe something was going on with her nose or her lungs. Out of desperation, he used the mint oil.

Saint shook her head. His explanation had nothing to do with Maria and Nala. She had room for nothing else in her mind.

"Come with me," he said. "I'll teach you what I know and what I don't know."

IN THE WORKSHOP, he redrew the sembie theory. "Here," he said, pointing to the figure of the human, "is the vessel. It's what me and you have. Bodies. Inside the vessel is the spirit." He moved his finger to the far right, touching the end of the horizontal line. "This where sunrise is. If I trace up like this, making this arc, we get to the top of the line that go up and down. That's noontime. Over here on the left, that's sunset. Everything down below is nighttime until the sun rise again and it's morning once more. Sunrise is birth. Noon is midlife, where we are right now in our living. Over here, sunset, that's old age. All beneath here is the

Otherside, afterlife. Underwater, where spirits like to be. That's why you not supposed to try talking to spirits you don't know by the water cause they'll snatch you up." He tickled Saint's side. She swatted him away, smiling, then fell contemplative, focused.

"What's the tree, then?"

"Tree where the big spirits live. Some folks call them gods. They was never alive so can't really be called dead. Everything meet in the center, the Otherside spirits from below and the godlike spirits at the top. Right at the bay, or where sand meets ocean. They don't follow time like we do, cause they live outside of it. Or, no that's not it. They live inside of it. Deep, deep inside, in the middle, where time don't move. The sembie at the center of time. It's a theory telling us that if we can get man to be right here instead of out here with the sun, then there's no death for him. But that means we must believe ain't no life, either. This not about raising the dead. It's about freezing somebody up in time. And if you freeze somebody in time, keeping them in the present, you can tell them what to do and they can't do nothing about it. Cause you locked them up and really just using the body. The soul still inside, waiting to move on, but you locked them up between life and death, tree and water, east and west, north and south, past and future. I don't know how to do this and if I did, you best believe I'd never do it to my own children. Eloise was lucky, not resurrected."

"And you're sure about all this? You're really sure?"

"Sure as my left foot not my right," Sebastian said. His smile was half-hearted.

That night, Saint stayed up in the workshop studying the pages. She looked for her notebook, having written "Mine own" inside to more quickly tell if it was indeed hers, but it was missing. Last time she saw it was in New Orleans. She decided she would just borrow Sebastian's notebook and rewrite her own when there was available time. Until then, she scoured Sebastian's pages, reading and rereading every sentence.

But something else plagued her. "Why didn't you bring back our babies?" echoed in her head. 'Because the dead stay dead,' Saint thought, tracing the circle counterclockwise with her middle finger. "Why your feet with the dead but your mind ain't? Turn." Who had said that? "Turn. Turn. Turn." Essence's voice rang out in her mind. "Turn, girl." She turned the drawing upside down and caught herself smiling. It frightened her.

[8]

March 1831, and a knock at the door. Sebastian opened it and there stood a man smelling like alcohol but not drunk. Not even a little. Focused beyond retrieval from the depths of his obsession. Saint entered the room and saw the man some feet away. Light snowfall brightened the view behind him, which darkened the man into silhouette. The man spoke loudly, spitting, a fire in his throat. Something about Perry. "What you do to make Perry not like me no more?" or "I reckon you done did something to Perry that keep him away from me," or "Make him like me again. Make it easy for me to be around him again. I can't go anywhere near him. I try but something keep pushing me away. You did it." Not drunk. Clear as hunger. Clear as thirst. Sebastian tried to close the door on the man, but he wedged his foot in the doorway and shouldered into the house.

Saint wondered why he was able to reach them with ill intent, why her sickness stones hadn't stopped him. She must've carved them wrong, placed them in the wrong locations. It hit her that maybe they didn't work because she felt safe, and the possibility that she could only be protected if she felt unsafe horrified her. She looked to Sebastian, expecting his blame, but the visitor had his focus, such that he quickly put himself between her and their intruder.

The man was as big as Sebastian, so when Sebastian punched him in the face, the man punched him back. They wrestled in the open doorway, snow blowing in from the outside, fire in the fireplace frantic and flailing about. "Make him love me again," the man said. He didn't stop saying it. Neither while Sebastian socked him in the kidney nor when Sebastian punched him one last time in the jaw, sending him reeling to the ground.

"That's enough," Sebastian said. Then, a pop. Like every bone in Saint's body cracked at once. She hadn't seen the man pull a gun from his pocket while lying on the floor. She only heard the sound, then saw her husband lean back until he hit the floor. And as the man tried to stand up, Saint saw a flash of light enter through the roof and into the shooter.

When she came to, the shooter convulsed on the ground and snow that had fallen just outside her door had melted away, revealing the road and dead grass beneath. Steam snaked up from both the earth and the man's cooked body.

Sebastian was still breathing, eyes shut, a hole in his stomach. She moved his suit jacket to the side and tore open the shirt at the bullet hole. She rubbed alcohol all over her hands, then fished around the wound for the bullet. It clinked to the floor after she tossed it. "Sebastian." No response. Saint pushed the furniture out of the way, grabbed a bag of salt from the pantry, and drew a circle around him. Her arrows mimicked those in the theory, but instead of drawing the waves for the water pointed up, she drew them pointed down. Sebastian stopped breathing. The upper center node that was meant to represent the treetop lay at his feet. "How do I do this?" she asked. "How do I make you stay? Stay. Just stay. I will not lose any more of my people. Stay. Stay. Stay . . ."

SAINT JUMPED WHEN she heard Madame Jenkins call her name. "You went off somewhere just now."

"I'm here," Saint said. "May I borrow a dress and a shawl? I have some things to take care of. Watch over Selah for me till I return? Won't take too long."

"Chile, it's raining harder than when you first got here."

Thunder shook the house. "I can't help it," Saint said.

"Can't help what?"

"I can't help how I feel."

Miserable how rainwater blurred everyone's doorway. It fell and wind blew it diagonal, giving everything Saint saw the illusion of leaning. She knocked on the first door and when someone opened it, she said, "I am so sorry for hurting you. Please forgive me." She went to the next door. "I am so sorry for hurting you. Please forgive me." Then the next, "I am so sorry . . ." and the next, ". . . for hurting you . . ." and the next, "Please forgive me." Door after door, she visited everyone in Ours, apologizing, head bowed, sobbing sometimes, calmer other times. "I am so sorry." Who knew that apologies were little fires? "for hurting you . . ." Each time she apologized, her mouth dried up, her throat burned, and her lips cracked. Each word a hard baptism. ". . . please forgive me."

Mr. Wife opened his door and Saint knelt before him. She apologized, then added, "I couldn't save her, Miss. I couldn't save her. Please believe me. I couldn't save her. I couldn't . . ."

Inside, he dried her off and opened a trunk full of Mrs. Wife's old dresses. He offered one to her.

"Y'all bout the same size," he said. "Don't sit in them wet clothes."

But Saint shook her head and let the heat of his hearth do its job.

Mr. Wife was chatty, hoarse but energized having not had an audience for days. He spoke about how things had been for him since Mrs. Wife died and he had taken in Justice. He used his hands a lot to speak, throwing his arms around his body, over his head. Animated, interested. Then his voice became soft. "I still can't read, Saint," he said, and that's when Saint saw all the scraps of paper on the floor. Mr. Wife picked up a tear of paper and showed it to her. It had been written all over until the letters bled into and over each other. She noticed how his alphabet never resolved: all this time, Mr. Wife had been practicing his letters but couldn't remember past the letter *T*. "Luther-Philip was teaching me, but . . ." He stopped and wiped his eyes for a good while. "If you see my son, tell him I miss him?"

Saint wrote *U, V, W, X, Y, Z* on the paper, saying them aloud as she wrote them. She didn't know Luther-Philip was missing and felt guilty for yet another loss. Moments later, Saint headed out, weighted by a forthcoming apology that she didn't have the strength to give.

Saint knocked on doors and swallowed hard each time a concerned face turned belligerent upon seeing her. She believed it was because she wasn't there to fight alongside them when the militia arrived; however, that was only part of it. Saint apologized and the Ouhmey's lips trembled, their eyes flew open then squinted as they sucked their teeth, and some made quick sounds behind their closed mouths that made their heads bounce in short spasms of outrage. "Hmph! Hmph!" and a quick nod, a soft-spoken "All right," an acidic "Thank you." Even still: an offer of soup, tea, a moment to dry off in the presence of their ire, all of which Saint refused. Then the door closing against Saint's lowered head. 'Sent them babies here to die,' they thought, and each person wondered where she was that day and why she decided to send those two girls to do such dangerous work that she should've done herself, could've solved easily had she been there.

It had been two hours by the time she reached Aba's house. She knew Joy was in there. Under the porch shade, Saint listened to water assault the tin, like it wanted to do the knocking that she couldn't do for herself. It must have worked, because Joy opened the door, her deadpan stare under lamplight the only greeting she gave. A mare passing gas would've gotten a stronger reaction.

"Aba's dead," Joy said. "What you need, Saint?"

"I was told about Aba. I'm sorry. For everything, Joy."

Joy looked over Saint's shoulders, spoke at that wet dark. "Why'd you make him dream about that white woman taking his manhood? The other dreams were something else, but that one? That one?"

"I never—"

"That one, Saint? Why do that to a man you called your friend? That one?" Each time Joy said "that one," her voice went higher.

Thinking back, Saint didn't plan on what dreams to send Aba, just that they would be punishment for leaving dead snakes at her bottom step. She only meant to spook him a little, just enough to make him come visit and tell her he got it and that he was sorry. A little fall off a cliff or losing all his teeth or getting bit by a snake wearing her face. Nothing, nothing ever, involving his so-called master, whom she had killed on her own volition along with her husband. Why, indeed, had she sent such nastiness to Aba? This cruel mistake, one she hadn't known about for years while she assumed Aba still wanted to punish her for the snakes, took all language from her. This was not a failure of conjure, but of friendship.

Seeing Saint had no words for her, Joy shook her head. "Frances well, at least?"

Saint didn't respond. She saw Joy holding her belly like Essence had all those years ago. It was dangerous for Saint to be there.

"She dead, too?"

"No. She left."

"Left where?"

"I don't know."

"You make her leave?"

"Yes."

Joy looked over Saint's head, hummed one long and loud note, then shut the door in Saint's face.

Who knows how long Saint stood on that lonely porch while the storm plowed through Ours. Embracing herself, she turned toward the storm that was her endless sorrow and wondered if this, too, deserved an apology. It smelled like the swamps of her past, one of the lasting memories from that time. Essence's face was leaving her, she had already forgotten Hu entirely. The rest of her past flickered firefly slow from her mind. It had become a reflex at this point. New memories took the life of older memories. Washed them all away with the rain, along with her footprints in the mud leading to Thylias's home where Naima opened the door and looked frightened when Saint appeared. 'You too,' Saint thought. Saint smiled, bowed her head, then went back down the road. It began to hail.

"Who was that at the door," Thylias asked from her bedroom. Her back had been killing her all day and she blamed it on the rain.

"Was hail, ma'am," Naima said. She closed the door to keep from getting hit.

[9]

The storm ended when Saint fell asleep in Madame Jenkins's chair. In the morning, Madame Jenkins asked a young man to drive Saint and Selah back to their home. The two women hugged goodbye as the boy unhitched the horse and attached the wagon. "You have a fever?" Madame Jenkins asked Saint, touching her face and forehead with the back of her hand. Saint shook her head. "Hmmm, but it could come later. Take this with you." She handed Saint a jar of herbs. "Wet it just enough so that it gets like mud. Stir it then rub it on your chest if you get sick." She hugged Saint once more. "I love you."

On the ride back, overcast darkened the ground below. She looked back and saw Mr. Wife, carrying what looked like a cake, walk over to Madame Jenkins's home and be let in.

God's Place stood in the distance in a furious gown of white flowers on the bottom half, the top half dark green and full of birds whose song she heard from the road. She asked the boy to stop for a moment. She hopped out the wagon on her own and headed to God's Place. Someone had hammered a sign into the ground that said, "For Aba Greyson." 'They spelled his last name wrong. It's an *A* not *E*,' she thought, touching the splintered wood. "Thank you, Aba," she said, and touching the ground with both hands she apologized three times. She must've been there for a while because when she looked down the hill, she saw the boy waving at her.

Back in the wagon, the wheels had trouble turning. Damp, the land would remain muddy until the sun was allowed reentry by the clouds. For now, Saint's somber mood relegated the usually crisp morning air to a dull yawn of dank air smelling of soaked earth and ripe plant life perspiring in a humidity she wasn't prepared for. She wiped sweat from her brow and from Selah's face lying on her lap. The boy had helped Saint lift her onto the wagon and lay her across hay bales lined up against the wagon's railings. Hay pricked Saint's thighs as they bumped through the woods and into open field leading to Creek's Bridge. She rubbed Selah's forehead with her thumb and stared out across the endless bed of wildflowers and tall grass, uncultivated land sweet-smelling enough to make one delirious. She repeated Selah's name to herself so as not to forget it. Then she repeated Naima's name. In rhythm, she said, "Selah. Naima. Selah. Naima. Selah. Naima." After a while, she started repeating her own name to herself, then Sebastian's.

When she reached back into time to find the names of her dead children to add to the song, nothing came to her. Soon, she would forget she had once given birth to twins. Oblivion rode with her across Creek's Bridge, and once they crossed the water and made their way to her house, a breeze touched her across the neck. Light broke through the trees from behind while overhead clouds sat squat in the ether.

Before Saint went to Ours in search of the twins, she had undressed Sebastian and sewed up the bullet wound. She cleaned up the blood with a floor brush, removed her bloody bedsheets, washed Sebastian's body, then wrapped it in a cocoon of clean linen. He was too heavy for her to lift, so she dragged him carefully down the stairs and outside just beyond the garden. Right there on the road—moon as witness, stars as audience, the secret lives of beast and bird awakening in the radiance of Saint's grief—she grabbed a fistful of black powder from her dress pocket and set Sebastian's corpse aflame. When it finished burning, she laid the serpent staff over his charred body and covered the remains in dirt, building a mound over him. She laid across the mound, dictating all the memories she shared with him into the dirt until she was breathless and story-less. Then it began to rain.

Now, she stopped the boy just before reaching the garden. She gave him every coin she had on her, and he thanked her. He helped Saint get Selah down from the wagon and rode off.

Nothing remained for her in Ours. Already discovered and invaded, the Ouhmey proved they could make it without her conjure, that her conjure may have caused more harm than good. She carried Selah past the mound over which she had placed calla lilies, Queen Anne's lace, and some of the roses the night before; past the garden that survived the deluge; past her house that had kept her for over a decade; past the animal pen now unlocked and empty; past where the path became a thin lane of dirt that spilled over with grass; through the woods' spectacular appetite as its branches and thorns rubbed against her arms a rough seduction; up into the world of creatures mingling with shadows as she moved through those shadows and broke through to the other side of darkness and into a scattering of shacks standing on dry land unaffected by the storm that had pounded Ours. She stood there in welcoming sunlight and the unwelcoming squint of Aurora who, hanging laundry on a line, let an immaculate sheet drop to the ground.

· CHAPTER 29 ·

Homeward

[1]

Sit her down here," Aurora said, pointing to a line of pillows on the floor. They were covered in a soft, thick quilt Aurora said she had sewn herself with shards of color and miscellaneous patterns cut into boxes, pentagons, trapezoids, circles, and everything else. Up close the thing looked a mess, so much so Saint swore she heard a cacophony of chimes ring out from the assortment of mangled, previously worn scraps. The ringing settled after she placed Selah over it, the girl's weight a gravity against the din.

It had been over thirty years since Saint saw Aurora. Not since Ours was founded had the two been in each other's close company, and the division still tasted bitter in both women's mouths. It was their time in the wilderness, right before the move into Graysville. They had built something real nice out there in the woods. Quiet. Good land. Plenty of space within the trees without needing to cut any down, so the shade fell perfectly. Nobody for miles. Potential for paradise.

But Aurora could hear the insides of people when they were hurting.

Not thoughts, just echoes of emotions. Early on, she wasn't impressed much by Saint because she had gifts of her own that Saint didn't have. She could make sense of the leaves and knew the difference between a spirit and a god. What she had was more practical, more invasive in Saint's eye than any conjure could ever be.

Aurora promised not to listen in on Saint's interior after revealing she could do such a thing, but she couldn't stop herself from hearing a nasty roaring in Saint's companion that made her nose bleed the first time she heard it. She asked Saint, politely as possible, "Why won't he stop howling inside himself?" Saint split off then, took over Graysville and left behind those who wanted to stay "out there," as she called it, to do what they wanted, but not to try to find her and her people because they wouldn't be welcomed. The whole time Aurora apologizing at the top of her lungs, "I didn't mean to. I couldn't help it. Saint. Saint! It's something wrong with that man."

It was all fear, not rage, that Saint felt back then and even now. Aurora knew this, because Saint sometimes snuck off from Ours to steal a glance at Turney and see how it was holding up. Those days, Aurora would hear Saint before she saw her, her poor sight making only Saint's general shape discernible in the distance. Saint's fiery interior roared, a sadness burning her up inside as she hid behind some bushes like a racoon.

Occasionally, Saint left baskets of food, seeds, herbs, and tools in the middle of the road for someone in Turney to find. Rarely did she let people who were new to Turney move into Ours, like how she almost allowed Foster in. But the originals, mostly Aurora, she didn't study, and it made Aurora laugh, the insecurity of it all. Saint's outlandish pride turned against her as Aurora had predicted it would the first time Saint snuck around the outskirts of Turney, lonely as the number one. 'Ours should've been named Hers,' she joked in her mind, believing Ours was simply another one of Saint's possessions, another private sword pretending to be everyone's shield.

"I heard about the troubles you been having in Ours. Watermelon troubles. Troubles with the spirits. The weather ain't right," she began, placing a warm towel over Selah's forehead. Saint remained quiet as Aurora spoke to her and managed small chores around her. "Watermelon meant for healing, not harming. Nastiest curse you could've put on somebody. I could've told you that. But . . ." She chuckled to herself. "And I heard about the spirit, too. Killed Mrs. Wife, is it? Way it was described to me, it sounded like you messed with the wrong one. What her face looked like when you saw her?"

"Whoever told you that much should've told you everything, since they had everything to say," Saint said.

"Oh, honey, don't be that way. I'm trying to help. It's too late but I can tell you what spirit visited you at least."

Saint breathed in hard. The image of the spirit's face had never left her. If a name could be applied, she wanted it. "He had red eyes, a gold tooth. Smelled like liquor—"

"Whiskey, rum, beer? Which one? It matter," Aurora cut in.

"Rum. And cigar smoke."

"And he called you out your womanly name? Then killed the woman he possessed? Sth sth sth . . ."

Saint said nothing. Drowsiness fell over her. Her eyes burned. Not much sleep reached her the night before and her pilgrimage through every inch of Ours and from Ours to Turney while carrying Selah had caught up to her.

"When you first was explaining it sounded like a spirit I'm familiar with, but those not his ways. I think you angered somebody I'm not knowing of. Probably a new spirit who took on the pain we feeling in this new land. You know names and feelings and ways change in the spirit world like they do here. What's hot come after what's cool, the way I was taught. A slave's anger can change a world. But what come after the hot?" Aurora smiled. "Some think Br'er Rabbit used to be a spider back in Africa, but he ours. Ever heard of 'Nansi? Chile, a trickster if there ever was one. But for Br'er Rabbit, we had to be here for him to come. Go to Louisiana, they got Compère—"

"Lapin," Saint said. Sebastian had told her those folktales back when they were courting. And the scent of him came rolling back, his hands playing in her hair, how he made a door of himself and let her in, how he made a house of her heart that he kept clean and slept in for years . . .

Aurora continued. "It matter where a thing born." She picked her teeth with a pinky nail and flicked the residue behind her. By the hearth, she slapped a pillow and sent dust flying. Then she swept her house back to front. By the time she finished speaking, she had tossed the dust into the hearth and set it ablaze and boiled water with that same fire to wash the floor. "Honey, how you go and open The Gate without permission? I'm glad you ain't say nobody name. You would've saw that spirit's face and said 'Daddy Lobo? That you?' and made whoever it was madder." Aurora bent over in laughter. "Chile . . ." and wiped tears from an eye.

"He felt familiar." Saint hadn't pulled her gaze from Selah. "Like I knew him from somewhere before."

"Maybe he not new, then. Just got new ways split off from the old. You know where you was born?" Aurora yawned and cleaned her teeth with her tongue.

"Why does that matter?"

"I suppose it don't. We all just souls that keep coming back, keep getting called back here for who knows what. Nothing die, really." Aurora kept her eyes low but had been watching both Saint and Selah with every sweep and now with every swish of the rag against the floor. Saint caught glimpses of the woman's looking from the corner of her eye but stayed her full looking on Selah. After a few minutes, the large room smelled of peppermint and lemongrass.

When Aurora lit a bundle of sage, Saint glared. "You calling me evil?"

"No. But who knows what you done brought with you." Aurora hobbled to each corner of the room, saying, "My home is protected from any misbehaving spirits, from any evil trying to make its way into my home. The Devil is a liar and I'm protected." Then she threw open each window, letting cold air enter. "When the last time you washed yourself?" When Saint didn't respond she told her to stand up. Saint stood and lifted her arms out beside her. Aurora danced the sage stick around her silhouette, repeating the same words as before but replacing "I'm" with Saint's name. Saint sat down when Aurora finished. "Where that man that was with you? The one who made my nose bleed with his heart?"

At this point, Saint carried no regrets of not letting Aurora into Ours. Her nonstop talking, the questions she asked with a cadence of someone who already knew the answer. That knowledge without effort. Saint never liked that about the woman, but here Aurora was helping her. It felt like a punch to the face. "Have you seen Frances? I know you know who she is. You know every damn thing."

"I heard it feel like summer over where you are. You know it's been fall here for about a month. What year is it in Ours?"

Saint's head was spinning. "What you mean fall? It's spring."

"Now that you put Selah down, go look outside. You barely had your eyes open when you dragged yourself up to my yard. It's fall and 1872 here. What year it is in Ours?" Golden bangles clanked around Aurora's right wrist. Daylight cut across them and split into two blades of radiance.

Saint stood fast, became light-headed. Crisp air touched her face as she stepped outside and saw the leaves were already red and yellow, unlike the bright green and flowering trees in Ours. Blue sky. Thick, white clouds. The sun still with some strength to it. The grass felt dry beneath her naked feet. Birds practiced their Vs overhead, their squawks and calls an omen dropping anvil-heavy onto Saint.

"What year is it in Ours, Saint?"

"How do you know what's going on in my town? You never been there. You never been welcome there. You never cared to be there—"

"You ain't welcome me. You forbade me. You ain't ask me what I cared about ever in my life and ain't bout to start now, it seem. But I know it's still spring in Ours. Y'all probably still think you in the Civil War, too. Did you even know there was a war? Negroes been free almost ten years now. Lincoln was 'sassinated. Or maybe y'all even further back than that. Was Ours just founded? Honey . . ." Aurora paused, shook her head. "Close my door and have a seat. You don't run nothing this way. I'll answer your questions, but you need to hear a thing or two with your feet on the ground and your ass not far from it."

Saint closed the door and sat down. The room spun around her, shifting Selah in and out of her gaze.

"When we first arrived in the woods back in, I think it was 1831 or so, I noticed that whenever you was around, nature got confused. It rained when it wasn't 'sposed to. The winters was destructive. Felt like nobody knew what day it was or nothing. I slipped away one day, went to see some folks who lived in a little house east of here. The farther I got from Turney, the warmer it got. By the time I reached my destination, honey, I was soaked. You hear me? Wet as a fish back.

"I spoke with them for a little bit, Timothy and his son Hazel. Cutest boy I ever seen. Palest too. Looking like he never saw a drop of oil in his life, he was so ashy. But tell me why they say it was a year past what we thought it was back in Turney? I said, 'What you mean 1833?' So, it was 1832. I was wrong earlier. We thought it was 1832 and winter in Turney. It was 1833 and summer everywhere else. When I came back to Turney, it was freezing. We had our fires going. Frost was all on the flowers. You hear that? The flowers wasn't dead. They was covered in frost. Dying, maybe. I don't even think they was dying. So, I knew then we wasn't gone be together long. I made up my mind not to be near you. I just didn't know when I was leaving. So, when you got angry that I heard that man's insides, it blessed me so. I was hurt, but it blessed me." Aurora refreshed the heat on the towel on Selah's forehead. "You like for things to be how you like them, and you don't like for them to change. But everybody else got to deal with how you feel, what you want, and when you want it. No future for us cause no future for you." She stopped, then said, "1872."

Now that she thought about it, Saint had no idea what year it was in Ours. Last she heard, the Civil War made everyone in Delacroix paranoid, but after that? Rage against people in her house trying to tell her how to run a town that she learned didn't need her running it, that she never really ran in the first place. She had wanted to use Creek's Bridge to erase all memories of whips and screaming in the cotton, smell of blood cursing the air. She had wanted to mind her business and let the folks in Ours figure out for themselves what they wanted and how they wanted to go about getting it. Just occasional conjure for favors. A patrol to make sure the stones remained in place. But she got caught up in fear, a fear she always claimed she never had. What once made sense to her—a clinging to vengeance as warning and punishment regardless the width of the act—was now senseless.

"Something must've happened to you to make you stop time like that, Saint. Something break your heart? Some-*body*?" Aurora said. She sat on the floor beside a large plant, leaves like hands with holes in them. "Frances here. He not doing too well. His memory off. Maybe the cry you need is over there with the cry he need. But, please, let Selah rest for the night. You will stay here and go to Frances in the morning. I'll help you carry Sel—"

"I'll carry her myself. Soon as the sun rise. Just tell me which house and we'll be out of your way."

Saint wondered what moment had frozen Ours up in the past and figured it must have been when she gave up on the concept of time altogether; the hands of her clock had come to have a mind of their own anyway. And who would notice their own temporal torpor with no more trips outside of Ours? No newspapers with the proper date blew into their territory, landing on a man's face as he dozed on the porch, sticking to a child's foot as they ran through the mud, or even a shred of news falling from a bird's beak on its way to making a nest with torn-up dates and events, timelines in fragment beneath a quartet of eggs.

Late afternoon, and Saint hadn't moved from that spot. A thump against the glass. Aurora went outside and returned holding a cardinal in her hand. She showed the unconscious bird to Saint. Black neck and mask, a bandit in her palm.

Aurora lifted a wing with a finger. "Still alive. You can see it breathing. I just like to mess with the wings cause what wings of my own I got to mess with?"

"You say this like this a habit of yours," Saint said.

"Cardinals fly into my window all the time. I try to keep the windows open but it's getting cold and y'all here with no coat or shawl. Poor little baby."

"The bird will be all right."

"Oh, I was talking about you, honey." Aurora smiled a genuine smile that melted away. "You haven't aged in forty years."

From outside, a spicy smell wafted into the house. "Somebody making curry. I'll go get us some."

Curried goat, collards, and rice enough for lunch and supper. By the time evening came along, Saint had grown somewhat comfortable in Aurora's house that felt like outside. The potted plants strewn about the sweet-smelling room reminded her of—what did it remind Saint of? She dug around her mind for the remembrance but returned with absence, despite knowing there used to be a memory there in the emptiness. Disembarking from the fruitless journey in her mind, she settled her thoughts back on Selah, making sure she remembered the other child's name, too. 'Yes, it's still there,' she thought. 'Naima still there. As is Thylias. As is Aba. And Madame Jenkins. Everyone in Ours.'

GOOSE FEATHER STABBING her back from the floored bedding, Saint rolled over in the middle of the night and awoke to Aurora, lit by the hearth, with Selah's head on her lap. Aurora had her back to Saint, which made the moment painfully private. The shared stillness between Aurora and Selah startled Saint, who locked her eyes on this nurturing and became overwhelmed by shame. Aurora's silhouette appeared as a woman-shaped opening in the fire, a doorway to step through, and what on earth waited on the other side?

The first time Saint saw Aurora's back was when she first met her. Aurora was standing in the middle of a road facing a horseless covered wagon where the horse had been released. It wandered off nearby. There, just north of the Louisiana and Arkansas border. Saint had cleared her throat to make her presence known and when Aurora turned around, Saint saw splattered blood all over her pale face, like paintbrush bristles covered in red paint had been flicked on her. "He in there," Aurora said. "He in there."

By "he" she meant her so-called master, an older man of mixed African and French blood. Before they set off for the trip, Aurora had put a sleep root on him and after ten minutes in the wagon, before he could assault her, he fell into a drooling sleep. On that road, splattered blood drying brown on her, Aurora had told Saint how she watched him sleep, trying to figure out if she should kill him first or the wagon driver who knew what their so-called master did to her and never blinked about it. Never even said he was sorry for what happened to her back there while he drove them. When she decided to kill the driver first, she chose to shoot him in the back of the head with their so-called master's gun. For the sleeping so-called master, she bludgeoned him repeatedly with a rock she had found after jumping out of the wagon and calmly exploring the area.

"He in there," Aurora had said. Saint hadn't seen the dead driver right away. It took the horse running back toward the two women for her to see that he had been tied to the horse, his corpse dragging behind.

Now, looking into the ingress Aurora's unlit back made against the fire, Saint closed her eyes before the horse in her memory dragged that corpse from the inky entrance and in front of her once again.

WAS A ROOSTER that woke her the second time, hearth burning away the morning chill. Then she heard Aurora inventing a song outside, screeching, juvenile for a woman in her sixties, but ascending beside morning, her voice lifted the sun on its shrill back. Saint ignored the pain in her feet and sat up so sunrays could warm her face. On a small plate beside her bed, Aurora had left mint sprigs and a handful of blueberries. Saint took them in, the fruit refreshing her mouth, the mint telling her she needed it.

She used a heavy stone to prop open the front door, gathered Selah into her arms. When she made it to the center of Turney where the outdoor cooking occurred, circled by a menagerie of stray goats and a single strutting, proud-chested black rooster, she locked eyes with Aurora, who pointed to her left with a cock of her head at the only house that had a fence, the raggedy door already open. Saint nodded and mouthed "thank you."

[2]

The house wouldn't let her in. Saint stepped through Frances's doorway and instantaneously returned outside the door she had just stepped through. She tried again, thinking hunger delirium had overcome her, but the moment her foot touched the floor of the house, she appeared back outside the door, her foot's full weight on the front porch facing Aurora as she casually cleared leaves from around the hearth. Saint realized she had been flipped around when her heel landed outdoors, Selah in her arms, the entrance behind her, and a cold breeze between her ankles.

"Gone in, honey," Aurora said, dipping her battered hat over her eyes and now sweeping around the chicken coop. The black rooster paced behind Aurora, peered at Saint, and strutted off back how it came.

Had Saint less sense she would've sworn she had gone mad. Madness, that incredulous aspect of the mind's possibility to be so wounded that it wounds the world in return, that it makes inside out and outside in, that it makes a prayer sob-worthy while making laughter the impetus for murder—madness was her natural state, she believed. She wasn't going mad and had not gone mad. She existed there from the start, on the edge of everyone's center, peripheral such that when she tried to move center the world pushed her away.

Essence had rejected her, knife and apple, baby safe inside her bound to come any time. Frances and Joy had done so, too, their own individual offenses paired against her singular resistance. Her now dead friend, Aba, burned her house down and maybe hoped to burn her inside, too. And her own tempestuous mind pushed her out by slapping away memories it deemed too burdensome for her to carry. And not even her own mind pushed her out cleanly, for it left residue of recollection all in her thinking, which allowed her to know she should remember Essence but didn't let her hold on to the name, just some empty space where "Essence" was meant to be. Saint's memory acted as the ultimate trickster, a grin with missing teeth and she the tongue easing into the gaps, wondering when they got there and if they could ever be filled.

Saint felt Selah's weight and cringed when it crossed her mind that she carried the poor child like a mere sack of grain in her arms. Meanwhile, Frances's doorway remained opened just to loop Saint back outside if she stepped through, back into the continuous labor of holding Selah, back into the wilderness of Aurora's gaze and judgment, into the line of sight of an arrogant black rooster that turned its neck up each time it looked in her direction.

After several attempts, each time Aurora saying, "Gone in, honey," Saint stood dumbfounded at the open threshold. Her arms burned from carrying Selah. Brushing beside her, the black rooster strutted up to then past her, and on through Frances's dark doorway. Its black feathers melded with the dark room until it stepped into the light pouring in from the window, circled Frances, who sat at that very window looking out at the garden, then headed back outside, puffed up its chest, and brushed against Saint's leg as a haughty goodbye. Its black cockscomb wobbled teasingly before the bird disappeared behind a barrel.

Saint tried to enter Frances's home three times more and all three times found herself exiting the door after having already entered it.

"Gone in, honey," Aurora said. She was bent in the same position each time, the words coming out with the same cadence and rhythm, repeating exactly each time.

Saint cursed loud, stomped, and screamed Frances's name. "Stop sending me back," she said. Blue jays responded from their perches with pulsing laughter, a tantrum of watercolor as they flew away.

Standing before the doorway through which she could see Frances enthralled by the view outside, her three central fingers on both hands pressed against the window glass along with her nose that with each exhale fogged the pane, Saint's deepening vexation became weariness. Holding Selah in her arms, feeling heat from Selah's body travel into her own as would a nourishing soup down her throat, she brought the girl's head up to her own and held her like a baby, one arm under her bottom while she pressed Selah's head onto her shoulder with her free hand. She had never felt the girl's cheek touch hers, had never felt Selah's hair rub against her locs and tickle the inside of her ear. Standing there tired and sweaty, the weight of a forever-asleep girl humbled her.

Saint flashed a determined glare into the house, watched Frances slowly turn her head toward her. Saint held Selah fiercely and asked to please be let in. "Please, Frances." Behind her, the black rooster crowed. She tried entering again after Frances looked away and succeeded, only to be punched in the face by a stench that burned.

INSIDE FRANCES'S HOME, the smell of salt and shit pierced the air and stung Saint's nose. Overwhelmed, she looked back over her shoulder at Aurora, who shook her head and looked away. Frances continued sitting in a chair, enamored by the window, staring blankly out of it. Her breath clouded the glass, covering the view in a mist of a distant memory forever leaving the mind.

Humidity sealed the brackish air inside the creaky house. Saint lowered Selah onto the bed and rushed over to the windows to throw them open. She hurt her shoulders trying to open one that remained stuck to the windowsill. She called out for help from Frances, but the window before Frances was like a demonic aperture that sucked her gaze into its fogged-up pane. The house creaked again then leaned. Gravity closed the front door. Furniture slid from one side of the room to the other, except the chair Frances sat in, which stayed fastened to the floor as it tilted to the right with Frances stuck in it, staring out into oblivion.

Saint's breath shortened, the burning in her lungs relentless. When the house pivoted in the opposite direction, she grabbed a chair and slammed it into one of the windows, which rejected it and sent it flying across the room. Then everything stilled. The house leveled out. The hearth lit aflame with a blue fire that drew in the putrid air and replaced it with the softer smell of lilac. Soon after, the flame extinguished, the air grew cold and dry and musty, and every window except the one Frances peered through flew open.

"They want me back," Frances said. She hadn't turned to face Saint. The window. The window. "They want me back cause I didn't save you."

Saint crept toward Frances, waiting to hear more, if there was more, about who this *they* was and what *they* wanted.

Frances lowered her fingers to her lap, dragging them down the windowpane so the fog of her breath left streaks of clarity on the glass. "I thought if I stayed my head in the then then I would remember then for the now to bring it back to you, but the more I stayed in the then the more the now took over and now I can't save you because the you now need something from the me then that the me now don't have no more. The you then was closer to getting saved when I was farther from the here that's always here. Here kept coming and the then-you kept changing into this now-you, your here-now easier to save in mind but my mind harder to save you in this time. If you was the you then that you is now and I had the mind of always-had-happened then . . . then . . . the waters"—Saint held her chest as Frances gulped water not in the room—"ahh water come again today. Through the fire, the elements confused. The waters come again through the fire and our people visited and pulled me up from this chair and dragged me to the flames to send me back to the water where our people at. My leg—" Saint saw that Frances wasn't wearing shoes and her right pant leg had been rolled up to the knee, revealing burnt skin blistering from her foot to the circumference just below the calf. "They grabbed my leg and slid me back into the fire-water but I fought back and said I had to wait for you cause I knew you was coming. I knew it. But"—Frances placed her fingers back on the glass—"I can't seem to touch the past like I used to. Today keep getting in the way of the ways and the way. I failed helping you get back to you and now now is all we got. That's nothing." Saint listened, covering her mouth with her hand, petrified by what was supposed to be inside coming out—this unstoppable mourning of seconds past, the soul made liquid and pouring from the leg. "This now is all there ever is."

Frances let her forehead fall onto the glass, her face muddled with tears and snot, still rapt by the goings on outside though nothing of note went on out there: a pair of deer crept along the outskirts of Turney, their faces buried in the bushes. Two young boys ran past the window, two birds fleeing the wind. Dogs barked after being chained to their posts and left there. Goat screech. Gusts raking the trees naked. None of it new, but maybe it was beautiful together, enough to watch closely. Frances kept repeating "they want me back, my people" vocalized, then pantomimed by her mouth warping into the shape of words that without sound were merely a relay of voids.

'Speak, damn it. Speak the words,' Saint thought. She looked outside the glass that blandly mirrored her into a ghost over Frances's shoulder and, too, hovering over the gardener and dying vegetable garden outside, putting her in two places at the same time. She put her hands on her hips and outside her hands clenched tomato vines to her thighs. She opened her mouth and a blue jay outside entered her head and flew out.

'The past is always escaping us, Frances,' Saint thought. Floorboards creaked then the walls and ceiling followed. The smell of salt returned, the dark abysmal mouth of the empty hearth burst into blue flames. Whatever Frances looked for in the once-before needed to wait. Selah's breathing grew audible behind them, loud enough to break through the sobbing house rocking on its foundation.

Quickly, Saint needed Frances to bring Selah out of this endless sleep, needed Frances to wake her up, to bring her back into the now neither Saint nor Frances understood. And every present eventually unpeels and spirals into the past, so it didn't matter what harm Frances had caused before, Saint thought, because it'll all end up dead in time.

"Frances. Listen to me. Frances. I need your help. You can still help me," she said, kneeling beside Frances on both knees, trying to get her to look in her direction, to stop appraising the damn window and the nothing-going-on outside. "Frances . . . Frances . . . I can still use your help. Frances."

"No, no I got to go back. I got to get ready. They coming to get me."

"Who?"

"I don't remember," Frances said, hitting herself on the forehead with two fists. "I can't help you now cause I don't know how. I'm so sorry for what I did to your husband. I didn't mean to, Saint. He just started bleeding after I touched him. I didn't mean to open him up like that. Please believe me. I . . ." The house moaned like a weary elder around them.

"Frances. Look at me. Look at me." Then the blue flame burst forth in the hearth once more, brighter than before, blue whips of fire gone serpentine to the ceiling. Frances began to sob hysterically. Without thinking, Saint grabbed Frances around the shoulders from behind, a hug, rocking side to side, holding on tight, rocking wider and wider with the rocking of the house. "Frances. Frances. We will get your leg together. We will clean you up. Get you fed. And you will help me with

Selah. We will get you right, first. Wash your leg so you don't get sick. Then we will help Selah."

Frances started to hum. Without thinking, Saint followed. They hummed in unison. Their two voices filled up the room so that the wood groaning all around them muted beneath their song. They hummed together, the same song swimming from their mouths, one they never practiced together, had never heard the other sing, the song swelling up in them both, memories rushing back, the blue flame gone out, the house still.

'Essence. That's the woman's name. Essence. How did I ever forget?' Saint thought. She squeezed Frances tighter as a storm lit up her mind. It was the dream she had of the ocean at night, birds flocking around them, floating planks of wood and upturned barrels bumping into fresh corpses in the water. And there, in view, Frances floating faceup in the water, eyes-closed, moonlight a lantern on Frances's wan face. Sting of salt. Sting of remembrance becoming once again remembrance, breaking free from the dreamworld. 'What is this when?' she thought.

A void made itself known inside of her. She wanted to hold it as she had held Selah. For the first time. A child whom she could love on. Love? She wanted to hold herself and fill all that was empty inside of her. Love? All of this just by hugging and humming with a woman, an intimacy she needed badly, had kept herself from feeling but why, why? Breathing eased. Her heart extolled. The void throbbed inside her head. A sweet smell overpowered the room. Lilac. Lilac. Salt. Lilac. Love? She had been hugging Frances from behind, around the shoulders, and holding her own arms to secure the embrace. Then, there were France's hands limp at her sides. Lifeless. Trained never to touch. Never to feel. Never to know Saint's skin, not as lover, not as friend, not even accidentally.

Saint touched Frances at the elbows, the shirt sleeve damp with sweat. The bones charged with sorrow. Such thin musculature.

"Frances," she said, soft enough to barely hear herself. "You remember, don't you?"

Frances nodded. "I do."

"What do you remember?"

Frances merged her upturned palms into a bowl before her. Saint kneeled before Frances and laid her head inside the bowl, the hands warm, damp. Light filled the void. Then darkness attenuated the light, breaking it into thin cracks. When Saint opened her eyes, she was on a ship surrounded by people she knew she had once loved, the vision of a burning island shrinking in the distance.

FIRE SMELLS OF freedom and she wants more of it. She was, is here. At the head of the ship. They had stolen it from their captors. On that burning island called Casa Verde, fifty miles south of what would be called Barbados. The British who brought them there in chains on a ship named the Divider. *A treaty between ocean and slave captor signed with blood. Enslaved African blood. Sugarcane stalks clamor. She can still hear them this far out, their sweetness entering the salt of the ocean. And here on the* Divider, *her people, her family survives. Dozens of them heading home. Back to ______. Back to where they were taken from. And here is Solomon. He is holding two babies and bringing them to her. Her daughters with the same face. They are safe. They made it, all together. No one left behind.*

Blade to belly soft, fire feasting on the false thrones of their enslavers, Christian idols kneeling in the sand—on the island she taught her people how to hold their breath in the shadows, to lay waste to guard dogs spraying the air with their livid barks, and to sculpt a lesson from failure and a weapon from fear. She is trusted, is machete and gold glistening against a wrist. There is no magic other than her flesh and wits, her wet teeth throwing back sunlight like a shield.

She sings a song because this is the time for singing. Water waves at them as they sing. But what they thought was the water fitting with their song was instead a warning. In the distance, there is another ship. The island is on fire. She sees the smoke from here. Sugarcane calling on the wind. She grabs her babies and tells everyone to prepare for a fight. Grab your artillery. Grab your blades. No, not sugarcane. Englishmen crying in the wind. Reaching all the way here from their burning bodies. This ship ours, she says. Keep it ours. Someone says the other ship come closer. She says let it. They head east without stop and if the ship tries to stop them, they will behead everyone on board. If her people can see the smoke, then they assume those on the other ship can see the smoke ribboning into the sky its endless black tail. A whole island burning, the hill of it lit up like sunrise because they said one sun is not enough.

Her people gather on the deck. Strong winds break across their bodies, but they do not bend. She kisses her daughters on their foreheads and hands them to Solomon once more to put away where there are beds. She asks Solomon to lead a team to survey the ship for supplies. The ship across the water nears. They are ready.

But the ship passes them and does not follow. Bright sun corrupting the sky, gulls circle, a halo beneath a halo. Masts flagged proper, sails swell with the breath of their ancestors. The ship rocks against the water like a cradle. Below the weather, she dozes. She deserves this. They all do.

Solomon has not returned with his party. She asks her closest comrades, Ebele and Afua, to help her find her children and Solomon. They open the door and already an aura of dread lashes at them from the dark. Ebele leads them and Afua protects the back. Solomon's party had already lit the lamps in the rooms leading to the great cabin, throwing haunting light over tattered manuscripts and corroded maps pinned to the wall and stretched across a table. Inside the room, an open hatch door leads to the crew space below. Ebele stops them, rounds the opening suspiciously, holding over the hatch a candelabra she has pulled from the table before returning it to the wall and nodding at them that it is safe to push forward.

At the door of the cabin, a dark aura falls over them. When the boat moans, it sounds like an old man upset with his lot in life. There is no joy in the voice of the wood here, and it sickens her that they must use this ship. But they will bless it before going too far toward their destination. Every room will know their name before long, turning that miserable creaking into music of their own.

Ebele stops suddenly and stretches her arm to block the rest of the party from continuing behind her. She draws her weapon, and the others follow suit. Something crashes on the other side, then familiar voices, accented wrong, accented in a key of violence, sugarcane warping the throat. They know this sound. It is the sound of God disappearing.

When the boat tilts hard, Ebele opens the door, she throws her machete before anyone else can see a target. She has split open a puppet's head hanging from the ceiling, a room full of wood-carved dolls with jester faces, bright red cheeks, long noses pared to a point. In a cage, two parrots mimic their British owner and flap so hard the cage swings and bangs against the wall behind them. Someone has been hiding them here so they would not be stolen or eaten. Ebele laughs to herself. Bitterly. They leave that room and return to the stairs and Solomon appears below, shushes them, then leads them downstairs to a room where he has taken her daughters, Nzuzi and Kalunga, and laid them on a blanket. Lilac hangs from the ceiling, carried in by Solomon. The room smells sweet, what her babies deserve.

She sits alone with her children and falls asleep while Solomon, Ebele, and Afua return to deck. This is the first time in a while she has felt this peaceful, this safe with herself. She hears the boat creak along the water, soft rocking lulling her deeper into herself as she wraps her arms around her babies, who, facing each other, are a mirror to each other.

She returns to the ship's deck and assists with bundles of sugarcane that the British planned on sending elsewhere with African sweat and blood on it. Someone has found rice. There is enough fresh water aboard to keep them till they reach their destination. Already, she can hear the sighs of those who had been waiting for her return. She is on the brink of tears.

Overhead, sky blows black and they smell rain coming on, soft warning scraping the salt stink from the air. The drizzle eases down, then pelts them, what should nourish having grown teeth. Then the rain stops and the wind stops. The air dead. A swell of birds flees northwest, and they wonder.

Nighttime come, and wind picks up, a little at a time, then in open palms of air, then fists. The sails had already been lowered. They knew what was coming but had never been through it while on water, and the water rises and falls, rocking the boat on its roaring back. Then lightning come, and they know danger lurks in the light, that the wind would only get stronger in the rarity of lightning crashing down through the wind howling its hunt. Ship bobs and as it curtsies, a wave opens its mouth and closes it over the ship. She returns to her children and holds them as they cry against the wind's ferocity beating to get in. Then a crack and explosion overhead. Water seeps through the ceiling in small waterfalls, wind kicking and stomping down the ship with unnatural hatred. Babies crying in her arms. What the wind does not destroy, the waves do. What the waves cannot break, the wind takes. She runs from that room and heads lower into the ship, down into the hold, the way barely lit by candles dangling from the ceiling, many blown out from the ship's swaying. In the hold, she finds the rest of her people and smells the familiar reek of filth and rot. The British had not cleaned the ship since their last journey and the waste of other slaves surrounds them in that place they promised never to return to, loose chains sliding across the floor with nuggets of dried shit rolling after. The few livestock they managed to corral add their waste to the floor and she can't tell their shit from the people's. A goat cries out, but it sounds like a baby as the ship rocks and moans. No! She screams. No! And runs back toward the babies' room to find it flooding, water spraying down the hatch, Nzuzi and Kalunga howling in her arms. The wind is set to drown them out. Water gathers around her shins until the wall becomes the floor and her shoulders switch places with her feet. She crashes into a pool of salty water with more pouring in. Her babies scream out. She hears her people calling out to her, hears them pray for the storm to let them be, to leave them for the freedom they fought and killed for, earned with rage and pike, gun and fist, with their running, running, running, running, running, running, ru— sky . . . she can see the sky, then a hammer made of water falls over her. When she opens her eyes her babies are gone, washed away with the water that fell over her and she can't hear them crying anymore, can't hear them crying, but her arms still feel their weight and warmth as a flash of lightning illuminates the ship's cracked ribs, and floating a few meters off are two bundles she cannot reach fast enough. Then the ship makes a tearing sound. Her feet lose the world.

The moon is what wakes her. Her head hurts and rings from the pain. Her daughters are no longer in her arms, but she still feels them there. The sky is dark. She floats on a bed of wood. The moon unclothes from behind the passing storm and washes over the ocean with its easy light. She can see the lines of things. It is how she can tell her body from the rest. She tries to move but is stuck where she is. Everything hurts. She looks down and sees a wooden pole has entered her stomach from behind. Her body is the dropped sail of a broken raft. It is clear to her she will die soon. She thinks she is already dead. A body slides from a floating plank and sinks beneath the sheet of water. Four hooved legs bob, then disappear near her.

The animal corpse cuts through the calm dark water, a disappearance into the hunger of the world. Then she sees someone she had not seen before. The person does not look like her, but she knows that person somehow is her, a part of her she no longer wants. She sees her face looking back at her. She reaches to her and she watches her. She does not sink like the others. She floats away, wearing a face that is not her face. But it is yours, Frances. You are the face that is not her but belongs to her. You, like blood, have come from inside her.

THUS IT BEGAN and ended in the grief-swelled shack made vessel floating and tilting over riptides ghosting in the grass, leaf clamor a sea sound hissing its haunting through unchinked slats of a shack's wood walls taught to sing a ship's song. How else would a house learn to moan oceanic but from the dead? Saint and Frances caught in the vestibule of their grief, between living and living-dead, even now while one laid her face in the coarse hands of the other and wept. Even now, Frances caught in the window's reflection, looking at herself looking out, looking through herself.

Saint, in the hold of recollection, felt Frances's fingers curve into and away from her cheek, luring her back to the present. Touched this way, Saint abandoned those visions of a storm that had tossed her onto the Apalachicola coast, amnesiac because she forced her memories out of her body so fast that they made a body on their own just to get back to her. Essence was right. Saint had been locked up, but not because someone feared her "energy"; rather Saint herself did the locking. Then the key that was just a part of her looking to return, a key called Frances, moseyed into her town with a smile.

Frances, fragment of storm and horror, of what the water held and what the heart couldn't hide, floated up the Mississippi River looking by instinct alone for the woman she belonged to. The pull on her heart all along was Saint, as though Saint's grief-warped mind tugged for closure without her knowing. All Frances had to do was touch Saint, no more than a casual brush of her fingertips against Saint's while complimenting her dress, hand holding while walking through town, an accidental bump between two pinkies while reaching for the same biscuit.

And what if she touched Saint's mind, to know that she loved the scent of just-cut apples and how freshly fallen snow caught sunlight like a mirror, that she hated secrets and missed adult company, that she fell asleep on the porch because the buzz of bees soothed her, and—most important—that she didn't know what most of her loves were. There was a time Saint knew she loved onyx over ruby, before both became merely a tool for survival, then citrine and turquoise like an unripe lime floating beside a birdless sky—all these gemstones weighing on Sebastian's fingers who hummed when he removed each one and carefully placed the rings in a silk-lined drawer. After he was killed and Saint sealed his soul into endless quiet, she promised herself she would find a way to bring him back. No matter the source of the conjure needed, she would supply, be it the last drippings from a honeysuckle beneath the ghost lamp of eclipse, her own blood boiled with the blood of ten wolves and its malicious tea sucked down, or collecting her own breath into a pigskin bag and floating its contents along the surface tension of the nearest ocean. As days became months and his every atom lost incandescence, her patience grew volatile, and she began to resent Sebastian, his blank stare into a cosmic abyss she had only read about, every non-blink a dutiful reminder of her failure. Still, she remained loyal and believed in a righteousness to call her own.

Then Frances had said, "You can't just leave people behind," with the sound of the roiling Atlantic spilling from her mouth. It wasn't clear where Frances had found her fury, why she chose at that moment to cut to the quick, shout, "You can't just leave them to die," then wipe out Delacroix's militia while wearing white.

"You can't just leave them to die" became clear once Saint opened her eyes from Frances's lap, but she had already chosen not to have her infants perish in the hold, had chosen to run away from the stench and loose manacles sliding across the hold's floor and summoning her with a chain's dragged hiss to return her to her own shackling. Away, away from her people's moans indiscernible from cattle and wood warped by water. She left them to die for the chance to give her children a life beyond towers of sugarcane and the absence of drums, beyond African heads on pikes as warning and décor, beyond insatiable water that all her life left nothing but screams in its wake. Away, away only to lose both children and comrades in the splinter and suck of the storm-ripped ship. And because Saint didn't want to carry any of it anymore—losing her babies, abandoning her people, the guilt of having done so—Frances had to carry it, invisible in her heart and a ghastly fear, carried it right on to Delacroix so that those in Ours would never have to face a storm, would never have to run away with gunfire at their backside and exile at the front.

Had there been no fear, Frances would've long ago offered the inverted cupola of her warm hands to hold Saint's glistening face like a fresh painting come to life. Instead, she waited, hid her touch in hot gloves, holding close the very gift she was meant to offer Saint. Now, her hands' warmth brought Saint to sweating, and Saint's tears warmed Frances's hands in return.

Feeling around for the wound, Saint felt the crease in her stomach with fresh understanding. Surely, she had died on the water when the wooden stake entered her, but here she was with her head resting on the lap of her own memory made flesh. A "Here I am!" she couldn't explain even if she tried. The wall and floor that once creaked and rocked her bilious settled beneath her feet, and the blue flames dissolved in the hearth's ashen mouth.

After seeing the image of her twins float away toward the dark recesses of a ship, Saint missed her daughters and wanted to say the word "daughter" again knowing two voices would reply, "Yes, ma'am?" She wanted to feel the word open her mouth with its occasion. There was no telling how long a daughter would last, let alone two. How can one predict the weather? "Daughter" a storm cloud occupying the sky, then overtaking it. "Daughter" rain from a cloud, quenching the grass beneath. She wanted to run outside and bathe in the thought of her body bringing new life into the world, even if that life, those lives, chose not to stay. Even when those lives left and came back, like Nzuzi and Kalunga had come back, somehow, as Maria and Nala, and in the arms of a man with a boy's face who called himself both Husband and Son of the water. Where else could he have found Selah and Naima but from the water?

The best she could do was love with no expectations. An unbridled love. She had spent eleven affectionless years keeping from Selah and Naima the only thing she could rightly give. Now, one slept an unbreakable sleep while the other beheld her with horror in her eyes from Thylias's decrepit doorway.

'Too late to love them in body, so I will love the memory,' Saint thought. 'Now that I have my memory back with me. Now that I have a little more *me* back.'

With Frances's knees, she pushed herself to standing. She had many questions, but for now, the present was all that mattered, and for once it brought with it a tomorrow she wanted to see. If only she could see that tomorrow with both Naima and Selah in it. In this life, however, both twins seemed determined to live on their own terms, to live at all, and that meant Saint had to let them go. In every instance of their return in which she held on, she lost them. No more. She didn't have to stop loving them to stop the pain of losing them. She only had to let them go and love them still.

Watching Selah rest, Frances and Saint held hands, skin to skin, living memory and keeper of memory.

"Should I try to wake her, bring her up out her sleep?" Frances asked.

Because Saint didn't know what Selah wanted or needed, she didn't answer.

Outside, Aurora heard from behind the cabin's closed door a sound she had never heard before, not from those who dwelled inside, not ever, a chorus of distinct voices becoming a singular, interminable, and warm note that swallowed the world that once held it. She rang the bell for breakfast. "A new nation born!" she shouted. "A new nation born!"

The year was 1872.

Coda

If you ask the historians, they will say that Ours's future was decided the very moment development began for the first airport in St. Louis County, quickening Ours's transformation from hidden Negro haven to poor Black town as future wars and industry demanded more from the airport, therefore demanding more land for expansion. This demand encroached on Ours's acreage every decade beginning in 1920 and solidifying in 1980 as more than 75 percent of Ours's residents lost their land and their homes to tens of thousands of feet of landing tarmac, hangars, plane docks, and highways. The rumble of flying planes eviscerated birdsong.

But if you ask the dead, they will say Saint's disappearance decided Ours's fate. Madame Jenkins discovered Saint's absence after she went looking for her to tell her she was getting married to Mr. Wife. What welcomed Madame Jenkins, other than the house's chipped blue paint, was Saint's garden overrun with weeds that had crept up the porch and overtaken the banister and chairs. The front door gaped open, and waves of colorful fabric stretched from the threshold in gossamer rivulets that poured down the steps. But lilac growing from a mound in front of the house made Madame Jenkins think Saint was dead, which is what she reported when she returned to Ours.

For years after Saint went missing, the Ouhmey assumed the stones still worked because no one bothered them for decades to come. Then the axe men came.

The axe men had leveled the trees just south of Ours, pushing northward until their closeness to town and the noise of their labor attracted the Ouhmey to investigate. They saw dozens of men with axes relieving the trees from their trunks. Leaf crash on the tumble down. A spray of hares escaped from their burrows into the hunger of shadows.

Powerless, the Ouhmey listened as the leveling of trees drew closer, each branch crack and trunk split echoed the cracking and splitting of their lives. By the turn of the century, Ours was incorporated into St. Louis County, the surrounding woods cleared out for roads on which a white man in a suit arrived by car, the first anyone in Ours had ever seen, discussing with them insurance payments, tax payments, deeds, and other concepts foreign to them. Paperwork needed to be signed. A certain amount of money was owed. They couldn't live there for free. As one of the oldest and keenest in Ours, Joy handled most of the paperwork and debated with the man about certain procedures and legalities. She wished her son was there to assist her, but he had died several years prior from natural causes, leaving her with three grandchildren to help raise with their mother.

Joy failed at getting most of what Ours needed during negotiations with the man in the suit but succeeded in securing the land just east of Ours's mainland and west of Saint's abandoned home as part of Ours. When she signed her name, she dated it 1912. The man shook his head—"It's 1922"—and laughed. "Happens to the best of us, kitten," he added, and before Joy could ask what he had called her, he was dashing back to his car and speeding off.

By 1930, new roads were paved through Ours and the adjacent field, a post office set up, addresses given, a census taken (520 residents, all Negro, varying ages between two months and ninety years old, near fifty-fifty split male and female, limited if any education, no income, no birth records).

For the most part they were left unbothered, until 1939 when World War II began and the airport expanded by adding nearly 10,000 feet of runway. James S. McDonnell, an aviator and engineer and man no one in Ours cared about, formed the McDonnell Aircraft Company at Lambert, and thereafter the airport produced military resources. More woods west of Ours faded in under a week and the war-readying noise increased, machine screech the endless screams of a civilization birthing an end.

Eventually, the money they had saved dried up. They looked for work in nearby towns, avoiding Delacroix as historically unsafe. Paid a pittance, they barely made it each month. They survived this way for two more generations; each decade, more and more of Ours disappeared in the mouth of industry and eventually luxury as passenger flights became most flights in and out of Lambert Airport. By 1980, Ours had 25 percent of its original land and fewer than 250 residents.

The early fears of strangers encroaching on their space hardened into resentment and complacency. Petitions to stop building factories and landing strips went ignored. Poverty increased with no new jobs created. Neither the factories nor the airport wanted or needed to hire them. Their schools went underfunded, the unasked-for roads built decades ago hadn't been maintained since they were built. Sewage pipes backed up. Lead in the water. Closest hospital two miles away. The Ours cemetery the only remnant from the 1800s, its population growing more quickly than the town's.

Folktales about a woman who freed enslaved Africans with magic, then disappeared, circulated during the early 1900s. By 1990, only a few remembered how it went but had turned Saint's name into a Candyman-type game, where saying her name five times while looking into a pool of water would summon her to forcibly take you to "freedom" by pulling you in and drowning you, the idea being that she had no idea slavery had ended. "Aight, keep playing and I'mma get

Saint to drown you" became a joking threat parents used to quiet their children. God's Place was gone by 1992, over which an empty field meant for recreation was built. No one called it a park because there weren't any swings or slides or woodchips, no field house and hardly any trees, and certainly no maintenance. But they barbecued there, held birthday parties there, put up tents to block out the sun and drizzle for baby showers, and played football using the ends of the long fence as touchdown markers.

It took almost a century for things to begin to level out. Jobs came, schools were renovated, and town leaders successfully rallied for a hospital to be built nearby. Though by that time, some would've said it was too late, would've said the drug dealers had more say than the pastors. No one in Ours felt that way. They kept the streets clean, their lawns mowed, flowers growing around the outlines of the houses. They greeted each other as best they could and felt no slight when a greeting wasn't returned. They held block parties, rent parties, party parties, sliding up and down one another's bodies, reminding them they had their own skin, tendon, muscle, and bone, and that it felt damn good to touch and be touched, licked across the pasture of their neck, focused on, enmeshed.

Marvin Gaye asked "What's going on?" from one record player down the street, while up the block, TLC sang they "ain't too proud to beg" from a car stereo. Children danced beneath a rigged hydrant, rainbows flashing their flipped grins overhead. Out of breath, the children sat on the curb, sipping from juice jugs and sharing a sandwich bag of Frooties. Their tongues the color of wildflowers, breath ripe as an orchard.

Every decade offered a new beginning. Even dressed, the adults became nude to each other, a cascade of shea-buttered arms backlit by streetlights dressed in moths. And none rushed to hide themselves while the ground, the earth that had once haunted them, felt softer beneath them. They lived, as they had always lived.

Acknowledgments

I owe my life to Spirit, the ancestors, and my family and friends.

Thank you, Mom, for your patience. You've been asking for this novel for almost twenty years. It's here! I wrote this for you, especially.

I'm thankful to my agent, Bill Clegg, and the Clegg Agency, whose early and enthusiastic support energized me to finish this book that had been long in the making. Your involvement, faith, and ready-to-fight attitude have changed my life.

I also want to thank the incomparable Paul Slovak, whose editorial eye and attunement to my vision made this process not only smooth but inspiring. Thank you to Allie Merola for getting me. Thank you to Andrea Schulz for believing in my work enough to support it within and outside the walls of publishing. Endless thank you to the Viking team and copy editor Joy Simpkins.

Thank you to my Bennington College family, especially Benjamin Anastas and Michael Dumanis, for checking in with me and offering emotional support.

To my Randolph College colleagues and students for yearly encouragement, check-ins, and helping me build confidence in this work, I thank you all (there are so many of you!!) for being a part of this journey. Big thanks to Gary Dop for supporting my genre-hopping.

Thank you to Kathryn Davis for years of support, starting at Wash U!

Thank you to Crystal Wilkinson for believing in my undergraduate potential all the way through adulthood.

Big thanks to Brittany Allen, Alex Chee, Bill Cheng, Mira Jacob, Luis Jaramillo, Tennessee Jones, and Julia Phillips for reading very early passages of this novel, all of which have been removed but advice for which has been applied to every chapter that exists in this book. I learned about clarity and easing a reader, and about kindness and generosity as comrades from our time together.

Major thanks to Elijah Bean, the best roommate anyone could ever ask for. You made my life bearable with your presence.

Thank you to Preston Anderson, Brit Bennett, Jamel Brinkley, Aricka Foreman, Hafizah Geter, Kaitlyn Greenidge, Rachel Eliza Griffiths, Ashaki Jackson, Robert Jones Jr., Stephanie Land, Evan Mallon, Airea D. Matthews, Jamila Minnicks, Jon Jon Moore Palacios, Justin Phillip Reed, Maurice Carlos Ruffin, Safiya Sinclair, Jayson Smith, UGBA, Javier Zamora, and anyone I am missing (please forgive my memory and spatial limitations of the book itself), who have all offered various forms of support, from early readership, to listening to me read excerpts so that I might edit, and/or for public enthusiasm about the novel.

Thank you to the National Endowment for the Arts, the Harvard Radcliffe Institute, and the Whiting Foundation for support over the years.

Author's Note

Ours began as a short story. I had written it as a submission to an undergraduate creative writing contest my sophomore year. The judge that year was Crystal Wilkinson, an Affrilachian writer and early influence. She selected it as a fourth-place winner, and in her note she wrote that the story felt more like the beginning of a longer piece. I had been found out! I did not see my submission as a short story but took the risk to see if I could win some money to supplement my student budget. This short story and the novel that grew from it are inspired by a family story that I included inside the novel itself. My paternal grandfather, Joe Francisco, was a pastor who grew up in Alexandria, Louisiana, before moving to Gary, Indiana. The story (a Gary, Indiana, story) is that a woman had come to visit my grandaunt, Tea, who lived with my grandfather at the time. My grandfather had the habit of salting his thresholds to keep out evil, so by the time the woman had come to visit Grandaunt Tea, the doorway and the windowsills were covered in salt. Long story short, the woman made a move as if she were about to come in then stopped herself, refusing to enter the home even after my grandfather invited her in a few times. This woman, not wanting to cross the salt because she was unsure of her own status with the powers of good or was an evil spirit fully aware of what salt would do to her, refused to enter my grandfather's protected house.

My interest in African spirituality, hoodoo, conjure, and mythology has accumulated over the course of many years, starting with the eloko when I was in grade school. My mother had purchased an encyclopedia on African mythology to broaden my then obsession with Greek mythology. I read about uchawi haramu, a kind of dark sorcery used to make people ill, and about the Bakongo goddess Nzambi, who made the children of the first man and first woman mortal because they buried their dead child in the earth against Nzambi's wishes. These stories added breath and breadth to my imagination and later made it easier to read *The Black Book*, edited by Toni Morrison; *Toni Morrison and the Idea of Africa* by La Vina Delois Jennings; *A Refuge in Thunder* by Rachel E. Harding; *Echo Tree* by Henry Dumas; and many others. The encyclopedia offered an early foundation for my ability to understand other spiritual and mythological possibilities, seeing signs and symbols of Africanaity in Black literature that otherwise would have gone unnoticed.

Virginia Hamilton's book *Her Stories: African American Folktales, Fairy Tales, and True Tales,* illustrated by Leo and Diane Dillon, planted the seed for supernatural stories centering Black people. I learned that even in our true tales, stories founded in real life with no supernatural elements, there is a string of magic, of the mundane swirling into itself to unfold on the other side of real: fantastic, uncanny, sometimes frightening. I read this book incessantly as a child, even copied one of the drawings in the book as an art project. *Her Stories*, another book gifted to me by my mother, is one of my earliest memories of discovering that Black people had a rich history of imagination, fantasy, spirituality, and a gift for exploring the surreal.

Ours is my attempt at creating a contemporary mythology for Blackness in the United States of America and acts as a continuation of such investment that began with my previous book, *Mutiny.* I aimed to write an epic taking place during the antebellum period where slavery is not the main antagonist without disregarding or disappearing the enslaved. I mean to trouble the ever-present depictions of violence against Black people that purportedly toe the line between revelation and spectacle. What I hope to see happen is an offering of mercy to each other as we navigate this history together.

I wrote a book of this length to give a full-life perspective of characters who may often go overlooked. In my opinion, there is no main character and therefore no side character. The story is one of freedom and slavery, and like stories of slavery, stories of freedom require the investigation of a range of figures as well as an understanding of how they all relate. The town itself is a character, and the evolution of the experiences and relationships between characters are to be read as a unit. Everyone has their time and their say, their archetypes and their nuances, and I've given them space to have full selves in a freedom they deserve.

On October 12, 2022, at the Free Library of Philadelphia, Drs. Saidiya Hartman and Keeanga-Yamahtta Taylor discussed Hartman's seminal text *Scenes of Subjection.* Dr. Taylor asked Dr. Hartman to speak to the recent mode of saying "enslaved" when referring to slaves, calling this motivation a "softening of our understanding of what slavery was." Hartman's response encapsulates my own feelings: "I think people want to maintain the idea of the dignity of the enslaved and that Black life isn't simply totally exhausted by the category of slave. To me, to say slave isn't to exhaust those practices; it's just to name the structural relationship." As for my decision to use "enslaved African" versus "slave" versus "enslaved," I do not fall into the camp that believes the word "slave" takes away from the lives of those who were slaves/enslaved.

My use of "enslaved African" is to point to the diffusion that is diaspora. I use both "slave" and "enslaved" interchangeably as nouns throughout the book, choosing one over the other usually for aural reasons. I use "enslaved" as an adjective, as in "enslaved cook."

"So-called master" is a critique of coloniality, not a denial that those who were called "master" had power over their slaves.

Chapter 2: The phrase "and now even the hollow is gone" is a nod at Janice N. Harrington's poetry collection titled *Even the Hollow My Body Made Is Gone* (BOA Editions, 2007).

Chapter 8: Eloko (plural Biloko) is a dwarf-like creature that lives in rainforests of the Democratic Republic of the Congo. They are sometimes described as envious of the living and deeply greedy regarding their treasures. Differing from my own interpretation, biloko live in hollow trees that they disguise with vegetation, leaping onto unaware travelers. They are known to wear small bells that can cast a hypnotic spell on prey, making prey easier to devour whole. Magic protection, such as a charm, could protect against this sound. Along with the bell, biloko are known to have childlike voices used to deceive potential victims.

Chapter 18: "'You've known places,' Frances said. 'We all know somewhere inside ourselves we never thought we'd know. Dusky places. Places more ancient than God'" is a nod to Langston Hughes's poem "The Negro Speaks of Rivers."

Chapter 21: The story about Here and There that closes this chapter is my take on a traditional tale about Eshu-Elegba. For more information, please see "The Sculpture and Myths of Eshu-Elegba, the Yoruba Trickster. Definition and Interpretation in Yoruba Iconography" by Joan Wescott, published in *Africa: Journal of the International African Institute* 32, no. 4 (October 1962): 336–54, https://doi.org/10.2307/1157438.

ALSO AVAILABLE

Mutiny

In poems that rebuke classical mythos and embrace spiritual imagery and Afro-Diasporanfolk, Phillip B. Williams conjures the hell of being erased, exploited, and ill-imagined and then, through a force and generosity of vision, propels himself into life, selfhood, and a path forward. With a ferocity that belies the tenderness and vulnerability at the heart of this collection, Williams honors the transformative power of anger and the clarity that comes from allowing that anger to burn clean.